On Forbidden Ground

They sprinted across the uneven grass, skirting rocks, finally slamming into the stone wall of the fortress. Rosie couldn't get her breath, and her mouth was dry. As they entered, she had the tangible feeling of crossing a threshold into a different realm. Everything felt cold and sharp. Behind her, Lucas kept treading on her heels.

"Where now?" she whispered.

"It'll be in his bedroom. That's where I'd hide it."

The broad wooden flight creaked under them. They turned a corner into a passage stretching to infinity before them. She glimpsed the half-seen shadow beasts around them. Lucas grabbed her hand. His was icy.

"Oh, damn!" Matthew gasped, sounding completely terrified. "I don't like this. We have to get out."

They froze in their tracks as a figure stepped out of a doorway and stood glaring at them. Her face was pallid, her eyes terrible with menace and rage. She must have seen their terror. She seemed to be drinking it in, Rosie thought, relishing it.

"Do you know where you are, child?" she said, staring at Rosie. "See how cold this kingdom is. Leave while you can. Don't let him suck you in, or he'll keep you here until the blood freezes in your veins."

Rosie clearly saw four translucent black shapes around her; they were dark hulks, ghostly and threatening. Rosie felt Lucas shaking, hanging onto her.

The woman stared from Rosie to Matthew to Lucas. She looked demented. Her green eyes shone bright and glassy. Then the women gave a shake of her head. "I haven't got time for this," she hissed. "Go home."

The spell broke and they fled. The madwoman's quick sure footsteps echoed behind them all the way, and the four dark guardians flowed after them, herding them out . . . down through the chill spectral heathland, empty-handed.

Praise for Freda Warrington's *Elfland*

"*Elfland* is an absorbing and gripping journey into a world where the otherworldly shivers alongside us, unseen."

— Storm Constantine, author of the Wraeththu Chronicles

Turn the page for more praise for *Elfland*.

More Praise for *Elfland*

"A literally enchanted story of magic, love, loyalty, and hope."
—Liz Williams, author of *Darkland*

"Romantic in every sense, richly imagined and richly told, *Elfland* is a complex fantasy of the heart, of the faerie heart; and it's a delight. Immediately engaging and intensely satisfying, this is a class act from a fine writer."
—Chaz Brenchley, author of The Books of Outremer

"Her writing is supple, and her characters have that annoying edge, so difficult to do, that really makes them (you should pardon the expression) human. . . . Sensuous and intense—buy it, read it, love it!" —Melanie Rawn, bestselling author of *Spellbinder*

"A heady cocktail of urban fantasy and wild romance, invigorating and intoxicating. Warrington's writing has lyrical beauty, and her characters are a delight to discover."
—Justina Robson, author of *Keeping It Real*

"Prolific British author Warrington puts a distinctive spin on human/nonhuman relations in this sensuous, relationship-driven story. Solid wordplay, great pacing, and a thrilling conclusion will definitely earn Warrington some new American fans."
—*Publishers Weekly*

"This sort of hidden-race-among-us storyline is becoming rather commonplace in our genre, but Warrington makes it her own, and even the most jaded fantasy reader will quickly fall under the spell of her characters and the warm, intimate voice Warrington uses to tell us their stories. Highly recommended."
—Charles de Lint, *The Magazine of Fantasy & Science Fiction*

"Cross Elizabeth Hand with *Fire and Hemlock*, and you might end up with something like Freda Warrington's *Elfland*. This is the kind of big, sweeping modern faerie tale that you don't see often on the adult shelves anymore. *Elfland* is complex, rich, sensual, beautifully written, and sometimes heartbreaking. . . . It's a sumptuous feast of a novel, I'll definitely be looking up Freda Warrington's backlist." —*Fantasy Literature*

"Anyone who has ever felt the real world might suddenly waver to reveal a glimpse of Otherness will find the reason why in this erotic and colorfully evoked mix of glamorous gothic faerie and modern values. A glittering treasure trove and a stunning read for Warrington's multitude of fans."

—Tanith Lee, bestselling author of
The Silver Metal Lover

"Do you ever have the feeling that certain places are imbued with a kind of magic? Then you'll have an affinity with the way *Elfland* captures that impalpable sense of otherness. A dark yet strangely uplifting tale."

—Stan Nicholls, author of *Bodyguard of Lightning*

Praise for Freda Warrington's
Other Fantasy Novels

"Fantasy doesn't come much better than this!" —*Starlog*

"One of the best young British writers of fantasy."

—*Publishing News*

"Warrington has a real gift for playing fair with her readers and nonetheless pulling the feet out from under us, more than once; the real success is that routine fantasy plot maneuvering always enables something genuinely shocking to creep up on us."

—Roz Kaveney

Books by Freda Warrington

*A Tor book

Freda Warrington

ELFLAND

TOR®
fantasy

A TOM DOHERTY ASSOCIATES BOOK
NEW YORK

This is a work of fiction. All of the characters, organizations, and events portrayed in this novel are either products of the author's imagination or are used fictitiously.

ELFLAND

Copyright © 2009 by Freda Warrington

All rights reserved.

Edited by James Frenkel

A Tor Book
Published by Tom Doherty Associates, LLC
175 Fifth Avenue
New York, NY 10010

www.tor-forge.com

Tor® is a registered trademark of Tom Doherty Associates, LLC.

ISBN 978-0-7653-5840-0

First Edition: August 2009
First Mass Market Edition: June 2010

Printed in the United States of America

0 9 8 7 6 5 4 3 2 1

This novel is dedicated with love to Jenny Gordon,
who was with me every step of the way.

The Charnwood Forest of Leicestershire, England, is an uplands forest area characterized by some of the most ancient volcanic rocks in the country, rolling landscapes, charming villages, and country parks such as Beacon Hill and Bradgate Park. Cloudcroft, however, is a fictional village loosely based on real villages around which I've spent most of my life. Likewise, Ashvale can be seen as a geographically shifted tribute to that market town of noble fame, Ashby de la Zouch.

ELFLAND

PRELUDE
Life with the Cold Prince

A demon screamed and Ginny woke, heavy with fever. She was alone in bed. Outside the monsoon rain fell and she saw drenched, glistening blue light shining in the open doorway. She tried to rise but a shadowy weight pressed her down. Webs of mosquito netting held her.

She saw her husband on the verandah, framed in the doorway against the light. Rain fell silver around him. Beyond, the dense coils of the rain forest gleamed and dripped in a sinuous dance. With his black hair streaming, he roared soundlessly into the storm, summoning all the denizens of the Otherworld, all her nightmares. His hands wove a white spell. She felt his terror and defiance as he called upon them to do their worst; felt the jungle shudder as it disgorged horrors. The hot wet air swelled as they came.

He was in league with them, wild and mad. The invisible weight that pressed her down was terror. She tried to scream—

Ginny woke. Rain fell but all was dark, the door closed. Her husband lay breathing quietly beside her under the tent of netting. She sat up, gasping for a wisp of air in the humidity.

She looked down at Lawrence's serene, carved face and knew that she couldn't stay any longer. She had tried and tried but it was killing her. She was starving for England, with its cool green landscapes and kindlier faerie realms. Famished.

"Ginny?" he said, stirring.

"Something here hates us," she whispered. "I can feel it."

"Not this again." His voice was heavy with weariness.

"I know." She dragged her fingers through the raven tangle of her hair. "This isn't me. I'm a grown woman, a mother, a fully paid-up life member of the wise and ancient ones. In a way, that's the point."

"What?"

"When I say that something wants to destroy us, it means it's true."

She heard him sigh. "And you would let it win by running away?"

"I am not the one running away, Lawrence," she said softly. "I want to go home."

His eyes were shining slivers, fierce and cold. Her beloved cold prince; her husband, and she didn't truly know him. "We can't go home," he said. "Our life is here. Our business."

"Your business is in New York and London. Your life, in England. Others could run this place for you, but you won't let them."

"You know why. I have to protect it . . . from Barada."

"But he's the one destroying us!" On previous occasions she had backed down, but now she was past caring. "Swallow your pride," she hissed. "Sell it to Barada."

"Not in a thousand years." His voice was hard. "He couldn't afford it."

"The money doesn't matter!"

"It's not about money," he answered, quiet as a razor. "You of all people should understand. I will not abandon my workers, or my birthright."

"Is this truly about protecting your interests? Or about hiding?" Her words were vicious; he answered with the knife-edged hostility of his eyes. Ginny shrank a little inside. "I know the mine is everything to you. But Sam and Jon need us, too. Think of them."

"They're strong," he said.

"No, they're not." Every time she put her toe under the waterfall of guilt, it tore her skin off. "They're little boys."

"Who must become strong, in order to survive in this world. I'm not taking them out of school."

"I'm not asking you to." Ginny reached out to touch his arm. He was stone under her hand, a statue of ice. "But I have to go home. This place is killing me."

He did not respond. Her heart sank and grief congealed in the back of her throat. She let her hand fall away. The silence was an ocean of steamy rain and there were hours of sleepless fever dreams to cross before daybreak.

After a time, Lawrence's voice came softly out of the darkness. "When humans dream, they create elves and angels, devils and vampires. But when we dream . . . when *we* dream . . . what do we create for ourselves?"

INTERLUDE
Zeitgeist

"The fantasy of unconditional love," Rosie said to her reflection, "the *lie* of unconditional love is that you can love someone from afar, someone who never even looks at you in return, and it's okay; it's pure and virtuous and noble. But it's not okay. Fuck the fantasy!"

She was twenty-three; a perfect age, perhaps, to walk away from her youthful dreams and harsh disillusionments. Her Aetherial parents claimed that age meant little in the Otherworld, but it counted here on Earth, where she'd always lived. So, it was time to admit that if she kept offering her heart to someone who didn't care, she shouldn't be astonished to find it so bruised and broken. Time to grow up.

The face in her dressing-table mirror was deceptively serene; a creamy oval with bright silver-grey eyes outlined by kohl and plum eyeshadow, a strong nose and mouth, glossy burgundy-brown hair falling to her shoulders. She'd been told there was a touch of the Pre-Raphaelite about her, but she considered herself too short, and usually too scruffy from gardening, to be any kind of siren.

Pretty or plain? Depended who was looking at her. Human or Aetherial? Impossible to say. It was just her familiar self gazing back. Surprisingly calm, after what she'd witnessed. So this was the face of a young woman who knew it was time to discard all romantic delusions and make a practical, adult decision.

The luscious greens of the garden were framed in the window behind her. Outside, oak trees swayed serenely, oblivious of the quiet collapse of her world.

"How did it all go so wrong for us?" she asked. "Was it the closing of the Great Gates, or is that just a convenient scapegoat for everything?"

She touched a fingertip to a scar on the side of her neck, a thin, reddish mark the length of a finger. Still there, after all these years. She rarely thought about it, but today, for some reason, it disturbed her. She arranged a lock of hair to conceal it.

Rosie looked around the bedroom that had always been hers, with its stone fireplace and treacly wood paneling, thick cream carpet and king-size antique bed. On those bedcovers, she thought wistfully, she should have had wild sex with some demon prince—but she never had. Behind the door of her wardrobe, she'd once found a secret passageway into a chamber where a magical tree grew, its roots bursting the floorboards. Not a dream, but a manifestation of Aetheric reality.

The Dusklands had always been fluid, capricious as waves. Of late, she rarely dipped into them at all. Did the Aetheric realm fade for those who turned away from it? Or was she turning away because she couldn't bear to see it fade?

Rosie didn't know anymore.

Idly, she opened an old bottle of nail polish and began painting her fingernails. The color was dark and multi-hued, like a peacock's feather. As she worked, she thought about her brother Matthew. Was he right to claim it was time to forget the Otherworld, since it was now lost to them? To accept that although it had been their parents' birthright, it was not theirs? To dismiss it all, even the Dusklands, as a dream? We must go forward, he insisted, and live fully in the mortal world.

Making the decision to go Matthew's way felt like an ax about to fall. Yet the other way was mist and darkness, and had brought her nothing but tears.

"What am I waiting for?" she murmured.

A memory surfaced. She'd been very young, five or six.

She was playing in the garden . . . discovering the innocent wonder of the Dusklands, of stepping sideways into a world that was like this one but watery and full of mystery . . . then hands had grabbed her shoulders and yanked her back into the real world, and Matthew was shouting at her as if he'd snatched her out of danger.

She remembered her fear and confusion. To this day, she didn't know why he'd been angry. It had been the first time, but not the last . . . Not that Matthew's warnings had ever stopped her. Perhaps, after all, he knew something she didn't.

Rosie sat back and studied the gleam of her painted nails. Each nail was different—navy, green, purple—and each one changed in the light, flashing magenta or bronze. She examined the bottle. The color was called Zeitgeist. German, literally "time ghost." So, the spirit of the age was oily. Many-colored. Fugitive.

"Figures," she said out loud.

"Rosie?" Her younger brother, Lucas, put his head around the door. "Are you okay?"

He looked worried. "Come in," she said, smiling as she displayed her iridescent fingernails to him. "That's us, that is."

"What is?"

She moved her hand to show the color change. "Aetherials are like that. No one sees us as we really are."

Lucas looked at her with a half-smile, and went to sit cross-legged on the end of her bed. At twenty-one he was dark-haired, good-looking and coltishly long-limbed. His presence soothed her. Of all her family—and despite the argument she'd had with him earlier—she was closer to him than to anyone. "Seriously, are you still furious with me?"

She sighed. "No, of course not."

"I'm really sorry," he said. "Don't sit up here brooding, Rosie."

"I'm not brooding."

"What are you doing, then?"

"I'm standing at the crossroads. Deciding which way to go. Remembering everything that's happened and realizing that I need to walk away from it."

"And?" He sounded anxious. "Come on, what are you thinking?"

Brushing her hair aside, Rosie touched the scar on her neck. "About the day I got this." She breathed in and out. "About the Wilders. Do you think we'll ever be finally, completely free of them?"

A long pause. Lucas looked steadily at her, frowning slightly. "Do you want to be?"

1

The House of Broken Dreams

On Rosie's ninth birthday, her father gave her the most beautiful item she had ever seen; a sparkling crystal heart that had captivated her in a jeweler's window. It wasn't her nature to demand things, but her parents had remembered. When she opened her present, there was the wonderful pendant, blazing on black velvet.

She wore it proudly on a sturdy silver chain. It was too dressy with her blue T-shirt and jeans, but she didn't care. Its hard little angles bounced on her chest as she ran, playing football with her brothers.

It was a warm and gleaming spring day. The lush greens of their garden formed enveloping caverns, drawing them from the main lawn to smaller bowers, through the rose garden, the herb garden, to the wild places where their property blended into the borders; into huge oaks and sprawling hawthorn hedges. They abandoned the ball. Matthew led the way through a gap in the hedge to the woodland paths beyond.

A stream snaked its way past their garden. They knew full well they were supposed to stay on this side. Matthew, however, led the way across stepping-stones and began to climb.

Hearts pounding, Rosie and Lucas followed.

Matt was fourteen and always took the lead. He was bursting with energy, climbing fast through the steepest part of the woods so that they could barely keep up. Lately, Rosie noticed, he'd become restless and resentful, too old to play with his younger siblings but still constrained to watching out for them. Lucas, two years younger than Rosie, was their shadow.

At nine, everything was eternally new to her. Eons stretched between one adventure and the next. There were always new twists in the paths, rocks she'd never seen before, amazing patterns in the trunks of silver birches.

Although the Dusklands manifested most strongly in twilight, on intense days like this she could see the deeper reality shimmering like a heat haze over the surface world. The eyes of elementals peered from between the leaves, vanishing if she tried to look straight at them. She could feel Aetheric energies brushing her skin, tingling like nettles. Knowing she was part of it—able to enter this subtle dimension as ordinary children could not—thrilled her.

She and Lucas shared the experience without words. They'd learned not to discuss it in front of Matthew, who only growled and called it foolish.

Rosie came to the foot of a squat, majestic oak that spread a gleaming canopy over her. Instinctively she began to climb, her breath fast with exertion.

"Rosie!" came Matthew's voice. "Get down, before you break your neck!"

His voice was distant; she slipped all the way into the Dusklands without thinking, entranced by the landscape turning bluish, mysterious and full of rainbow gleams. Leafy elementals snaked around the tree limbs, smiling at her as she smiled back . . .

"Rosie!" The voice was loud and angry. The next she knew, Matthew was grabbing her off a branch in a shower of twigs and leaves and setting her on the ground. "How many times have I told you not to do that? It's not safe!"

"Get off!" she retorted, shaken and indignant. "I wasn't doing anything wrong."

He pushed back his fair hair, glaring at her until the blue fire of his eyes softened. "Look, as long as I'm in charge of you, you'll behave," he said firmly. "Follow me, and don't wander off."

Grumbling, she obeyed. Above the tree line, they waded through knee-high bracken, coming out onto heathland high above the village. Rosie and Lucas were gasping for breath. It was wrong to trespass, they knew, but a guilty pleasure. Even Matthew had never dared come this far before.

He climbed a spar of ancient rock and posed there. Massed clouds created an eerie light in which the greens of spring turned luminous against an iron-grey sky. From here they commanded a spectacular view across Cloudcroft and the Charnwood hills. Their own house, Oakholme, nestled below them, broad and friendly with cream-washed walls and black beams. The scattered thatch and slate roofs of the village were visible through a sea of budding oak, ash and birch, strung along the meandering length of a valley.

On the opposite side of the valley, green farmland gave way to the stark hills of High Warrens, wild with rocks as ancient as the Aetherial race itself. Beyond stood Charnwood's main peaks; Beacon Hill, Bardon Hill grey with distance, Old John with its stone beer-tankard folly. Dark green pine forests spilled into the folds beneath, mixed with softer woodland and hedgerows.

On this side, the hilltop behind them was bleak. The grass was wiry, the soil fragrant with peat. Clusters of rock thrust out of the ground, wreathed in bracken. On the long, rugged backbone of the summit, there stood a house. It was built of granite and looked like a fortress. The roof was black slate. Behind it, rain clouds massed angrily.

"Is that Stonegate Manor?" Rosie said, startled. She'd only ever glimpsed the house from the road. It looked different from this angle.

"Of course it is, idiot," said Matthew. "It's where the Wilders live. The neighbors Mum and Dad talk about in whispers."

"Isn't it weird that we never see them?" she said, suddenly consumed by a sense of mystery.

"I have," Matthew said loftily. "A few times, swishing around in massive cars. The father's abroad a lot."

"How d'you know?" said Lucas.

Matthew shrugged. "I know everything."

Rosie studied the Manor, shivering to think of it standing empty, haunted. "Are they like us? Old blood?"

"So Dad says." Matthew looked at the sky. "It's going to piss down. Let's go back."

He jumped off his rock, hitting the ground with a flat-footed thud. Rosie and Lucas struggled to keep up with his long strides. She grabbed her little brother's hand and pulled him along. "Matthew! Wait for us!"

Suddenly he was out of sight and the footpath was unclear. There were vague tracks forking through the bracken, some young birch trees in front, more rocks to their right. She started to feel nervous. Which way had he gone?

Don't cross the stream, she heard her father saying. *Our neighbors are very private and it may not be safe.*

Two shadows appeared, drifting towards her through the birches. They seemed to come in slow motion. Rosie was paralyzed. Two skinny figures in dark clothes, with bright hair blowing behind them. At first she thought they were ghosts or elementals from the Dusklands, menacing; then—she didn't know.

Lucas clung tight to her hand. The figures came on, confident, threatening. Two boys. One was close to her age but the other looked as old as Matthew, a lithe teenager with a harsh face and bright sea-green eyes.

"Where d'you think you're going?" said the older one. The smile that played on his face chilled her. Mocking, probing.

"Nowhere. Home," said Rosie.

"You're on our father's land, you know," said the younger boy, in a precise tone. He hung back, not glaring at her as the older boy did. His eyes were brown, his face softer, more aloof than aggressive.

"Yes, you're trespassing," said the green-eyed one. "You want to know what we do to trespassers on the Wilder estate?"

Rosie pushed Lucas behind her. "No," she said, trying to sound brave. "We don't mean any harm. We got lost."

"That was careless. There's a price to pay." The cold eyes glinted with cruelty and she knew a terrifying game was being played that could only end in pain and humiliation. The boy slipped a fingertip under her beloved new pendant. Tears of rage oozed onto her lashes, but she daren't breathe or speak. "This is nice," he purred.

"HEY!" The shout came from a few yards away. Matthew appeared over the shoulder of the hill near the rocks. He came charging at them like an enraged ram and his voice was as gruff as a man's. "You get away from them!"

The taller boy legged it. He barged past Rosie and as he went, he grabbed the silver chain and jerked it so hard it burned into her neck as it broke. She yelled in pain. He was gone, running madly along the slope of the heath with her precious crystal heart in his hand. She heard his mocking laughter.

Through her tears, Rosie saw her brother come rushing up and knock the younger boy onto his backside. "You little shit!" he yelled. Then, after the thief, "You! I'll get you for this!"

The answer came as a fading echo. "You and whose fucking army?"

The younger boy staggered to his feet. For a moment, he caught Rosie's eye and something passed between them like a physical shock. Recognition, unspoken apology? He coughed, so shocked by Matthew's violence that Rosie felt sorry for him. He started to back quickly away, saying, "You don't want to upset my brother. He'll kill you."

Matthew laughed out loud. The boy turned and fled after the older one, who'd circled up the hill to wait for him. Rosie heard her attacker growl "*Jon*!" as he caught the smaller one by the shoulders; then both boys stood for a moment like a pair of wraiths, coats flapping, so eerily hostile that even Matthew lost the nerve to pursue them.

He put his arm around Rosie and pulled her away. "Wankers," he growled.

"He took my pendant," was all she could say through her sobs.

"Come on, let's get you home."

The way back seemed endless, drizzle turning the paths to glass. When Rosie's tears subsided, Matthew said, "Don't tell Mum and Dad."

"Why not?" said Lucas.

"Because we shouldn't have been up there. If Dad finds out, he'll go mental."

Rosie felt aggrieved with Matthew for leading them into danger; but she'd known, and joined in with the adventure regardless. "Who are those awful boys, anyway?"

"Samuel and Jonathan Wilder. The young one is Jon. The thieving bully is Sam."

"Do you know them?"

"No, but I've heard stuff. They go to some posh boarding school miles away. They say the older one's off his head. He's always in trouble."

Rosie shivered. Her neck was sore. She touched the place and felt a raw weal. She licked her fingertips and tasted blood. "Mum's going to notice."

"Put a polo neck on. Tell her the heart's safe in your jewelry box."

She struggled not to cry again. It was true, she couldn't possibly admit she'd lost the heart through being plainly disobedient.

"Why don't they go to our school?" Lucas asked.

"'Why, why, why?'" Matthew parroted. "The Wilders are so high-and-mighty that they look down on everyone else, human or old blood alike. They're massive snobs. Dad hates that sort of thing."

Rosie thought of how they'd come drifting through the trees, two menacing specters. "Dad's not scared of them, is he?" She shook her head vigorously, thinking of her father's broad frame, his strength. "No, he's not frightened of anything."

"Look." Matthew turned and gripped her shoulders. "We cannot tell Dad about this because he's going to blame me. Anyway, all Mr. Wilder would do is deny his sons are thieves. There's no way you'd get your necklace back."

"I know," she said miserably.

"So we have to sort it out ourselves. I'll get it for you. Next time I see Sam, I'm going to beat the living crap out of him."

"What?" Rosie's stomach turned cold. A resolute anger rose in her. "No, you mustn't! I'll get it back myself."

"How?"

"I'll sneak into Stonegate Manor and find it. Lucas will go with me, won't you?"

He nodded eagerly, but Matthew looked furious. "No way. That's the most stupid idea I've ever heard."

"You're scared," Rosie taunted, roused enough to defy him.

"Am not."

"Prove it."

"I'm not scared of the stupid Wilders!" Matthew paused and stuck his hands in his jeans pockets. "All right. But there's no way you're going in without me, Rosie."

"And you're not going without *me*," she retorted, folding her arms. "Three musketeers?"

Matthew looked back at the rugged shoulder of the hill. The house was a bare grey shadow in the mist. "Two and a half musketeers," he said. "Okay. Tomorrow."

In those days, they did everything together. However burdensome Matthew found his younger siblings, he needed an army to lead, an admiring audience.

The next morning brought the sun pouring golden into their garden. Rosie hadn't slept, and bitterly resented the Wilder boys for ruining what should have been an idyllic day. Yet she was madly excited. Nothing now would stop them entering the forbidden realm, Stonegate Manor.

As they trod the paths through the woods, Rosie couldn't sense the Dusklands. The world was plainly three-dimensional, closed and solid. She kept thinking about the younger boy, Jonathan. She'd never seen anyone like him before. He'd been so pretty, like a cupid in a painting. She wondered what he'd meant when he looked at her. That he was sorry about his older brother's behavior? That he secretly wanted to be friends? Would they meet him again in the house? Would they meet *Sam*?

The thought spun her into knots of terror. The theft— although devastating—was only a symptom of the jeering malevolence she'd sensed when Sam had slid a cold fingertip onto her breastbone, to sever her from a beloved gift. As they climbed the hill, the sunlight wavered. Mist hung up here as if rolling from the house itself, turning every rock and tree into a ghost. Stonegate Manor loomed like a fortress with prison windows. She imagined hostile eyes watching, crossbows or rifles trained on the intruders.

At nine, she suspected that she knew very little about Aetherials. Her mind latched on to the idea that the Wilders were rarefied Aetheric lords, glaring icily down upon their subjects. A family of unearthly aristocrats, dwelling in a castle, so forbidding that even her father dared not approach them.

Around the rear of the house lay an informal garden with broad lawns, rhododendron bushes spilling over natural rock. There was no fence. She wished with all her might to turn into a fox—her namesake, an earth elemental—so that she could sneak into the house fearless and unseen; but it was only a wish.

A dog barked. Matthew grabbed her and Lucas by the arm, pressing them back into a waxy-leaved rhododendron. "If there's a guard dog, we can't do it," he whispered. Rosie saw he was anxious, and that unnerved her completely. Looking up at the heavy slate and granite bulk of the house, she felt overwhelmed.

No dogs appeared. When the bark came again, it sounded far away. A lawn lay silver-green between them and their destination. There were French windows in the center of the building and, near the left-hand corner, a back door.

"This is it," said Matthew. "Crouch down and run. Now!"

They sprinted across the uneven grass, skirting rocks, finally slamming into the stone wall of the fortress. Rosie couldn't get her breath, and her mouth was dry, sticky.

No one saw them. The place felt desolate. Only the house itself kept watch.

She'd imagined Matthew prizing open a window or breaking glass, but the door was unlocked. He pushed it open and they all walked in; as easy as that.

As they entered, she had the tangible feeling of crossing a threshold into a different realm. Everything felt cold and sharp. The sensation was so strong it made her dizzy. Behind her, Lucas kept treading on her heels. They entered a narrow hall with coats and boots; then a kitchen with old-fashioned units and a big oblong sink. Rosie was shocked at how shabby it looked compared with their warm and friendly kitchen at home. Leading from the kitchen was a corridor with stone walls and a bare lightbulb. They crept along the wall, as if that could make them magically invisible.

The corridor brought them into a great baronial hall, a frigid space so cavernous that they stopped in awe. Anxiously they scanned the galleries for hostile eyes. There was dark wood, grey stone, a huge dusty fireplace with crests carved above it, chilly daylight winking through leaded windows. Her hopes fell; they'd never find her treasure in this vast place.

"Where now?" she whispered.

Matthew answered at the top of his voice, "No need to whisper. There's no one home."

"Shush!" she gasped, horrified. "How do you know?"

"Can't you feel it? There'd be music or the TV on, or people talking. Nothing."

His voice echoed. "Shut up!" she hissed. "It'll be in his bedroom. That's where I'd hide it."

"Stairs," said Lucas, pointing.

The broad wooden flight creaked under them. Rosie felt the frosty whisper of the hostile realm all around them, like the Dusklands but cruel and cold. From the corner of her eye she saw a four-legged shadow pacing beside them; the impression was so clear that she turned in shock to look—and saw nothing there.

"What was that?" whispered Matthew, his bravado vanishing.

Upstairs, the house seemed all corridors, all arctic light on stone walls. How would they ever find the thief's bedroom? They'd be trapped here until they died. This was a terrible house and it hated them.

They turned a corner into another passage stretching to infinity before them. Rosie's dread of meeting Sam here became agonizing. The fear was out of all proportion, as if they might meet some horrifying spectral essence rather than an actual person. Again she glimpsed the half-seen shadow beasts around them. Lucas grabbed her hand. His was icy.

"Oh, shit," Matthew gasped, sounding completely terrified. "I don't like this. We have to get out."

She'd never seen him scared like that before. His terror was infectious. There was a faint noise from above, like claws scraping and a thin, animal moan. Then, from along the corridor, someone coughing or crying. They froze in their tracks as a figure stepped out of a doorway and stood glaring at them. Lucas let out a short, high yelp of shock.

It was a woman. A madwoman, Rosie realized a second later as she began to advance. Her face was pallid, her eyes terrible with menace and rage. Thick wavy black hair flowed around her shoulders. She wore black; a long skirt under an enveloping coat. In one hand she carried a suitcase that itself seemed full of menace, as if it contained a torturer's instruments.

As the apparition reached them, the case dropped from her hand and landed with a sharp thud. She must have seen their terror. She seemed to be drinking it in, Rosie thought, relishing it. She would have been beautiful, but for the terrible cold light in her face.

"Do you know where you are, child?" she said, staring at Rosie. "Is it the Spiral, Elfland, the land of Faerie? Or the dream realm, the Crystal Ring? Or Dumannios, realm of demons? All those circles overlap here. I used to call it home." Her gaze swept around the gallery. "See how cold this kingdom is. That isn't dust falling down from the rafters, it's ice. Leave while you can. Don't let him suck you in, or he'll keep you here until the blood freezes in your veins."

Rosie clearly saw four translucent black shapes around her; great dogs, gryphons, lions? There was no detail to them; they were simply dark hulks, ghostly and threatening. The moment stretched on, like a path into a realm of incomprehensible madness. This woman of pale skin and black hair was a sorceress who would lure children with candies and kindness . . . until the pretense evaporated, and her true ferocity blazed.

The sorceress stared from Rosie to Matthew to Lucas. She looked demented. Her green eyes shone bright and glassy. Rosie felt Lucas shaking, hanging onto her.

Then the woman gave a shake of her head and said, "Have you come to see my boys?" Her voice sounded hoarse. "I'm sorry, they're not here. They've gone back to school."

When they only stared, she said, "Did you hear me? You're Jessica's lot, aren't you?" None of them dared answer. "I haven't got time for this," she hissed. "You've had a wasted visit. Go home."

She stooped gracefully to pick up her case, starting towards them in the same movement. The spell broke and they fled. Matthew was gone first, oblivious of Rosie's and Luc's desperate efforts to catch up. The madwoman's quick sure footsteps echoed behind them all the way, and the four dark guardians flowed after them, herding them out. Along the frigid corridors they ran, down the creaking slope of the stairs, across the haunted cavernous hall, the passageway, the drab kitchen . . . down through the chill spectral heathland, empty-handed.

At home that evening, Rosie sat close to the fire crackling in the marble fireplace, but she couldn't get warm. The welt on her neck stung. Everything was ordinary: cooking scents wafting from the kitchen; her father browsing a newspaper, his feet stretched out and a glass of red wine in one hand; six o'clock news chattering on the television. Matthew was frowning over his homework, Lucas reading a book. Rosie sat shivering on the rug, clutching her knees to her chest until heat burned the back of her hands.

What a relief to be in her own home. She'd never appreciated it so intensely before.

The most frightening thing of all had been Matthew's plain fear. He was supposed to be the brave leader, yet he'd fallen apart. Afterwards, to cover his embarrassment, he'd been abrupt and dismissive, pretending nothing had happened.

She longed to tell her father everything, but words wouldn't come. She couldn't bear to admit she'd lost his gift. It had meant the world to her. She'd wanted to wear it to show her father how pleased she was; now he might think she didn't care, and that was so far from the truth it nearly broke her heart.

Auberon was the center of their world. He owned a house-building company, Fox Homes, as befitted his deep connection to the elements of earth and rock. No one who worked for him would suspect he was not human. His customers, however, found walking into one of his houses like coming home—as if they sensed the age-old roots of the earth itself through the house. They couldn't leave, but had to buy. That was Auberon's magic. It had made him very wealthy.

Their mother Jessica was a musician, teaching harp, guitar and piano. Once she had been lead singer of a folk-rock band, Green Spiral. Rosie had heard all her CDs, but the group was long disbanded. Apart from the odd few notes while teaching, Jessica didn't sing anymore. No one could persuade her to sing a complete song. Nevertheless, Rosie's school friends regarded Jessica as fantastically glamorous.

Although they were of ancient blood, they lived as humans on the surface world. We must not put on airs and graces, Auberon insisted. Special, but not superior—a contradiction, but Rosie could only accept it.

They called themselves Aetherial, and sometimes Vaethyr—meaning the ones who lived on Vaeth, the ancient name for Earth—and she'd heard whispers of a much older name, *Estalyr*. There were others in Cloudcroft, although none of her own age—unless she counted Jon Wilder, which she couldn't, since she didn't know him. Other Aetherial families sometimes came to the house for private meetings with her parents. It was only when she saw them in groups that Rosie glimpsed an aura that she didn't normally see in her own family. An indefinable glow; a knowing, feline shine in the eyes. Whatever they did or talked about, Aetherial children were not party to it. Rosie could wait. She didn't feel ready to explore these brooding, unfathomable layers of secrecy.

She remembered once seeing a book in her father's study, with a design embossed in silver on the cover; a five-pointed star with a spiral behind it, like a star caught on a cobweb. There had been a strange word at each point of the star. She hadn't seen the book since, but recalled the arcane image with a delicious shiver.

She heard the phone ring in the hall, her mother's voice murmuring for a few minutes.

"Bron?" said Jessica in the doorway. Her golden hair was pinned up in a messy halo, her clothes gracefully bohemian. "That was Phyllida. Incredible piece of gossip going around the village."

"Oh yes?" As her parents looked at each other, Rosie watched them closely. Her mother's grey eyes were concerned, her father's brown ones patient but guarded. It was one of those meaningful secret looks they were always exchanging.

Her mother spoke in soft disbelief. "Apparently Ginny Wilder walked out on Lawrence this morning. She went while he was taking the boys back to school. So . . . she's finally done it."

Auberon knew something was wrong, even before the ceremony began.

There were nearly two hundred Vaethyr gathered in the warm summer night. Cloaked and hooded in the subtle colors of dusk, masked with stylized animal faces, they waited near the top of a hill in a dip that formed a natural amphitheater. Firefly lights glimmered around them. Aetherials had gathered like this, on sacred nights, for centuries.

Auberon waited with one arm around Jessica's waist. They wore fox masks; his was embellished with swirls of garnet and jet, hers surmounted by crescent moons. Her sister Phyllida stood close by with her husband, Comyn, both wearing the gold-and-onyx faces of bulls. Amid a sea of jeweled heraldic masks—all focused on Freya's Crown, the rocky outcrop of the summit—they awaited the Gatekeeper.

The Dusklands gave the landscape an inky cast and turned the stars to veils of frost. The beauty felt fragile with tension. Living like humans for so much of the time, it was easy to forget they were anything more; but on nights like this, Auberon felt the shimmer of power all around him. He sensed Vaethyr forms trembling to change shape, perhaps to stretch great wings or simply to glow with supernatural light; Vaethyr perceptions expanding to see through multiple layers of reality. His own body ached to unfold into a more imposing shape, that of a forest deity, stronger and wiser than his human form . . . They needed this ceremony, in order to reconnect with their true, ancient selves. After dancing in the beauty of Elysion, they would bring back its healing energies to Earth, as if trailing cloaks of green and golden light in their wake.

If Lawrence ever came.

This was the Night of the Summer Stars, the great ritual that fell every seven years, when the Great Gates to the inner realms would be thrown open. Many times in the past, Auberon had witnessed the heel of the Gatekeeper's staff striking the stone, the rocks of Freya's Crown shining and shifting as the Great Gates opened. He'd relished the crunch of a hazelnut on his tongue as he stepped through the infinite archway to the Otherworld. There were only adults here. When his children reached sixteen they, too, would be initiated.

Auberon frowned. Rosie and Lucas seemed happy to accept their Aetherial blood. Matthew did not. No one had pinned him down to a reason. Perhaps it was teenage rebellion that made him roll his eyes and turn away if Aetherial matters were mentioned. *Perhaps,* thought Auberon, *it's my fault. Have I told him too much, or too little? How is a parent to judge?*

Freya's Crown remained a dark, volcanic bulk against the stars. The Gatekeeper did not come. The crowd began to grow restless.

"Something's definitely wrong," said Auberon. "Lawrence hasn't been right since Ginny left."

"She left him because he's *never* been right," said Jessica.

"And should never have taken up the staff," said Comyn, his voice muffled by the bull mask. "I suppose you know the Lychgate has been closed against us for three weeks?"

Lychgate was their name for the small portal that was always open, a tiny doorway within the Great Gates. "I didn't know," said Auberon.

"No, because you're too busy with earthly business as usual," Comyn said gruffly. "What the devil is Lawrence playing at? Right, that's it, I'm going to find him."

"No," Auberon said firmly. He knew Comyn's temper. "Let me."

"There's no need." A figure rose up beside the rocks. The voice came from behind the haughty beak of a hawk. "I'm here."

The Gatekeeper stood before them in full majesty, cloaked in black, blue and white, the applewood staff shining in his left hand, his hawk face that of a glaring deity. Four wolfish silhouettes padded after him. Silence lay on the Vaethyr, a collective held breath. Lawrence raised gloved hands and spoke. "My friends, the rite of the Summer Stars cannot take place. The Great Gates cannot be opened tonight. Go home."

There was a ripple of dismay. It grew louder as Lawrence began to turn away. Comyn's angry tones carried over the rest, "What's going on?" No answer. "Gatekeeper! Don't you dare walk away! You've no right to deny us access! Hoi!" Comyn's voice rose. "Who d'you think you are? You're a doorkeeper, Lawrence. Do your job!"

Jessica made a noise of agonized embarrassment in her throat. Lawrence stopped. Auberon saw the vulturine shoulders rising. He turned to face them again. "A doorkeeper? Let's say a concierge, then. My job is to protect you." The voice behind the mask was hollow.

"From what?"

"The inner realms are not always safe. You know that." He seemed to falter. "At this time there are disturbances of energy . . . Storms."

"We'll be the judges of the danger," Comyn retorted. "Let us in."

The four shadows arranged themselves around Lawrence, becoming four corners of a square that contained him.

"I'm not your servant." Lawrence Wilder's voice grew hoarse. "I was appointed Gatekeeper by the ancients of the Spiral Court. I am answerable only to them. I decide when it's safe to open the portals; that is my duty. It's in my gift to judge, not yours."

"What storms?" called Auberon.

His reasonable question only seemed to make Lawrence angrier. "I have no choice but to seal the Gates for your own safety. Disperse."

The crowd swayed, defiant. Comyn squared up aggressively even though Lawrence, on higher ground, towered over him. Auberon stepped forward, hoping to calm things before a riot ensued. "Lawrence, please. This is a sacred night. To deny us is a devastating breach of tradition. It's not just for our own benefit—the Earth needs the flow of Elysian energy as much as we do."

The impassive raptor face turned on Auberon. Lawrence seemed to stare down from a great height. "What, you think this will starve the Earth of magical blessings? Coming from you, intent as you are upon covering the landscape with brick and concrete, that is absolutely priceless."

Auberon drew back, stung. "At the very least, please explain."

"I owe you no explanation." His voice rose, fierce and rasping. "Have you all grown so arrogant that you cannot trust the authority placed here to protect you?"

"You've no authority!" Comyn tore off his mask and yelled, "How long have we known you'd pull a stunt like this? Open and stand aside!"

There was a pause. To Auberon's eyes, Lawrence seemed to waver as if in a moment of panic or doubt. Others began to shout too, only to fall silent as the Gatekeeper drew himself straight again. Then he held the white staff aloft and his voice cracked out, "As you wish it!"

Lawrence extended the staff and touched it to the flank of Freya's Crown. Lightning tongued the rock. A thin black split appeared.

"There," said the hawk mask. "The Lychgate is open. Those who want to pass through, go now, quickly. Be warned, however, that I will shut and bar it behind you, and the way shall not be opened again until I deem it safe—which may be a month, a decade, or a century. Your choice."

No one moved. Not even Comyn, who stood trembling. Auberon's and Jessica's arms tightened around each other. The collective aura of Vaethyr power seemed to shrink back, leaving them all diminished.

"I can only assume," Lawrence said thinly, "that, from your silence, you have decided to put your faith in me after all." With that, he broke the applewood staff across his knee. The snap was like a detonation. The portal slammed shut at the same instant.

"Now you will leave," he said.

Around him, the shapes of his four guardian *dysir* were swelling in size, becoming monstrous. Auberon had never seen such a sight before. If the change was illusory, it was still unutterably menacing. They became hellhounds, with glowing eyes and jaws dripping fire. The gathered Vaethyr began to retreat in shock. It appeared their Gatekeeper had declared war. Unthinkable.

The soft blues of the night turned to harsh, red-rimmed black. Lawrence was drawing down the nightmare realm of Dumannios around them, filling the air with fire and demons.

"Go." His cloak became a flapping wing as he raised his arms. "I offered you a choice and you have chosen. Now go!"

Comyn stood his ground for a few moments, until a *dysir* swung its great head at him, drooling flame. Even he could not withstand the illusion. With a curse he caught Phyllida's hand, and they fled. As they went, Phyll looked back over her shoulder at Jessica, the frozen face of her bull mask perfectly conveying blank bewilderment. Auberon reached for Jessica's hand, began to draw her away.

The flight seemed to take place in slow motion. Turning in to the flow of Vaethyr streaming away down the hill, they ran in horrified panic and disbelief; and whenever they glanced back, the four huge hounds loomed like glowing coals, filling the sky, watching over their frantic flight.

2

Rosie in Wonderland

For years afterwards, Rosie had recurring dreams about Stonegate Manor. Sometimes it loomed above her, a glacial castle without doors or even the smallest window to let her in. In other dreams, she would be inside, lost and frightened. Corridors changed, rooms moved. She searched, always with dread that a faceless presence lay in wait for her. When she tried to escape, in an ecstasy of panic, doors opened onto walls or staircases collapsed. Never once in her dreams did she escape the house.

Five years had passed since the failed invasion of Stonegate. Since then, Rosie had glimpsed the house and its inhabitants only from afar. During school holidays, the boys were abroad with their father, or sent away somewhere, or unseen behind the walls of the manor. A few times, she'd been startled by a black limousine sweeping past, and realized with a shiver of fascination that the strangers behind the tinted windows must be Lawrence, Jonathan and Samuel.

One encounter had been enough to leave her with a scar, as if someone had tried to cut her throat.

There had been a horrible day in the winter following her ninth birthday. Matthew had come home bruised and bloody, his face swollen and knuckles raw. He'd fallen off his bike; that was the story he mumbled to his parents. Later, Rosie had found him in a corner of the rose garden, huddling behind the frosted skeleton of a hedge. "Did Sam do this?" she asked warily.

His face was stone, his eyes red with angry tears. "Leave me alone, Rose."

"Oh, Matt, I asked you not to!"

"Sod off!" he growled. "I met him in the lane. I demanded your necklace back. He laughed. We fought. End of story."

She knew that if Matthew had won, he would have been strutting despite his injuries. Anything she said—angry or sympathetic—would only compound his misery. It was all there in his posture: utter, anguished humiliation. "Come in, it's freezing," she said. "I won't tell anyone."

"I'll get him back for this," he snarled, wincing with pain. With an ocean of suppressed rage, he added, "You keep away from him, Ro. He's crazy."

Five years carried those events away from them. Rosie was fourteen now, Matthew nineteen. Looking back, it seemed that something had changed around that time; she remembered her parents being gloomy and preoccupied, serious-looking groups of Aetherials coming and going from the house and Uncle Comyn arguing with her father . . . They'd never told her what it was about. It had passed, but she couldn't help associating the memory with spectral, impenetrable Stonegate.

And then came the invitation.

Rosie was in the sitting room in her party finery. She held the oblong of creamy card between her fingertips and read, for the tenth time, the curling italics.

To Auberon and Jessica, Rosie, Matthew and Lucas.
Lawrence and Sapphire Wilder request the pleasure
of your company
at Stonegate Manor for a Yuletide Masquerade.
Date: Saturday 17th December
Time: 8pm.
Dress: Festive. Masks desirable but not compulsory.
Bring your friends, all welcome!

On the back, a handwritten note had been added. *"Please do come! L. tells me it's been too long and I'm dying to meet you all. It will be very informal and lots of fun. Let's start a festive tradition! Love, Sapphire."*

"I still think it's weird," said Rosie. "You don't speak to them for years and then they invite us to a party?"

"What's weird is the words *fun* and *Stonegate Manor* anywhere near each other." Matthew leaned in the doorway, blond hair flopping over his forehead. "They'd better have lager. I'm not drinking anything with fruit floating on top."

"God forbid any fruit should pass your lips, Matt," said Jessica. She stood at the mantelpiece mirror as she tried to pin up her unruly hair, sliding hairpins in, impatiently pulling them out again. "I'd hate a vitamin to sneak inside you in the Trojan horse of alcohol. Ouch! Oh, bugger."

"Mum, stop messing," said Rosie. "Why don't you leave it loose?"

"Because I don't want the new lady of the manor thinking I'm a hippie chick."

"But you *are* a hippie chick," Rosie said, giggling.

"Rosie, you are terrible." A smile hovered on her mouth but she gave Rosie the comb. "Matthew, make sure this child drinks nothing stronger than gin tonight, won't you?"

He rolled his eyes. "Oh, I'll watch her," he said ominously. It was rare to see him out of a rugby shirt, but his suit gave him the look of an elegant, spoiled undergraduate. "We driving up?"

"Well, I'm not walking up that hill in these heels. Will your friends be there, Rosie?"

"Mel and Faith, I hope. There," said Rosie, happy at last with the gilded flow of her mother's hair. "You look amazing."

Jessica was splendid in a white medieval-style dress with embroidered gold panels and fishtail sleeves. Rosie's dress was of similar style, in burgundy velvet that echoed the red-wine glow of her hair. "So do you, dear."

"Apart from the makeup she's troweled on," said Matt, "for that fourteen-going-on-twenty look."

"It's a tiny bit of lip gloss and eyeliner!" Rosie retorted. "No more than you're wearing."

"Ha ha." Matthew grinned. "Yes, I'll bet the Wilders would *love* the pleasure of our company, all right—if the company in question was Fox Homes. I don't trust 'em further than our cat can spit."

"Go upstairs and see if your dad and Lucas are ready, would you?" said Jessica.

Matt obeyed, hands in pockets. Jessica turned to Rosie and spoke quietly. "It's not true that we haven't spoken for years. Your father and Lawrence are perfectly civil. Just not close, that's all. Lawrence is . . ." She frowned and trailed off.

"Have you met Sapphire?" Rosie asked.

"Not yet. He was away for ages, then turned up a few weeks ago with a new wife. It's strange. After Virginia left, I never thought he'd marry again. Never."

"Why not?"

Jessica's full lips thinned. "Lawrence is a recluse. If this woman's persuaded him to throw parties and start festive traditions, she must have worked some kind of miracle upon him."

In Cloudcroft, Aetherial festivals were often held alongside human ones; a natural merging, since Vaethyr liked to celebrate the changing seasons as humans did. The death-and-resurrection cycle of the year, the sacred dance into the heart of the Spiral and out again, the sun's rebirth in December, the arrival of spring or the riches of harvest—Earth and Aetherial realms, although separate, still lay closely interwoven.

Auberon swung the car between two sentinels of rough-hewn granite and onto a driveway that swept uphill between rhododendrons. Cars lined the sides, so they had to park some way down and walk the rest. The air was chill and sharp with drizzle. Other guests were converging on the house. Rosie could smell rain on their coats.

She looked up at the house and shivered. Seen from this new angle, the manor was no less imposing. It reared into the night, but the leaded windows were aglow. Anxiety coiled in her heart.

"Hey, Rosie," whispered Lucas, pulling her arm so they dropped behind their parents and brother. "Remember that time we broke in?"

"Yes, I still have nightmares about it."

"Me too," he said.

"Don't say anything, will you?"

"Course I won't." He looked solemnly up at the house. "What's with our parents and the Wilders? They go all thin-lipped and huffy when Lawrence Wilder is mentioned."

Rosie spoke close to his ear. "I don't know. All I can make out is that they think they're too superior to associate with anyone, human or Aetherial. Dad hates that."

"It must be more, though, don't you reckon?" said Luc. "There's an ocean of things we're not allowed to ask about until we're, like, fifty years old."

"You noticed that?" Rosie laughed. She was constantly startled by Lucas's perceptiveness. Intuition shone in his eyes. He was growing into a beautiful youth, with porcelain skin and black-brown hair. He had a quality of inner stillness and innocence, and not a cruel bone in his body. Rosie was proud of him. Everyone loved Lucas.

Light from the broad, stone-pillared portico flooded out to capture them. Auberon, with his black beard and twinkling eyes, his sweater patterned with holly and red berries, was like a dark Santa Claus, a Holly King. "Masks!" called Jessica, turning.

Rosie felt the cool satin lining grow warm against her face as her mother slipped the mask onto her. It covered eyes and nose, making it hard to breathe. Through the eye slits she saw her family transformed. They each had the muzzle of an exotic fox with red-silk fur, slanted eyes, black nose. The eyes were outlined with gold and red crystals, the ears tipped with jet.

Rosie grinned. Matthew suddenly pulled off his own mask and said, "This is daft. I'm not wearing it."

"Oh, Matthew!" said Jessica.

"As you wish," Auberon said lightly. "Come on, troops."

They passed under the porch and into the light. An intense atmosphere enveloped them. Thrumming, heated air, shifting light, voices, the church-scent of stone threaded with the fragrance of pine needles; all coalescing in a great shimmering veil of sensation. The threshold of another world.

The last time Rosie had seen the grand reception hall, it had been desolate. Now it was lit with thousands of sparkling fairy lights. Four massive Christmas trees, glittering and glowing, stood as high as the galleries that lined the heights of the hall. Candles gleamed on the linen and silver of long buffet tables. There were masses of guests in costume or cocktail dress, fabrics shimmering in the softly flattering light.

When she began to notice animal faces scattered among the human ones, her heart skipped in excitement. Unknown jeweled eyes glanced her way from the symbolic visages of cats, hares, reptiles. She recognized most of the Vaethyr clans from Cloudcroft—among them the Staggs, the Tullivers, the copper-haired Lyon family—but she knew little about them. Aetherials kept their children strictly apart from adult mysteries.

As the crowd parted, she saw four figures at the far end of the hall, holding court before a huge stone fireplace. Elusive Aetherials who had haunted her dreams for years. Lawrence Wilder and his family.

There was an elegant woman in a figure-hugging white dress, her hair a sleek dark brown waterfall almost to her hips. With her stood a tall, imposing man in a cobalt-blue Nehru suit. Black hair, chin held high, long fingers slightly clawed with tension.

Beside them, the two boys that Rosie had so dreaded

encountering were now lean young men. The younger one
was in a white shirt and black trousers. His chestnut hair
had grown long and hung in shiny waves on his shoulders.
The older one, as if he couldn't be bothered and wanted
everyone to know it, wore faded black jeans, a charcoal
T-shirt with a tie-dye pattern on it and a spiky steel chain
around his neck. There had been whispers of him in trouble with the police, but no one knew the full story.

The woman was unmasked and smiling, but the Wilder
males wore the faces of hawks, silver and haughty.

"This is weird," said Jessica, tucking her hand through
Auberon's arm.

"It should be interesting," he murmured from the side of
his mouth. "You okay, Jess?"

"All ready with the smiley politeness," she answered.

The walk gave Rosie a vision of dignitaries visiting a
foreign court. When the two families met, there was a moment of ritual; an inclination of heads—then all masks were
removed in a flourish.

The legendary Lawrence Wilder stood revealed. He had
the same emphatic, stark features as his son Sam—handsome,
but hard and threatening with it—and glacial eyes, thick
ebony hair swept back from a high forehead and cheekbones. Rosie couldn't believe he was real.

"Auberon," he said. His voice was deep and quiet. "Jessica. I'm so glad you came."

Her father leaned in to shake hands. "Happy Christmas,
Lawrence. Yuletide greetings, blessings of the sun's rebirth, and all that. It's been too long."

"Indeed it has. Allow me to introduce my wife, Sapphire."

Sapphire was the antithesis of Lawrence, all smiles and
quick movement, glossy hair swinging around her shoulders.
Blazing white-rainbow gemstones flashed on her cleavage.
Matthew couldn't take his eyes off her. Rosie was tempted to
poke him so he would shut his mouth.

"It's wonderful to meet you all . . . heard so much about
you . . . Don't you all look splendid?" She came forward

with air kisses, her fingers stroking them like butterfly feelers. Despite the cut-glass perfection of her English, there was an exotic trace of accent that suggested it was not her first language. "Matthew, so handsome . . . oh, Rosie, such lovely hair . . . and Lucas. What a fine young man."

Jessica and Auberon were plainly startled by this overture, but responded in good heart. There was a moment, when Jessica leaned in to kiss her, that Sapphire's smile slipped and Rosie heard her say, "I'm sorry?"—then the moment was lost in the general chatter. Meanwhile, Lawrence and the two boys stood back, detached. They were unreadable.

"My sons, Samuel and Jonathan," said Lawrence. "I don't believe you've met, at least not formally."

There was a round of handshaking that Rosie couldn't avoid. First came Lawrence's icy impersonal grip, then Jon's, soft and shy. Rosie didn't want to touch Sam, but she had no choice. She looked away as she felt his alien hand in hers, bony and hard; felt his eyes slipping over her, chips of green-blue ice. It was over quickly. The world didn't end.

When Matthew and Sam shook hands, they held the grip a little too long and she saw the tension of their mouths, their faces tilting belligerently towards each other. Matthew was a good six-footer now, fit from rugby. Sam was a couple of inches shorter and somewhat leaner, but in the war of aggressive stares, he won; his eyes held all the amusement of a hardened gangster.

"I can't believe such close neighbors never see each other," Sapphire said, placing possessive hands on her stepsons' shoulders. "Ours are always away at school, poor things."

"I like my family around me, where they belong," said Auberon. "Nothing wrong with the local schools, you know. Excellent sixth form at Ashvale; Matthew got all the grades he needed for university."

"Oh, what are you studying?" Sapphire leaned towards

Matt, passionately interested. Her perfume wafted over them.

"Architecture," he stammered.

"Sooner he graduates, the better," said Auberon. "I need him on my team."

"Oh, so Fox Homes is a real family firm, how marvelous. People like yourself and Lawrence are in a position to be such great benefactors to the community. Well, do help yourselves to drinks, won't you?" Sapphire gently pointed them at the buffet tables. "We'll talk later."

"Looking forward to it," said Auberon.

"What do you think?" Jessica asked as they moved to the drinks table. There were bottles of wine and champagne in gleaming rows, huge crystal bowls of jewel-red punch, uniformed caterers poised to serve. Rosie spotted her friends, Mel and Faith, and waved.

"Lawrence hasn't changed," said Auberon, passing cups of punch around. "All this is just his new wife being nosy."

"Not *us* being nosy, oh no," Jessica laughed.

"She's very glamorous, isn't she?" Rosie put in. Matthew grabbed a bottle of beer and was scanning the crowd.

"Very," said Jessica as they moved away from the table. "She's wearing about half a million pounds' worth of Elfstones around her neck. She's making a fantastic show, but does she know what she's let herself in for?"

"Gossip?" said Aunt Phyllida, gliding up to them in an ivory Grecian-style dress, her gold bull mask hanging over her arm. Groomed and poised with glossy caramel hair, she was the opposite of bohemian Jessica. Phyll was the village doctor and had an open, no-nonsense manner that made Rosie feel shy around her. In her spare time she sang opera, and seemed to look down on Jessica's folk-rock leanings. Rosie wondered if that was why her mother had stopped singing.

Jessica greeted her sister with a kiss. "You're talking about the replacement, aren't you?" Phyll murmured from the side of her mouth. "Human. Definitely."

Meanwhile, Phyll's husband, Comyn, crinkled his eyes at

Rosie and Lucas; it was the closest he ever came to a smile. He was a farmer, a wiry man with Celtic-pale skin and dark eyebrows; black hair cropped short, and watchful green eyes. He wasn't bad-looking as uncles went, Rosie thought, but so serious and intense. No one quite knew what Phyll saw in him. To most people, he was a fearsome misery, but he always had a friendly word for Rosie and Luc.

"You agree, she's not Aetherial?" said Jessica. She and Auberon exchanged glances. "That was our feeling, wrong aura, but you can't always tell for certain. I could be mistaken."

"You're not," said Phyll. "No color change in the Elfstones? She's mortal, all right."

"Even odder," Jessica said, with an edge. "Lawrence is such a purist. I never thought he would look twice at a human."

"I never could work the devil out at all," Comyn said grimly. "And he'll have hell to pay if he carries on like—"

"Comyn," said Auberon, interrupting. "Not tonight."

"Perhaps he's gathered us for an announcement?" said Phyll.

Rosie took the chance to slip away into the company of her girlfriends. She heard her uncle complaining, "In the old days this would have been a full-blooded winter ritual that meant something. Now we're reduced to ruddy cocktail parties," and then his voice faded into the general murmur.

High up on one of the galleries, Rosie and her friends commanded a bird's-eye view of the hall.

Mel was skinny and pretty, with platinum-bright hair and dewy skin. In khaki pants and a rainbow T-shirt she looked exquisite. Faith wore a charity-shop floral dress, her mouse-brown hair scraped back in a ponytail, spectacles perched on her nose. Rosie's friends were human, but next to Mel she felt dowdy and lacking in Aetherial glamour.

"What's with the fox face and medieval getup?" said Mel. "You didn't tell us it was fancy dress."

"Oh, it was optional," Rosie said, touching the mask that hung at her hip. "It's a family tradition thing. Like announcing, 'Here comes the Fox family.' I can leave it off now."

The party was growing loud beneath them, music competing with conversation. Heat shimmered up from below. Her velvet dress was sticking to her.

"I've always said your family's weird." Mel grinned. "Nice, but weird."

"I wish mine were weird in a *nice* way," said Faith.

"Yeah, I'm lucky," Rosie said quietly. "Really lucky."

"I thought there'd be more decent boys here." Mel was craning over the balustrade. "See anything you fancy?"

"Honestly, Mel, you never stop," Faith remarked in admiration. Mel was already on her third or fourth boyfriend. Rosie and Faith weren't ready to do more than spectate and dream. "My mum used to be Ginny Wilder's cleaner, years ago," Faith added, looking at the high gothic shadows of the rafters. "She reckoned this place was haunted. That's why she quit." Rosie had heard that Ginny had in fact sacked Faith's mother for drinking on the job, but she said nothing.

"Hey, *he's* not bad," said Mel.

Rosie saw Sapphire chatting to her parents far below, hair swinging around her creamy shoulders as she laughed. There was no sign of Lawrence. She looked for Jonathan but couldn't see him, either. "Which one?"

"The guy in the grey T-shirt. He had a hawk mask on earlier. Sam, is it?"

"Ew, no, not him," Rosie exclaimed.

"You are kidding," said Mel. "He's *gorgeous.*"

Rosie turned her back to the party and folded her arms. "Only if you like psychopaths. Sam's a really nasty piece of work." She pushed her hair back to show the scar on her neck. "He did this to me."

Mel was taken aback. "You said a twig hit you in the woods."

"I know, that's what I told my folks. Actually Sam ripped a chain off my neck. When Matt tried to get it back, Sam nearly killed him." She shuddered at the memory. "Seriously, Mel, don't. You only have to look at him to see he's not right."

Mel looked horrified. "Come on, it's just a laugh. Okay . . . what about that guy with your brother?"

Rosie turned, saw Matthew below with a ginger-blond man; similar height, broader build. "That's his mate, Alastair Duncan. They're at uni together. He's okay."

"He's more my type. Nice and rugged."

"He's a bit old for you."

Mel shrugged and grinned. "So? We're only window-shopping. Come on Rosie, there must be someone you fancy."

She surveyed the scene, earnestly searching. "Nah. Don't think so."

"Can I tell you who I like?" Faith said unexpectedly. Her voice was intense and tremulous with embarrassment. Her cheeks flushed pink. "Matthew."

"Good grief," said Rosie. "As in, my brother?"

"I do, I like him. It's stupid, I know. But I think he's fantastic."

Rosie gave a hollow laugh. "You don't have to live with him."

"Don't worry, he'd never look at me in a thousand years."

"Oh, Fai," Mel sighed. "You know, if you colored your hair, and wore trendier clothes—"

"I couldn't. My father would kill me."

Rosie couldn't face another session of Mel advising, and Faith finding a zillion reasons why she couldn't change. "I'm going to find the loo. Won't be long."

As she walked into semidarkness, she heard Faith's voice fading on a question, "Mel, have you ever, like, you know, *gone all the way*?"

Rosie found the bathroom without difficulty, but when she came out, she got lost. There was one broad corridor after another, high windows letting in chilly starlight. No sight or sound of the party, only desolation. Everything seemed to shift, as if the house had taken off its mask. Duskland strangeness prickled her skin, sinister in a way she'd never felt outside these walls. Prowling beasts seemed to stalk her, only to vanish when she looked round.

She stopped, took a deep breath and retraced her steps. This time she turned in to a different corridor; this one held a row of bedroom doors standing ajar. It was familiar. She saw a ghost image of Ginny Wilder, storming along with her mad black hair and her suitcase.

Possessed by curiosity, she tiptoed to the first door and peered into a huge room with a four-poster bed and muslin curtains flowing across the windows. It must be the master bedroom, where Lawrence and Sapphire slept. The next room was plain, with a computer desk and shelves full of files. Then a library with towering bookshelves, tables and armchairs set in acres of empty space.

Rosie stepped in. It felt cold and empty, all dust and moonlight; like one of her dreams. She went to the window to convince herself the real world still lay outside. The voices and footsteps came softly, hardly giving her enough warning to hide. At the last moment she pressed herself into an alcove, heart racing.

"Whiskey?"

"Very small one. I'm driving. Well, how are you?" It was her father's warm deep voice. "You know, I miss the talks we used to have."

The second voice was measured, gentle but icy. "You're very gracious, considering all the circumstances." Through a gap in the bookshelf that concealed her, she saw Lawrence and her father, clinking whiskey tumblers. "That always was a commendable trait in you, Auberon, one I lack."

"So what's changed? Why the party?"

"It's Sapphire, of course," Lawrence answered. "Convinced me that I should reopen the lines of communication."

"I'm glad." There was a silence. She saw her father with his arms folded, shuffling his feet. "How did you meet her?"

"Oh, she was working for me." Lawrence spoke with brisk distaste for personal questions. "Marketing manager . . . she's very good . . . we became close."

"She's lovely, but I wouldn't have seen her as your type. Not old blood, eh?"

"Quite. We've absolutely nothing in common." A glint of amusement showed through the ice. "Except that we each like our own space . . . somehow it works."

"Didn't even know you and Ginny had divorced."

"Well, I was as surprised by Sapphire as no doubt you are. But she has been . . . good for me."

"Obviously. Does she know . . . who you are?"

"I told her everything."

"Good heavens." Another silence. "We've been wondering if the party meant a change—a thaw—a special announcement, or—"

Lawrence interrupted, "Nothing's changed, in fact." Rosie saw the eyes shining in the imperious face like flecks of light in a glacier. "I know what you want to ask, and the answer's still no."

"Lawrence, it's been five years."

"An eyeblink to Aetherials."

"Not to our children."

"And it's for the safety of the next generation that I do this. It's still not safe. I can't guarantee it ever will be again."

"Never?" Auberon sounded anxious.

"There's nothing I can do. It's too dangerous."

"Still?"

"You have no idea."

"If you'd be specific about the danger, perhaps I could help?" No answer. Auberon exhaled. "Since you refuse to speak to them, it's me they come to demanding answers. All I can explain is that there are energy shifts between realms, like earthquakes or storms, and until you decide it's safe, we must be patient. I don't even convince myself. Is it so hard to tell me the truth?"

"That is the truth," came the soft chill of the voice.

"And what about the inner realms? I wonder if the Aelyr are as distressed as the Vaethyr about this? Are they in danger, too? Why doesn't the Spiral Court act?"

"A lot of questions," said Lawrence. He paused to sip his drink. "I *am* the Spiral Court's authority when it comes to the Gates. Keeping them closed keeps both sides safe. It keeps the flood still, as it were, like a dam. Since you ask, I don't suppose the Aelyr much care, since they take little interest in Earth. It's only the Vaethyr who insist on making this undignified fuss."

"Because it's gone on so long, and we need to visit our home realms," said Auberon.

"Then they should have gone through when I gave them the chance!" Lawrence's gleaming eyes narrowed. "Does no one believe me? Not even you?"

"Strangely . . . yes, I do," Auberon said heavily. "I don't know why. Intuition tells me that you would not do such a bizarre thing, except for a genuine reason."

"Thank you for that, at least."

"And I hope I'm wrong! God knows, Lawrence, I've supported you—but this isn't the answer they'll want to hear out there. They'll be clamoring for different news. They think it's why you've invited them tonight!"

Lawrence Wilder spoke in the same remote tone, unmoved. "And they'll swiftly find out that no, in fact, they were invited because they deserve the courtesy of an apology."

"And I suppose I must be the one to deliver it. Again." Her father's anger startled Rosie; it was so rare. "They won't easily forgive what you did that night. It caused outrage."

"It was the only thing that would make them leave. If a

child puts its hand near a fire, you shout at it first and explain afterwards."

The two men glared at each other. "This explanation has been a long time coming," said Auberon. "So I get all the flak, while you retreat behind castle walls. You really presume a lot on friendship."

"I know." Lawrence dropped his gaze. "And I'm grateful, Auberon, but you've done enough. This time I'm going to speak to them myself. Support me, please. Trust me. It's all I ask."

Auberon looked down at his own tapping foot. "Of course," he said at last. "Out of respect for Liliana—what choice do I have?"

They finished their drinks and left. Weak with relief, Rosie waited a few seconds before following, but when she reached the corridor, she found it deserted. She came to another bedroom, this one overflowing with posters of Pre-Raphaelite paintings, with framed photographs and books everywhere.

Jon's room.

Rosie stepped into the doorway, aware that she was trespassing, not to mention being insufferably nosy. The room felt warm; it drew her like an oasis of sanity in a hostile land. She longed to go in, to touch the satin of the bedspread and the peacock feathers in a vase beside the bed.

Terrified of getting caught, she dragged herself away and went on.

Next she found an odd little turning staircase of eight stone steps, and at the top, a gothic-arched doorway into another bedroom. She glimpsed the shapes of bed, wardrobe, a poster of some wild-haired rock band. This could only be Sam's room.

A perverse impulse made her step over the threshold. Somewhere in this room might be . . .

"Looking for something?"

The voice, casually menacing, made her jump violently. She turned. Sam stood blocking her escape. His face seemed older than his seventeen years, all severe chiseled lines. He leaned casually across the narrow stairwell with one hand braced on the opposite wall, the lean muscular angles of his shoulders and arm forming a barrier. He was so close she could smell the faint spice of his sweat, and some patchouli-scented soap or shampoo he'd used. His hair was short, disheveled, dark at the roots and tipped with bleach at the ends. He leaned down, his face almost touching hers, staring hard into her eyes.

Rosie stepped back. Sam's glare broke into a mocking smile. She wouldn't have been greatly surprised to see the white teeth turn into vampire fangs. Her heart was stumbling over itself, but she was too proud to let him see her fear.

"Yes, I am, actually," she said, folding her arms. Her attempt at authority came out sounding, at least to her, like the bravado of a twelve-year-old.

"And what is that, actually?" said Sam.

She raised herself to her full five-foot-two and tilted her chin. "You stole something from me."

"What?" He had the nerve to be affronted.

"You do know who I am, don't you?"

"Yes, Rosie Fox, I know exactly who you are."

"So don't pretend you've forgotten!" She was vibrating with anger and emotion that had built up for years to this moment. "You took a chain with a heart on it. You ripped it right off my neck. Maybe you've stolen so much stuff in your time that you really *don't* remember!"

"Oh, bloody hell," he said. He folded his arms, turned his face away from her. "That was years ago!"

"That doesn't make it all right! I was nine!"

"Right." His eyes narrowed, gleaming with amusement. "And that's all you've done since you were nine, is it? Thought about me and plotted revenge?"

"No," Rosie said through her teeth. "I've had much better things and people to think about than you."

"I bet."

She glared at Sam, her whole being whirling with visceral hatred of him, hating him even more for the reaction he stirred so easily in her. Suddenly he sighed. "Okay, look, I'm sorry. It was a stupid, nasty thing to do. I'm sorry."

Trapped between him and the dark room, she was certain he was mocking her. "Well?" she said.

"Well what?"

"I want it back."

"Bossy, aren't you?" Sam pushed himself off the wall and edged past her. She moved quickly out of his way, considered fleeing, decided it would look idiotic. He prowled to a chest of drawers and halfheartedly opened the top drawer. She followed him.

"So," he said, rummaging in a heap of socks, "your folks told you the facts of life yet?"

"Excuse me?" Rosie gasped. "I'm fourteen, not ten."

In the semidarkness, his teeth glinted with sadistic amusement. "I don't mean biology lessons. I mean the facts of *our* lives." He opened another drawer. She saw books, a box of dark carved wood and what looked suspiciously like a large knife in a black leather sheath.

"What, Aetherial traditions?" Rosie spoke coolly. "Of course. We've always been part of it."

He gave a knowing laugh that made her angrier. "Oh, so you don't know, then. They'll tell you when you hit sixteen. It's like a coming-of-age thing. It can be a bit nasty, I've heard. Or not, since my father's put the whole thing on hold."

"What on earth are you talking about?"

"You'll find out."

"My parents don't keep secrets from us. They treat us like grown-ups. I don't suppose your family is as close as ours, though."

That struck a nerve in him. He glared at her, eyes full of coldly furious hatred. "You don't know anything about us."

"And I don't want to. Just give me my property back."

"I don't know," he said, making a show of searching the drawer. "It was a long time ago. God knows what happened to it."

"What the hell did you do with it?" she exclaimed. She'd never hit anyone in her life, but it was all she could do not to take a swing at him. For Matthew, if not for herself.

He shrugged. His eyes glittered. "Probably gave it to some girlfriend. Or just threw it out as a piece of tat."

"You bastard," Rosie said viciously. "You absolute bastard!"

"Yeah, I am, aren't I?" He raised his right hand in the air and she saw silver links glistening between his fingers. He lifted the hand out of her reach, letting the chain drop into a loop, and down the loop slid the crystal heart, blinking with shards of white fire. It hung above her head, pulsating.

"Hey!" She made a grab for it but he swung it out of her reach.

"Real Austrian crystal, that," he said. "Nice. Worth at least a tenner."

"Give it to me!"

Sam seized her upper arm. Her rage almost burned away her fear of him, but he was so much taller and stronger than her. "You have to give me something in return."

"No."

"Only a kiss."

"No! You're off your head! Let me go!"

"Just a kiss, Rosie," he said reasonably. "It won't hurt. I'll be gentle. You might enjoy it."

For a moment his mouth hovered near hers, coming closer. Then she jerked free. Her palm smacked into his face and he stepped back, shocked.

"Ow. Karate lessons? That stung."

"Good. I wouldn't kiss you if you were the last boy alive."

"No kiss, no necklace," he said, closing his fist around the crystal. "Shame, though."

"Go to hell." She backed towards the door, rubbing her bruised arm, terrified he would make a sudden rush and stop her.

Sam spoke, his voice low with menace. "You know why I hate you and your stupid family? Because you think you're better than us. All smug in your cozy house with your perfect picture-book life. You think you're above us."

Rosie glared back. Confusion and rage warred in her. Without answering, she turned and skittered down the eight steps, found the corridor even longer and more sepulchral than it had seemed a few moments ago. A misty blue light seeped through the windows like frost vapor.

Just as in her dreams, Rosie ran for her life.

Lucas found the party dull. There was hardly anyone of his age there. He wandered around, ate some cheese, chatted with a couple of younger boys from the village. Then there seemed nothing to do but go in search of Rosie. When he couldn't find her, the thrill of exploration drew him on.

Upstairs, the gallery brought him to a set of tall double doors with a sort of dining room beyond, and on the far side a rooftop conservatory. A glimmer of light drew him and he slipped through the doors into a glass-domed space with fairy lights winking among potted ferns.

There were some Aetherials in there, cloaked in blue-grey with sea-serpent masks. He wasn't sure who they were. One noticed him and said, "Off you go. No children allowed at the meeting."

Lucas froze, but more Aetherials came in and distracted the first group. He took his chance. He lost himself behind foliage, slipped through an outer door and found himself on a small roof terrace.

The rain had stopped and stars appeared. Crouching, he watched through the window as Vaethyr guests streamed in, a mass of color and finery amid tiny sparkling lights. He felt the magic of the Dusklands charge the air around him, clearly heard their voices through open vents above the windows. He saw his parents come in with his aunt and uncle, masked. He was effectively trapped now. Cold air needled through his shirt. Whatever was happening that he was not supposed to see, he had no choice now but to watch and wait until it ended.

———

At the far end of the corridor, Rosie came to high double doors standing ajar. A soft alluring light and a murmur of sound fell through the gap. She caught her breath, checked that Sam wasn't following her and entered. Inside, she found a high-ceilinged room with a dining table, unlit Tiffany lamps on a sideboard, leaded windows. The light came through a pair of glass doors at the far end. Cautiously she walked towards them, listening intently as the sound resolved into the chanting of a young male voice.

No one looked round as Rosie slipped into the rooftop conservatory; a bower of light, walled and roofed with glass. All the Aetherials were gathered here; no humans. They wore their masks pushed back on their heads like crowns, a strange congregation of animal-headed deities. Their faces glowed, eyes ashimmer with the jewel fire of their nonhuman heritage.

Palms and ferns threw shadows in the enchanted light. Hundreds of tiny white fairy lights had been strung through their foliage and the air was thick with incense. Rosie was spellbound. She had walked into a dream.

Their attention was held by a dais that stood against one wall, bathed in sparkling light, where Jonathan Wilder was reciting a poem.

I am a stag of seven tines
I am a wild flood on a plain
I am a wind on the deep waters
I am a hawk on a cliff . . .

It was the most haunting thing she'd ever heard. With the hawk mask rearing above his head Jon looked unearthly. His lovely face and intense brown eyes shone in a transport of passion. His long wavy hair, the brown of burnished hazelnuts, moved beautifully on his shoulders.

Rosie felt dizzy. This was more than a dream. She'd stepped into the Dusklands and become someone else. How had everyone known to come here—had they all known but her?

It didn't matter; there was only Jon. His face and brown eyes were captivating, framed by the softly moving hair. He must be fifteen or sixteen now and there was a youthful softness about his face, the look of an androgynous saint from a Renaissance painting.

Rosie fell in love.

She watched his long agile fingers moving for emphasis and wondered what they would feel like touching her. She remembered the look that had passed between them as children. Sam had menaced her, but Jon had wanted to help, and would have done so if he'd been older. Finally she knew what the look meant.

The recognition of souls.

If Sam had torn her to pieces, Jon now healed her. She trembled and her heart raced. As the chant ended, Jon glanced straight at her through the crowd and gave a slight smile, enough to heat her with embarrassment and hope. She was dying to tell Faith and Mel, but they weren't here, and there was a delicious ache in hugging the secret to herself. Her whole being tingled with red fire.

"Now my father wishes to address you," he said quietly, and slipped to one side of the dais.

Rosie wondered if she dared speak to him. It would look so obvious to push through the crowd. No, it would be like trying to chat to a prince in the middle of a solemn royal ceremony. Impossible.

Lawrence stepped up to the dais. The crowd fell silent. Rosie moved to see better and there, at the front, stood her own parents. She'd never realized before that they could appear *magnificent*.

As Lawrence began to speak, the air shimmered and she saw him differently. He was taller, sleek and black and silver with a streaming feathered cloak—or wings. Truly unmasked. It seemed to Rosie that everyone into the room had changed, turning into the true, essential self of which the mask was only a symbol.

"Beloved siblings of the old blood." His tone was stilted. "My family and I welcome you to Stonegate Manor and we wish you blessings of the newborn Yuletide sun. I regret that it has still not been possible to throw open the portals for the celebrations we enjoyed in the past. However, we hope you appreciate our intent this year to carry on in the spirit of our heritage."

There was some stirring among the Aetherials at the front. Lawrence went on, "You are aware that for the past five years or so, it has been impossible for me to open the Gates."

"Impossible?" called out a male voice. "No, all we know is that you refuse to do it!"

Rosie recognized the voice as Comyn's. She heard the menace of his anger.

"And for good reasons, which I'll explain, given the chance." Lawrence's gaze went over their heads. Rosie shifted, afraid he would see her. "There is still a dangerous disturbance behind the Great Gates. Until it abates, I dare not reopen even a Lychgate."

"Lawrence, you've had five years to cobble together a better press statement than this!" shouted Comyn.

There were grumbles of agreement. Rosie felt the spiky tension of the room. Lawrence's mouth hardened. "It is all I can tell you," he said harshly.

"It's not good enough!" rang Phyllida's voice. "Your grandmother Liliana never treated us with such disdain!"

"Please." It was Auberon; Rosie could just see him, facing the gathering with his hands spread to calm them. "Lawrence is the appointed Gatekeeper. He would not take this action without good reason."

"You still support him?" said Comyn. "Do you know something we don't?"

"No," said Auberon, "but I believe he's telling the truth. Don't leap to rash judgments. Be patient." His words had a solid, calming quality, but the atmosphere continued to seethe.

"I swear on Liliana's life, I swear on the Mirror Pool itself, the peril behind the Gates is genuine," said Lawrence, voice growing ragged. "I do this for your protection. The danger is too great."

"Well, damn the danger!" Comyn shouted back. "Let us through and we'll deal with it!"

"Impossible," said Lawrence over the rising voices. Even those at the back near Rosie, who had been quiet, began to shout.

"Be careful, Gatekeeper," Comyn said sharply. "We have already been patient for five years. Danger? What about the potential disaster to us if the Gates stay closed? We could take you down and open the Gates for ourselves."

Auberon began to speak again, but Lawrence stepped forward and leaned like a figurehead over Comyn, Phyllida and their supporters. "No, you cannot," he said. "The power of the Gatekeeper resides only in me, as it resided in Liliana before me. You know it. Harm me and no one will open the Gates again, ever. Have you such short memories? I opened the Lychgate and I gave you a choice: Go through now, or trust me. You stayed. You made your choice!"

Even Comyn seemed unable to answer that. The protestors seethed, defeated.

"Now I hold you to that decision," Lawrence went on, his voice calm, his authority regained. "Yes, in easy times I am your doorkeeper. In difficult times, I am your protector. Let the man or woman who knows better step up here and relieve me of the burden—if any can. No? Then trust me."

Silence. Rosie sensed a shift in mood, a grudging acceptance

"You know he's right," said Auberon. "Let's not say anything we may regret. Let us all keep calm and enjoy the rest of the evening."

"Please," Lawrence added, opening one hand to gesture at the doors. "Eat, drink and dance. It is the season of goodwill, after all."

He turned away. It was over.

As the grumbling audience began to break up, Rosie was caught in the stream of people. Outside in the corridor again, she felt a distinct jolt and a wash of cold reality. She was desperate to speak to her father, but couldn't see him. She craned for a glimpse of Jon and suddenly saw him go past—but he didn't notice her, and when she tried to follow, she lost him in the throng. Bewildered, she was carried along with jostling strangers until a hand gripped her arm and pulled her out of the flow.

It was Matthew; no mask, no jacket, collar undone. He looked annoyed, and somewhat the worse for beer. "What were you doing in there?"

"I don't know, I just walked in."

"Where's Lucas?"

"No idea."

"For god's sake, couldn't you watch him instead of skipping off with your girlfriends? Come on, back to the party."

She jerked free. "Why shouldn't I have been in there?"

"Because . . ." He pushed his hand through his hair. "You're too young. You should be mixing with people your own age, not that crowd."

"Matt, were you in there? Did you hear what was said?"

He sighed through his teeth. "Yes, most of it. I knew we shouldn't have come."

"I have to ask Dad about it."

"No, you don't." He grabbed her arm and pushed her into an alcove. His fervency alarmed her. "No, Rosie, you will not be asking Dad anything. Keep quiet."

"You tell me, then," she said, defiant. "What's going on? What Gates?"

"You don't need to know."

"Why? Because I'm too young to understand?"

"No," he said, groaning in exasperation. "Because it's not what I want for us, Rosie. This Otherworld business, it's living in the past, it messes with your head. I mean, look at them, getting agitated in there when they could be concentrating on the real world. I told Dad, I want nothing to do with it and I never have. It sucks you in, wrecks your head with mad dreams and then spits you out. I don't want you and Luc to go through that."

"Have you finished?" she said, shaken to the bone.

"I care about you," Matthew said intently. "Someone has to stand up and state that we don't need it. We can have a better life, a normal life in the real world without that stuff. Let the bloody Gates of Elfland stay closed! It's the best thing that could possibly happen!"

Lucas had witnessed the meeting from outside, his face pressed to the corner of a misted pane. When it was over, someone went around the inside shutting the vents. He squeezed down into the shadows, waiting for them to finish. When he looked again, all the lights were out and the door through which he'd sneaked earlier was locked.

Wonderful. He was trapped on the roof. Only now did he notice how very cold it was. On one side was a narrow terrace and parapet with the abyss of the night beyond; in front, a blank wall . . . behind, another strip of roof leading to a sort of storm porch.

He went in and found a wooden door, unlocked; and behind it a staircase, leading up.

Lucas was trying hard not to panic. If he could find his way up to the next floor, there must be a way back down into the main body of the house. Blind and clinging to a wobbly banister, he ascended.

At the top, he could smell the thick dust and damp of a roof space. It was ink-black. There could be anything in here or he might stumble and put his foot through the ceiling . . . He froze. He had a vision of being found up here in fifty years' time, a skeleton.

His eyes adjusted, drawing dim shapes on the darkness with Aetheric sensitivity. Cautiously he began to edge through the space. There was an occasional floorboard but otherwise he was stepping on rafters. Trunks, boxes, hat stands and piles of musty curtains loomed nightmarishly around him.

Away to his right, half-concealed by heaped material and old lampshades, he noticed something pale—luminous—actually glowing with its own light. He swallowed a yelp. Two more steps and he saw clearly the curve of a naked back.

A body, human in shape. The thighs were folded underneath, the head bowed on the knees, arms lying loosely back along the floor, face hidden by a flow of hair. From the slumped shoulders a pair of wings curved into the air. All drawn in faded gold and bronze.

The figure was breathing. It uttered the faintest groan.

Lucas was transfixed. He said, "Hello?"

No response. The glowing creature sobbed. Its voice roused such dread that he ran, stumbling and teetering, to the far side of the attic. There his hand found a doorframe, and the dome of an antiquated light switch. In a paroxysm of terror, he flicked it. A naked light bulb oozed a reluctant glow.

A painting. He was looking at a life-sized framed oil painting of a disconsolate Eros, brown with layers of old varnish.

Lucas fumbled at the door. It gave onto a small staircase down to a deserted landing—but he was inside the house again, and could hear the far-off murmur of the masquerade. He stood there gasping with fear, relief and laughter at his own idiocy.

A painting. But he had seen it breathing. He had seen breathing, living flesh.

3

King of Elfland

After the party, Lawrence sat in an armchair in the library, hands dangling over the sides and a cold breeze blowing over him through the open window. From here he could see the Great Gates. In the surface world, the sight was nothing remarkable; a rugged hill encircled by trees, crowned with folds of Precambrian rock, a characteristic feature of the Charnwood Forest.

It was when he shifted his sight into the Dusklands that it became something else. A dolmen mound. A monumental structure, silvery and solid yet alive . . . set there by the Ancients, a crossing point between this world and the Underworld.

His jaw taut, he looked away.

It had been a wondrous labyrinth leading into the rich, layered realms of the Aelyr. Now it seemed a fortress, a series of gigantic doors, one inside the other, each locked, barred and impenetrable.

He had barred those doors himself. Every time he closed his eyes he was there again; running, running as if against a flood; and the great unseen beast, the vaporous shadow giant Brawth was pursuing him. It filled the sky and it would be sated only by him. It had to punish him for some great transgression he could not even remember; had to destroy him, simply for existing. And worse; to flame everything in its path, to pierce the skull of every Aetherial with its burning sword of ice . . .

His sons. It wanted his sons.

The ice giant kept coming no matter how many gates he closed against it. Parts of it pushed through and were severed by the slamming gates, and came skittering after him in the wispy form of nightmares. Again and again in his memory, he crashed the last barrier shut and the tumblers of the combination span and everything went silent.

Then Lawrence had fallen to his knees with exhaustion, and he had known.

He would never dare to open the Gates again.

Never.

Fragments of the beast had leaked through and they hunted him still. Even as he sat here in the silent library he could feel them. They lived in dark corners of the house, mindless spies for their master. He could not tell them apart from the *dysir,* his own house guardians sent from the Spiral Court to protect him. He wasn't safe.

No one was safe, but however hard he tried to explain, he could not make them understand.

He was walking with his grandmother in Ecuador, through the wilds of the Oriente rain forest. Lawrence was young, fifteen or so; his grandmother, Liliana, ageless. They'd discovered a narrow gully and were exploring along the bank of a creek that came clear and cold from the mountains. Liliana went ahead, rangy and athletic, her hair silver-white like the mist that rose around them. There were places on Vaeth that blended with the Dusklands, she was explaining, overlapping so strongly that even humans might stray there without realizing, and this was one such place. Too elusive to be mapped.

She was showing him the world, teaching him how to sense such hidden places. This valley cast an immediate spell on him. Tree trunks coiled around each other, festooned with tumbling bromeliads and orchids. Lawrence smelled the rotting richness of the air, heard the echoing bell calls of birds and monkeys. A tiny purple humming-bird whirred past. Toucans watched from the branches. Everywhere he looked, he saw jewels; turquoise butterflies, bright green crickets, tiny poison-dart frogs.

The pouch of stones he'd collected on their trip bumped against his thigh. Even as a boy he loved minerals, loved the solitude of cutting and polishing.

The flash flood hit so fast that even Aetheric senses had little warning. Birdcall ceased. There was a terrible noise, a moment of confusion. Then the bank crumbled under Lawrence's feet and he was being carried off in a deluge. Water the color of blood foamed and roared in his ears.

Above the torrent, he heard his grandmother's faint yell. "Lawrence! The Dusklands!"

He panicked like a human for a few seconds. Then instinct kicked in. He held his breath and shifted himself fully into the first layer of the Aetheric realms.

Around him, he felt the world change. The flow became smooth, enabling him to push his head clear. He grabbed onto a flat boulder midstream, hung there panting for a few moments, then hauled himself up.

The stream had turned the color of midnight. The world was cooler, bluer. He could see the stars, lamp-bright. The bank looked too far away for him to jump, but Liliana was there, holding out a creeper-festooned branch to him. The branch shone silver like a fork of lightning. Lawrence seized it and leaped. On firm ground, he stood swaying and gasping.

"Don't forget," Liliana said, "We always have this. We can skew reality, as surface dwellers cannot. It can save your life. Forget at your peril."

Then she called the names of the local elementals and said with good humor, "Desist! Let us pass in peace."

That remained Lawrence's most vivid image of his grandmother; gaunt and silver-haired like some fairy-tale sorceress, calling the elements to heel; the forest steaming behind her. It happened with older Aetherials, that they began to seem stretched, translucent. Then they would turn away from the surface world and look ever deeper into the Spiral until their feet were bound to take them there.

Liliana had been Gatekeeper for untold decades, and Lawrence was her heir. He carried what she called the lych-light within him. Lawrence grew afraid when he saw that translucency, knowing she would soon leave—might even abandon him here, if the call grew too strong. He was not ready to become Gatekeeper.

As the solid world refocused around them, they saw that the bank had crumbled away all the length of the gully, revealing fresh red earth. The flood was slackening. Small rocks carried from the mountains tumbled in the flow. Lawrence saw a gleam of pure, clear glass. A nodule of quartz, he thought, torn from the mountain roots and washed here, to his feet. He leaned down and plucked it from the current.

Not quartz. It turned pale violet at his touch and there were fragmented rainbows inside, like opal. The longer he looked, the more it revealed of its gorgeous, flashing fires.

It felt, to his experienced fingers, as hard as diamond. A chill shivered through him; he'd seen such a stone before, but only in the Otherworld. Specifically, in Sibeyla, in his father's hand, the day they'd parted.

"What have you found?" asked Liliana.

He'd never told her what his father, Albin, had done, what he'd said that day. But she would recognize the type of gem, of course. "It's an Otherworld stone," he said quietly. "Birthed in the Spiral. An Elfstone."

They climbed farther up the gully, balancing on the precarious bank. At the head, where the two valley walls converged and the water surged from underground, they found the place; a red cleft in the rock that lay within two realities, a thin place between the surface world and Naamon, realm of fire. A breach, a minor portal. He removed his boots and waded into the stream, feeling fragments of Elfstone beneath his feet, dislodged by the flood. The scarlet rock felt hot and burning cold to his touch, richly veined with minerals.

"These stones have never been found on Earth, to my knowledge," said Liliana, amazed. "The lych-light within you is for more than opening the Gates. It drew you here, called by the fire of Elfstones. You were meant to find them, Lawrence."

And she thought it a happy discovery, not knowing the torment the sight of the stones wrought in him. He wanted to destroy them. At the same time a compulsion surged through him, utterly irrational but irresistible, to dig out every last fragment in vain hope of finding the one Albin had stolen from him.

Lawrence called the place Valle Rojo. And he named the mineral albinite, in tribute to his father—as if such a tribute could draw the approval he'd never yet won. The name was fitting. The gem, untouched, was cold white ice.

Where was the lych-light now?

There were no wages for being appointed Gatekeeper; it

was a duty. The gemstone, however, brought him an earthly fortune. Years of experience made him a master jeweler, but it was albinite on which he built a small empire. Later, when he was able to return to Ecuador and claim Valle Rojo, he kept the operation closely guarded. He trained a tiny workforce of Vaethyr to pan and dig for raw mineral. He cut and set the stones himself, and displayed them in two exclusive stores, one in London, the other in New York. Externally, the stores were all black lacquer, with subdued interiors where jewelry sparkled in glass cases like rows of aquariums swimming with light.

Albinite was unique, with a hardness of nine on the Mohs scale, and unparalleled luster and fire. Its brilliance was richer than that of diamonds, the rainbow lattice in its depths hypnotic. Now it graced some of the most outrageously expensive pieces of jewelry on the planet. He couldn't stop humans from buying it, of course, but only his Aetherial customers truly appreciated its provenance. On their skin, its curious properties became apparent; it changed color, taking on a beautiful blue-violet gleam that would reflect flashes of red or green in response to an Otherworld portal. Elfstone wasn't magic; it was simply reactive to different conditions, rather as the rare gem alexandrite showed green in daylight and crimson by candlelight.

It had been a secret, sacred stone within the Spiral. Here on Earth, thanks to Lawrence, anyone who could afford it could wear it. Puritan Aelyr, like Albin, were bound to be outraged.

The jewel had even brought Ginny to him. He was standing in the air-conditioned coolness of a trade show in Arizona when she had walked in from the burning heat, her black hair streaming against the sunlight, her skin sheened with sweat, masses of turquoise at her throat and wrists. The cosmic sparkle of albinite drew her. Then they laughed together, discovering they were both English and both Vaethyr. But Lawrence was from cold, mountainous Sibeyla, Ginny's ancestry a mix of watery Melusiel and mysterious Asru; perhaps that made them incompatible from the start.

So many years ago.

He grew attached to Ecuador. He built a colonial-style ranch near the mine, his refuge from responsibility. A haven, until Ginny admitted she loathed it and could not stay. He had tried to blame her state of mind on illness, on Barada or Dumannios; but the truth was, it was Lawrence himself who drew the darkness down, and they both knew it.

Albinite was not a magic amulet. It made him money but did not make him a better Gatekeeper. It could not protect them from the shadowy horrors of the Abyss.

Years later, the gem also brought Sapphire to him. She worked in his New York and London stores before becoming his marketing manager. In the dark days after Ginny had fled, he had thought Sapphire could bring him back to life. Back to *light*. She soothed him, brought energy into the house, paid his sons the attention he'd never found it easy to give . . . but she could not defeat the demons. She was an innocent.

Lawrence remembered lifting the river of her hair and sliding a necklace around her throat . . . her gasp of sensual delight. Gleaming ovals of albinite clasped in platinum—a fortune adorning her body, richer than diamond, rarer than tanzanite. Her delight had pleased him, but even then he should have known better than to drag her into his dark undeclared war.

Now Lawrence stared at the derelict portal and felt nothing. The Vaethyr of Cloudcroft were out for his blood and he didn't care. Auberon could not hold them back forever—and why should he try? So they would come for him at last, and perhaps then he would fling open the Great Gates, step aside and let the roaring beast devour them all. Let it be over, the Spiral laid waste, Aetherials destroyed, humans abandoned. Then would Albin be satisfied?

Lawrence gripped the thick arms of his chair. No. He must go on protecting them, however much they hated him for it. For his sons' sake, if not his own. He felt the darkness of the Abyss rising inside him. Leaning forward, he picked up his glass and felt whiskey running down his throat like hot tears to quench it.

A silky movement behind him made him tense. Her reflection was a ghost on the dark window. "Darling?" said Sapphire. "Are you ever coming to bed?" She sat on the arm of his chair, her thigh warming his hand, her perfume sliding over him. "So, the party was a great success, despite your reservations."

It was hard to drag his mind back to the surface. He tried to sound gracious, not icily harsh. "Everything you did was magnificent."

"I told you it would be. Next year will be even better. Perhaps in the summer, a garden party . . ."

"No," he rasped. "No more parties."

He heard her indrawn gasp. She said reasonably, "I thought we agreed it was a success."

"I can't fault the festive atmosphere. However, it was no pleasure to be listening all night for the first poisonous whisper about Sam."

"No one could fault you for trying to keep his difficulties secret," she began, but he spoke across her.

"Nor do I call it a success to be openly accosted by guests who used it as no more than an excuse to criticize the way I carry out my duties."

Again he heard her breathe carefully in and out. "I agree, it was unfair. But if you give them no other chance to speak to you . . ."

"Well, I tell you, they won't be given the chance again. That's the first and last time I open my house, to humans or old blood alike."

"But I've told everyone—"

"I don't care what you've told them. No more parties."

She paused, said softly, "Is this about Sam?"

"No. It isn't."

"Lawrence . . . We were going to start a new life."

"Unfortunately, the old is still here." He spoke grimly,

unable to look at her chiding, disappointed face. Her frustration was a powerful force, but it left him unmoved. "I must bear this burden alone. However hard I try to explain, you will never truly understand. You can't."

"Well, you told me a human wife was what you needed. If you now consider it a problem, you should have married another Aetherial." He felt her withdraw, quietly hurt and matching his chilliness. "No, I can't understand, Lawrence. Not unless you learn to trust me."

Coolly she slipped away and left him alone on the lip of the Abyss.

Rosie approached her father's study with the sensation that the oak-paneled corridor was lengthening as she walked. Lucas was at her side. It was the day after the party, and all morning they'd been gathering courage to ask their questions. Echoing from another part of the house came the clear sweet notes of her mother's harp, an eerie lament. Light shone from the half-open door and she could hear her father moving about, humming to himself.

As she pushed open the door to his sanctuary, the noises stopped. There was no one there. Only an empty desk, a large black book lying in the spotlight of a desk lamp.

Lucas walked to the desk and touched the book's leather binding. "*The Book of Sepheron*. I've seen this before."

Rosie looked over his shoulder and realized that she'd seen it, too. There was a five-pointed star embossed in silver on the cover, a pentagram superimposed on a spiral. At the top point was the word *Asru*. Moving clockwise, the word at the next point was *Elysion*. *Sibeyla* and *Naamon* labeled the two points of the base. Moving up again, the word at the left-hand point was *Melusiel*. And back up to *Asru* again. The words were also interconnected by the straight lines of the pentagram.

She noticed that the spiral was double. As the line reached the center, it turned on itself and came out again; and at the outside, it curved to recommence its inward journey.

"Oh, this book!" she gasped. As Luc opened the cover, she saw the diagram repeated in black ink on the frontispiece, and below it the words in curling script, *A translation by Auberon Fox*. The paper was handmade, thick and untrimmed. "When did we see it before?"

"We sneaked in here when we were small," said Lucas. "It was on the desk. Then Dad came and told us off and took it away. I don't know why, I couldn't understand a word of it anyway."

Remembering, she felt a guilty thrill. "Does it make sense now?"

He began to read out loud. " 'First there was the Cauldron, the void at the beginning and end of time. As if the void brooded upon its own emptiness, a spark appeared like a thought in the blackness. That spark was the Source. For the first time or the ten millionth time—we can never know—the Source exploded in an outrush of starfire.

" 'As the star-streams cooled they divided and took on qualities each according to its own nature: stone and wind, fire and water and ether. From those primal energies, all worlds were formed.

" 'On that outrush came Estel the Eternal, also called Lady of Stars, who created herself with that first spark of thought. Her face is the night sky, her hair a milky river of stars. For eons Estel presided over the birth of the sun and planets and hidden realms. She watched as the Earth roiled with liquid rock and white-hot fires, until the molten torrents birthed Qesoth: a vast elemental of fire and lava. Qesoth brought with her a dark twin, Brawth, a giant shadow that breathed ice. These two fought battles that shook the planet until Estel, to make them cease, took a great rock and smashed Qesoth into pieces. Her shadow twin Brawth dissipated with her, scattering fragments of fire and ice that rained into the boiling oceans. Those fragments seethed with wild energy and rose to become the first Aetherials, who were called Estalyr; forged in fire, washed in rain and infused with the breath of life.

" 'At first, Earth had only its Estalyr name: Vaeth. Wo-

ven of star and sun, ocean and storm, those primal Estalyr
were the first sentient manifestations of pure energy unable to contain its urge for life. Curious and watchful, they
bestrode the infant Vaeth like divinities. They were the
color of night, darkest indigo, with sun-golden eyes that saw
into other layers of reality.

" 'The primal Estalyr shaped the Spiral. Like spiders spinning silk they wove new realities from the raw materials.
That is how the Otherworld came to be a reflection of Earth,
for they were woven of the same substance. Siblings.' "

Rosie was spellbound by Luc's light, gentle voice. Closing her eyes, she thought, *I know this.* In the spaces when
Luc paused, a strong pure voice began to sing the story in
counterpoint; her mother's voice, far away but clear.

> *The blackest point of heaven,*
> *The swirling cup of blood*
> *Poured forth its life,*
> *Poured forth its fire*
> *Blinded angels with its force,*
> *The womb of us,*
> *The source of us,*
> *The Source.*

" 'The Estalyr freely wandered all the realms. As life
evolved upon Earth, the Estalyr changed too, tasting the
new life of vegetation and animals, taking the qualities
that enriched us. We became the fully living yet semidi-
vine other-race; Aetherials. We became proud, ruling all
the realms like angels walking in Eden or gods in Val-
halla. We answered to no authority except our own—why
worship divinities when we *are* divine?' "

The shifting enchantments of song and prose turned her
dizzy. When her father's voice broke in, she and Lucas
nearly hit the ceiling in shock.

"Hardly the best-written translation of our origins, but I
was aiming for clarity."

Auberon was sitting on the leather couch behind the

door as if he'd been there all the time. As they turned to him, the room transformed into a dazzling space without boundaries. A great tree stood where wall and door should have been; the couch was one of its thick roots. Rosie clearly saw her father in a different shape, robed in crimson, green and brown, a proud and powerful fox deity enthroned on the Tree of Life.

Oakholme was never predictable.

"That's a book you're meant to read when you turn sixteen," he said. "Don't try now, it goes on and on."

As he spoke, he became their father again. The other-form remained visible, a translucent cloak, but she could see the kind eyes behind his glasses, the unruly black hair and beard, the rosy apples of his cheeks. She let her breath go in relief. He'd been waiting for them. "Dad, we came to ask you something."

"I know. Sit down. You want to know about last night."

They obeyed, sitting cross-legged on the satiny roots, Luc cradling the book. Rosie hesitated. Matthew's dire warning made her nervous, as much as it had spurred her into action. "The secret meeting of Aetherials—we didn't imagine it, did we?"

Auberon looked amused and disapproving. "No, you didn't."

"We weren't supposed to be there, were we?"

"Not strictly speaking, but never mind, it's done now."

"So what's going on?" Rosie asked simply. "We're not children anymore."

Auberon inclined his head. He was more bear than fox, she thought, solid and protective. "We normally keep the full story until you're sixteen. It's a delicate matter, when we live in the mortal world, knowing how much to tell our children."

Rosie smiled. "So we don't gossip at school and get labeled as weird? I think it's too late for me, Dad."

She loved the way his eyes twinkled when she made him laugh. "Well, that's part of it. Tell me what you know, then I'll know how best to answer."

Rosie sat up straight. She hadn't expected to be put on the spot. "Only what you and Mum have told us. We're of an older race . . . we look human so that we can live among them . . . we can step into the Dusklands . . . and I thought I knew everything, but obviously I don't."

Auberon smiled. "Some humans know or suspect we dwell among them, but most have no idea."

"If they knew, they might be jealous or afraid of us?" Rosie put in.

"True, and good reason for being discreet about our nature. The inhabitants of Cloudcroft view us as the locals who've been here the longest, still clinging to ancient festivals that exclude outsiders. We gather in Cloudcroft because the Ancients sited the Great Gates here—and that happened because the borders were thin here."

"But we can go into the Dusklands anytime," said Luc. "What do we need Gates for?"

"The Great Gates guard the deeper realms, which we call the Spiral, where curious Vaethyr fledglings have been known to vanish." There was a grave note in his voice. "The inner realms are not safe, not for the uninitiated."

Rosie and Lucas exchanged a look that burned with questions. Every word their father said seemed to stir a lost memory, unraveling everything she'd been certain of. She murmured, "And the Dusklands are separate from the Spiral, how?"

"Think of the Dusklands as part of the Earth," said Auberon. "It's like a veil over reality, or an extra dimension that only Aetherials can perceive—and a few sensitive humans, who might call it the land of Faerie. It's a warping of perception, a mirage over the landscape on burning hot days or at dawn or dusk; transitional times. It's usually benign, but occasionally, when it becomes deeper and darker and less friendly, we call it Dumannios."

"Like the difference between dreams and nightmares?" said Lucas.

"That's a fair comparison. It is somewhat like the realm

of the subconscious—only, to us, it's real. If you approached an Aetheric portal while in the surface world, it would look like a natural feature, say a rock, a hollow tree or a spring. Only if you entered the Dusklands would you see the way through."

"To the Otherworld?" Rosie asked softly.

"One distinguishing feature of our ancestors, the Estalyr, was that they could perceive dimensions of which humans aren't aware. It's said that, although they didn't actually *create* the Spiral, they shaped it from the raw material of those hidden layers." Auberon's voice was low, his eyes introspective. He was talking to them as equals, as true Aetherials, at last. "Pass through the Great Gates and you find yourself in Elysion, the first inner realm. The realms are easy to remember; think of the five-pointed star, and the five elements; Elysion is associated with earth, Sibeyla with air, Naamon with fire, Melusiel with water and Asru, with ether or spirit. Asru is the innermost realm, the most elusive and mysterious. It's Asru we're drawn to as we grow older. It contains mysteries such as the Spiral Court, the Mirror Pool, and the Abyss itself."

Rosie felt a chill roll down her spine like black ice. Although she didn't understand all he was telling her, she felt she'd grown up very suddenly. "Have you been there, Dad?"

"Not yet." He smiled slightly. "To the other realms, yes, and many times to Elysion; the Fox clan originates from Elysion, the realm of earth and rock. But . . ."

Rosie saw that he was struggling with how much to tell them. Lucas broke in and gave him a way to continue. "So, do any Aetherials live in the Spiral? Or do we just go there to die?"

"What made you think that?" He gave Luc a half-amused, admonishing look. "No, it's a real, living place. The Aetherials who live on that side are called Aelyr, but they're quite remote from us now. They're scattered in city-states, like the network of ghostly spired cities that they once built across prehistoric Earth. Others live in rural or nomadic fashion . . . Aetherials were never much for central authority or laws, although there was a time when Naamon, the realm of fire, rose up to conquer the inner realms. The great Queen Malikala of Naamon ruled for centuries until one Lady Jeleel of Melusiel led a rebellion against her. The story is that Jeleel's son, Sepheron, became Malikala's lover, and betrayed her. He kept her from the battlefield, thus giving his mother, Jeleel, a chance."

"Wow, he must have been persuasive," said Rosie, imagining Sepheron with long flowing hair, like Jon. All at once, she heard Jessica singing:

> *Fingers blue as sea or dew*
> *He wound into her fiery hair*
> *And moist as rain his comely face*
> *And fair moist lips he placed near hers,*
> *And whispered, "Maliket of Fire,*
> *The golden rivers of the sun*
> *Cannot compare, cannot compare*
> *With richer glories of your hair—*
> *And thus the time has fled that we*
> *Have idled on your fiery couch.*
> *My mother's armies—oh, the clock*
> *Betrayed us—oh, your face turns cold—*
> *Her armies on the desert gold*
> *Face yours, and there she lifts her staff*
> *To strike the stone, to strike the rock . . .*

She became dizzy, trying to capture both her mother's voice and her father's at the same time. The room whirled with flowers of light.

"After Naamon's empire ended, the realms fell into their usual chaotic state of self-rule. On Vaeth, Earth itself, different Aetherial branches such as the Felynx had established civilizations while mankind was still evolving. They must have appeared godlike to humans; you can see their footprint in legends about angels, elves, vanished races. Sadly they lacked divine foresight to predict how humans would swell in numbers and aggression. They simply weren't prepared. Eventually, human tribes overwhelmed Aetherial civilization and it fell. Driven out, they flooded back to the Spiral. Unfortunately, they'd grown too used to dominating Vaeth. Their leader, one Jharag the Red, last of the Felynx, decided he would conquer the Otherworld instead. The Aelyr formed a hurried alliance to defend their freedom, led by the extraordinary Lady Violis, an archmanipulator of the fabric of the Spiral. The legends say that battle raged on the borders of Vaeth and Elysion—not with weapons, but with the raw matter of creation itself. Earthquakes and volcanoes, ice, storms and floods. The war went on until it seemed the fabric of the Spiral would be torn apart."

Auberon sat forward, folding his hands. "Finally, the elder Aetherials who had long ago passed into Asru stirred themselves to intervene. They formed the Spiral Court to keep watch and curb such conflict. They decreed that the damage would be limited by forming a seal between Earth and the Otherworld. The barrier was porous, with many portals which were to be controlled by one great master portal, the Great Gates. All sides were so shaken by the war that they agreed. Lady Violis and many other adepts labored for years before the work was complete; there were objectors, of course, but in the end the Spiral Court had its way. And there the Great Gates stand, much weathered by time; a guard against conflict, and a statement of will to peace. Also, it's quite hard to mount an invasion when your army can only squeeze through one at a time."

Lucas grinned at the image. "But Aetherials were still allowed to cross over?"

"No one was forbidden to move either way, but many had 'gone native,' as it were, and preferred the human world. We're all Aetherial, but those who live on Earth are called Vaethyr and those who dwell in the Spiral are called Aelyr. Since we tend to absorb the qualities of the life around us as camouflage, we have taken on humanoid bodies and lives. After our early civilization fell we went into hiding, but if you know how to look you can see Aetheric hands all through history . . . Aetherials have been there all the time, adepts at manipulation and secrecy. When we enter the Dusklands, or the Spiral itself, our true selves begin to be revealed . . . but that really is a talk for another time."

"And Lawrence controls the Gates." Lucas frowned as if trying to remember something.

"Twenty years in the post," said Auberon. "He succeeded his grandmother Liliana, who was a hard act to follow, as it were. He's always seemed troubled in the role . . . concerned about doing a good job, perhaps, but where she was easygoing, Lawrence has been controlling and has alienated many. The term *gate* is misleading. The structure is really more of a labyrinth, a configuration of different passageways. Usually, most of it is kept closed, with only a tiny way called the Lychgate left open for us to come and go as we please."

"Oh, that's why you kept it secret." Rosie's eyes widened. "So that we didn't try to sneak through!"

"And you won't be sneaking through anytime soon." Auberon had that dark, troubled look again. "There's a festival that falls every seven years, the Night of the Summer Stars, at which the Gatekeeper flings the Great Gates wide open. Five years ago, without warning, Lawrence stopped the ritual and refused to open the Gates. He drove us off in a regrettably aggressive fashion that many can't forgive. We found that he'd closed even the Lychgate against us. Sealing the Great Gates like that locks all portals, everywhere. No one can go in or out."

"He kept saying it was too dangerous," Rosie murmured, recalling the meeting. "People didn't seem to believe him."

"That doesn't mean he's wrong," her father said quietly.

"Can't you appoint a new Gatekeeper?" asked Lucas.

"It's not a job you can apply for." Auberon chuckled. "It's a power granted in higher realms. Also, he is a guardian who must be trusted. He can't be forcibly removed. Celebrating the Night of the Summer Stars is an incredibly important tradition. Losing it is painful, but the prospect of losing contact with the Spiral altogether is devastating. Many Vaethyr are angry but Lawrence refuses to back down; and here we are; stalemate."

Rosie felt a cold, pale pressure in her solar plexus, as if she might faint. Eyes closed, she felt herself swooping over an unknown landscape, the Abyss yawning beneath her as she curved in flight and plunged downwards. Her whole body jerked and her eyes flew open. In the same moment, Lucas uttered a cry.

"What did you see?" their father asked gently.

"I don't know," she gasped. "I feel I already know everything you've told us, but I can't quite grab the memory. Like a nightmare where you're in an exam and can't answer a single question."

"The hill beside Stonegate," said Lucas. "The rocks called Freya's Crown. They're the Gates."

"Who told you?"

"No one." Lucas looked bewildered. "I saw it."

"And we're meant to be allowed into the Spiral when we're sixteen?" said Rosie. "That's two years for me. Perhaps Lawrence will have changed his mind by then."

"Perhaps. Or you could call it a lucky escape, since initiation has its own dangers." Auberon's expression darkened. For all his kindness, there was an edge of flint in him that made her wary. "It's a difficult situation. You saw how frustrated the Vaethyr are with Wilder's stubbornness. If he won't budge, I don't know what will happen."

"You think they might lynch him?" said Lucas hopefully.

Auberon laughed. "In a cowboy film, yes, quite possibly. In reality, no. His position is sacrosanct. It would be a devastating breach of tradition. Sacrilege."

Rosie bit her lip and watched her father's troubled face. "He must have done it for a reason."

"There's a precedent; Liliana twice sealed the Gates to protect us from storms raging on the other side. Only for weeks, though, not years. Now Lawrence claims a similar danger."

A chill went through her. "Do you believe him?" she asked.

"You can't believe a word the old bastard says," Auberon answered with unusual venom. "However . . . this time, yes, I suspect there is something behind it. And that it's worse than he will admit. That's his trouble: he's honest with no one, least of all me. He is the appointed guardian and we have no choice but to trust him, however obstructive and bloody-minded he is. As for his sons . . . their father isn't their fault, but you can see the damage it's caused the older boy. Always in trouble at school, and Lawrence making prodigious donations to smooth things over."

Rosie's heart jumped at the mention of Jon and Sam. Dozens of questions clamored inside her. "Dad, do you know exactly who is human and who is Vaethyr in Cloudcroft? Can you always tell?"

The question seemed to throw him. "Usually, but . . ." He hesitated. "You'll learn. Some of us are better camouflaged than others. There's an aura, however subtle, that you'll pick up, but it's not infallible. There's a vein of snobbery among some Aelyr who insist that Vaethyr are not pure; that interbreeding has put too much human blood in our veins. Usually our identity is clearly defined but there may be the occasional individual in whom the borders blur. There must be a tipping point, a certain balance of genes where a potential Aetherial simply never "wakes up," as it were; has no idea they're anything but human. Likewise, if we lost our connection to the Spiral, we might all fall asleep and forget what we used to be . . . We need Elysion as we need water, we *must* go there to refresh our essential natures, but . . ."

He trailed off. Again Rosie heard the eldritch voice and suddenly realized, with shock, that Jessica was not singing in reality; that her song was entering her mind from the ether of some lost place and time.

All the demons of Dumannios
All Maliket's fire and Melusiel's flood,

All the stern towers of Tyrynaia
Cannot keep me from you, my love, Elysion.
As if I lay down with a lover, I will lie down in Elysion
And drink your sweet dew . . .

The voice faded. Auberon cleared his throat. "Those matters aside, I'm trying to keep things calm between Lawrence and Comyn. Alienating Lawrence Wilder is not the way to resolve this. Apparently my role is to play the diplomat, as usual."

"What about Matthew?" said Lucas. "Was he . . . initiated at sixteen?"

"No. Nor the Wilder lads. The Gates were shut by then."

"Is that why Matt tells us to forget the Otherworld and live in this one?" asked Rosie.

Auberon exhaled. "I suspect that Matthew's trying to protect you. As am I. Understand, there's one thing I put far ahead of Aetherial politics, and that's the safety of my family. Believe me, there's no harm in concentrating on the human world, rather than yearning for what we can't reach. Ah, I didn't mean this talk to frighten you; but you deserve the truth." He reached out to ruffle their hair. "You're a good girl, Rosie. You and Luc and Matthew are the best children any man could have, mortal or Aetherial."

Jessica's eerie music ceased and the study resumed its normal boundaries, the tree root a leather couch, the flowers of light simply embers in the grate. Rosie sat at his feet like a child, but she was a child no longer. What else was being kept from them? Sam's knowing mockery stung. She understood more now, but the talk had left her more disturbed than reassured. Her father's frowns and silences were gaping dark holes in which fear swirled.

Auberon seemed the center of the Earth, the axis around which the Spiral revolved. Everything flowed from him as he sat secure on his throne at the heart of the Tree of Life: Auberon, King of Elfland. She had to trust him. Yet, because he *was* the center, all the unsaid things were a thousand times more terrifying.

Two days after the party, the Christmas trees remained like icy sentinels in the great hall, but the festive atmosphere was ash.

Sam stood in the doorway between his father's study and his workshop. Lawrence was sitting with his back to the door, silhouetted against the concentrated pool of light at his work station. A grinding machine buzzed, spraying a mist of water from the gem he was shaping.

"Dad," said Sam in a low voice. "I'm sorry. That is, not about what I did—I had to—but I'm sorry I let you down."

As if he hadn't heard, Lawrence said, "Is albinite a hologram, do you think? Every single piece containing the whole? The macrocosm in the microcosm. If it is so, why can't I find it?"

"What?" said Sam. "Dad, did you hear what I said?"

"I heard." Lawrence did not turn round. He didn't even look up from his work. "You have narrowly avoided a custodial sentence and acquired a criminal record that will follow you for the rest of your life. It's an utter miracle that we kept it quiet this long. I cannot begin to imagine how your mother would have felt."

It was so rare for Lawrence to mention Ginny at all that Sam couldn't speak for a moment. "I know, I've disgraced you," he said. "Totally screwed up this time, haven't I? Ruined Jon's life, as well as my own."

Lawrence replied in a thin and final tone, "I cannot disagree with anything you've said."

Sapphire was alone in the sanctuary she'd created on Stonegate's top floor. Disused servants' quarters became a stylish relaxation zone where she now sat and looked out over the estate in icy winter sunshine. One hand fondled the matte black cover of a catalogue. The only image on the blackness was of a solitary tear-shaped stone that glittered with incredible rainbow fires. It was like a galaxy in space. Even in a photograph you could see layers and layers within the crystal, whole worlds into which you could fall forever.

The catalogue was from Wilder Jewels. She'd designed it herself. Although Lawrence sold to anyone with money, he preferred his jewelry to adorn the necks, wrists and brows of Aetherials. Sapphire touched the ice at her throat. The albinite stones were so cold and smooth they were actually arousing. She didn't mind that they stayed white, marking her as human.

She knew about albinite long before she met Lawrence. She even knew about the secret mine, Valle Rojo. She had heard strange stories of Aetherials and dreamed of infiltrating their circles, working for them . . . hardly dared to dream she would actually marry the man himself.

She'd dreamed of wealth and jewels, the shiny magazine lifestyle she deserved. And now she had it, but it was only a gloss on her true goal. She had known Lawrence would be difficult. That was a given. When he was in a dark mood, she couldn't easily get round him with sweet talk or sex. And sometimes all it took to put him in a dark mood was a single misplaced word; she was allowed to refer to *Aetherials,* even *Vaethyr,* but heaven forbid she should ever utter the sacred term *Estalyr.*

She also hadn't bargained on his appalling sons.

Still, she was more tenacious than he dreamed. The voice of Marilyn Monroe slipped silkily through her mind, making her smile. "*Square-cut or pear-shaped, these rocks don't lose their shape . . .*"

She had to understand what Aetherials were. If it was the last thing she did, she had to *understand.* She'd been striving to do so for years, through meditation and observation. There must be a way to break through, to reach the heart of the infuriating mystery, even to *become* Aetherial if that was what it took. The hypnotic effect of albinite on all who saw it proved it was more than decorative; surely she could use it to change herself, channel its energy through her own chakras, something, anything to transform her own consciousness.

You can break through to their plane, she told herself. *It's so close.*

You can make him open the Gates for you.

4

About a Bull

"I don't know why Dad couldn't have told us before," said Lucas. The Christmas break over, he and Rosie were walking along a lane towards the bus stop, school bags on their shoulders, their breath clouding the air. It was an iron-hard winter day and the hedgerows glittered with frost.

"Well, if there were no adult secrets to discover, we'd have nothing to look forward to, would we?" Rosie answered. "They think they're protecting us."

"Like, if they don't tell us there are scary things out there, we'll never find out? But we will. There are things in Stonegate you don't want to meet at night."

"I know," Rosie said darkly. "So, we still have the Dusklands, because it's part of Earth, part of us . . . but we can't go into the Otherworld proper. I can't bear to think we'll never see Elysion."

'D'you remember how Matthew would get mad if we entered the Dusklands in front of him?" said Luc. "Maybe it is dangerous, but he can't protect us forever."

"Matt says that being Aetherial doesn't matter in the human world. It holds us back and stops us being part of things."

"Really?" Lucas kicked a frozen pebble. "Why can't we be human and Aetherial at the same time?"

Rosie huffed a vapor cloud. "I suspect Dad agrees with him. As if to say, we mustn't worry our little heads about the Gates being closed, it's not our concern."

"But it is," Luc said, frowning.

They reached a tight bend in the lane, where her favorite tree stood proud on the inside of the curve, a glorious oak of great girth and age called the Crone Oak. She stopped to look up into the frosted limbs. Doubt needled her. She trusted her parents—but what if Matt was right, and they were living in the past, and there was some vital reason for abandoning their origins and embracing the human world, because it was more . . . real?

"I love this tree," she said. "It looks like it's been here a thousand years, and seen everything."

"Rosie, come on, we'll miss the bus."

He walked on but she hesitated. There was a face looking down at her from between the branches. A small heart-shaped face, green as lichen, with straggling leafy hair.

"Come on then, ducky," said the green woman. "Climb up to me. I've got something to tell you."

Rosie took a step back. "I can't," she gasped.

"You've climbed up before. I've seen you."

"I know, but it's slippery . . . and there isn't time . . ."

The dryad slithered headfirst down the trunk and reared out from the branch like a snake to put her face near Rosie's. She was semitranslucent, sinuous. "I will not have blood on my tree," she hissed.

Alarmed, Rosie backed away. "I love your tree, Green-lady. I'd never harm it."

"I know you wouldn't, but I see blood and broken limbs." The dryad's cracked voice was fervent. Rosie had glimpsed elementals before, but this was the first time one had spoken to her. "You make them keep their blood off my tree! I won't have it!"

Rosie ran. The dryad came after her, snatching at her blazer and hair. Lucas was farther up the lane, almost at the intersection with the main street. She saw her friends at the bus stop, heard the rumble of the Ashvale bus. With cold air searing her throat, she ran until she shook off the clawing mist of the Greenlady's fingers.

———

Later, she sat with Faith and Mel on a wall under the horse chestnut trees at the edge of the school quad. They were wrapped in gloves and scarves, their legs mottled purple. Pearl-grey rime sheathed the twigs; puddles cracked with ice.

"Your explanation for vanishing midparty is the weirdest thing I've ever heard," said Mel, amused but sceptical.

"Oh, Dad said it was some sort of, er, neighbourhood dispute." She was uncomfortable. To pacify her abandoned friends, she'd described the clash with Sam and the strange Vaethyr gathering. It was natural to confide in them—especially about Jon—but Rosie knew it sounded fantastical. So now she backtracked, to make herself sound less mad. "He wouldn't tell us much, really."

"Sometimes parents keep things to themselves," said Mel, "and there's nothing you can do about it."

"Oh, I wish mine *would* keep it to themselves," Faith said under her breath. "When they fight, the whole street hears. They were awful over Christmas." Her head drooped. Faith had a difficult home life: squalid house, no money, a mother and father who drank and fought like demons and sometimes even vanished for nights on end, leaving Faith to fend for her two younger sisters. The others gave her pats of fellowship.

"You sure you didn't have a drop too much punch, Rosie?" Mel teased. "Nothing weird happened to Faith and me at the party."

"Maybe." Rosie nodded. "That's it, I was drunk."

"Don't say that," Faith put in. "I love the idea of people with animal heads and a beautiful boy reciting poetry. It was scary there, but so magical you could taste it. We saw the masks, Mel."

"Mm. Still sounds crackers." Mel smiled to herself, gazing across the quad, where dejected groups of teenagers shuffled around, blowing on their hands. "Funny, these peculiar events only seem to happen to you, Rosie."

Mel was cheerfully dismissive, but Rosie was crushed.

"I didn't make it up, honest," she said, deciding not to mention the dryad who'd terrified her just this morning.

"The Cloudcroft Mafia," said Mel. "That's what my mum calls people like Lawrence Wilder, the Lyons and the Tullivers, all that lot. They swan about as if they own the village. They think they're special, but all they are is far too rich. Nothing against your folks, Ro, they're great—but some of the others . . ." She shook her head.

"It's not like that. I know you don't believe me, but it's only trying to keep old traditions alive, like . . . speaking Cornish," she finished lamely.

Mel raised her eyebrows. "So now you're Cornish?"

"Er. No. For example."

"I see how it is," said Faith. "Rosie has to keep it secret, but there are people in the village who are different, a mysterious older race who look human but can change shape and walk in other worlds. They're called Aerials."

"Aetherials," Rosie said automatically. Then she paused, certain she'd never spelled it out that plainly. "Where did you hear that?"

"I don't know." Faith reddened. "Sorry, I'll shut up. I'd really like it to be true, though."

"So Rosie's a fucking Cornish elf," exclaimed Mel. "Yippee. I love you two, but you're the bloody limit. Can we talk about something normal, please?"

"Fine by me," said Rosie.

"I mean, your parents look as human as anyone. Okay, Lawrence Wilder is rather gorgeous in a scary way, but still human. Looked like he'd got everything in the right place, if you know what I mean."

That set them laughing. "You think everyone's gorgeous," said Faith.

Mel didn't respond. She was suddenly wired, sitting forward with her hands braced on the edge of the wall. "Oh, my god!" she whispered, her attention on the school gates.

Then Rosie saw. Her jaw dropped. Utter disbelief, excitement and panic surged through her.

Jonathan and Samuel Wilder were prowling across the

quad, wary and predatory like two dark panthers unleashed from a cage. They were wearing the school uniform; black trousers and jacket, white shirt, black and silver striped tie. "I don't believe it," she said.

Mel laughed. "Close your mouth, Ro, you're drooling icicles."

Rosie's teeth began to hurt with the cold. She snapped her mouth shut and accidentally bit her tongue, causing her eyes to fill with water. "Fuck," she said, remembering to breathe. "*Fuck*."

The bell sounded and chilled students began to stream towards the school building. Jon and Sam, moving with the flow, would have to come past the wall where Rosie was. They vanished behind other students for a moment. When they reappeared, Sam had moved off with a group of sixth-form boys and Jon was on his own, walking straight towards her.

Her pulse quickened. Their eyes met, disengaged, met again. He paused as if not sure what to do. Mel poked her in the hip and the next thing she knew, she was on her feet in front of him.

His long hair was tied back and he looked more beautiful than she remembered; perfect face, dark long-lashed eyes, sensual mouth. Her heartbeat shook her whole body as he approached. She'd thought falling in love would be wonderful; no one had warned her it could be painfully mortifying. Her watering eyes made her nose run, while her mouth was glued shut.

Jon wore a slightly startled, *do-I-know-you* expression, which she hadn't expected. This seemed a good moment for a chasm to open beneath her.

"Hi, I'm Rosie."

He gave a small frown. "Rosie . . . ?"

"We live down the hill from you." Her tongue felt clumsy. "We met at the party, do you remember?"

"Er . . . yes, you're really familiar," he said, still looking blank.

How could he not remember, when she'd obsessed about

him ever since? Her fingers described a muzzle in front of her face. "In the fox mask."

"Oh yes, yes." Light dawned at last. "Rosie Fox. Course."

"That's it," she laughed in relief. "My father knows yours . . . anyway . . . I really liked your poem."

"I didn't write it. It was 'The Song of Amergin.'"

"Er, I know, I meant the way you performed it."

"Thanks." His gaze drifted away from her—scanning for Sam, she assumed. He wasn't making this easy at all.

"I thought you were at boarding school," she struggled on. "What are you doing here?"

"Uh," Jon said, and looked at his feet. "We were. Dad decided to take us out and send us here instead."

"Oh," she said, and thought it extraordinary that Lawrence actually might have listened to her father's throw-away advice. "Do you mind?"

"I don't know yet." The sweetness of his face and the fall of his hair was playing havoc with her insides. He caught her gaze with those melting brown eyes as if he wanted to confide something vital, and would if she could only win his trust.

"What subjects do you like best?"

"Um . . . English is okay, and biology . . . I'd better go." He started to turn from her, hands in pockets, head down. A sudden small flame of courage lit inside her and, on an impulse, she stepped after him.

"Jon, could I ask you a favor?"

He stopped, met her eyes again with a wary frown. "I suppose so."

"Your brother Sam has something of mine."

"What?"

"Ask him," she said more confidently. "He'll know what it is. It's not much, but it's important to me. Could you get it from him, and bring it round to my house? Please? When you've got time."

He looked perplexed, then gave a quick smile that lit up his face. Her heart sprang like an elated lamb. "Yes, okay. No problem. See you later."

"*I've found out everything, got all the gossip.*"

Mel's words circled around Rosie's head as she trudged home with Lucas, damp grass squelching beneath their feet. Ghostly clouds turned the twilight luminous. She could smell snow. She glanced anxiously at the Crone Oak as they passed it, but nothing moved.

"So, you think any of it's true, then?" asked Lucas.

"What have you heard?"

"All sorts. The kids in my class have talked about nothing else all day. Sam was expelled from his posh school for fighting," said Lucas. "There are so many rumors flying around, I don't know what to believe."

"Sam took on three boys and put them in hospital," Rosie said flatly. "That's the truth."

"How d'you find that out?"

"Mel, of course. Her mother has sources. Sam was already on umpteen warnings."

"Wow."

"I hope that's not admiration I can hear in your voice."

"No, no," Luc said quickly. "Why did our school let him in, then?"

"Why d'you think?" said Rosie. "Lawrence is loaded. That's why his school took so long to expel him, and why ours was so eager to take him on. *Money.*"

Lucas gave her an eloquent sideways look of disgust. "I know one thing. No one dares say anything to Sam's face. Everyone's scared witless of him."

It had been a strange day, with Sam's incongruous presence and tantalizing glimpses of Jon. It was as if they'd already webbed the school with the tangled atmosphere of Stonegate Manor. "I'm not afraid of him," she said.

"Brave Rosie. I'm not scared either, then."

"Good," she said, "because if he lays a finger on you, I'll kill him." The comforting bulk of Oakholme shone behind webs of winter trees. After a moment, she asked, "Lucas, do you like Jon?"

"Seems all right," he said, offhand. "I don't know him

yet. Bit quiet. If we were in the same year, we'd probably dodge sports classes together."

An hour later, when Rosie came down from her room, she heard her mother talking to someone in the kitchen. Her heart skipped. She'd changed into jeans and a soft wine velvet top, brushed her hair to a deep shine . . . just in case Jon came.

She walked steadily down the hall towards the glow of the kitchen, saw her mother leaning against the warm bulk of the Aga cooker with her hair in a loose ponytail over her shoulder. She was smiling and chatting to someone concealed by the door. Rosie bit her lower lip to redden it, swallowed hard, and strode casually in.

The young man sitting at the farmhouse table was not Jon, but Sam. He was out of school uniform and in jeans with a grey cable sweater, looking older than seventeen and perfectly angelic.

The world juddered under Rosie's feet.

"Hello, sweetheart," said Jessica. "You've got a visitor. Can I leave you to it while I do things upstairs? Kettle's boiled." She was gone, not waiting for Rosie to answer, let alone ask her to stay. Sam stood up, edged to the kitchen door and casually pushed it shut.

"Hi," he said.

"Would you please leave?" Rosie stood stiff and hostile in the center of the room.

"In a minute. Jon said you—" Sam's shoulders were drawn up in contrition and his eyes were somber, not mocking. He held out a closed hand. When she didn't respond, he placed an object on the table. There was a waterfall of hard little clicks and her crystal pendant lay there, glittering on its chain. "You asked for this, so . . ."

"I thought he was going to bring it himself." The dismayed words were out before she could stop them. She groaned inwardly. Damn, *damn*.

Sam's eyebrows flickered. "I see." He sighed and fidgeted, looking uncomfortable. "Sorry to disappoint, but he didn't seem that bothered when I offered to come instead. I mended the chain, by the way. Look, Rosie . . ."

She stood with her arms folded against him, furious and helpless.

"I'm sorry," he said. "Really, truly sorry. We got off on completely the wrong foot."

"I don't think we did," she said. "It looked to me like you started exactly as you meant to go on."

"No, no, I didn't. I'm an idiot. I want to make it up to you."

Her kind nature wanted to believe his apology, but her memory called up the bruise he'd left on her arm at the party, his sadistic pleasure in taunting her. "You could try explaining why you changed schools," she said crisply. "I heard bullying with violence and grievous bodily harm."

"Who told you that?"

"Who didn't?" she retorted.

He looked away from her, his voice low and flat. "Yeah, I got expelled for fighting. So? They had it coming."

The easy way he admitted it shocked her. "And that made you feel big and tough, did it?"

"Not really, no."

"What about Jon?"

"He didn't want to stay on his own, so Father took us both out."

"And are you planning to start roughing up everyone at our school instead?"

"No," he said, with the trace of a laugh. "Only if they piss me off."

"You're really charming, aren't you?"

"Just honest."

Rosie didn't know what else to say. He made her jumpy and angry and she desperately wished he would leave. Perhaps she could perform some cleansing rite on the pendant, so she could wear it again. "Anyway, thanks for bringing back my property finally, although I don't know why I'm thanking you."

"I understand." He moved towards the back door, stopped. "Rosie, would you, er . . . How about going for a coffee with me sometime?"

She stared at him in complete shock. "Are you asking me out?"

"No!" Sam said quickly. "Well, yes. Only for a coffee."

"What for?"

He appeared tongue-tied for a moment. "So I can say sorry properly. And, you know, you're not completely repulsive." He smiled.

The suggestion floored her. She turned hot with panic. She was ready to fantasize about a gentle boy with the eyes of a poet—but not ready to put herself at the mercy of a rogue with a reputation and fresh blood on his hands. He'd already tried to kiss her—what else would he do?

No—god, no. The potential for fresh humiliation was boundless.

"You must be joking." All the rejection in the world blazed in her voice. He actually flinched.

"Right." The cruel, intimidating glitter reappeared in his eyes. He gave a twisted grin, angry or embarrassed at her refusal. She'd sounded harsher than she'd intended—but she was thinking of schoolboys bleeding on hospital trolleys, the raw sting of the chain breaking across her throat, Matthew crouching bloodied and wretched behind a hedge, saying, *He's crazy, keep away from him.*

"It was worth a try," he added. "Plenty more girls at school. In fact, your mother's pretty fit."

"Get out," she said, panic turning to outrage.

"What happened to my cup of tea?"

"You're asking for boiling water over your head. Could you be any more obnoxious?"

"Haven't even started yet." He crossed to the outside door, paused with his hand on the doorknob and said, "You like Jon a lot, don't you?"

"He's okay," she said defiantly. "I can't believe you're related. He's nothing like you."

"No kidding." Sam opened the door onto darkness and

she tasted needles of ice on the air. Slipping away into wintry gloom he glanced back at her, his face pale in the closing gap. "You do know he's gay, don't you?"

Auberon was walking along a footpath towards Comyn's farm. Around him the afternoon was chill and wrapped in all-day winter twilight; but he loved Charnwood in all its masks. The trees were clawed ghosts in the mist. As he walked, he remembered . . .

Lawrence at Freya's Crown; hair jet black against his robes, the great stone mound looming behind him. He held the applewood staff and a bronze dish of hazelnuts. The sky above the Dusklands was black glass scattered with snowdrifts of stars. A throng of Vaethyr waited, their Otherworld forms already emerging; hair growing longer and brighter, eyes becoming feline, human bodies elongating. On some shoulders, ghost wings rustled.

Candle smoke curled into the air like soft breath. When Lawrence lifted his staff and struck the stone, the ground trembled; one Gate turning inside another until they all came into alignment and there was the portal, stretching like an infinity of mirrors; the Way to the Inner Realms, the Gate of Gates.

Then Lawrence offered each Vaethyr in turn a hazelnut, and they ate, and passed through.

It had been a beautiful night, that last Night of the Summer Stars twelve years ago; crisp and glowing. It was shortly after Lucas's birth, a time of renewed happiness . . . Auberon and Jessica had felt the cool grass of Elysion beneath their bare feet as they danced . . . but, later, they'd sat out of the Great Dance itself, content to watch, sipping honey wine.

A perfect, peaceful night. Auberon wondered if he'd missed some hint of the coming darkness. Lawrence's high-handed abrasiveness had given no clue, since it was his usual manner . . . or was it?

Wilder came from Sibeyla, realm of air, and of course the Spiral-born often found it hard to adjust to Earth. In his twenty years as Gatekeeper he'd proved capricious about the lesser festivals, sometimes not turning up. He'd become feared and disliked. Auberon had reason to hate him; but at a younger age, he and Lawrence had been friends. He had seen Lawrence in moments of weakness that made hatred impossible.

Lawrence had twice opened the Great Gates for the Summer Stars rite. The first time, nineteen years ago, Liliana had been there to support him. Second time, twelve years ago . . . yes, he had looked uneasy. If you ruled out personal matters or stage fright and attributed it to foreboding instead, his grim demeanor took on new meaning.

Third time—Gates locked in their faces, *dysir* set upon them, Lawrence intransigent.

Auberon felt a dark wave shudder up through the roots of the earth, and through his body. He opened his eyes, tasting soil like death in his mouth. In that moment, he knew that Lawrence was telling the truth. The very rocks, connected to the Gates, pushed the knowledge into him. An amorphous peril slumbering within the Spiral, some formless terror that he couldn't grasp . . . the image was gone, leaving a dark trail of fear behind it.

Sighing, Auberon continued his walk. The grass squelched under his boots as he followed the lane towards Comyn's farm. He wondered about other Vaethyr communities around the Earth, their network a delicate spider's web with nodes concentrated around portals, and all those portals controlled by the Great Gates of Cloudcroft. Really, the Aetherial population of Earth was tiny, and mostly too distant to give Lawrence any trouble. The majority, although they might be uneasy about their Gatekeeper's actions, still trusted him.

After all, it was Lawrence's role to be vigilant, to sense threats that no other Vaethyr perceived. It was his gift and his duty. If he'd sensed this gathering shadow from the beginning . . . well, it did not excuse his behavior, but might explain a lot.

Auberon climbed a five-bar gate into a pasture, check-

ing for the massive bull, Brewster. The pasture was empty.
The bulk of farm buildings appeared on top of the hill. As
he drew closer, Comyn came to meet him, fitting the role
of gentleman farmer in a green waxed coat and cap; a natural denizen of the landscape. His rubberized boots left
deep imprints in the mud.

"Found a moment out of your busy schedule?"

Auberon had learned not to take offense at his brother-
in-law's bluntness. "You said come up for a chat. Here I am.
Is this a friendly cup of tea, or something more serious?"

"It's serious," replied Comyn.

He led Auberon across the farmyard to a barn. Inside,
the air was wreathed with the steamy stench of cattle. Railed
in a pen stood Brewster, Comyn's pride and joy, the magnificent brown bull that had triumphed in the show ring
and earned him a fortune at stud. The concrete stall was
swept clean, the straw fresh and golden. Brewster, however, stood with his head lowered, no fire in his eyes. His
coat was dull, muscles wasted. Auberon was shocked to
see him.

"He's dying," said Comyn. "We've kept him going but
the last couple of days—" His hand sliced the air to indicate sudden decline.

"What does the vet say?"

"Hopeless. We've tried everything." His voice was gruff.
"End of the line."

"He's quite an old man now," Auberon said gently.

Comyn let himself into the pen and stood stroking
Brewster's once-hefty neck. The bull huffed, swiveling
cloudy eyes towards him. "He's not a mortal bull, Bron. He
came with me from the inner realms. A wedding gift from
my clan."

Auberon had always lived in the surface world. His family had owned this farm for generations. Comyn, however,
had been Aelyr, Spiral-born. He came of an Elysian clan
called the Fheylim, a tough, fierce, dark-haired people from
which Auberon's family had also branched. That made him
and Comyn distant cousins.

Long ago, during a solstice rite in Elysion, Phyllida had met Comyn and brought him to the surface world. Since Auberon had his own business and no desire to be a farmer, he'd asked his parents to leave the farm to Comyn instead. Despite the gift—or because of it—Comyn had an edge of disdain towards him, an Elysian who'd rejected his farming heritage to build houses for humans. Auberon tried to ignore the needling.

"I know," Auberon said, leaning on the top rail of the pen. "There's such vigor about Brewster, as if he's the very archetype of a bull."

"That's precisely what he is." Comyn stroked the bellowing flank. "Human myths overflow with bulls. He is the sun, the fire of life. Can you guess when he began to lose his health?"

Auberon exhaled. "When Lawrence first closed the Gates?"

"Exactly then. Brewster hasn't eaten the grass of Elysion for five years and this is the result. How long before we fade, too?"

Phyllida appeared from the gloom of the farmyard. Her hair, falling over the collar of her waxed jacket, blazed under the barn's fluorescent lights.

"It's the way things are, Bron," she said. "My skill to diagnose and heal is no longer as instinctive as it used to be. I feel I'm only half a doctor. We take for granted those Spiral-connected energies that give us an edge over humans, until they fade."

"Everything is affected," Comyn said fiercely. "Everything."

"I know," said Auberon, "but we're strong. We still have the Dusklands. Even if Lawrence keeps the portal shut for fifty years, we'll survive."

"As what?" Comyn turned to face him. "Mortals with our memories gone? No chance of rebirth, just plain old death? Is that what he wants? Is that what *you* want for your children?"

"No, but there are worse things than living in this world—"

Comyn cut him off with a growl. "It's our birthright, as Aetherials, to have free access in and out of all realms—regardless of the rules the self-appointed jobsworths of the Spiral Court try to impose upon us. Bron, if he doesn't get those Gates open, whatever these supposed dangers, he'll have no choice. We'll force him."

"No." Auberon made a placatory gesture. "I understand, but forcing him would be wrong. Whatever we think of Lawrence, he's acting to protect us. He may open the Gates tomorrow."

"That will be a day too late for Brewster," Comyn murmured. "Why do you, of all people, defend him? Are you afraid of him? Happy, are you, for your children to be denied their birthright and turn into human drones?"

"Of course not!" Despite himself, Auberon was angered. "But what possible reason could Lawrence have for lying?"

"Who knows?" Comyn flared, striking the rail with the flat of his palm. Brewster snorted, showing a flicker of fire as he swung his great horned head. "Conflicts like this led to our fall, our influence fading from human history. Now we live in secret, like fugitives! Left to me, there'd be no Gatekeeper and no Gates, either. D'you think I can watch my bull dying and not think the unthinkable? If we have to depose the almighty Lawrence Wilder, so be it!"

Auberon waited for the outburst to end. "No," he said firmly. "If we do that, we might unleash the very peril that Lawrence fears. We could lose the Spiral for all time."

"That's a lot of mights and mays to be afraid of," Comyn growled.

"Comyn, he's telling the truth. The danger's real. We must trust him."

"Well, I say to hell with the danger," Comyn spat back. "Bring it on."

"And I would agree with you, but I have children to think of."

"And how is this slow, fading death better than a quick, violent one?" Comyn breathed out through his teeth, rage subsiding. "Vaethyr trust you, Bron. If you don't help us, who will?"

"That's what I'm trying to do," Auberon replied. "To avert conflict, and stay in friendly communication with Lawrence. If we're too quick to declare him the enemy, where's the ruddy sense in that? We'll only resolve this by negotiation, not war."

Phyllida said gently, "He is right, Com."

"I know." Comyn turned to Brewster and slid gentle hands over the sunken rib cage. Phyll watched him, her face somber and haunted. "Don't worry, Bron, I have the patience of mountains." His voice tightened with pain. "I won't do anything rash. But I'll never forgive him for this."

"I'm sorry about Brewster. I truly am."

No one spoke for a minute or two. When Comyn turned again, there were tears in his eyes. Never in his life had Auberon seen him in tears.

"We're waiting for the slaughterman," he said. "Will you wait with us?"

After Sam had gone, Rosie lifted the crystal heart and held it up to the light. She'd been certain it would be a disappointment, a glass trinket. Instead, its sparkling fire enchanted her all over again.

Could she wear it again, and pretend to her dear father that she'd had it all the time? Strange, that Sam had kept it safe all these years. Perhaps it was a magpie mask he needed, not a hawk.

She pocketed the heart as Jessica came back in and slipped an arm around her shoulders. "Am I right in suspecting that the infamous Sam has a crush on you?"

Her mother's body felt warm and safe and her hair smelled beautiful. "And on you, apparently," said Rosie. "Probably on any female who can't sprint away fast enough. Did you hear why he was expelled?"

Jessica nodded. "It's a shame, the way he's turned out. Such a good-looking boy, and as charming as anything to me. I don't want to judge him on hearsay, but you're wise to keep your distance."

Rosie bit her lip. She'd never admitted her previous encounters with Sam. Her mother might have been less relaxed if she had. "I'm not afraid of him."

"Nor should you be. Never forget, we're Aetherial," Jessica went on firmly. "However human you look or feel, your core is Aetheric. When you feel ready for a lover—"

"Oh, Mum." She tried to squirm away, mortified, but Jessica held her shoulders and looked straight into her eyes, deadly serious, equals.

"When you're ready, Rosie, remember what you are. Nothing can take that strength away from you. Unlike humans, we have conscious control over certain of our physical processes. It's our power."

Embarrassment fell away as Rosie remembered the talks—more from Aunt Phyll than from her own mother— about sealing her own inner chambers, controlling pleasure, secreting protective juices that would repel microscopic invasion of any kind. Learning awareness of her body, until it was as instinctive as breathing. "I know. I was taught well."

"So you can choose whoever pleases you—but no one can invade you, infect you, or impregnate you against your will. The power is yours."

The kitchen faded and they were two warrior queens in an older, more vivid world. Rosie felt a shining fire inside herself, as if her spine were made of gold. A handful of eccentric memories—her mother taking her out at dawn to bathe in dew, or to lie laughing and ecstatic under a full moon—now fell into place. It was about maintaining their Aetheric nature, regardless of the masculine barrier of Gates. She sensed green leaves all around them, flowers and ivy twined in her mother's hair. She felt truly *other*.

"Aetherials are layered beings," Jessica went on. "There's our human shape in the surface world, and the changed forms we may assume in the Dusklands or Spiral.

There's our core or essence, which equates to the human heart, soul and mind, but includes instinct, our sense of the flow of right or wrong. And then there's the *fylgia*—the shadow soul, which dwells in the Spiral and always connects us there. It may take a smoky animal form, if you ever glimpse it at all."

"Mine would be a fox, then." Rosie smiled.

"Not necessarily. You know, your blood realm doesn't always define your elemental leanings or character. I'm Elysian like your father, but I feel Sibeylan, drawn to air, birds, music . . ."

"So yours is a bird?"

"Oh." Jessica looked startled. "Well, they're hard to see clearly and the *fylgia* is very personal. You can think of it as a guide, the part of you that knows best . . . usually." Her gaze lost focus. "It is hard, being unable to visit the inner realms to replenish those energies. So we have to make more effort to nourish our Aetherial side here on Earth. Nurture the animal, divine and elemental as well as the human. There's no division in us."

"I feel I know this," said Rosie. "It's like a dream that I'd forgotten until you reminded me."

"Yes," Jessica said sadly, "that's how it is."

"So we've done sex, can we do death?" Rosie said, wry but serious. "I don't see any white-haired bent Aetherials around. What about your parents?"

Her mother's shoulders drooped, expressing sadness. "Some Aetherials raise their children like birds; fling them out of the nest early and fly away. The moment Phyll and I were old enough they were away, touring with their orchestra. Cello and first violin. The house was always full of music . . . but they were gone too soon. Maybe that's why I'm too possessive of my children, and Phyll has none. They aren't that old, but . . . Didn't your father talk about this?"

"No, he didn't. I don't believe we're immortal."

"Nothing's immortal, sweetheart. Call us semimortal.

We don't age so much as fade, and then we're drawn towards the Spiral. We *need* to go there. That's why the older ones vanish. If my mother and father decided to go, I doubt they'd even tell us. They lose themselves deep in the heart of the Spiral and they're transformed. They may come out again in their original shape, or they may rest in elemental form for a century or two, or be reborn entirely."

Rosie took this in, thinking that it sounded desolate, not comforting. She had a sudden, chilly vision of arriving home one day and finding Oakholme deserted, her parents simply gone . . . "And what if a mad axman bursts in and chops my head off?"

Jessica pulled a face at her. "Then you die, and leave a mess on my floor, but your essence travels to the center of the Spiral and may, sooner or later, be reborn in a new form. You wouldn't necessarily remember who you were. That depends on the individual's strength of will."

"It sounds frightening. A kind of open-ended journey without a proper shape."

"But it's exhilarating, too. I used to sing a song about it, 'Kiss the Mirror.' "

"I sometimes hear you singing, Mum, in my head. Maybe I'm nuts, but it's kind of comforting. I wish you'd still sing. In reality, I mean."

Jessica gazed narrowly at her. "I can't. My voice went. And you're lovely but weird; a true Aetherial. Anything else you want to ask, love?"

"Yes. Initiation?"

"No. Not today. Not for two years."

"And will the Gates be open again by then?"

"Who knows?" Her mother's eyes darkened, as her father's had. "I don't know."

"Mum, everything you've told me has been about the Otherworld, about going in and out of the Spiral," said Rosie. "But we can't anymore. So what happens instead? We just die, end of story? Matthew might think he wants that, but I don't. I want the journey."

As Sam trudged up the hill in the dark, he looked back and saw lights shining in the windows of Oakholme. Ice sifted around him and he was wet, freezing, but he didn't care. All he could think about was Rosie, Rosie, Rosie and it made no sense.

He wasn't sure when it had happened. He'd noticed what a nice shape she was as she entered the great hall, of course. Then finding her in his room—that was it. One moment she was just a spoiled Fox to mock and torment. The next, her plum-red mouth and sultry eyes and glorious burgundy hair and fearless spirit had plunged inside him and exploded every shred of common sense into a torrent of molten desire.

Oh, yeah. That was purple but absolutely true. Hopeless. Every word he said only made her hate him more. Never mind putting his foot in it, he was chest-deep in crap every time he opened his mouth. He didn't even know why he couldn't stop thinking about her.

Close to the manor, he heard something in the bushes to the left of the house. He stopped and watched, owl-silent, until he saw the moving shadow. He stalked at a distance, all the way up the hill, creeping closer until he was at the summit, an arm's reach away. The figure was sitting cross-legged with its back against the bulk of Freya's Crown, eyes closed. Sam bit his lower lip. Then he reached out and clutched the figure's shoulder.

Jon gave a strangled yell, jumped so violently he almost launched himself off the earth. "Jesus, Sam!" His hair was stringy with sleet, his skin stone-cold.

"What the hell are you doing, you prat?" said Sam.

"What do you think?" Jon said angrily. "Leave me alone."

"A couple of points," said Sam. "One, how the hell are you going to see into the Otherworld, when you didn't even sense me two inches away?"

"Fuck off."

"Two, if Father catches you here, he'll kill you."

At that, Jon turned even paler in the darkness. "You won't tell him, Sam."

"No, but one day he's going to catch you. If he thinks you're trying to open the Gates, oh my god, you'll wish you'd never been born."

"I wasn't trying to open the Gates," Jon said. He jumped nimbly to his feet and stood there, a skinny bedraggled angel. Sam rose with him, saw scratches on his hands and face. On the ground lay a wreath of thorny twigs, inter-twined in a rune.

"No? Don't leave the evidence lying around."

He kicked the object so it flew into the bracken and dis-integrated. "Hey!" Jon exclaimed, trying to pull him back. Sam held him off easily with one hand.

"Now get inside before you freeze to death."

"You don't understand," Jon said angrily. "I wasn't try-ing to break through. I just wanted . . ."

"What?"

"To see Mother. To see where she is."

At that, Sam put one hand round Jon's throat and pressed him back against the rocks. "You fucking idiot. You think she went through there? How and why? I suppose it's as likely a place as any!" He let go, shoving Jon away. The touch was only to shake Jon up, not to hurt him. Sam took a few paces away, calming himself; then came back and said, "So . . . you actually have any success?"

"No."

"No," echoed Sam. "Because she's dead."

"She is not dead!" Jon cried. "How can you say that?"

"She must be dead," Sam said quietly. "She would never have left us without a word for all these years, unless she'd died in the meantime. Even if she was in the Spiral, she wouldn't have just forgotten us. You simply can't face up to it."

"Oh, yes she would," Jon answered with venom. "She just doesn't care, that's all."

He flinched as his brother turned on him again; but Sam

let his hand drop, let the anger bleed into nothingness like the sleet. He walked away with Jon's wounded voice following him. "You're the one who can't face it: She never cared about us."

5

❦

Not Quite Narnia

Jon. Jon. Rosie wrote his name over and over again in swirling ballpoint letters. *Jon & Rosie, Rosie & Jon.*

First love, unrequited love; it was a powerful drug. If she'd thought that the rest of her schooldays would be haunted by frustration, her heart would have broken on the spot; but she couldn't think it. Not when each day brought fresh hope of seeing him, of reading volumes into the briefest glimpse or smile.

Jon was friendly towards her, but always distracted, as if he had somewhere more important to be. He wouldn't let her any closer. Rosie convinced herself that he was concealing some great secret pain. If he'd only confide in her, the barriers would crash down and they would be twining hands and whispering secrets.

"Mel, do you think he's gay?" Sam's unkind revelation haunted her.

Mel did a double take. "What? No chance."

"How d'you know?"

"Having long hair and being a poser doesn't make him gay, Rosie," Mel said with conviction. "We need to make him notice you."

Easy for Mel to say. Radiant and sun-blond, she chose and disposed like a princess. Rosie felt invisible, like the earth-spirit she was. Her abiding impression of Jon was of him hurrying along school corridors away from her, pre-occupied, his hair streaming around his sharp, dancer's shoulders. He'd gathered a clique of hangers-on by then. Rosie tried to join in but she was always on the fringes, couldn't find the key to the inner circle. The effort wounded her pride. She felt idiotic, like a fan stalking a film star, yet she couldn't stop dreaming.

Sam, meanwhile, had only a year or so left at school. He hung around with a bad crowd and, although she tried to keep out of his way, she was forever turning around to find him watching her from a distance. He was like a stalking panther, still and predatory, an ice carving in black-and-white.

He'd taken up with a girl from the rough end of Cloud-croft, a stocky, ebony-haired creature covered in tattoos. Mel nicknamed her the Pit Bull. Every time Rosie went out, Sam seemed to be lurking with his gang, draping him-self over this square-faced girl with her short, hard little fringe, and all of them glaring menacingly in Rosie's direction.

"He's trying to make you jealous," Mel said one day.

Rosie was horrified. "Never. He's trying to scare me. He once admitted he hates my family. He must hate me even more for standing up to him."

"So ignore him," Mel said sensibly. "Let's plan how we can get you and Jon together."

The usual thrill of misery fell through her. "I don't think it's going to happen."

"Well, there are plenty of other guys who aren't so in love with themselves, if you'd only give them a chance."

"I don't care about them. You don't know how I feel."

She tried, but never could shake off the image of her perfect soul mate in Jon's limpid brown eyes, his shy grace and long, artistic hands. She had only to glimpse him and it all started again.

Oh, the drama. Mel tried on boys like shoes, but when Rosie loved, it was forever.

Rosie turned sixteen, the age of knowledge and initiation. The Gates, however, stayed closed; there was no magical rite of passage for her; life went on as before.

That summer, she and Lucas threw an end-of-exams party at Oakholme. It was an excuse for Rosie to invite Jon—but Jon, to her dismay, didn't come. Instead, Sam arrived without invitation. When she took him outside and coolly explained that he and his gang weren't welcome, he simply left; sardonically glowering, but resigned and gracious enough.

"Still worth a try, pet," he said, tilting one eyebrow at her as he went.

The next evening, as Rosie was walking home alone from Mel's house, a bulky figure stepped out from the shadows of a hedge. It was Sam's girlfriend, the biker chick, all muscle and studded black leather. She was no taller than Rosie but could plainly bend her in half like a hairpin.

"You stay away from Sam," she said.

Rosie didn't know how to react. The winding lane was deserted. "I haven't been anywhere near Sam," she protested.

"I saw you with him last night."

"Yes, telling him to get lost!"

This only seemed to make the Pit Bull angrier. She swaggered forward, all menace and simmering violence. "I know your game. Every time Sam and me are out, I turn around and you're there. You think you can take him off me. But he's with me, you bitch."

"Yeah, you rich bitch," said another voice behind Rosie, and there were two of the Pit Bull's female cronies, both as big and tough as bodyguards.

Fear flashed through Rosie. She knew she was doomed and nothing she said would save her. "I don't want your stupid boyfriend!" she hissed.

The first punch knocked her back into the arms of the bodyguards. As the second came she twisted to evade it and dived to the ground, gravel scouring her palms. A kick to the kidneys took her breath away. Part of her was paralyzed with disbelief that it could be happening; what use was her heritage if it lent her no powers to defend herself? More kicks. Winded, bruised and helpless, she curled up and tried to roll out of range. A hand grabbed her collar and dragged her half-upright. Her legs gave way. She tasted blood.

The Pit Bull punched her in the stomach.

As she collapsed, she instinctively fell sideways into the Dusklands. The world turned lavender and cobwebby. The three females were still laying into her but now the blows landed like gossamer. They looked less substantial, smaller and paler. In a trance, controlled by a deeper self, Rosie rooted her feet in the ground and stood up.

What did her attackers see? Something translucent, she imagined, wild and wolfish with twigs for hair, rising like a specter between them. They froze. She heard one of the girls say, "Jesus."

The Pit Bull took a swing at her, which made enough impact to drop her to her hands and knees again. Then the attackers were fleeing in a welter of rubber-soled boots, the Pit Bull shouting over her shoulder, "You stay away from my bloke, you fucking freak!"

When she staggered upright, almost disintegrating with delayed shock, a gentler voice whispered above her, "You all right, girl?"

She looked up and saw the leafy face of the Greenlady, high in the branches of the Crone Oak. This must be what she'd meant about blood on her tree; a warning that she wouldn't tolerate violence near her beloved oak. "I'm sorry," Rosie choked.

"You go on home," said the dryad, sounding kind, not angry. "Go on. Can't leave my tree, but I'll watch you home."

Rosie told her parents she had fallen in some brambles. They seemed to believe her. The next day, she marched up to Stonegate Manor and presented Sam, who'd opened the door to her, with her black eye and torn hands. He stood openmouthed and incredulous as she brusquely described what had happened.

"You call your bodyguard bitch off," she finished furiously, and strode off without giving him a chance to respond.

"Rosie!" he called after her, but she kept walking. For once she felt strong and fearless, and it was a good feeling.

That night, she lay in bed and thought about the Greenlady, and Jon, and what it meant to be an Aetherial trapped in the human world. A golden summer moon glowed through her curtains. What if she and her brothers—and Jon and Sam, come to that—were never able to enter the Spiral or partake of the experiences their parents had known?

A memory rose: She was about seven, sitting on Brewster's broad back as Comyn led him, gentle as a lamb, around a paddock. They'd often visited the farm as children. She remembered her father and brothers watching from beneath sunlit trees. Her uncle was saying as they went, "You'll notice things about certain people, Rosie. Adults who don't seem to grow any older. No comfortable grey-haired grannies for us; no, our grandparents look as fresh as our parents until they simply disappear. Mysterious, eh?"

Rosie had been disturbed. Had the half-remembered adults who'd doted upon her as a tiny child been her grandparents? All she'd been told was that they lived far away now. Her uncle continued, "Don't be afraid of it, girl; it's what we are, Vaethyr, not human. Your family lives in the human world but you'll feel the call of the Otherworld, a need to run under the stars like a wild animal. You'll know what it is to be both huntsman and hound, tearing into the raw flank of your prey . . ."

At that point, her father had appeared beside them, saying, "That's enough, Comyn."

He'd sounded angry. Her uncle had grunted, "You've no

right to shelter your children from the truth of what they are," and Auberon had retorted, "And you've no business telling them anything; that's left to me and Jess, not you."

Strange, that the memory surfaced tonight. The news of Brewster's death in winter two years ago had saddened her. Had her grandparents made it to the Spiral—her mother's musical parents, Auberon's farming family—or were they trapped on Earth? Would the Greenlady die too as all links to the Spiral faded? She remembered the terrifying image she'd had of coming home to find Oakholme deserted, her parents gone without a word. At least, if the portal stayed closed, Jessica and Auberon would surely have no reason to vanish.

Lying in her bed, she let her awareness slip into the Dusklands, felt the changed perception swelling like honeyed moonlight into the room. It was easy. Surely nothing could be wrong when the Dusklands still saturated Oakholme so deeply?

Her bedroom was bathed in light, glistening as if coated with golden dew. She rose and went to her wardrobe, finding not clothes inside but a twisty corridor of dark walnut leading to a chamber where a shining tree thrust up through the floorboards and vanished in the vault of the ceiling.

In an enchanted state of consciousness, Rosie circled the tree, climbing over its roots. The leaves were flakes of green light and the trunk was silvery, thick and swollen with rounded excrescences, slippery as silk and warm to the touch. In her strange waking dream she trailed her fingers over the undulations. She rested her face on its silken bark. Her arms went around the trunk and as she pressed the length of her body into it, its hard warmth seemed to swell into her, molding perfectly into the strange urgency that transported her.

Rosie floated, breathing hard as she dissolved into golden fire. The Dusklands softly exploded. She came awake in bed, gasping, hands flung back on the pillows as she convulsed. For once there was no thought of Jon in her mind, only the simple wonder of ecstasy. She slid one hand between her thighs to make the feeling linger.

What lay behind her wardrobe door was not quite Narnia, but it was hers. Her beautiful secret tree of knowledge.

School terms and seasons rolled by. Rosie never saw Sam with the Pit Bull again. The girl was still around the village—keeping a safe distance from Rosie—but Sam had left. Gone, said the rumors, to backpack around Europe. Lawrence apparently was not pleased. Rosie wasn't sure what she felt; relieved, mostly.

One firm conviction anchored her; her love of trees, earth and living things. She was a true Elysian, a natural gardener. To be affiliated to earth meant going into the natural world, to the greenwood, to silver lakes where willows kissed their reflections; being absorbed into rock and the moist wormy soil . . . and rising out again, remade. She tended Oakholme's rambling grounds, speaking softly to the shy elementals who peeped down from the branches as she worked. She began to redesign the neglected rose arbor, taken with an idea to create a sacred space. Always when she passed the Crone Oak she bowed and greeted the Greenlady, even though Luc teased her, and the dryad herself was rarely in evidence. It was a matter of respect.

At eighteen, she left school with good grades and a place at horticultural college. Jon was now at art college in Nottingham and rarely seen, yet Rosie's obsession lingered. She couldn't bear the thought that she'd never have a renewed chance of what should have been.

One day in August Lucas came running to find her, breathless. "I just met Jon in the village," he said. "He's having a birthday party next Saturday. Everyone's invited—all his mates from college, school and the village. D'you want to go?"

Rosie nearly said no. She was annoyed at herself for the wave of yearning, heart-pounding excitement that swept over her. If Jon wanted her, he knew where she lived and he'd had an open invitation for the last four years. She did not need to humiliate herself at a wretched party. *But,* she thought helplessly, *but . . . what if this time . . . ?*

Every time she entered Stonegate, it was different. This time, the house became a dim and smoky morass of adolescents, lit by candles and saturated with the odor of spilled beer. Guests were dancing in the great hall, sitting on the stairs and along the galleries. Factions spilled into bedrooms; there was a ghost-story session in the rooftop conservatory, wreathed in incense. There were a few locked doors, but no sign of Jon's parents. Mel, Faith and Rosie all had to agree, it was a damned good party.

Apart from the elusiveness of Jon.

Wherever Rosie went in the house, he was elsewhere. She no sooner entered Jon's presence than he had somewhere more exciting to go. She ended up sitting on a rug in his bedroom, drinking cider from a bottle, her ears full of trance and indie music. She started college soon. This could be her last chance with him. Certainly, at this rate, her only chance to see the inside of his bedroom.

How drunk would Jon have to be to find her suddenly enticing? How drunk must *she* be to fling away caution and grab him?

Faith was beside her, sipping lemonade and clearly out of her depth; Mel was in a corner kissing a boy she'd known for quite some minutes. Others were sprawled over the floor and bed. It was too noisy to make conversation. The bedroom was dark, but misty light spilled from the corridor and she saw Jon out there, talking intently to someone, half a dozen student friends around him. She felt a bite of envy. What did they do in their secret circle? Smoke pot, talk politics, play truth or dare?

Rosie saw that the person talking to Jon was Lucas. She rose unsteadily to join her brother, but in the four seconds it took her to reach the corridor, they had all vanished.

Lucas saw Rosie in the doorway, her hopeful face appearing from the darkness, and he wanted to wait for her; but it was too late. Jon and the others, oblivious, were herding him away and the moment when he should have said something was lost.

Outside, the night was summery, with a hint of cool breeze. Jon led them through tangles of rhododendron and birch to a hilltop where a volcanic crag thrust from the heathland grass. Below the rocks lay a shallow, ridged dip in the ground. The night was sourly fragrant with bruised grass and bracken. Oak trees shivered against a midnight sky.

Lucas knew this place. Freya's Crown. In the dip, Jon threw down a red velvet cloth and sat cross-legged on it, his hair flowing over an Indian patchwork top. He looked like a beautiful shaman seated there, ethereal and self-contained.

The others were four lads and three girls from Jon's college, all human as far as Luc could tell. Some had musical instruments. Warily Lucas sat in the circle, facing Jon. There was a hush, a sense of ceremony. Jon produced a packet of brownish, leathery disks; mushroom caps. Placing them on a red enameled plate, he took out a penknife and cut each one into thick slices. Then, holding the plate as if it held communion bread, he offered it around. Lucas watched the others taking slices, holding the stuff on their tongues with closed eyes. When the plate reached him, he hesitated.

Jon's gaze met his. "Go on," he said.

"What is it?" He immediately felt idiotic, marked as a virgin.

"Dream agaric," said Jon, his eyes intense and compelling. "It grows in the Dusklands. It opens the corridors of the imagination. It's strong stuff. Are you scared?"

"No," Lucas said quickly. He took a thick slice and slipped it into his mouth. It tasted musty and bitter, its texture rubbery with a hint of sliminess. Wincing, he chewed and swallowed quickly. It went down whole and he almost threw it back up again. Only pride and panic kept it down. Everyone sat cross-legged, eyes closed, waiting for it to take effect. Fighting nausea, Lucas waited with them.

A chalice of syrupy wine came around, followed by a foul-smelling joint. Jon began weaving leafy twigs into a crude shape: a spiral threaded through a pentagram. One of the students was playing a flute, while a spiky-haired girl tapped a rhythm on a bodhran.

Nothing happened. Lucas frowned, feeling trapped in this absurd situation and wishing Rosie were there. He didn't know why Jon had taken to him. They'd met on the stairs and Jon had begun talking to him with a steady gaze—as if he'd suddenly registered Luc's existence.

Nothing happened, but he noticed how soft the ground felt, friable as if he could feel all the space between the atoms, like soil fragments on a cobweb. He lay down to feel it more fully. The sky was the face of a goddess with blue-black skin and star-streams for hair. Estel, Lady of Stars, staring down at their tiny forms exposed on the hillside like a sacrifice.

Lucas suddenly understood the Dusklands as a state of altered awareness, as opposed to a physical Otherworld. Of course! He couldn't fathom why he hadn't got it before. The humans around him became indistinct, but Jon glowed red and gold, like a religious icon.

Freya's Crown was huge and bright, covered in silver snail trails. The trails were runes glimmering on the surface. Everything around him went shadowy but the rocks grew more solid and he began to hear their insides moving. Huge cogs were grinding like millstones, like Russian dolls, one inside the other.

Lucas felt that grinding inside his body. The whole crag was turning, drilling the earth like machinery chewing through rock. He felt the ground fall away as the churning vortex sucked him in. With a scream he fell right through the Dusklands, down into a chasm of fire and steaming ice . . . down through an endless corridor of arches, until he saw a vast, mausoleum door of granite waiting for him. It was so real he saw the spirals and runes engraved on its surface. He was going to smash into it—and when he did so, he knew he would die.

White light crackled around him. He felt the heavy shudder of the door cracking open—and that was worse. There was something terrible behind it, gigantic and so dazzling that it blinded.

He felt the immense pressure of a flood straining to break through—only the flood was not water but shadow, utter darkness and blinding fire. As he fell towards it, he knew he must will the door closed again, even knowing the impact would kill him. Death was preferable to letting that hideous force burst into the world.

He fought, shadow-boxed, twisted his fingers in magical gestures but nothing helped and he could only fall, helpless. Then out of the whirling chaos a pale and terrible face surfaced. It was far away but huge—glaring at him with blazing, mad eyes, reaching for him—all he knew was that he must slam shut the Gates before this horror burst through—and suddenly it was not far away after all but human-sized and close. "*Lucas*," a voice hissed in his ear.

His whole self turned inside out on a scream as he saw that the terrifying face looming over him was that of Lawrence Wilder.

He came to, lying flat on a couch. He was gasping and dizzy, his stomach sore. Sapphire Wilder was bending over him, wiping his mouth with a damp cloth.

"It's all right, Lucas. Can you hear me? Open your eyes, that's it."

Lucas managed to sit up. His limbs were softened wax. The walls around him glowed red and gold. He had no idea where he was, but it didn't matter. He'd closed the Gates, hit the hard surface, and lived. Sapphire gave him a glass of water and he drank, coughed, and drank again. He was shivering violently.

"Good lad." Sapphire turned away and said, "Has he taken something?"

Jon was a vague figure near the door. He shrugged. "Only if he took it before he got here." He looked levelly at Lucas as if daring him to contradict.

"Funny, I didn't think he was the type to take drugs."

"Me, neither," said Jon. "He was drinking cola. Maybe someone spiked it."

"That would be extremely serious," she said, turning back to Lucas. Her hands with their long nails were warm on his, and she exuded a fresh, exotic perfume. "How are you feeling, dear?"

"Okay," said Lucas. He knew it was essential not to admit anything. The world felt as sharp as glass. "I'm sorry, Mrs. Wilder."

"I'm thinking you should see a doctor."

"No! No, I don't want my parents to worry. Honestly, it was just cider. I'll be fine."

"Cider? Jon, this party was supposed to be soft drinks only. We agreed."

Jon rolled his eyes. "Some of them smuggled it in. For heaven's sake, we're all over eighteen."

"Lucas isn't. Anyway, that's not the point. We had an agreement; I kept out of the way as long as everyone behaved." She looked at Lucas with her head on one side, her lovely mane hanging over one shoulder. A gem at her throat held a universe of tiny rainbows. "Still, we do these foolish things as teenagers and there's no need for parents to know every humiliating detail, is there?" She stood up. "Jon, would you watch him while I make tea?"

Jon stood to one side of the door, thumbs hooked in his jeans, until his stepmother had gone. Then he came to the couch and looked down at Lucas with dark, intense eyes. "Are you all right?"

"I don't know."

"It made me sick the first time I tried it, too," Jon said with a twisted smile.

"Sorry," said Lucas, compelled to apologize for acting in an uncool manner. "I feel a right idiot."

"It doesn't matter." He squatted down by the arm of the couch, his voice falling to a whisper. "My father cannot find out about the mushrooms. Promise you won't tell anyone. He'd go ballistic. Promise?"

"I promise," said Lucas, startled. "I wouldn't, anyway."

"You don't know him. He's terrifying when he's angry. He's forbidden me to even think about the Gates, let alone try and see what's on the other side. If he found out what we were doing, he'd kill me."

Lucas looked at him, startled. At the same time he became mesmerized by the luminosity of Jon's face and the incredible bronze-copper texture of his hair. "That's awful."

Jon shrugged. "We have to be careful, that's all."

"Is that what we were doing?" said Lucas. "Trying to look through the Great Gates?"

"Yes, you know, through visions."

"You didn't say."

Jon grinned. "I know. It's better that way, then people don't make things up to impress me. So, what did you see?"

Lucas hesitated. He liked Jon and wanted to please him. "It was a muddle. I was falling. The rocks turned silver and opened up to let me through, but I hit this massive stone door . . ." He didn't want to describe the nightmare. It made no sense, and the fear was too raw. "It sounds lame."

"No, that's really interesting. You saw more than I ever do, even though I've tried and tried. There are forces that want to stop us and we must learn to see through their illusions."

"And your human friends . . . do they see anything?"

Jon shrugged. "Not really. Humans haven't got the wiring. Y'know, they'll report seeing all sorts of exotic garbage, but nothing *real*."

"Why do you bother with them, then?"

He gave a one-sided smile. "I enjoy being a guru. It makes them feel special. And you never know, one of them might have a genuine revelation. But we're different, Luc. We're Aetherial so we're tuned in; it's already there inside us, waiting to be channeled. We can try again sometime, if you're up for it?"

"Here's tea," Sapphire interrupted brightly, bearing a

tray. Jon rose, putting a fingertip to his lips. "Anything else you want, Lucas?"

He smiled, grateful for her attention. "Just if you could find my sister, please?"

Rosie looked at her watch. Half past midnight. Mel and her latest conquest had vanished, Faith had fallen asleep in a corner and Rosie was frankly bored. There were a few necking couples and semicomatose loners around the room; no one she could actually talk to. Apparently it was expected for guests to stay overnight, but Rosie wished she could go home. How annoyed would Jessica be if she walked down the hill in the middle of the night and left Lucas behind? She sighed. Perhaps she would find Jon's party crowd in the conservatory, but knowing her luck, this would be the night Sam chose to come home and she'd meet him, or something worse, in a darkened corridor.

And then her dream strolled in.

Jon was in the doorway. He was coming towards *her,* ignoring everyone else, hair flaring around his shoulders, his face serious and radiant in the semidarkness.

"Rosie, could you come with me? I need to talk to you."

"Sure," she answered, affecting nonchalance.

In silence, he led her along the passages where she always got lost. Her heart was lurching. Jon's presence beside her was so vivid, warm and silken, it was all she could do not to grab him. This tactic usually worked for Mel, but Rosie was too nervous to risk the utter hash she knew she'd make of it.

"So, what's up?" she asked lightly, to break the silence.

"Lucas was taken ill," said Jon. "He threw up and sort of passed out. He seems okay now, but he's asking for you."

Rosie's heart plunged. Her dream shattered; fear filled the void. "What's wrong with him?"

"Too much cider, he says."

"The stupid idiot!"

Jon brought her to a staircase she'd never found before and led her to the top floor. The scent of flowers and candles wreathed the landing. Everything was ivory with touches of green, and Japanese calligraphy on the walls.

"He's in here," said Jon, smiling apologetically as he opened a door to a Chinese-style red sitting room with two sofas.

She was furious, but when she saw Lucas, bone-white and shivering, with Sapphire tending to him, her heart melted. "What's all this?" she said, sitting beside him. "You can't start knocking drink back like a Norse god, you know. You're not even old enough."

He gave a wan smile. "I know. Promise you won't tell the parents."

"I'm really sorry, Mrs. Wilder," Rosie said, feeling awkwardly responsible. "He usually knows how to behave."

"Not your fault, dear. All part of growing up, unfortunately."

Jon said, "Is it all right if I go, Sapphire? I should get back to the others."

Sapphire turned coolly to him and said, "Your guests might want to think about going home or to bed. Sort them out and I'll look after these two."

"Thanks." Jon sidled out, to Rosie's dismay. He was obviously relieved to escape, and not remotely interested in spending time in her company. Nothing had changed. Something died a little inside her.

"I could phone my father and ask him to collect us," she said.

As Sapphire leaned forward, all gloss and serenity, Rosie had a strange mixed feeling of being cosseted and trapped. Her creamy voice was enchanting. "No need for that. We don't want Lucas to land in trouble, do we?"

"Dad's not an ogre," Rosie said sharply. "He'd tut a bit, then it would be forgotten."

"Still be embarrassing," said Lucas. "I'd rather stay, Rosie, honest. I'm fine."

She sighed, her nerves wavering at the thought of a long, haunted night in the manor. If she were pressed close against

Jon all night, of course, that would be different—she suppressed the thought. "As long as you're feeling better."

"I've made camomile tea," said Sapphire, pouring from a bamboo-handled teapot. "It's so nice, having this chance to know you better. We've never really talked, have we?"

"No, not really," Rosie said guardedly. Sapphire was so charismatic and confident. Her presence filled the room like the fragrance of jasmine, and Rosie still wasn't convinced she was human. With some Aetherials, as Auberon had said, it was hard to tell. They held their aura in so tight you couldn't sense it. Why would someone like Lawrence marry a human?

"It's lovely to see such a happy, close family as yours," Sapphire went on, handing Rosie a cup and saucer. "I'm afraid Jon and Sam have suffered from the absence of a mother or a proper home life. I'm trying to make it up to them."

"Um—yes. I can't imagine life without our mum." She sipped the scalding honeyed tea to cover her awkwardness.

"You're a cautious soul, aren't you, Rosie?" Sapphire smiled. "You don't give much away. I hope you'll open up once we know each other. Unfortunately, Lawrence and I have been too busy with the jewelry business to socialize as we planned, but I'd like that to change."

"Oh . . . I know my dad and Mr. Wilder are acquainted, but we've never seen much of him—I mean, we don't know what our parents get up to, it's like a different world." Rosie smiled weakly.

"But you're quite close to Jon and Sam?"

"No, we never had the chance. They were away at boarding school and . . ."

"Yes, it's such a shame. Sam's a law unto himself, of course, but you and Jon seem to get on well, don't you, Lucas?"

"Yeah, he's great," said Lucas, looking startled.

"He really likes you too, dear. I think Jon and Lucas are like peas in a pod, don't you, Rosie?" Sapphire smiled, showing perfect white teeth. "A pair of truly fine-looking young men."

Lucas squirmed, coloring. In other circumstances it would have made Rosie laugh. She said, "I hadn't noticed, but I suppose they are."

Sapphire's smile became knowing, confidential. "Of course you've noticed. Women do. We understand, at a deeper lever, things that aren't apparent on the surface."

There was a strange moment in which Sapphire's gaze hung on Rosie's; probing, implying, watching her reaction. Puzzled, Rosie frowned. Sapphire caught the look and the probing abruptly stopped.

"You know, dears," she said, smoothing over the moment, "if there's one thing I'd advise young people to do, it's to talk to their parents. Honest communication is the key to happiness."

"We do talk to them," said Rosie, concerned that Sapphire was implying a problem where none existed. "They're great."

Sapphire's perfect eyebrows twitched. Her full pink lips parted. "Good," she smiled. "We'll talk again. Now, you should sleep. We have spare rooms, but not many with actual beds in them; Lawrence's ex-wife wasn't much for homemaking, as you've probably gathered. Will you be all right on the sofas here? I'll bring duvets and pillows. That way you can keep an eye on your brother."

"Thanks so much," said Rosie. "It's really kind of you."

"My pleasure, dears." Sapphire blew them a kiss.

Lucas was in the attic with Jon. The winged being was there in front of them—not a painting, but alive and hiding its face in its hands. Now and then it uttered a faint, anguished sob.

Sapphire was there too, bending over the angel's head. She was barely visible among the heaped shadows. "This is your father's business," she said.

"We have to let it go," said Lucas, distraught. "You can't keep it prisoner here, it's wrong, it's cruel!"

"There's nothing I can do," said Sapphire. She put her hand beneath the being's face and caught a large, shining tear. When she held it up, Lucas saw that she was holding a tear-shaped Elfstone. "This is where albinite comes from. It's the tears of the caged god."

"Why's it crying?" said Jon.

"For all the unrequited love, dear," said Sapphire.

Lucas woke violently, his heart racing from the horrible, haunting dream. It took him moments to work out where he was. He looked up at the ceiling and wondered if the attic was above him, the angel in the painting still up there weeping?

He tried to sleep, but the room spun and he was falling into the stone jaws of the Gates again. His sister was fast asleep. Thirsty and starving, Lucas decided to go in search of the kitchen.

Rosie didn't stir as he slipped from the room. He tiptoed into the corridor, barefoot in pajamas, and felt his way down to the middle floor, where chill moonlight lit the long gallery. Rosie always complained that the house shifted and played tricks, but to him it felt all too solid, like a fortress.

Carpets prickled his feet; the stair treads were cold and waxy, then came the flagstones of the great hall, like walking on ice. The drug was still working through his system, making every sense too vivid. Perhaps he was still dreaming.

The kitchen had been expensively refitted and smelled of new wood—Sapphire's touch. Lozenges of moonlight fell on blond wood and black marble. He found the sink under a window, put his mouth under the tap and took a long cold drink of water. Then he groped his way along a countertop until his hands found a china cookie jar.

As he removed the lid, he had a sudden impression that the jar was mounded to the rim with human brains—or mushroom caps. He recoiled. No, only oat cookies. He took one and it tasted incredible.

He ate and wondered about Jon—what he'd truly intended by handing out magic mushrooms—but he couldn't think straight. The moonlight was solid like crystal, and the darkness had a furry texture against his skin. Nothing felt right. Only the mealy warmth of oats on his tongue anchored him to reality.

Then something touched him in the dark.

There was a shadow by his thighs, nosing for the crumbs he was dropping. He pushed forward with one knee but it went through thin air. The shadow had no weight and no scent, yet it was *there*. Not animal, but something sinuous and hungry, with a touch like damp leather.

Lucas was petrified. His arm flattened along the wall and found a light switch. A blaze of light dazzled him, but through it he saw there was no demon at his feet.

There was, however, a man in the room with him.

An island unit stood in the center, and the man was on the far side, staring at him. Pallid skin molded over harsh bones, black hair swept back, narrow eyes colorless. The face from his drug nightmare. "Turn out the light," he hissed.

Terrified, Lucas obeyed. Now he was blind in the darkness. "I—I—I'm sorry, Mr. Wilder," he choked out. "I didn't know you were—I'll go."

"No." A hand fell on Lucas's left shoulder, making him jump as if a live electric cable had lashed him. "It's all right, Lucas." Lawrence's deep, quiet voice rolled out of the velvety darkness. "I didn't mean to give you a fright. I'm sorry."

"'Sokay." He knew Lawrence could feel him trembling but he couldn't stop.

Another hand came behind him to grip the right shoulder as well. "Are you all right? Take deep breaths. I think that's the advice."

Lucas shuddered, mortified. He felt his heart slowing as the wave of shock faded.

"Couldn't sleep either, eh?" Lawrence asked. He sounded friendly.

"No, sir," Lucas mumbled. "I was hungry."

"Absolutely. Help yourself. I was about to make tea."

The massive hands fell away. Silhouetted against the

window, Lawrence filled a kettle and switched it on. Then he leaned on the countertop beside Lucas, in darkness in the weirdest silence Lucas had ever experienced. He didn't know how to escape. Again he sensed a gryphon shape moving around the room. He daren't say anything, but he stared, trying to see it.

"It's only a *dysir*," said Lawrence. "One of my household guardians. Trouble is, they're of dark Aetheric substance from Asru, so how can one be sure they're not fragments of Brawth? I suspect they're the same thing."

Lucas had no idea what he was talking about.

"Making no sense, am I?" said Lawrence. "They're like guard dogs but only there to warn, not to hurt. I command them, since the official *dysir* keeper deserted me, but that's not to say I want them here, these compulsory trappings of office. Guardians or spies?"

If Lucas had been human, he would have been convinced that Lawrence was utterly mad. Since they were both Aetherial, Lawrence seemed only three-quarters mad. "I've never seen anything like that in our house," he said. "Not even in the Dusklands."

"Well, you wouldn't," Lawrence said softly. "Your family are happy and wholesome and they live as creatures of Aether should, with their roots in the earth and their branches in the light. Such haunts don't plague your household."

"I—I should go back to bed."

"No, stay. Have some tea and talk to me." Lawrence's tone was impossible to disobey. He poured boiling water into mugs. "I'll take a little whiskey in mine. Would you like some? For the fright?"

Lucas coughed. "No—no thank you."

"Just a drop. You're not a child."

"Oh, oh—all right then, sir, thanks." Lucas began, rather innocently, to suspect that this was not Lawrence's first drink of the evening.

"You're sixteen, aren't you?"

"Yes." The tea was black, sweet and fiery. If Rosie

smelled it on his breath in the morning, she would have a fit. At this moment, though, he felt that morning would never come. Lawrence Wilder would surely drink his blood, or smother him.

"Sixteen. Old enough for initiation rites. Old enough for knowledge. I suppose your father has painted a very grim picture of me?"

"No, not at all," he said. "I always got the impression he admires you—grudgingly, sort of, but he does."

Lawrence gave a bark of laughter. "Extraordinary. Ever the diplomat, the philanthropist, the backbone of our community, your father. I say *your* father . . ."

Another silence. The laced tea was floating Lucas even further from reality. He watched the slithering *dysir* and waited for Wilder to continue.

"Of course, the thing you should have been tóld, which you're now old enough to be told, which no doubt your lovely family hoped to sweep under the carpet forever, is the fact that I am your father."

"You're what?" Lucas laughed involuntarily. Lawrence laughed too, his barely visible face contorted with mirth.

"You are my son, dear boy. Not Auberon's. Mine."

6

Battle of the Demons

The next morning Lucas was quiet as they walked home; not companionably so, but deathly, lip-bitingly quiet. He'd insisted on leaving before anyone else got up. Rosie had to say everything twice to get his attention and then he looked through her with cloudy eyes.

"What's up with you?" she said. "Still nursing your hangover?"

"No," he retorted. He scowled, pushed his hands in his pockets. "I'm fine."

"So what did you get up to with Jon?" She couldn't quite keep the envy out of her tone. "How special d'you have to be to join his secret clique?"

"God, Rosie, are you obsessed? There are more important things than whether you can get off with Jon!" His outburst startled her. Then out of the blue he asked, "Do you think I look like him?"

"Like Jon?" she said, thrown. "Not really."

"Do I look like Lawrence at all?"

"No. Why would you?"

"Because . . . last night I . . ." Lucas stopped in his tracks, sat down on a rock and rubbed his face with both hands. He sighed and stammered, and then the story came spilling out. Rosie absorbed it in disbelief. "I've got to ask Mum if it's true," he finished, agonized.

She was staring at him, her mind reeling. "No, it can't possibly be."

"Then why would Lawrence tell me such a massive lie?"

"I don't know! But think—you can't ask Mum if she had an affair!"

Lucas raised pained eyes to hers. "No, you're right, I can't. It's too horrible."

After a moment of heavy silence, Rosie said, "All those strange hints Sapphire was dropping last night . . ." They stared at each other.

"No. How could Sapphire know before me? That's not fair. That would make it real and it's not."

"Come on," she said gently. "It's probably a misunderstanding."

They pushed through the hawthorns into Oakholme's garden and Jessica was there, throwing scraps to the birds in the soft morning sunshine. She was graceful and barefoot in a long skirt, her hair a messy golden veil. She waved, called them into the kitchen and poured coffee.

As they sat at the big pine table, Lucas sat close to Rosie, silent as if waiting for someone to slap an explanation out of him. Jessica looked inquiringly at her daughter, who looked back without expression. "Are you both okay?" asked Jessica. "Good party, was it? Late night?"

"It was odd," Rosie answered when Lucas didn't. "Which I suppose is normal for the Wilders."

Lucas went on gazing at his fingers wrapped around his coffee mug. "Has someone upset you?" Jessica asked more firmly. She touched his wrist but he pulled away.

"No." He chewed his lower lip, sighed and said, "I had the weirdest dream."

Rosie's heart lurched into her throat. She shook her head, but he took no notice. "Yeah." He looked his mother in the eye. "I dreamed I met Lawrence Wilder and he told me that he was my father. What sort of a dream was that?"

"A completely ridiculous one," said Rosie.

Jessica didn't laugh. Dismay shadowed her face. "Oh, my god," she breathed.

"It was a dream, though, wasn't it, Mum?" Lucas focused intently on her. "Why would he lie about a thing like that?"

"Oh my god," Jessica said again. "Tell me what happened."

Lucas described his descent into the kitchen, a man in the darkness, a surreal conversation. Color came back to his face and he was almost gabbling with the relief of confession. "I tell you, it was like *Star Wars,* 'I am your father, Luke,' only without the costumes and heavy breathing. But why would he say that? I don't get it."

"Bastard," Jessica whispered. "He had no right. This wasn't meant to happen."

"Mum?" said Rosie, alarmed.

"Oh, god." Jessica pushed her chair away and stood with her back to them. She put her hand to her mouth, let it drop. She walked about, hugging herself.

Hard flakes of disbelief settled in Rosie's heart as she watched her mother pacing and struggling. "He had no business . . . Lucas, I always meant to tell you, but the time was never right. This is wrong, you should have heard it from me, not him."

Rosie and Luc stared, seeing a different person. She returned to the table and looked down at them, her face serious and intense, her eyes alight with distress. "I'm so sorry," she said quietly.

"No," said Lucas, his forehead creasing with angry pain. He sounded so bereft that Rosie's heart broke. "I don't want to be Lawrence's son. I want to be Dad's."

"And you are, in every other way, but—"

"What happened?" Rosie asked in a small voice. "Did you have an affair?"

Jessica's gaze fell. "I made an awful mistake," she said.

"And that's me, is it?" Lucas cried, rising to his feet. "An awful mistake?"

"No, no, that's not what I meant." Then Jessica was holding his hands and protesting how much she loved him and he was trying to pull away and all three of them in tears. Horrible.

"Rosie," Jessica said grimly, "let Lucas and me have few minutes alone."

Shock like that made the whole world spin. Sitting on a chair at her bedroom window, Rosie cried a little and wasn't sure why. Lucas was still her brother, no one had died. Still, it felt like the death of something.

After an hour she heard the click of her door, and Jessica's footfalls on the carpet. "Are you all right, love?"

"Is Lucas all right?" said Rosie, turning. "That's the real question."

Jessica perched on the side of the bed, facing her. "Not yet, but I hope he will be. We're still the same people."

"Are we? Thank goodness." Rosie wanted to be angry, but she was too bewildered.

Jessica asked softly, "Your level of boiling fury, on a scale of one to ten?"

"About a nine," said Rosie. "It's all right, Mum, I'm not going to yell at you."

"You've every reason."

"Yes, but we don't do things by yelling, do we? We're civilized. But . . . I can't believe it. Dad adores you."

"And I adore him."

"Then *how could you*?"

"Sometimes it's not enough." Jessica looked at her bare feet, rubbing one on the other. "When things seem too perfect, you can get restless. I had a moment of insanity long ago, which only made me realize how much I loved Bron after all."

"And this moment—without details, please—what brought it on?"

Jessica met her gaze with steady eyes. "There's nothing I can say to excuse myself. It was impulsive and selfish, that's all."

Rosie was grateful for the lack of information. "Does Dad know?"

"Yes. He's always known."

"And he forgave you?"

"Eventually." Jessica smiled wanly. "He's a good man. He has a heart the size of the Earth. He decided on the spot to treat Luc as his own, and he always has."

"And there's no chance Luc could be his?"

"None. He was away for some weeks on business at the crucial time, so . . ."

"So when were you planning to tell us?"

"I don't know. It was easier to put it off. Why make an issue of it, and make Luc feel different? Bloody Lawrence! But it's my fault. The last thing I wanted was for you to find out like this, but it was bound to happen. *Mea culpa*, I'm so sorry."

"Boiling fury now down to a six," Rosie murmured. "Sapphire, last night—she was hinting at how alike Jon and Lucas are. Very strange. When I tried to ask what she meant, she looked all serious and gave us a lecture about communicating with our parents."

Jessica groaned. "Oh, great, so Sapphire knows."

"I suppose everyone in Cloudcroft knows, except Luc and me."

"No. Only Phyll and Comyn, and they'd never tell. Whether Lawrence has told his own sons—I've no idea."

"Oh god." Rosie realized that the shock wave would go on spreading outwards. More ammunition for Sam, more reason for Jon to disdain her? "Mum, remember the advice you gave me . . . about our power to control our fertility? So if it wasn't an accident—why would you decide to have a child with Lawrence?"

The question hung in the air between them.

"I can't answer that." Jessica's voice went hoarse. "Yes, I let it happen but to this day I've no idea why. An impulse. As if Lucas insisted on being born and I had no will to prevent it. And who'd want to be without him?"

"No one," Rosie said emphatically.

Jessica tilted her head to one side. "Can you forgive me?"

"As long as Lucas can." She moved next to her mother and hugged her. "It's not the end of the world."

They held each other for a long time. "You're a wonderful girl, Rosie. You have Auberon's kind heart, for sure. I must phone him, and there's still Matthew . . . Come on, let's face the day."

Rosie stood up, calmer now but shaken. "Mum . . . your, er, moment with Lawrence . . . It's not why Ginny left, is it?"

A long pause. Eventually Jessica answered on her way to the door, "Let's just say it didn't help."

Later, Rosie found Lucas by the sound of a tennis ball slamming against the garage wall. He grinned at her, turned away and went on throwing the ball harder than ever.

"Stop it," she said, pulling at his arm. She took him to an arbor with a moss-covered sundial and a stone bench, and sat him down beside her. "How was your chat with Mum?" He sighed and looked away. "Come on, we have to talk."

"What for?" he said. "Mum thinks she can make it all

better, but she can't. I thought I knew who I was, and now . . . I feel sick."

"It was unbelievably cruel of Lawrence to tell you like that. Why did he do it?"

Lucas shrugged. "First time he'd ever met me alone, and he'd had a few drinks. At least he was honest. It's the deceit I can't get my head round." He sat with his hands braced on the edge of the bench, dark hair dangling forward. He did resemble Lawrence in a way, she thought, long-limbed and skinny like him. "I don't want to think about how it happened."

"Me neither," she said, and they fell quiet, determinedly not thinking about it. "Only Mum knows, and she's not saying."

Lucas chewed at a thumbnail. "You want to know what I was doing with Jon last night? We were trying to get through the locked Gates to the Otherworld."

Her jaw dropped, even as Jon's name sent an electric pang through her. "*What?* How?"

"Not literally." He gave an uneasy laugh. "Through a sort of . . . trance."

"And did you?"

"No. I think he expected me to have incredible visions, being of the old blood and that." Luc's head drooped lower. "D'you think he knows we're . . . ? God, I can't say it. Brothers. Is that why he expected more of me? I wanted to please him. I don't know why. There's something about him . . ."

"Yes," Rosie said helplessly. "I know."

"But if no one's told him . . . Will he be angry? Will he still want to be friends with me?"

Rosie grabbed his hand. "There's no one who wouldn't want to be friends with you, Luc. If he doesn't, that's his loss."

He grinned, looking briefly like his old self. "Thanks. I bet you've forgiven Mum already, haven't you?"

"Pretty much," said Rosie. "Why?"

"Because that's how you are. A bleeding angel."

"Can *you* forgive her?"

"Don't know. She and Dad let me spend my life thinking I'm one thing, then I find I'm something else entirely." He looked as she'd never seen him before; desolate, lost, and suddenly older. "What the hell am I supposed to feel or do about any of it? What do I say to Dad tonight?"

"Dad will be fine," she said firmly.

"He might, but will I?"

Jessica paced the familiar rooms of Oakholme, thinking of everything that she could have told Rosie, and hadn't. In the bedroom, she opened the box that contained her albinite bracelet and draped the chain of sparkling gems across her palm. Lawrence had given her the bracelet after Lucas was born.

Auberon knew she had it. He'd never demanded she give it back; in return, she never wore it. It wasn't a gift given in affection—that wasn't Lawrence's style—but a sort of respectful goodbye. Typical of Lawrence; no words, just cold jewels—but an acknowledgment of Lucas, all the same.

Music had been Jess's lifeblood, her home the stage, her life the passion of her songs. At home with two young children, she'd missed it. Sometimes she felt that she'd lost her real self. It wasn't that Auberon took her for granted; rather, he loved her too much, protecting her like some rare egg wrapped in silk tissue. Her bird spirit had rebelled. She'd wanted someone not to protect her, but to admire her with raw lust.

It had been during an icy stretch of Lawrence and Virginia's volatile marriage . . . An Elysian ritual to celebrate the luscious spring, with dancing and too much honeyed wine . . . Jessica had happened to dance with Lawrence, and the dance had left them both hotly aroused in a way they dared not admit.

Couples would often slip away into the forest, not always with their usual partners. Auberon, however, wasn't wild like that; he liked to stay in the center of things. That night, Jessica had rebelled against his decorum. Instead of returning to his side she wandered into the woodland and there she met Lawrence again, alone by a tree as if he'd been waiting for her.

To claim she'd been bewitched sounded lame. She'd certainly been drunk. No words; just a look of reckless, mutual heat. And away into the woods, with the peaty earth, the fragrant bracken and springy grass, clouds sailing across the stars, tree branches trembling and owls haunting the night as they devoured each other.

It had been incredible.

The one thing she'd never spelled out to Auberon because he hadn't asked—although he obviously knew—was that it had happened more than once. Gods, many times that summer. The coincidence of Auberon's long business trip had made it all too easy. So exciting, to see Lawrence's stone-cold exterior thaw for her. Delirious, she'd opened herself completely to him, opened every last gate within herself until conception was inevitable, as if to keep him inside her forever. She still felt a guilty throb of heat, remembering.

But it was only lust. Lawrence had no tenderness in him. In the end it burned itself out with its own arctic chill. Finally she understood what she truly wanted, and Auberon had waited patiently for her to come back.

She still questioned the flood of madness that had led her to conceive Luc—and led Lawrence to collude, because he had. Vanity? Look how beautiful we are, we should have a child? Or some shadowy manipulation by unseen Aetheric powers of which they weren't even aware? No, that was evading responsibility. The fact was, Lucas was here and she wouldn't change a thing.

Dignified to the last, Virginia had never said a word to Jessica, but the frigid hauteur of her eyes said it all. Another seven years had passed before she actually left Lawrence, but it must have added unbearable strain to their fragile relationship.

No, nothing Jess said to her children could possibly make it sound acceptable.

Strangely, it was Matthew, returning home that afternoon, who took it hardest. He blanched as his parents haltingly explained. They were all stiff, measured dignity, while he looked close to tears. Rosie, curled next to Lucas on the sitting room sofa, looked out at the summer evening and longed to escape.

"You know what? I sort of knew," Matthew said tightly.

Lucas gasped, "What do you mean?"

"You look like Lawrence. Can no one else see it? And I always knew there was something going on, some secret buried. Being Aetherial, nothing's ever straightforward, there always have to be layers underneath. Why can't we be normal?"

"Whatever normal means," Jessica replied, eyelids lowered and arms clasped across her waist. "I can't justify what happened . . . things happen in the Otherworld that sometimes shouldn't."

"Good job the blasted Gates are shut, then!" Matthew turned on Auberon. "And what about you, Dad? Don't you want to knock Lawrence's teeth out?"

Auberon stayed deadly calm, but Rosie saw the color rising in his face. "It's not the way we do things."

"Who's we? The noble Vaethyr? We behave no better than humans! Why didn't you kill him?"

"We make free choices," said Auberon. "We don't own each other. Do you not realize that your mother and I made peace on this issue years ago?"

"I'm not talking about Mum! I'm talking about Lawrence Wilder springing it on poor Luc in the middle of the night! Are you going to let him get away with it?"

Rosie felt tension in the air like wire about to snap. Jessica took a step towards him, saying shakily, "Matt, I know you're upset—"

"*I'm* upset? What about Luc? You've just told us something that's destroyed everything I thought we were supposed to be! So much for the perfect family! Lawrence must be in stitches! Jesus!"

There was a split second of awful silence. The whole room trembled. Then, an explosion of glass. Auberon hadn't moved, but a Tiffany lamp on a table four feet from him burst into fragments, showering the room in rainbow shards. The lightbulb exploded. The heavy stem of the lamp hit the carpet.

They all flinched. Matt gave a sharp cry of pain and sat down heavily beside Lucas, one hand flying to his face. Rosie saw blood spill between his fingers. A piece of glass had struck his lip. Wincing, he probed the wound and looked at the blood on his fingertips. Jessica was there at once, solicitous, but Auberon fixed him with a firm stare.

"And there you've exactly hit the point. Lawrence attacks my family because he's jealous of us. He cannot hold his own household together so he seeks to disrupt mine. If ever I stormed up there to confront him, he would read it as victory. That's why I don't retaliate. Jess came back to me, and I have his son, and I will never let him see that he's hurt us. *That* is my revenge."

"Well, you're a bigger man than me, Dad," Matt said, muffled. "Me, I'd want to knock seven shades out of him."

Lucas groaned. "Matt, shut up, will you? Don't make it worse."

Shaken, Rosie got up and began picking bits of glass out of the carpet. When she heard a quiet knock at the front door, she rushed into the hallway to open it. Matthew's friend Alastair was on the doorstep, looking startled when she answered. "Oh, Matt didn't tell us you were coming," she said.

"He didn't know," said Alastair. "I only dropped in to see if he fancied a pint." He glanced curiously at the glass fragments in her hand, inclined his head at the raised voices behind the half-open door. "Have I chosen a bad moment?"

Rosie let out a breath and gave a half-smile. It was a relief to see a different and friendly face. She didn't know Alastair well but he always seemed cheerful, and he was antithesis of Jon; reddish-fair, his face broad, freckled and smiling, with hazel eyes and fair lashes. Not bad-looking, really, in a generic, sporty way. She liked his Aberdeen accent.

"We're having a family crisis, that's all," she said, embarrassed. "We're not normally like this."

"I know."

"I'm sure it'll blow over, but . . ."

"Look, I'll go. Tell him I came by." He stood looking at her. "Rosie, you look upset."

"It's unbelievable," she said, her throat suddenly aching, "how a handful of words can tear up your life, spin you round and drop you into a world entirely different from the one you thought you were living in. What are you supposed to do?"

"I don't know," he said, bewildered. "Whoever's upset you, hurt them back, only worse. Really hit them where it hurts. Me, I usually punch a wall so I only harm myself, but . . ." He trailed off with an uncertain half-grin. "Are you all right?"

"Not really," she said. "D'you mind taking me to the pub instead?"

After two large vodka-tonics, she told Alastair what the quarrel was about and watched his reaction. He was plainly surprised and went quiet, his eyes unfocused. Then he shook his head, took a drink of beer and said, "Your father's amazing."

"Forgiving Mum, you mean? Couldn't you?"

"Oh, I suppose I could. It hurts, like being stabbed; I know that. An ex of mine, once, she . . ." His hesitation woke a pang of empathy in Rosie. "Anyway, she wasn't worth forgiving. But someone like your mother, how could a man not forgive her?"

Rosie sighed with relief, feeling on safe ground again. "I wish Matt had taken it that well. He blames anything that goes wrong on us being . . . different."

"I don't get it. You're a great family."

"I know." The admiration in his tone amused and

warmed her. "And Matt knows it. He has our best interests at heart, but he can't resist telling us all how to behave, even our parents, even though he's out of line and knows it." She paused while Alastair bought her another drink, then went on, "I'll tell you what he's like. Matthew is like a boy from an arty, eccentric bunch of bohemians, who's embarrassed by them because he wants to be a city slicker in a suit."

They laughed together at the image.

"Your parents seem normal to me," said Alastair. "At least they're together."

"Yours not?"

He had that quiet look again; sorrow under the cheerful exterior. "Father's dead now. Mother's long gone with some bloke or other. It's history. Matthew and your folks are more family to me than they ever were."

"Oh, Alastair, that's so sweet."

"So, your parents used to be hippies, then?"

"Undoubtedly," Rosie giggled, "but that's not what I meant by 'different.' Suppose we were from another country, and even though we've been British for centuries, we still practice the old traditions. Matt finds it tedious and backward, that's all."

"Yes, so he says, but I'm not sure what he means." Alastair leaned forward, looking intrigued. "So, what's your mysterious background, then? Irish, Romanian, Viking? Are you Russian émigrés or something even more romantic?"

"Better, we're the faerie folk," said Rosie, laughing even harder. "Oh dear—Matt really hasn't told you, hasn't he?" And suddenly she stopped laughing.

Later, Lucas slipped through the gap in the hedge and Jon was on the other side, waiting for him. He was a soft silhouette in the twilight, hands in pockets, hair blowing around his shoulders. "Hey," Lucas greeted him.

"Hey," said Jon. "You okay?"

"Had to get out of there. I, er . . . found out some stuff."

"Me too." They looked at each other. "About my father and your mother?"

"Um, yeah, that," Lucas said awkwardly.

"Let's walk," said Jon. They took the thin footpath along Oakholme's boundary, making for the village. "They told me when I got up. Which was at lunchtime. I don't think Dad would ever have admitted it if Sapphire hadn't made him. She's known for ages, apparently. I bet he'll put off telling Sam too, but he needn't think I'm doing it for him."

"Are you angry?" Lucas's greatest fear was that Jon would reject him.

"No. Annoyed with my father, that's all."

"It's horrible," Lucas stated. "I can't imagine my mother . . ."

"Why not? She's incredibly pretty." There was a touch of mischief in Jon's remark. "Father says *my* mother knew, but he swears it's not why she left. He said he's not proud of what happened, but not ashamed either. Shame is for humans."

"Right, he's so 'not ashamed' that he had to get drunk first and tell me in the dark," Lucas sighed.

"At least he did, finally." Jon smiled. "He and Sapphire are *dying* to get to know you. How scary is that?"

"It's weird."

"The point is, when they told me, I wasn't surprised," Jon went on. "It was as if I'd always known. I feel a link with you. We're brothers."

Lucas laughed. "Yes, we are."

"I'm glad, aren't you? I've acquired a brother I can actually get on with. When I go back to college, you should come with me."

Their walk brought them to high ground above Cloudcroft, the ridge called High Warrens. Below them lay the undulations of Charnwood landscape with outcrops standing rough against a wild sky. Across the valley, they could see the roof of Stonegate Manor, with the crag of Freya's Crown to its left.

Lucas thought about his parents; a mother he didn't

know anymore, a father who wasn't really his. He put his head back, feeling that a gust of wind would take him into the sky, weightless. "I feel strange," he said. "It's as if I don't belong anywhere. Except for Rosie, I could walk away from the lot of them."

"They don't matter anymore," said Jon. "There's just you and me now. We have far more important things to do."

Jon took his hand, pulling him bodily into the Dusklands. In the oceanic light, they entered a glade of birches with a wide tree stump in the center and a steep slope curved like a horseshoe to one side. The trees moved fluidly, like underwater corals. Jon began to climb, bending now and then to investigate wild plants in the grass. Lucas followed him in a dream, thinking, *We're brothers, linked by seed.*

Jon's ghostly, graceful figure cast a gradual spell over him. Suddenly he saw why Rosie was in thrall to him, albeit in a different way. With his slim form, long legs and rippling fall of hair, he seemed the mysterious essence of an Otherworld that was tantalizingly out of reach.

"Did you know that plants gathered in the Dusklands have different properties from those in the surface world?" Jon turned to him, displaying a domed black toadstool. The surface was as velvety-delicate as moleskin, with a ragged hem drooping over purple gills.

"No, I didn't."

"I've experimented with all sorts." Jon leaned on a tree, one foot up on a mossy stone. "Ever wondered why I was so popular at school? I always had the best drugs." He grinned, teeth white in the gloom. "If we can't break through the Gates physically, we should at least be able to send our mind and essence through."

"Lawrence ever caught you?"

"Not yet. Sam did and went nuts, but he can't stop me. It's our birthright, Luc. My father doesn't own the inner realms. We're shamans and we can find our own way in." He tore off a piece of fungus and held it out teasingly. "So, are you up for trying again?"

Lucas looked at him and said nothing. Fear snaked through him.

"Humans are useless visionaries, and I'm not much better," Jon went on, "but you're special. I know you can break through, given the right substance, the right guidance. I believe in you. Our secret?"

Luc took a deep breath. Then he peeled off fear like a cape and threw it away. He wanted this. He wanted his new brother to accept him, wanted to prove to Jon that he was courageous and would not let him down. The nascent secret between them was the most wonderful thing he'd ever known. The world trembled with magic.

Looking straight into Jon's eyes, he accepted the purple-black flesh from him. "Dream agaric?"

"This one's called devil's nightcap," Jon answered with a smile as Lucas tried the spongy bitterness on his tongue and, without flinching, slowly chewed and swallowed.

After the storm, nothing was the same again. It passed, but the truth had pressed their world into a different, spikier shape.

Jessica loved Auberon, and yet she'd slept with someone else. While Rosie was still a toddler, her mother, for reasons only she understood, had turned away from Auberon and twined herself around cold, mad Lawrence. *Lawrence and Jessica naked, gleaming like marble in a wash of iced moonlight, joined and thrusting* . . . Rosie cringed in embarrassment at her own imagination. Why, why?

All was peaceful again, but the buried tension was like a physical force that wanted to push her out. So Rosie would take long walks around the village at twilight, climbing until she stood shivering on High Warrens, hunched against the wind. From here she could see all of Cloudcroft, a sprawl of houses strung along lanes that wound in all directions up into the Charnwood hills. The village was an inky blur with flecks of light; the woods and hills indistinct blue-grey masses. Tonight the sky hung low, painted orange by the lights of Leicester, Loughborough and Ashvale around the horizon.

She was worried she'd said too much to Alastair. Three large vodkas and she'd begun to let slip words like *Aetherial*. Alastair had been an attentive listener; the attention was flattering, when she got so little from Jon. Her concern was that Matthew would tear her to shreds for saying too much.

She took a breath. The air tasted harsh, like metal, the night cold, wild and brooding. She could feel the closed Gates. Couldn't define how she felt it exactly, but it was like a pressure, a blind spot in the vision, nothingness where something rich and solid should have been.

The great festivals that her parents had enjoyed were no more. Small groups of Aetherials still gathered to mark those occasions, and at the annual Cloudcroft Show each May, they still held a carnival-style dance called the Beast Parade—but the climax, the ceremonial entry to the Spiral, was missing. These events were no more than wistful tributes to what had been. What they felt like, Rosie thought, was arriving at a party with gifts but never being let through the closed door.

Fear blew through her. We need Elysion, her mother had said. Brewster the bull had starved for lack of it; it broke her heart to think she'd never see it . . . and then she remembered the darkness in her father's eyes when he said that he believed Lawrence. The Great Gates had become their barricade against some hideous, unspeakable threat. Oh, but to step into the Otherworld, to face the danger regardless . . .

The wind grew stronger and she tasted rain. Double-wrapping her scarf and pulling on gloves, she began to descend. Trees lashed around her. As she reached the first of the houses and the sanctuary of streetlight, there was a blackout. The world turned to swirling rain and darkness.

Rosie swore and hurried on, barely able to make out the footpath beneath her feet. She felt spooked, disoriented. She couldn't tell if she was walking in the surface world or

Dusklands, and there was some creature snarling in the storm . . .

Right by her ear.

She froze. All around her was boiling cloud with lightning flickering inside. Then the cloud split like a fruit and out fell two demonic, spiny-tailed beasts, screaming and growling and tearing into each other with fangs and claws. Yellow fires flickered around them.

Rosie scrambled up a grassy bank that ran between the footpath and the houses. There was an ash tree there and she pressed behind the trunk, staring as the creatures wrestled. She saw rain and blood glistening on their scales. They were fighting, with yellow-eyed hatred, to the death.

All right, she told herself. I'm definitely in the Dusklands. Just have to step sideways into the surface world . . . She couldn't do it.

Surely the creatures' battle must rouse the whole village. Their screeches were deafening. One demon fell and the other crouched over it, piercing the armored throat of its enemy with curved claws. The screeching ceased. The victor's tail lashed, scraping the gravel of the footpath and gouging the turf.

The eerie fires vanished. Now Rosie couldn't see a thing and she daren't move. Was the demon still there in the dark, raging and hungry? She saw the faintest hint of light sliding over rain-wet, scaly haunches as the victor sloped away from the body of its rival.

Streetlights and house lights flicked back on, making Rosie jump. She looked down at the scene of the fight. There was nothing there.

"Fine," Rosie murmured under her breath, head down into the rain as she ran the rest of the way home. "All right. This must be what Matthew means. Walk in the Dusklands and we start seeing things we shouldn't. We start to go mad. So he's turning his face against the Otherworld and living on the surface, to save himself from insanity. Fine. I get it."

Even their own garden seemed threatening tonight and

she hurried along the front path as if specters were waiting in the greenery to ambush her. The warm lights of Oakholme spilled out. As she put her key in the lock, a pale hand came out of the night and grabbed her arm.

Rosie let out a short, heartfelt yell.

"Rosie, I'm sorry," a small voice whispered. "It's only me."

A pallid face moved into the porch light. It was Faith. She was soaking wet, hair plastered down, rain trickling down her thin face.

"Oh, shit," Rosie gasped. "Wait until my heart starts beating again. God." She took a breath. "What's up, mate? Are you okay?"

Faith was plainly not okay. Her eyes were wide with trauma, a thousand years past crying. "My parents," she whispered. "They had a fight, the worst ever . . . The police and ambulance came and . . . I think my father's dead." Faith stumbled forward and Rosie caught her. "I can't go back there, Rosie. Can I stay with you, just for tonight? I'm so sorry to be a nuisance. Only tonight."

7

Self-Defense

Faith stayed.

Neither of her parents was dead, but after a spell in hospital, there were police reports and restraining orders, separation, her two sisters taken into foster care, the crumbling family demolished. Faith, although shell-shocked, was old enough to decide her own fate. She took refuge at Oakholme.

Soon she became Jessica's shadow, always running around dusting, washing up, offering to mow the lawn or shop. Her eagerness to help was painful, but no one could stop her. Every single day Faith had to show them her gratitude for their love. When they asked her if she wouldn't like to try for university, she backed away like a frightened horse. She wasn't ready, she insisted. In her family, any hint of ambition had been mocked and crushed.

After a while, Faith got a part-time job in the village post office and seemed content with that. To pay her own way—even though the Foxes didn't need her to—was essential to her pride.

Rosie, meanwhile, began college. The school of horticulture was in the Cotswolds, based in an old stately home surrounded by magnificent gardens, with orchards, vegetable plots, acres of greenhouses. There she shared a cottage on the estate with four other students. Although it was drafty, basic and in the middle of nowhere, she enjoyed her new life. Losing herself in work, she could exorcise recent memories.

She tried not to think about Jon. She'd bumped into him and explained that she was going away and lightheartedly suggested they write to each other; and Jon had agreed yes, that was a great idea. She'd written one letter—probably giving too much away—but he'd never replied.

Meanwhile she dated a handful of men and had pleasant sex with two of them. Each reminded her of Jon, but neither was him, so in the end it was worse than nothing. Virginity lost, experience gained, fine—but not with the man she'd dreamed of. No one moved her heart.

One lover was so upset when she dropped him that he staged a protest outside the cottage, armed with roses. Rosie watched him from behind voile curtains. She wondered if he saw her as coldhearted, ethereal and untouchable, regarding his pained longing from behind her windows without a trace of compassion. In other words, did he see her as she saw Jon?

It was a relief when he gave up.

When she visited home, it was lovely having Faith there, like a sister. Matthew and Alastair were often around and the four of them would go to the Green Man together. Alastair was easy company and kept the jokes going when Matthew was moody.

It was always a battle of wills between them. Matthew telling her how to behave and who to see, trying to control her as he always had; Rosie blithely defying him. When he'd had a few beers, he would put his arm around her and tell her what a great guy Alastair was, causing Alastair to turn red in embarrassment. Meanwhile, Faith would gaze at Matthew with the sort of look Rosie reserved for Jon—while Matt sat equally oblivious, managing to bask in her admiration yet ignore it at the same time.

"I had to tell Alastair about Luc," Matt had told Rosie on her first trip home from college. "Didn't want to, but it would be worse if he found out later."

"Oh, right." So Alastair hadn't revealed that she'd already told him. She mentally awarded him a gold star for discretion.

"But let's keep the weird side out of it, shall we? Humans get funny ideas about us. They either think we're delusional, or they get star-struck."

"What does Alastair know about us, then?" Rosie asked, desperately affecting innocence.

"Same as most people in Cloudcroft; eccentric family traditions, sort of thing. No big deal."

She laughed. "Fine. Is that what you told him?"

Matthew's eyes sparked with anger. "Have you any idea what I'd give not to be forced to explain my family? I don't want his face rubbed in it, that's all."

"You want him to think we're ordinary, normal and not odd in any way?"

"Exactly."

"But we are!" Rosie exclaimed. "If he wants the flaming Addams family, let him take a stroll up to Stonegate Manor."

Matthew grimaced. "You said it."

"Look, Matt, he probably knows more than you realize. I know I've said things in unguarded moments. He's still around. You won't scare him off that easily."

"Fine, I'm just pointing out that he's a good mate and I want to keep it that way. His last girlfriend gave him hell, sleeping around and doing drugs. He was close to a breakdown over it. He deserves better than that."

"I'm sure he does," she said, pointedly ignoring the implication. She felt relaxed in Alastair's company because he never tried to make a clumsy pass at her. He was just Matt's friend, as reassuring as a teddy bear. "Hey, you're not trying to get him and Faith together, are you?"

Matthew rolled his eyes. "Send me a postcard when you wake up, Rose."

Rosie thought Lucas and Faith would make a sweet couple, both shy and kind-natured. However, as her first and second years at college slipped by, no one behaved as they were supposed to. Faith still worshipped Matthew, while Lucas spent more and more time at Stonegate Manor.

Since the revelation Luc had grown distant. It worried her. If she questioned him, he would simply smile and slip away. Rosie was perhaps the only one who could have enticed him back to Oakholme; but, selfishly, she didn't try too hard. Lucas's newfound friendship offered her chances to see Jon.

"It's what I feared," Jessica said softly to her daughter one day. "That the moment he found out who his father was, they'd take him away from us. It's exactly what I dreaded."

A chill breeze blew into Jessica's face, laden with the scent of wet woodlands. She and Phyll and a handful of other Aetherials were gathered around a hollow tree a few miles from Cloudcroft. Tea lights in green glass holders made an eerie glow in the dark. It was the summer solstice; even though the way to the Otherworld was barred, they still kept alive the tradition of gathering around an ancient portal on such festivals. It was their quiet way of keeping the flame of hope alive.

Jessica looped the albinite bracelet over her middle finger and held it up. In the Dusklands the stones glowed violet, but there was no flash of scarlet or green to indicate the presence of an open way. She sighed. She didn't need Elfstones to tell her that the portal was still sealed.

The auburn-haired Lyon women and Maeve Tulliver with her sad dark eyes—all looked resigned. Led by Phyll, they began to sing softly,

> *All the demons of Dumannios*
> *All Maliket's fire and Melusiel's flood,*
> *All the stern towers of Tyrynaia*
> *Cannot keep me from you, my love, Elysion.*
> *As if I lay down with a lover, I will lie down in Elysion*
> *And drink your sweet dew . . .*

Jessica mouthed the words, not trusting her voice. She felt overwhelming sadness. She and Phyll had walked mountains in Wales and Scotland, landscapes as high and airy as Sibeyla; they'd explored forest glades and sea caves, springs and ancient paths, every place they knew that had been a minor portal. Each one was dead, sealed shut along with the Great Gates. There was no leakage. In one way it was a good thing, proving that the system protected them. But it was also very hard to bear.

Small groups of Aetherials still gathered around the trees or springs that had once held minor portals. They did so all over the country; all over the world, as far as Jessica knew, in tribute to their ancestry. They brought gifts of flowers, fruit and wine for their Aelyr cousins; but the Aelyr seemed impossibly distant now, untouchable, as if they were ghosts in the Underworld. *Or we're the ghosts,* thought Jessica, *unable to reach the land of the living.*

She'd brought Faith with her, and Faith sat nervously on the edge of the circle, wide-eyed and silent. The girl had been at Oakholme for nearly two years now. Perhaps it was wrong to bring a human to this hidden, Vaethyr rite. *Perhaps I'm treating her as too much of a Rosie substitute while Rosie's away.* Yet Faith seemed a natural part of it, and no one had objected.

When the song was done, they each placed their gifts inside the hollow trunk, murmuring a few words to their Aelyr clans or lost relatives in the hope that, somehow, they might hear across the ether.

"For my son, who vanished during his initiation," whispered Maeve Tulliver. "For all those who went before us, in the hope that we'll meet again."

"You know," Phyll murmured very softly into Jessica's ear, "I quite understand why you and Auberon want to keep out of Comyn's anti-Lawrence campaign. As long as the Gates are shut, your children are safe and you don't have to worry about them ever vanishing."

"They can vanish in the surface world, too," Jessica replied tartly. "Anyway, there is plenty to live for on this side." She smiled at Faith, who smiled shyly back.

They sat in meditation for a while. In everyday life, they were so well camouflaged it was easy to forget they were anything but human. When they came together like this, though, Jess saw the shine of their combined aura and caught hints of their strong, graceful Otherworld shapes, hints of animal elements, ghost wings, or fugitive colors. The glow even reflected off Faith, making her seem part of it.

A far-off echo broke into her thoughts. It was a vibration, like a battering ram striking stone deep underground. A wintry-cold mass of air settled over them. The albinite in Jessica's hand turned pitch-black and she felt the hairs on her neck stand up.

The moment passed. "What was that?" said Jessica. "Did you feel it?"

She saw from their shocked expressions that they had. "If Lawrence is right, if there is something on the other side," said Phyll, "I'm damned if we're going to let it frighten us off."

"We're with you, but let's call it a night," said Peta Lyon, the mask maker. "Now, how about we all retire to the Green Man and get hammered?"

"Faith," said Matthew out of the shadows as she headed towards her room. "You know, Mum means well but she shouldn't be inviting you to those little coven meetings."

"Why not?" Faith stopped. His disapproval startled her. In the time she'd been at Oakholme, Matthew had evolved from ignoring her completely to being quite attentive, talkative, positively civil to her. She might almost say they were friends, if only she hadn't found his glamour so intimidating. "Anyway, it's not a coven. Just, er . . ."

He came close to her. "I know, it's Aetherial tradition stuff and she really has no business taking an outsider."

Her heart fell. "No one said they minded."

"They may not have said it, but . . ." His blue eyes softened. "Hey, I didn't mean 'outsider' in a bad way. I'm one too. All that stuff can mess with your head and do serious damage. All I'm saying is that you can never be a real part of it, because you're human, and I want nothing to do with it either. So let's stay out of it together, eh?"

His arm slid around her waist. It wasn't the first time he'd touched her but the touches had always felt brotherly before. She caught her breath, nodding vehemently. "Yes, okay. I didn't mean any harm."

"I know," Matthew said in a quiet tone that wouldn't accept refusal. "But next time Mum asks, you just say no, right?"

Then his arm did not fall but tightened insistently around her; and Faith, trembling, wondered if he yet realized that she was incapable of refusing him anything.

Lawrence stood at the Gates; or rather, at Freya's Crown, the great stone marker that kept the place in the closed book. It was August, the weather cloudy and humid. He was about to make a trip to his New York store, and before he left he had to check over and over again, like an obsessive-compulsive, that the Gates were truly locked. The albinite gem in his hand stayed pale, but he didn't trust it.

He closed his eyes and reached out to touch the rocks.

For a blinding second he saw clear through all realms to the heart, the vast engulfing Abyss. Its immensity fell away from his feet and he was staring into it, teetering. And he saw the giant rising out of it, a huge shadow horned and silhouetted against a blazing icy light. It was coming for him. In silence it came, smashing the Gates in its path like eggshells.

He fell before it. A scream broke from his throat, a low-pitched jagged scream of despair, of surrender. It was searching for his sons, mouth gaping to drink their souls. He'd tried so hard to protect them and failed . . .

"Lawrence?" He was on his hands and knees. A woman was standing over him, shaking him by the shoulder. "Dear, what happened?"

She loomed against the sky. She was in gardening clothes; jeans, an old shirt, hair escaping from beneath a waxed hat. He couldn't see her clearly against the glare and for a moment he thought she was Ginny. "You should never have made me come back here," he gasped.

"What?" She crouched beside him and he saw it was Sapphire. For a moment, unable to help himself, he reached out and clung to her. "Lawrence, what's wrong?"

He let her help him up. An impulse gripped him to pour out all his fears—but the image of himself as a gibbering hysteric horrified him. He savagely mastered his weakness, turning back to glacial stone. "Nothing. I tripped."

"Don't treat me like an idiot. You seem to forget that you told me everything, a long time ago."

"I should never have told you. You don't feel the shadows. You don't understand."

"It's not my fault I'm human." Her voice was warmly chiding. "I'm not any human; I'm your wife. So tell me the truth."

Her eyes were bright and intense, the pressure of her gaze a physical weight. Lawrence felt suffocated. Sapphire didn't belong here. It was his mistake to remarry, but that gave her no right to demand answers. "No," he said impatiently. "It was a vision. The point of a vision is not what it can do, but the *implication . . .*" The words came up heavily from his stomach. He had to stop.

"Were you trying to open the Gates?"

"There is no hope of that."

"What, then?"

"Making sure they're locked fast. So everyone will remain safe while I'm away."

"It's only New York for a couple of weeks. I won't let anything happen."

"It's not in your control," he said, looking away.

"You can't keep shutting me out of your life like this, Lawrence." Frowning, she placed her hand on his forearm. "You'd better decide what I am to you—a wife, or a glorified housekeeper? What do you want?"

Sapphire, beneath the veneer of control, was angry. The more he closed her out, the more she tried to force her way in, and the farther he withdrew in response. His eyelids fell. "I want peace. I want Sam to come home."

Her lips bowed in a tight smile. "We all want that. I was right in persuading you to tell Lucas the truth, wasn't I? You've gained a son."

"Indeed." *Another son for Brawth to hunt down,* he thought bleakly.

"So you owe me. If you'd only let me into this secret world of yours!" Her voice became impassioned. "We could open the Gates together, side by side. That's how it should be. You and I, conquering the Otherworld together, king and queen."

He covered her hand with his own, and plucked it off his arm. As he bent to kiss her cheek, he whispered, "Never, my dear. The Otherworld was never on offer."

Sapphire sat in her apartment at the top of the house, fuming. Even in her gardening outfit she was elegant in her setting, like a tousled film star about to be photographed for a magazine feature. One bare toe tapped repeatedly at the air.

Things were not supposed to be like this.

It was her nature to operate with sweet reason, not anger. That was how she'd trained herself. If it were otherwise, she would have punched Lawrence off his feet.

"He will swallow you and spit you out," Jessica had murmured sweetly in her ear the first time they'd met. Sapphire had thought her jealous—poor chaotic earth mother—but she'd been right. Sapphire had dreamed of the social scene she would create; opening up the house, presenting herself plus perfect new family to the world; becoming queen of a shining court.

But Lawrence would not play.

At the start he'd tried, until the anger of the Vaethyr community had thrown him back into brooding, self-imposed solitude. She was exasperated with him for giving up so easily—but saw now that she'd been a fool to think he could change. Meanwhile she'd forged on, acting the hostess, fond mother, glamorous face of Wilder Jewels, general pillar of the community—but while he refused to support her, it was a hollow masquerade. And that's exactly how Lawrence was using her: as his mask.

Some years ago—long after Virginia had left, for it had taken Sapphire an age to win his trust—he'd taken her to a conference. In the hotel suite, he'd let her demonstrate her massage skills upon his back, and that had flowed into hours of sex and champagne. Drunk, he'd confessed that he was of an older race, charged with keeping the Gates between worlds; told stories of a kind but demanding grandmother, a hostile father, a child by another man's wife . . . of his own wife leaving, because she could not forgive him for loving his business more than he loved his sons.

He spoke of Eugene Barada, a brutal human enemy who had tried to take the mine from him.

"What happened to him?" Sapphire had asked, her head close to his on the pillow.

A pause. "He lost. I proved the more ruthless. Gems are all I trust; they're solid, they don't demand fear or love. They are worth protecting, at any cost. I don't expect you to believe my story—I don't *need* you to—but it's the truth."

Sapphire, however, had believed him. She'd made herself a student of Lawrence Wilder, long before she ever met him. It was the first and last time he opened up to her like that, but it was enough. He proposed to her that night.

On paper, it was a perfect arrangement: two attractive, glamorous people who formed the ideal couple. *Arrangement,* however, was the key word. Yes, he'd gained a glossy companion, substitute mother and homemaker, and she'd gained wealth and a fabulous mansion. But love?

Sapphire fingered the teardrop of albinite at her throat. It was worth a fortune, this hard cold lump.

Sometimes life had been good. Promoting the business, poring over jewelry designs and gemstones. Making plans for the house; trying to drag its curmudgeonly bulk out of the eighteenth century. As long as she played the innocent, everything was fine; but step on his territory, dare to mention Gates or matters Aetherial, and she became an instant pariah.

Sex had been amazing—and suited Lawrence since it was a chance to avoid talking—but even that was sporadic now. Mostly she kept to her rooms and he kept to his. She had her tranquillity zone and yoga to keep her sane. He haunted the big drafty library or shut himself in his workshop with his gem specimens, his only companion a bottle of single malt.

Sapphire bit her lip. She wasn't sorry for herself; simply frustrated. Lawrence's last marriage had failed because Ginny didn't know how to handle him. *With me,* Sapphire had thought, *he'll be different, because I'll prove my smooth creamy perfection to him every single day.*

She never forgot her background, how she'd clawed her way out of poverty in Brazil to remake herself. And the man who'd helped her do that, the one man she'd truly loved, had been taken away from her by his obsession with Aetherials. She'd made promises to him. She had made it her life's mission to find out what Aetherials *were,* why the fascination, what lay behind the Gates.

The triumph of marrying Lawrence had been incredible. The problem was she hadn't planned on falling for him. In that honeymoon glow, her life could have gone a different way. She could have discarded her bitter feelings, abandoned her mission, truly loved her husband. Their life need not have been a masquerade. It could have been real.

How swiftly she was disillusioned, when Stonegate unsheathed the cold flint core of Lawrence. He used her; he wouldn't let her near his secrets; he would not open the damned Gates, even for her. She wasn't special to him after all. He wanted a beautiful servant, not a partner with thoughts of her own.

Amazing, how abruptly love became hate. Wounded, Sapphire withdrew in turn, angry with herself for losing sight of her quest. Her need for answers flamed into a drive for revenge—but she kept it hidden. Her poised control was her only weapon. When she removed her real self from him and replaced it with a smiling facsimile, Lawrence didn't even notice. Didn't notice! That self-centered blindness made her despise him.

It was good, though, that he didn't notice. As long as she presented a chilled, smooth surface to him, he didn't suspect a thing. She must bide her time.

So much for playing the perfect stepmother. Sam had loathed her from the start and the feeling was mutual. Whatever Sam thought, he came straight out with it, and that was never going to make him popular. Sam come home? Over her dead body. Sapphire half-hoped he might

be murdered on his foreign travels, or at least catch something exotic, if Vaethyr were vulnerable to disease; ma-
laria perhaps, or Ebola.

Jon was the opposite; insecure, secretive. He tolerated
her with that fey, indifferent manner he had; but he'd come
to rely on her. He turned to her for advice and approval; he
was vulnerable. His need was her power.

She knew she'd pushed Lawrence too far today, but his
reaction had made her furious. He'd been so contemptuous. How dare he? Who was he, anyway, to forbid her from
the Otherworld?

So her life had taken this path instead, the way of cold
vengeance. Ultimately more satisfying than mere love, she
suspected. After all, her promise had been made to someone far more important than Lawrence. If she couldn't control Lawrence Wilder—well, there were others she could
control, and other ways to hurt him.

Sapphire threw her hair back and grinned. King and
queen, indeed. One of these days she'd seize his kingdom
with one hand, and with the other stab him right through
the black flint heart.

"It doesn't look much," said Rosie. "It looks neglected."

"That's kind of the idea," said Jon. "It's meant to be discreet."

The fabled entrance to the Otherworld was a crag of
folded diorite and tumbled blocks, its bedding planes deformed and striated with quartz from the vast forces that
had thrust it from the ground half a billion years ago.
Bracken sprouted around its roots. The flanks of the mound
fell away steeply behind and gently in front, where the
shallow dip cupped a handful of Jon's college friends.
Masses of oak and beech encircled the summit, glowing
green in the dawn.

Lucas added, "You can't have a huge golden arch with
neon arrows flashing 'This way to Elfland' on it."

"Or every Tom, Dick and Legolas would be in and out

as if it was Las Vegas," said Rosie. To her delight, Jon actually laughed. Wow, she'd made him laugh!

It was the summer break at the end of her second year. Now Jon was at art college in Nottingham, Lucas had been spending weekends there—against Jessica's wishes, since she was fretting about his education. He and Jon had started a band, as students did. Rosie had been to see them last night and they weren't bad; slightly pretentious, mercifully in tune, with Luc in the background on guitar, three others on drums, bass and keyboards, and Jon singing cryptic lyrics that only Vaethyr would comprehend. His voice was nothing special; but his charisma in the spotlight held the audience.

Afterwards, they had partied. Rosie had been first indignant, then wretchedly unhappy, to see what she could only describe as groupies draping themselves around Jon's neck. All evening he'd been the center of attention, as if caught in a beam of light. She didn't like the look of his hangers-on. The idea of Luc associating with them made her uneasy. Jon was so close, yet she couldn't get near him, and instead had to endure bleached-blond freaks throwing themselves at him. So she'd drunk enough to make the evening blur and, in the early hours, the hard core had climbed into taxis and headed for Stonegate. Lawrence was in New York, Jon explained, so it was safe.

The groupies had fallen away by then and the only constant at Jon's side was Lucas. He'd grown his hair and started to dress like Jon and even to stand like him, shoulders up and hands in pockets. She still couldn't see them as brothers but they looked wonderful together, like a pair of gorgeous young actors in a costume drama. They spoke softly so the humans wouldn't overhear.

"I'm surprised you two never knew this was the portal," said Jon.

"Well, it's in your back garden, not ours," said Rosie. "No one said."

"It's wrong." Jon looked straight into her eyes. Despite

herself, she thrilled to his attention. "All Aetherials have a right to pass in and out. Instead our parents kept us in the dark. We've been cheated. They held their ceremonies in secret—then by the time we're old enough for initiation they tell us, tough, the Gates are locked."

Rosie nodded. She was sober now, her eyes sore with tiredness, but she couldn't stop gazing at him. She only had to glimpse him for all the painful feelings to start again. It was like looking into the delicious heart of life and finding it looking radiantly back at her. It's no good, she thought; I'm not over him at all. *Damn.*

Had he slept with any of those girls who hung around him? If with them, why not with her? She shuddered at her own tormenting thoughts. She tried not to feel ungraciously jealous of her own brother for being close to Jon, but it was hard. She couldn't shake off the bittersweet longing to be in Luc's place, cherished and chosen; the anguish that it wasn't so.

"And you think you can travel through in a trance?" she asked.

"We can," Jon said enigmatically. "We have. Want to try?"

"Is it safe?"

Jon pulled a face at her. "Of course it isn't. So?"

"What do I do?" she asked. He and Luc exchanged a glance.

"Er," said Luc, "oh, we meditate, like you would in yoga. Imagine the rocks opening, and what you might see on the other side. That sort of thing."

"Green Elysion," said Jon. "Sibeyla, realm of air. Naamon's fiery deserts, Melusiel of the lakes. And Asru, the mysterious heart."

She felt the dawn breeze winding around her, smelled the fragrance of bracken. Every sense warned her that this was a bad idea—but it was a chance to involve herself with Jon. Feeling self-conscious, she sat cross-legged before the rocks and closed her eyes. She visualized . . .

The guy she'd slept with who looked the most like Jon,

but wasn't. A project she must complete on hybrids. What color to help Faith dye her hair. Her growling stomach, gods, she was so hungry how could she think about anything else?

There was no sense of a deeper self or the latent powers an Aetherial should command. The rocks remained solid. She tried to blend into the Dusklands, but the rocks gave off a furry buzz like static that physically pushed her out. She felt as earthbound as any human.

Someone laughed.

A sharp feeling that they were laughing at her, humoring her naive desire to help, brought her up short. She opened her eyes; Jon and Luc had gone to sit with the others, and no one was mocking her, or paying her any attention at all. She sighed in relief.

The morning light shone like thin honey. Through it, she saw Jon gilded by the sunrise, hands resting loosely on his knees, hair streaming around his perfect profile—she'd never seen him look more beautiful. He looked like a da Vinci angel, porcelain-pure and untouchable, long lashes veiling the liquid darkness of his eyes. That image burned itself into her memory, sublime and golden, and she almost wept at the sweet pain. She knew she daren't hope for anything; yet she was powerless to stop herself yearning.

Jon opened his eyes, saw her looking at him. "See anything?" he called.

"No, sorry. Think I'm too tired."

"Not to worry. You tried," he said, and rewarded her with a radiant, laughing smile that bathed her with heat like the sun.

There was something about flying that Lawrence found soothing; the drone of the engines, and the clouds drifting beneath reminding him of his home realm, Sibeyla. On his flight home from New York, he sat half-remembering, half-dreaming, and he was there again, among the airy heights of Sibeyla's mountains with its spired cities . . .

He'd hardly known his mother, Maia. She had followed

her own call deep into the Spiral when he was tiny; he recalled her dark red hair, nothing more. He'd been raised by his father, Albin, a tall man of marble-pale skin and swan-white hair. Albin, though, was a cold, complicated, withdrawn man who brooded about Maia and gave Lawrence only discipline and criticism—when he acknowledged him at all.

Love came from his grandmother Liliana; but she was the Gatekeeper, and lived on Earth, so he rarely saw her. One day Liliana came to them and said that when her time was over, the mantle of Gatekeeper would pass not to her son Albin, but to Lawrence.

Albin had greeted the news in steely silence. Lawrence, still a child, had argued with her; surely his father was her rightful heir?

"It doesn't work in that way," she'd answered gently. "The lych-light is bestowed by the Spiral Court. It usually stays within our branch of the House of Sibeyla, yes, but not in direct line. It means that you must come with me to Vaeth, the surface world, so I can teach you."

Liliana was full of life and wisdom, Albin glacial and distant. Of course he wanted to go with her. He was torn by guilt; it seemed wrong to leave his father when Maia, too, had abandoned him. But he knew he must follow Liliana . . .

The figure of his father stood luminous against shifting bluish gloom, as Lawrence made ready to leave. "You really mean to go?" Albin said thinly. "Turn your back upon Sibeyla for the easier pleasures of Vaeth? In becoming Vaethyr you become lesser. You degrade yourself. If I had my way there would be no Gates, and no contact with the human world at all."

Lawrence was in agony. Nothing he said or did had ever pleased his father. Whatever he chose he couldn't win; but Liliana's call on him was stronger. "I have to go with Grandmother," he said.

"Then know this." Albin opened his hand and showed him a tablet of pale crystal with symbols carved in its surface. Lawrence recognized them. Dread pooled in his limbs. "I hold your heart, soul and core hostage within this Elfstone. Your soul-essence. If you leave, you leave without it. If you do not come back, you will live on Vaeth without your heart and soul for the rest of your existence."

Darkness rushed up around him.

As small child . . . far back in the fog of Otherworld time . . . he'd been haunted by a ghost face that rose over his cot when he was alone. It was two-dimensional, the color of ice in shadow, and it never spoke. It simply appeared, telling him without words that it would always haunt him. A childhood fancy? No, it was too terrifying to be so dismissed. He couldn't explain it. From infancy, he'd simply understood that he was confronting a lifelong enemy, a terrible, irrational, ravenous tormentor.

His very existence meant he had an opponent hell-driven to challenge that existence—like Qesoth, the fire elemental who couldn't exist without casting a shadow, Brawth. Lawrence knew that his only protection against it was his own essence—and Albin had stolen that away.

He'd never told another soul what Albin had done to him that day. He'd simply lived with it in desolate silence, knowing that he could never be the Gatekeeper Liliana wanted; that he was doomed to fail both her and his father. But part of him thought, *Damn you, Albin. If I displease you by leaving, by mining and selling sacred stones, by possessing the lych-light that you think should have been yours—good. May you choke upon your displeasure.*

The dream twisted towards nightmare and Lawrence was back in Ecuador again.

From his chair on the verandah, he could see the head of the cleft valley where albinite oozed like petrified tears from the scarlet rock of Naamon. In twilight Valle Rojo twinkled with tiny lights like the eyes of dryads. All around, the rain forest writhed and chirruped with life. The heat was soporific, the chair beside him—empty.

It was shortly after Ginny had stormed out on him. He'd fled back here, away from the chill of England, the shadows of Stonegate, the formless monster that menaced him. Without Ginny's discontent, he could stay here forever; but without her, staying seemed pointless. Living in the enveloping cocoon of heat, or existing on the chilly edge of death—it was all the same now.

He saw someone approaching; a heavyset man dressed in khaki like a big-game hunter. The shine of the bald head was unmistakable. As casual as a tourist, the man paused to admire the view before padding up the verandah steps.

"You should really have a bodyguard, Lawrence," he said, puffing. Sweat gleamed on the fleshy red face set on a bull neck. The eyebrows quirked up like demon horns. "I could be anyone. I might have had a gun."

"So might I," Lawrence said thinly. "What the hell are you doing here?"

"Just passing." Eugene Barada dropped into the chair beside him with the *whumph* of a small hippo. His accent was staccato South African. "On your own?"

Lawrence showed no reaction. "Drink?" he said, pouring whiskey.

"If you haven't poisoned it." Barada took the tumbler. "How is your lovely wife?"

Lawrence gazed at the steamy shadows of the valley. "Virginia and I are no longer together."

"I'm sorry to hear it, old man," said Barada. "Amazing she stood you as long as she did."

Lawrence didn't answer. The jungle seemed to expand and contract with his heartbeat. Slow rage roiled inside him. "What do you want?"

"The same as I always want. How much more reasonable can I be? I could charge you rent or throw you off the land. Instead, I'm offering to buy you out. Name your price."

Eugene Barada was a land speculator who claimed ownership of this obscure strip of rain forest. Years ago, he'd stumbled upon the hidden valley and threatened Lawrence's workers. Lawrence had seen him off, but Barada had come back with armed men and tried to take the mine by force. In contempt, Lawrence had called up the horrors of Dumannios to drive them mad and screaming into the jungle—but Barada simply would not give up.

It had been the start of a long, bitter feud. Lawrence didn't care about Barada's legal title. Valle Rojo was of the Dusklands, the mine an interstice to Naamon, albinite an Otherworld gem; none of it the concern of any mortal. Barada, though, persisted; legal action, armed force, nothing would shift Lawrence, but the South African wouldn't give up. They were like two bulldogs locked on each other's throats.

The more he feared failing as Gatekeeper, the more the shadow that haunted Lawrence had grown in power. Fear had made him obsessive. That obsession was, in part, what had driven Ginny away. She could no longer live with the darkness that possessed him. Since she'd left, though, the shadow had increased a thousandfold and he felt it haunting the Spiral beyond the Gates, waiting for him.

Sweat began to trickle beneath his collar. "You can't afford it," he said.

At that, Barada's eyes lit up with orange fire reflected from the verandah lamps. He carefully put down his glass. "One day I'll take it from you like *that*"—he snapped his fingers under Lawrence's nose—"and you will never see it coming."

Lawrence laughed. "Learn your folktales. 'The Goose That Laid the Golden Eggs?' The cleft is an interstice to the Otherworld and I have the power to close it. Claim the mine and you'd be looking at barren rock—if you could find it at all. How much more will you sacrifice on this pointless quest?"

Red with anger, Barada hauled himself out of his seat and clumped down the verandah steps. "Leaving so soon, Eugene?" said Lawrence.

Barada turned and looked back. "Speaking of folktales, there is a type of fairy who thieves and steals," he said through heavy breaths. "But she only does it to those who deserve it, because they are so careless of their possessions."

Then Lawrence made his great mistake. It came from Ginny leaving, from fear, and from complete exhaustion. He simply wanted this to end. He clasped the heavy handgun that lay at his hip, raised and aimed it at Barada's heart . . .

To Lawrence, murder was utter weakness. It had become the Aetherial code, after the ancient conflicts, to use any means but physical violence against your enemies. Not that everyone abided by it, far from it, but that was the ideal. To pull the trigger was to slide into the absolute black pit of moral depravity, an invitation to the great shadow to break its chains and rampage across the universe . . .

He aimed the gun at Barada's chest and fired. The bullet exploded into his enemy's flesh. Barada toppled, staring at Lawrence in blank amazement that he'd done something as prosaic and final as shoot him.

Lawrence staggered to the place where the body had fallen and uttered a scream of anguish. Too late, he grasped a hideous possibility, that Barada was not merely human but an entity in mortal form sent to test him. Sent by Albin, by Brawth, by all the dark powers arrayed against him—and he'd failed the test. All he'd done was set Barada's shade free to join his shadowy tormentors.

That was his descent into darkness. With that act his doom was sealed, the shadow giant Brawth set free to rampage. There was only one thing he could do to stop it and that was to go into the Spiral and confront it . . .

He realized the dropping sensation in his stomach was the plane descending through the clouds. He woke in panic, convinced he was still in the past, flying home from Ecuador to make that last expedition through the Gates—meaning to confront the Shadow, only to find himself fleeing in terror, panicking to seal and lock every last Gate behind him.

Lawrence gasped in his first-class seat, waiting for his heartbeat to subside. Same memories, same torment haunting his sleep, slowly but inexorably driving him to the brink. He had to push the madness out, think of business instead.

Sealing the portal had meant that the flow of albinite ceased. He still paid his miners, and they still searched; but they found only fragments in the streambed now. Once his stockpile ran out, that would be the end. He'd visited the New York store to prepare his staff. They still had diamond, sapphire, ruby and all the rest, but the one gem that had made Wilder Jewels unique would be no more.

Albin must be smiling. Barada had taken the Elfstone mine from him, after all.

"Sam's coming home," said Jon. Standing against the light from the leaded window of the dining room, he was wearing an Indian patchwork shirt too big for his slim body. He looked so young, Sapphire observed, as beautiful as any Pre-Raphaelite vision of a god.

"Soon?" she asked, her mood clouding. Lawrence was due back that day, and she wasn't looking forward to that, either.

Jon flexed a postcard between his long fingers. It held a montage of bright coastlines and olive groves. "Mid-September, he says. I'll be back at college then, so you and Dad can have him all to yourselves."

"Oh." As Sapphire moved closer, she noticed the dark crescents under his eyes. Idly, she adjusted the table display of ikebana, pebbles and candles. "Your father will be pleased. It's been rather peaceful without them."

"You don't like Sam much, do you?" Jon said.

"Quite the contrary," Sapphire answered smoothly. "We can only hope that he's overcome his dislike of me in— what is it? Four years?"

"Must be."

"And never been back."

"I don't blame him," Jon said waspishly. "We always

had to fend for ourselves. Once I was old enough to look after myself, I suppose he found life better elsewhere."

Sapphire tensed at the implication; clearly, since she was not their mother, her presence in their lives counted for nothing. Her suppressed rage at Lawrence banked a little higher. "I suppose he hasn't been told about Lucas?"

Jon gave a silent, pained laugh. "Not as far as I know."

"Then let Lawrence tell him. I'm not doing any more of his dirty work." A dish slipped in her hand and hit the table, making her jump. She sighed, hair tumbling forward as she rested on the table edge for a moment.

"Something wrong?" said Jon.

Sapphire swept the silky river back over her shoulder, strolled over to him so they were face-to-face. "You'd better tidy yourself up for your father." She pressed her thumb beneath his left eye.

He jerked away. "What?"

"I don't know what you've been smoking or sniffing with your student friends, but it needs to stop." He stood glowering at her. *He's so easy to scare,* she thought, *bless him.* "Just bear in mind that Lucas is a lot younger than you and that gives you a responsibility to keep him out of trouble."

Jon frowned, indignant. "He's eighteen, not a kid."

"He's as naive as they come," she sighed. "Some of your friends are nice enough, but some, quite frankly, look as if they've stumbled out of a methadone clinic. I don't know why you and Lucas hang around with such people. I don't like it. Your father wouldn't, either."

Jon shook his head, pupils dilating. "It's none of your— why have you turned on me all of a sudden?"

Sapphire exhaled, stroking his lovely hair. "I haven't, dear. I'm trying to look after you."

"Well, don't. I'm twenty-one. And you're not my mother."

"No. I'm not." She was thrilled at how easy it was to rile him. The feeling of power gave her a warm rush. "You know, even Aetherial beauty may tarnish if you abuse it. I want you clean and healthy, Jon."

Jon looked more suspicious than ever, but didn't try to move away; not that he could, pressed against the stone windowsill. "What's it to you?"

"Don't you think a human spirit could feel what it is to be Aetherial?"

He gave a low, contemptuous laugh. "Please. That's sacrilege."

"You think you're so special, don't you? I think if I broke you open and looked inside, there'd be nothing there. Is there anything inside you, or inside the Gates?"

He stared as Lawrence did, offended that she'd trespassed on their territory. "What are you saying?"

"That it's not fair, living in an Aetherial family but never being let into your secrets. I need to see and feel and taste and understand. Lawrence won't help me, but you can. Or are you all afraid I'll find out there's nothing to discover?"

His face revealed fear, anger, helplessness, but he couldn't form an unattractive expression if he tried. "I don't know what you want."

"Yes you do, dear. I want to *understand*." She fondled the front of his patchwork shirt, felt the bony ribs and his heart beating fast, like a bird's. "Lawrence has been no husband to me and no father to you for quite some time. I feel cheated. Who can blame us for seeking consolation?"

"We weren't going to do this anymore." Jon's voice was shaky.

"Well, I say we still need it," she answered huskily. "You wouldn't want me to draw Lawrence's attention to your friends, would you? There's so much we wouldn't want Sam or Lawrence to find out . . ."

When she kissed him, her lips were warmly demanding, his dry and hesitant; but he didn't try to stop her.

It was dark by the time Sam approached Stonegate Manor. He was exhausted from the long journey. He half-wished he could have stayed on the Mediterranean for good—with sunshine, olive groves and casual work to sustain him— but an ever-stronger impulse drew him home. Family, guilt, the hope that things might one day get better. Images of a slender, curvy, beautiful girl with masses of plum-brown hair and bright silver-grey eyes . . . the hope that her contempt for him might have mellowed.

There had been a couple of passing girlfriends and empty one-night stands. Finally he'd spent a disastrous few months with a stunning Greek girl, all honey skin and blue-black hair. Unfortunately she'd turned out to be a devotee of high melodrama, with a keen interest in shotguns and a tendency to fire indiscriminately at walls and ceilings when she was angry. In the end, preserving life and sanity, he'd fled.

Never for one moment had he stopped thinking about Rosie.

The late bus from Ashvale was long gone and there were no taxis to be found, so he'd walked the last few miles. The hill was as steep and the wind as cold as ever, Stonegate Manor looming like Wuthering Heights. He looked to his left as he walked up the drive but couldn't quite see Oakholme from here.

He thought of Rosie in her cozy house, which glowed like an inn on a Victorian Christmas card. Safe with her family around her, a fire roaring in the grate, all of them probably gathered around the piano having a bloody singalong. His own house looked cold, dark and deserted. There were no lights on. Jon would be back at college and Sapphire in her apartment, perfecting her ashtanga yoga or whatever she did up there. His father would be in the library, brooding over whiskey.

No—Sam checked his watch and it was gone midnight. With any luck they were in bed. Good. He felt even less like speaking to them than before he'd left.

He detoured down the side of the house into the back garden, and let himself in through the kitchen door. The familiar arctic atmosphere wound around him and reeled him along the passage. None of Sapphire's desperate renovation projects had dented it. As he entered the kitchen, something crunched under his boot.

Broken glass.

Sam was about to switch on a light when he heard the clunk of something falling, followed by a whispered curse. He could see in the dark better than any human, so he left the lights off and walked slowly, warily into the great hall. Freezing cold as always, full of crawling shadows. He felt the ghostly *dysir* sniffing at him, recognizing his scent, melting into darkness again. In the far corner to his left, beneath the upper-floor gallery, there was the door to Lawrence's study. He saw a hunched figure lurking there.

Sam wasn't nervous by nature, but the intruder startled him. Even as a dark shape on blackness, it was plainly not his father. It was too bulky, and when had Lawrence ever worn sports gear? A tracksuit and black woollen hat made the man all but invisible—an effect marred by luminous green flashes on his trainers.

Sam watched, grimly fascinated. The stranger was struggling with a bag, swearing to himself as he tried to hoist it onto his shoulder. The strap kept slipping off the synthetic material. Still fighting with it, the man sniffed loudly, glanced around and began to stroll towards the staircase like the squire of the manor.

Why hadn't the *dysir* done their work? Because . . . this was a human, and couldn't see them.

Sam wasn't frightened. He was furious. If this moron expected him to cower while he helped himself, he was about to be severely disillusioned. The intruder reached the foot of the stairs and paused, scouting up the treads with the pencil-thin beam of a flashlight. Then he let the bag slide to the floor, and began to climb.

Sam's fury leaped into protective rage. Criminals these days would murder people in their beds for ten pounds. They thought nothing of raping, shooting, taking hostages. He must put himself between this bastard and his family, whatever it took.

Silently he moved to the bottom of the staircase and watched the man climbing. For a couple of heartbeats he

stared at the shapeless back. Then he cleared his throat.
The burglar froze, turned, and stared.

He was young, twenty at most; a potato-faced lad sweaty
with nerves. His chin was unshaven, his eyes dull and soul-
less. The cheap tracksuit sparked with static in the darkness,
and the thick woollen hat was pulled almost down to his
eyelids.

"Nice shoes," said Sam.

The intruder squared up to him, startled and dangerously poised. "You wanker," he said, shining the torch into
Sam's eyes. He slipped his free hand into a pocket and the
shape that formed in the fabric could have been a hammer,
a gun, anything.

"I wouldn't go up there if I were you," Sam said, blinking.

"Fuck off."

"Trust me. My father keeps a gun under the bed." He
called out, "Dad!"—not loud enough to wake anyone, but
loud enough to make the thief panic.

He glared at Sam, glanced at the rucksack, and apparently decided to cut his losses. "Get out me way," he rasped.
His lips hung open around large front teeth. He looked desperate, blank-eyed with violence.

"You're not going anywhere, mate," said Sam.

"Get out me fucking way or I'll cut you."

"With a flashlight?"

"With this." The burglar's right hand appeared from the
folds of his tracksuit and in it he held a huge carving knife.

The staircase was too wide for Sam to block. He was
insane to try, but too angry to think about getting hurt. As
he took a step and spread his arms, the man rushed him.

The impact took Sam down and they rolled together.
The attacker's breath was loud in his ears and odorous.
Sam felt the knife tip at his stomach, caught the wrist that
held it. The arm was monstrously strong. He strained to
force it back. Still he felt the blade trembling nearer, the tip
nicking his shirt, a cold sting in his abdomen.

Sam slammed his head into the intruder's nose. Warm

drops spattered. As the youth jerked in reflex, he wrenched the wrist and got the knife from him.

They wrestled, struggling in a clumsy tangle of limbs to get blows in. Disarmed, the thief still wouldn't stop. Panic or drugs made him ferocious. Sam found himself underneath with the man swearing and spitting on top, hands groping around his throat. Sam shoved upwards and felt a yielding sensation, like cutting into heavy sponge cake . . .

The man gave a horrible choking yelp. He rocked back onto his heels and for a second he crouched above Sam, clutching his gut and staring at the dark liquid spilling out. "Jesus," he hissed. Then he rose and staggered towards one of the tall windows.

"Oh, no you don't," Sam said, rising up after him. He was in a fever of rage in which he acted with calm, precise clarity. Glass smashed. The thief was hanging over the ledge in a mass of shards and twisted lead. He was screaming now. Sam seized a handful of his tracksuit and began to drag him back.

He struggled, shrieking in terror. "Didn't mean anything," he squealed. "It were just a laugh. I'm a friend of Jon's! *Let me go!*"

"No, you don't, you little shit." Sam got his forearm round the throat, dragged him back, and squeezed until he felt the warm, struggling beast in his arms go limp. The weight slipped down to the floor, almost taking him with it.

"Who's there?" His father's voice came from above. Lights flicked on, spilling weak amber radiance down the walls. The hall's three great chandeliers made an anemic impact on the darkness.

Sam stood back, gasping. The knife hung in his hand. "We had a break-in. I stopped him."

"Lawrence? What's happened?" Sapphire came along the gallery behind him, tying a Chinese silk dressing gown. "Oh my god."

Lawrence was coming down the stairs quite slowly. Sapphire rushed past him. Sam held his hands out to stop her but she stepped around him and stared down at the youth. Blood was pooling under him. His mouth moved weakly.

Sapphire looked from the intruder to Sam, her face dropping in horror. "Sam, have you done this?"

"After he tried to knife me, yes." He could hardly find his voice.

"He's still alive. You stop the bleeding while I—" She turned and ran towards Lawrence's study, blue silk flying. Sam had never seen Sapphire upset before. Was this what it took to dent her composure, a man bleeding to death under her nose?

"Yeah, uh, we should try to stop it," Sam said faintly. He grabbed a cushion, knelt down and pushed it into the wound. The lad groaned weakly.

Lawrence only stood there, looking down without expression. "Are you hurt, Sam?" he asked.

"No. Jon at college?" Lawrence nodded. "Thank god."

"It's from the Abyss," said Lawrence, staring fixedly at the man.

Sam looked up with a frown. "What? He's human."

"But the ice giant sent him, as it sent Barada."

"Dad?" A shiver went through Sam. Had his father lost his mind? This was a nightmare. Coming home was like stepping into hell. "He's probably a junkie. Check his bag. He said he knows Jon, but everyone knows you're loaded and you won't even fit a sodding alarm system! If you will keep a million quid's worth of precious stones lying around, what d'you expect?"

Lawrence bent down to the man's rucksack. He rummaged, then shook it until the contents came clunking out onto the floor. Hammer, chisel, crowbar, flashlight batteries, a packet of cigarettes and an empty potato chips bag. Lawrence stood looking at the sad debris as if he didn't believe it.

"There you go, he didn't get anything," Sam said hoarsely. "Your safe passed the test."

"But what was he looking for? This can't be a simple thief." He stood over the intruder and gave his shoulder a push with his foot. The swollen eyes came open. "Who are you working for?"

The mouth moved, but the eyes were unfocused. He began to shiver.

"We could torture him," Sam said casually. Then, off his father's gimlet look, "What? You're the one kicking him. You really think I could do that? Is that what you think of me?"

"I wouldn't know," said Lawrence. "You're never here."

Sam turned his head away, biting down on his anger and frustration.

Again Lawrence rocked the man with his foot to rouse him. "Who are you working for?" He bent down, suddenly shouting into his face. "Who sent you?"

The man let out a grunt that could have been a word but was probably pain.

"Dad, for fuck's sake! He's an opportunist, he got nothing!"

His father ignored him. "I knew it," he said, straightening up. "Brawth, Barada, Albin, all hand-in-glove. Of course. What did they tell you to do? What do they want? Answer!"

The man's eyes rolled under heavy eyelids, but he couldn't speak anymore.

"This isn't working," said Sam. "He's still bleeding. Oh, shit." Horror danced around him but he couldn't connect to it, couldn't feel anything. His mind turned over mad plans to hide the body and with each second he knew more clearly that nothing could ever be the same again after this moment. The enormity of it thundered around him but he couldn't feel its weight. Not yet.

Sapphire came back to them, looking pale.

"I've called an ambulance," she said. "I've called the police."

8

Dumannios

Rosie's car tunneled through darkness. Sheets of rain swept over the windshield, sparkling in her headlights, mesmeric. The lane was narrow with high wooded banks on either side, making it impossible to drive fast. It was late on Sunday night and she was tired out, body and soul.

She was glad to be returning to college. The last few days had been surreal; the sky behind Stonegate Manor blazing with blue lights and sirens one night, police swarming over the estate, a flow of horrible rumors—an intruder stabbed and strangled to death, Sam under arrest.

Cloudcroft was in shock. Sympathy for his son's arrest was tempered by dislike of Lawrence and Sam's reputation. There were debates in the media about homeowners' rights to defend their property. Weeping relatives appeared on the TV news declaring that *"Gary was no angel, but 'e was trying to get off the drugs. 'E didn't deserve to die."*

Lucas had been restless and moody. Rosie had never known him to argue so much with Jessica as he had today. "I can't understand why they won't let me see Jon," he'd kept saying. "He must be having a hellish time. Surely he needs his friends. What's wrong with them?"

"It's their decision." Even Jessica was frazzled. "If it had happened to us, I'd want to shut myself away, too. Let them deal with it. What if you and Jon had been at Stonegate that night? I can't bear to think of it!"

"Well, we weren't," Lucas had said defiantly, so unlike his usual self. And then Matthew couldn't resist joining in, saying that the Wilders were all mad, a road crash waiting to happen, and the only wonder was that Sam hadn't pulled a stunt like this before.

In the end, Rosie had thrown her clothes into a bag and driven off. Her small Volkswagen, a birthday gift from her father, gave her that freedom; strange freedom, to escape the home she loved. But she needed peace, soil under her fingernails, rooks cawing and dryads whispering in the trees above her. Even their green-eyed gossip was preferable to her family at the moment.

Much as Rosie distrusted Lawrence, she felt sympathy for him. And for Jon, of course, and Sapphire . . . even a little for Sam himself. What a hopeless, horrible mess.

The car bounced on potholes as the lane wormed through the night. A shape moved, just beyond the range of her headlights. A deer in the road? No one would be out so late in this weather. She slowed down but saw nothing through wavering sheets of rain.

Then a shambling figure peeled out of the shadows and staggered in front of her. She yelped and stamped on the brakes. In the eerie rain-light of her headlamps she glimpsed wild hair, a gaunt face. Swerving for good measure, she narrowly missed the man, skidding as he lurched aside. Disheveled and feral, the figure turned to watch her as the flank of her car slid past.

Quickly checking her mirrors, she saw that he was still on his feet, unharmed. He swayed in the middle of the lane, shapeless in a dark overcoat, hair dripping. A tramp. Drunk or drugged, and staggering god-knows-where. Rosie put her foot down and accelerated away. She was too shaken and scared to stop. At least she hadn't killed him, only given both herself and him a hellish fright. However, he was still out there, wandering towards the isolated cottage. Great.

She pulled into the driveway. There were no other cars, no lights on. It looked as if her housemates wouldn't be back until tomorrow. Checking that no one was lurking in the garden, she leaped out and locked the car, ran to the front door and struggled in a fumbling panic to get her key into the lock.

She was inside. Door closed, locked—then she went around switching on every light. She took her bag upstairs; checked each small, crooked bedroom for intruders—feeling foolish, but compelled to do it. Downstairs again, she put music on, filled the kettle. No; wine was in order.

It's at this point, she thought, *that someone cuts the electric and phone cables.*

No, she told herself, taking deep breaths. *This isn't a film. Calm down, idiot.*

Her panic eased, but she stayed on edge, aware of the false cheer of light and music, the size of the night. *Please don't let him come to the cottage,* she thought. He might only want shelter, but there was no guarantee he was harmless.

Trying to act normally, she pulled off her boots and settled on the sofa with a full glass. The familiar room with its flaky white walls, ancient rugs and sagging furniture felt cold and shabby.

There was a knock at the door.

"Shit!" she yelped and shot bolt upright, spilling wine all over herself.

Should she turn out the lights out and pretend no one was home? Too late. Her skin crawled. Perhaps if she passed him some money through the letterbox to go away . . . Another knock. She swore, angrily willing him to leave.

"Rosie!" came a thin voice she didn't recognize. More thumping. "Rosie, open up, it's only me!"

Confused, she warily went to the door. She made sure the chain was on, took a breath, and opened it. The tramp stood on the doorstep. Shabby coat, stringy hair, rain running down ghostly skin, eyes deep with shadow.

The tramp was Jon.

"Can I come in?" he said. "Is it okay?"

Speechless, she took off the chain and let the damp apparition over her threshold. He stood dripping on the carpet, sniffing and pushing his hand through his hair. He looked dreadful. His face was haggard, eyes sunk in brown shadow. He wasn't drunk; just tired and desperate, perhaps ill. Rosie was so shocked she couldn't move. "What are you doing here?" she said at last.

"Is it all right? You don't mind, do you?" He lurched toward the sofa, nearly tripping on the curled-up edge of a rug.

"No, of course not—hang on, let me take your coat," she said as he made to sit down in the wet garment. "It's such a surprise."

The coat weighed a ton. As she hung it on the newel post at the bottom of the stairs, a smell of damp and smoke wafted from it. "Yeah, I know. Sorry."

"No, really, it's all right. Was that you"—she waved at the outside world—"walking down the lane?"

"Yeah. I couldn't find a bus. Didn't realize how far it was."

"Oh god, I nearly ran you over. I'm so sorry. If I'd known it was you, I would have stopped."

"'Sall right." Jon dragged his hand through the strings of hair again, a nervous gesture. "I didn't know where else to go," he said, shaking his head. He seemed twitchy, one knee bouncing under his elbow.

"Really?" she said cautiously. "Why on earth didn't you come to Oakholme?"

"You must be joking. I couldn't face anyone there. Wasn't thinking straight, anyway . . . I just went."

"Oh . . . Do you want a cup of tea?"

"The wine looks good."

"No problem." She rushed to fetch a glass and the bottle, nearly tripping up the step from the kitchen as she came back.

"Thanks," he said, and half-emptied the glass without drawing breath. Rosie sat on the arm of the sofa, watching him. She had no idea what to say or do. The person she'd pined for with such desire and adoration for all these years— this wasn't him, and yet it was. She couldn't imagine anything less appropriate than making a pass at him now.

"You must have been having a dreadful time," she said gently.

"It's all so stupid," Jon muttered. "The guy that died—he said he knew me. I don't remember, he wasn't from college. Maybe he came to see the band, that's all. But my father went mad, blaming me . . ."

"I'm sorry. That's horrible."

"I couldn't stand it at home any longer."

"Is there anything I can do?"

He hesitated, shaking and pushing his hair back only for it to fall forward again. "Yes, I need to ask you a favor, a really big favor."

"Of course." Rosie felt overwhelmed that he was even here. His sorry state provoked a wave of protective love. "Anything."

"You heard about Sam?"

"Yes. I'm so sorry. It must be so hard for you and your family."

"He's in jail on remand, and they sent him to Yorkshire because the local prisons were full. The thing is, I'm supposed to be visiting him tomorrow, and . . ." Jon shivered. "He refuses to see my father or Sapphire, so there's only me. Luc and me, we thought it was ecologically friendly not to own cars or learn to drive, but now it's just a bloody nuisance."

"Do you want me to take you?" Rosie offered with ready warmth.

She was already planning every detail. She'd drive Jon to the prison, wait for him, console him when he came out again. They would have time alone in the car together, perhaps a stop for supper on the way back . . .

"I can't face it," Jon was saying, oblivious of her thoughts. "I just can't do it, Rosie. I couldn't bear to see him locked up in there. I wondered . . . would you go instead? For me?"

"Instead? Can I do that? I thought you needed a visiting order, or something."

"No, it's all right. On remand, anyone can see him until

he gets sentenced . . . *if* he does . . . Please. I know it's a lot to ask, but I just can't."

She was startled and dismayed. He looked so wretched that she couldn't refuse. "So you," she struggled, "you don't want to come with me?"

"I'm sorry," he said, looking crushed with misery. "I would if I could, but I can't face it."

"It's all right," she heard herself saying. "Don't worry. If you feel like that, of course I'll go." He rewarded her with a smile of such relief and gratitude that her heart swelled. She was a pushover. Anything for him.

The closer Rosie drew to the prison, the bleaker the landscape grew, as if some dark lord of fantasy had scoured the land. It was on the north edge of the Yorkshire Moors, a good four hours' drive. Her small car steamed bravely on. A sharp headwind slowed her speed and she felt isolated, exposed and tiny, with the peat and heather of the landscape sweeping to the horizon in every direction. But she was doing this for Jon, proving the depth of her love even if he never loved her back.

He'd spent the night in the room next to hers and she'd barely slept, conscious of him so close to her but untouchable. This morning he'd emerged looking exhausted, refusing breakfast, only smiling wanly at her as she left. He looked absolutely broken down with guilt. At least she'd persuaded him to take a shower.

On the outskirts of a small town, signs appeared for the prison. She followed the route through the charming old town center into an estate of seventies houses. Then came runs of electrified fencing topped with barbed wire, rows of floodlights. And looming through the storm-light, the walls of the prison itself. She'd visualized a grey edifice on the moors, all gothic towers and tiny barred windows. Instead she was confronted by a vast modern expanse of sandy-colored bricks. The sweep of the wall took her breath away, stretching upwards and onwards forever, blank, institutional and deadly serious.

Rosie quailed. She could hardly blame Jon for not wanting to come. If not for him she would have turned the car around and fled. Instead she drove to the barrier, showed her ID and was waved through.

She parked in the visitors' area and began to walk slowly towards studded iron doors. She felt cold, dizzy with dread. The fortress sucked her in, one gate, one security check after another, and with each step she was more aware of the weight of brick and metal around her.

A female officer searched her, sweeping her over with a wand then patting her clothes as she explained the rules. Rosie looked around at the tired, sad faces of other visitors and realized what a sheltered life she'd led. This was all so mundane and yet hostile, soul-stealing.

"That way," said the officer. At that moment, Rosie was seized by a hallucination. The woman's face changed; the skin turning to scales, eyes bright green and lidless. Shock struck her dumb. "First time, love?" the woman said. "Don't look so worried." As she spoke, she turned human again, with a pleasant, weathered face, curly brown hair.

"Yes," Rosie managed to say.

"Husband, is he?" Her voice was reassuring, full of seen-it-all worldliness. "Boyfriend?"

"No! Just a—a neighbor, really. He's got no one else."

"Well, that's kind of you." The guard's face gave another human-to-demon flicker. "All clear on the regs? Good. Follow the others and give your name to the officer on the door."

"Thank you." The featureless corridor trembled around Rosie. She could taste the tension in the air. She heard the voices of other visitors farther ahead; but as she turned a corner, the corridor was empty. It looked all wrong.

The light turned dim and she felt the floor shaking as if from the rumble of underground machinery. This isn't the surface world, Rosie thought as she walked on, and I've never seen the Dusklands like this . . . She glimpsed narrow tunnel mouths glowing with red fire. Lights strung along the walls emitted an ominous hum. The stench was of stale urine, sweat and disinfectant, laced with cabbage.

She entered a smoky grey cavernous space with an officer waiting just inside. With his reptilian face and bright green eyes, he didn't even try to look human. She held her nerve as he summoned her in. "Table four, love."

She took a step, and the visiting room shook itself square, with white walls, barred windows, red plastic-topped tables.

Another few steps and the room warped again. The transitions were making her dizzy. Now the room resembled a dusty medieval cathedral filled with small round tables. Each table had two chairs like gothic thrones, most occupied by translucent human ghosts. The hubbub of voices echoed off the high vault of the ceiling. Looking up, she caught an impression of convoluted arches far above, with bats or tiny demons fluttering in the sooty shadows.

Rosie's mouth was ash-dry. These illusions felt so real and solid. Prisoners, visitors . . . they looked far away, as if seen through gauze.

She found her table and sat down. The gothic seat and table were bleached and cracked like driftwood. Around the walls were alcoves occupied by gargoyles wrapped in dark leather wings . . . not statues, but living guards.

It's all right, she scolded herself. I'm Aetherial. Weird things happen.

Then she saw Sam threading his way towards her through the crowd. Slender, light on his feet, wearing a green prison tabard over grey T-shirt and jeans. His hair had been cropped close to his skull, which emphasized the sculpture of his face. He was all cheekbones and bright, dazzling blue-green eyes. The eyes were beacons against the monochrome of the walls.

Seeing her, he stopped in his tracks. He stared, gave a silent laugh of amazement. Rosie stood up and waited for him to reach her. "Rosie? What on earth are you doing here? Where's Jon?"

He stood gaping at her. His obvious astonishment and pleasure embarrassed her. He smiled, his teeth as white and feral as ever. "Who cares where he is?" he added. "I can't believe it."

She had absolutely no idea what to say. Her throat was burning. Sam went on staring. "It's amazing to see you." He glanced quickly around, and down at himself. "Not that I ever wanted you to see me like this." An officer took a warning step towards them. "Oh—sit down."

The gargoyle folded into its alcove again as Sam and Rosie took seats on opposite sides of the table. She couldn't find her tongue, wished herself anywhere but in this nightmare place. "They don't like you standing up," Sam explained. "No touching, kissing, hugging or passing items, either."

"Well, none of that's going to happen," she said.

"No, of course not." He folded his arms and gazed at her. His eyes were lasers. "You must have had a hell of a journey. They'll bring tea round; fifty pence a cup, though, sorry about that."

"No problem. I can raise a pound."

"I dreamed about seeing you. Never thought it would be in this situation."

"I don't know," she said thinly. "It suits you."

"Cheers. I should have expected that." He spread his hands, still grinning. "Abuse me all you like, I enjoy it."

"I'll do my best." Rosie wanted to be fair and helpful, but she was struggling. She didn't trust Sam on any level. She didn't know him. His rapt attention made her uneasy, needling through her defenses. One minute of conversation and they were falling into the usual pattern of sarcasm; but perhaps it was better than pretending. "Am I your first visitor?"

"Dad came once. It was horrible. I told him not to bother again. I can't believe you're here. So, how come? I didn't know you cared."

"I care about your brother," she said. "Jon asked me. He

said he couldn't face it, so I'm here instead as a favor to him."

"Right." The light went out of Sam's eyes and he looked away from her. "At least we cleared that one up. The one member of my family I could face seeing, and he can't get off his backside to make the effort. But you'd crawl across Death Valley and stick your head in a tar pit—as long as it's for him. Figures."

"He was scared," Rosie said sharply. "He lost his nerve."

"He knew you'd do anything for him. He knew I'd be pleased to see you. He's really a monumental creep and archmanipulator; I'm bloody impressed."

"He was distraught! If you'd seen him—" Rosie sighed through her teeth. "Great, so I've driven two hundred miles to listen to this for an hour?"

Another prisoner leaned between them, so sudden and quiet that she nearly jumped out of her skin. He placed two teas on the table. The reek of sweat from his armpit as he leaned over nearly knocked her out. Behind him, reality and illusion morphed in and out, mundane to cobwebbed gothic.

"Thanks," she whispered, giving him money and holding her breath until he moved away. Sam grinned at her.

"You've never been here before, have you?"

"Prison?" she said. The tea, served in Styrofoam cups, was scalding and full of sugar. "No. My family manages to stay on the right side of the law."

"Not prison," he said, the grin darkening. "Dumannios."

She put the cup down, spilling it. "We're in Dumannios?"

"The lower layer of the Dusklands, gone bad. The home of nightmares, living gargoyles, pseudo-demons and burning cathedrals. Molten lava and hellfire. Great, isn't it?"

Rosie looked around at the dripping fortress walls, the ashen guards. It wasn't exactly fear she felt but intense, cosmic unease. She thought of stormy skies and boiling black clouds, the moors stretching forever outside, miles of electric fencing sizzling in sulfurous rain. The dead eyes of the staff, their skin sucked dry by the heat of volcanic vents. The whole prison edifice trembling over a lake of fire.

"Oh, fuck," she whispered.

"Although, if you've been in Stonegate, you can't be that surprised."

"I suppose not, but I've never been trapped inside it like this."

"Hey, don't panic." Sam reached across the table and touched her hand; Rosie snatched it away. "They say it's a perception thing. Stuff that's always there but we don't see it. I'm sure you can drive out, same as you arrived. It's only the inmates who are stuck here."

"How?" she said. "The others look human. And how can humans build a prison in Dumannios?"

"Oh, it was built in the real world. I reckon the other inmates and visitors are looking at plain walls and fluorescent strips and cheap plastic tables. I catch glimpses. It's only Aetherials who are stuck with the deeper dimensions and the H. P. Lovecraft nasties."

Her eyes widened. "Is it just you? Us, I mean?"

"There are a couple of other Vaethyr in here," he said softly. "And yes, we all get the slimy dungeons and interesting visits from the night staff who no one else sees."

"All the time?"

"No, but the unpredictability factor makes it that bit more exciting."

"Why is it happening?"

"I have no bleeding idea, love." He tilted his head slightly, eyes narrow. "Some sort of shadowy Spiral Court justice, I think. The Ancients don't like us stirring it on Earth, so we get a double punishment. Things go on in the inner realms that we don't have the faintest clue about. Jon had every right to be scared."

"I don't think he knew it would be this bad."

"Maybe not. Gates are locked, it messes up our instincts."

"Are you here until the trial?"

"Apparently. I was refused bail. I've had issues with the police before, and this time someone died. Also, they seemed to think I might skip off abroad again."

"Any idea how it will go?"

"I'm looking at five years for manslaughter," Sam said bluntly. "Probably get out in three. You were hoping I'd say life, weren't you? Sorry to disappoint."

"Of course I wasn't." Cold, delayed shock sank through her. "It's not fair, is it? You were defending your family."

"D'you know, if we were in America, it would have been okay for me to shoot him? But not here. Apparently I used unreasonable force. Dragging the guy back into the house when he was trying to escape; never a good idea. Helping him along with a bit of strangulation while he was bleeding to death; not advisable. Plus, I have a record."

Rosie sat back in her chair, looking at him. Sam had a beautiful, cruel face, like his father. His eyes were jewels, glittering and glacial. He'd never seemed to give a damn about anything, even himself; and for that she couldn't warm to him. Even now he was sitting there trying to make himself look as wicked as possible, purely to shock her.

She didn't realize she had any kind of expression on her face until he said, "You really hate me, don't you? It must be killing you to sit here trying to be social."

"I've had better days."

"I don't know why you bothered. Jon won't be a tiny bit grateful."

"I'm not doing it for gratitude," she snapped.

"Just in it for the martyrdom, then?" He sat back with a groan as if giving up. Then impulsively he leaned forward again. "Rosie, maybe I'm a masochist, but I think the world of you. You're the most beautiful girl I've ever seen and you've got no idea. You think it's any fun for me to sit here being loathed by you? I'm in love with you."

"You're *what*?" She gaped at him, completely thrown. "You have to be kidding."

"No, I'm not." He leaned closer, his expression luminous with sincerity; but he was such an actor, she didn't believe him for a split second. "I mean it."

"You don't love me—you don't know me! I haven't even seen you for four years! I didn't come here to play stupid games."

"I'm not." He drew back. "I wish I could have done things differently so you weren't sitting there despising me. I'd rather have hostile Rosie than no Rosie at all—but this isn't you. It's not the real you."

"Tough. It's all you're getting. You don't love me, you're just nuts from being in this place."

"That must be it," he said flatly, making her more annoyed.

"'Unreasonable force,' that's the story of your life! You wonder why I don't like you? D'you want a list?" She swept her hair aside to expose her neck. "I've still got the scar from the first time we met."

He winced. "I'm sorry."

"You stole from me, beat up my brother, threatened me, lied to me—"

"When did I lie?"

"You told me Jon was gay! God knows what you've told him about me!"

"Come on, teasing—"

"No. A decent person knows the difference. You've bullied and beaten people and you set the Pit Bull on me."

"The who?"

"That little tattooed biker you used to go out with."

His forehead creased. He looked part guilty, part amused. "You mean Sue? You called her the Pit Bull? That's priceless."

"Oh yes, it was bloody priceless being set on by her and her mates!"

"Rosie," said Sam. "Two things. Try to smile and look happy while you're hissing at me so the warders don't intervene. Second, I did not set Sue on you. She knew it was you I really wanted and she was jealous. I had no idea she was planning to hurt you. I was horrified, but you never gave me a chance to make amends. I told her what I thought and I dumped her, end of story. By the way, you do know you terrified the crap out of her, don't you?"

"Good! You keep such great company, too."

Sam waved a hand. "Look around; you've got me where you've always wanted me. I'm doing my penance now. Give me a break."

She gasped, "Do you even care that you actually killed someone?"

"Can I tell you what happened?" He leaned forward, elbows on the table, face serious, eyes shining.

"About the murder?"

"I didn't murder anyone!" he exclaimed. "Manslaughter!" People at the neighboring tables fell silent and looked. "What?" said Sam, turning to them. "Our conversation more interesting than yours, is it? Fine, pull up a chair!"

They all looked away and resumed muttering. Rosie dropped her head onto one hand. "All right," she said. "I'll give you a break. Tell me."

"I came home and there was a burglar," he said very quietly. "He was about to go upstairs and do god-knows-what to my father. I didn't even know if Jon or anyone else was in the house. What was I supposed to do? So I tried to stop him and he attacked me. I'd like to tell you that the magical mist of Dumannios came down and turned us into demons, but it didn't. It was just ugly.

"He had a huge knife. If I hadn't got the knife off him, I'd have been dead—and I didn't intend to stab him, but it happened." Sam leaned farther forward. She strained to hear him, moving closer but looking at the tabletop, not at his face. She felt his breath on her ear. "He tried to get away by throwing himself through a window, so I pulled him back and throttled him. Don't suppose you've ever experienced the red mist like that? Only he was ten times more scared than me, and that's why he fought so hard and why I ended up killing him. What do I tell the court, except the truth? He took the knife from our kitchen so I can't prove he had it first. It was only when he lay bleeding and my father put the light on that I realized what I'd done."

In the eerie light, all color bled out of his face "I'm not very good at remorse," he added. "But I didn't get up that morning intending to kill anyone, Rosie, I swear."

"You were defending your family," she said.

"If I'd let him go, so he bled to death on our lawn instead of on our carpet, I might have gotten away with it. But I didn't, because I was too furious at this fucking toe-rag for invading our house. So, five years looks pretty lenient. What do you think?"

"I don't know." Rosie groaned. "What are you angling for, forgiveness or condemnation? Part of me thinks it's completely unfair, because he shouldn't have been there. Part of me thinks that if you hadn't ended up here for this, it would have been for something else."

"God, you really think I'm that scummy, don't you?"

"Don't pull that face," she said. "Anyone could see it coming."

"And you're probably right."

"What are you going to do when you get out?" she asked angrily. "Carry on as you have been until you finally talk yourself into a life sentence?"

"Rosie," he said acidly, "can you guess what I was doing while I was away? Not beating, robbing or murdering anyone. I was trying to forget about bloody Stonegate and being a flaming Aetherial. I've been picking olives, oranges, apricots, you name it, I've picked it. Then I come home, filial duty and all that, and I walk into this."

"I don't know what you want me to say. This situation is crap for everyone."

She folded her arms and looked away, but from the corner of her eye she saw his regard on her, cool and steady. "Don't let's talk about it any more," he said. "How are you? What have you been doing? How's your little brother?"

She let her arms drop and composed herself. Arguing with him was pointless and yet it was incredibly hard to stop, like the excruciating thrill of scratching a rash. "Luc's fine, but he doesn't say much about . . . you know. We've all got used to the idea now, but it was a hell of a shock at the time. You probably thought it was a big laugh, and I expect you've known for years."

"What are you talking about?" said Sam.

She frowned at him. "Lawrence telling Lucas that he's his father, of course."

"What?"

He looked genuinely confused. Rosie's mouth dropped open in shock. "Oh my god, they haven't told you? All this time and they haven't—?"

"You tell me. I have absolutely no clue what you're on about."

She began, then shook her head. "No. You know, all right. You're just playing games."

"Rosie, I swear to all the gods I'm not! All we've talked about is my stupid trial! My father said what to Lucas?"

A bell shrilled. The physical shock seemed to tear loose a veil, and she suddenly saw the room in its square, banal reality, with ordinary prison officers standing about. This time the change held. Only Sam looked the same. "Five minutes, ladies and gentlemen, thank you," said an officer.

"That was never an hour," Sam said, jumping to his feet. "Rosie, please tell me."

There was noise around them as chairs were pushed back and tearful farewells made. Rosie tried to speak over the hubbub. "Apparently Lawrence had a fling with my mother—look, you'll have to ask him yourself."

"Fuck!" said Sam. "This is crazy. You can't just tell me that and walk out."

"Thank you, ladies and gentlemen," came the command. Rosie glanced around at the glaring lights, disoriented. Sam saw her expression.

"It's all right," he said. "Go out the way you came, don't look back, and you'll be fine. Thanks for coming."

"It's okay."

"Rosie, you have got to come back and finish the story," he added softly. "Please."

She hesitated. "No," she said firmly, turning away. "It's your family you need to see, not me."

When Rosie reached the cottage that evening, Jon was still there. He looked better, eyes bright and skin radiant, and he'd washed and combed his hair back to shiny chestnut glory. He thanked her profusely for making the journey.

"Is it all right if I stay the night again?" he asked.

"Of course," she said, stunned. "Stay as long as you like. I'm knackered. Let me freshen up then I'll tell you all about it."

She ran upstairs, showered, dressed in her best peasant skirt and clingy black top. She dabbed her mouth with lip gloss, brushed out her hair to a softly swinging, burnished veil and had to admit that, for a ten-minute makeover, she looked okay. However horrible the situation, she couldn't return to Jon looking a wreck.

As she left the bathroom, she bumped into Clive, one of her housemates. "Wow, look at you," he said. "Is that for"—he aimed his thumb at the stairs—"your boyfriend down there? Lucky him."

"He's not my boyfriend. Just a friend."

"Right." Clive gave an insinuating grin and a wink. "Mind you, he's a bit strange, isn't he? Looked like he'd slept in a hedge. Just lay on the sofa all day."

"Has he had anything to eat?"

"Jill did him some soup. Doesn't say much, does he?"

"He's having a difficult time. His brother's in prison."

"You go and take his mind off it, then." Clive gave her a conspiratorial pat on the shoulder. "I'll keep the others down the pub for a while, know what I mean?"

"You're a saint," she said.

Rosie opened a bottle of wine, sat beside Jon all swinging hair and perfumed skin. She felt spacey with tiredness, yet managed to be cheerful and consoling as she told Jon about the visit—giving him a selectively edited version without gargoyles, hellfire or sniping—in the hope that he would feel better. She moved closer as she answered his questions. She became the warmest, most seductive Rosie she could possibly be. If love would comfort him, she was ready to do anything.

Jon did not respond at all. He didn't even seem to notice. He looked pale, preoccupied and shivery. She felt as sexy as a block of wood.

"You're so good to do this," he told her. "I'm sorry, d'you mind if I go to bed? I can't keep awake."

She jumped up. "Urm, there's only my room tonight. Everyone's home, so no spare beds."

"I can sleep on the sofa."

"No, you can't. They'll come in from the pub, make a noise and sit watching TV for hours. And it's freezing down here. Come on. This way."

She led Jon upstairs to her tiny room. She felt unreal. She'd dreamed for years of doing this and it was nothing like the dream, nothing. They stood awkwardly in the doorway, looking at the narrow bed. Moonlight dazzled through the window.

"I can sleep on the floor," he said.

"No, no," said Rosie, "you have the bed. You're obviously not well."

"Thanks. Getting a cold, I think. There's probably room for us both, anyway," he said. "Yes, come on Rosie, we'll both fit in there fine."

"Oh. Okay. I'll just, er . . ." She went to the bathroom, cleaned her teeth and slipped into blue cotton pajamas. She was shaking. This was surreal.

When she returned to the bedroom, Jon was already asleep.

He lay in her bed, on his side facing away from her. Jon, naked in her bed.

He was so thin that he left acres of space and she could easily lie beside him without touching him. She couldn't sleep a wink. The room felt close and alien. She lay there listening to her housemates coming in, messing about, finally going to bed. Then the cottage was quiet, but she was wide awake.

Rosie sat up and looked at Jon. The bronze waves of his hair spread over the pillow and down his back. She'd never seen him naked before and he really was slender, barely a hint of muscle on his body. Every notch of his spine showed. His skin looked colorless.

She reached out stroked the silk of his hair. Her hand touched his shoulder. He twitched but didn't wake. His skin felt cold and clammy; he had hardly any scent, except the faintest hint of fresh sweat.

What would he do if she turned him over and started kissing him? Would he fight her off with protests that he didn't feel like *that* about her? Or would she awaken some sleeping serpent of passion, make him realize what he'd been missing?

The most disturbing thing of all was that she didn't want to.

He looked vulnerable. He looked unhealthy. She just . . . couldn't.

Rosie slipped off the bed and went downstairs. It had been an experiment, the sexy clothes, the perfumed hair; something she'd had to try, even though her heart had not been in it. She looked back on it with a stale taste in her mouth. If you truly love someone, she thought, shouldn't you love them no matter what?

She spent the rest of the night on the sofa, hugging her knees to her chest. Perhaps she slept, but when morning came she could only remember staring at the darkness.

When Jon appeared the next morning, he didn't comment on her absence from bed. He was quiet, nervous and kept sniffing. He refused Rosie's offers of tea or coffee.

"You know, if you've got a cold, you need fluids."

"Have you got any cola? I need the sugar," he said with a wan smile.

"Clive might. I can't stand the stuff. Very unhealthy."

"I'll be okay. I've really got to go."

She rose, worried now. "I think you should stay in bed. You look awful."

"God, will you stop fussing?" he said with a flash of temper she'd never seen before. "You're worse than Sapphire. I have to go."

Rosie withdrew to the kitchen and put the kettle on, to steady herself. "Can I give you a lift somewhere?" she called.

"No, it's okay. I'll get a taxi to Gloucester station."

She was too tired to argue. As she poured a glass of cola, hoping at least to keep him alive, she heard him making a phone call. Then he appeared in the doorway in his coat, smiling sheepishly.

"Be about fifteen minutes. Thanks for everything, you're a real friend," he said. "Thing is, Rosie, I'm a bit stuck. You couldn't lend me some money, could you? Say thirty quid?"

9

Blackdrop

"What was I thinking?" Rosie groaned. "Please shoot me."

"Ro, it's not that bad." Mel leaned over to refill her glass with white wine.

"It's worse," said Rosie, tucking her feet under the hem of her long burgundy skirt. "What's wrong with me? How could I be so selfish?"

Mel's apartment in Nottingham was tastefully minimalist, open-plan with cream decor and subtle lighting; the fruit of a well-paid job she had landed as a conference organizer. Rosie and Faith were curled in the corners of a big leather sofa, Mel cross-legged on the rug. She was perfectly groomed in white trousers and pink top, fingernails and toenails varnished pearly pink to match, her golden hair aglow.

"Selfish?" Mel gasped. "You offered him your body and that was selfish, how?"

"What I mean is that Jon was in a state, distraught about Sam, and yet all I could think about was getting him into bed and in love with me. I'm vile."

"No, you're not," said Faith, cradling a full glass that she hadn't touched. Living at Oakholme, she'd picked up Jessica's taste for hippie-ish dresses, favoring rustic browns and blues. Her hair was brunette and sleek, her glasses stylish with thin black frames. Despite the changes, her shyness lingered. "You love him. You wanted to comfort him."

"Yes," said Mel, "and if the roles were reversed, what man wouldn't take advantage of a female in distress if he fancied her?"

"That's exactly my point!" Rosie exclaimed. "I'd like to think I'm better than that, but apparently I'm not!"

Mel topped up her glass and waved the bottle. "Come on, Faith, you're slow tonight."

"Oh, you know me," said Faith, turning pink. "One drink and I'm plastered."

Sliding the bottle onto the coffee table, Mel continued, "So, to recap—you took Jon in and comforted him, you drove four hundred miles to visit a horrible prison on his behalf, you offered him a night of passion and then, to top it off, you gave him money? Pure evil, Rosie. Yes, someone was taking advantage, all right, and I don't think it was you."

Rosie felt the glow of wine loosening her tongue. "I don't know what to think. I always had this hope that he'd open up to me, and we'd talk and talk, and the sex would be wonderful and natural because there were no barriers between us . . . And you'd think any man would be glad of an affectionate female to take his mind off things, wouldn't you? But not Jon. He didn't even notice. I felt about as sexy as a lump of concrete. A rock in a frock."

They laughed. Rosie sipped her wine, savoring its cold, sweet acidity. "When he was there in my bed, though . . . I didn't even want to. He looked so thin and lifeless."

"Oh, no kidding," said Mel.

"I mean, what is love? It's hard to keep feeling passionate about someone who gives you nothing back. If I truly loved him, I wouldn't have been considering my own desires at all. The Jon in front of me wasn't the Jon I'd fantasized about, but if I don't desire him, all I feel is sorry for him . . . I'm so confused."

"Rosie, will you stop beating yourself up?" Mel said fervently. "The guy is a loser! He doesn't deserve all this agonizing. You must know it's not you. I think he's one of those people who's not that bothered about sex. They do exist."

Stung, Rosie said, "You've got strong opinions, considering you hardly know him."

She happened to catch Mel's eye and found the strangest light there. Mel's china-doll face blushed bright red. "What?" said Rosie. "*What*?"

Mel's lips parted as her color continued to rise. She blurted out, "Rosie, I've slept with him."

Rosie felt the blood draining from her head, the room spinning. "With Jon? You can't have. When? How?"

Her friend's head dropped as she made the quiet confession. "About six months ago. He turned up here one night looking bedraggled and I felt sorry for him. So I fed him and let him stay. I suppose we had too much to drink and it just . . . happened."

All Rosie could do was stare at her. Faith stared too, one hand over her mouth. "The point is," Mel went on, "to be blunt, he wasn't much good. He was terribly skinny and kind of passive, almost squeamish about touching me. Quite honestly, I had to get myself off, because he didn't try at all."

"But he wanted you," Rosie whispered.

Mel shrugged. "Apparently, but he seemed to find the whole experience as thrilling as a cup of tea. Okay, he's sweet and angelic-looking, but it's not enough. I need a bit of enthusiasm."

"Are you saying he didn't feel anything?"

"I suppose he did when he was, you know, climaxing, but otherwise he was about as dynamic as a length of wet spaghetti."

Rosie felt an urge to laugh. If they'd been talking about someone else, she would have. The laughter congealed in her throat. *Jon climaxing inside Mel,* taunted her imagination. *Jon, climaxing. Inside Mel.*

"How could you, when you knew how I felt about him?"

"Rosie, I'm sorry." Mel sounded devastated. "I wouldn't have hurt you for the world."

"Have you seen him again?" she asked, keeping her voice steady.

"He came round a couple more times uninvited, sat on my sofa and lit a joint without even asking, and you know how I hate smoking! Oh, nothing else happened." Rosie believed her; the image of dainty, house-proud Mel falling for a scruffy art student was ludicrous. "It was a mistake, Ro. I told him it wasn't going to work and he just shrugged and left." Mel bit her lip. "Please forgive me. It didn't mean anything."

"It did to me," said Rosie. Calmly she got up and walked into the bathroom, where she stood at the sink breathing hard and pressing cold water onto her face until the welling tears subsided.

"You okay?" said a cautious voice after a few minutes. Faith came in and sat down on the closed loo seat. "Mel's upset."

"*She's* upset?"

"Are you furious with her?"

"No, not really." Rosie breathed in and out, looking at her blotchy face in the mirror. "It's not as if Jon and I were together and he cheated. I don't own him. It's just—what's Mel got that I haven't? I can't believe Jon's so shallow as to prefer blondes, but maybe he is. I would have done anything to be with him. Instead he wants Mel, and she's not even interested!" She growled, low in her throat. "Did I want to hear that he and Mel are blissfully happy together? No. Do I want to hear that Jon's a hopeless sponger who's also rubbish in bed? No, I don't. Life refuses to fit my vision. Big deal. But it still hurts."

"I know," said Faith, stroking her arm. She sat pigeon-toed, looking worriedly up at Rosie.

"I'll be fine," Rosie sighed. "Hey, your roots are showing, Fai. Do you fancy a different color? How about black underneath and blond on top? Go wild."

Faith frowned, self-consciously pushing her hair behind her ear. "Matthew likes me to keep it natural."

"What the hell's it got to do with Matthew?" Rosie exploded. Then she managed a laugh. "We're a sad pair, aren't we? Look at us. Both pining after men who couldn't care less."

Faith frowned harder. Her eyes were glittering.

"What?" said Rosie. "Don't tell me you've slept with Jon as well!"

"Of course I haven't! I'm not pining. We're getting married."

"Who is?" Rosie was floored.

"Me and Matthew, of course. Oh no, I knew you'd have that expression!"

"What expression?"

"Complete disbelief!" Faith stood up, as animated as Rosie had ever seen her. "He'd never look at someone as mousy as me, that's what everyone thought, isn't it? Well, they were wrong. I was wrong."

"No, I—I believe you," Rosie gasped. "But it's so sudden. You and Matt—how did I miss that happening?"

"Life at home doesn't freeze while you're at college, you know," Faith said tightly. "Things go on when you're not there."

"Obviously." Rosie found a smile, and Faith visibly relaxed. "Tell me, then."

"We just sort of . . . started getting close. We tried to pretend nothing was happening at first, but I kept ending up in his room and it was so amazing . . . The first time, I was really nervous, but when I told him I'd never done this before and that I'd been saving myself for him, he was so thrilled I thought he was going to cry." Her eyes shone. "I wanted to tell you ages ago, but I was . . . embarrassed. Trying to find the right moment. It seemed insensitive, when you were unhappy over Jon."

"You don't have to tiptoe around me, ever."

"Well, you'd better make it up with Mel, because I need bridesmaids."

Rosie took this in, steadying herself. "Oh . . . how soon?"

Faith touched her own stomach. "As soon as possible, because this baby's due next May."

Rosie gaped, washed away on the tide of other people's lives. Once the power of speech came back, she said, "Do my mum and dad know?"

"Yes. Jessica was the first person I told. She's thrilled."

"That's great but—gods, Fai, are you sure about this? We're hardly twenty. A child is a huge responsibility. I'm nowhere near ready for it."

"Well, I am," Faith said firmly. "It's all I've ever dreamed of. A real family of my own. Please be happy for us."

Tears flowed down her cheeks. Rosie wrapped her arms around her. "Oh my god, you were planning to announce it tonight, weren't you?" She groaned. "Instead you get upstaged by my drama-queen whining. Forgive me, honey, I didn't know."

Mel appeared, leaning in the doorway, red-eyed. "Are you two speaking to me?"

"Yes." Rosie sighed, turning with one arm around Faith's waist. "We're fine. Fai's got news."

"I heard," Mel smiled. "Surely you realized I was listening? I just need to clear things up with you first, Ro. About Jon . . . It was as if this demon of curiosity inside me said, let's have a taste of what Rosie wants and see what the attraction is. It was a kind of envy, if I'm honest."

"You—envious of *me*? What for? You're the man-magnet!"

"It's not about men." Mel looked at the floor. "It was more about the magical tradition stuff you had going on. I never wanted to believe it, but I could see it was real for you. I felt left out. This selfish bit of me thought that having Jon would be like stealing a piece of it."

"And was it?"

Mel met her eyes. "No. It was just bad sex."

"Jon's not an experiment, not a door you can go through to a higher state of consciousness." Rosie sighed. "He's a person. Maybe that's the mistake I made, thinking he was some demigod."

"I know what I did was cruel and thoughtless," said Mel. "If you can't forgive me, I don't blame you, but I wish it hadn't happened. Please don't let this be the end of our friendship."

Rosie felt the hard edges of her pain softening. She couldn't forgive overnight, but knew she would eventually. "I'm not mad with you, Mel. More just . . . *disappointed*. Everything you said about Jon is true, but I didn't want to believe it. If I can't trust my own judgment, what can I trust? I needed some sense slapped into me and you've done it. Thanks." She smiled sourly at Mel, who grinned back in relief. "Men come and go, but friends are forever."

"I'll get that tattooed around my navel," said Mel.

Afterwards, Rosie wasn't angry with Mel or Jon. She felt as if someone had taken her heart out with a wrecking ball, but no one was to blame.

The next day she was in the center of Ashvale, doing a little shopping and lost in her own thoughts, when a figure in a dark overcoat stepped in front of her. She started violently and looked up at the pale, carved face of Lawrence Wilder. "Rosie, might I have a word with you?"

She couldn't remember him ever speaking directly to her before. His tone, although polite, allowed no possibility of refusal. "Of course," she said warily.

"I understand you went to see Sam."

She felt stupidly tongue-tied, like a child in front of a

high court judge. Had she committed some hideous faux pas by making the visit? Interfered in his private family shame? "Yes, I did."

"You appreciate that the only reason I didn't go myself was that Sam refuses to see me? And I am ashamed of Jon for asking such a thing of you. He will be admonished."

"No, don't do that," she said, horrified. "Really, he's upset enough as it is. Mr. Wilder, I'm so sorry this has happened, but please don't blame anyone. I didn't mind going. It's a difficult time for you. Anything I can do to help . . ."

Her words dissipated, like sea foam on a tall, cold rock. "How is Sam?" he asked.

She told him. As she spoke, she began to see Lawrence as not simply aloof but forlorn. She guessed that it was against all his natural inclinations to seek her out like this; an immense effort for him to utter the next words. "I must ask a very great favor of you, Rosie. If Sam continues his refusal to see me, would you go instead, on my behalf? He says he will see no one but you."

A dark shiver went through her. "If he knows you've sent me, though, he might refuse my visits, as well."

"Then don't tell him."

"Then I'd be deceiving him."

"I would not ask you to go against your conscience." He turned very slightly away, the cold grey eyes under the dark brows still watching her. The shiver became a surge of icy, thrilling dread. It wasn't fear of Lawrence that made her decide; it was his obvious, stark pain.

"Mr. Wilder, it's all right, I'll go," she said.

"Truly?" The faintest spark of light caught in his eyes. "Why?"

"Because I can see how painful this is for you, and I hate to think of Sam stuck there with no one at all."

Lawrence broke eye contact and looked down. She could see aspects of both Jon and Sam in him, even though all three men were so different from each other. She could understand why, for all his iciness, her mother had found him devastatingly attractive.

"You must think it absurd that I, of all people, would dare to ask for a trace of compassion," he said. "Especially in such a situation."

"No—I don't think that. The, er, the issues between you and my family . . . well, they're separate. I want to help you."

"And you'll keep me informed of how he is?"

"Yes." She hesitated. "If you'll do something for me in return? Mr. Wilder, would you please tell Sam about Lucas? Everyone seems to know but him. If he won't speak to you, write a letter."

Lawrence drew and released a quiet breath. "I meant to, of course, but events intervened . . . yes, I'll tell him. Call me Lawrence, not Mr. Wilder."

That would not be an easy change for her. Carefully not using either form, she asked, "Does Sam's mother know what's happened?"

She sensed a closing-off inside him. He looked into the middle distance, his face clouding. "Unfortunately I have no means of contacting her. The day Ginny walked out was the last day I saw or spoke to her. She vanished. She might be in London, Australia or the Spiral itself, for all I know; I can't open the Gates to look and in any case, what is the point if she doesn't want to be found? It's too late."

"There must be ways to look for her—I'm sorry. You must have been through all that. It's none of my business."

He spoke softly. "Who could blame her for going? The darkness drove her away. She blamed Ecuador but the darkness was always part of me, and wherever we went, I dragged it with me . . . Now you are staring at me as if I'm mad, Rosie."

She resisted the temptation to quip, *You must get that a lot.* "No," she said, "I just don't understand."

"And I can't explain. It's inappropriate of me to try. Suffice it to say that after Ginny left things grew worse for me, very much worse. The force that dwells behind the Gates makes it impossible for me to open them, even to look for her, even now. I've learned to live with how unpopular this makes me. Understand that I'm doing it to protect you." He looked at her with special emphasis.

"Me?"

"Yes, *you*. And all Vaethyr. Even your reckless uncle. And especially my sons."

"Can't you tell us . . . what it is?"

She held her breath, waiting for his answer. Lawrence seemed to run out of words; she almost physically saw him close up, as if a gap in his armor plating had sealed shut to keep blood from spilling out. It struck her that it caused him mental torture to talk about it, and she felt bad for asking.

"I'm inexpressibly grateful to you," he said, "about Sam. Take this." He was holding out a handful of twenty-pound notes to her. She recoiled, drowned in the ghastly implications of being given money in the street—but Lawrence only gave a thin smile. "To cover your travel expenses. Please."

"It's too much."

"No, it isn't. You will have to stop for gas and wretchedly overpriced refreshments on the road. Or I could hire a car and driver for you. I'd even drive you there myself . . ."

"No!" she protested. "No, really. I like to be independent. It's fine."

"Then take the money," said Lawrence. "And give my good wishes to Sam."

He was gone in a swish of black fabric, leaving her with a handful of bank notes and a vaguely sick, shaky feeling in her stomach.

Later, she was at Fox Homes, where Auberon had offered her work experience designing gardens for show homes. She told no one she'd seen Lawrence; it felt like a guilty secret. From the window of the architects' office, three floors up, she could see the uplands of Charnwood. Even the weather was different there; shafts of sunlight slicing dramatically through cloud. It was like some fantastical painting, cloud and light appearing to form a vortex of energy swirling around the Great Gates.

Rosie wondered if it was her father's master plan to employ the entire family. Alastair was working at a drawing board on her left. To her right, Matthew sat at his computer, firing off emails and appearing generally busy and important. When Alastair left his work station to fetch coffee, Rosie sidled up to her brother and said, "So, you and Faith, then?"

Matthew turned a 3-D projection of a house on his monitor. One side of his mouth rose in a white grin. "She told you."

"Well, uh, yeah. She's ecstatic. Never thought I'd see anyone made ecstatic by *you*, but it takes all sorts. Jolly well done getting her pregnant, by the way."

"Cheers."

"That's not why you're getting married, is it? Never thought you were that old-fashioned."

Matthew sighed and swiveled his chair to face her. "What's up? We thought you'd be pleased."

She was watching him for every nuance of body language; twitches of mouth or eyebrows, failure to meet her eyes. "I want to be. I'm making sure I've got something to be pleased about."

"What's that supposed to mean?"

"I didn't think she was your type, Matt."

"Right." He scratched his head. "That's a bit insulting to your best friend, isn't it?"

"Oh, like you're such a catch! She's so vulnerable. I thought you'd prefer a glossy career girl with a big personality, so you could pose around being the alpha couple. Someone like Sapphire, maybe. Why Faith?"

"I like Faith," said Matt. "She's always around. You wouldn't think it to look at her, but she is *incredibly* enthusiastic in bed."

"Too much information, Matty."

"Really," he continued with relish. "She saved herself for

me. How great is that? I dated a few of those alpha girls at uni, and they were stone-cold, too much in love with themselves to care about anyone else. Faith, though, she was like a flower opening up in the sun. Just amazing for the ego."

"She loves you." Rosie folded her arms, leaned in closer to him. "Do you love her?"

He shrugged. "Sure. Whatever love is. She's happy, so what's your problem?"

"I need to know you're sincere."

He looked at her, still with the same lazy smile and narrow eyes. "What the hell's it got to do with you?"

"I'm watching out for her, that's all. You concealed the fact that you were seeing each other. That looks like you were ashamed, or hedging your bets."

"Rubbish. We've got a right to privacy, haven't we? We decided to tell the world in our own good time."

"Come on, what's in it for you?"

His smile grew narrower. His voice dropped. "Look at her, Rose. Aside from the fact she can't get enough of me—she's a fantastic housekeeper. Be a great mother. She's never going to be unfaithful. And the icing on the cake: she's human."

Rosie gasped. "You're marrying her because she's *human*?"

"I never wanted an Aetherial wife. You know that."

"Yes, but she loves you. She hero-worships you."

He laughed, impervious. "Yes, and? That's a plus, isn't it?"

"You can't marry her as a human slave!" The more Matthew grinned, the more furious she felt. "This is Faith, Matt. Don't do this to her."

He leaned towards her, face tilted. "What are you going to tell her, then? 'Oh, Faith, don't marry the man you love.' What d'you expect her to say? She'll wonder why you're trying to sabotage her happiness. She might even think you're jealous."

Rosie exhaled sharply. "I'm warning you, if you don't treat her properly—"

"Touched a nerve?" Matthew said, eyebrows rising. "I've told you before, if you keep chasing air-brained Aetherial idiots like Jon, you'll get your heart broken."

"What's wrong with Aetherials? *We're* Aetherial!"

His eyes became serious. "Let's just say that some of us—not all of us—are away with the faeries. Do I want a partner who's preoccupied with the Otherworld, changing shape, having affairs with people like Lawrence Wilder, or even vanishing altogether? Do you? No. I want a sweet-natured all-human woman who thinks only about me and our children."

"Put like that, you sound almost reasonable," she said grudgingly. "Perhaps you could get her to wear one of those little Amish-style headscarves while you're at it."

"Shut up," he said. "I want to see you happy too, Rosie. With someone straightforward and dependable."

She followed his pointed gaze and saw Alastair returning with a tray of coffee, a grin broadening his cheerful face. He looked as wholesome, solid and comforting as a cushion. Everything Matthew was suggesting she needed. Everything, perhaps, that he'd found in Faith.

"Rosie," Alastair said, "there's a new curry house opened up. You don't fancy giving it a try, do you?"

Rosie woke up with a start in the middle of the night, in Alastair's bed.

A vague dismay went through her. The sheets felt waxy-cold on her body. The sleeping mound of Alastair reminded her . . .

It had been . . . fine, really. Slightly awkward and embarrassing, as sleeping with your brother's best friend was bound to be . . . no fireworks, but she couldn't have handled violent passion . . . not earth-shattering, but certainly not dreadful. It had seemed a good idea after a few glasses of wine. Sturdy and friendly must be far better than malnourished and neurotic. At least he wanted her.

She thought back on their wine-hazed conversation at the restaurant. He was easy company, cheerful with an edge of sadness. A bit on the staid side, but that was okay; she didn't have to struggle to impress him. She liked his soft Scottish accent and his self-deprecating sense of humor. Pressed, he'd touched on the ex-girlfriend who'd left his self-esteem a mangled pulp. The way his eyes turned dark had aroused her sympathy, which was largely why the evening had ended in bed.

She'd found herself fantasizing while they were in the act. She had begun to think about Jon, but couldn't; it was too raw. She'd always been drawn to skinny men but it was time to move on, she told herself, and learn to appreciate the attraction of a big, solid, rugby-playing physique instead.

Now she thought, *Oh god, was this really such a good idea?* She imagined facing Mel across a dinner table and asking, "Pilsbury Doughboy or wet spaghetti?" Involuntary mad laughter shook her. Alastair woke and turned over. Seeing her awake and smiling, he smiled back. "You and me, eh?" he said lazily. "We kind of drifted together. I always hoped we would."

He wasn't bad. He was kind. He was safe. It was bound to get better.

"Oh my god, you came back!" said Sam, his face luminous with shock and pleasure.

Rosie sat down, facing him across the table. She tried to ignore the eerie morphing of the room. It was like being on the set of some gothic horror film, fiery and overblown. When bleak modernity peeped through, it made her jump every time. "I should tell you, I'm only here because your father asked me to come."

"Oh right. So he's just as persuasive as Jon, is he?"

"He's worried about you. I have to report back to him. And he's paying me."

His smile twisted. "So you're a spy, and you take money for it. Glad we got that established."

"I'm just being honest, so you can tell me to bugger off, if you want," she snapped. He said nothing, but his grin became narrow and wicked. "Oh, wait . . . you're in on this, aren't you? You're deliberately refusing to see Lawrence to get me here instead."

"Aren't you flattered?"

"You're sick! This isn't a game. He is really distressed, even though he tries to hide it."

"Well," said Sam, leaning forward on his elbows, "haven't you got a high opinion of your charms? The truth is I really *don't* want him here, because he's crazy enough as it is and he does my head in. Thanks for being honest. You have my permission to go back and tell him I'm absolutely fine."

They sat in silence for a few moments, not looking at each other. Finally Sam said, "Since you've come all this way, can we at least have a cup of tea and fake a civil conversation?"

"Of course." She tried to let go of her tension. "I don't need to fake it."

"I bet you don't." His eyebrows rose a little. She looked stonily back at him until he shook his head and said, "Okay, I'll start. So, what's new?"

"Well, my brother's getting married."

"The nice one or the blond bastard?"

"Matthew, to my friend Faith."

His face lit up demonically. "Faith, the little cross-eyed waif?"

"God, you're a terrible bitch, Sam."

"No, just observant. That's terrible. He'll kill her."

"Pardon?"

"Metaphorically, I mean. Yes, it figures. He needs someone to crush the life out of. Poor her. What?" he said, reading her expression. "Sorry, rewind. What wonderful news, give them my congratulations."

"Thanks," she said through gritted teeth.

"What else?"

"I won't tell you, if you're going to react like that."

"Sorry. Mouth-brain connection, not great." His gaze intent on her, he asked, "So, where would you be if you weren't here?"

"At college," Rosie answered.

"And what would you be doing?" He sounded genuinely interested, yet there was an edge to him, as if he were playing a game at her expense. Kind behind a cruel mask or cruel behind a kind mask—she couldn't work him out.

"Greenhouse work today. Potting on seedlings, taking root cuttings, that sort of thing."

"I always had you down for an artist, or maybe a psychologist. But you like that hands-on stuff, don't you?" A slight lifting of one eyebrow.

"Yes, I do. It's real and worthwhile."

"Plants don't answer back, eh?"

"Well," Rosie couldn't help smiling, "not in the surface world."

Sam grinned. She couldn't remember sharing a joke with him before. The sudden intimacy made her uneasy. "It's good of you to come, whatever the reason."

"The stuff I started telling you . . . Have you spoken to your family?"

Sam folded his arms and looked down. His sleeves were rolled up. Rosie couldn't help noticing his beautifully shaped forearms and long-fingered, strong hands. She tried not to look. "I asked my father straight out on the phone and he told me the truth. Or his version of it, anyway. It's weird, isn't it? Your brother is also my brother. I still can't believe it. Still, it's bloody typical of my father."

"What, to have affairs?" Rosie was indignant on Jessica's behalf.

"No—I mean to disrupt other people's lives. Not to care about the consequences. Maybe that's where I get it from."

It was a throwaway remark, part of his mask of bravado that so antagonized her. "I don't know what my mother was thinking, but I suspect your father resents mine, because mine is content with life and yours isn't. Lawrence wanted to take that away from him. Jealousy, revenge or something. It didn't work."

"Didn't it? Not even a bit?"

"No," she said firmly. "Not in the long run."

"There didn't have to be a child, though," Sam said, resting clasped hands on the edge of the table. "We don't have accidents. Surely your mother's told you that?"

"Of course." Her eyes narrowed. To hear feminine wisdom coming from Sam's mouth made her uncomfortable.

"So, Lucas wasn't an accident," Sam continued. "They meant to have him. Or . . . they couldn't stop him."

"For heaven's sake," said Rosie. "You make it sound like some Otherworld conspiracy. I'm sure it wasn't that. You don't believe Aetherial births are preordained, do you?"

He shrugged, a teasing glint in his eye. "Not really."

"No," she said. "I asked Mum and she couldn't answer. It's like she had a premonition of Lucas and that's why she let it happen. We wouldn't be without him for anything."

"That's sweet, the way you throw the best light on things. Good job he didn't turn out the black sheep of the family, eh?"

"Don't tell me you're jealous of Lucas," she said acidly.

He paused, expression darkening. "Maybe I've got cause. Dad gets himself a shiny new son, and I'm stuck in the trash can here. Jon can't stir himself to come and see me because he's too busy with his super new brother."

"Are we getting to the bottom of why you're so bitter and twisted?"

"Haven't even started," Sam answered, with a crooked grimace. "I'll tell you what really chokes me, though." He leaned towards her. His blue-green eyes turned harsh. "Seeing people shipwreck themselves on the hope of Jon's friendship."

Rosie drew back. "What's that supposed to mean?"

"You and Lucas aren't the first, you know. All his life people have fallen in love with him, and his problem is that he just doesn't give a toss. He doesn't even see it. There's only room for one person on Planet Jon, and that's Jon."

Her mouth opened as if he'd kicked her. "I can't believe you feel like that about your own brother."

"Just telling the truth."

"Do you really hate him so much?" She was recoiling

inwardly, her distrust of Sam reaching new depths. "I can't believe it. No wonder your family are crazy. You all hate each other, don't you?"

Sam leaned back, his eyes freezing her. "Wow," he said dryly. "That's quite a set of conclusions you've come to."

"After several years' observation."

"Well, you're absolutely wrong," he said. "Of course I don't hate Jon. I love the stupid sod. But you know, if you float around like a Renaissance cherub reciting Spenser and Tennyson at public school, you attract all the wrong kinds of attention. You get the crap beaten out of you. You get pestered by huge sixth-form boys who won't take no for an answer. You get made to stay behind by masters who are one grope away from leaving under a cloud of shame. And so on."

Sam had shocked her into silence. After a moment she found her breath. "Did he really have such a bad time?"

"Not quite. I protected him from it as best I could. Trouble was, I couldn't be with him every moment and a few things happened—but once I found out, I made sure the bastards never went near him again."

Rosie let out the breath she'd been holding. "That's why you were expelled?"

He finally broke eye contact. "Yeah. That's what it was all about. By the end, most of the school understood that if they touched Jon they would get their head pulped by me. But there were three boys who hadn't quite got the message and they thought they could take me on. Yes, I put them in hospital. Not proud of it. I'd had enough and I lost it. Even my father couldn't donate his way out of it that time."

He'd dropped the mask. He was telling her the truth. Rosie said, "Why didn't you tell the school what was going on?"

Sam gave a grim laugh. "Wasn't the culture. Making complaints marked you out as weak. So you sorted things yourself. That's what I thought, anyway; maybe I got it all wrong."

"Couldn't you have got your father to take you away?"

"Nah. He was busy and didn't want to be bothered. He'd

view it as a sign of failure. Besides, there was no point. It was my duty to protect Jon and that's all there was to it."

"I didn't realize," she said warily.

"You had me down as a psychotic thug?"

"Something like that."

He shrugged. "Maybe I am. I can't pretend it didn't feel good making those bastards scream. I like people to be scared of me. That's kind of sick, isn't it? But sometimes necessary."

"What did Jon feel? Being bullied, and you protecting him? He must have been damaged by it, too. You can see he has."

"There's the thing," Sam said very quietly. "I don't think I helped him at all, because he got to thinking he was untouchable. And when something did happen, he had no idea how to deal with it. I should have left him to sink or swim. But I couldn't. When it was happening under my nose, I simply couldn't. And now, he's not even grateful; I think he resents me for it."

"Is that why he won't visit you?"

Sam didn't answer. He stared at the table and said, *"Fuck,"* under his breath. Then, "I don't want to sound like I'm blaming Jon for everything. I'm not, Rosie. I only wanted to explain a few things."

"And you have." She shifted on the hard seat. She wanted to ask more about Jon, but it was too personal. Too obsessive, and she didn't want to obsess any more. "Anyway, you were away for four years. Don't assume I'm still pining after him."

"Really? Good. By the way, I swear I never said a thing to keep Jon away from you."

She frowned. "Like what?"

"I could have made up anything," said Sam. "Told him you had a nasty rash, or an unnatural interest in farmyard animals, anything. The point is, I didn't."

"I never thought you did," she said tightly. "He wasn't interested and why should he be? Perhaps I'm too . . ."

"What?"

She shrugged. "Intense, needy, or something. Unattractive."

"Come off it." Sam gave a huff of exasperation. "Jon's off his head. You love him and he doesn't notice? He deserves a kicking. Some Vaethyr, though . . . They feel threatened by other Aetherials. They go with humans because it's less of a challenge."

"You think Jon's like that?"

"I don't know," Sam said wearily. "Who knows what goes on in his head? Yes, I was jealous as hell of the way you felt about him, but I hated to see you hurt. I'm sorry."

"No," she said hurriedly. "Don't. I've moved on."

His sharp eyebrow rose again. "As in seeing someone else?"

"No. Yes. Sort of."

"Okay, stop. That's news I don't want to hear."

"It's early days," she said lamely.

Sam glared at the table. After a moment he looked up again and said softly, "Tell me what else you do at college. I can see all that physical work is keeping you amazingly fit. I can just picture you in a sleeveless T-shirt, running around with a loaded wheelbarrow, your arms all golden and glistening with perspiration. The T-shirt's riding up your tight little waist and your hair's all over the place. You'll have your own TV show in no time."

She rolled her eyes. "God, is that what you fantasize about in your cell?"

"Well, yeah," he said, opening his hands. "Got any photographs?"

"I could bring you a photo of a cold shower."

His eyes glistened with a mixture of mockery, lust and affection that made her blush. "Come on, embarrassing you is all the fun I get. Tell me something really boring about plants. Otherwise I won't be able to stand up."

"You are disgusting," she said mildly.

"Go on. The difference between annuals and perennials. Anything."

"What for?"

He shrugged. "I like the sound of your voice."

As she began to speak, delayed shock hit her. It was suddenly hard to accept that when she left, Sam couldn't walk out with her. Horrible, to think of leaving him in this place; she almost couldn't bear it. She felt it out of simple humanity, even though she could never let him through her defenses. She kept a powerful barrier of distance between them and he was always trying to break through it; that was the game.

"Is there anything you need?" she asked as time was called.

"I'm in prison, not hospital," he said. "I don't need sympathy."

"And you're not getting it. I'm trying to be helpful, that's all."

He gave a wicked grin. "Well, okay, if you insist. How about making your next visit a conjugal one?"

"How about in your dreams?" Rosie retorted.

"Always worth a try." He sighed. He looked at her through dark eyelashes. "Actually, there is something. Since you're such a keen spy, fancy being a double agent?"

"What do you mean?" It took her a moment to realize he was serious.

"Part of the reason I came home was that I started wondering about Sapphire. Just . . . who the hell is she? Because I don't actually know, and I don't think Dad does, either. I was going to do some digging around, but I didn't get the chance. And she could not *wait* to see me taken away in handcuffs."

"So you want me to dig around for you?" Rosie was stunned.

"Would you mind? Only don't go up to her and say, 'I have to be straight with you, I'm spying for Sam.' It's supposed to be secret, you see." He winked. "I'll pay you."

"You've got to be kidding," she gasped.

"Well, who else can I ask? Jon's too flaky. How about Lucas? He's at Stonegate quite a bit, he could poke around and report to you . . . Split the fee?"

"I'm sorry, *what*? You want my little brother to do your dirty work? Just when I was almost starting to like you!"

"Okay, bad idea." He seemed to realize she was genuinely outraged, but his expression stayed serious. "This isn't a joke, Rosie. If she's up to something, I need to know, because it could hurt my family. If you care enough about Lawrence and Jon to visit me for them, you must care enough to find out if there's a problem with the wicked stepmother."

"No," she said. "It's none of my business and I can't believe you'd try and involve me. Absolutely not, Sam." The last call came and she moved into the stream of departing visitors, glad to leave because she was fuming. She realized she'd barely noticed the prison on any level of reality while they'd been talking. On his feet, Sam called shamelessly after her, "Hey, did you say starting to like me?"

The night sky was the goddess's face, arching above him. Lucas was falling into her. Always falling into blackness, in thrilling terror. A half-seen cat led him along sinuous streams until he met an Aelyr man with long snowy hair. A gemstone gleamed in the pale man's outstretched palm.

Lucas was someone else in the vision. He felt that he was Lawrence, and that the white-blond man was his father Albin, and that their argument had been going on for years.

"You hold open the portal for the Vaethyr, the exiles who sold themselves for a taste of Vaeth's riches, then still expect to be welcome here?" said Albin. "Aetherials will never be strong again until we all gather back in the Spiral. There is no place for us on the surface."

"I'm doing what my grandmother asked of me," said Lawrence-Lucas. "I can't refuse. The lych-light's branded in me."

"Then you'll have nothing of it but sorrow." Albin held out the gem, then closed his hand, withholding it. The gesture was incomprehensible, yet it seemed the moment around which the universe revolved. Lucas felt that some vital part had been ripped out of him, leaving him defenseless.

What he'd taken for a cat now appeared as a mass of smoke that was gradually swelling, reaching amorphous arms towards him. As it grew, Lucas's fear swelled with it. It was going to suffocate him. He struggled to escape, rooted to the spot as the fog blanket overwhelmed him. He tried to scream. Then out of the fog came a ghost-white figure, thrusting a spear of burning-black ice towards his eye—

He burst out of the vision with his heart thundering and cold sweat pouring over him.

"Luc, Luc, it's all right. What did you see?"

He was looking at the cracked ceiling of Jon's room in the shared house in Nottingham. Jon sat cross-legged on the floor in front of him, a tin and cigarette papers in his hands. The room was an amber cave of candlelight.

"A black cat," said Lucas, struggling for breath between words. "Only it wasn't a cat, I couldn't see it properly."

"Your *fylgia*," said Jon. "Your twin soul in the Spiral. It was guiding you."

"It attacked me."

"It can't have done."

Luc sat up and put his head in his hands. The trip was a blur. All he could remember was the suffocating, bone-crushing fear. "I'm telling you what I saw. It was a mess."

"Did you see anyone?" Jon bit the end of his pen. "A woman with long crinkly black hair?" He sounded so hopeful, Lucas hated to disappoint him.

"No. There was a man . . . I don't know what it meant. Jon, we need to be at Freya's Crown to do this. It's never going to work here."

"But we can only do that when my father's away. And even here, you see things."

"And even at the Gates, I can't get through. I don't think I want to. Your father's not lying; there is something awful on the other side!" Luc's heartbeat shook his body like an animal trying to break out of his rib cage. He clutched at his chest, gasping.

"You all right?" said Jon, frowning at him through skeins of red-brown hair.

"Whatever the hell you gave me—it's too strong. I can't do this."

"You're just hyperventilating. You need a smoke to calm you down."

Lucas hung on as Jon's agile fingers sealed cigarette papers together, sprinkled a line of tobacco and added parings of waxy black resin. It was Aetheric blackdrop, an opiate sap that Jon harvested in the Dusklands and cooked to a resin. Expertly he rolled and lit the spliff. Luc took it, bringing it to his mouth with shaking hands. He struggled to inhale, but once the smoke hit his lungs he felt the anxiety recede in a wash of sweet dizziness.

"Are you going into college tomorrow?" Lucas asked after a while, clawing damp hair off his face.

"I might." Jon took a drag, holding it in his lungs as long as he could. Smoke wreathed from his mouth as he spoke again. "Why d'you ask?"

"Because you don't want to do anything lately. Go to college, rehearse the band . . . or even make the effort to visit Sam."

Jon huffed a last wisp of smoke. "You know, if you're going to carry on like Sapphire, you can sod off," he said flatly.

"I'm not, but brooding like this is not going to get Sam home any faster. Anyone can see you're in pieces but you won't admit it. All you do is drown it with drugs. You can't keep saying fuck it, let's get stoned instead."

"I haven't noticed you arguing much." Jon's eyes narrowed. The brown irises turned crimson. "Unless we can break through the Gates, it's all pointless! Unless we discover what Lawrence is hiding, there's no point in college or bands or anything. I thought you were with me!"

His anger wounded Lucas. "I am," he said softly, "but we're not getting anywhere."

"Yes, we are." Jon looked at him with that demanding, irresistible light in his face. "Every trip, you're seeing more."

"More horrible things I can't understand."

"That's a matter of getting the dose right. You can't give up, Luc; you're too strong for that. And I need you."

Sighing, Lucas took the joint and sucked in its bitter perfume. "And if we get through, what then? What did we miss by not being initiated when we should?"

"Wisdom," said Jon. His pupils were large now, his expression relaxed, radiant in the candlelight between waves of auburn hair. "Experience."

"Auberon said there are dangerous beings that carry off tender innocent Vaethyr." Luc's own words struck him as funny. A wave of blissful heaviness went through him. A few more drags and he had to lie flat on a heap of floor cushions.

Jon lay down beside him, smiling. "What we've missed is our lives. Our true selves. That's what my father's stolen from us, but we can get it back, if we keep trying."

"Next time," said Lucas, unsure if he'd even spoken aloud. Jon leaned over him, his hair making a glowing red silken cave over them. His mouth brushed Luc's, claiming the smoke as he breathed it out.

Lucas knew he should do grown-up things like go to college, learn to drive, find a girlfriend . . . all the real-world things that his parents and Matthew wanted him to do . . . but while Jon was there, like some woodland god tempting him with the never-ending promise of Elysion . . . when the lazy ecstasy of drugs filled him . . . it all drifted away. There was only Jon.

10

September Will Be Magic

"He's fine, considering the circumstances," said Rosie. "He's bearing up really well."

Usually, Lawrence phoned her for a progress report. This time—when she'd been visiting Sam for about six months—he'd invited her to Stonegate and taken her into his study, where he sat behind his desk with a small black velvet tray of gems in front of him. While Rosie stayed carefully on safe, mundane ground such as prison routine, she could see from the shadows and drawn lines of his face that Lawrence was not bearing up well at all.

"And you're happy to go on seeing him?" he said.

"If it's what you both want, yes."

"I'm inexpressibly grateful," said Lawrence. "Rosie, do you own any albinite?"

"Er, no. It's rather expensive and I don't wear much jewelry . . ."

"Choose one," he said, pushing the tray towards her. The cut gems sparkled, spilling rainbows like dragonfly wings. "It's a stone of unusual properties. On humans the color is stable, but it responds interestingly to Aetheric wearers. The mine's exhausted, which means the value will only ever increase."

"No," she said, taken aback. Traveling expenses were one thing, but accepting jewels from the man who had been her mother's lover—? "No no no. Thank you. I really can't."

He nodded. "I understand. If you change your mind, let me know."

As Rosie saw herself out, she glanced around the cavernous hall and sensed Dumannios in the air, a burning chill full of ghost shadows. This was where Sam had . . . she tried not to visualize it.

As for Sapphire, how was Rosie supposed to root around Stonegate for incriminating evidence, and what would she be looking for? Sam hadn't mentioned it again, but the idea still played on her mind.

Sighing, she entered the kitchen and walked straight into Sapphire. "Rosie, I've made us a coffee," she said with a friendly, confiding smile. "Let's drink it in the garden. I know you're quite the gardening expert and I need your advice on my azaleas."

Her voice was velvet, her fingers smooth on Rosie's arm as they walked down the broad lawn until they were out of sight of the house amid trees and shrubs. Sapphire was wearing a floaty pastel silk trouser suit and a single round Elfstone at her throat. They examined plants and sipped their coffee while Rosie wondered what this was really about.

"Your azaleas are lovely," said Rosie, playing along. "I could test the Ph of the soil if you like, but they look healthy to me."

Sapphire took both empty cups and set them on the grass. "I'd love to grow plants or flowers impressive enough to enter a class at Cloudcroft Show. I do enjoy that little show every May. I love the parade at the end—reminds me of the Rio Carnival. Different every year."

"Rio? Have you been there?" She seized the chance to pry, despite herself.

Sapphire smiled enigmatically but didn't answer. "What you are doing for us by visiting Sam is wonderful. Rosie, I owe you an apology."

"What for?"

"Persuading Lawrence to come clean about Lucas. I

only wanted to help, and the truth needed telling; but I apologize for the distress it must have caused."

"It might have been an idea to speak to my parents first," Rosie said stiffly.

"That's what I expected Lawrence to do, but he's unpredictable. I'm so very sorry." Sapphire suddenly unclasped her Elfstone pendant and held it out to Rosie. "Here, I'd like you to have this. A peace offering. Albinite belongs more on you than on me."

"Er, no!" Rosie gasped. As she pushed Sapphire's hand away, the stone turned briefly violet. "No, please, you don't have to give me anything."

"Oh, did you see the color change? You're Aetherial like Lawrence, and I'm so close to you, but I can't see inside you." Her expression was hungry, yearning.

"Why would you want to see inside me?" said Rosie, her eyes widening.

"I don't mean literally, dear. My problem is that I want to help my husband, but to do so, I need to understand Aetherials. I'm an outsider." Sapphire took her arm as they walked slowly along grass paths between rhododendron bowers. "You wouldn't know it, but I've experienced poverty, Rosie. Yes, I know Rio; I grew up in Brazil. My mother was a servant on a big cattle ranch and she had nothing. The owner would invite his rich friends to stay and one of them got my mother pregnant. Oh, she did her best for me but her health was poor and she died when I was five."

"God, I'm sorry."

"Don't be. I was very fortunate. The man who fathered me came back and lifted me out of the dust, quite literally. He took me to America, paid for my education. His own children were long grown up and gone, you see, and I was a little princess for him. Oh, he was no saint, I know, but I worshipped him. He was my king. Only something took him away." Sapphire swept back the dark waterfall of her hair. "Aetherials took him. This was a tough businessman without a sentimental bone in his body, and yet he became obsessed by a hidden race who gave rise to stories of elves, angels and demigods. He was forever searching for them, coming back fiery-eyed with excitement, disappearing again. As I grew up he made me promise that if anything happened to him, I'd continue the search. I simply wanted to know what these creatures were that so fascinated him. In time I went to work for Wilder Jewels, and I met Lawrence. However . . ."

Sapphire sounded wistful. Rosie thought she glimpsed genuine vulnerability beneath the glossy exterior. "I suppose—long after his first wife had gone, I must add—I fell rather in love with the glamour of Lawrence. Even married to an Aetherial, I still only see you from the outside."

"And what do you see?" Rosie asked warily.

"I'm not sure." Sapphire compressed her lips. "You are mysterious, complex and infuriating. But then, so are humans. You have so many masks; an ordinary one, a glamorous one, an animal one . . . one mask under another, but who knows what's really underneath? Is it masks all the way down? Rosie, I have longed as passionately as any Aetherial for the Great Gates to open and the transforming magic to spill out."

"Really?" Rosie laughed nervously. "Hasn't Lawrence told you all about it?"

"He's told me, but how do I know it's the truth? I thought you might offer some insight that would enable me to help him."

The Elfstone shone in Sapphire's manicured fingers. Rosie wondered what secrets she thought the gem could buy. "I'm Vaethyr, a surface dweller," she said. "I've never been through the Gates. I have no arcane mysteries or magical powers. I'm virtually human."

"No magic? Come on. You all have that glamour, even you, Rosie, though you don't seem to realize it. Everything Aetherials touch turns to gold and you can step into realities humans can't see. No powers?" Her eyes held Rosie's, warm, demanding, threatening not to release her until she spilled some revelation. Then she broke the tension with a sigh, letting her hand fall. "Please forgive me, dear. I shouldn't have put you on the spot like this. You can't blame me for the fascination that I absorbed from my father. If I seem overcurious, you must understand that it stems entirely from love."

"Bullshit," said Sam when Rosie related the encounter on her next visit. His face was luminous; ghostly white against a dark, cobwebby background. Dumannios manifested strongly today, warping the space to resemble a derelict, soot-caked Victorian factory full of pillars and arches and ghosts. No matter how hard she tried, she couldn't shift back into reality.

"I'm just repeating what Sapphire said," she retorted. "What's the point of asking me for information if you're not going to believe it?"

"Sweetheart, I meant *she* was bullshitting, not you."

"I know," Rosie said thinly. "And I meant that you shouldn't make assumptions. You can't know she wasn't telling the truth."

"So, Agent Fox, what other news from behind enemy lines?"

"This isn't fair, Sam!" Rosie said curtly. "All I tell your father is the safe stuff. No controversy. Expecting me to spy on your behalf—it's completely out of order!"

"Joke," he said softly. "I know, and I apologize. I just want to know how my father is."

"I'm sorry." Rosie shuddered, folding her arms around herself. "This place is really freaking me out today. Lawrence is all right but he looks stressed to hell, in that very dignified, understated way of his. The way he and Sapphire both tried to thrust albinite jewels on me—it was seriously creepy."

Sam tilted his head. "Did you accept? I know how you love sparkly things."

"Of course I didn't! Lawrence was trying to reward me, but I don't want gratitude. As for Sapphire, trying to bribe me for Aetherial revelations . . ."

Sam exhaled, sitting back. "The sob story about Brazilian poverty—that's a new one on me."

"Really? She always gets my back up, somehow. Always gives me the power look."

"The what?"

"You know, that condescending gaze that says, 'I'm the boss of you, and don't you forget it.' But underneath that, she seemed genuinely lost. Out of her depth but trying to hide it."

"You're saying she's just another Aetherial groupie," said Sam with an acid grin. "A very accomplished one, but a groupie all the same—like Faith and your ginger boyfriend?"

"If you have to put it like that." Rosie groaned. "How did I get tangled in this infernal triangle? Lawrence has me reporting on you; you've got me watching both him and Sapphire, and she's trying to make me spill secrets about Lawrence! I'm nothing to your family but a go-between."

"You could tell us all to fuck off."

"I could."

They glared at each other, and she saw nothing but hostility in the green-blue scintillation of his eyes—as if he'd torn off a mask and revealed the demon underneath. Then he broke the stare. Without warning, the visiting room gently, disturbingly, shivered into plain reality.

"But you won't, will you?" said Sam. It was half plea, half statement. "I think you're enjoying it too much, Agent Fox."

The dancers of the Beast Parade whirled past the village green, costumed as firebirds enacting a chaotic courtship display. Phyll and Comyn always organized it, choosing only Aetherials to take part and ignoring village grumbles about elitism. Once, the procession would have led to Freya's Crown and Elysion. Now there was nowhere for them to go but around Cloudcroft and back to their starting point, the slate-and-granite pub called the Green Man.

Jessica tipped her head back, basking in the last rays of

the setting sun. She was sitting on the green in front of the pub with Faith—who was days from giving birth—beside her, their shoulders lightly touching. Auberon, Matthew and Alastair were inside the pub, buying drinks; Rosie and Lucas, Phyll and Comyn somewhere among the costumed dancers.

Around May Day each year, Cloudcroft swarmed with visitors who came for the annual show. Comyn gave several fields over to marquees and show rings, with classes for cattle and sheep and horses, displays of jousting and birds of prey. Steam engines and tractors chugged around in shiny majesty. Giant vegetables wilted under hot canvas. There was Maypole and Morris dancing, a brass band, hot dog stalls, a real ale tent; every tradition expected of an English country fair.

Jessica liked the evening best, when the main events ended and the visitors flowed up to the Green Man to watch the Beast Parade. For centuries, Vaethyr had dressed up in masks and finery to dance in procession around the village. To the human crowds it was an old fertility rite, one of a handful still preserved around England. They didn't know the deeper meaning, the reference to the journey into the Spiral, back to the heart, to their essential being . . .

But now it was only for show. Disheartened, fewer Vaethyr took part each year. Without the true climax to the parade—the journey into Elysion, after the human crowds had departed—it felt hollow.

Jessica used to sing the songs and lead the musicians for the Beast Parade. After her affair with Lawrence, she'd stopped. No one had told her to stop, least of all Auberon. She'd simply lost the heart to sing and leap about in public, after the way she'd hurt him.

"Jessica, do they really change shape?" Faith's question was so soft, it took her a moment to realize what she was asking. "The Aetherials in the dance? Underneath their costumes?"

Jess laughed. "That's the mystery. Because they're costumed, you can't tell." Seeing the concern in Faith's eyes, she relented and gave a fairer answer. "Well, I didn't. Mostly not. However, if you entered the Dusklands, you might see a change of sorts."

"What do you mean?"

"Some Aetherials may transform dramatically, others hardly at all. Some say that those 'changes' are different aspects of us that are always present, but only visible in certain circumstances."

"Like in the Dusklands?"

"Yes. Or a heightened emotional state, maybe. And some of us, like Phyll and me, hardly change at all; but that's all right. We are what we are. Hasn't Matthew told you any of this?"

Faith sighed, looking down at the curve of her stomach. "I'm not supposed to talk about it, to him or you. He gets annoyed if I try."

"I know he stopped you coming to our private circles," said Jess. "It's too bad of him. You shouldn't let him push you around. Don't be afraid to have your own opinions."

"Rosie tells me that, too, only I worry . . . that he'll find me out as an impostor."

Her manner wasn't that of a nervous, rescued orphan any longer. Faith had changed; she was calmer, more self-contained. When she made these remarks, they no longer came from anxious insecurity but from somewhere darker and more reflective.

"Why?" Jess said impatiently. "Because you're not Aetherial? But he made no secret of not wanting an Aetherial wife. I could smack him for that because it's a ridiculous distinction. Or I could blame myself for him preferring someone who would not run off into the Otherworld or sleep with Lawrence Wilder." She saw Faith's cheeks redden. "Whatever, he chose you. So stop worrying, love, please. And now I'm bossing you around, too. Sorry." She gave Faith a quick hug. "I know your parents gave you a hard time, but it's over. You're with us now."

Faith frowned. They'd talked about this in the past, but

it kept clawing at her, as if there was something she couldn't manage to express. "When they fought, it was like they were possessed. Like something from Du—Dumannios?—took them over. My mother used to clean at Stonegate. Could some bad spirit have got into her? Is that possible? What if it affects the baby?"

"Love, of course it won't." Jessica bit her lip. The only spirits that got inside Faith's mother at Stonegate, she thought, were vodka and whiskey. "Is that what's worrying you? Has Matt been frightening you with stories?"

"No. Sorry. Blame it on my hormones." Alastair was coming towards them with a tray of drinks as Faith went on. "I'm looking for reasons for them being like they were but there aren't any—they were just horrible people with an alcohol problem. I want to be a good parent, not a useless one."

"Hey, if you're talking useless parents, can I join in?" Alastair said amiably, settling on the grass on Jessica's left. "You're so sweet and quiet, Faith, I thought your folks would be the same."

"No, they were loud—always drunk and rowing. They called me a freak, because I worked hard at school and made friends with Rosie. They thought I was getting above myself. I'll never go back to that life, thank goodness."

"So that's why you're quiet—always getting shouted down, eh?" said Alastair. "Mine just shouldn't have been together. Dad was a miserable devil and mother always threatening to leave. I thought it was my fault and if only I was better behaved, she'd stay."

"Yes, that's what I thought, too!" Faith exclaimed. Matthew strolled up with beer in hand and leaned on a nearby tree, nodding as if he'd heard his friend's story before.

"It didn't matter how good I tried to be," said Alastair. "She went anyway. She had all these other men on the go and she didn't seem to give a damn about anyone but herself." He sighed, adding cheerfully, "I got my own back, though. I squashed her wee dog."

Faith and Jess both stared at him.

"Not on purpose!" he added hurriedly. "I was about eleven—I went to the house where she was living with this low-life. The low-life had a motorbike and he let me mess with it—only it was too heavy for me to handle and it fell over. Landed straight on this wretched little terrier she had and killed it stone-dead. God, she was absolutely wailing like I'd had murdered her baby. Afterwards I realized it was the only time I'd ever seen her truly in pain. I looked at her and I thought, Finally, lady, you know how I felt when you walked out. I swear, she loved that dog more than she ever did me. She never let me forget it, either. I decided to leave her to it. After my dad died, that was it—I moved to England, never saw her again."

"Alastair, what a sad story." Faith blinked tears away.

"It cracks me up," said Matthew, grinning. "Okay, I know it's not supposed to be funny, but when you think of the terrier's face as a ton of motorbike descends towards it—oh come on, it's hilarious. That's Alastair—looks harmless, but he's lethal to family pets."

"Keep him away from our cat," Jessica said dryly.

The dancers were returning, the parade over. Two of the Lyon sisters strutted past, dressed in flimsy, flowing scarlet and obviously loving the attention. Matthew watched them, sneering. "God, are we ever going to give up these cheesy old traditions?"

Even as a young boy, Matthew had expressed an aversion to Aetherial matters. *I wonder if we did something to scare him,* thought Jessica, *without even realizing it.* "Those cheesy traditions are part of our heritage, thank you," she said, sipping the white wine Alastair had brought her. "Something to keep our identity alive."

Matthew shook his head. He'd been in the real ale tent all afternoon, which made him even more forthright than usual. "But you only ever look at the pretty side, Mum. Dad never wanted us to go through the Gates in case all sorts of horrors happened to us on the other side. And you know what? I agree with him. Look what it does to people; you end up nuts like Lawrence, or locked up like Samuel."

"Oh, as if that never happens to humans?" Jessica arched her eyebrows at him. "We can also end up perfectly grounded and adorable, like your father and Rosie and Luc."

"Oh, right. I'm sorry, but nobody sane hangs around with Jon Wilder. And not content with having a crush on him, what's with Rosie and this prison visiting lark?" Matthew caught Alastair's eye and suddenly seemed to realize that deprecating Rosie was not the best idea. "Yeah, I know she's adorable, but she shouldn't be acting like a social worker for that crowd. She's too kindhearted for her own good."

"I don't like her going either, but she won't listen to me," said Alastair in the background.

"All I'm suggesting is that every time you criticize Aetherials, you're criticizing your own family," said Jessica.

Matthew kneeled behind them on the grass, putting one arm around his mother and one around Faith. "No, I'm not. I don't mean it like that, Mum. You're gorgeous and glamorous and so is Rosie. You're faerie princesses and that's fine. But it's not for me and Faith. Is it?" He stroked his wife's bump with an affectionate hand; she smiled. "The surface world is enough for us."

Rosie came running up in her firebird costume, out of breath and exhilarated, oblivious of their conversation. Jessica smiled at the affectionate ease with which she and Alastair put their arms around each other. Sensible girl, recognizing at twenty-one the advantages of stability over heart-tearing passion.

"Strange, how we always want what we haven't got, isn't it?" It was Sapphire who spoke. Drifting elegantly past them, she stopped and fixed Jessica with a thoughtful look. "I would love to dance in the Beast Parade. It gets the blood flowing, like a hunt, doesn't it?" She gave a broad smile. "But I'm not allowed, so don't worry, Faith— marrying an Aetherial doesn't make you one."

An icy wind whipped up from nowhere, blowing grit into Jessica's eyes. Grey cloud smothered the soft golden light, and then came the sting of hail. People around them began groaning and running for the shelter of the pub. Sapphire didn't move and the moment stayed in Jessica's mind afterwards like a cameo: Sapphire's words, and the way she stood alone and lost in thought, oblivious of the white ice swirling around her. And Jessica thought in sudden sympathy, *Lawrence is killing her.*

Sam pleaded guilty to manslaughter and received five years, as he'd predicted. Rosie watched him grow thinner, quieter, harder. He observed the other inmates with eyes of steel. There were men here twice his size, with far worse crimes to their names, and she knew he survived only by playing tougher than them. Between them and Dumannios, she wondered what would be left of him when he came out.

Faith gave birth to a girl, a perfect blond cherub they named Heather. Rosie was so caught up in the glow of aunthood that she even forgave Matthew everything. He and Faith seemed content. The baby had a touch of eczema, Faith complained, but Rosie could see no soreness on Heather's chubby arms, only a faint iridescence, like butterfly scales.

Over the next two years, Rosie graduated from college with honors and began work as a landscape designer for Fox Homes. Auberon had been persuasive, insisting he needed her talent. She created gardens with an enchanting faerie quality that helped to entice his home buyers.

Alastair was renting a small apartment in Ashvale but she stayed at Oakholme, refusing to move in with him. She was deeply fond of him, and almost couldn't imagine her life without him. They'd been together for two and half years—yet still, annoyingly, the residue of her yearning for Jon held her back, like an acid fire in her heart. *Yes, heartburn, literally,* she thought with a grimace. When Alastair started hinting about marriage, she would cheerfully evade the subject. Then the war would start inside her: *He's not feckless and uncaring like Jon. He's reliable, he's kind, he wants me. Life with him would be simple. Stop being a child! Stop dreaming about dancing barefoot in the wild-woods of Elysion. Yes, yes, I will grow up . . . but not yet. Not yet.*

Her visits to Sam were only a small part of her life but each one haunted her; strange, artificial yet so intense. Separated by the table, she and Sam would look into each other's eyes, talking endlessly. However unflattering the baggy jeans and sweaters she wore as armor, she would sense his gaze sliding over her, hot and speculative. His attention never failed to make her uncomfortable. And that, obviously, was why he made no attempt to disguise it.

"How's Ginger?" he asked sardonically, meaning Alastair. "How's Captain Normal and his spawn?"

"If you mean Matthew and Heather, they are fine."

"I hope he realizes that he can wed humans until he's blue in the beard; it won't make his children human."

Rosie felt heat in her face. "No one would dare say that to him. Heather's one hundred percent human as far as he's concerned."

"And Faith buys it?"

"Faith would buy any policy of Matthew's, even if he decided the sky was yellow."

Sam tilted his head, looking serious. "You ever talk to her about what we are?"

"Kind of," Rosie said with a half-grin. "I told her things when we were younger. Then I'd remember I wasn't sup-posed to, and try to cover it up. Faith so wanted to believe it, but now she's married to her Aetherial prince, she has to pretend none of it's real."

"What is Matthew's problem?"

"I don't know." She sighed. "He's always been full of opinions. He takes no interest in our nonhuman side, but he has a right to feel like that if he wants. What about you?"

"Whatever we are, I can take it or leave it." Sam leaned closer, resting on folded arms. "Don't you ever wonder *what* we are, Rosie?"

"Oh, yes," she said softly. "Did your parents ever talk to you?"

Sam uttered a soft *huh* and looked down. "My father's never talked much at all, except to express disappointment with us."

"Did you ever go through the Gates?"

She was ready to be envious of Sam's answer, certain he must have sneaked through illicitly, but he said, "No. Dusklands or Dumannios, that's all. I quite like Dumannios." He glanced around at fungal darkness punctuated by glowing reptilian eyes. "It suits me."

Rosie didn't even try to make a joke. Pale and gaunt, Sam looked part of it.

He went on, "It's said that we're born knowing everything. Our history, all about the Spiral and our elemental natures. But we forget and have to learn it again. That's why we're all so screwed up."

"I can see it in Heather's eyes," said Rosie. "Two serene blue pools. Sometimes I expect her to speak like an adult."

"As long as she keeps her mouth shut in front of her daddy." A corner of his mouth curved up. "Problem is, we'll never understand the Otherworld until we go there. Reading all the travel guides in the world is no substitute for the moment you step off the plane."

Rosie had expected this to be a point-scoring, *"I know more than you do"* conversation, but it wasn't that at all. She asked, "Do you know why your father closed the Gates?"

He chewed at his lower lip and was silent for a moment. "You're expecting the big revelation?"

"Hoping," she replied with a ghost smile.

"Something happened to him on the other side that completely freaked him out. He won't talk about it. He drinks, and has nightmares, and thinks no one knows."

"Couldn't your mother shed any light? Your real one, I mean?"

A cold glitter flashed into his eyes, startling her. She felt his anger physically, like a mass of cold air between them. "Don't even start down that road," he said.

"Why not?" Rosie exclaimed. "I refuse to tread on egg-shells with you, Sam. Why won't you talk about her?"

"Because she's dead."

Rosie was taken aback. "I'm sorry. No one told us."

"If she isn't, she might as well be."

"She isn't, then."

"We don't know! That's the point! She vanished one day while Lawrence was taking Jon and me back to school. Not a word since. I can understand her not wanting to speak to Dad, but her own sons?" She saw his arm muscles tensing to cords.

"Maybe she went into the Spiral."

"Maybe. That's what Jon hopes, but I still think she would have found a way to contact us. We only have Lawrence's word that she walked out. He may have murdered her and buried her in the shrubbery for all we know."

"But she did walk out," said Rosie.

The blue fire grew fiercer. "How the hell would you know?"

"Because I saw her leaving." She described the raid she, Lucas and Matthew had made on Stonegate, years ago.

Sam sat very still. Eventually words stumbled out. "Thing is, as long as I believe she's dead, I can forgive her. But if she's alive and never . . ."

"I'm sorry," Rosie said faintly. "That was meant to help, not make things worse. It never occurred to me you didn't know."

"No," he said, swallowing. "I never seriously believed she was dead, not in my heart. I needed to believe it wasn't her decision to ignore us. I mean, what did we do to . . . ?"

She almost reached to touch his hand, curbed the gesture. "D'you know why she left?"

"Endless arguments. My father wanted to live in Ecuador near his mine. Mother insisted they come home. Lawrence never forgave her for . . . forcing him to face his responsibilities."

"That must have been horrible for you and Jon."

"If I *ever* find out he was seeing Sapphire before Mum left, she is dead meat."

"She said not," Rosie said quickly. "Like I told you, she's as foxed by Lawrence as anyone. And she thought the gems would be a key to unlocking him, but they're not."

Sam's lowered gaze swept up to meet hers. "Albinite originates in Naamon, according to my father. The mine was an interface, a minor portal."

"The realm of fire. Volcanoes, massive pressures, hence fabulous crystals," said Rosie.

"As soon as I break out of this hellhole, I'll take you there, sweetheart."

"I've heard it's a bit warm at this time of year."

He smiled thinly at her. "My father had this enemy called Barada who reckoned he owned the land the mine was on. They fought about it for years. It crossed my mind that my father closed the Gates purely to keep Barada out of his mine."

"He told me that the mine was exhausted." Rosie frowned. "Isn't that like cutting off your nose to spite your face?"

"Like I say, my father is unfathomable."

"Then why tell lies about storms?"

"Telling the truth makes him break out in a rash, apparently."

Rosie felt strange being in this sinister, whispering dungeon with a trickster who'd tangled her in nebulous rumors of conspiracy. When she went home—when Dumannios released its tendrils—she would go to the pub with Alastair and everything would be cozy and normal again. "Why can't he simply secure the mine, open the Gates and get on with life?" she asked.

"Of course, why didn't I think of that?" Sam exclaimed. "Pop up to the manor and tell him, will you? Then everything will be fine."

"I'm only asking. There's no need for sarcasm."

"Sorry, love." Sam rubbed his face. The sculptural lines

were gouged deep with weariness. "He can't. He's paralyzed. Psychologically, I mean. What I'm trying to say is that the struggle over the mine was only a symptom of something much worse. A while ago he stopped talking of Barada as a human nuisance, and started referring to him as some kind of cosmic enemy . . . like people refer to the devil. What does that sound like?"

"Paranoia."

"Exactly. When I stabbed that intruder, my father was convinced that some dark supernatural enemy had sent him."

Rosie was puzzled. "That's not possible . . . Is it?"

He was silent for a moment. When he spoke, it was a near-whisper. "No. It was a druggie who tried to rob us because he knew my father was loaded. I warned Jon about hanging around with garbage like that but he'd never listen."

"I know, Sam," Rosie answered. "Jon told me. He was absolutely cut up with guilt. He attracted some dodgy people but he can't have realized they were dealing drugs or wished him harm."

"Not realized?" Sam blinked eloquently. "Why d'you think they hung around? Jon was the one selling god-knows-what to them. He thinks I don't know, but I have sources." His expression turned hard and angry.

"*Jon* was selling . . ." Her mouth fell open.

"What? You don't still think he's some perfect Botticelli angel, do you? He is pretty naive, though. Too precious for this world. Didn't occur to him that some low-life might see him as no more than a dumb rich kid with a big house: an easy target."

"You're saying this is all Jon's fault?"

"No," said Sam. "I would never blame Jon. It was just a chain of events. But that's how I know it was nothing supernatural." He opened one hand, indicating the eerie morphing of their surroundings. "Whatever's going on with my father is only getting worse. I can feel it here. Dumannios, getting dirtier and really outstaying its welcome."

His words sent chills crawling over her. As difficult as she found roguish, sniping Sam, this troubled side of him was even harder to handle. "Lawrence is so hard to talk to. One moment he's rational; the next he lets something slip that makes you think he's lost his mind."

"I know. God knows what I'm going to find when I get out of here."

"Is there anything I can do?"

His gaze, resting on her, softened. "You've done enough. Just talking to you helps. The anger's not aimed at you, sweetie."

"I think it was, a bit," she replied tartly.

"And still you want to help me." He paused. "Hey, I almost forgot to wish you happy birthday."

"How did you know it was my . . ."

"I've always known. Just turned twenty-three, haven't you? If age means anything to Aetherials. And if I could, babe, I would give you the *biggest* bloody birthday present you've ever had in your life."

His grin turned her hot all over. "Shut up," she groaned. "We were discussing if there's a way I can help you."

He exhaled. "Okay. There is one thing that would help, love. A photo of my mother."

It would mean another visit to Stonegate. "You want to be careful, Sam. You'll have me thinking you're not as tough as you make out."

"No chance." He began to smile, blue-green irises glinting with mischief. "Hey, bring me one of yourself while you're at it. A lingerie shot will be fine."

The next day, Rosie was climbing steadily towards Stonegate Manor with Lucas at her side. The stone battlements reared up in front of them, awakening memories. "The sight of it still gives me shivers," she said. "Doesn't it do that to you?"

"No, of course not." Lucas tossed back his long dark hair.

"I don't believe you," she said teasingly. "I think that, no matter how many times you come here, you still get a little frisson of dread."

"Shut up," he said, between a sigh and a laugh. The view unfolded as they climbed. Rugged hills with swaths of spring-green forest and, above them, the tilted rocks of Freya's Crown. "What are you going to say?" he asked.

"Simply that Sam wants a photo of Virginia. I'll keep it brief. I don't want to get involved in any more weird conversations. Sapphire doesn't give a damn about Sam, and I don't think Jon does, either."

"Yes, he does," said Lucas. "He's just really bad at handling it."

A little farther on, Rosie asked, "How is Lawrence with you?"

"All right," said Lucas. "I don't see him much. He's friendly, but very formal. Tells me about gem-cutting or the history of Stonegate, things like that. Nothing personal."

"Do you like him?"

Lucas seemed to find the scenery fascinating as they entered the rear gardens. Eventually he answered, "Yes, I do. He's not approachable like Dad. He can be incredibly intimidating. But I do sort of like him, anyway."

Reaching the kitchen door, Rosie knocked. When no one answered after a few seconds, Lucas tried the door and opened it. "I usually walk straight in," he said. "Come on."

There was no one in the kitchen or the great hall. The house was silent and cavernous, impassively watching them. Lucas stood in the middle, looking up at the galleries. "Hello, anyone home? Jon?"

"Looks like there's no one here," said Rosie, deflated. "What sort of family has a break-in, then still leaves doors unlocked?"

"I'll try the library," said Lucas, sprinting up the broad staircase.

"If you find a photo, just grab it," she called after him. She went into a living room off the hall, where leaded French windows held a glimmering view of the wide lawn sloping into tangled green bowers of rhododendron and birch. Feeling like a thief, she went to a cabinet and opened a couple of drawers. There were notebooks, pens, paper clips; the normal detritus of any house. In the second drawer she found a small framed photo of Lawrence with a dark-haired woman; hearing a noise she guiltily stuffed it into a pocket, and went to the glass doors. She exhaled, her breath clouding the diamond panes.

She saw someone moving in the garden. Figures, half-hidden by greenery . . . Jon and Sapphire. She was about to call, "Luc!," but the word died in her throat.

Jon was leaning back against a birch tree. Sapphire stood facing him, talking intently. She was too close, crowding him; Jon's arms were folded against her. The conversation went on, intimate and intense, as if Sapphire were delivering a lecture. Her right hand came up to rest on a branch beside Jon's head. Then her left, to stroke the hair over his ear.

Rosie was caught there, staring, as if watching a film. Time ran slowly. She saw Sapphire moving in, giving what might been a motherly kiss on the cheek . . . until her right hand moved to cup the back of his head and his folded arms fell to his sides . . . no, *no* . . .

They were plainly, unmistakably kissing.

Sapphire pressed against him. Jon's hands rested lightly on her hips.

Rosie stood behind the veil of glass and watched as if transfixed by the climax of a horror film. She thought she might be sick. When she heard Lucas breathe in and out by her shoulder, she nearly jumped out of her skin.

"Oh, *fuck*," he said succinctly.

Rosie's head swiveled and she found her brother staring back at her, eyes stretched wide to reflect her visceral shock. Neither could speak. Eventually he made a feeble effort to pull her arm and said, "Don't look, Ro."

"Right, because that will make it not have happened?" She turned her back to the window. Her heartbeat was heavy. "Please tell me they're not doing anything else."

"They're not." Lucas released his breath in a rush. "They're coming this way."

"Did you know?" she asked tightly.

"What?" His face turned the color of porcelain. "Of course I didn't! Do I look as if I knew?"

"All the time you spend with him, and he's never mentioned it?" She took a shuddering breath, laughed. "That's great, that is. Can this family get any more dysfunctional?"

"I swear, I had no idea. Maybe it's just a . . . one-off."

"Oh yes, because who hasn't French-kissed a stepparent in their time? Body language, Luc. That wasn't the first time."

Lucas looked helplessly at her. "What are we going to do?"

"Nothing," said Rosie. "Let's go."

Like thieves, they retraced their steps. They were too late; as they entered the kitchen, Jon was coming through the back door. Seeing them, he started like a nervous colt. "Oh, hi," he said. "Didn't know you were here. Hi, Rosie."

In the passage behind him, Rosie saw Sapphire dragging off her gardening boots. "Hello, my dears," she said brightly over Jon's shoulder. "What a lovely surprise. Tea?" She moved Jon out of her way—Rosie cringed at the sight of her hands on him—and crossed the room towards the kettle.

"No, it's okay, we're not stopping," she said quickly.

"Oh? You can't leave so soon."

"We didn't think there was anyone in," said Lucas.

"We were just doing a few things in the garden," Sapphire said breezily. "It's so rare I manage to drag Jon outside."

"I bet it is," Rosie said under her breath. "Actually, I need to see Mr. Wilder. Is he here?"

Sapphire looked taken aback at her brusque tone. "No, he's in London. Can I help?"

"Yes, Sam asked me for a photograph of Virginia," Rosie said evenly.

The way they both stared and blanched seemed to give

Rosie the upper hand, which she hadn't expected. "Er, yeah, no problem," said Jon. He went to a kitchen drawer and produced one almost immediately; a six-by-four of a smiling woman with gothic-pale skin, raven hair, ropes of turquoise at her throat.

"Thank you," said Rosie. She tried not to notice his finger brushing hers as she took it. Jon's face was pallid, pupils dilated, hair disheveled but as deliciously autumn-colored, thick and silky as ever. Knowledge lay congealed inside her of him sleeping with Mel, and all the rest. How was it fair that he could look so unhealthy and still so heartbreakingly beautiful? "I thought you might like to hear how Sam is, if you're even interested."

Her words came out flat with scorn. For the first time, Rosie felt her disappointment with him turning to anger. For the first time she looked at Jon and felt not love, but hatred.

"That's not fair," he said, forehead creasing. "Of course I'm interested."

"Is that right?" She folded her arms, wouldn't let him escape her eyes. "You care so much that you can't even phone or walk a few hundred yards down the hill to ask after him?"

He looked shocked, completely floored by this new, furious Rosie. "But I see Lucas all the time."

"Lucas isn't the one who sits with him in that horrible place for two hours every month. Lucas isn't the one who knows him!"

His expression clouded. "Hang on. Where's this come from?"

Rosie caught her breath. "You're right. I should have said something before. I was too busy trying to be nice and obliging."

Sapphire put in, "But Rosie, you know full well that Sam refuses to let us visit him. We'd go if he let us, of course, but he won't."

Jon's eyes turned hard. "You know, if you've got a problem making those visits, fine. We thought you didn't mind.

All you had to do was tell us, not come in here out of the blue ranting at us."

"I do not have a problem visiting Sam!" Rosie flared. "I'm happy to go and I'll do it to the bitter end! All I want is for you to give a flying rat's ass about him!"

There was a frozen, very English silence.

Jon and Lucas were both apparently struck dumb. Sapphire came forward and leaned on the central isle. Her mouth looked red from kissing. "Rosie," she said in a pained tone, "you have no idea what we've been through or what we feel. To come in here suggesting that we don't care about Sam is preposterous. Why don't we sit down over tea and have a civilized discussion?"

"No," said Rosie, feeling warmth in her cheeks and water stinging her eyes. "Thank you. It's a bit of a poisoned chalice, isn't it?"

"I beg your pardon?"

"Excuse me. I'd better go. I hope you realize that Sam won't be in prison forever. I hope you're ready for how much he's changed."

She took in Sapphire's outraged expression as she walked towards the back door, not even glancing at Jon. A few seconds later, as she crossed the lawn on her way downhill, Lucas caught up with her. "Wait for me," he said. "Are you all right?"

"No, of course I'm not. This isn't a tantrum about seeing Sapphire with her tongue down Jon's throat. There's other stuff. Did you know he's been supplying drugs?"

Hidden behind bushes, they stopped and faced each other. She saw from Lucas's guilty expression that he knew, all right. "Rosie—I swear—it's nothing serious. It's only herbal stuff, not even illegal."

"Herbal? And cannabis isn't? It must have some pharmacological effect, or why would people buy it? Luc, you should have been two years into a music degree by now! Instead you've been doing what with Jon? Selling drugs and playing in a not very good band? Fucking hell, Luc. I never thought I'd feel ashamed of you, but I do."

She started to walk away again. She didn't expect him to follow, but he did, almost on her heels. "I was so in love with him," she said. "All he's done is make my little brother waste his life. He doesn't care about anyone but himself."

"Rosie, I'm sorry." Lucas sounded distraught. "It's not like that."

"Are you blind, or is it me? Luc, I'm not going to lay down the law or forbid you to see him. You wouldn't listen to me anyway."

He was quiet for a few steps, then said, "He's my brother, my friend—I know he's difficult, but he's not a bad person. He gets too focused on things . . ."

"Like his stepmother?"

"I can't explain that." Lucas put his hand through her arm.

A few paces on, she asked, "Luc, has Sapphire ever questioned you about being Aetherial?"

"Er, yeah, she has," he said, looking troubled. "I told her how the Dusklands can manifest anywhere but the Spiral is a separate dimension, that sort of thing . . . She nodded and said that was what Lawrence and Jon had told her."

"So she was checking that they hadn't lied to her? Why wouldn't she trust them?"

He shrugged. "I've no idea. We've got nothing to hide, have we? I only told her the truth."

"And did she seem satisfied with that?"

"Not really, but I don't know what else she wanted me to say. Surely Lawrence could tell her everything she needs to know?"

"Quite," said Rosie. "So what's she up to? Asking questions . . . messing around behind Lawrence's back with her own stepson . . ."

She fell quiet, and several steps further on, Lucas said, "Ro, I can't bear seeing you hurt like this. I'd rather never see Jon again in my life than see you upset. You're right, I need to keep away from him for a while. I will, I promise."

In the midst of her misery, she felt a thrill of relief. She turned and hugged him. But this was sweet, loyal Lucas; she should not have been amazed for a moment.

"The fantasy of unconditional love," Rosie said to her reflection, "the *lie* of unconditional love is that you can love someone from afar, someone who never even looks at you in return, and it's okay; it's pure and virtuous and noble. But it's not okay. Fuck the fantasy!"

She was twenty-three; a perfect age to grow up, at last.

Rosie thought she'd taken it quite well, in the end. After all, where Jon was concerned, she'd had a lot of practice. She sat at her mirror, looking at the scar Sam had left on her neck, knowing it was time to leave beloved Oakholme and dreams of Elysion behind.

"What am I waiting for?" she asked herself.

She was absently painting her fingernails with the dark rainbow of Zeitgeist nail polish when Lucas came in, anxious to know if she'd forgiven him. They talked about the past, about Jon and Sam and Lawrence, but the talk was all about letting go, about giving Matthew's outlook a chance instead.

"The Wilders . . ." she said softly. "Do you think we'll ever be finally, completely free of them?"

And Lucas said, "Do you want to be?"

Yes, yes I do, she thought, after Luc had gone. *It's time. I'm at the crossroads and I need to choose the best way forward—using my head this time, not my stupid heart.*

She would continue visiting Sam, of course—but once he was released, she could leave the last of it behind and fully embrace the human world instead.

The small framed photo she'd pocketed, which she'd hoped was a picture of Lawrence with Virginia, turned out to be a wedding shot of Lawrence and Sapphire. Sam would definitely not want to see that. Taking the back off, she found another, passport-sized image of a much younger Sapphire with an older man—some sugar daddy, no doubt. Sighing, she reassembled the frame and threw it in the back of a drawer. Wedded bliss, indeed.

Then she turned her thoughts to Alastair. There was no pain when she thought about him, only warmth. His kind nature and steadiness . . . that would be nice to come home to. She'd grown to appreciate his stocky, rugby-player physique, and sex with him was good. True, he wasn't wildly passionate or imaginative, but that was okay; it wasn't his nature. Their love life was gentle, companionable and satisfying, and that was all she could ask. Temperamentally, he had his grumpy moments, like anyone, but he was slow to anger and his rare explosions of temper were over quickly. In short, he was wonderfully normal. If Jon was a tortuous, thorny path, the broad clear road of Alastair looked increasingly desirable. In fact, he'd become such a fixture in her life, it was impossible to imagine a future without him.

The next day, Rosie opened her bedroom window and leaned out to bask in the shimmering fresh greens of spring. She felt strange; numb, emotionless, abandoned. Yet there was no pain. That was good. It was almost a pleasant feeling, letting go, not caring anymore, floating free.

It was time for a new start.

Still, it was hard to forget the image she'd fallen in love with; Jon's soulful eyes, shy smile and flowing hair. The vision of him in the early morning sun, head back, hair streaming.

Doesn't matter what Jon's done, she told herself. *There's only one thing you need to know, which is that he doesn't want you. Not because there's anything wrong with you, or with him, but because he sees the world differently; doesn't see the soul-light in you, the gleaming other half of himself.*

Jon did not break my heart.

Fantasies broke it.

Matthew was right. The Otherworld was dead. The Gates were locked, derelict, the key rusted and thrown away. Vaethyr were beautiful shells; cold, mad and empty inside. Humans were warm and safe. She would pack away her fantasies and go with Safe.

The next time Alastair asked the question, he would be in for a shock.

One evening in July—some three months since Rosie had quietly confided her engagement to her human boyfriend, news to which he was largely indifferent—Lawrence was driving home in the summer dusk, thinking painfully about his visit to London. It was hard to put on a confident mask for his staff and explain that the supply of albinite had come to an end. Their morale was low. There were other gems—but if the one that made Wilder Jewels unique was gone, what was the point of continuing?

As he rounded the last bend he braked, startled by a mass of people all over the lane at the entrance to Stonegate's drive. He pipped his horn, but they only looked at him. Losing patience, Lawrence climbed out to remonstrate and saw that they were Vaethyr.

Striding among them, he entered the Dusklands without intention. They carried it with them like an aura that revealed their Otherworld forms; elegant, jewel-eyed, some with a hint of tendrils or gossamer wings. Their hair was living light. As he approached, their piercing eyes turned to him and a ripple of intense emotional pressure passed over them.

Rigid, Lawrence halted and surveyed them. Some had masks and others were bare-faced but he knew them all. Not just locals, but some he hadn't seen for years. In the middle of the drive between the two granite sentinels stood the ringleader, Comyn. A black and white sheepdog sat wrapped around his legs, nose pointed up at its master.

"What the hell is the meaning of this?" said Lawrence.

"A peaceful protest," Comyn answered mildly. "It's the seventh day of the seventh month of the sixth year. A reminder that in the seventh year, the Night of the Summer Stars falls."

"I am well aware of that. As you are well aware that I will open the Gates only when it is safe to do so."

"Then make it safe."

"Remove yourselves from my land, before I summon my *dysir*."

"We're not on your land," Comyn replied. "We're on the public highway."

"You're obstructing my right of way. Disperse." Lawrence was trembling, too angry to admit he was powerless. Glancing around, he saw scarlet-haired Peta Lyon and her sisters, the Tullivers with their sea-serpent masks . . . but no sign of Auberon Fox. He wouldn't associate himself with this undignified display.

Comyn raised his hands. "Long before mankind appeared, Aetherials held dominion over all the realms. There were no Gates, no barriers."

The bastard was making a speech. Jaw tight, Lawrence had no choice but to let him finish. "We call those times to return. The Gates have severed us from the flow of life and power! Our young have missed their initiations. They have lost their festivals and their connection to the Spiral, lost their right to taste their true nature. This is a crisis that will turn to utter disaster unless the Great Gates are reopened. We assert our right to pass freely among all the realms without hindrance!"

All the Vaethyr breathed in soft agreement, a sound far eerier than applause. A cool female voice added, "Some Aelyr despise the Vaethyr and might want to keep us from the Spiral out of sheer spite. Is that the way you feel, Lawrence?" It was Peta Lyon who spoke, a slender chalk-faced artist who wore blood red, a shade darker than her hair.

Lawrence could barely find his voice. "Have I not explained a dozen times that I am protecting you all from danger?"

"And we say to hell with the danger!" growled Comyn. "We'll arm ourselves and march in and deal with it. What danger is a match for us?"

"Idiots," said Lawrence, but the word was drowned by the cheers of Comyn's followers.

"Our point is made," said Comyn. "Take a valium, Wilder. We're leaving."

He grinned as he shouldered past, his sheepdog trotting with him. The protestors streamed away towards the village, bowing to Lawrence—respectfully, with no hint of mockery—as they passed.

Moments after they'd gone, Lawrence was speeding up the long drive. He abandoned the car in front of the house, and ran the rest of the way through woodland and undergrowth until he reached Freya's Crown. Breathing hard he circled the rocks, one hand hovering inches from the surface as he clambered around the rear of the mound, then came down into the hollow at the front. The grass was spongy under the soles of his shoes.

Someone had been here. A cigarette paper; a bottle top; a little wreath of twigs that hadn't woven itself by accident. He pocketed the litter and shook the twigs apart. Not Comyn; the *dysir* would ward off outsiders. Someone from his own family, then, which meant Jon or Lucas. He felt a trace of annoyance, a blip in the flat line of his emotions. Boys, playing. No one would dare to interfere with his Gates.

He remembered his earliest awareness of the entity that had always haunted him; a face or a cloud shadow, always there in the corner of his eye. No bigger than a cat at the beginning. Then—after Albin had taken his heart and soul hostage—it had begun its monstrous expansion. The gun kicked in his hand . . . the shadow giant broke its bonds . . . and he knew then that what he had summoned was Brawth, the ice giant that would consume his race.

Locking the Great Gates was all that had stopped it. It kept the Otherworld safe as well as Earth because, like a dam, it stopped the dark current in its tracks. But even those who claimed to believe him did not *understand,* because only he could truly feel it . . .

Lawrence shut his eyes. He felt his chest constricting, breath rapid. His hand hovered closer to the stone but he couldn't bring himself to touch it. He braced himself for the onslaught; the face from the Abyss, the rushing darkness, the Gates slamming and shattering and all the realms crashing one into another . . .

His palm met rock.

He felt the surface, chill and gritty under his fingertips. He held his breath—

Nothing.

No visions, no terror. No silvery runes, no rumbling in the earth as the Gates strained to slide open. All he felt under his hand was cold, impenetrable stone.

Dead.

The Great Gates were dead.

Even the lych-light inside him, the flame of the Gate-keeper, no longer yearned towards the stone. He'd repressed it for too long. It had burned away to ash. All the Gates to the inner realms stood like dead shells one inside the other. Fossils.

Lawrence recoiled.

Sudden, complete terror overwhelmed him. What had happened? Was it his fault, his failing that had killed the Gates? Was it permanent? Had the lych-light been confiscated, or had his fear destroyed it?

In the next breath he felt wild relief. It was so strong he almost fell. If he simply *could not* open the Gates, then it all went away, the guilt, the responsibility, the danger to his sons—

No, that was delusion. Black panic surged over him again, bringing him to his knees. Looking up he saw a young Aetherial woman standing in front of him. Slim as a willow with long rippling hair, she was a ghost, a church-yard angel, pointing a crumbling stone finger straight at him. Her eyes were blank orbs without pupils. When she spoke the whisper pierced his brain, *"We warned you it would be taken away from you."*

He cried out. He opened his eyes but she was gone, leaving him alone with his desolate knowledge.

The loss of his lych-power was the loss of everything. While he had the authority to keep the Gates closed, he was in control. But without the power to open or close, he had nothing. No mandate from the Spiral Court. No status. Nothing.

His panic, having reached its peak, began to subside. Lawrence climbed shakily to his feet and made a pact with himself; no one must know he'd lost his power. It would be the end of everything. He must behave as if nothing had changed. No one must ever know.

Three years.

That was how long Sam had served when his parole was granted. Even without the warped time and illusions of Dumannios, it had felt like the full five.

He stepped out of the prison gates and breathed fresh September air. This was strange. Almost a letdown. He'd always had release to look forward to; now there was nothing. His possessions were few, and the only one that mattered was the photograph that Rosie had given him. He began to walk towards a bus stop.

A blue Volkswagen Golf was parked a few yards away. He thought nothing of it, until Rosie suddenly leaned out and waved.

"Are you getting in, or what?"

As Rosie drove she was powerfully aware of Sam in the seat next to her. His physical presence, his strength, the faint spicy warmth of his body that seemed to bypass her higher reasoning entirely. However, she could also smell the prison on him. She sat tense, deeply uncomfortable and not knowing what to say. She'd never told him about the Jon-and-Sapphire incident in April . . . all she'd seen was a kiss, but who knew what storm would be unleashed if she mentioned it? At the same time, she felt hideously guilty for keeping it from Sam, and that set her even more on edge.

"You're not scared of me, are you?" he asked.

"No, of course not."

"So what's with the shiny white knuckles?"

She tried to relax her hands on the wheel, annoyed that she couldn't seem to hide anything from him. "This feels weird, that's all."

"Yeah, having a convicted killer fresh out of prison all alone with you in the middle of nowhere—I'd be nervous, too. Sorry. I was going to catch a bus, didn't expect you to be there. Don't be uncomfortable. It's only me, Rosie. All I'm interested in is getting home."

"I know," she said through her teeth. "I am not nervous. Will you please shut up?"

She heard him exhale. For a time he stared through the windshield. It wasn't fear she felt but unease—for all the reasons he'd named—and there was a well of other emotions that she couldn't begin to untangle. It was impossible even to tell him a perfectly simple piece of news.

He said, "Don't know whether going to Stonegate is a good idea. My father won't want me. The stepmother definitely won't. In fact, if you could drop me in the nearest city . . ."

"Then where would you go?"

"I dunno. I'd find something."

"Don't be ridiculous. Isn't it a condition of parole to tell them where you're living?"

"Aren't you the expert?" he retorted.

"Well, I'm not abandoning you in a strange city. Of course Lawrence will want to see you."

"It's a shame you and I don't get on better," he said in a low voice. "You might have let me sleep on your sofa."

She gave him a sideways frown.

"'Sall right, I know that's never going to happen," he sighed. "I'll have to face the music. If it goes badly, I know where the door is."

"It will be all right, Sam. And there'll be people to help you, won't there? Counselors, parole officers?"

"Fuck that," he said flatly. She glanced sideways and saw his eyes gleaming narrowly with anger. "I'm Aetherial. Things happened to me in that place that they couldn't conceive of. What the hell do they think they can do for me? I don't need rehabilitating! Sod their help!"

"I'm sorry," said Rosie. "That sounded really patronizing. I didn't mean to. I'm just worried about you."

"Wow," Sam said quietly. "Are you?"

"Yes, of course. Why d'you think I kept coming to see you? I hated leaving you in that place. Every time I left, I wished I could take you home with me." She felt herself turning hot with the intimacy of the confession. "I don't mean—I just meant—"

"I know." There was a rueful smile in his voice. "That's sweet of you, Foxy, but I don't need you to worry about me. Last thing I ever wanted from you was sympathy. I'm a grown-up. Hey, I'll miss our assignations. You got a last secret report for me? Anything I need to know before I get home?"

She swallowed, caught on the impossible edge of what she should and shouldn't say. "Your father seems worried about his business . . ."

"Don't tell me anything else," he said, letting her off the hook. "I know it's not fair on you. I can find out for myself now."

"Fine," she said, breathing out.

The landscape around them was dark and warped. She had never known it to take so long to pass out of Duman-nios before. It was as if Sam brought the second realm with him, like a cloak. Sulfur-yellow fires rolled across the land-scape around them, and she saw burning cars and armies of apelike demons.

"Just keep going," said Sam. "They're illusions. We'll be out soon."

"Feels like we're going deeper in," she said. Red fires glowered in her rearview mirror. On the road ahead a gar-goyle crouched, pointed wingtips curving high above its head.

"Keep going. It's not real."

"You pay for the damage if it's as solid as it looks!"

The creature stayed put. An instant before she hit it, Rosie closed her eyes. The car passed through thin air.

Then with a horrific thump, the thing landed on her hood and sprawled there.

"Jesus!" she shouted, narrowly keeping control of the car.

It was real. She saw every detail of its face leering through the windshield, every scale and tendril. Its breath clouded the glass. Rosie braked. She started as it brought a fist down hard on the glass. Its claws scrabbled and squeaked, trying to reach her. Surely the glass would shatter. The car jerked to a halt and the creature rested there, panting.

Sam started to open the passenger door.

"What are you doing?" she cried.

"No, you're right," he said, slamming and locking it. "I get out and kill it, it turns into a human, the police come and this time they take me and throw away the key. Just drive!"

Holding her breath, Rosie slammed into gear and put her foot down. The car skidded, showering gravel as it pulled away. There was a clear slot below the fog of its breath and she focused on that, saw the bend in the road—

She flung the steering wheel hard over. The car slewed. The beast lost its grip and went tumbling off into a ditch.

Rosie steadied her speed, clenched her teeth and drove on. Her heart was racing but she willed it to slow down, willed herself calm.

"Brilliant," exclaimed Sam, glancing behind. "That was a great bit of driving, Rosie."

"Thanks."

"You okay?"

"Yes," she gasped. "Dumannios, realm of illusions? That was one realistic illusion."

"You have to give it that," he said. "Great special effects."

Ten long minutes later, the world returned to normal. The change felt nonchalant, as if nothing had happened. Tarmac, hedges, grass, road signs. Late-summer sunlight fell beautifully over the landscape. "Told you," said Sam.

A couple of hours later they reached Cloudcroft unscathed. He hadn't tried to pounce on her; he'd been as good as gold; she'd survived. As she turned into the drive of Stonegate Manor, Sam said, "You can drop me here, okay?"

She stopped the car. "Are you sure?"

"Yes, I'll walk up. It'll give me a few minutes to collect my thoughts."

"Okay," she said.

He turned to look at her. "Thanks for everything, Rosie," he said gently.

"That's all right." He always embarrassed her when he was sincere. The sniping and sarcasm were much easier to parry.

Hesitantly he reached out and took her hand where it lay curved on her thigh. His forefinger pressed into her palm and the feeling sent a tentacle of warmth through her core. "I'm crap at sounding like I mean it, but I do. You kept me alive in that place. You saved my life. It meant everything to me."

Rosie couldn't look at him. She looked at his hand in hers. She couldn't clasp it in return, but she didn't try to pull away, either. "Thanks."

"Er, Rosie, when I've got my life into some semblance of order, d'you think we could maybe see each other sometime?"

Her breath came out somewhere between a gulp and a sob. "No, no I don't think we can."

His touch slackened. His face and body turned dull with resignation. "Thought we were getting on quite well. I knew in my heart you were just being kind, but I hoped—no, you wouldn't touch soiled goods like me with a ten-foot pole and why would you?"

"It's not that," she said hurriedly. "I'm getting married."

"You're what?" He released her hand and stared at her. "Who to?"

"Alastair, of course. The one I've been seeing for three years, as you know perfectly well."

"What? You can't marry a fat ginger geek!"

"He's not fat, and he's not ginger!" Rosie cried.

"He's not Aetherial, either."

"I know," she said, nodding vigorously. "That's the idea. I've had enough of Aetherial men."

Sam caught her gaze and she couldn't look away. His eyes, shining with pain, pinned her down and searched her. "After Jon and me?" he said.

She mentally kicked herself for saying it. "It's nothing to do with him, or you."

"Oh, god, Rosie, please don't do it." The shine of his eyes grew brighter. He looked away from her, blinking.

"It's all arranged," she said. "It's happening next week. I'm sorry, Sam. I didn't know how to tell you. But life went on while you were away."

"I knew you were keeping something quiet," he said hoarsely. He opened his door, hesitated. "Do you love him?"

"He's right for me."

"That's not what I asked you."

"I thought I loved Jon. I was wrong. I don't know what love is. Once I've worked out what the question means, I might be able to answer."

He shook his head and said bitterly, "Then what the hell are you doing this for?"

"Because I want a normal happy life," she said, staring ahead through the windshield.

"And I want to be Pope! Bloody hell, Rosie, *please*."

She couldn't speak. After a brief, horrible pause he said, "I thought there was more to you than this, sweetheart. Now I look at you and see someone who's dead inside. Matthew's put you up to it, hasn't he?"

"No. I can decide how to run my life without—"

"I know my father's a bastard, but he's nowhere near as poisonous as your brother with his phoney Sir Galahad act."

Rosie bit her lip until she tasted metal. "Cheap insults not helping, Sam. I thought you'd take it better than this."

"There's nothing to take, because it's not about me. I know you can't stand me, let alone love me. I live with that every sodding day. It's about watching you make a horrible mistake."

Sam swung out of the car, hauled his bag off the back-seat. He looked at her, tried to say something, gave up and turned away from her in a kind of disgust. Tasting blood, she watched him walk away.

There were smears of reddish slime from the Dumannios creature dried onto the windshield. She pressed the wipers to clear it. The soapy rush of fluid turned Sam's retreating figure into a slim, wavering shadow.

11

❦

Sleepwalking

Sam dropped his bag and stood looking around the great hall; first time he'd seen it for three years. The scent of flowers and incense couldn't mask its underlying mustiness. No one came to meet him, except the creeping shadow forms of the *dysir*.

He'd been dreading this moment. Every sound and sensation came back. There was the spot where the man had died . . . he half-expected to see bloodstains and crime-scene tape. Sapphire had bought new rugs. Their jewel-fresh glimmer was an accusation, worse than the sight of an old blood-rusty carpet would have been.

He hadn't expected to feel anything but he did. Cold inside and slightly sick. "Hello? Anyone home?"

The study door opened. His father stood there, dark and angular.

Then there came light footsteps on the gallery, and Sapphire appeared at the top of the stairs in a kingfisher-blue kimono. Lawrence-and-Sapphire formed a quite different entity to Lawrence on his own. They both halted and stared as if they'd turned to wax.

"You knew I was coming home today, right?"

He sensed their unease as they watched him, wondering what it meant to have this stranger in their home, a released prisoner, as alien as a soldier home from war. Sam felt drained, empty, a grey rag.

"Sam," said Lawrence. "Yes, yes of course." Reaching him, his father clasped his shoulders at arm's length. A proper embrace wasn't his style. Sam studied his face. He looked more gaunt and aquiline than Sam remembered, his grey eyes remote, like some lonely dark tyrant in a folktale. "I would have fetched you, if you'd let me."

"It's okay, Rosie came for me." Sam felt a pang as he spoke her name. "Anyway, I won't be staying. Just came to say hi and see how things are."

"Of course you're staying," Lawrence replied. "You're home. We're not letting you go anywhere. Are we, Sapphire?"

Sapphire came forward cautiously, as if approaching a dangerous dog. "We wouldn't dream of it," she said smoothly, touching his arm. "Welcome home, dear."

Her surface was serene, her manner warm and polished, but underneath she was brittle china. She'd never liked him; she couldn't phone the police fast enough, that night, and see him handcuffed and taken away. Relief and triumph had emanated from her. Now her seething discomfort was equally tangible. Sam smiled at her. She instantly broke eye contact, seamlessly shifting her gaze to his father.

"Well," said Lawrence. "Make yourself at home. Your room's ready for you as always."

"I'll make coffee," said Sapphire, whirling away to the kitchen. The heavy dark swing of her hair made him think about Rosie's hair, and the rest of her . . . he sighed. He'd definitely been locked up for too long.

When she'd gone, Sam relaxed a little. There was something wrong, he knew—you could slice the tension with a cake knife—but then, there was always something wrong at Stonegate. It was normal. His homecoming suddenly felt ordinary, an anticlimax. "This is so weird," he said, looking around.

"I know," said Lawrence, looking gravely at him, "but we can put it all behind us now, can't we?"

"I don't want to sit raking over it for hours on end."

"Neither do I," said his father, the master of brooding silence. "It's over. We won't speak a word of it unless you want to."

They looked at each other for a moment or two, but neither of them was good at that and Lawrence was the first to break the gaze, clearing his throat as he turned away. "Suits me," said Sam. "I'll go and dump my bag. Is Jon here?"

"I believe he's upstairs," Lawrence answered.

Jon was in his room, sitting cross-legged on a chair at an open window with his back to the door. He was smoking a reefer. The smoke drifted around him in lacy layers. Sam sat down silently on his bed and watched him for a couple of minutes.

"Hey, asshole."

It was worth it to see Jon levitate in shock. He swung round violently, staring. Sam was startled to see how rough he looked; eyes sunk in bruised skin, hair uncombed.

"Oh my god, Sam."

"I've escaped. You've got to hide me."

"What?"

The panic in his eyes was priceless. Sam spoiled it by starting to laugh; he couldn't help it. Jon sighed and grimaced. "For fuck's sake, Sam! You frightened the hell out of me! Jesus!"

"Well, you know, it's time for the reckoning now. I'm out, and I'm not going back—unless I do something really stupid, like killing my brother."

Jon unfolded his long legs and stood up, putting the palms of his hands out. "Look, Sam, I wanted to visit you. I really did. I just couldn't face it."

"Relax. I understand. It was no fun there; anyone would have freaked out. Thanks for sending Rosie instead. Come on, sit down."

"No, you don't understand." Jon turned paler, shaking. "I couldn't come because it was my fault that guy broke in. You don't know how bad I've felt, what it's been like for me . . ."

"Like I said, I understand," Sam replied, low and firm. "You're a prat, but you didn't invite him to come and rob us, did you? If you feel bad about it, that's up to you. But I've never blamed you. Sit down, idiot."

Jon obeyed, sitting on the end of the bed at right angles to him.

"So, how have things been here?" Sam asked. "What's up with Morticia and Gomez?"

"Just the usual." Jon drew nervously on the spliff.

Sam beckoned, and Jon passed it to him. Sam took a drag and nearly choked. "Christ, what are you smoking? So, have you managed to sneak through the Gates yet?"

"Not yet."

"Still trying, though?"

Jon's eyes burned with sudden life. "I tell you, Sam, if the Gates had been open, no prison could have held you."

"Well, I spent at least sixty per cent of my sentence in Dumannios and that held me quite nicely, thank you," he said quietly. Needling Jon was a habit all too easy to slip into. "Have you contacted Mum? Any messages from beyond?"

Jon ducked his head. "No."

"I appreciated the photo, anyway." Sam tried another drag, and his head whirled. "Bloody hell, Jon, what *is* this?"

"Just weed." Jon took the joint back.

"Keep it, it's disgusting." Sam reached out and clasped his bony shoulder. "You ought to knock it on the head, you know. You look bloody awful. If Dad smells it, he'll go nuts."

"I'm fine. It's just . . . you don't know what it's been like. Everyone thinks I don't care about you, but I do. Dad's under pressure about the Gates, and Sapphire . . ."

"What?"

Jon shook his head, grimacing. "The more Dad shuts her out, the more curious she gets about Aetherial stuff, and now she seems to think I'm her passport through the Gates. Pestering me with questions, wanting to go up to Freya's Crown with me . . . It's nothing to do with her! It's mine, it's private, she's got no business interfering. And she's going behind Dad's back."

"Oh, and you're not?"

"It's different. I'm allowed to rebel. She's not, it's grotesque." Jon drew in smoke, held it, blew it out. Sam watched, disturbed, wondering what dark tangle lay under the surface.

"Tell her to sod off, then."

"It's not that easy," Jon murmured. "You haven't been here, and it's been awful without you."

"That's nice. Never thought you'd miss me for two seconds." Sam grinned. "Hey, I'm back, mate. Home sweet home."

"Yeah. Thank the gods." They shared a quick, awkward hug. Jon felt too thin, as always.

"By the way," said Sam, trying to sound offhand, "did you know she's getting married?"

"Who?"

"Rosie."

He looked blank. "No."

"She didn't tell you?"

Jon made a movement between and flinch and a shrug. "I don't think she's speaking to me. She and Luc came up here, let me think, about six months ago. Out of the blue she went crazy at me, and I've no idea what it was about. I haven't seen either of them since."

"Ah. Maybe not long after I told her about your sideline in herbal medicine? Don't deny it. News travels. You were at it in school, anyway."

Jon glared at him. "Thanks. What she didn't know didn't hurt her—now she's stopped Luc seeing me because of it? That was my best friend you've driven off!"

"Well, I'm sorry," Sam said sharply. "I was sick of covering for you, trying to protect Rosie's feelings because she believed you were a saint. She deserved the truth. Now she's marrying this friend of her brother's."

"Oh, right."

"Don't you care?"

Finally Jon reacted, catching and holding Sam's gaze, a frown line indenting his forehead. "It's none of my business. What's it to you?"

Sam jumped up and paced on the threadbare Indian rug. "If there's one thing that is your fault, it's this."

"Excuse me?"

"It's your fault she's marrying some jerk! You broke her heart!"

"What? When? What are you on about?"

"She's in love with you, you dolt!"

Jon looked affronted. "No, she isn't."

Aware he was close to shouting, Sam lowered his voice. "Maybe not anymore. I don't know. But she was, and you treated her like she didn't exist. You could have had the most wonderful thing in the universe and you didn't even notice. You prick!"

Jon was wide-eyed. He put out his hands. "This is not my problem. Yeah, she used to follow me around, but lots of people did. I never gave her any encouragement. I didn't even know."

"No, that figures." Sam rubbed his forehead. "You have got to help me stop her getting married."

"How?"

"I don't know. Go and tell her you've been an idiot, beg her not to go through with it. Tell her you love her."

"But I don't." Jon looked bewildered. "Sam, you need to calm down."

"Please, I'm desperate."

"Why me?"

"She'll listen to you."

"No, she won't. I tell her a load of lies and then what? Oops, sorry, didn't mean it? And if she was with me instead of this other guy, how does that help you?"

Sam leaned on a chest of drawers, head in hands. "Yeah. I'm going nuts. But how can you not?"

"How can I not what?"

"Love her."

"Fuck it, Sam, I don't know. She's just little Rosie, she's great, but I don't fancy her. I liked that blond friend of hers, Mel? But you know what, I can't do girlfriends, I can't stand people fussing over me." He shuddered. "I just want to be left alone."

Sam took a deep breath. "You're going to be more left alone than in your wildest dreams, at this rate."

"Look," Jon said, his voice hardening, "if you've got the hots for Rosie, it's your problem, not mine. I reckon this is all because she's the only female you've seen for three years."

Sam slumped back onto the bed, defeated. "Yeah, that's what it is."

"Go in any pub in Ashvale tonight and you'll pull any woman you want within ten minutes."

Sam shivered in distaste. "Thanks for the vote of confidence, but all I'm interested in is Rosie. I'm screwed, aren't I?"

"You've definitely been in prison too long," Jon said sagely. "We all have."

"Fuck the fantasy," Rosie said to her reflection.

Two hours until the ax fell. She looked down at her hands and wondered if she had time to paint her fingernails. Against the dark oak of her dressing table, her splayed fingers were pale and still.

"Steady as a rock," she said. "That's good. I can do this."

Her dressing-table mirror reflected a serene ivory face, grey eyes bright and inscrutable beneath plum-shadowed lids. Her hair was swept up with pearls and lilies; pearls encircled her throat and stiff ivory silk clasped her shoulders. She looked immaculate. Definitely a siren today, and no hint of scruffy gardener. Her face was expressionless and she felt calm. Outside her bedroom window, the greens of late summer were brushed with September gold. She could smell bonfires.

"Rosie?" A gentle knock and her father came in, smiling warmly. Her heart lifted. "Where's your mother?"

"Gone to panic about flowers, I think," said Rosie. "Dad . . ."

She held out her arms and he came to hug her, very delicately so as not to disturb her hair and makeup. His kind face beamed into hers. She basked in the solid glow of his presence, the clean earthy smell of his aftershave, so familiar. As long as her father was there, everything was fine.

"I can't believe it," he said. "You look quite the princess."

"You're not going to cry, are you?" Rosie said sternly. "They've got me dressed too early and now I daren't move. I should have stayed in my dressing gown, downing sherry with Auntie Phyll."

He chuckled. "D'you want a drink? You're bound to be a bit—"

"I'm not nervous. I'm really not."

"That's marvelous. That's a sign that you're really sure."

"I am," she said firmly.

"And you look wonderful. Hang on, a quick photo . . ."

"I feel a complete dog's dinner," she said, giggling as the camera flashed. The small digital image on the camera's screen showed a perfect bride; petite in her tasteful silk dress, smiling radiantly. It looked like someone else.

"Let me take one of you, Dad," she said, wanting to keep him there, her guardian to ward off the future.

When he'd gone, Rosie looked around her familiar bedroom with its dark antique furniture and the Waterhouse prints on the walls. She would be sad to leave. The big bed

had never hosted the wild demon sex she had often fantasized about. Sad.

One hour until the ax fell. On the landing she could hear
chattering voices; Jessica, Phyllida, Faith and Mel . . . If
only they would keep talking and let her have this last
island of time alone. She contemplated a suitably bland
oyster-pink nail polish, but a mischievous impulse made
her choose the dramatic, oily rainbow of Zeitgeist.

It was a small act of rebellion. She sat back and grinned
at the multihued gleam of her nails.

"All right?" Matthew poked his head around the doorway. "Can the best man come in and wish the bride luck?"
He strolled in, statuesque in his dark suit; a fair-haired
prince. He stood grinning down at her, nodding slightly,
hands stuffed into his trouser pockets. "You scrub up quite
well. At least you resisted the temptation to let out your inner masked goddess and scare the crap out of Alastair's
family."

"What?"

"I mean, you chose a nice conventional dress. Suits
you."

"Sod off." The words came out more angrily than she'd
expected, but Matthew's attention flew to her hands.

"You are joking," he said. "You can't get married with
black fingernails! What the hell are you doing?"

"It's not black. It's any color you want, in the right light."

"Typical. You can never do anything normal, can you?"
He looked at his watch. "Want me to pierce your lip with a
safety pin before we go? Still got time."

"Shut up." Rosie bit her tongue until the urge to retort
had died down. "How's Alastair?"

"Fine, apart from dashing to the loo every five minutes."

"Oh god, he's that nervous?"

"Shitting bricks," Matthew said delightedly. "I offered
him whiskey, told him it got me through my wedding day,
but he says he can't swallow."

"Why's he in such a state?" Rosie felt irrationally guilty.

"Because this means everything to him." Matthew leaned down to her, his eyes narrowing with sincerity. "Alastair's a fantastic bloke. This is absolutely the best thing for you, Rose. A full life in the real world."

Half an hour until the ax fell. Her mother floated in and out, golden and beautiful in a white hat with pale roses, tearful but collected. Mel and Faith appeared in their bridesmaids' outfits with Heather—a tiny angel in a halo of flowers. Mel was teasing Faith for being even more excited and panicky than she'd been on her own wedding day.

Rosie sat patiently as her nails dried and her family drifted in and out. Lucas pulled up a stool and sat at the dressing table beside her, leaning on his elbows. He was sweet; he didn't fuss like the others, just wanted to be near her. She said, "The way everyone's coming in and out, it's like being visited on my deathbed."

"Hence the gothic fingernails?" he said with a lazy smile.

"It's symbolic of the multicolored Aetheric spirit," she said wryly.

Lucas only looked at her with a mysterious half-smile. After a minute he said very softly, "Are you sure about this?"

"Well, I'm stuck with it. You don't think I'm organized enough to possess nail polish remover, do you?"

"Not that," he sighed impatiently. "I meant . . . you know . . . getting married, it's huge."

"I can't back out now," she said lightly.

"Rosie . . ." He reached out and touched her neck. "I can see the scar. Only because your hair's up."

She leaned towards the mirror, putting her fingers to the reddish line. She found a tube of concealer and passed it to him. "Mum missed it. Would you?" She sat patiently as Lucas dabbed makeup onto the scar with a fingertip, his tongue protruding a little in concentration.

"There," he said. "Invisible." She resettled her necklace

and the scar was gone. The milky beads felt warm against her neck and a single pearl teardrop lay on her breastbone. The picture of icy perfection was complete.

Princess for a day, she thought, staring at her unfamiliar self.

I feel like the King of Elfland's daughter, marrying my father's most favored knight. Everything is as it should be.

I'm a gardener with dirty fingernails.

I'm just me. Which is—what?

"Car's here!" her mother's voice sang from the landing.

"You're quiet, Rosie," said Lucas. "Are you scared? It's only Alastair."

"I'm not quiet, I'm serene."

"So what are you thinking about, then?"

Rosie breathed in and out. "The future," she said.

Here it came, the fairy-tale wedding with tumbling sprays of lilies and the eager strawberry-blond-not-ginger bridegroom in his kilt and a new future in the surface world. *No more Wuthering Heights with its deranged inhabitants,* she thought. *We are all smiling and going forward.*

The few hours in her bedroom had been her last oasis of peace. The moment the wedding limousine came, she was cut adrift.

The venue was a Georgian mansion refurbished as a conference and wedding center, all marble majesty with cascades of white flowers. It was like every dream wedding there had ever been. There was Alastair, handsome and trembling, the archetypal nervous bridegroom; there were his uncles and cousins from Aberdeen in their kilted finery, and all, Alastair included, a clan of strangers.

Rosie drifted though the ceremony as if tranquilized. She seemed to be witnessing the proceedings from outside; a disembodied spirit, watching a serene, composed young woman making her promises before the registrar. When Alastair kissed her, she hardly felt his lips on hers. It all floated past like a play.

"Do you think we'll ever be finally, completely free of

them?" she'd asked Lucas not long ago, meaning the Wilders, the web of Stonegate. Already it seemed like a past life.

As photographs were taken on the sweep of marble steps outside, she noticed that her family looked as plainly human as Alastair's. There was no difference at all. It was as if they'd crossed a barrier and become mortal, losing all memory of the Otherworld. A tiny thread of denial went through her. She saw Matthew smiling.

Rosie chatted and laughed her way through the reception. Glasses were clinked, humorous speeches made. She felt blissfully detached. Nothing could hurt her anymore and so she was free to laugh all she wanted. From the outside, it was a flawless rendition of happiness. The guests looked on and approved her radiance. The past tipped away and the future rose on this fulcrum, the joyous point of rebirth, and not one of them knew the journey that had brought her here.

When Alastair claimed her for the first dance, beaming with pride, she felt like two separate beings. One was the elegant, smiling bride, swept up in the ocean of massed family joy. The other stood apart, not recognizing herself. Who was this man in her arms, with his big unfamiliar body? He seemed nice, but she didn't know him. Everything felt strange and unreal.

Much later—the meal long over, tiers of cake demolished, guests dancing to the cheesy classics of a live band—Rosie joined Mel at a corner table. The ballroom felt overcooked. It was at the rear of the mansion, with a shiny dance floor and a long spread of French windows along one side. Outside was a path, a strip of lawn and then woodland with amber sunlight falling through leaves, a tantalizing refuge she couldn't reach.

Floating on too much champagne, they raked over history and confessed thoughts that they probably wouldn't remember in the morning.

"Alastair looks happy," Mel remarked. "And intoxicated."

Rosie glanced at her husband—*husband,* how surreal—where he stood surrounded by family she barely knew, all roaring with laughter. His father was dead, mother estranged, and he only had these distant relatives from Scotland. No wonder he'd attached himself so readily to Matthew and Oakholme.

"Oh, he can hold his drink. Unlike some." Rosie nodded at Lucas, who was prettily asleep on the next table amid carnations and crystal glasses.

"Don't get left behind," said Mel, pouring more champagne. "To be honest, I'm astonished you ended up with Alastair."

"What d'you mean?"

"He's a nice guy, but so straight. Like the anti-Jon."

"Safe," said Rosie. She twirled her glass, her fingernails flashing bronze and purple. "He's not deep or difficult. I don't have to prove myself to him."

"Mm, there's a lot to be said for that," said Mel. "I never thought you'd go for the traditional works. I imagined you'd do something new-agey in a forest."

Rosie smiled. "I went along with Matt, Faith and Alastair. They had such fun planning everything, I wasn't bothered. A wedding, so many people get involved it sweeps you with it like a juggernaut."

"Not bothered?" Mel gave her a probing look, head tilted.

"No, I went with the flow. It's fine."

"Why? So you could fast-forward to the mind-blowing sex?"

"God, you're dreadful." Rosie laughed, took another drink of champagne. It frothed deliciously on her tongue, tasting of lemons and new-baked bread.

"Come on. You must be having fun under his sporran, or what's the point?"

"Oh, the sex is fine," Rosie said, aware she was slurring.

"Five times a night?" Mel grinned.

"Twice a week, if I'm lucky. Half the time we're too tired or lazy to bother. We're so busy with work, pub, baby-sitting Heather . . . so much stuff to do, you know. It's no big deal."

"My god, you're already an old married couple!" Mel cried.

"Kind of. Yes, we're a fixture."

"But are you sure it's enough? Does he do the right things?"

"Pretty much." She was giggling; it all seemed so ridiculous. "He's not the most imaginative lover in the world, but it's fine."

"It doesn't sound it! Be more demanding, get the whip out, insist he makes more effort!"

Rosie laughed even harder at Mel's outrage. She wiped tears away. "No, it's not an issue. I'm happy the way we are. He's a sweetheart."

"That's all very well, but what about passion?" Mel bent close, quiet and serious.

"Oh, sod passion. It's overrated. I have definitely had too much to drink."

"You know what this looks like, Rosie?" Mel said very softly. "Going through the motions."

"Oh," said Rosie. "Does it? Well, it's only a ritual. I had to make a decision to leave all the old stuff behind and this is it, the point of no return, the guillotine."

"Wow," Mel said dryly. "That sounds extreme. As in, guillotine through Jon's neck?"

Rosie gave a pained grin. "Through everything," she said. "Mel, what are you trying to say?"

"That I don't think you're in love with him."

The words sent a cold flash of denial through her. " 'In love,' that's meaningless. Yes, he's not Jon and I feel totally different—secure and peaceful, instead of torn up in agony. What's wrong with that?"

"Nothing, but . . ."

"Look, there's more to life than passion. I tried following my heart and look where that got me. Sometimes you have to look at things coolly and make a sensible decision with your head. And that's the right thing to do."

"For some, perhaps," Mel said, with a slight frown. "Not for you, honey."

Rosie gulped more champagne. "Stop it. You're being absolutely mischievous."

"No, I'm not," Mel whispered, putting a hand on Rosie's. "I'm saying it because I know you."

Rosie pulled her hand free. She was trying hard not to be cross, but Mel's words were picking away at her serene detachment. "Well, it's done. Alastair's part of my life and we're married, end of story."

"Oh, Rosie, I know. Just ignore me. I really hope it works out for you."

"It will. It has to." As she spoke, she became acutely aware of the guests, surface dwellers on the thin skin of reality, growing happy and oblivious with alcohol. There were disheveled aunts dancing with red-faced uncles, children running through the debris of fallen napkins and flowers. Rosie stared at the scene as if watching a film. A bizarre pantomime, nothing to do with her. She looked for Alastair and he was part of it, a red-faced drunk roaring with his mates.

He saw her looking and came for her, dragging her onto the floor again to slow-dance to some cloying song. "You're my angel," he murmured. "Your family is amazing. I finally found people who won't let me down." He laughed. "I was in such a mess before I met you. This is everything I never had. *Everything.*"

She was an icicle in a steam bath, dissolving. Alastair with his hot hands and blissful grin was only part of the suffocating mass. "This is it, Rosie Duncan," he purred, his alcohol-laden breath hot in her ear. "You and me, forever."

A shaft of panic pierced her.

"Just going to the loo," she said, fighting out of his arms.

She slid around the perimeter of the room, fending off friendly hands, until she reached the doors to the foyer and saw green parkland outside; but there were guests on the front steps, gossiping and smoking. Retracing her steps, she found a side exit. It brought her onto a path that led to the back lawns, and there she found another track winding into the woodlands. Gathering up her skirts, she plunged into the cover of trees, almost running until she was certain no one could see her.

Gods, what a relief. Sweet fresh air, the warmth of the sun. Nothing around her but nature. The first fallen leaves crackled like bronze coins under her slippers. She glanced back and the building was out of sight. Trees sheltered her with veils of green, brushed with early red and copper.

At last she could breathe. She leaned back against the thick silken trunk of a beech tree, closed her eyes and sighed. The wedding music was faint. Rosie began to shake, wave upon wave of shock trembling through her.

"What have I done?" she groaned to herself. "What the fuck have I done?" She rubbed her forehead. "Bloody hell. *Shit*."

The rustle of feet was so soft, she thought it was a bird, until she sensed a more substantial presence. Her eyes snapped open. Sam was standing an arm's length from her. Dark blue jeans, a green-blue batik T-shirt and over that a black biker's jacket, unfastened. The contrast with her cream finery made her feel she was in fancy dress.

His hair had grown longer and the dark brown was tipped with gold again, brushed back off his face but trying to fall forward.

"Hail, the Queen of the May," he said.

"What the hell are you doing here?"

He stared at her, eyes narrow, the hint of an unkind smile curling the corners of his mouth. "No invite, so I'm holding my own little private wake out here."

"For pity's sake." The thought of him lurking here, when she'd imagined him to be miles away, was disturbing. "Sam, you're too sad for words."

"What about you, then? Why aren't you inside holding court? It's your big day, princess."

"It's too hot in there," she said, averting her face so he couldn't pin her with his eyes. "I needed some air."

"Right." Even without looking, she sensed his attention all over her. "You'll mess up your lovely dress."

"I don't care." Her palms felt sweaty, her face hot.

"And this fit of the vapors is because you're so happy at becoming Mrs. Bob-the-Builder, is it?" He moved a fraction closer. "Cursing and swearing a sign of marital bliss? I saw you, Rosie."

"You have got to go, Sam," she said, infuriated. "You shouldn't be here."

"You're so fucking happy that you're in the woods, banging your head on a tree?"

"I was not—" She stopped and met his stare. His gaze pushed into her, demanding the truth as always. The contemptuous smile wavered. His green-blue eyes were sad, intense, his expression grave. Almost stunned. Catching reflected light from her dress, Sam's face was luminous, like a sculpture of a heartbroken saint.

Rosie thought savagely to herself, *If he makes me cry in front of him, I'll kill him.*

"Sam, you can't be here. Just go."

"No." He took a step closer. Reaching out, he touched the hair on her left temple; she flinched. "Come on, Rosie. How long have we known each other? I know a panic attack when I see one. You're scared witless that you've made a mistake."

"How dare you?" She tried to sound outraged but couldn't force conviction into her shaking voice. "This, from the person who told me I'm dead inside? It only shows that you don't know me at all. I'm with Alastair. It's what I want."

"Bollocks," he said softly.

"No," she said, anger heating now. "I'm sorry if this has upset you, but you have to accept it."

Sam was quiet for a moment. He laughed under his breath. "What the hell is this about, Rosie? You don't love him. You think you can be Mrs. Normal? Mrs. Happy Human, with one-point-eight children and no strange bright blood in your veins? You think you can turn your back, pretend the Otherworld never touched you? Yeah, you can try, but you can't beat it. It'll reach out in the night and grab you right back. Who are you kidding, Rosie? This isn't what you want. It's what Matthew wants."

Her breath rushed in and out. She was fighting tears with all her strength. "I'm not listening to this. We had a few conversations across a prison table. That doesn't mean you know me, and it certainly doesn't constitute any kind of relationship." She made to move away but he braced one hand on the tree trunk, blocking her. The pleasant leathery fragrance of his jacket reached her, blended with whatever delicious cedarwood-scented potions he'd used, warmed by his body. His legs made folds in the thick silk of her skirts.

"Right, and it's not so easy to be civil without the protection of a table between us and guards all around?"

"I'm not scared of you!" He was right, though. In the safety of the visiting room, it had been possible to talk to him. By contrast, this was pure chaos, as their old encounters had been.

"I know," he said. "It's the truth that's scary, isn't it?"

They stared at each other, breathing hard. He was so close, hard and real as no one else had seemed real today; and the aphrodisiac scent of his body, clean, spicy and shockingly familiar, made her head swim. Then he let his arm drop. "Go on your merry way, then. Enjoy your new life. Congratulations. You need anything—a toaster, wineglasses?"

Rosie couldn't move. Horribly, she realized she didn't want to stop fighting with him. It was a hard, bright release from the pain.

"I'll prove you wrong," she said, lifting her face close to his. "You've spent your life putting me down, trying to control me. How's that make you any better than Matthew?"

"No," he said, frustrated. "Only because you're so far above me—I never meant—"

"I will prove you wrong," she said vehemently.

"Yeah?" He leaned defiantly closer. "Want to put money on it?"

Their faces were almost touching, tilted at just the right subtle angle to each other. He raised his hand to her cheekbone. She let him. His mouth was beautiful, she saw, the lower lip full and expressive.

"What color are his eyes?" Sam whispered.

"What?" Rosie frowned. "Er . . . sort of hazel."

"You had to think about it," he said, very low.

They stood there for a few moments. She felt her lips parting, her whole body softening. Doing absolutely nothing to end this. "If I could kiss you once," he whispered. "Just to say good-bye and have a nice life."

He hovered, as if waiting for consent, but she was already moving towards him, making the kiss her decision. As she felt the warm pressure of his lips between hers, she felt him shudder from head to foot with astonished delight. A hot wave went all through her, opening her up like an orchid. His mouth felt wonderful, like warm silk. She parted her lips, drew him deeper in, felt his tongue probing gently to touch hers.

Gods, they were kissing. A jolt of mild horror and disbelief went through her—*what the hell am I doing?*—but she couldn't stop.

A flood of madness took her. Anger, panic, hunger; it was all the same flow. The kiss intensified, and she curled her hand around his head, feeling the soft springiness of his hair; opening her mouth to him, consuming him. It was the best kiss she had ever tasted.

Sam leaned into her, his weight pressing her into the tree's smooth trunk. The pressure of his body was warm, slender and muscular. Her other hand strayed around the small of his back, feeling under his T-shirt until she could caress the bare heated flesh as she pulled him harder into her.

Now his mouth was moving over her neck; incredible sensation. She was lost. Honeycomb melting in flames. It was the first time she'd been truly in her body all day. At last, her true self, which had been a floating, detached observer, dropped back into its sheath and turned her into a column of rose-red fire.

And her body didn't care what her intellect wanted. Her hands clawed at his shoulders. Her lips caressed his neck and jaw. When she found his mouth again he uttered a groan and she felt his hardness through the layers of her dress, pressing into the crease of her hip with the ache of long-accumulated desire. His arousal melted her. She writhed and stroked him and tried to undo his belt. Nothing mattered but this. There was no way back.

His hand groped for the hem of her skirt, lifting what seemed yards of silk and net layers. It was awkward, frantic. They started laughing. Then he found her thighs, looked down and gasped, "Oh my god, white stockings," and he went on laughing and gasping with wonder against her throat, raising the hairs on her neck. He stroked her naked skin above the stocking tops, traveling upwards. His fingers played deliciously on the white lace thong she wore, then slid and played beneath it.

Rosie dimly knew that this was the worst thing she could possibly have chosen to do. Even as his fingertips chased the electric ripples of desire, she knew it. But she was past the point of no return. Sightless with desire, she couldn't see past the fulfilment of this wonderful, terrible dance . . .

Some dim flame of awareness was whispering to Sam, *This isn't how it should have been,* and he knew it was wrong, that he should stop, couldn't understand why she suddenly opened up and devoured him; but gods, this was *Rosie.* Might be all of her he ever had. She tasted wonderful. She was all around him, scented with rose and musk and jasmine; he felt her heat through the bodice of her dress and he wanted to tear it off so he could kiss her breasts and all of her; but he couldn't have everything. So little time. When his hand found her at last beneath what seemed yards of fabric, she cried out, responding, folding one leg around his hip. The feel of her was beyond his most lurid dreams.

He tasted her throat, caught the slight bitterness of perfume on his tongue, the smooth globes of her pearl necklace between his teeth. He found the texture of the long scar on her neck that was his fault; he licked it, wanting to kiss it away.

Her breathing now high and sharp, she unzipped his jeans, drew out the straining stem of flesh. Her touch brought him close to passing out. He couldn't wait. With the steady guidance of her fingers, he pressed into her incredible silken warmth and . . . oh gods, he was inside her. Inside Rosie.

She shuddered and trembled. Her breath flowed hot against his ear. There was a sort of anger between them; savagery, frustration, and this blood-hot urge all merging into a single molten force. And they poured it into each other. There was nowhere else for it to go.

Mouth open, Rosie felt Sam sliding into her, all the way in, gliding exquisitely over nerve endings, flesh enclosed in flesh; and yes, he was everything she'd secretly imagined, and it mattered, as sex with Alastair had never mattered; and it was sorcery, a living sorcerer's wand enchanting her, seducing her with the dark excitement of the one thing in all the world that she should not be doing . . .

She entered a sharp, wild plane of existence beyond the Dusklands. The sensations were so intense that she could no longer breathe. This deep, oiled and burning pressure was all she needed in the world. The faint thought came to her, *I've never had an Aetherial man before, he's the first . . .* and she felt herself cresting a magical wave as he moved convulsively into her.

The world swam and dissolved. Her awareness of his pleasure intensified her own beyond bearing. She saw colors. It seemed that Naamon, the realm of fire, was whirling around them, coalescing to a glittering diamond peak that left her straining and wordless with its intensity; then pulsing strongly outwards, ecstasy flowing like oil, curling and leaping as he gasped her name; then ebbing at last into delicious rainbow trails.

Release. Thank the gods.

Peace, just for a few seconds.

They stood holding on to each other, shaken and trembling, caught in a golden moment before reality set in. Sam sighed, "God, Rosie," against her neck. She only exhaled, openmouthed as the last trickles of pleasure faded. She clung for him for a moment; then remembered where she was.

Oh fuck. Oh hell, what was I thinking?

Within seconds, the chill stickiness of regret began. They were in a hideously undignified position, straddled against a tree trunk with her dress billowing around him like a meringue. Awkwardly they began the process of disentangling themselves and rearranging their clothing. Rosie tried to straighten the layers of her skirt with damp hands.

There were rows of curved creases that wouldn't shake out. Blood inflamed her face and she couldn't look at Sam. In a flash of horror she imagined all the wedding guests encircling them, beginning a slow handclap—she glanced around, but the woodlands were deserted. Shuddering, she wondered how she could avoid speaking to him and escape—preferably into a chasm in the ground.

"Are you all right?" he asked quietly.

"The dress isn't," Rosie snapped, shaking the hem.

"It's fine. Just a few leaves—" He brushed her hip. "That's it."

"Get off. I can manage."

She was aware of his silence as she went on fussing with the fabric. Then he said, "Run away with me, Rosie."

"What?" She straightened up. Sam was looking at her, his head tilted and the tip of his tongue touching his upper lip. His eyes glittered and his hair was in a spiky mess.

"I mean it. Come on. I've got a motorbike . . ."

"How unbelievably corny."

"Yeah, whatever." He glanced over his shoulder to indicate escape. "Please, let's just go."

He came close again but she put out her hands to ward him off. "Don't be ridiculous. I have to go back."

"To the reception?"

"Where else?" She began to walk but he came with her. "Don't follow me."

"Don't walk away!" Sam caught her shoulder. She knocked his hand aside but stopped, afraid he would follow her all the way back to the hall. Rosie was in shock; surely if anyone saw them together, they would know exactly what had happened and the world would end.

"What, Sam? You thought one moment of complete madness would make me abandon my marriage? I have to make it work!"

"Oh yeah, it's already working so well that you jump me and practically eat me alive? Not that I'm complaining, but what was that about?"

"I don't know!"

"Oh, I do," he said grimly. "It wasn't all one-sided, Rosie. You felt something."

"Disgust and revulsion."

"It's a start," he said. "So, does revulsion normally make you that hot?"

She took several deep breaths. The only way she could think of to make him go was to be ice-cold and cruel. He'd never give up otherwise. "Look, Sam, I've had too much to drink and an overload of emotion. It was a fit of nerves, that's all. Nothing happened, okay? Nothing happened."

He put his hands in his pockets. "Yeah, well, you can try and kid yourself—"

"You could have been anyone," she hissed. "Yes, all right, I panicked and did something unforgivably stupid. But you were just—a body."

At that, he recoiled. He looked at the ground and then at her again, eyes darkening. "You don't mean that."

"Oh, I do. You had no right to come here and—What the hell can I say to make you leave me alone?"

Sam's expression grew remote, withdrawing from her. She wondered, with a wisp of anxiety, what he might do in revenge. He asked levelly, "Are you really going to go and play the good wife, after what we've done?"

"I really am," she replied.

This time when she stepped away, he stood white-faced and let her go.

Rosie spent her honeymoon night in a hotel bed, listening to Alastair snoring. He'd been in no fit state for sex and she was relieved. His safe, friendly flesh seemed as lifeless as lard and she couldn't have responded if she'd wanted to. She hated herself for it. Would he have smelled Sam on her, realized that another man had spilled himself inside her, even after she'd half-drowned herself in the shower?

Random images of the day clamored in her mind. Talking to Lucas as she painted her nails this morning, feeling calm and certain that she was taking the right path—it seemed centuries ago. Jessica and Auberon slow-dancing, blissfully content in each other's embrace. Aunt Phyllida, merry and flirting with the Scottish party. Her uncle Comyn, watching everything and everyone, watching all the time like a raptor.

And after she'd made her flustered return to the reception . . . The glowing faces of her family, especially Matthew with Faith on his arm like a kitten . . . Rosie frantically smiling back, feeling that she must be red-faced and wild-haired with guilt. When she caught a glimpse of her reflection in a huge gilt mirror, she couldn't believe how composed she looked. Surely she was staring at someone else.

Not at a bride who had just run out and shagged another man.

It was one thing she could never confess to anyone, not even Mel. She couldn't believe she'd done it, let alone understand what had possessed her.

Sam was right. Her marriage was a hopeless act of desperation. She hated him for being right.

No, Sam was wrong. She could create a life and be happy; not like Jon, obsessed with the unobtainable, not like Faith in her doormat devotion. Open-eyed, clearheaded, she'd made a sensible choice to live in harmony with the human world, and who the hell was Sam to come along and say she couldn't?

Alastair was solid, kind and faithful. He didn't deserve this. Sam was—what? A force for chaos. He was untrustworthy, and to Rosie, there was nothing worse. There was something twisted in him, an abyss in his soul. The Wilders all had that black hole inside, Lawrence and Jon and Sam; and in each it was of an interestingly different kind, but in all of them it was there.

Rosie lay seething. Sam couldn't simply send a card with good wishes, oh no; he couldn't concede graceful defeat and let her go. No, he had to lie in wait and sabotage her life in the worst possible way. That was not gracious. That was selfish and destructive. Sam existed only to disrupt her life and then stand gloating.

Then she turned the beam of anger on herself. If Sam had behaved disgracefully, so had she. *I started it,* she thought, not him. *Be honest. I knew exactly what I was doing. What's the worst thing you can do on your wedding day, short of stabbing an in-law? And what made me rush out and do it?*

"You're so good, Rosie," she heard voices saying. Even Jon had said it. *"You're an angel."*

No, I'm not.

I'm wicked. I'm scum.

She looked at the shape of her husband's back in the darkness. He slept unknowing, oblivious of what he'd married. Shame consumed her. She wondered, was this how Mum felt, after she slept with Lawrence?

No, this is nothing like that. It was a moment of insanity. A mistake, and it's over.

Yet when she closed her eyes, it was not Alastair's kind, freckled face she saw as they made their vows. No, all she saw was Sam. All she felt was his hot mouth on her, the wonderful pressure of his hands and his narrow hips between hers. Remembering, she sighed and turned restlessly. Ah, the searing thrill of him inside her.

"I'm so happy, Rosie," Alastair had said as they danced, his guileless face shining. "Finally found the place I belong."

When she slept at last, she dreamed she was running across an open mountainside with a shadow figure beside her. She knew it was Sam, and they were racing together like wolves through a bright rainstorm. The dream was distorted, as if projected onto an oblique screen, and it glistened with shadow and light all night long.

12

Queen of Fire

Lucas walked across High Warrens, where sedimentary rocks pushed out of the bracken and the lower slopes were thick with oak and sweet chestnut. He'd often come here with Jon. It was their place.

He followed a path through the trees into a hidden glen, with a steep horseshoe-shaped slope on one side, a dry stone wall with birches and brambles on the other. It was late November, a soft misty day gilded by weak sunlight. Rags of leaves clung to the branches, making a web of yellow and russet lace.

He saw a spectral figure halfway up the slope. It appeared to bend and flow over gnarled roots, around fallen logs encrusted with fungus. Lucas felt reality shift into the Dusklands. He never knew how he made the transition, since it was as natural as walking. A veil rippled away. The light turned royal blue, trees and shrubs shone ultraviolet. The specter solidified into Jon.

Seeing him, Jon straightened up and waved. Over skinny jeans, he was wearing a brown velvet jacket that he'd owned for years, and there was an old-fashioned wicker shopping basket on his arm. "Finally," said Jon. "Where the hell have you been?" He stood smiling, hair blowing around his shoulders, as Lucas climbed up towards him. He looked ethereal, like a beautiful consumptive. "I thought you weren't speaking to me."

"I'm not," Lucas retorted.

"Why were you looking for me, then?"

"I wasn't."

Jon nodded. "So you're not looking for me in a place we always used to hang out together?"

Lucas sighed, looking at his trainers, trying not to smile because it felt like betraying Rosie. "Okay, I hoped I'd find you. Thought it was time we made peace."

"Fine by me. I never understood why we fell out in the first place."

"I think you do," said Lucas. "Rosie found out about the dealing."

"It was only a few mushrooms!" Jon rolled his eyes. "I don't know why everyone gets so agitated about it." He began to climb slowly again, searching the wet grass.

"And the rest," said Lucas, following him. "It drew the very worst kind of people around us until Sam ended up in jail over it."

Jon glared sideways at him. "Whenever someone attacks us, Sam loses it. He always goes too far, but that's not actually my fault. You know how bad I felt."

"Well, I had to get away from that scene. So should you."

"I have," Jon said icily.

"Look, she's my sister. She didn't forbid me to see you, but if I had, she'd have been really hurt. I stayed away because I love her, not because I don't like you."

"So why are you here now?"

Lucas kicked at a loose stone and a finger-sized elemental fled from underneath with a tiny shout of anger. "Oops. Must remember not to do that in the Dusklands."

"Don't change the subject. Why?"

"Furor's died down. I missed you." He tried a smile. Jon put down his basket and wrapped slim arms around him. Startled, Lucas hugged him back. Jon stroked his hair, slid his hands to hold Lucas's face between his palms. They kissed each other lightly on cheeks and lips.

"I missed you too," said Jon. "Here, carry this while I harvest." He pushed the basket at Luc. It was heavy, containing a stone pestle and mortar beneath a collection of blood red fungus and fat seedcases. An earthy scent rose from them. Jon resumed his search, squeezing berries between his fingers. "How is Rosie, by the way?"

"She's great," said Lucas. "All happily married. Went on honeymoon in Italy for two weeks, came home and moved into her brand-new Fox Home in Ashvale. And she's set up a whole new department for Dad, Fox Landscapes. She's really happy."

"That's good." Jon smiled. Eerie light reflected off his face, smoothing shadows and making him look as spellbinding as the night he'd first offered Lucas the dream agaric. "So that's why you're here. Rosie's not in your hair anymore, telling you what a bad person I am."

Lucas felt sudden anger. "I'm here because I want to be. I needed time to think. Your whole answer to Sam's situation was to drag me off to get so stoned that I lost three years of my life. I just want to know why."

Jon gave him a pained look. "I went off the rails, okay? I didn't expect the Spanish bloody Inquisition."

"It's not. You don't look like you're back on the rails yet."

Jon dragged a hand through his hair. "Well, try having someone stabbed on your carpet and your brother taken away for it, and your stepmother—it was a bad time and I couldn't deal with it. That's all. It's over."

"Really?"

"Yes. Sam's back, life at Stonegate is no more crappy than usual. I'm fine."

"You don't look it. You're still using, aren't you?"

"For fuck's sake don't go moral on me, Luc. Nothing I harvest or sell is illegal. Botanists couldn't even identify it." His face came closer to Luc's. "Their petty human standards don't apply to us."

"It's not about morals," Lucas retorted. "When we were in Nottingham, we were so busy and creative, weren't we, saving the world? Only we weren't. All we actually did was get high."

"You didn't have a problem with it at the time."

"Obviously I should have."

"That's why you abandoned me?"

"You were destroying yourself! I didn't have the sense to see it. Now it looks like you're doing a great job of messing up without any help from me. You look like hell."

Jon stared at him, eyes turning hard and glittery. Lucas expected to be told to fuck off. Instead, Jon seemed to collapse inside.

"I thought you understood." Turning, he sat on a mound of grass, facing down into the glade. He leaned his elbows on his knees, utterly dejected. "There's been so much crap in my life. College was a farce; I'm no artist. You can bluff your way through, but my heart wasn't in it."

"Why did you go, then?" Lucas sat down beside him.

"I thought art might be another way into the Spiral, you know? But it didn't happen." Jon was so wretched, heartbroken almost, that Lucas softened. "You've got your music but I've got nothing; can't paint, write, play an instrument, any of the things I dreamed of. Even my songs were shit."

"That's not true."

"Don't you understand that the purpose of blackdrop is to make the pain go away? You don't need it like I do, because you're a sane and happy soul, and that's why I love you. I know it's wrong but I need it, just to feel I'm floating in Elysion—and to lose the fear that I'll never, ever, go there in reality. I don't blame you for walking away."

"It wasn't just that," Lucas said softly. He finally let the words out, low and hesitant, "Rosie and I saw you kissing Sapphire."

Jon's head snapped up. He looked haggard. "Uh," he breathed. Lucas had never before seen him so plainly, viscerally shocked.

"It broke Rosie's heart. That's why I left with her."

"Oh my god." Panic entered his voice. "You haven't told anyone, have you?"

"Of course not. Jon, er . . . Was it really what it looked like?"

"Oh." Jon leaned on one hand, rubbing distractedly at his forehead. After a few seconds he said, "Yes, I've been fucking my stepmother, what about it?"

Lucas sat gaping at him.

Eventually he managed to say, "That doesn't sound like the best idea in the world." After another minute, "I know she's attractive, but *she's your stepmother.*" And eventually, weakly, "Why?"

"I don't know," Jon sighed, putting his head in both hands. "She was having trouble with Lawrence. Obviously didn't realize what a cantankerous devil she was marrying. She wanted to get back at him with a nasty little secret and I was something she could control. I was too young to understand that at the time. I was sixteen when she started on me. I honestly didn't want to, I was terrified of her. But she's so persuasive, and . . . dominant. And she was always so kind and warm to me, you know? I didn't want to lose that. I was confused. So I sort of let it happen and then I didn't know how to make it stop."

"Did you try saying no?"

"Yes, later, but somehow she'd always talk me round, find reasons to carry on. 'I'll tell Lawrence about this or that, we're in too deep,' and so on."

"Christ, Jon." Lucas was almost gasping for breath. "*Sixteen?* But that's . . . when you first came to our school . . . when Rosie got a crush on you . . ."

"I know, it's sick, isn't it?" Jon gave a ghostly grin.

"But that's like nine years . . ."

"Oh, it only happened occasionally, like if she was mad with my father and needed a whipping boy. Not that she literally whipped me . . ."

"Stop!" Lucas exclaimed. "Too much information."

"Yeah, well, who the hell can I tell, if not you?"

"As long as I can get my memory wiped afterwards." Lucas pulled an expressive face. "But surely you could have stopped it by now? You're an adult. You don't have to keep going home. What, are you enjoying it too much?"

Jon grimaced. "That's the problem, isn't it. It's complicated."

"Do you love her?" Lucas asked, frowning.

Jon's voice came softly out of the twilight. "I sort of love her, and I sort of hate her. I always knew it was wrong, worse than wrong, disgusting actually, but your body's got other ideas . . . so the disgust and the pleasure get mixed up until you can't tell them apart. I hated her so much but I was entranced. I could never bring myself to touch her, really, but that's what she liked; a boy to lie there like a sacrifice while she enjoyed herself. It was vile but it was exciting . . . afterwards you feel contaminated. The pleasure isn't worth it and the revulsion is way off the scale. No, I can't let it happen anymore."

He sat chewing his lower lip, eyes blank. Lucas said, "You need to find someone else."

"I've tried." Jon gave a soft laugh. "I slept with Mel once and I didn't know what to do, because I was so used to Sapphire . . . using me. Hopeless, isn't it?"

"I don't know what to say."

"Well, now you know why I was always hiding in Nottingham and permanently stoned. D'you remember, when we had the band, we'd wake up with strange girls in the house and I couldn't even remember if we'd done anything with them? I couldn't wait to boot them out so I could just be with you."

"And get stoned again," Luc said dryly.

"With Mel, it wasn't what I'd hoped for at all," Jon said

sadly. "I thought she could rescue me, but she couldn't. It would never have worked in a thousand years. She wouldn't wipe her shoes on me."

"Yeah, you are kind of chalk and cheese . . ."

Jon grinned bitterly. "Drugs are better than sex, any day. The pleasure lasts longer, and they never complain that you haven't phoned them."

"The sad thing is that you mean it," said Lucas. "Plus it's incredibly hard to find a girlfriend while you're either hallucinating or unconscious. Thanks for that."

Jon reached out to touch his cheek. "You never did a single thing with me that you didn't want to, Luc." He let his hand fall. "What finished me is Sapphire's quest for Aetherial enlightenment. It's like she's trying to soak it out of me. Everything precious I shared with you, she inflicted this hideous parody on me. But I humor her, because every time I say no, she threatens to tell Lawrence."

"But how could she tell him? She'd ruin herself as well as you."

He exhaled, shivering. "Because she's fearless, and I've got more to lose. She can easily get another husband, she says. I can never get another father."

Jon rose to his feet and began to hunt plants again, a rangy silhouette in the blue dark. Lucas went after him. "Jon," he said. "We're still brothers, aren't we? We can be strong together."

Jon halted and fixed him with intense, demanding eyes. "I need you more than ever, Luc. I wish you hadn't left when we were so close to unlocking the Gates."

"We were never close!" Lucas exclaimed. "All we had were hallucinations. We never got one millimeter into the Gates."

"That's not true," Jon said. "Your visions were genuine. Is that why you stopped—because you were scared?"

"I'm not scared! Only I think Matthew's right, we should let it rest. It's not meant to be."

Jon's eyes glowed chestnut, almost red in the eerie light. "I can't believe you feel that. This is what's wrong with everyone! Tangling themselves up with the surface world, marriages, businesses, instead of concentrating on what truly matters. Your uncle Comyn is right. Unlocking the Otherworld is the only thing that can save us!"

He spoke so passionately that Lucas lost his own conviction. What if Jon was right? He tried a different view of the world in which Matthew, Auberon, Rosie, even Lawrence were walking around in a dream because Elysion was lost, while only Jon and Comyn were keeping the flame alive. The idea was frightening enough to be real.

Jon went on, "Imagine you've been looking through gates into the most beautiful garden, and all your life you've been promised that you'll go inside one day . . . Then, when it's time, they turn around and say oh, sorry, we forgot to mention there are wolves and lions loose so you can't go in after all. Ever. We can't let them do that to us." He rested his hand on Luc's shoulder. "We can't let them kill the dream."

"But we tried and failed."

"No. We haven't started yet. With the Gates open, everything can be healed. You said it—we're brothers, strong together. Are you with me?"

Lucas felt the world pulling out of shape. He loved Jon, needed to believe him, wanted with all his heart to rescue him. And Jon's passion was as persuasive as ever, netting him with enchantment. "Yes, completely," Luc said with a sigh. "You don't have to ask."

"I'm useless without you. Now you're here, we can achieve wonders."

The twilight thickened, and pairs of luminous eyes gleamed down from the branches. Eventually Lucas asked, "What are you looking for?"

"A little sign saying 'Eat Me,'" Jon answered. "Shush." As the slope began to flatten near the top, there was a hollow where the grass grew thick with wild plants. "Ah," said Jon. "Here it is."

He bent to a plant and lifted drooping berries. It resembled deadly nightshade, but this was larger than life, the stem glowing with its own pale green light and berries bulging like blood clots.

"Every plant in the Dusklands will bring dreams of some kind. I found this a few months ago. It's called night splinter, for the blaze of light when the darkness splits open. By the way, when you harvest something, always remember to thank it." Plucking berries, he murmured, "Forgive me, mistress, for taking your fruit. In thanks I'll scatter some for the seeds to grow."

"How the hell do you know all this?"

Jon shrugged. "It's basic Aetherial herbal knowledge. Of course, they don't want us to know, any more than human parents show their children how to grow cannabis."

"Have you tried it?"

The berries clustering tenderly in Jon's palm were black, with a dusting of blue that fluoresced in the twilight. "I wouldn't give you anything I hadn't tried. This, combined with devil's nightcap—it's the key, I'm sure." Jon's conviction shone out of him, contagious. "Do you trust me? Will you try for me?"

Once more, Lucas was snared by the terrifying, irresistible thrill of the unknown. He looked into Jon's eyes and said, "When do you want to do it?"

Jon gave him a look of gratitude and faith that made his heart swell. "Now, if you like."

The blue of the Dusklands faded to lemon-streaked grey and the sharp, surface world breeze blew over them as Jon led the way downhill. On the floor of the glade, Jon sat on a broad tree stump, took the basket from Luc and brought out the pestle and mortar. In went the berries and a scrap of bruise-colored fungus.

"Grinding it first brings out the full potency." Jon began to work the pestle, creating a blue-black foaming mush. Lucas sat cross-legged on the grass in front of him, entranced. "Break down the cell walls, crack the seeds, squeeze out the sap." He grinned. "This is the one thing I'm good at. Okay, I can't sing or write and I faked my way through art college."

Lucas watched the swing of Jon's hair as he worked, the strange crimson flash of his eyes. Meanwhile, his own hands wove a pentagram of twigs, the points symbolizing earth, air, fire, water and ether in balance; a token of intention. Through it he wove a spiral of ivy. He felt cold to the core.

"But this is instinct," Jon went on. "I could be a purveyor of designer cocktails to the adventurous. I could be as rich as my father." He tipped the mush into a tea strainer, then forced it through with the pestle until a few teaspoons of thick inky liquid had dripped back into the mortar.

He held it out like an altar cup to Lucas. "If you take it now, it will be working by the time we reach Freya's Crown."

"Aren't you going to—?"

Jon shook his head. He dipped a fingertip in the juice and sucked it clean, a token. "One of us has to keep watch."

Lucas took the mortar. A rim of lilac bubbles clung around the sludge. He remembered the first time Jon had fed him dream agaric, and his stomach twisted. Fear of being poisoned gripped him, but he pushed it away. He raised the cup to his lips and swallowed.

It tasted of blueberries and bitter almonds.

He stood up. Joining hands they walked together, Lucas looking up through the trees and waiting for the darkness to split open.

"I'm so glad you're here," Jon whispered, leaning over to kiss him on the mouth. "Everything will be all right now."

Lucas found himself alone at Freya's Crown. The bluish light of the Dusklands saturated the landscape. He knew Jon was there, but couldn't see him. A panicky chill ran through him.

The outcrop towered like a cliff face. It crawled with runes that whispered to him. The sound was silver and tasted sweet, like mint. The world dissolved; he was suddenly inside a fissure, looking out at a woodland glade. A doe looked back at him. Her coat was creamy-beige, her head delicate with huge dark eyes. As Lucas went unsteadily towards her, she turned and trotted away. He followed.

She led him deep into the greenwood until they came to a pool. There she dipped her head to the water, drank, and changed shape. Now she was a girl sitting on the ground in a billow of cream fur. Her face was heart-shaped, young and sweet. Her eyes, like the doe's, were completely black. "Let me show you our story," she said.

As she spoke, Lucas turned dizzy. Her words became a spell, a summons into a chaotic nightmare. The world swam horribly around him and he saw volcanoes erupting from the earth, the mountains rolling like the sea . . . He found himself on a desert plain beneath a mountain, the landscape burning with sunset colors. He saw the troops of Naamon pouring across the bright sand with hair of flame, armor of scarlet and gold. The sides of their chariots bore stylized designs, lynx, salamander, phoenix. And waiting to engage them were the rebels of Melusiel, the realm of water. Glittering silver and palest blue, greenish and slender, they were fluidly soft, too few to withstand the onslaught . . .

The end of Queen Malikala's empire, the doe girl's voice told him without words. And he was caught in it. The ground boomed like a drum. Lucas's face burned with raging heat. Sand flew into his eyes and he cried out, choking. Flaming arrows began to fly. The watery Aelyr were crying out, falling, defenseless.

High on the mountainside stood the Melusian sorceress Jeleel, Queen of Water—a column of pale iridescence. Her hair rippled with ropes of pearl and seaweed. She struck the mountain with the heel of her silver staff, and from it flowed a spring . . .

Lucas saw the staff strike, saw the glassy trickle burst from the rock. In seconds the spring became a torrent, a river in full flow. Paralyzed, he watched the foaming current thundering past him.

The deluge crashed into the Queen of Fire's army and swept them away. Their lethal lines broke up into a panicking mass of horses, broken chariots, drowning men. Suddenly Malikala herself was there in front of him, real as life and aiming a flame-tipped arrow at his heart.

She looked far from human, her head and body that of a crested dragon, her armor glowing like lava. Her eyes were golden ice, but the scaled body beneath the armor was blue-black obsidian. Unleashing all the anguish of her defeat upon Lucas, she let the arrow fly. From short range, it thudded into his breastbone, flinging him backwards into the deluge. The wound burned, a ferocious circle of acid. Water roared in his ears and he flailed, forced deeper and deeper. He was carried off, drowning.

When his head broke water, he glimpsed drenched and struggling fire warriors in the torrent around him. The excruciating pain in his chest made breathing impossible.

A shape grazed the edge of his vision. He looked up.

There were boats in the sky.

A flotilla of long, flat-bottomed boats with curved prows drifted overhead. Soldiers of Naamon were being lifted out of the water on ropes, rising to safety like spiders on silk. The boats bore the hawk emblems of Sibeyla, realm of air; Malikala's allies . . .

There was a boat directly above Lucas. A rope unfurled towards him. Choking, fighting the swift tumble of the current, he reached up, gripped the rope and began to climb. It was a slow, hard ascent. The arrow had vanished from his chest, but the wound throbbed, making each movement agony. The rope shook and swayed. The boat began to fly and the wind buffeted him.

All elements must act in balance, like the five points of a star, came the doe girl's soft voice. *When they quarrel, the storms rage on for centuries . . .*

As he drew nearer to the boat he saw his rescuers; four tall, slender, muscular men, naked to the waist. They had the heads of birds. Long curved beaks, blue feathers, proud eyes. *Eyes like Lawrence,* he thought. They were all avatars of Lawrence, unfeeling deities. He hung below the boat, unable to climb farther. They made no move to help him.

He glanced below and saw the flooded desert dwindling into gloom. He was alone with the bird-headed gods.

The boat began to fly at speed. He clung to the rope, feeling the prickle of ice on his skin, the ache of trembling muscles, the shaft of pain through his breast. Vast landscapes yawned and tilted below him. Sulfurous volcanoes, glaciers, mountains dropping into immeasurable valleys. A plain of lakes, rolling into violet and blue infinity.

It was beautiful beyond words, terrifying beyond comprehension.

They passed over a city carved entirely of black onyx. He saw graceful, not-quite-human beings, extravagantly dressed, gliding through the fantastical streets, untouched by the distant battle . . .

The rope jerked. From the boat, a face thrust itself down at him, almost touching his: an elongated demon face, bony, white and hard as arctic ice. It had bright blue eyes and a bright blue gem in the center of its forehead. Lines of frost ran from the ends of the fingertips, crackling all through the Spiral to the Earth, freezing and fracturing everything.

He realized that the rope to which he clung was the creature's own snow-white hair, plaited.

"Do you know what your father has unleashed?" said the frost demon.

Lucas looked down and saw a vast fire creature, the size of a mountain, breathing flame and hot gas—trailing a shadow ten times its size, which swirled like a great tornado. *The fire is Qesoth, the beginning, and the shadow is Brawth, the ending,* murmured the doe girl. *The Shadow was there at the start of time and will return to end time itself, tearing apart all Aetherial life with no more thought than a hurricane.*

"Is this what you want to happen?" said the frozen face above him. "Let Vaeth and Spiral remain separate. Let the Great Gates be sealed, a flood barrier. Otherwise . . ."

Lucas writhed and protested, but no sound came out of him. There was nothing he could do to end the vision. He could not shut his eyes against it. He saw everyone he knew standing in its path—his beloved sister, his parents, everyone—oblivious. Only at the last moment did they see the shadow boiling towards them—falling in horror as it pierced each skull with a spear of burning-black ice.

A structure loomed, so immense he did not recognize it as a tree until they were swooping between branches, each of which was the arm of a nebula. Lucas couldn't breathe. Then they were beyond the Tree of Life, and now there was nothing left except the darkness that contained it . . .

The Abyss.

Lucas looked down and screamed.

Two chasm walls filled the universe, one flowing with ice and the opposite with lava. Between them, blackness yawned and dropped forever.

The blackness was oblivion, the end of all things. Yet it held more; a soup of stars and gas and dark matter. At the same time it was a sentient beast with a shape. He saw it rising, saw the bulk of its great shoulders and head blotting out the stars. Cosmic terror overwhelmed him. *Brawth*.

Impassive, the frost demon in the boat leaned down and, with the slash of a fingernail, cut the rope of its own hair.

Lucas began to fall.

He flailed, spread-eagled on the darkness, mouth wide, screaming.

The Abyss did not care. It swallowed him and he fell and fell forever.

13

❦

Over the Threshold

He was screaming and screaming, but his throat would make no sound.

Someone was holding him. Patterns whirled around him, black and white.

"Lucas! For fuck's sake! Calm down. You're okay. I'm here, I've got you."

He heard the words but couldn't understand them. The hole in his chest became the burning chasm through which he was falling. The world had broken into shards of ice that tumbled through the Abyss with him, and it was all his doing. "I broke it," he gasped. "The ice giant is coming."

"Luc, you're all right. You're having a bad trip."

He saw Jon in front of him, like a wraith, all bones and eyes. Lucas flinched backwards, warding off the apparition with outstretched hands. Jon's voice was far away, murmuring without meaning, while worlds shattered around him.

Time jumped. The voice became suddenly clear, sounding tired and desperate. "Come on, Luc, you're safe. Can you hear me? Listen to me, Luc, please."

"Where are we?"

Jon sighed in relief at his response. "Dumannios. Hold on, try to relax so I can take us back."

"I can't. It's all broken." He clawed at the fire in his chest.

"Take this." Jon held a bottle to his lips. It was blue and ridged, like an apothecary's poison bottle. A syrupy, bitter liquid went down his throat.

"Why are you giving me cough mixture?" said Lucas.

Jon laughed. "It's tincture of blackdrop. Wonderful stuff, calm you right down. Are you with me now?"

"They cut the rope," Lucas said, feeling this would explain everything.

Then the world seemed to stop, and pulse, and wash away into a glorious warm light. Lucas felt his heart beating slow and heavy, like the heart of the Earth. The pain of his wound eased to throbbing soreness. The light, softening to blue, entranced him.

"We're in the Dusklands again," said Jon. "You really scared me. What did you see?"

"I don't know. Everything. Terrible."

"Tell me."

Lucas tried. "The doe told the story, but it was real. The white demon cut the rope—he was in the boat with the gods. They were bird-heads like Lawrence."

"You're making absolutely no sense," Jon said gently. He began to craft a joint, shaving blackdrop resin along its length.

Lucas took a deep breath. He felt distant from the terror but it was still there, a motionless shape in the corner of his vision. "I fell into the Abyss. That's why I was screaming." He rubbed at his breastbone, wincing as he found a tear in his T-shirt and raw flesh underneath.

Jon looked up, frowning. "God, Luc, what *is* that?"

Lucas pulled his coat open and raised his T-shirt. On the breastbone was a red-raw circle, two inches across. To his distorted senses it seemed a bomb crater. "I don't know. It's as sore as hell."

"It's only on the skin. How did you get it?"

"Malikala shot me." He laughed. "No. That's crazy. I must have fallen over. I—I saw the rebellion of Jeleel against Malikala, like I was actually there . . ."

Jon was staring intently at him. "You really went through," he said, soft with awe. "It worked. Next time, if we get the dose right—"

"No, no." Lucas felt rising panic. "Never again."

"I don't mean now." Jon lit the joint, took a drag and offered it. "Let's chill and talk it over."

Lucas, who rarely lost his temper, became violently angry. From the burnout of drugs or fear, he didn't know. He struck the joint out of Jon's hand. "Are you trying to fucking kill me?"

"What?" Jon flinched back, astonished.

"Keep it all away from me! I've had enough." He pointed wildly at the rocks of Freya's Crown. "Your father's right. There's something terrible in there. If we disturb it, we could all die—the world could end!"

Alarmed, Jon raised both hands as if to calm a startled horse. "Luc, cool down."

"Am I still not making sense? Lawrence knows what he's doing! There's some appalling force behind the Gates. I don't know what the hell it is, but the Gates keep it still, like a dam. If he opens them, it will wake and surge out like a flood. He was right to lock them. He had no choice. Are you satisfied?"

Jon stared at him. In the silence, Lucas looked up and saw the Gates in their true form, a great, raw monolith. All his rage and emotion rushed out like fire and hit the stone. He couldn't stop it. The ground trembled. He saw flame running over the surface like ignited petrol, runes flashing in its wake. He felt heavy segments of rock grinding against each other, shifting an inch or two before juddering to a halt. He saw a thin dark split down the rock face that wasn't there before.

Lucas held his breath, trying to grasp what he'd experienced. Hallucination. He closed his eyes and when he opened them, the crag had returned to its usual self. It contained not one crack but hundreds along its sheared planes.

They were in the surface world. A colorless, dewy dawn.

Jon hadn't noticed anything; all his attention was on Lucas. "I wasn't trying to poison you," Jon said, reaching out to clasp his arm. "You know that, don't you?"

"Yeah. I'm shaken up."

"I see that," Jon began, but his voice was drowned. A

towering, raging figure came out of nowhere, his overcoat flapping like crow's wings.

"What are you doing? *What the hell have you done?*"

Lawrence.

Intent on each other, they hadn't seen their father storming up the hill. The shock reawakened Lucas's terror and sent it spiraling like a flock of birds. Lawrence seized them both by the scruff of the collar, like boys caught thieving, lifting them almost off their feet. Then he threw them hard onto the ground.

Lucas's drugged heart stumbled, refusing to keep up with his panic. He was in the Abyss again, drowning in nightmares. "Who would dare to interfere with the Gates?" Lawrence ranted above him. "After all I've said, all my warnings. *How dare you?*"

"We haven't done anything," came Jon's voice, high with alarm. "Dad, honestly—we were only talking."

"Don't lie to me! What were you doing here?"

Lucas climbed to his feet, saw Lawrence hauling Jon up by his jacket lapels, clutching handfuls of his Indian shirt with them. Jon stared sideways at Lucas, eyes huge and pleading. "Dad, we were only—"

Lawrence's face was frozen stone, as furious and heartless as the frost demon or the giant in the Abyss. "What's the matter with you? Are you drunk, or drugged?" He shook Jon. "You reek of smoke. You think it's a game to come here and weave your foolish twig tokens? Did you actually think you could go through? *How dare you try, how dare you even think of it?* You're going to tell me everything and, by the gods, you're going to be sorry you disobeyed me and set foot on this sacred place." Lawrence's head swiveled slowly to take in Lucas. "Both of you."

His expression was the most horrifying thing Lucas had ever seen. He began to back away, stumbling on the rough ground. The growing impulse flared. His nerve broke and, in blind panic, he turned and fled.

———

The house was a wedding gift from Auberon. A perfect three-bedroom detached Fox Home on the edge of Ashvale. With a small garden front and back, it was set on a curving road arranged to capture the feel of a charming old village. Ideal start to a new life.

Rosie knew she was spoiled rotten. Other couples struggled for years to afford the most basic home. She felt guilty that she couldn't love it.

Each day she drove to the office with Alastair and worked between him and Matthew under Auberon's benevolent eye. It was a pleasant life and she drifted through it as if sedated. She felt cocooned between husband and brother; simply letting it happen because it was so safe and warm.

Sometimes too warm. Hot, stifling. She was struggling to burst out of a too-tight skin; but when she looked for the cause of her distress, the world was serenely ordinary. No one was imprisoning her. She was free to walk out of the door and see anyone she chose at any time. Then she'd wonder if she was going insane.

Most weeks she was on site, working on the gardens she'd designed. That was her escape. Yet she never touched the Dusklands while landscaping these new, bare plots of earth. She'd walked along golden beaches with Alastair, soporific with heat, and never sensed the Dusklands there, either. They were closed, gone, as if she'd become human; and the worst thing was that she couldn't talk to Alastair about it, couldn't turn to him and say, "Is it me, or do you feel it too?"

On honeymoon she had longed for home, but when they came back, it seemed the Dusklands had turned sideways like a sheet of paper, folded away and vanished.

Married to a human, banished from the faerie realm? That was how it felt.

Alone in the new house, she would walk around searching for a taste or scent of the Dusklands, for hidden rooms to appear as they did at Oakholme, for her secret tree and mystical fiery lights. The rooms, however, stayed solid and prosaic, as though sneering at her search. She couldn't bring herself to decorate the plain white walls. That would feel like surrendering to the house.

Alastair, of course, was oblivious. She knew that if he became aware of her behavior, he would quite reasonably think she'd gone mad.

There was almost a hint of Dumannios in the atmosphere . . . not even that, because Dumannios at least had a malign energy. This house had nothing. It was dead.

And then, one Saturday morning, she realized what was wrong.

"Can you feel it, Dad?" She'd asked Auberon to come round while Alastair was at rugby practice. "Or rather, not feel it?"

At work he was very much the boss in his suit; but today, in causal trousers and earth-brown sweater, he was her father again. She followed as he went from room to room, pausing in each one to consider the atmosphere. At least he was taking her seriously. He looked carefully over the whole house, then said, "Any chance of a coffee?"

As they sat together in the small bright kitchen, Auberon asked, "Well, what do you feel is the problem?"

"I don't want you think I'm ungrateful," she said hurriedly. "It's not that at all; we like the house, it's great. But Dad, people buy Fox Homes because they walk in and it feels like home. That's your magic. You bring the earthly, homely part of the Otherworld into the building, and even humans feel it and fall in love. But it's not here. It's because the Gates are closed, isn't it? The magic's failing."

He put his large hand over hers. "Don't worry, I'm not about to go out of business." He smiled, but his eyes were serious. "Selling houses isn't sorcery. It's all about design and materials. We mimic that feel for human buyers, it's true, and they fall for it, but I can't create actual magic for them. Rosie, are you sure it's the house?"

"How do you mean?"

"This is all new for you, love. It's only been two months. It's bound to take time to settle in."

"Of course," she said. "I miss Oakholme. I took the Dusklands for granted. It didn't matter that the actual Gates were closed, because I couldn't miss the deeper realms if I'd never been there."

Auberon nodded. He was the one person who made her feel safe without stifling her. "But we bring the Dusklands in ourselves," he answered. "I can't build them into a house, love; either they seep in or they don't, rather like a stray cat sensing where it's welcome."

She took a sip of her coffee. "So a human in the house might be a barrier?"

"Perhaps. An Aetherial might be, too, if she was unhappy. Rosie, is anything bothering you?"

"No! No. Dad . . ." She caught a breath and was on the point of spilling it all out.

That nothing felt right and she'd made a mistake, living with Alastair was like rubbing along with a friend, comfortable enough but that didn't mean you wanted to live and sleep and eat and work with them and because her life was so perfect on the surface, she had nothing to struggle against and that made her feel trapped and if she loved Alastair why was she so numb and indifferent to everything, why was she sleepwalking through what should have been her life . . .

"Dad, I, er . . ."

The phone rang, making her jump. She went to answer it and Faith was on the other end, sounding nervous and too cheerful, as she did when something was wrong. "Rosie, can we meet up sometime? I can't tell you on the phone . . ."

"Course, what is it?"

A soft sigh. "About Matt . . . I don't know . . ."

"Is he okay? Is it urgent? Only Dad's here and . . ."

"No, no, not urgent at all. I just need to talk something over. It doesn't matter, really."

"Yes, it does," Rosie said firmly. "I'll call you back later, okay?"

When she returned to Auberon, the moment for confession had passed. "Sorry, Dad," she said. "It's just . . . I can't stop thinking that we should have paid you for the house. You're too generous."

"Nonsense. If I can't give my daughter a gift, what can I do? Let's hear no more about it." He patted her shoulder. "Give yourself time to settle in, Rosie. And any problems, don't hesitate."

After Auberon had left, she headed towards the phone, meaning to call Faith back. Just as she touched the receiver, someone knocked at the front door. She opened it, and Lucas came spilling through like a wraith.

He was dressed completely in black with a long overcoat pulled around him. Underneath it he was hunched and shivering like a man caught in a storm. "Luc?" she said. "What's up?"

"I need to talk to you." He looked jumpy, haggard and exhausted.

"Come in, come in." She closed the door and pulled him into the front room, all thoughts of Faith flying out of her mind. "Dad was here a minute ago . . ."

"I know. I waited until he'd gone. He can't hear this." He collapsed on the sofa.

"Why not? You look awful." Suspicion flared. "Have you been with Jon?"

"We've had a massive row with Lawrence, Jon and me. He's going to kill us."

"*Lawrence?* Why?"

He closed his eyes and shivered. Briskly, Rosie prised his coat from him, finding it damp with mud and grass. He sighed shakily. "We were at Freya's Crown again. Lawrence caught us. He went absolutely crazy. I panicked and ran for it, jumped on a bus."

"Oh, Luc!" She clasped his shoulder. "He didn't hurt you, did he?"

"No," he said, touching her arm in return. "It wasn't the shouting. It was the look in his eyes." He rested his head back, skin bleached against the blackness of his hair. He looked like an ethereal black-and-white image from an anti-drugs poster.

Sitting beside him, she asked, "When did you start seeing Jon again?"

"Yesterday."

"For heaven's sake," she sighed. "You were fine, all the time you kept away. Now you're with him for one night and you look like death!"

"Yeah, you told me so. God, I hope he's okay. I should have stayed, but I was so scared . . . You know how there's this light in your head that should come on but won't, for some reason?"

"Oh, yes," said Rosie. "I know that one. Please tell me there weren't drugs involved." Instinct had told her long ago what Jon's shivering and shadow-haunted eyes had meant. She hadn't wanted to admit it. "Oh, Luc!"

He looked away. "Not street drugs, I told you, only Duskland stuff."

"Natural doesn't equal harmless! Christ, you could have poisoned yourself!"

"I know that," he flared back. "We thought the risk was worth taking. Shamans have always done it, Jon said. It was to see through the Gates."

"And did you?"

He paused. Slowly he unbuttoned his black shirt and pulled up the T-shirt beneath to reveal his chest. On the pale and hairless skin was a disk of blistered flesh, lividly red and weeping. "I went through," he said hoarsely. "I came back with this."

She was staring. "That looks sore. What is it?"

"I don't know." Before her curious fingertip could reach him, he pulled his shirt down again, wincing as fabric touched the wound. "Every time I'm with Jon he pulls me into this nightmare."

"That time you were ill at his party?"

"That was the first time, yes."

"God, I might have known," she exclaimed.

"I believed in him. He's so compelling, it took me forever to see what a problem he's got." In response to her questioning look, he went on, "Aetheric blackdrop, it's a resin he cooks up from the sap of Duskland poppies. Makes all your problems float away, like opium. He said if it was good enough for nineteenth-century poets, it was perfect for us."

"Well, that sounds romantic and every bit as nasty." She drew up her feet and sat cross-legged, holding on to her toes. "Is he an addict? Are you?"

"He said our bodies are more resilient than humans', so it's easier to stop—if we want to. It makes all the pain go away . . ." His dark head drooped. "I stopped, but he won't. I feel sorry for him, really."

"When he came to the cottage about Sam, I thought he was all pale and shaky because his brother was in prison. What kind of idiot am I?"

"One with a decent heart," Lucas put in.

"Great, my supposed soul mate and your brother—You could have said no."

Lucas's dark eyes flashed. "Like *you'd* have said no to him? He didn't force me, I wanted to—to prove I had the guts to travel with him."

"Doesn't sound like he's going anywhere," she said bitterly.

He took her hand and held it hard. "He was like some mystical shaman with all the answers. I didn't want to let him down. Last night was horrendous—I saw things so real, so horrible . . . When I came out of it, I looked at Jon and realized: The reason he wants to escape through the Gates and the reason he uses drugs is the same. He's empty inside. And he was taking me with him. This morning I looked at him and thought, *I can't go back to this. We'll both be dead in a gutter within a year.*"

Lucas wept, head turned away from her. She reached for him and drew his face into her shoulder. "Don't. He's not worth it," she said.

"But you love him."

"No, I don't, Luc. Not anymore."

"So why are you crying?"

"I'm crying for you, idiot," she said.

He pulled away from her, sat wiping his cheeks with his hand until she reached for a box of tissues and handed one to him. "There's this fantasy that when you meet your soul mate, you'll *know*," she said. "When I saw Jon I thought I *knew,* but I was so wrong. And it's nothing to do with his behavior. If he'd loved me back, no doubt I'd have let him get away with murder."

"Like I have?" Lucas put in.

"Yes, dear, like you have. Instead I had a lucky escape. We saw through him in the end, and it hurts." Luc nodded. He closed his eyes in a brief, sharp expression of pain. She said gently, "D'you want to tell me about this vision?"

"Yes. No. It was . . . It seemed real, but . . ." He gave a violent shudder. "I just want to forget it, Ro. Any chance of a drink and a shower?"

She sent him to the bathroom, made coffee. When he came back, in a shirt and baggy jeans of Alastair's, he was calm. "Jon's not all bad," he said. "He's had . . . tough things to deal with. I shouldn't have left him with Lawrence. I hope he's all right."

Looking up, Rosie saw a movement outside the window, a haunted face looking in at her. She gave a small gasp. "I think you'll find he is."

Jon was on the doorstep, a terrified refugee. He had his arms wrapped around himself and kept glancing over his shoulder. He smelled of the outdoors, of damp grass and bonfires. "Is Lucas here?"

"Yes," Rosie said coolly. "No thanks to you he's still alive."

"I've got to see him. Please."

Sighing, she stepped back and let him in. She watched numbly from the doorway as Jon stumbled to the sofa and flung himself down beside Luc. "I got a taxi. Phoned your mum for the address. I guessed you'd be here. If in doubt, run to Rosie's."

"You useless bastard," Lucas grumbled under his breath.

"Me?" said Jon. "You're the one who ran away!"

"D'you blame me? Not enough to poison me, you nearly get us killed."

"Are you really mad with me?" Jon looked ashen.

"Fucking fuming," said Lucas. "No, I'm just glad you're okay. I thought Lawrence was going to kill us both."

"Me too." They embraced like shipwreck survivors. Then Jon pulled his feet up and sat cross-legged, oblivious of his dirty boots on the seat cushions. "He's thrown me out. My father's thrown me out!" He put his head in his hands.

Rosie stood with folded arms. She wanted to yell like an outraged parent, but didn't. They were both in such a state, there seemed nothing more to say.

"I'll make some lunch," she said. "You both look starving."

"Thanks, and can I ask a favor, Ro?" said Lucas. "Can we stay for a bit? I can't face Mum fussing." He and Jon looked expectantly at her.

"You can, Luc," she answered quietly. "I don't want Jon here."

"But he's got nowhere to go. Please."

She felt suddenly cast in the role of carer to two delinquents. Still, it was preferable to them ending up in more trouble. "All right," she said, relenting. "Only for a day or two. Then he has to go. And no drugs in my house."

Jon began earnestly, "No, you don't get it, it's not recreational—" but Lucas gripped his arm and said, "Shut up. Of course we won't, Ro. It goes without saying."

Rosie withdrew to the kitchen and tried, as countless generations both human and Aetherial had always done, to heal things with food. She was shaken, but what was the point of anger? Lucas needed a safe haven, not a lecturing parent. As she buttered bread, she heard the front door opening. There was a pause, then Alastair came into the kitchen, dropped his sports bag and stood there. Rosie felt a sense of dislocation, as if she'd forgotten he existed.

"What the hell's going on?" he asked at last. He looked irritated, verging on livid.

She decided to simplify. "Lawrence caught Jon and Lucas smoking pot, and threw them out."

"Good grief! This is our home, not a doss house for druggies!"

"That's my brother you're talking about. Where can he go, if not here?"

"Er—his own home?" Alastair said with sarcasm. Solid in a red rugby shirt, he looked the opposite of Lucas and Jon. They were skinny, scruffy students, wild spirits out of the Dusklands. Alastair seemed by contrast heavy and prosaic, a bit baffled, set in his ways, so ordinary you could sell him by the pound.

"Mum will fuss, if she finds out," said Rosie, grating cheese. "He knows he won't get hassled here."

"Right, but they're not kids. They can look after themselves. I want them gone." One thing she'd leaned about Alastair since marriage was that he hated his routine being upset.

"And they will go," she answered reasonably, "as soon as Lawrence calms down. We've got spare bedrooms. What's the problem?"

"*One* spare room! You needn't think they're taking over my study! Look, I know you care about Lucas—"

"Yes, I do," she said pointedly.

"But that thing you had about Jon is no big secret."

She grated a fingernail, and winced in pain. "Oh, come on, that was a million years ago. They know they've been idiots. They need to sort themselves out."

"Have you still got feelings for him?"

"Don't be daft." His sudden, needling questions made her uncomfortable. His eyes looked bloodshot. "Alastair, have you been drinking?"

He didn't answer. "It was supposed to be just you and me, Rosie," he said. "You think I want some guy around that you used to drool over? This is the sort of thing *she* would do." He meant the ex-girlfriend, she who made his eyes go blank with hurt anger.

"I'm not her."

"Letting dodgy friends stay, up all night snorting coke like it was perfectly normal and there was something wrong with *me* for objecting." A heavy pause. "All of them laughing at me, the idiot who didn't realize she was sleeping with most of them."

Coldness flashed over her. Alastair's expression was wild, disturbing. "This is totally different. I'm not about to do any of that, especially not with my brother."

"How about your old flame?"

Rosie laughed. "Have you seen the state of him? I think he'd break if I jumped on him." She meant it lightheartedly but Alastair's expression only turned madder. *He couldn't suspect about Sam, could he?* She asked in shock, "Is that what you think of me?"

"Fucking hell, Rosie, I don't know what to think!" Suddenly he flung open the kitchen door and stomped out into the garden. She heard a strangled growl, then the dull *thunk* of something breaking. Tense, Rosie continued preparing food. A few minutes later, Alastair came back in, his face flushed, expression sheepish, his big shoulders hunched with contrition.

"I'm sorry, Rosie," he said quietly. "I kicked a plant pot. I've calmed down now."

"Not my little bay tree?"

"Sorry. I'll help you repot it."

"God, Alastair!" she cried, furiously cutting up sandwiches. "What the hell is wrong with you?"

"It's not you. I've been dropped from the team for the next game. Apparently I'm not fit enough. I was bloody fuming at the coach so yes, I went for a pint. Then I come home to find this! Sorry, sorry, I lost it for a moment. I know it's your brother, but we really don't need the lazy pair of them lying around messing up the house. That's all. The stuff I said, I didn't mean it. I'm sorry."

He put his arms around her, so apologetic that she softened, and kissed his warm cheek. "Hey, you'll get back in. I know it's disappointing, but Ashvale Tigers will soon realize they're useless without you. And I'm sorry, too, about the invasion, but you have no reason to be jealous."

"I can see that," he said, his brawny arms tightening possessively. A smile entered his voice. "If you seriously had the hots for that scarecrow in there—well, everyone's allowed a wee lapse of taste, but thank goodness you got over it, eh?"

"Yeah," she breathed, untangling herself from him and piling food onto plates. "I know it's a nuisance, but they'll only be here for a day or two. You don't mind, do you?"

"No, no, it's fine," said Alastair, clearly not happy but at pains to be obliging and tolerant. "Whatever you need to do."

"Thank you," she said crisply, heading for the door with a loaded tray. Once she'd thrust food and drink at the strays, she left them to it and dealt with the tension of the house in the best way she knew. She escaped outside and attacked the front garden.

"Hey, sweetie."

Rosie was on instant alert at the familiarity of the voice. For twenty minutes she'd been so absorbed in digging a flower bed that she hadn't noticed his noiseless approach. She sat back on her heels and saw Sam a few yards away on the footpath that bordered her front lawn. He was very still, as if he'd been watching her for a few minutes.

In a split second, every part of her mind and body swirled into chaos; stomach thrilling with anxiety, heart leaping, warmth rushing up her spine and blood rioting though her. An instant replay of erotic ghost sensations mingled with general embarrassment, panic, guilt, and a truly disturbing flash of excitement . . . She'd always wondered how it would be when they met again, as they were bound to; what on earth she'd say or do. She'd decided on a stance of cool, detached politeness. She'd even rehearsed it in her head but now, faced with reality, she was hopelessly flustered and drowning—just as she'd always known, wretchedly, that she would be.

All of that flared through her and was smoothed over in the second it took her to stand up. "Hi, Sam."

He was observing her, head tilted a little to the side, gauging her demeanor. He was dressed simply: black jeans, blue T-shirt, black leather jacket, a steel and leather cord around his neck. His clothes hung neatly and beautifully on him. Worrying, that he looked better every time she saw him; lean and compact, with light shining through the ends of his hair, making an aura around him so that he seemed dark yet gilded at the same time.

Rosie didn't know what she felt, but it wasn't angry or defensive. They'd both behaved badly but it was over; the playing field was level. So her greeting came out with a slight smile. He gave a very tentative smile in return. Oh, he was wary, all right. Holding back, so as not to give her reason to lash out at him. She thought, *Perhaps he's put it all behind him and moved on; which was only what I wanted* . . .

"How are you?" he asked.

"I'm great," she said. "How about you?"

"Couldn't be better. So this is it, *chez* Rosie." He glanced over the house. "Nice."

"Thank you. Well, thanks to my dad, really."

"All settled in?"

Again heat prickled her skin like warm fur. "Yes, lots to do of course, and, er . . . why are you here?"

"Don't worry, love, I'm not stalking you." One eyebrow arched suggestively. "Much as I'd like to. I'm looking for Jon. Did you hear, he had a huge fight with Lawrence, and got the boot?"

"Yes." Removing her gardening gloves, she walked closer so they could speak quietly. "He's here."

"I guessed as much." Sam nodded, looked down at his feet. "Where else would the beggars go to ground, when they're in trouble? I need to speak to him. Is that all right?"

"As long as he wants to see you." She folded her arms, shook her hair back over her shoulders. "Did Lawrence send you, and are you going to give him a hard time?"

"No to the first question, and to the second, probably. All I want is to know what the hell's going on. Come on, I'll be gentle, I promise."

"Mind you, Jon deserves a hard time," she said. "Okay, but no fighting or yelling in my house."

"There won't be." Sam remained at the edge of the lawn, a half-smile on his lips. "Aren't you going to invite me over the threshold?"

"Why do you need inviting? Have you turned into a vampire?"

"Not a vampire. I'm just trying to work out how mad you are with me."

"I'm not mad with you, Sam."

"Really? You were well and truly seething, last time I saw you."

"And that was two months ago. I can't seethe for that long. Anyway, there's nothing to be mad about, is there?"

"Oh, right," he said, nodding. "Because nothing happened."

"Exactly. Nothing happened," she repeated firmly, then spoiled it by holding his gaze a bit too long. Coloring, she turned towards the front door. "Come on."

"By the way, you look amazing," he said over her shoulder. "I prefer it to the wedding dress. I always knew how hot you'd look, slaving over the soil."

"Shut up."

"Just making an observation, sweetheart."

She stopped at the corner of the porch and faced him. "And please don't call me sweetheart in front of Jon and Lucas and Alastair."

"Alastair's here?" Sam blanched.

"Well, yes. He happens to live here."

"Of course he does. And hey, he's in. Great."

"What difference does it make?" They were close together, whispering. The more Rosie looked at Sam's face, the more unstable the earth felt beneath her feet. "You're here for your brother, aren't you?"

"That's right. All I'm interested in is Jon. Honestly,

Rosie, I'm not going to embarrass you. Do you think I'm an idiot?"

"I know you're not an idiot, Sam. I don't trust you, that's all."

"Thanks. That's bloody charming, that is."

"Don't be disingenuous. You've always liked making mischief. I'm simply asking you, please don't. Don't even think about it."

"What? You think I'm going to make a pass at you in front of Alastair, or ask him if he's ever had you up against a tree so we can compare notes?"

Rosie gasped. She stood speechless.

"Give me some flaming credit," Sam went on. "Do you think I've spent the last few weeks pining for you? I've got other fish to fry. I've been good, I've stayed away from you like you wanted, and I'm only here now for Jon. I'm not going to drop you in it. What more can I do?"

She found her breath again. "I knew this would happen. Only together five minutes, and we're scrapping like a pair of hamsters."

"This is not a fight." Sam moved imperceptibly away from her, his tone cooling. "I'm trying to say that you're right, it would never have worked between us. The little taste I had of you was an eye-opener, and very nice, thank you, but it's over. You're safe. Stop worrying."

She stood glaring at him. "Is that all it was? All the faked emotion and tears, just to prove you could have me? One shag and you've won the game? Just walk off smiling with the cup, Sam one, Rosie nil? I might have known."

"Since we're not arguing, and since I'm a gentleman, I really shouldn't point out that you kissed me first. But what the hell? *You* kissed *me*."

"All right, we were as bad as each other. That's why I'm not angry, or only with myself. But—no, we can't talk about this now. Or ever. It didn't happen."

"Whatever. Can I see my brother now?" he said, looking pointedly at the front door.

"What fish?" said Rosie.

"Pardon?" His gaze came back to her face. Although she could see through his bravado, she didn't actually trust her own eyes. She couldn't cut straight to the truth, like Mel could.

"You said other fish to fry. Are you seeing someone?"

"Bit too late to be jealous, love."

"I'm not. I only wondered what you've been doing."

"Every woman in the county, young and old alike," he said thinly, "trying to get over you."

Rosie felt as if someone had flung a heavy ball into her stomach. Of course he'd been sleeping around with one female after another; what else would he do after three years in jail? Worse, she could picture it vividly. This was horrible, miserable. Meeting Sam again was a thousand times worse than she'd ever dreamed it could be.

"Is it working?" she asked as she opened the door for him, her voice cold and thin.

He looked at her. The look seemed to go on forever. At last, as he stepped lightly inside, he said, "No."

"You plank," said Sam, sitting on the edge of an armchair facing Jon. He sounded more exasperated than angry, Rosie thought, hovering in the doorway. It was weird to see Sam in her living room; unnatural to the point of alarming. Jon sat glowering back at him, shamefaced but defiant. He'd lit a thin roll-up, filling her pristine room with smoke. Lucas stared at the carpet.

"Great, this is all I need," said Jon.

"So, are you going to take him home, or what?" Alastair said, over Rosie's shoulder.

Sam turned to Alastair with the most sublime look of contempt and loathing Rosie had ever seen. "I would if I could," he said, his conversational tone bearing no relation to his expression, "but Dad's thrown him out and I don't know how long he'll take to relent."

"Why are you here, then?" Jon asked sullenly.

"To make sure you're all right, knob-head," said Sam. His face changed completely when he looked at his brother.

"I don't know what to say. I warned you, over and over. You can't claim this is any big surprise, can you? If anything, you've got off lightly."

Narrow-eyed, Jon sucked on the roll-up. "I suppose. I'm just pissed off. Not with you—well, a bit with you, Sam. With everyone for not seeing that we're doing something important, absolutely vital, and if Dad can't hack it anymore he should think about retiring."

"What the hell's he talking about?" Alastair said, genuinely puzzled. No one answered him.

"Instead we get treated like a pair of kids," Jon went on. "Like idiots. I'm not an idiot, Sam."

"Yeah, well, that's a matter for debate. By the way, Sapphire wants to see you."

At that, Jon virtually levitated, dropping ash everywhere. Lucas's head jerked up and he looked at Jon, half-frowning. "No! No, Sam, no way can I see her. Make her stay away."

Sam shrugged. "My feelings too. What are you going to do now? Hole up here while you think up a different way to save the world?"

Jon shook his head, lips thin. "All I want is to be left alone."

"Might be an idea to talk to Dad, once he's calmed down."

The head-shaking became more emphatic. "I can't. It's too late."

"I want to see him," Lucas said out of nowhere. He sat forward, all nervous energy. "I really need to talk to him."

Everyone looked at Lucas in surprise. "And say what?" Jon exclaimed.

"I don't know." Lucas looked sideways at Jon. "Nothing about . . . anything. I just need to tell him . . . that we're sorry."

"I thought Lawrence scared you out of your wits," Sam said dryly.

"I'm not scared. D'you think he'll see me, Sam? Will you give me a lift over there?"

———

Rosie wouldn't let Lucas go alone, so she had the uneasy experience of sitting beside Sam in a metallic blue cabriolet—Sapphire's, apparently—with Lucas silent in the backseat as Sam drove through the twisting lanes towards Cloudcroft. She wished she'd taken her own car. Too late now.

As soon as Sam let them in through Stonegate's imposing oak doors, Sapphire appeared. She wasn't her normal glowing self, Rosie observed; she looked tired and harassed, and had applied too much makeup to compensate. She spoke to Sam only to ask about Jon; then focused her attention on Lucas, ignoring Rosie completely.

"He's in the library. I'll go and ask if he'll see you," Sapphire said when Lucas made his nervous request. "Don't hold out any hope, dear. He may not even speak to me, in this mood."

They waited in silence. The musty weight and ice of the atmosphere fell heavily on her, darker and more warped than ever. She looked at Sam, but he only gave her a cynical, speaking glance, as if to say, *Lovely, isn't it?*

Sapphire came back, all brisk poise, and said, "He'll see you."

Rosie went upstairs with Lucas, aware of every footstep echoing through the vault of the great hall. When they reached the door to the library, Lucas turned to her, his face so bloodless it shone. He looked fragile but certain of himself. "Have to do this alone," he said. "I'll be fine, Ro."

The door was ajar, leaving a tall narrow chasm of semidarkness. He slipped through and the door closed. She hovered outside for a few minutes, couldn't hear anything. By the time she decided to go downstairs again, Sam was nowhere to be seen.

The house was oppressive. Rosie went out into the garden and made her way down the sloped lawn to a bower of rhododendron bushes. She wasn't consciously looking for Sam, but instinct led her and when she found him, it felt inevitable. There was a clearing like a leafy cave, with yellow birch leaves scattered on the earth and a large flat boulder in the center. Sam was sitting on it, resting his elbows on his knees.

Rosie cleared her throat. "There you are," she said.

"Well," he said, "this family gets better and better."

Softly, Rosie went and sat beside him. "You're really worried about Jon, aren't you?"

Sam exhaled. He didn't react to her sitting there; didn't turn towards her or move the braced arm that made a barrier between them. She wondered if he'd got over her after all. It was what she'd asked, but now it seemed to have happened—she felt awful, as if she'd been dropped in midair.

"I am and I'm not, love. He puts on this aura of being a pathetic mess and yet he's the one who always bounces back like some pouf in a shampoo advert, while I end up with the split lip, black eye, blood all over the pavement and handcuffs."

"Poor you," said Rosie, with the gentlest hint of mockery. "Hang on, I'll get my violin out."

"I'm much more worried about Dad. He's holding himself together by a cobweb and no one seems to see it but me."

"We see it, but he won't let anyone near him, will he? No wonder Jon's a mess."

"I don't know to do about Jon," Sam said wearily. "It's like talking to a brick wall. It's one thing derailing himself, but taking Lucas with him . . ." He dipped his head and ran his hands over his hair. "Where did I go wrong, Rosie? Is it my fault for protecting him too much? Not telling him to stop?"

"Sam," she said gently. "You're his brother, not his parent. People have minds of their own and they do stupid things, whatever you say to them. You can't control him or Lawrence. Matthew can't control me, no matter how hard he tries."

"Is that right?" He looked sideways at her. "So, how's married life, Mrs. Bob-the-Builder?"

"He's an architect. There's a difference. It's fine."

"Lots of mad passion and romantic gestures?"

"It's peaceful. Which is nice."

"Good. I never wanted you to be unhappy, Rosie."

"I'll give you the benefit of the doubt on that."

They sat in silence for a few moments. The inch of space between them became charged with their body heat. Sam always smelled good and now his scent was redolent of long intense conversations and heated arguments and delicious lust. She only had to catch that spiced fragrance and it bypassed her common sense altogether. Warmth crept over her. She was all too aware of the lean firmness of his shoulders and arms and hands so close to her, the heavy ache of desire that she'd never felt for Alastair. Her breath was unsteady.

She tried not to think of the other women, all the dozens of other women sighing and convulsing underneath him. They didn't exist.

"Sam," she said, "do you think that the locking of the Gates makes Aetherials go mad?"

He turned a little, his arm falling to his side. Their knees touched lightly. "I'm damn sure it does. Why?"

"Because I think that either I'm mad, or people around me are. I feel like I'm in being kept in chains somehow. Soft chains. By Matt, Alastair, even my father. Bounced between work, home, marriage like I'm in a little padded cell. I didn't expect Alastair to be so . . . possessive. Is it them or me? What do they think is going to happen to me?"

"I don't know." He frowned, his eyes dark aquamarines. "Me, perhaps?"

"But they don't know about us. They don't even suspect."

"There's an us?" he said, mouth softening.

She ignored that comment. "No, I mean it's as if there's a conspiracy to keep us from even thinking about the Spiral. Like if we only think about the surface world, eventually the Otherworld will fade to nothing and we won't even remember. I expected that from Matthew, but not from Auberon . . ."

"I don't think you're mad." He turned more towards her, so that his thigh pressed hers along its length. "I don't know what it means, but we've got a duty to find out, don't you reckon? They can only make you feel trapped if you let them."

"I know, but . . . Oh look," she said with a nervous laugh. "We can have a conversation without arguing. That's a relief."

"Let's write the other one off, then, shall we? At least it broke the ice."

"With a sledgehammer," Rosie said, raising her eyebrows.

"By the way, about what I said before . . ."

"You said a lot before."

"About sleeping with every woman I could get my hands on?"

"Oh, that."

"It wasn't true. It was total bullshit. For what it's worth, I've not been able to look at another girl. I did try, but it was only window shopping. Nothing happened."

Rosie felt a ridiculous wave of relief. *I'm definitely not thinking straight,* she told herself. *If he's still obsessed with me I should be concerned, not glad . . .* Her body, however, was not listening.

"Oh," she said unsteadily. "Didn't meet anyone you liked?"

"That's the trouble." His hand slid onto her knee. "I've already met her. As you know damned well."

"Sam," she groaned. "Oh god, don't . . ."

He moved towards her and whispered in her ear. The tickling heat dissolved her. "When we were in the woods, I know it was wrong, it was wicked and I'm sorry, but wasn't it the best thing you ever felt? How can you think that once was enough, Rosie? It was only the first taste . . ."

Their mouths came together and here they were again, devouring each other, hands everywhere. She sensed the Dusklands at last, shimmering around them like flame.

His body was so slim and hard, his clean scent so warmly enticing, she wanted to seize and consume him with her mouth and with every other part of her . . .

"No, no, stop," she said, pushing him to arm's length and holding him there. "I can't. I'm not doing this again."

He held on to her forearms, gently struggling to stop her pulling free. His face was radiant and intent. "You know what this is, Rosie. It's the Otherworld calling you. This is what happens when you try to deny it."

"No. This is lust. Don't try and dignify it."

"And whatever insipid thing you have with Alastair, that's love, is it?"

"We made vows."

"Since when do human vows hold us?"

"You've got no morals," Rosie said vehemently. "That's what's wrong with you, Sam."

"You still want me inside you, though." His velvety, urgent whisper unraveled her. "We can't go through the Gates, but can we reconnect to our Aetherial nature through each other. You could say we have a duty . . ."

"God, you're unbelievable!"

"Tell me you're enjoying incredible passionate ecstasy with Ginger and I'll walk away. But if you are, why are you here with me?"

She tried to sit very still, to cool her own arousal so that Sam wouldn't sense the warm musky waves flowing towards him. "I don't know. I shouldn't have let it happen. We can't keep doing this."

His hands moved gently over her. He touched her hair. "You've got me, Rosie. You know I love you."

"I don't know any such thing. I know you say it, to wind me up."

"It's such fun winding you up, though."

She stood abruptly. The molten pull of desire was so strong, it was almost impossible to walk, let alone walk away from him, but she must. "Sam, I'm sorry. I don't know why this keeps happening. I never meant to lead you on. I'm married and I don't love you; it's as simple as that.

I think we should just keep apart from now on and get on with our own lives."

"Fine." He rose and faced her, panther-lean. "So why are you crying?"

"I'm not." Quickly she swept moisture out of her eyelashes.

"Don't go, Rosie. Stay and talk, I won't lay a finger on you."

"No, I'm going to find Lucas. Don't try to see me again," she said helplessly, beginning to walk away.

"Oh, all right." Arms folded, he stood at the entrance to the bower and looked at his watch. "So you won't be wanting a lift home in a few minutes, then?"

"Always with the smart answer," she said over her shoulder.

He smiled. "Don't forget, you invited me over the threshold."

14

In the Garden

The library was dim, dusty and apparently without boundaries. Light diffusing through white nets made a tall, blurred silhouette of Lawrence standing at the far window. Luc's heart stumbled as he crossed the room. He reached the edge of a polished walnut table and halted beside it for support, ten feet from Lawrence. He had no idea what to say.

"I am amazed you have the nerve to come back here again," came Lawrence's voice out of the heart of shadow, infinitely scornful. "What do you want? A pat on the head? Absolution?"

His face was gaunt and implacable. Lucas felt an inch tall. He'd been mad to think he could do this. "No, sir," he said, stiff and formal. "I've come back to tell you what I saw."

Lawrence was silent, breathing in and out. Then he said, "Go on."

Lucas looked him in the eyes and told him everything. "This dead-white, frosty, cruel face was staring down at me . . . warning me . . ."

"Albin," Lawrence whispered.

"At the end, a great shadow rising out of the Abyss . . . It saw me, too. I don't know what it was—I can't describe it—but it's there now, waiting for us." His heartbeat quickened as he spoke. "I understand—that is, I *don't* understand, but—I saw it."

"Yes." Lawrence—his real father—loomed slowly towards him. Lucas held his ground. Whatever happened now, he was beyond fear.

"I see why you closed the Gates, sir," he said. "I didn't know and I'm sorry."

"You saw it." Lawrence's eyes shone with an alarming light. It struck Lucas that he, too, was intimate with terror but keeping it under stern, practiced control. "You saw Brawth, the enemy. You believe me. At last, someone else has seen it!" One hand came up and gripped Lucas's shoulder, his head tilting as he studied him more closely. "You did something stupid, dangerous beyond reason, yet you survived. What am I missing? Who are you?"

"No one." Lucas drew back, trying to shake off his scrutiny. He'd delivered his apology, but had no idea how to leave. "I should go now."

"Must you?" said Lawrence. "It would mean everything to have someone who knows what this means, who is on my side. How would it be if you stayed in Jon's place?"

Lucas floundered, alarmed. "No, I could never take Jon's place. And he's not against you, no one is, they're just . . . confused."

The grip tightened. Pain lanced through his neck. "If

only things were different . . ." He was like a vulture, looming above Lucas with fierce eyes and talons. Then the grip loosened. Lawrence seemed diminished to normal height again. "No, Lucas, you're right. I'm no fit company." He ran one thumb along the edge of the table. "I can't forgive Jon. He knew the rules and defied me. You, however, were easily led. I wish I could give you more, but I can't. I daren't. Look at my sons; I don't want you to become like them, aimless, empty and destructive. You're my one hope, Lucas, and you'll only remain safe if you keep away from me. Stay with Auberon and Jessica, but know that . . . that I *would* love you, if any part of me were still capable of love."

Lucas was stunned, confused. Lawrence fascinated as much as frightened him. "Can't anything be done about . . . Brawth?"

"Can humans stop a tornado? No. The barrier keeps us safe for now. The danger is to all of us—to Jon and Sam, to you, to everyone, but it is *my* enemy, so the further I stay from you, the less I draw Brawth's attention to you. You'd better leave now, Lucas."

Last night's fear woke and slithered horribly down his spine. *Brawth's attention.* The words were out before he knew they were coming, "Will the Gates ever be opened again?"

"Never." The word fell like a tombstone. Lawrence trembled as he whispered it. "Never."

The storm passed, but days later Jon and Lucas were still camping out in Rosie's spare bedroom. For the first three days, Jon barely emerged. Then on the fourth morning she found him alone in the kitchen, dressed in cargo pants and a khaki shirt that were clean, if un-ironed. She frowned to see him smoking a roll-up but she could hear her own voice in her head, *"No drugs. No smoking,"* like a clucking landlady, so she sealed her lips.

"I suppose we should pay you some rent," he said.

"Why?" Rosie couldn't look him in the eye. He looked far better than he'd any right to; tangled hair flowing over his shoulders, pseudo-military clothes flattering his lean body, shapely forearms like Sam's. The bruising around his eyes only enhanced his pallid beauty. "Rent is paid by tenants, not emergency guests. How long are you planning to stay?"

"I don't know. Even if my father relents, I won't go back to Stonegate."

"What about Nottingham?"

"Father stopped paying for my room there, so I can't."

Rosie busied herself washing mugs, trying very hard not to lose her temper. "I hardly dare suggest it, but how about finding a job?"

He gave a flat laugh. "You've really bought it, haven't you? The human world. Marrying a human, working, pretending the Spiral never existed."

She turned on him, stared into his narrowed eyes. "It's where we live. Maybe if you got used to the idea, you wouldn't be so discontented."

Jon was silent, blowing smoke. Then he said, "You don't like me, do you?"

He seemed baffled, to her amazement. "At this moment, no, I don't very much. It's nothing to do with my feelings, but everything to do with the way you've treated Lucas."

"Lucas never did a damned thing he didn't want to," Jon retorted. Stubbing his roll-up on the draining board, he walked out, leaving Rosie on the verge of throwing a heavy object at his head.

Two months later, the refugees were still there. Lucas got a job in a music shop; Jon came and went like a stray. Sometimes Rosie would hear them arguing through the bedroom wall, voices murmuring until the early hours. She knew she should make them leave—but to go where? Jon wouldn't consider living at Oakholme, and Lucas wouldn't leave him. At least being under her roof kept them out of trouble.

Alastair expressed regular irritation with them, but Rosie soothed him by ignoring his complaints and rewarding him with affection when he mellowed. Rather like training a child, she thought, disliking herself for being so manipulative. Christmas was difficult, with Jon refusing invitations, Lucas restless without him, awkward questions from Jessica and Auberon. Rosie and Luc gave a carefully edited version of the truth: that Lawrence had overreacted to an innocent situation. No one who knew Lawrence would disbelieve it.

Lucas gave Jon a guitar for Christmas. A few days later, she found Jon in the kitchen complaining bitterly that the guitar was broken and it could not have happened by accident. He accused Alastair, who cheerfully denied it and called him paranoid.

She knew Jon and Luc had to go, but how and where?

Winter was damp, grey and mild. During the dark days of January, Alastair went to a weekend conference with Matthew, and Rosie found herself relieved at his absence. Three days in which to relax, and not be constantly policing her guests and soothing tensions. She hadn't realized how exhausting it was.

On the Friday evening, she made a date with Faith. "Jessica and Auberon are going out," Faith told her, "and I don't want to spend the evening on my own. Can you come over, please?"

About seven, Rosie arrived at Oakholme with a bottle of wine. Under a long jacket of umber velvet, she wore an autumn-hued patchwork skirt and a russet sweater, with a long turquoise-blue scarf for extra warmth. Faith, letting her in, was dressed for invisibility; flowery dress, enveloping blue cardigan. She was nervous, hands bunched inside the overlong sleeves. Her face, with her glasses perched slightly askew, was so sweet that Rosie seized and hugged her, overwhelmed with love.

Faith burst into tears.

"What on earth is wrong, babe?" Rosie asked, embracing her ever harder.

"Nothing." Faith pulled back, wiping her face on her sleeve.

"Drink," said Rosie, raising the bottle. "Talk. Is it Matt?"

Faith took the wine from her and put it on a table. "Will you help me bathe Heather and put her to bed first?"

The warm beeswax scent of Oakholme wrapped around Rosie as they went upstairs. She always felt the same rush of nostalgia, a physical longing for the dark oak paneling, creaking floorboards, wide corridors running at quirky angles, and always the promise of mysterious extra rooms that might reveal themselves.

"How are things with Alastair?" Faith asked as she ran the taps and poured in bath foam. Steam misted the tiles.

"We're supposed to be talking about you." Rosie sat on the closed lid of the loo.

"We are," Faith said. "Indirectly. Is he . . . Are you happy?"

"Yes." The question took her by surprise. "Pretty much."

Faith exhaled, her posture radiating misery as she tested the bathwater. She'd always found it torture to admit anything was wrong. Once Heather, all pink and blond, was splashing happily in a meringue of bubbles, Faith asked, "What's Alastair like? I mean, has he changed? Does he take you for granted? Can you tell him absolutely anything?"

Rosie knelt on the bathmat and wound up a clockwork frog for her niece's delight. "Look, it's no good comparing Alastair with Matthew. Do you think I have a perfect marriage?"

"I don't know. Do you?"

"No, Fai. I don't know what I expected." The truth came easily with her friend, as it hadn't with her father. "We got on great until we were married, because we didn't make demands on each other. I'm really fond of him, even when he has his little tantrums. He's a big handsome man, what's not to like? But the moment we got married, I panicked. It's like . . . imagine you have a really good friend whom you occasionally sleep with and it's a nice, comfortable arrangement. But one day you sign a contract saying you'll spend every moment of the rest of your life with them and never look at anyone else—wouldn't you break out in a sweat and think, *Oh fuck, what have I done?*" She paused for breath. "We're okay. I just feel a bit . . . stifled."

Faith stared. "So why did you marry him?"

"Delusions about romantic passionate love messed my head up. I was trying to be levelheaded and sensible instead."

"But you made a mistake."

"No. I made a choice. And after the huge fuss and expense of the wedding, and our lives being tangled up together for so long—I've invested too much in it not to make it work."

"Does Alastair know you don't love him?"

The bluntness of Faith's question startled her. "He . . . He means a lot to me." She frowned. "We don't discuss it. Alastair slumped into marriage like it's a comfy chair. He's not interested in ecstasy. I think it scares him. He just wants a safe, quiet life."

"With the boss's daughter, no less," Faith remarked.

That threw Rosie off her stroke. She'd never even thought of it before. "Oh my god," she whispered. "The boss's daughter. Am I really that blindingly stupid?"

"No—oh no, Rosie, I didn't mean that the way it sounded! I'm sure he loves you for yourself. How could he not?"

"Well. I expect we'll be fine in the end; I need time to adjust, that's all. I know I should try harder, so one day I wake up and think, wow, I'm happy, we did the right thing after all . . . but I'm finding it such an effort. I know he's pissed at Luc and Jon being there and I should make them go . . . but I'm sort of hiding behind them, so I don't have to face this . . . making-it-work thing."

She sighed. Faith said worriedly, "I had no idea."

"Fai, I'm only saying that if something's wrong, join the club. I know how difficult Matthew can be. Is your love life still okay?"

"Fine," Faith said with a blush. "It's the one thing that always has been. He can be so sweet, especially in the dark . . . but . . ."

"Daylight turns him into a big posturing ego on legs?" Rosie suggested. "It always has. So what's he done?"

"Nothing." Faith gave a shiver. "It's what he might do if . . ." She swept bubbles away from Heather's waist, leaving a clear window of water. The child's top half was plump, pink and awash with bubbles; but her legs and tummy, submerged, shone with blue-green scales like a mermaid's. Her small hands flashed in and out of the water; now iridescent green, now pink again. "Can you see, Ro?"

"Yes," Rosie murmured.

"I can't let Matthew see this." She sounded anguished.

Rosie said gently, "Darling, this isn't altogether a surprise to me. She's half-Aetherial. Sometimes it shows. Mind you, being of an earthy persuasion, it's usually leaves in the hair or furry legs with us, but . . ."

Faith didn't smile. "Matthew can't know."

"Are you sure he doesn't already? He must have bathed her himself."

Faith gave a firm shake of her head. "No. He's old-fashioned, he's happy to leave it to me. I've got quite clever at covering her with foam or a towel if he comes in. Jessica knows, of course, but he can't. He mustn't."

"But he'll guess. He's Aetherial. He won't be amazed that his daughter shows signs of it."

"No," Faith groaned. "That's not the point. You know what he's like. In his own mind he's human, and so are we. This would spoil the illusion. It wouldn't be perfect anymore. Rosie, I want more children, but how can I? I daren't, I can't . . ."

"Honey, are you scared of him?" Rosie had never seen her so distressed before. "He's not going to turn against his own daughter, is he? The only way to deal with Matthew is to give as good as you get."

"I can't. I'm not like you. If I was, he wouldn't have married me—oh, I didn't mean that like it sounded. I know I do everything his way, but it pleases him. That's what he loves about me, he says."

"And meanwhile, you're making yourself ill with worry trying to disguise his faerie daughter as human? You think that if you tell him something he doesn't want to hear, he'll stop loving you?"

"Yes," Faith said, white-faced. "I know it's ridiculous, it's all wrong and I should stand up for myself, but I can't change, it's what I learned from my parents, keep them sweet or they'll leave. They left anyway."

"Hey. Don't. D'you want me to tell him?" She placed a firm hand on Faith's shoulder. "Before Heather decides to announce it herself? She already talks more than a politician. Look, Matt's got a decent soul in there somewhere. He'll come round."

"No." Faith sponged her daughter's back. "It's not just Heather. That's the point. It's worse, much worse."

"How?" Rosie lowered her voice. "Matthew's not her father?"

"Of course he is! He's the only man I've ever slept with. You know that."

"Whew. That would be a wild leap out of character. Sorry. But what could be worse? Come on, tell me."

Faith rose, lifted Heather out of the bath and wrapped her in a fluffy white towel. Rosie emptied the bath and tidied up, joining them in the nursery until her niece fell charmingly asleep. Then Faith pulled Rosie along the landing into her old bedroom. They closed the door, switched on a bedside lamp and sat on the bed together. The room glowed warmly and its scent of wood and polish was so familiar that Rosie felt homesick. "Go on, then."

Faith's head drooped. She said, "It's too hard. I can only say if you tell me one in return. A deep, dark secret that no one else knows."

"It's that serious?"

"It really is." Faith looked up, eyes glimmering, face intense.

"Can't think of anything," she laughed.

"You must. It's a pact." Faith leaned forward and took her hands.

"Okay," Rosie said slowly. "This is the deepest darkest one I've got. I've slept with Sam."

A beat. "Is that it?"

"What do you mean, is that it?"

"Well, it's not exactly earth-shattering, as secrets go, is it?"

Rosie gave a tight smile. "You didn't mention rules about what secrets qualify! Okay. I had sex with Sam—in my wedding dress."

Faith's eyes grew large. "Come on, Rosie, that's bizarre. Don't make things up to humor me."

"I'm not," she said, quiet and serious. "In my wedding dress. Up against a tree. Four hours after the ceremony and during the reception. Is that deep and dark enough for you?"

Now Faith believed her. Her face was a picture. "Whoah, bloody hell," she said, making Rosie smile. "How, why?"

"Tell you later. I've kept my half of the bargain. Now you."

"Right." Faith stood up, white and shaky. "Open the wardrobe."

Puzzled, Rosie obeyed. The built-in double doors creaked as she pulled them wide. She caught her breath. Beyond the old clothes she'd left behind snaked the Dusk-lands tunnel she remembered. The walls were sheened like beech bark and shone with alluring silver light.

Emotion burned Rosie's throat. She hadn't found it for years. "Faith, can you see this?" she asked. In answer, Faith stepped into the wardrobe and walked into the tunnel.

Rosie followed. A couple of gentle curves brought them into a little cavern, its boundaries blurred by shifting light. In the center was the thick, gnarled bole of her secret tree. She touched it. The bark was satin-smooth, like the skin of a lover.

Pools of rainwater sparkled in pockets between the thick roots. Faith put her bare toes in the water. She dipped her fingers and anointed her own forehead.

She changed.

Her skin turned to gleaming blue-green scales, her hair to waterweed. Even her clothes became dragonfly wings. She looked translucent, too delicate to be real. Her face was still recognizably her own, but it glimmered with scales, reptilian yet eerily lovely.

Rosie cried out loud, as if she'd been kicked. "Faith? How?"

"I'm Aetherial," Faith whispered. "Only I didn't know until I came to Oakholme. Being here brought it out of me."

"Why didn't you tell me?"

"I tried—you were going to phone me back, remember? Only you didn't, and I lost my nerve."

"Oh my god, I'm sorry. It was when Luc turned up—went right out of my head." Then Rosie remembered. Two demons battling in a storm, the night Faith had fled to Oakholme. Rain-light flashing on scales, one demon falling, the other slithering away. Faith's mother and father, in their deeper Aetherial form? "Your parents must have known."

"Either they'd forgotten, or they were in denial. They never said or did a thing that wasn't horribly human. I'm sure they didn't know."

"Auberon spoke about this once," said Rosie, thinking fast. "Humans and Aetherials can interbreed, can't they? Usually we are either one or the other but sometimes the balance tips. What if your parents had just enough Aetheric blood to make you, but not your sisters, Aetherial? Same as if you got two recessive genes for green eyes while the rest of your family got brown. Does that make sense?"

"I suppose so. Odd things have always happened to me but I kept it secret, in case people thought I was weird. That's why I was always asking you questions! Ro, help me."

"Honey, don't be scared," Rosie said, finding her breath again. "You look beautiful, by the way."

"You don't look any different."

"You're more Aetherial than I am, then," she said with a bittersweet smile.

"I'm a demon."

"No, you're not. Your affinity is water. Melusiel. You're a water nymph, Fai, an undine."

She looked distraught, pinned like a butterfly. "How am I going to tell Matthew? I'm sure Jessica's guessed, but I daren't discuss it. How am I going to keep it secret? A mortal wife, a human wife—that's all he wanted. If he ever finds out what I am—he will kill me."

Much later, Rosie walked alone through the streets of Ashvale, brooding.

She'd stayed with Faith until Jessica and Auberon came home. As Rosie left, Jessica slipped out to the car with her. "I gather you know about Heather's, er, skin condition," Rosie said softly, fishing keys out of her jacket pocket.

"Of course," Jessica breathed. "And about Faith, too, though she won't admit it."

"That she's one of us? I've only just found out myself. Can't believe I didn't see it."

Jessica nodded. "She's a deep girl. I can't bear to see her so afraid of Matt finding out. I'm in an impossible situation. Heather needs to learn about matters Aetherial, and Faith won't tell her so I must . . . but if Matthew's against it, what can I do? I can't go behind his back. Neither can I watch her grow up in ignorance, it's not right."

"Someone ought to stand up to him," Rosie said grimly, "but I don't want to be responsible for holy hell breaking loose."

"I'm afraid he'd actually take them away," Jessica said worriedly. "I couldn't bear that."

"And if he knew about Faith, what else might he do?"

Rosie had driven nearly home, but couldn't face the moribund house, haunted by twin wraiths Lucas and Jon. Since Alastair was away, it didn't matter if she was late. She parked near the center of Ashvale, locked her car and began to walk, hands in pockets, towards the main street.

She was now fuming with thoughts of Matthew. Who the hell did he think he was? So set in his ideas that Faith was terrified of admitting the truth. Instead she would hide her real self until she shriveled away. What kind of love was that?

Rosie walked down the lively main street. Shoals of shaven-headed lads poured from one pub to the next. Groups of girls with bleached hair went staggering along shrieking with laughter, hands spilling food wrappers. Rosie walked slowly among them, hypnotized by acres of bare bellies and white thighs. It was mild for late January, but still far too chilly for such a bravura display of flesh. No one took any notice of her. Covered up in her velvet jacket, scarf and long skirt she was apparently—thankfully—as enticing as a traffic officer.

She thought, *If Matt says one word to hurt Faith—*

"Rosie?" Sam's voice came from an alley on her right. She looked round and saw him in the darkness, almost invisible in a long black coat. He was leaning against a wall in the shadows, a predator contemplating the night hordes.

"We have to stop meeting like this," she said, folding into shadow beside him. "What the hell are you doing here?"

"I could ask the same of you," he said.

"I asked first."

He shrugged. "Somewhere to go. Don't want to go home."

"Pretty much the same here," said Rosie.

"How come?"

"I just found out something . . . devastating, actually."

"Really? Tell your wicked uncle Sam."

"It's not me, it's a friend. I can't tell anyone."

"I know the feeling," he said thinly.

There was something wrong. Sam was wax-pale and unsteady, eyes lifeless. He had none of his usual spark. "Are you drunk?" she asked.

"Not yet," he said grimly, producing a hip flask. "D'you want to try?"

Rosie accepted and took a sip. Whiskey. She took another, closing her eyes at the delicious burn. "It's good stuff," he said with a ghoulish grin. "One of my father's zillion-quid-a-bottle single malts." He took the flask, drank from it and used it to indicate the Friday-night masses. "Do you ever feel like you've just stumbled in from another planet?"

"Try another universe," she said.

"Too right." Sam fell quiet, unlike his usual self. She saw faint lines drawn in his forehead, a cold burning of his eyes. The prospect of lager-fueled yobs colliding with a drunken Sam gave her chills. She knew who'd come off the worse.

"Are you okay?" she said, more brisk than sympathetic.

"Great," he said, then sighed. "No, not really."

She paused. "Is this about me?" she asked softly.

"No," he laughed. "No, it's not. Amazingly enough, not everything is about you, Rosie."

He wouldn't look at her. Usually he couldn't take his eyes off her. "What is it?" She took his arm and tried to pull him deeper into the alleyway. He resisted. "Come on, Sam, tell me, please."

She pulled again, and this time he went with her. Around them were shuttered shops, and farther down, a jumble of old buildings split by a maze of small courtyards. He veered into one of these, reeled back against a wall and stood there, ashen. "I can't tell anyone," he said. "I'm stuck with it."

"This is me you're talking to." She moved closer, touching his arm. "You told me every grim detail of a fatal stabbing; how can it be any worse?"

"It is." The words were almost a sob. "That's it, it's come back." His eyes closed. "The body. A few nights ago when I went home, the house was dark and no one up. And the corpse was back. The man I killed. Lying on the carpet exactly as I left him, only stark naked and glowing white."

"Oh, god," said Rosie, picturing it. "An illusion?"

"Not really white, more this horrible yellowy color . . . You can see all the veins, and his eyes . . ."

"Sam, it must have got to you more than you'll admit. It wasn't real."

"That's what I thought. But it was still there the next morning. It's still there now. I poked it with my boot, and it was solid. Fuck, this sounds ridiculous."

"Dumannios playing tricks on you."

"I suppose. Doesn't make it any less real to me."

"Can anyone else see it?"

A pause. "Lawrence can, I swear. He won't say, of course, but the looks he's been giving me, like he knows . . . I don't know what to do. It won't go away."

She'd never seen him in shock like this before. Sam wasn't the sort of person you could hug in sympathy. His arms were folded against her, one palm to his forehead. She let her hand stay on his arm. "I know what to do," she said gently. "Just acknowledge it."

"What? Give it a friendly kick each morning, 'Thanks for ruining my life, you bastard?' "

"No. That's not what I meant. Instead of pretending it's not there, go and look at it. At him. Talk to him. Ask what he wants, say you're sorry, or whatever you need to say."

"That's ridiculous. I can't, I'd feel a complete prat."

"So be a prat," she said stiffly. "It's all I can think of."

"There you go, being nice to me again."

"I'm not. I'm being practical." A pause, then she said cautiously, "D'you, er, want me to come home with you?"

He unfolded his arms, brought one hand to catch hers where it pressed his upper arm. Now he looked at her, and the cold fire in his eyes changed, turning hot and intense. The look was more demonic than tender. "There's an offer I can't refuse."

"I only meant . . ."

"I know, love. No, I don't need to you hold my hand. But thanks. You're certainly helping to take my mind off it."

The burning pressure of his eyes melted into her. She felt herself rise to meet it, aware of the danger yet unafraid—not able to resist, either. That was all it took, the unbreakable gaze. It dissolved the world. She was inclining towards him so it only took the slightest shift and she was leaning into him, her body pressed along his. Too easy. *Let's carry on where we left off.* His hands slipped around her, warm on the small of her back. Hers slid under his coat and shirt, onto the heated skin beneath and that was unambiguous, you didn't delve under someone's clothes and caress their naked back unless you were thinking *Gods, yes, I want you now* . . .

Rosie became someone else in the dark. No ties, no conscience. No more words.

Sam's hand enfolded the nape of her neck. She stood on tiptoe as he leaned towards her and the kiss began, hot and sweet as honeyed opium. She opened her mouth to him. Pulses of golden electricity shot through her.

For a long time they only kissed. It was too delicious to stop. After a time, it grew deeper and hungrier. The feeling was hot and dark, flooding her from head to toe. Slow at first . . . then a deluge. They were drowning in it. This time she would not push him away, couldn't. Sam groaned. As their eyes met, he seemed as astonished as she was.

She'd wondered how it would be a second time, oh gods, yes, thought about it all the time, and now she was starving to find out, so aroused from imagining it and now from his hardness and the heat of his mouth, the urge was uncontrollable. Dimly she was aware that they were reeling along the wall, clutching at each other, devouring.

Sam dragged her into a doorway behind a shop. He braced himself across it, leaning back, pulling her over him to straddle his hips even as they fought with clothing. It was that urgent, that crude. She was already sliding onto him, couldn't wait. He pulled her hard against him and the sensations were beyond heaven, so delicate yet so extreme. The roughness of fabric against her thighs contrasted astonishingly with the delicious fire where their bodies were joined.

Some confounded part of her mind wondered what she was doing with a creature who hung about drinking whiskey in alleys, who was haunted by the corpse of someone he'd killed, who reduced her life to wretched chaos . . .

Who was now turning her inside out with the most intense orgasm she'd ever experienced. It sucked all the breath out of her. As she came back down, Sam moved slowly, minimally under her. He looked straight into her eyes as he came, didn't even blink, only caught and held her soul with his gaze.

Enveloped by the velvety darkness she felt safe. No one could see them . . . unless they had Aetherial eyesight. Her legs were shaking so hard she couldn't stand, let alone climb off. She became aware of bare bricks, the door with its chipped paint and grime. How sordid this was. Utterly, unredeemably sordid.

Then it started to rain.

Sam held her up. His face was radiant with a faint smile of disbelief and, perhaps, a hint of smugness. "You're incredible," he breathed. He slipped one hand under her jacket to stroke her waist. "Rosie . . ."

"This was not meant to happen," she said helplessly.

"No, really? There I was thinking it was part of my rehabilitation."

"Don't. It's not funny. It's awful."

"I know. Never tried it in a doorway before. I think I'm stuck. What if they find us like this in the morning?"

"Yes, that would be hilarious," she said.

That's it, we've crossed the line, she thought. *Once might be written off as a forgivable mistake. Twice, and it's deliberate. I don't know how to put the barriers back between us. The barriers are gone, like a bridge washed away in a flood, and I'm lost.*

"Gods," she groaned, dropping her head. He pushed back her hair.

"Hey," he said. Then he began to kiss her, all over her lips, cheeks, temples, neck, the kisses so delicate and tender she came close to dissolving.

"Why are you doing this to me?" She meant the tenderness, not the sex.

"Why are you letting me?"

She couldn't answer.

"You're a mystery, love. You give your heart to my brother and the rest of yourself to Mr. Safe. I'm like a stray dog that came within an inch of being put down. What are you doing with me?"

"This is just sex."

"Is that all it is?" he asked, very soft.

"It can't be anything else. You know that."

"Well, I'm not complaining. If that's the case . . . When am I going to see you naked, Rosie?"

"Never. No way. That is definitely not going to happen."

At last she found the strength to climb off him, without much grace. He tried for a moment to keep her there, then let her go with a sigh. She smoothed her skirt, Sam zipped his jeans. Then it was as if nothing had happened. Again.

"Why not? Have you got a terrifying birthmark? Goat legs? A giant tattoo of Shrek? I don't care, love."

"It's not happening," she repeated.

"Right," he said. "Because if we only do it fully clothed, it doesn't count?"

Rosie said nothing, only looked at the falling rain. Sam put his arm around her shoulders. "Can we go for a drink?" he asked, without much hope in his voice.

"I should be getting back."

"Let me walk you home, at least."

"My car's only . . . Two sips of whiskey won't put me over the limit, will it?" They walked in silence, getting wet. As they reached the car, she said formally, "D'you want me to drive you to Stonegate?"

"Only if you're going to stay there with me."

"You know I can't."

He nodded, resigned. "No, I'll be fine. I'm a big boy."

"I can't argue with that," she said, with a glimmer of a smile. She looked into his eyes. "Promise me you'll go home, Sam."

"I promise."

It was something he had to do alone, he knew.

The last thing Sam wanted was to return to Stonegate, but because he'd promised Rosie, he went. And to drag it out, he walked. Only six miles, a good hour and a half to think about her.

Sam had done his best to keep away from her, even though it had almost killed him. She was always in his mind; her hair moving like glass on satin, the chestnut strands lit with sparks of red and gold . . . expressive rosy lips, silver-grey eyes shining from plum and kohl shadow. Her face, shining across table four: the light of his world. Even angry, she was so luscious. Her eyelashes, fluttering and falling as she gasped against him, and the heat of her body through her wedding dress . . .

Rosie working in her garden, her petite body all taut curves. Sweaty and earthy, she looked better than all his fantasies put together. Who could see those beads of sweat on her throat and not want to lick them away?

Of course, they'd been bound to meet again. Only a question of where and when. Taken him by surprise, though, how hard she made his heart beat. How hard she made everything, in fact . . . And tonight, floating out of nowhere, autumn-brown and ragged like a wood nymph. Her mouth tried to say no, but her eyes said yes . . .

Why am I treating her like this? he wondered. *I'm supposed to love her. I should be sending flowers and love letters from afar, I should respect her wishes and keep away. I should not be screwing her in alleyways. Does she get love from me? No, she gets insults, sarcasm and filthy rough sex up against walls. No wonder she despises me. Why am I doing it?*

Because it might be all of her I'm ever going to get.

He was home. He looked up at Stonegate's forbidding frontage and his soul failed. With a sigh he fumbled for his key and let himself in as quietly as possible so the creaking of the door would not wake his father and Sapphire.

The apparition was there as he'd left it, spread-eagled on its back in the great hall. He saw it clearly in a faint wash of moonlight. Reaching it, Sam stared down at the bloated limbs, the luminous pallor of the skin. The hands were flung outwards, fingers fat and softly curved. The eyes were half-open, watching him.

"Look, Gary," said Sam. "I'm sorry I knifed you through the gut. Just get over it, okay? Oh, this is fucking ridiculous."

He paced up and down. He was cold, heartsick and close to unraveling. He thought of Rosie. After a while, he forced himself to calm down and try again.

He lit five candles around the body; one each at feet, hands and head. He sat cross-legged at the feet, watching the eerie play of light on cyanosed skin. It was the first time he'd simply sat with the corpse instead of cursing it and running away. After a time he began to speak.

"I call on the powers of Elysion, Sibeyla, Naamon, Melusiel and Asru to protect this space. I call on the powers of Aether to bear witness." He paused, realizing that however foolish he felt, it didn't matter. "Look, mate. I truly am sorry. You took a risk and you came off worst; it could have gone the other way. You know that, don't you? Yeah, you probably didn't deserve to die. Wrong place, wrong time. But I'll tell you something, I am never going down this road again. I don't want to be a killer. You taught me that, if nothing else." Sam settled there, ready to keep a long vigil. "Right, I'm just going to sit here with you now. You're not alone anymore. I'm not going until you do. We'll see which one of us can last the night, shall we?"

Rosie tried several times to phone Sam over the next week. The first time, to her dismay, it was Sapphire on the other end. "I'm afraid Sam's not in, dear," Sapphire answered, sweetly smooth, a world of speculation in her tone.

"Has he got a mobile?"

"If he has, I don't know the number. Is it about Jon?" Her voice became too interested. "You can tell me."

Rosie hesitated, cursing the fact that Sapphire had proved a false friend. She wouldn't trust her with the weather forecast. "No. Jon's fine," she said, switching to icy briskness. "If you see Sam, would you ask him to call me at work?"

"Of course," came the bright answer, but Sam never called. She only wanted to make sure he was okay. That was all.

Now she sat at her computer, aimlessly moving digital

trees around a ground plan to look busy. She couldn't concentrate. The background murmur of the office seemed far away. How ridiculous to worry about Sam, when it was Faith who needed her; yet she couldn't stop. Matthew and Alastair were on the far side of the room, talking to a group of colleagues. Their chatter washed in and out of her awareness.

Then someone breathed on the back of her neck. "Hey, you."

Rosie jumped, shocked out of her reverie. Sam was standing behind her, grinning. She swiveled her chair to face him. Relief flashed through her, followed by the usual thrill of panic.

"God, what are you doing here?"

"It worked, Rosie. It worked!" He was pale with tiredness but his eyes sparkled and she saw the teasing white gleam of his smile. The sleeves of his black denim jacket were rolled back and he held a folded newspaper under one arm. "I did what you said. Five nights I sat up with that bloody corpse. Sixth dawn, he faded and vanished. I waited a couple of days to be sure, but—you know how when you're certain of something, you feel it right in here?" He put a fist to his chest. "It's over."

She became aware that his arrival had caused a mild stir. All her female coworkers—not to mention a couple of the men—had stopped work to check him out. She saw the general exchange of glances and suggestive smiles between them.

"I'm so glad to hear it, but Sam—"

He rested on the edge of her desk, face alight with pleasure. "I had to come and tell you. Thanks so much, Rosie. I know I sneered, but you were right. I can't thank you enough."

"It's okay," she said, leaning towards him. "But—"

"I think it was a—a sort of Aetheric balancing. Not a haunting, not guilt, but something . . . higher. Like a trial. I had to face up to what happened until he was ready to go. And I got through it, because of you."

"And I want to hear all about it—but not here." She scanned the office. Matthew was staring, to her dismay. "I meant you to phone me, not actually turn up."

He looked puzzled. "How d'you mean, phone?"

"You know, the plastic device with the buttons? Didn't Sapphire tell you I called?"

He frowned. "No, she didn't."

"Bitch," said Rosie. "I might have known!"

"You phoned me?" he said, face lighting up. "*You* phoned *me*?"

She saw Matthew and Alastair heading back towards their workstations. Smart trousers, shirt sleeves, all easy confidence. Surely they must be able to hear what Sam was saying. She tensed like a bird about to take flight, no idea what to say or do. "Yes," she whispered. "I was worried."

"Bloody hell. I didn't know you cared. I would've called straight away if I'd known, but I had to tell you face-to-face."

"Not here, you shouldn't be here," she said through her teeth.

"Why not? If you've got a guilty conscience, no one knows it but you." He lifted one eyebrow, half-teasing and half-sinister. He leaned closer. "I've got a perfectly legitimate reason for being here."

"You have?"

"So stop acting as if there's a big screen over your head replaying your naughty secrets."

"Samuel!" Matthew called cheerfully, "How the devil are you?"

"I'm great, thanks." Sam settled more firmly on the edge of her desk and folded his arms.

"How's life on the outside?" Matthew's voice was pitched to carry. The hum of the office faded as everyone pretended not to listen. "I'll bet you miss the old institutional lifestyle. Must admit, you're looking fit on prison food; they obviously fed you too well in there."

"Oh, you know. Had to keep myself in trim," Sam said quietly, eyes narrow. "Survival of the fittest."

"Well, it's great to see you. Alastair, you remember Sam, don't you?"

"Oh, aye, we've met quite recently." Alastair stood next to Matthew, sharing the same belligerent stance—feet apart, hands resting loose and low on the hips—and the same mocking smile.

"Which reminds me," said Matt, "any chance of you removing your scrounging brother from Rosie's house?"

"That's Rosie's decision."

"She's too softhearted," said Alastair. "Wouldn't mind if Jon would do an honest day's work and pay his way."

"Ah, well, that runs in the family," Matt said jovially. "Neither of them have done an honest day's work in their lives, that I can remember. Correct me if I'm wrong, Sam. Jon's a dropout. Only university Sam made was Her Majesty's university of hard labor."

Sam simply looked at him. Aggression hung so heavy in the air, Rosie was tempted to make a remark about bottling and selling it. When had Alastair become Matthew's henchman? He couldn't match Matthew's effete venom, but his attack was more subtle, a quiet goading and smirking.

"As a matter of fact, that's why I'm here," said Sam. He unfolded the newspaper he'd brought. "Situations vacant. 'Gardener to assist busy landscaping arm of the East Midlands' premier house builder, Fox Homes. Experience not necessary as full training will be given.' Broke plenty of rocks on the chain gang, didn't I? Well . . . dug the prison garden, anyway."

"You've got to be joking." Matt looked stunned. "Christ, man, you must be desperate."

"Oh, I am," Sam said grimly. "You try finding employment after you've been jailed for murder."

The office went absolutely silent.

"Manslaughter, I thought it was," blundered Alastair.

Sam shrugged. "Whatever."

"You're seriously here begging Rosie for a job?" Matthew threw his head back and laughed. "That's the most pathetic thing I've ever heard."

"That's how desperate I am." Sam smiled thinly. He gave both men an icy look. Matthew went on smirking, but Rosie saw sweat break out on his forehead.

"Well, I wish you all the best," he said. "However, surely she's explained that you need to fill in an application form, and ripping it up would give us all a damn good laugh."

"No, it's all right," Rosie said, standing up. She was so angry with Matt and Alastair she could hardly speak. "Are you serious, Sam?"

"Yeah," he said, looking startled. "I want to work."

She knew she was taking a huge risk, that it was crazy to make a split-second decision based on anger, but their attitude deserved no less than a sharp, cold slap. "All right, I'll give you a trial."

"What?" said all three men together.

"I'm giving him a chance," she hissed. "I'm taking him to the site right now. And you two ought to be bloody well ashamed of yourselves."

"This is it," she said, jumping out of the truck. "Five-bedroom show home, the star attraction. It has to sell the dream lifestyle, inside and out. When the viewers look out of the back windows, they'll see a perfect little fairy glen, fall in love and never want to leave."

"Ah. So your father enchants people to part with their money. Just like mine."

The development was on the far side of Ashvale. All through the ten-minute journey, Sam had sat laughing in the passenger seat. Still cross and resolutely businesslike, Rosie tried to ignore him as she led him down the side path. The back garden was an oblong of churned soil. Inside, the house was unfinished, all plaster and dust sheets.

"We can go inside to make coffee," she continued. "There are usually workmen around."

"Oh, good," he said. "My virtue's safe, then."

Rosie prodded his arm to make him look at her. "My

fairy glens don't happen without a lot of hard work," she said gravely. "It will be tough."

"Are you serious?" he said. "You'd really consider me?"

"Looks like it. You asked for it, you've got it."

Sam grinned. "Anything to piss off Matthew."

"One of these days," she said tightly, "I am going to chain all three of you to a bloody great rock and drop you in the river. Jon too, while I'm at it."

"I've got the picture, sweetheart. Matthew grooms Alastair as his devoted protégé. Then he marries you off to each other and hey presto, he's in complete control of his tiny empire. Foxy cunning."

"And you think you'll have a go at pulling my strings too?" she said crisply. "Get the tools from the truck. You can turn the soil and pick out all the stones and builders' crap. I'll fetch my plan and start marking things out."

"Yes, boss," he answered, startled.

She made him work hard. It felt good to watch him digging the winter-heavy soil. She was punishing him a little. Sam was fit, she had to concede. He uttered not a word of complaint but his eyes gleamed sardonically at her, as if he knew her game and was defying her to break him.

There were two workmen inside, fitting kitchen units. After a couple of hours, one of them stuck his head out and called, "We've finished here for the day, Mrs. Duncan; can you lock up when you go?"

"Sure," she called back. When they'd gone, she went inside and switched on the kettle. She needed a break. The house felt strange with no one there, raw and echoic. It was like stepping into another world. "Leave your boots outside," she said as Sam followed her. "They get mad if we tread mud on their nice new tiles. Coffee?"

"Thanks, *Mrs. Duncan*," he said mockingly.

As she made drinks, she was acutely aware of Sam's presence, the sweat of his work-hot body and of her own, mingling with the smell of new wood and plaster. They stood sipping their coffee, Sam leaning against the sink,

Rosie at right-angles against a worktop. Now she had calmed down, she felt tongue-tied. Funny, she'd never been lost for words with him before.

"This is different," he said.

"The coffee? Is it bad?"

"No, this situation. Being your employee." He winked at her. "I rather like it."

"I'm not working you hard enough, then," she said.

She meant it to be a quick break. The slate tiles felt cold through her socks. Sam was behaving impeccably, but what was he thinking? She saw an awful vision of the future; a pleasant secure life with Alastair on the surface, but in secret—in the underworld—snatched frantic moments with Sam, rough and hot, almost violent, compelling, decadent and rotten with guilt. God, it would be so easy. And in the end, it would kill her.

"Come on, we can do another hour." As she leaned past him to put her mug in the sink, pain caught her left shoulder. She lifted her opposite hand to soothe it.

"What's up?" Sam asked.

"Pulled something. Must have been bending over for too long."

"That would be impossible."

His eyes gleamed so wickedly that she had to bite down on a smile, despite herself. "Can I say anything without you finding a lascivious innuendo in it?"

"You have to seize every chance you get, love," he said. "Turn around."

She did so, presenting her back to him. His hands came down on her shoulders and began to knead. The heat and pressure felt amazing. The sweet pain as his fingers worked into the ache was so exquisite that her head fell back and she groaned out loud. His mouth came close to her ear. "That good, eh?"

"Oh god, yes," she whispered.

The strong fingers went on working deep into her. She went weak at the knees, letting herself relax against him so

that their legs touched, half intertwined, her bottom nest-
ling into his hips. She realized that the hard ridge pressing
into the small of her back was not his hipbone.

After a few minutes his hands came to rest on her shoulders, transmitting heat, sliding gently around her as she
turned to face him. They looked at each other. He wasn't
smiling now; his expression was somber, his beautiful lips
parted. Everything changed. "Better?" he asked.

"I didn't know you could do that." Her voice was low, her
breathing steady but fast. Then they just stood there, looking softly into each other's eyes, neither making a move.

"I'm thinking that cold tiles and plastic sheeting don't
look very inviting." Sam's voice was unsteady. "Every time
I'm with you, I want you so badly I can't see straight. But if
it's going to end with you running away, tearing yourself
up with guilt and hating me, I'm not doing it anymore.
You're using me, Rosie. I suppose I deserve it. But even
scum has pride, you know."

"And you're not using me?" She drew herself taller, noticed his gaze flick to her breasts as she did so. "Laughing
at me because I put on this indignant pose of being a happily married woman, when you know that I collapse into a
complete mess every time you touch me?"

"I'm not laughing at you." He stroked her cheek. "Never
that."

"Don't tell me you don't get a malevolent thrill out of
what we've done. It's all over your face when you look at
Alastair. You love it."

"Well . . . yeah." He tipped his head to one side. "So?"

"This is a game to you."

"How else do I get to play with you?" His hands tightened on her shoulders. His eyes turned fiery. Blue-green
fire. "You think I'm dirt. You think I'm easy."

Rosie laughed. "You are easy, Sam!"

"Well, yes, okay, I'm a tart. For you. But I can't go on
being your sex slave, Rosie. I can't."

"You haven't even started yet." She stood gazing into his
eyes, pulling her lower lip between her teeth, feeling the

blood rush into it. Sam's eyes softened as he looked at the lip, entranced. Everything went still inside her. All of her good resolutions evaporated like mist—being honest, she knew they'd never been anything but vapor—and in their place a deeper, Aetherial self took over; one that could set aside human conscience in order to hunt down the truth. Her voice low, she asked, "Will you come upstairs with me?"

"Oh, I'll have to think really hard about that," he whispered. "Why?"

"I need to know," she said simply.

"Need to know what?"

Rosie didn't answer. Her other-self felt as purposeful as a wolf and slightly crazy, as if she'd entered a trance. She took his hand and led him into the hallway, up the sweep of the stairs. Sunlight sparkled through the windows, illuminating specks of dust. There was carpet on the landing, protected by a plastic runner.

"It's going to be the show house, you see," she said. "All beautifully furnished to attract the buyers. They've almost finished up here." She pushed open the door to the master bedroom. "Nice, isn't it?"

The room was inviting; simple yet opulent, glowing in diffuse sunbeams, with an acre of creamy carpet and plain silk curtains of palest gold. Three walls were painted biscuit, and the fourth—facing the door and framing a huge double bed—was deep burgundy. The bed was dressed with layered silken covers and scattered with cushions in the same shades of coffee, pale gold and dark rich plum. Beaded fringes glittered. The burgundy against the softer colors was emotive, almost visceral, like blood.

"I'd buy it," said Sam, a bit hoarse.

Rosie closed the door behind them, quickly discarding her un-erotic socks behind his back. "You still want to see me naked?" she asked. She was shaking a little now, hardly able to believe she was doing this.

"Uh," said Sam, his face a picture of astonishment. "Yes. Of course. God, please."

"I want to see you, too. Lie on the bed. Pull the covers

back first; we don't want to get into trouble for creasing all that beautiful silk."

He obeyed, and now he actually looked nervous, startled by a Rosie he'd never seen before. He pulled off his jacket and threw it on the floor, settled back against pillows and white linen.

"One condition," she said. "No touching."

"None at all?"

"Not until I say so. Promise."

"Fine, I promise. This isn't a horrible practical joke, is it?" he asked, half-smiling. "You get me naked and then all the workmen burst in with cameras?"

"Sam," she said, and pressed a fingertip to her lips. "Shh."

She began to peel off her clothes. Not the most glamorous garments in the world, but he watched enraptured. She slid her jeans over her hips, stepped out of them. Flexed upwards to remove her T-shirt, her hair falling in a static cloud as she discarded it. And it was like shedding the veil of her everyday self: the self that kept pretending she was fine and didn't want or need Sam. In her panic of denial, she'd relinquished mastery to Sam, given him free license to manipulate her desires and fears. All along, he'd been winning the game. Now it was time to reclaim her power.

In lacy bra and briefs of darkest crimson, she twirled, looking back at him over her shoulder as she did so. He must realize she didn't usually wear expensive underwear to work. *No, Sam, this was a mistake, this is never happening again,* she kept saying, and yet she'd taken to wearing satin and lace under her clothes . . . just in case.

Time to stop pretending.

She was self-conscious at first; but Sam's reaction, his parted lips and shining eyes, gave her confidence. She leaned over him, hands on either side of his chest. He tried to rise, his mouth questing for her.

"Ah-ah-ah. No touching."

"Oh god, Rosie . . ."

"Put your hands behind your head. Keep them there."

He was wearing a charcoal-grey shirt. She undid the first

two buttons and pushed her hand inside, palm flat against his chest. He smelled wonderful. Warm skin, fresh sweat, and the earthy, aphrodisiac fragrance he used that always drove her mad. She felt the quick rise and fall of his rib cage, the beating of his heart. She went on unbuttoning the shirt, then swooped to kiss his chest. He exclaimed in surprise.

As she slid the shirt off him, her eyes blurred. His torso was lovely, so lean and beautifully muscled, shoulders just broad enough. She pulled off his socks, and even his feet were strong and perfect, like those of a classical statue. Then to his jeans . . . she ran her fingers inside the waistband, caressing downwards until she grazed a fingertip over warm, tumescent flesh. He tensed. She looked back at his face and saw his eyes were closed. He was trembling.

Rosie caught her breath. This was too much fun. This was incredible.

His jeans and black briefs fell to the floor. As she stood back to admire him she felt tears in her eyes, gathering and spilling. Long legs and narrow hips and English-pale skin. Angular, sensual face resting back between his folded arms, his mouth and eyelashes feminine against the male planes. Smooth chest. Hair brushed back, dark at the roots then bronze, then tipped with gold and already a bit tousled. *Oh, dear gods,* she thought, *he really is gorgeous.* She studied the dark curls at his groin, the stiff, magnificent rise of the wand, a deeper reddish purple against the pale skin. She realized she'd never really seen it before; felt it, certainly, but never had the chance to admire it. It was all part of his beauty, and gods, so exciting. The sweet ache inside her was growing unbearable.

Sam opened his eyes. "Christ, I thought you'd left the room."

"Just looking." She smiled.

"I wish I could take a photo of you 'just looking.' Your face . . ."

"Am I what you hoped for?" she said, coming close to him.

"You know it," he said helplessly. "Can I at least touch the lacy bits?"

"Patience," she murmured. And she leaned down to take him in her mouth, gently tasting, finding the surface as smooth and delicate as the inside of her own cheek. Sam gasped and groaned, but she released him, smiling as he propped himself on his elbows to stare at her.

"Bloody hell, are you trying to torture me?"

"Oh, yes," she said with a grin.

She rose, put her hands to her hips and slid out of the wisp of lace. Control. That was what it was about. She'd given it all away to him and now she was taking it back. And realizing how complete her power over him could be, she felt a thrill of nervous excitement, felt herself blossoming into the true, wild, authentic Rosie she had never been before.

"Is this nice?" she asked.

Sam watched spellbound, as helpless as if she'd handcuffed him. Here she was at last—exactly as he'd dreamed but a thousand times better because she was really here, her compact body as neat and smooth as ivory, and the lovely lines of her stomach leading into the promise of that dark, fleecy triangle. Only her breasts were still concealed by crimson lace. Her scent was all around him, clean, warm and divine with arousal.

"Is this nice?" she asked, as if genuinely uncertain. That faint blush of innocence drove him beyond reason. She looked as if she had never, ever shown herself off like this before, and was startled to realize her own glorious power.

He guessed, almost in disbelief, that no one had ever told her how amazing she was.

"God, yes," he croaked. He couldn't find the words. "Understatement of the century. No tattoos. Where's Shrek?"

She ran her hands down her waist, hips swaying. "No scales. No leaves, no wing buds. Just my skin. Do you like it, Sam?"

"Rosie," he said, blood rushing haywire through him. "You don't expect actual words, do you? You can *see* how much I like you. As compliments go, will that do as a down payment?"

He smiled at her and she smiled back; a truly warm smile from the heart that he'd never had from her before. The tip of her tongue came out and touched her lips. "All right, you can touch me." Leaning down to his jacket, she picked up a black leather glove that had fallen from his pocket. She pulled the glove onto his right hand and added, "But only with this."

"You're crazy," he said, startled and strangely delighted.

"Yes, I am," she agreed. "Be creative."

He flexed the encased hand. "Oh, I will."

Rosie knelt on the bed and settled herself across his hips, gasping at the delicious rigid pressure of him against her. The sensations were almost unbearably sweet. Sam's gloved hand went everywhere, caressing, worshipping; tracing her shoulders, her neck, her collarbones. She leaned down to him and let him undo the clasp of her bra. As her breasts came free, he craned upwards to kiss them. Rosie moaned. Okay, he was bending the rules a bit, but she didn't try to stop him.

"Oh my god, at last," he murmured, teasing with lips and tongue until she was close to dissolving. "So beautiful . . ."

She sat up, arching her spine. The glove traveled up and down her arms, across her belly, creating thistledown lines of electricity. The leather felt incredible, like sensuous alien skin. Her head fell back. She began to move on him, couldn't stop herself. In a blinding rush of light they exploded on each other. Crimson light and zinging, muscular ecstasy, as intense as pain. Sam was moving under her, gasping. Probably the whole building site had heard them, but she was past caring. The outside world had ceased to exist.

In that golden, hallucinatory moment, Rosie drew her hand over the damp skin of Sam's chest, drawing swirls and spirals, then running her fingers in the same designs over herself from pelvis to throat. Drawing Otherworld runes.

"What are you doing?" he whispered. His eyes were

half-closed and shining. He clearly couldn't believe this wild, unsuspected Rosie.

"Anointing us," she said solemnly. "Covering us in each other."

"You know it will never wash away?" Sam pulled off the glove and threw it on the carpet. "May I touch yet?"

"Oh—yes," she groaned. "Please. Everything."

He was still as hard as ever. He gave a conspiratorial smile, as if to say, *Surely you didn't think I'd finished?* Dizzy and sensitized, she slid onto him, holding her breath as he filled her. Every nerve flowed with energy. She'd never known such bliss and it was scary, because how could any-one come back from this?

She felt cotton gliding against her back and realized he'd grabbed his shirt and was draping it over her. He was grip-ping the fabric on both sides, using it to ease her against him. "I'm not sure I'm ready to touch you yet," he said.

"Sadist," she breathed.

"It takes two." His thumbs brushed lightly against her arms. He held her shoulders, palms hot through the shirt. "Now you'll smell of me," he said. "And when I put it back on, it will smell of you. Hot, glowing Rosie. And I'll never wash it again."

"Nice," she said. Underneath the flippant asides an ocean was surging. *What does it mean, that we will always be covered in each other and never able to wash it away? Does it mean anything at all, or is this just sex, incredible sex, but nothing else? How can there be any such thing as just sex, when it's like this, like the whole universe turning inside out?*

"I'm no good, Rosie," Sam murmured as he moved un-der her, eyes lambent. "You always saw it. That's why you shied away from me. It's why I couldn't do the decent thing and leave you alone. I'm wicked."

"You're bad," she agreed, voice rough. "And you're proud of it. That's why I want you. And you want me be-cause you can't have me."

The second wave built slowly, agonizing in its promise.

"Years, I've waited for this. You've no idea how much I wanted to be inside you, untouchable Rosie."

"Didn't you know I wanted it too? I could have taken you across that prison table . . ." She writhed on him, liquefying.

"God, I wish you had." He began to move more forcefully, looking hard into her eyes. His voice was ragged. "We were always heading towards this. And we've both always known it."

"We're both wicked, Sam." The words came out of her core and she couldn't stop them, she was molten.

"Oh, yes. As bad as each other."

Release broke with such incredible power, such a long and complex fugue of sensation, that Rosie was amazed to survive. The shirt slid off her as she convulsed. Sam's hands came to her hips and held her, drawing out every last shock of sensation. Then she collapsed onto his chest, exhausted. He held her, his palms and fingers spreading delicious warmth across her naked skin, arms strong around her, whispering, "It's all right, I'm here, I've got you."

She lay beside him, dazed.

Sam rose on one elbow, stroking her face. He was watching her face tenderly, as intently as a cat. "What?" she said at last.

"Somewhere about now you go into a panic, tell me nothing happened and run for the hills. Don't even think about it."

"I'm not. I can't move."

Blue-green lights sparkled across his eyes as they took in every inch of her face. Satiated, but still wickedly speculating. "There's something I've always wanted to do with you that we've never done before."

"Oh yes?" She stirred and flexed, ready to rise to any challenge. "Shock me. Spiky metal whips?"

"Hey, you were the one with the glove. This," he said, sliding his arms more tightly around her. "The tender part. To lie in bed with you afterwards. I wanted this more than anything."

The ocean floor fell away and she was drowning.

So easy to duel with him. So very easy to have rough quickies in inappropriate places, or to play erotic power games. But to lie holding him, that was for people who loved and trusted each other, and it was a worse betrayal of Alastair than anything else she'd done. Suddenly she was terrified. Human again. Apparently her Aetherial-self hadn't thought this far.

"What have you done to me?" she whispered on the very end of her breath. "When I'm in bed with Alastair—"

"Don't," he said roughly, but she had to tell him.

"When I'm in bed with Alastair, I can only come if I think about you."

His mouth quested for hers. They began kissing and all the lovely melting fire was there again. She realized that, for all they'd done, it was the first time they'd kissed that day. *So, let's kiss for several hours.* It seemed a lifetime since they'd come upstairs. His mouth was delicious. They lay interlocked, moving sensuously against each other as they kissed at length.

He was so strong and solid, so bright with energy. It wasn't physical pleasure that made this so overwhelming. No. It was special because it was Sam, no one else, but her dark, dangerous, flaky Sam. His hands on her, his body against hers, his excitement and affection and complete attention all pouring into her.

"Did you find out what you needed to know?" he asked.

"I think so. But I'm scared to believe it."

"What is it?"

"Whether this is real. Whether it's any more than lust. Whether this is the end or the beginning."

"It's real for me." He paused. "What is it for you?"

"I want you, Sam. You know I want you."

"But you can't love me?" He lay still. "I never really expected you to. I know I'm not good enough for you. I try not to let it break my heart because, hey, you're lying in bed with me, but . . . no, why should you?"

"Because I—there's something missing. In me, I mean.

I thought I knew with . . . other people . . . but I didn't. I could so easily get it monumentally wrong yet again." She traced his cheekbone. "You're in paradise just being here with me, aren't you?"

He half-smiled. There was a slight frown there too. "Yeah. Completely."

"Have you any idea how seductive that is? But you've got nothing to lose. Do I give up my house, life, job, everything for you?"

"Sweetheart, no, I don't want that." He was distressed, reality dawning. "You think I was put on this Earth to torment you but I'm not, I just couldn't give up while I could see that spark in your eye. Never meant you to lose anything."

"But I'm bound to. If they ever find out about us, I could lose the lot. It's my career that means the most, being an important part of my father's business, making him proud of me. That's everything to me."

"You—you wouldn't have to leave work, would you?"

"Oh, I would. Matthew would disown me. He might stop me seeing Faith and Heather. How could I possibly expect to go on working alongside him and Alastair? Not in a million years. Even my mum and dad would be ashamed."

"So you want to know if I'm worth the sacrifice?" Sam said somberly. "Well, I'm not, am I? It's obvious. I'm no architect. What does it say on my CV? Expelled. Prison. Oh yeah, and dug garden for two hours then spent all afternoon in bed with the boss. I'm never going to be worth it."

"Hey." She leaned above him. A tear fell out of nowhere and landed on his face. "Why the hell do you think I'm even considering it?"

"You are?" His face was frozen, as if he were desperately hoping but not expecting anything.

"But what if I'm making a mistake? What if the minute I say yes, you lose interest—oh, got that one conquered, I'm bored now, let's move on?"

"What?" He gripped her shoulders, looking helpless. "If

you think that, you don't know me, you don't know anything."

"That's kind of the point. I don't really know you."

"Sordid life of crime," he said. "Thieving, drugs, violence. I could probably make it as a hit man. Bit of necromancy. Torturing hamsters for fun and profit. Rosie . . ."

"What?"

"That's where I would have been if I hadn't met you. You know me better than anyone. You rescued me. I'm your bloody slave. What can I do to convince you?"

She bowed her head, touching it to his. "Give me some time."

"All you want." His voice was a rush of hope and gratitude. "Anything you need, love, everything . . ."

He began kissing his way down her throat, tongue and lips feathering all down her body then working into her, setting the pearl of pleasure alight. Rosie cried out. Too much ecstasy. So intense now, she couldn't bear it. She drew his face up level with hers and kissed him, tasting their myrrh all mixed up together. She wrapped her hand around him, felt him firm and eager in her palm.

"Is this for me?" she asked.

"All for you," he said, pushing and gliding into her as she lifted one knee over his hip. "Always."

"I want you there, Sam," she said, crying. "As deep as you can go. Forever."

The world turned molten with sensation, red and golden. She felt the Dusklands burning around them. Felt herself changing, transforming, becoming the Aetherial she was always meant to be, meeting her *fylgia* on the other side and becoming her true self. They floated in a strange fiery heaven where pleasure was so intense it was close to pain. They wept afterwards.

Somewhere, control and power had all evaporated.

Then they lay together, knowing they couldn't stay much longer, but not wanting to break the spell. "It's only ten to three," Rosie said, looking at her watch. "They won't expect us back at the office until five."

"What haven't we done yet?" Sam asked lazily. "Haven't shown you what else I can do with my tongue . . ."

"Keep something for next time. I'm done in."

"Me too, sweetheart. Hey . . . did you say *next time*?"

"Apparently," she whispered.

Sam fell asleep for a few minutes. Rosie sat up, hands clasped around her raised knees, hair slipping over her shoulders, and watched him. He was truly beautiful, stretched out like sculpture with every muscle defined, lovely as marble but warm and living. She smiled.

No one had ever loved her like this before. No one ever would again.

And she felt a terrible ache in her heart, because she knew it was doomed. Neither of them truly felt worthy of that much love. And Sam was unstable, had nothing in his life except Rosie. Yes, he was wonderful for the forbidden demon sex in the dark. But if they tried to be together, they would fall to pieces. She knew it.

I still can't give him up, she thought, holding on to her toes. *I can't, I just can't. Okay, I'm going to be very careful. One day at a time. Oh my god, I'm having an affair.*

There was building noise from the house next door. Sam woke with a start, saw her looking at him. "Sorry, love, I dropped off. Told you I was up for five nights."

Noise from next door came again, a dull hammering, or the soft thunder of boots on scaffolding planks. Weirdly, she thought she heard a voice calling her name, but she dismissed it. Then a door opened, sounding oddly close . . .

Suddenly, horribly, and too late, they realized that the noises were inside the house. The door to the bedroom was wide open. A man was standing in the doorway, gaping at them.

Alastair.

15

The Crone Oak

No one said a word.

The lovers reclined in disarray on the tangled bed, frozen as if caught in stage lights.

Alastair stared. It was only for seconds, as long as it took him to process the scene. His lips began to form unanswerable questions—*What the hell?* or, *How could you?*—but nothing came out.

His eyes glittered. Blood rose in his face. Then he whirled on his heel and walked out.

They heard him stomping down the uncarpeted stairs. A door slammed, filling the house with tense echoes. Rosie sat there in shock. There was no breath in her to speak or react. Arms, hands, legs, nothing would move.

"Oh shit," said Sam, sitting up. "Oh, god, Rosie. Bloody hell."

She put a hand to her face, squeezed her eyes shut and said, "*Fuck.*"

Sam got off the bed and began to gather their scattered clothes. She sat on the edge of the bed with her head bowed, then shook herself and began to dress, fumbling so much that Sam was fully clothed a good minute before her.

"Are you all right?" he asked gently, one hand hovering near her shoulder without actually touching.

"Help me fix the bed," she said, hauling the covers over the sticky, rumpled sheets. Her mouth was dry, her heart trying to explode out of her chest, but all she could think to do was tidy away the evidence, too late. "Chuck me those cushions."

Sam obliged. "How did he know we were here?"

"He knew which plot I was starting. He often drops in, if he happens to be on site. I never thought he would today. God, I'm an idiot!"

"No. It's just crap luck."

The room was soon as pristine as they'd found it. No one was likely to disturb the bed again until the house was sold; but when they did, they were in for a fairly unsavory surprise. Rosie took a deep breath, shuddering. "Oh god."

"I'm so sorry, babe." Sam raked his hand through his hair. She'd half-expected gloating pleasure from him at being discovered, but she'd misjudged him again. "I never wanted this to happen. What are we going to do?"

"I don't know, Sam." She finally managed to meet his eyes. His hair was all tousled and he looked tender, beautiful and worried to death. "I'd better go after him."

"No, let him cool down first, I would."

She exhaled. "It'll be worse if I put it off. He deserves an explanation."

"Let me come with you. Face him together."

"Oh, he'd love that." Shock had turned the afterglow to ashes. They could barely touch each other. "Thanks, but no. I have to do this alone."

Lucas made his way towards Freya's Crown. He approached from the west, across the wildest part of the estate, where he wouldn't be seen from the manor. He pushed through drifts of waxy evergreens, through beech woods and brambles, climbing the steep rocky slope towards the great molar on the crest.

This was a huge risk. If Lawrence caught him, it would be the end. If Jon found out, he'd be furious—tough. Jon had done nothing for months, except sit on Rosie's spare bed, brooding and feeling sorry for himself. Lucas had finally worked up courage to seek the truth.

The tilted volcanic outcrop loomed over him. Reaching it, he pressed one hand to its surface and rested there to get his breath back. The wind was freezing up here. He'd had time to get over the frantic fear of his last visit here and now, although nervous, he was surprisingly calm. Again he glanced around the wild landscape to make sure he was alone. The grey shadow of a *dysir* began to sniff around him, but made no move to stop him.

Carefully, Lucas let himself blend into the Dusklands.

The world turned liquid blue. The Great Gates stood in stately glory; a structure created by the Ancients. The sight induced swooping dizziness and he paused to steady his nerve . . . then he began to work his way around, trailing his hands over the gritty surface. The ridged scar on his chest began to throb and burn.

He didn't expect to find anything. He must have hallucinated the rock face opening after the bad trip with Jon. There couldn't really be a crack, or Lawrence would have found it.

The rock spoke, making him jump. A deep, echoing *ah* of heavy stone shifting. His fingers found the rim of a fissure. It was a jagged line of darkness stretching from crown to base, just barely wide enough for a slim person to squeeze into.

Lucas sank to his knees, overwhelmed, staring into the dark. He could perceive nothing inside. Only inky blackness. Perhaps the hint of a cold draft.

It was true. The Gates had cracked open as he'd come out of the drug trance. Had the gap been here all this time, or had it sealed itself and just this minute opened again at his touch? Whatever—it meant he'd somehow *unlocked* it. Panic swelled under his heart. Why hadn't Lawrence found it? If he had, he would surely have mentioned it, raged about it—and, above all, relocked it long ago.

Did this mean that Lawrence, impossibly, did not know the crack was here?

It was only a sliver, hardly even a Lychgate. Not enough for anything to pass in or out, Luc told himself . . . not even Brawth. At least, he prayed with all his strength that nothing dangerous had crept through. "It can't have done," he said aloud. "We would have known, wouldn't we?"

He felt into the fissure with both hands, pressing his palms to the cold hard walls. He tried to imagine stepping in, but couldn't; it was too terrifying. You could stare off a cliff top, but—unless you had a death wish—you wouldn't jump.

Holy crap, I've unlocked the Gates, he thought, *but Lawrence doesn't know. How can he not know? He said they'd never be opened again. He said there was only one Gatekeeper and it was him. So how . . . ?*

Unless Lawrence has lost the power.

No, thought Lucas, *no. I can't be responsible for this.*

He sensed no flood, no storm, no ice demon rushing towards him. Only an intense, wintry chill. He snatched his hands out of it, rose to his feet and stared at the gap in helpless alarm. He had no idea how to open it any further—not that he wanted to—and no idea how to close it, either.

What the hell was he supposed to do now?

He shut his eyes and saw, all around him, figures in masks. Foxes, wildcats, wolves, hawks, lizards and jeweled fish—vast, transparent deities, watching him from another place as if from the tiers of a great amphitheater. They were ghostly, shining with their own eerie light; and they all simply stood there, staring at him. Waiting.

He had no idea what they wanted. He'd been seeing them in dreams for weeks. "*Come,*" breathed the wind. "*Come to us.*"

Lucas jerked backwards, stepped into the dip behind him and fell, lurching violently back into the surface world. Clear air, stark landscape. He rolled to his feet and stood there, head whirling with shock. He knew he should tell Lawrence or Auberon—but what drastic action might they take? How could he keep such a monumental secret to himself . . . but how could he even begin to confess it?

If the Lychgate had stood unlocked like this for months, was it possible that there was no danger after all?

Lucas turned and walked away. Head down, hands in his coat pockets, he was nearly running. And all the way down the hill the wind kept hissing at him, "*Come in, come to us. It's time.*"

The aftermath was a panicky muddle. Locking the house and loading the truck as if nothing had happened, even though the world was falling in. Driving Sam back to Fox Homes to collect his motorbike; watching nervously for Alastair's car all the way; persuading Sam to leave quickly, before anyone saw him.

"When am I going to see you?" he asked.

"I don't know. You'd better keep out of the way for a while."

"How can I?" Sam was dismayed. "What if he rants and raves?"

"I don't need protecting from him. Please, just over the weekend."

"And . . . what happens then?"

Rosie shook her head. "God, Sam, don't ask me that."

"Am I fired?" he asked so plaintively that she wanted to laugh and cry at the same time.

"Have you got a mobile?" she said. "Quick, give me the number. Then I won't have to get past Cruella again." And they stood inanely swapping phone numbers, while the dark hunt came thundering towards them through the cosmos.

Once he'd gone, Rosie hauled herself upstairs to the architects' office, steeled for disaster. Matthew greeted her with a feeble joke about Sam tunneling to freedom and never being seen again. When she asked if he'd seen Alastair, he looked innocently puzzled. "I thought he went to find you."

"We must have missed each other," Rosie said lamely, and rushed out.

So Alastair hadn't run straight to him—and why would he? No man would want to admit such humiliation, even to his best friend.

She looked for his car, checked the nearby pub. Finally

she went home, shaking with anxiety all the way—and there he was. Waiting for her on the living-room sofa; a solid mass of bewilderment, pain and simmering anger. His face was purple with emotion.

Rosie sidled in, as if making no sound would make her seem more contrite. "Um," she said softly, and perched on the arm of a chair.

Alastair said nothing at first. The atmosphere hung sour and awkward between them. Finally, as if they'd already had half an argument—which perhaps they had, inside their own heads—he said, "You know, I came to tell you I was sorry."

"About what?" Rosie said, startled.

"Matthew and me, being rude to Sam. I felt bad about it after. It was childish. I've got nothing against Sam, he's obviously a *great* fellow"—the word was loaded with sarcasm—"but when I say to Matt, 'Maybe we went over the top,' he sneers and starts telling me Sam's a troublemaker, a psycho and all that, and I start thinking, oh lord, even if Matt's exaggerating, I let Rosie go off on her own with him. Better make sure she's all right."

"You felt you needed to check up on me?"

"No. I thought, I'll apologize for being a prat, and see if she's all right. I was concerned about my wife, is that okay?"

Rosie bit her lip. Her throat ached. "I didn't mean to hurt you," she said, and meant it. She was fond of Alastair, perhaps more than she'd realized. No passion between them, but there had been *something*; affection, friendship, habit, something too solid to be thrown away lightly.

"No, they never do," he said darkly. His accent grew more Scottish when he was upset. "'It just happened. It's not you, it's me.' And so on. I've heard it all before. So, what was it, a spontaneous shag to get back at Matt and me?"

"No. It was nothing to do with that."

He pondered. His eyes shone with tears. That brought her close to the edge, too. Truth dawning, he said, "It wasn't the first time, was it? How long's it been going on?"

"A while."

"But we've only been married four months!" he shouted. He slapped his palms hard on his thighs, jumped up and paced around the room.

Watching him, Rosie felt a strange sense of resignation. She hadn't wanted this—but what had she planned instead? To deceive him, find excuses to avoid sex, then sneak off for heated liaisons with Sam? So her plans had been torpedoed. It served her right. She felt sad and wretched, but relieved that he knew.

"We should have stayed friends, Alastair," she said gently. "I shouldn't have married you."

"Then why the hell did you?" His voice was tight with anguish.

"It seemed right at the time. I made a mistake. It's my fault, not yours."

"You settled for me. I always knew, but I tried to kid myself it would work out. I thought you wanted that cretin Jon, so why are you screwing his brother?"

Then he started crying. He stood with his shoulders shaking, desolate. Tears ran down Rosie's face. Neither of them spoke for a time.

Eventually Alastair composed himself and said, to her complete astonishment, "We can put this behind us, Rose. You wanted to go a bit wild, maybe. I suppose that's in your blood. But you've got it out of your system now, right? Can't we forget it and make a new start?"

It was the hope in his voice that destroyed her. He was offering her a way back. Sam was a wolf in the dark, but Alastair was part of her family.

She realized that this was the moment of heartbreak. Not being discovered, but this.

"No," she said, quiet and firm. "I'm sorry, Alastair. I shouldn't have married you. It wouldn't be fair of me to stay."

"No, wait. You don't know what you're saying."

"Yes, I do. I want Sam."

"But he's a nutcase!" He began to pace again.

"No, he isn't. Even if I stayed with you, I'd go on seeing him, and I can't do that to you."

"I should never have let you go to that bloody prison!"

"*Let* me? It wasn't up to you!"

"You're not thinking straight. This isn't you, Rose. You're sensible, you're kind." His hands were shaking, his eyes growing wild. "You wouldn't do this to me."

"I would. I have," she said somberly. "And I'm terribly sorry."

Alastair paced a bit more. Finally he seemed to accept what he was saying. Then he lost it. "When did I strike you?" he cried. "*When did I strike you?*"

"What?" She was on her feet, startled by his sudden rage. "What are you talking about?"

"I've read the folktales. If a man takes a faerie wife, he knows the rules; if he once mistreats her, she'll vanish back to the land of Faerie. That's the deal. He can't control her like he would a human wife. He hits her, she's gone. One strike and you're out. I've kept my side of the bargain! So tell me, *when the hell did I strike you?*"

Rosie stood aghast. She wondered what she'd missed by taking him at face value. "What do you mean? Where did that lot come from?"

"Oh, I know what you are. The elder race. The *others*. You told me yourself, sort of laughing as if you assumed I wouldn't believe it. But I've had chats with Jessica. Words with Faith, who couldn't keep a secret if her life depended on it. Even Matt, who's almightily embarrassed by it, more or less sold you to me on the strength of it. Yes, you might be a wee bit wild, but the magic of you more than made up for that."

"He *marketed* me?" she said numbly.

"Special. More than human. All glamorous and mysterious, like a goddess."

"I didn't realize you were such a romantic," she said scathingly. "Oh my god, I never guessed. You really thought you were buying into a fairy tale?"

"Yes, it sounds idiotic, put like that. But I did, because I thought you'd be different."

"How? As compared to the coke-snorting hell-bitch who broke your heart before me?"

"Aye, different from her. Exactly. But oh, no. Human, Aetherial, you're all the bloody same! All women have this witch inside them!"

She stood incredulous at the volcanic rage boiling out of him. "And you married me, thinking that?" Outraged, she squared up to him. "Matthew was so desperate for me to marry a human, I never stopped to quiz *your* motives. You thought you were getting some kind of special offer, one faerie princess, slightly soiled, comes complete with rich father and chastity belt?"

"I never thought that. I loved you."

"Maybe it's all the love you're capable of, but it felt pretty bloody lukewarm to me."

"Well, I'm only a humble mortal. You're a princess and I treated you with respect. Now I'm not passionate enough for you? But you knew what you were getting! I thought you were happy. Satisfied. I didn't realize you secretly wanted some man all over you like a rutting hog. Just not me, eh?"

"I thought we were happy, too, but that's because I was dead inside. Sam brought me back to life."

Alastair glared at her, fury seething in his eyes. He took a couple of steps back, nostrils flaring. "Will you get yourself away from me?" he said, an ocean of disgust in his voice. "You stink of sex."

"Well, I have just had lots of it. I'll take a shower," she said icily. She turned away, heartsick. From calm sorrow to cheap, vicious insults—what had made her think they could do this with dignity?

As she went into the hallway she saw Lucas and Jon, hovering at the bottom of the stairs. Great, all she needed was the whole ghastly scene to have been witnessed. Lucas looked wide-eyed and upset. "Are you all right, Ro?" he mouthed.

She didn't answer. Jon's expression was closed, contemptuous. *Despising me for getting mired in a human mess?* she wondered. *I bet that's exactly it. He thinks he's above all this.*

"Come on, Luc," Jon said flatly, walking towards the front door. "I need to get out of here."

"Who's going to tell Matthew?" Alastair said as the door closed behind them. He stood with his hands on his hips. "You or me?"

"I will," she said. "He's going to be furious with me, whoever tells him."

"Where am I going to live? Because if you think you're moving Sam in here—"

"You can have the house," she said quickly. "I'll go to Oakholme."

"I don't want the bloody house!" he cried. "I want you. Rosie, please!"

She looked away. She couldn't bear his anguish.

"That's it, is it?" he said shakily. "You'd give up everything to fuck some loser who can't even get a proper job? It's really over?"

"I'll leave," she said faintly.

"No, don't stir yourself." His voice turned flat with anger. "I can't talk to you any more." And he was gone. She winced as the front door slammed.

Two hours later Rosie sat in the kitchen, numb. She was alone in the coldhearted house with winter darkness falling outside. She wanted to call Sam, but didn't. She needed to distance herself from him before she could even straighten her thoughts, let alone speak.

In the shower, she'd cried until she couldn't anymore. The water had washed away the essence of Sam and her tears together.

Now she was cradling a mug of tea. Thought of adding brandy, decided it wouldn't help. When she heard the front door opening, she went on red alert, steeling herself for another bout. Lucas's face appeared in the doorway, porcelain-pale and worried. She slumped in relief, asking, "Where's Jon?"

"We had an argument." Lucas came in, removing his coat and throwing it on a chair. He sat opposite her. "We met this mate of his, and Jon wanted to go off with him and get stoned. I was mad at him for thinking about himself when you're having a crisis, but getting mad at Jon only makes him more obstinate. So I left him to it."

"Great," Rosie sighed. "And Alastair's walked out."

"So it's just you and me." Luc sat looking anxiously at her. "That was a bombshell, you and Alastair. You want to tell me about it?"

"I don't know what to say. I've been seeing Sam. Alastair caught us in bed at the show house I was working on." She gave a sour laugh. "If I'd told him we'd taken our clothes off to have a rest after a tough morning's gardening, I don't think he would have bought it."

"Good grief, Ro, you're a dark horse. I thought you were the last person . . . d'you remember, the morning of your wedding? I knew your heart wasn't in it. I knew."

"Yes, you did." She gripped his hand across the table. "I've screwed up royally."

"Come on, you're not the first person ever to . . . uh," he trailed off as they caught each other's eye.

"Must run in the family, eh?" Rosie gave a sour grin.

"I'm confused. You don't even like Sam."

"I thought I didn't. Actually I was like a cat on a hot plate every time I saw him, and I never knew how to react, except to fend him off. He grew on me. I like him. A lot."

"Do you love him?"

"I don't know yet. That's the problem, I'm scared I've wrecked our lives for nothing. What if it's only lust in the end? Demon lovers promise the world then leave you high and dry. I don't know what to do."

"Don't worry, Ro. Don't rush into anything. It'll work out."

She smiled at Lucas, feeling an intense wave of love for him. He was pure-hearted, loyal, the light of his soul shining clearly in his eyes. A being of light, no less. "I'm so glad you're here. We've got each other, whatever else happens."

"I seriously need to talk to you," he said, eyes darkening. "Sorry I've picked a bad time."

"Oh, I'm tired of my own problems. What's up?"

His shoulders hunched. Skeins of black hair fell forward. "Don't know where to start. I daren't tell anyone. I—I—I think I opened the Gates."

"You've done *what*?"

"Oh—not wide open. Is there a word for not even ajar?" He held up his hands in prayer position, a few inches apart. "Just a sliver."

She sat speechless, listening intently as he explained. "I didn't intend to do it. I don't know how it happened. It was months ago, just after that bad trip with Jon—I sort of *felt* the Lychgate crack open, but I told myself I'd imagined it. Then today I plucked up courage just to go and check . . . and it had really happened. I'm certain Lawrence doesn't know, otherwise he would have gone completely insane about it, and reclosed it long ago . . . but he didn't. I don't know what I've done. I'm so scared."

Rosie knew her brother well enough to believe him. "So he was angry just because you were messing around at the Gates—not because he realized you'd unlocked something? Hold on, are you absolutely certain this crack hasn't been there forever?"

He paused, considering. "No. When it first happened, I felt it—inside." He touched his chest. "Today I felt it again. I saw these beautiful, ghostly Aelyr calling to me. I didn't sense danger, only this bitter cold. Perhaps it's all right."

"Perhaps you should talk to Lawrence again," she said quietly.

"I can't. God knows what he'd do." He looked imploringly at her. "I'm sorry to lay this on you. I feel like the world's falling apart. Then you and Alastair . . ."

"And I've been too busy to notice what a horrible time

you're having. I'm sorry. God, I've done nothing but apologize today." She blushed suddenly, remembering that it was far from all she'd done.

Luc squeezed her hand, to tell her it didn't matter. "Part of me is drawn to the Gates. Part of me wants to run like hell. I daren't tell anyone, not even Dad."

"What about Jon?" she asked. "I thought he'd be the first to know."

Lucas shook his head. "Not with the state of his head at the moment. I dread to think what he'd do. I know he's infuriating, but I still care about him."

"I know," said Rosie. "He's obviously in denial about what a mess he's in. Er, when Lawrence threw him out—are you sure that was all about the Gates, and nothing to do with Sapphire?"

Lucas flinched. "Gates, definitely. Lawrence doesn't know."

"About the French-kissing of the stepmother?"

"You're not still sore about that, are you?"

"No," she said. "Merely puzzled. All the girls or boys he *could* have had . . ."

"You don't understand. It was all Sapphire."

"Is that what he told you?"

"He told me the truth. She got hold of him when he was sixteen and he didn't know how to stop her. If she was a man, no one would think twice about calling it abuse."

"Sixteen?" Rosie was silent, shocked. Pieces fell into place. She felt sick. "Of course. That's why Sapphire's all over him. And it's why he's refusing to see her."

"You've got it."

"Oh," she gasped, heart accelerating. "Sam doesn't know, does he? I went into denial and told myself it was just a kiss, and I never mentioned it because, truly, it's none of my business. If he'd known, he'd have been raging on the warpath about it long before now."

Lucas's eyes shone with alarm. "You mustn't tell him! I was supposed to keep quiet, but stuff like this—it's too much."

"Great," she groaned. "Another bloody secret." She imagined lying in Sam's arms, knowing and not saying . . . "I can't not tell him, Luc! Oh, don't worry, I won't. But if Sam finds out I knew, and didn't say anything—I'll just go and live in a monastery, shall I?"

Lucas gave a sweet, tired grin. "We could slip away through the Gates together. No one would ever know where we'd gone."

"Tempting."

His smile faded to a frown. "Seriously, what are we going to do?"

"Sleep," said Rosie. "Nothing will seem as bad tomorrow. That's what they say, isn't it?"

Alastair did not come home that night. Next morning, there was still no sign of him. It was Saturday, so Rosie had two days' grace; two days to smooth things over so they could all—Sam included—turn up at work on Monday and behave in a civilized fashion and so avoid her father's wrath because his key staff were missing, and all because—she closed her eyes, mortified at the prospect of everyone finding out—she and Sam couldn't keep their hands off each other.

Not a hope in hell.

Rosie fastened her crystal heart around her neck; it helped her to feel safe, because it reminded her of her father. Then she switched on her mobile phone and found a dozen messages from Sam, each increasingly urgent.

RUOK?

Please call me.

Switch your bloody phone on!

Rosie what's happening?

Just let me know ur OK . . .

She dialed his number. He answered within one ring. "Rosie?"

"I've spoken to Alastair."

"How was it?"

"Horrible." She pressed her knuckles to her forehead. "As bad as it could be."

"Oh, Christ. Are you all right, love?"

"Yep." Her throat was in a knot. She tried to swallow past it. "He wants to forgive and forget. Thinks we can get over it, like it never happened."

Sam went quiet. She sensed his fear, like a cold wave across the ether. "And what did you say?"

"I said no. I told him it wouldn't work and I made a mistake marrying him. Should've listened to you, shouldn't I? I ended it, Sam. He walked out."

"Oh." He sounded shocked. A pause, then cautious hope. "Does that mean you and me can . . ."

"No, not yet. It's too soon. I don't know." She choked on tears, couldn't help it.

"Rosie, don't. Sweetheart, I wouldn't have upset you like this for anything. We were meant to take it slow, let him down gently."

"If not now, it would've been next week, or next year," she said. "It would never have been gentle."

"I have to see you, I can be there in ten minutes."

"No, Sam. If he comes back and finds you here, it'll make things worse. I need time to sort myself out. I'll call you later, all right?"

She ended the call and sat with the phone limp in her hands. Well, it was done. Her safe little world staved in, just like that. She couldn't leap out of the wreckage and into Sam's arms; it wasn't possible. Physically and emotionally, she couldn't. It had all happened too soon. Perhaps for him, too.

As she reached Oakholme an hour later, she looked past the house to the hill beyond. Sam was up there at Stonegate, desperate to see her. A pang caught in her chest, but she must put her family first. The day was chilly and full of mist. The Gates were up there, open a mere sliver, issuing a faint draft from the underworld . . . Her head swam and the world turned strange; a sudden waking vision that the Otherworld was lost, and where it had been was only the absolute zero of the Abyss leaking slowly into the surface world—she shook off the darkness, but it took a long time to settle inside her and let it go.

She found Matthew, Faith and Heather in the dining room, lingering over a late breakfast, a cameo of family bliss. Matthew looked up from his newspaper. He wore reading glasses and it suddenly struck Rosie that he and Faith wore glasses as if taking on human imperfections, stacking mortal props around themselves to ward off the Aetheric world. They looked like a pair of teachers, perfectly matched.

"Hi," she said in answer to their surprised greetings. "Have you seen Alastair?"

"Not today," said Matthew. "Hasn't he got rugby practice?"

She shook her head. "Mum and Dad not here?"

"Gone to Leicester for the day. Shopping, cinema, dinner." He tapped his watch. "You missed them by about ten minutes. So, how have you managed to mislay your husband?"

Rosie pulled out a chair and sat down. "There's no easy way to tell you this. We've split up."

His reaction was an explosive reflex. "Don't be ridiculous! How? You were perfectly fine yesterday, until you . . ." He slowed down, nodding. "Oh, I get it."

"Do you?" Rosie tensed, startled.

"I put him straight about Sam, so you've had an argument about it. For heaven's sake, Rosie, it seems to be your mission in life to help the socially challenged, but Sam Wilder? Have you lost your mind? No way on this planet is he suitable to work for us. You must see that. Alastair and I are trying to protect you, that's all. You don't split up over one little argument."

Rosie chewed her lip. She caught Faith's eye. "It's a bit worse than that."

As she explained, Matt's face was a diagram of disbelief and outrage. He threw his glasses on the table. "You and Sam? That's impossible."

"Perfectly possible, as it turns out."

"Why him? *What were you thinking?*" To her shock, he turned on Faith. "Did you know about this?"

"Of course she didn't!" Rosie exclaimed. Faith sat pale and frozen, gathering Heather on her knee as Matthew went predictably ballistic.

His tone was controlled but loaded with disappointment, like an exasperated schoolmaster. Sam was a criminal lunatic. His brother was a junkie, his father insane. Rosie must be possessed by demons. And so on. She listened wearily, wishing herself anywhere but here. What a glorious way to spend the weekend.

"Do you imagine you're going to discard Alastair for that jerk?" Matt continued, when he'd drawn breath. "Just wait until I catch him!"

"No," Rosie said firmly. "Don't you dare. It's not your problem."

"Oh, yes it is. That's my best friend you've betrayed. Look, Rosie, you've done something unbelievably stupid, but Alastair's daft enough to forgive you. Grovel. Promise you'll never see that bastard again."

"No, Matt," she said with fierce emphasis. "Why were you so keen to marry me to a human in the first place? When I was with Alastair, I couldn't touch the Dusklands." Matthew thinned his lips and looked away. "But when I'm with Sam, it comes rushing back and it's where I belong. I can't deny what I am. Especially not to suit you." She was aware of the weight of Faith's attention as she spoke.

"That's childish," he said.

"Is that your best argument? Because you were happy to talk me up to Alastair as some elven princess."

Matthew said thinly, "No one forced you to marry him, Ro."

She paused. "That's true," she said. "I don't expect forgiveness or approval, I'm simply being honest, so . . ." She trailed off. Matthew's hand, lying on the table, looked weird. Elongated, sheened with slate-grey fur—a paw with thick black claws. She blinked and the hand was normal again. "So that you know the situation."

Matthew produced a phone from his pocket. "Let's see what Alastair has to say about it, shall we?"

Sensing the atmosphere, Heather wriggled on Faith's knee and said, "Mummy, grow your wings. Let's play water fairies."

"Not now, dear," Faith said quickly. "Come on."

Matthew didn't look up as she gathered the child and swept her out, didn't register her pallor and tension. Rosie stood up to follow, glaring at her brother. "Call him, if you must. It won't make any difference."

"We'll see about that," Matthew said grimly. "Everything I've done has been for your own good, Rose. All I wanted was to see you happy and this is how you thank me, just throw it back in my face? I'm not having it."

"You can't control me," she said. "Sam may be everything you've said, and worse—but at least he's truly alive."

She found Faith in the kitchen, furiously running hot water into the sink. Heather was at the table with crayons and paper, drawing a figure with blue streaks in its hair, green tendrils flowing from its shoulders.

"Are you all right?" Rosie asked, rubbing her friend's tense, bony shoulder. "Matthew's too self-absorbed to notice anything a child says."

"No. He watches like a hawk." Faith put a hand to her forehead, leaving a blob of bubbles there. "It's nothing. I'm fine."

"Fai, he's all hot air. I've just told him the worst thing ever and what can he do, except bluster? You can't live like this, being scared of him. It's wrong. Heather will pick it up."

Faith only sighed. She soaped and rinsed crockery, passing it to Rosie to dry. "You said you'd only been with Sam once."

"I had, when I told you. Things heated up after that."

"What are you going to do?"

"No idea," Rosie said. "I don't know if Sam and I can last five minutes. I've tried unrequited infatuation, settling for a safe bet, and lust. I still don't know what real love is, or how I'd recognize it if I found it."

"We're a mess, aren't we?" Faith said, with a sideways grin.

Matthew appeared in the doorway, holding out his phone to Rosie, grimly triumphant. "I've persuaded him to speak to you."

Drying her hands on a tea towel, she reluctantly took the phone. "Thanks. Hello?"

"Hi, Rosie, how are you doing?" Alastair sounded subdued.

"Okay. You?"

"Bit of a hangover. Bruised ego. I'm all right."

"Are you coming home?" she asked.

"Have I got a home? Does that mean you've changed your mind?"

Rosie paused, heavyhearted. "No," she said quietly. "There's no point in pretending, or dragging things out. It wouldn't be fair."

"Have you seen *him*?"

"If you mean Sam, no."

"You're not seriously going to employ him, are you?" Alastair's dull tone took an edge. "That's going to be fun in the office, isn't it?"

"We'll sort it out on Monday," Rosie said wearily.

"Oh, you think it can be sorted, do you? You really hurt me, Rosie."

"I know. I'm sorry."

"I don't think you do know," he replied in the same soft tone. "I don't think you've got the first clue what you've done to me."

Rosie closed her eyes. He sounded wretched. "I know. It's raw. There's nothing I can say to make it better. We're not the first couple who've ever split up."

"Well, you know, I never thought it would happen to us.

I should have remembered; the faerie folk have no hearts, no souls and no morals, do they, Rose?"

She exhaled through her teeth, losing the will to argue. "Come home and we'll talk it over," she said. She heard him breathe in and out. Then he hung up.

"I'm going home," she said, handing the phone back. "To wait for Alastair."

Matthew gave a broad, menacing smile. "Good girl. *Sort it out.*"

She took her leave, got into her car and began to drive slowly out of Cloudcroft. She looked up through clouds of bare branches in the direction of Stonegate. Perhaps tomorrow she would see Sam, once Alastair was calmer. God, yes, she had to see him. The idea of making a date with Sam sent sensual thrills of anticipation through her, cutting deliciously through the morass of guilt.

She drove slowly around the bend where the Crone Oak stood. As she passed beneath its bare, spreading branches, she saw the Greenlady—coiling and dipping like a green snake through its limbs. The head lunged suddenly at the passenger-side window, causing her to swerve in shock.

"Blood tastes like iron," the Greenlady's hiss followed her. *"Now I can never get the taste out of my mouth."*

Night was closing in when Lucas went in search of Jon. He headed towards the run-down house of Jon's drug buddy on the far side of Ashvale, walking along a narrow street with houses on his right and a tall hedge screening a park on his left. Streetlights gave the scene a watery amber glow. As he rounded a bend, he saw Jon in a pool of light, talking to a woman whose dark hair cascaded almost to her hips over an elegant fur coat.

Sapphire. Lucas didn't know whether to interrupt and rescue Jon, or dive into the hedge. In the event he did neither; Jon saw and acknowledged him with a glance that Sapphire didn't notice. Feeling awkward, Lucas hovered in the shadows a few yards away.

"Finally I can speak to you without the Rottweiler seeing me off," she was saying.

"Rottweiler?"

"Rosie. She's a bit of a diva, that one."

"She was protecting me," Jon said. "I didn't want to see you."

Sapphire appraised him, her head on one side. She raised her manicured hand to stroke his face. "When are you going to end this sulking marathon and come home?"

Jon jerked his head away from her touch. "I'm not sulking! Father's disowned me. Any claim you had on me is long over. Find some other stupid boy to use."

"You think I want you back for that?" Sapphire laughed. "Don't flatter yourself."

"Thank god."

"Oh, don't tell me you got nothing out of it."

"It's like eating too much cotton candy, isn't it?" he said flatly. "Eventually it makes you sick to your stomach."

Lucas saw anger flare beneath her smooth surface. "I don't want your scrawny body, dear," she hissed. "Help me as you agreed, and I'll make things right between you and Lawrence. I know that's what you want."

Jon's shoulders rose. "I didn't agree to anything."

As he turned away, she slipped her gloved hands around his arm and stopped him. "Oh yes, you did. You promised that we'd break through the Gates together."

"Yeah, well, I would say anything to get you off my back," Jon answered, his eyes narrow with scorn. "The Gates are sacred! They're none of your business! Why the hell does it matter to you, anyway?"

Sapphire paused, then spoke so quietly that Lucas strained to hear. "Someone I loved vanished. Aetherials took him, I'm sure. Yes, he may be dead, but if there's the slightest chance he went into the Spiral, I have to know. I need to know if a human can go through, that's all I'm asking. Jon, it was my father. I have to know what happened to him!"

She was fervent, but Jon pulled out of her grip, unmoved. "Please tell me that's not why you married Lawrence."

"Don't be ridiculous." She gave a honeyed smile, belied by the desperate and ruthless gleam of her eyes. "Come on, who was there for you with your mother gone, your father always absent, your brother in prison? Me. Who else has been kind and loved you like I have?"

"Used me." Jon folded his arms to make a barrier. "I'm sorry about your father, Sapphire. But I can't open the Gates for you, and if I could, I wouldn't."

"You're as stubborn as Lawrence," she snapped. "You know what I think you're both afraid of? That when you take off your masks, I'll see that there's nothing, absolutely nothing underneath."

Jon's voice became hoarse with pain. "You've no idea what it's done to us, being forbidden to enter the Gates like normal Aetherials. When I was sixteen, I should have been discovering the Spiral—not trapped on your mattress. Years, you've been using me to achieve this quest of yours, and you don't even know what you're asking. Not the first clue."

He strode away, coming towards Lucas. Sapphire let him go. She watched him for a moment, her eyes glistening; then her lips tightened and she walked in the other direction, dwindling until she reached a parked car, got in and drove away.

Jon stared after her. "I suppose you heard all that."

"Keep away from her," said Lucas, shaken. "She seems . . . demented."

"She'd have to be, to marry my father," said Jon. "Forget her. I have."

They began to walk along the dark street. Presently Lucas asked, "Enjoy yourself last night?"

"Can't remember. I call that a result."

Lucas sighed. "Are you coming home?"

"Where's home?"

"Rosie's."

"Not if we have to sit through another round of marital bliss, no thanks." Jon grinned bleakly. "So, Sam finally got what he wanted. I knew he'd never do it without causing complete mayhem. That's Sam all over, that is."

"What he wanted?" Luc frowned. "To get her into bed, you mean?"

Jon shrugged. "He's had a thing about her for years. Didn't you know?"

"No. One of these days I'll write a book called 'What I didn't know because no one bothered to tell me.' I don't want her to get hurt again. She keeps picking the wrong blokes. No offense."

"Cheers."

"Anyway, Alastair's left. It's peaceful. I don't like you hanging about in drug dens, Jon. Please come back."

Jon's demeanor softened. "Yeah, okay. Since it's you." After a moment he added, "Everyone gets Sam wrong. He'll fight like a dog to protect you. The trouble is, he doesn't know when to stop."

"That's not completely reassuring," said Lucas. "Look, about the Gates . . ."

"I know, I need to stop obsessing and do something with my life. Charity work?" Jon said sardonically. "Helping drug addicts? Forget the Gates. There is no Spiral. We'll all be fully human in no time and won't even remember being Aetherial, and my father will be stuck in torment forever, but that's okay, because mundanes like your brother Matthew will be happy."

Lucas didn't know what to say. He bit his lip. He had to confess. "No, Jon, listen . . . About that time at Freya's Crown, something happened . . ."

A car swished along the road behind them, drowning his voice. Drawing level, it stopped and the window slid down. "Lucas!" called the driver.

It was Alastair.

"Oh—er—hi," said Luc, startled. "Where are you off to?"

"I'm on my way home. Do you want a lift?"

Jon and Lucas looked at each other. "No, we're fine, thanks. We'll walk."

"No, come on. It's a good twenty minutes for you and it's starting to rain. Hop in."

He looked his usual self. Slightly flushed and sweaty, but no worse than after playing rugby. "Okay," said Lucas, but Jon hung back.

"No thanks. Don't want an encore."

"Rosie and I are fine," Alastair said emphatically. "No more words, I promise. Come on. She wants you home." He leaned over to open the passenger door. "Hop in the front, Lucas. You'll be all right in the back, won't you, Jon?"

"Whatever," Jon said, and climbed in.

Lucas settled in the squashy seat and fastened his seat belt. The central locking clunked shut. He felt suddenly claustrophobic. The car moved off and Alastair drove with a ghost smile on his lips, humming to himself as he navigated towards the main road. When he reached it, instead of turning towards the house, he went straight on.

"Where are we going?" Lucas asked. No answer. "Have you seen Rosie today? She was worried."

"I've spoken to her, aye."

"This is really awkward. I don't know what to say."

"You don't need to say anything, Luc. It will all be evened out, don't worry."

Alastair swung off the main road, onto the long switch-back lane that ultimately led to Cloudcroft. Darkness rushed past and the car bounced, almost taking off over the high curves.

"Where are we going?" Luc asked again, nervous now.

"Rosie's at Oakholme," Alastair said in the same light, slightly manic tone. "She's waiting for you there."

"Oh," said Lucas, puzzled. "I didn't realize. Could you slow down a bit?"

"Yeah, d'you mind?" said Jon.

"You pair of wimps." He slowed minimally, beefy hands tight on the wheel.

"Why's she at Oakholme?" asked Luc. Catching a sour scent on Alastair's breath, he added, "How much have you had to drink?"

"Not enough." The car hurtled down a tunnel of trees, gathering speed, headlights making an eerie glow. After a minute or so, Alastair began, "I want to explain to her what she's done to me. But I can't put it into words. I want to say to her, 'If I could only make you understand one second of the pain I'm feeling'—but it's impossible. Words aren't adequate. She doesn't care. What would make her care, eh?"

He swung the car onto the lane that wound into the village. The road was far too narrow for speed. Lucas felt he was suffocating in the closed glass and metal capsule, the thick leathery scent. He felt Jon hanging on to his seat back.

"I swore no woman would ever do this to me again." Alastair's voice took on a strangled note. "No woman, human or faerie, has the right to do this to me. The bitch!"

"Hold on," Lucas interrupted. "You can't call Rosie that."

"Calling her as I see her. What else is she? I thought we were solid." His mouth trembled. "I thought I knew her, but I didn't. What were our wedding vows to her, a joke, a laundry list, what?"

Trees and a house flashed past. Lucas's head whipped round. "Alastair, we went straight past Oakholme. Where are we going? Stonegate?"

"You're after Sam, aren't you?" said Jon, alarmed. "What are you going to do?"

"I don't know, but if I see that bastard, if I catch him—" Alastair's voice caught with sobs.

"This won't help anyone!" Lucas exclaimed. "What are you planning? To run him over? Then what?"

"I don't know. I don't know!" Alastair braked violently, slewing the car around on the lane in a shower of gravel. Sweat and tears were pouring down his face. "I need to think."

"Well, can you let us out then," Jon said shakily, "because this is really wasting gas, and it's nothing to do with us." He fumbled with the door handle, but the locks wouldn't release.

Alastair moved off again, bumping the car over grass at the roadside. "Oh, isn't it?" He cruised back the way they'd come, passing Oakholme a second time. His driving was erratic but slower now. "Did you know, Lucas, she once told me you were the most precious thing in the world to her? Not me. You."

"What?" Lucas said faintly.

"I don't know if she loves Sam, but I know she loves *you,* and even that birdbrain in the back, more than she ever loved me. I gave her every chance to put things right. How many men would do that? I was ready to forgive her and she throws it back at me—like my forgiveness is worthless. She doesn't get it—I tore out my heart and my pride and offered them to her on a platter, and she doesn't even care, she just kicks them into the mud." His teeth were bared, his eyes glittering with tears. "What would it take to make her feel the pain, eh? Hurt something they love. Destroy some darling fluffy wee thing they love. It's the only language they understand."

"Excuse me," said Jon, "this is kidnap. What are you going to do with us?"

"I don't know! Shut up!" He pressed the accelerator, veering onto the wrong side of the road. "I don't want to hurt you. But while I've got you, I've got the power. Let me think!"

"Yeah, slow down," said Lucas. "You shouldn't be driving in this state. Let's stop and have a talk instead."

"Don't patronize me, you wee bastard." He swung left onto another unlit, winding lane, taking the bends without care as he wavered piteously between tears and rage. "We'll just drive around awhile, so I can think straight. I trusted your family! How could she, when I trusted her?"

"Look," said Jon. "I'm getting massively pissed off with this. I know you broke my fucking guitar! I know you hate me, but it is not my fault that Rosie decided to break her heart over me. She's flaky. She married you on the rebound and probably shagged my brother on the rebound, too. Reality check: She doesn't love you. Get over it. You want to find Sam, he's probably at your house doing Rosie right now."

Alastair turned, even in the gloom, deathly white. He pressed the accelerator. The speed flung them back in their seats.

"There's a sharp right bend ahead," gasped Lucas. He saw hedges racing past on either side, the tight bend approaching, the huge oak tree that Rosie loved standing proud, directly in their path. In a panic he unfastened his seat belt, fumbled uselessly with the locked door. Alastair's eyes were glazed, his mouth an oblong of pain and rage as he thrust his foot to the floor. The engine shrieked. Lucas and Jon were both shouting now. It was like shouting underwater.

Alastair screamed. He wrestled with the steering wheel, trying at the very last second to turn—too late. The Crone Oak came rushing at them. Lucas felt the tires slithering on the asphalt as the car went out of control. He flattened himself against the seat back, held his breath, watched paralyzed as the trunk grew huge in the windshield.

There was a violent shock as the car hit rough grass and became airborne.

Impact. Crunching metal, shattering glass. And Lucas went on flying; falling from the cliff edge, plunging through the Gates, diving into the blackness of the Abyss.

16

Transformation

Rosie was woken by a steady pulse of blue light across her ceiling.

For a moment she couldn't think where she was. It was dark and she was lying on the sofa. Her watch said nine o'clock. Then she remembered; she'd come home to wait for Alastair, waited and waited—until, exhausted, she'd fallen asleep where she sat. And still no one had come home.

The shrill of the doorbell brought her sharply to her feet.

From the hallway, she saw figures outside silhouetted against the glare of a police car. Nothing felt real. Her head was whirling as she opened the door. At the same moment, her phone began to ring. There were two policewomen on the doorstep, as somber as undertakers.

"Mrs. Duncan? I'm afraid there's been an accident . . ."

The next hour passed in a blur. Sitting in the back of the police car as it took her to Leicester, the illuminated blocks of the Royal Infirmary swimming into view. The musty-sweet smell of hospital corridors. Bright lights, bustle, the shine of metal and glass.

Then the dim and soothing green decor of the relatives' room. Matthew sitting with his head in his hands. Auberon pacing in shirt sleeves, Jessica rushing to meet Rosie, her face anguished and tear-streaked . . . Being held tight in her mother's arms, shrouded by her thick golden hair. The two of them weeping on each other's shoulders, and Auberon's arms wrapping around them both.

She had never seen her parents like this before, ashen-faced with grief. She never wanted to see it again. "Rosie, we're so sorry," they kept saying.

She was still struggling to accept what the police had told her; Alastair was dead, killed outright. Jon had escaped with injuries. Lucas . . . Lucas was not expected to survive.

He had been thrown through the windshield, straight into the tree, *her* tree, the Crone Oak. He was in intensive care, condition critical. It was all too much to bear. The knowledge of Luc lying near death left her choking with pain as if she'd been stabbed.

"It makes no sense," said Matthew, red-faced with shock. "He was a careful driver. He drove like a bloody snail."

"It must have been icy," said Jessica. "Was it icy? Where were they going?"

"I don't know." It was all Rosie could do to speak. "I can't understand why they were in the car with him at all. There must be a mistake."

Cups of tea. Doctors coming and going. More police officers, gently trying to piece together a statement from Rosie's utter confusion. After they'd left, Matthew looked at her, his eyes fierce and raw. "Hadn't you better tell Mum and Dad?"

"Tell us what?" said Jessica. She was sitting beside Rosie, firmly clasping her hand.

Rosie looked at the worn carpet tiles beneath her feet. "I broke up with Alastair yesterday . . . because I've been seeing Sam."

"Oh" was all Jessica said. Auberon took it in without comment.

"And you were going to put things right," said Matthew, pointing a damning finger at her. "Why didn't you?"

"Are you blaming me for this?" Rosie gasped.

"No, I'm only suggesting that Alastair wasn't driving carefully because he was a little bit upset."

"I asked him to come home! You tell me why he didn't."

"No one's to blame," Auberon said firmly. "It was an accident. Let's wait for the facts, shall we?"

They waited; time slowed to an interminable crawl. Rosie thought about Faith, alone with Heather at Oakholme. Earlier, she'd phoned Sam and arranged a guilty rendezvous at the Green Man for the next day, Sunday. That couldn't happen now. She pressed her crystal heart, which she'd put on that morning, between her fingertips for comfort.

Phyllida arrived, running to Jessica with hugs. Her presence eased the atmosphere, since she wasn't afraid to demand answers from the medical staff. At last a nurse came and said they could see Lucas. Her manner was grave and delicate, as if to discourage false hope.

There was a busy ward, a hissing glass door leading off to a white room with one bed. Lucas lay with closed eyes, tubes and drips connecting him to the last thread of life. Rosie and Jessica pressed close to each other, hands tangled so tight that it hurt.

He had a dressing on his head, swollen cuts and bruises around his eyes; otherwise his skin was as white as the bed on which he lay. He looked diminished, almost emaciated under the covers, mouth slack around plastic tubing, ribs bellowing in time with the ventilator that was breathing for him. Machines beeped and clicked.

A grey-haired senior doctor came and began talking about head injury. Coma. Brain-stem death. He was telling them that the machines were keeping Lucas alive. The longer it took him to show signs of recovery, the less chance there was. They might have to face the decision to switch off life support.

"Lucas?" Rosie whispered, sliding her fingers into his palm and squeezing. No response. He wasn't there.

When the doctor left, Phyllida bustled about finding chairs. Auberon sat beside Lucas with his head in one hand; Jessica, next to him, stared fixedly at her son's face. With his hair back he looked like Lawrence; not the harsh, aquiline one but a young, sweet and boyish version. Matthew stayed on his feet, restless.

"This can't be right," Rosie whispered to her aunt. "I thought Aetherials were more resilient than humans."

"We are," Phyll replied. "If he wasn't Vaethyr, he probably would have died instantly. But these bodies are still flesh and blood. We can be injured or killed, in a human sense. You know that."

"It's no good," said Matthew, "I can't stay in here."

As he turned to go, the glass door slid open and there were Lawrence and Sapphire, imposing figures in dark overcoats. Sapphire was pushing Jon in a wheelchair; it was an eerie shock to see her in possession of him like that. Rosie looked anxiously for Sam, but he wasn't there.

The two families gazed at each other.

"May we see him?" Lawrence asked. He looked as haggard as Auberon.

A pause; then Auberon answered, "Yes, of course."

"Where's Sam?" Matthew asked sharply.

"He's attempting to park the car," said Sapphire. "Traffic's a nightmare, even at this time of night. This is such an appalling shock . . ."

"There are too many of us," said Phyllida. "Come on, let's get coffee. Jess?"

"I can't . . ." her mother said faintly, then let Phyll, Matthew and Auberon shepherd her away. Sapphire went with them. Rosie hesitated and found herself alone with Jon and his father.

Jon and Lawrence, in the same room. Was this what it took?

Lawrence said not a word. He went to the far side of the bed and stood gazing down at Lucas. What thoughts were moving behind the cliff face, Rosie had no idea—but he must feel something, surely, or he wouldn't be here?

"Can you push me closer, please?" said Jon.

Rosie obliged, maneuvering the wheelchair. In a dressing gown the same shade of brown as his disheveled hair, he looked stunned, red-eyed. He had one arm in a sling, impressive bruising on his forehead and his left ankle strapped up. Rosie, all petty resentments swept away, could have wept with relief to see him alive. "How are you feeling?"

"How d'you expect?" His voice was hoarse. "Like complete shit. They give you nice morphine, but never enough. You?"

Rosie couldn't answer.

Jon sat gazing at Luc's swollen face, the closed eyes— the *absence* of him. He turned ghostly with loss. No one spoke for a while. Then Jon leaned forward and touched his half-brother's wrist. "Luc?" he said, his voice so rough it was barely audible. "Don't know if you can hear me. I'm all right, cuts and bruises. I'm still here, but where are you? You wouldn't go into the Spiral without me, would you? We always said we'd go together."

Jon's voice broke. A spasm of sobs overtook him. Lawrence glanced at him, eyebrows twitching, but made no comment. Fighting tears, Rosie thought, *Can't he even console his own son?* She placed a tentative hand on Jon's shoulder.

"Can you remember what happened?" she asked.

"I remember a paramedic dragging me out. There were

twigs everywhere." He turned to look at her, red eyes glittering. "Alastair did this," he said. "Your wonderful husband."

She gasped, shaken. "You know he's dead, don't you?"

"Yes. I'm sorry for your sake, but excuse me if I don't grieve too much."

"He meant something to me," she answered bitterly. "Not his fault I didn't love him like I should. This was an accident, wasn't it?"

The hiss of the door made her jump. A brisk and smiling nurse came in, asking gently if they wouldn't mind going out while more tests were done. *Tests.* What would they find—alien physiology superior to humans? Astonishing healing powers? Or were Vaethyr bodies so perfectly camouflaged that they were no different, the same fragile pulp? *Killed in a human sense,* what did that mean?

As they left—Lawrence wheeling Jon—Rosie stared back at Lucas until she couldn't see him anymore. That morning he'd sat yawning at her breakfast table, trying to mend a silver chain he wore while she moaned at him for leaving long hairs in the bath. This was surreal. It couldn't be happening.

Back in the relatives' room, the others were sipping coffee, Phyll gently trying to persuade Jessica to go home. Still no Sam. Seeing Rosie, her mother almost jumped off her chair, her face fraught with hope and anguish. "What's happening?"

"Nothing, Mum," Rosie sighed, finding a seat. "He's still the same."

Sapphire said, "Phyllida's right, it's late. I'm taking Jon back to the ward. He shouldn't even be out of bed, he's had a hellish experience."

"Wait a moment," Jon said grimly. "You need to hear this before I keel over. About what happened."

All their attention gathered on him, a poised, anguished hush. Even Lawrence, used to commanding attention, was listening. In a quiet, hoarse voice, Jon described the night's events. Rosie listened with her head in her hands, every word dripping torment on her.

"It wasn't coincidence that Alastair picked us up," Jon said. "He must have been cruising around looking for us. It was all about punishing Rosie."

Rosie was weeping convulsively. She tried to do so silently, to keep it contained. Auberon moved next to her and she felt his strong arms around her.

"Are you saying he drove into the Crone Oak on purpose?" cried Matthew.

"Maybe not, but he was completely irrational. Looked like he'd been drinking pretty heavily, too. He wanted to lash out at something and picked us. I don't think he had a plan, beyond driving around, ranting at us." Jon looked down, reddening. "Maybe it was something one of us said, I don't know, but he suddenly went nuts and drove at the tree. Like you'd punch a wall or break a priceless vase in a fit of temper and totally regret it a moment later. Maybe he just did it to scare us. It happened so fast. He was struggling to get control of the car, but it was too late. Who knew he'd go crazy like that?"

Matthew was on his feet, incandescent. "You're lying! How dare you suggest it wasn't an accident? Alastair was my best friend! He wouldn't do this to us!"

"What did you say to him?" Rosie asked in a whisper.

Jon looked straight at her and said, "I've no idea."

"You were supposed to talk to him, Ro!" Matthew raged, crimson. "He's ready to forgive you, and you just brutally tell him it's over? Why?"

"Because it was true!" she cried. "You didn't tell me I needed to lie so he wouldn't try to kill everyone!"

"Shh, Rosie," said her father, his arm firming around her.

"What, Matt?" she added shakily. "Did you know he might do a thing like this? Did you?"

"No, of course not! He was upset!"

"Upset?" said Jon. "Completely psychotic, for as long as it took."

Horrible silence descended. With supreme timing, Sam appeared in the doorway. His gaze fell on Rosie; she physically felt it, like sunlight, as they tried to look at each other while pretending not to.

"Here you are," he said quietly. "I've been all over the bloody hospital trying to find you. You've no idea how big it is. I've had to park miles away, and—"

"You bastard," Matthew growled, and launched himself across the room at Sam. He punched him, grabbed and flung him hard against the wall, hit him again.

Sam went down. He made no attempt to defend himself. Matthew was reaching down to yank him back to his feet when Auberon, Lawrence and Sapphire hauled him off. Rosie flung herself between him and Sam, pushing her brother back, Jessica helping. Phyll stepped into the corridor, calling for security.

"You bastard," Matthew repeated, struggling against their restraint. Their combined strength barely held him. "You're all poison. That's my best friend dead and my brother dying, because of what you've done."

Sam rose to his feet, nose and mouth dripping blood. He held up his hands, palms out in surrender. "I'm truly sorry about what's happened. But I'm not fighting with you, mate."

Sapphire put in, "Am I the only person here who doesn't know what's going on?" No one answered.

"You're going to pay for this," Matt persisted. "Come on. Outside."

"Nah," Sam said thinly. "If we go outside, I will kill you, and I'm a bit sick of prison. It's not happening."

"We can do it here, then." He surged forward, breaking loose. Sam leapt out of his way. In the same moment, four security guards piled in and grabbed Matthew. He stood panting like a captured bear between them.

"Might I remind you that Lucas happens to be my brother, too?" Sam said from halfway across the room.

An angry nurse appeared, demanding to know what the trouble was. "Nothing," said Lawrence. He pointed at Matthew. "It's just him."

"Sir, you'll have to leave the building," said one of the

guards. "You can walk out quietly with us, or we can call the police. Up to you."

"Fine," Matthew grunted, still glaring at Sam. "You can take your hands off me. I'm leaving. This is not over."

Rosie slipped out of the room and along the corridor to watch her brother being escorted away. Sam followed and stood beside her, making no move to touch her. "Should've expected that," he said, sniffing.

"It looks painful." Rosie handed him a clean tissue and he dabbed at the blood. "Well done, not retaliating."

"No one needed to see a fistfight on top of everything else," he said quietly. "There's my reputation as local maniac shot to pieces."

She gave a pale half-smile at his remark. "I should be furious with Matt. But . . . he's lost his closest friend."

"Any idea what happened?"

A shudder went through her from head to foot. "You missed Jon's speech. Apparently it's all our fault. Seems Alastair had a few drinks, kidnapped Jon and Luc to hurt me, then crashed the car in a fit of sheer fury."

Sam groaned under his breath. "You have got to be fucking joking."

"She isn't," said Jon behind them.

Sapphire was wheeling him. She pushed the chair to Sam and Rosie, stopped and looked them over. Her air of worldly-wise compassion made Rosie want to strangle her. "I'm the last to know as usual, but finally things are clear. Really, Sam, couldn't you find someone who wasn't married?"

His eyebrows flicked up and down. "Apparently not."

He plainly couldn't be bothered to rise to Sapphire's bait, but Rosie said icily, "This is what happens when affairs get found out."

She looked straight at Sapphire as she said it. Then she had the satisfaction of seeing Sapphire freeze for a moment, unsure of her ground, suspicious. She even had the grace to blanch. "I'm taking Jon back to his ward now."

"Let me do that," said Sam, shouldering her out of the way. "Haven't had a chance to see him yet."

"Thanks, mate," Jon said wearily, raising his hand in a vague wave to Rosie. "Night. See you tomorrow."

As they went, Sapphire caught Rosie's arm with a warm, firm hand, her bone-hard fingernails digging in slightly. "I truly am sorry, Rosie. This is a dreadful time for everyone. Lawrence is distraught."

"Lucas isn't dead yet," she said thinly.

"Still, you need to prepare for the fact that when people survive a coma like this, they may never be the same again." Sapphire moved closer, her voice overflowing with tender concern. "They seem alive and even conscious, but effectively, they are a shell. The person inside has gone."

Rosie bit her tongue until it sang with the iron taste of blood. "It's called persistent vegetative state," she said. "The doctors told us."

"It's a terrible outcome to—what? An impulsive little affair? Don't be too hard on yourself. What woman could suspect that her husband might actually commit suicide over her? I want you to know that you have our full support. And if it reaches the newspapers—you'll need it."

"I have to go," said Rosie, feeling she was about to lose it completely. "Thanks, but I can't talk about this now."

"I was trying to protect you," Sapphire said.

"How?"

"By not giving your messages to Sam. I knew he was up to something. He's unstable and untrustworthy, and he'll hurt you. You need to face it, for your own good. He'll break your heart." If Rosie was already on the ground, Sapphire had booted her in the stomach. She cursed her own eyes for spilling tears in front of her torturer.

"He'd have to be some kind of evil genius to beat this," she said with a vicious grin that finally silenced Sapphire. "You tell me what Sam or anyone else could possibly do to hurt me more than this?"

Rosie stood in the mortuary, looking down at Alastair's body, where it lay on a flat steel drawer. His face was all cuts, lesions and swollen flesh but the torn edges had shrunk on themselves, like lemon peel curling. The skin was a livid abstract of blues, purples, waxy yellow. A rancid chemical tang steeped the air. They had warned her the injuries were bad, that she might find it too disturbing, or not even recognize him. She did, however.

"Did you really love me so much you'd rather die than lose me?" she murmured. "Because I don't believe it. What was it then, hurt pride? Was it worth it?"

Snippets of the previous night haunted her: her parents' stoic faces as her aunt failed to persuade them to go home; Rosie trying to sleep across chairs with her head on Auberon's knee. Lawrence leaving at some stage—not that she'd noticed him go, but she'd felt his absence as if the shadow of a standing stone had vanished.

Waking drearily at six to a cup of machine tea, and realizing it was Sam who'd fetched it. He'd taken Lawrence and Sapphire home, then come straight back.

Being allowed to see Lucas at last.

No change.

That was the worst moment of all. Hope building up overnight, only to be crushed. The dreadful pallor of her mother's face . . . Lucas was stable. That was the best the doctors could tell them. Without life support, he was still effectively dead.

"How can you compare what I did to this?" Rosie asked Alastair's impassive death mask. "People survive broken marriages. It's not the end of the world. So why the hell did you have to turn it into the end of the world?"

"Rosie," said Sam behind her. "You shouldn't be here on your own."

She turned. His arms enfolded her. His chest received the soaking weight of her grief and anger.

"I wasn't on my own," she said eventually, indicating the kind mortuary attendant who was some feet away, discreetly not noticing anything.

"We were meant to be meeting for a pub lunch today," Sam said regretfully. "This isn't exactly the Green Man, is it?"

She sighed. "I can't understand why he did it. Life goes on, why couldn't he see that?"

"I don't know, love. Some people hurl their toys out of the playpen and only think, 'Oops,' when everything's wrecked beyond repair. Come on."

She hesitated. "I can't believe he's not going to walk in and dump his rugby kit, like he does. Bounce into the office with his hair all ruffled and say, 'Fancy a curry?' Joke around with Matthew. Ordinary stuff. I never meant him any harm."

"Everyone knows that."

"But they're always going to be looking at us and blaming us, even if they don't mean to. Why try to kill Lucas, and not me?"

"Or me?" he said.

She looked at the scuffed toes of her boots. She almost couldn't stand up under the weight of misery. "I feel so ashamed."

"Don't say that, Rosie," Sam murmured.

"What are we going to do?"

"Practical things. Eat breakfast. You'll be no use to your mum if you pass out. Organize shifts so everyone gets sleep and Luc always has someone with him. It's all we can do, isn't it? Come on."

"Thank you," said Rosie to the attendant.

He nodded, unfolded the white sheet to conceal the face of the corpse. Rosie let Sam walk her away, his arm around her shoulders; and even through two sets of doors, she heard the oily hiss of the drawer sliding closed.

Later, Rosie found her mother alone at Lucas's bedside, clasping his lifeless hand and intently watching the blank, closed face. She pulled up a chair and gently set about combing her mother's hair. The naturally thick blond mane had become a tangle overnight. Jessica said nothing. The only sound was the monotonous clunk of the ventilator.

"Mum, there's a lot I need to explain," Rosie began.

"Now isn't the time, I know, but you must wonder what the hell's been going on. You must think I've gone crazy, seeing Sam . . . I swear, I never dreamed this could happen in a million years . . . Mum?" Still no answer. Rosie felt worse. How could her parents ever forgive her? "Please say something. Even if you're furious. I can't bear silence."

Jessica turned to her and said in a cracked whisper, "I can't. I've lost my voice."

"Oh." A terrible feeling pushed up in her throat; the urge to laugh. Her mouth turned down with the effort of suppressing it.

"Rosie, it's not funny." Jessica's eyes crinkled and they shared a moment of desperate mirth. She put a hand to her throat. "It hurts."

"What made you lose it? The shock?"

"I suppose so," her mother whispered with effort. "We all react in our own way. Auberon's stoic. Matthew goes mad. I lose my voice."

"Oh, god. I feel so awful, I don't know where to start."

"Not now." Jessica shook her head. "I'm the last person in the world to judge you. Luc is all that matters. Would you do something for me?"

Rosie gathered her mother's hair into a ponytail band and smoothed the hank between her shoulders. "Anything."

The strained whisper was so faint, Rosie had to bend close to hear it. "Go to Oakholme. Make sure Matt and Faith and Heather are okay. And get some rest."

She found Sam in the next ward, beside Jon's bed. Jon was sitting up, looking as he had the previous night: pale, tired and worried. Rosie took the chair on the opposite side from Sam as she began the expected pleasantries—how was he feeling, how much pain, had he eaten anything?

"Stop fussing, Rosie," Jon said with a trace of grim humor. "I'm all right."

"I was talking to Sam," she retorted.

Sam grinned, despite a nicely bruised and swollen lip.

Jon only flicked his gaze at the ceiling. "Have you seen Lucas?" he asked.

"Yes, still the same. No improvement."

He nodded, his expression pained. "I'll go and sit with him soon. If anything happens to him . . . I don't want to be here without him."

Sam and Rosie looked at each other across the bed. "Don't start talking like that, you idiot," said Sam. "You're alive. So's he. Do I have to break into a chorus of 'Always Look on the Bright Side of Life?' "

"Please don't." Jon gave the faintest smile.

Rosie said hesitantly, "Jon, you know when you first visited Luc, you said something about him going into the Spiral? Was it a turn of phrase, or do you think he really could . . . ?"

"Your folks have told you, haven't they?" Jon paused. "It's said when Aetherials die, it doesn't mean we're gone forever. It means we change. If the body is dead, or near death, the soul-essence travels to the heart of the Spiral . . . but with the Great Gates closed, I'm not sure we can. Only I'm convinced Lucas *has* broken through, in some form. Luc being in a coma might mean his soul-essence has fled there and doesn't want to come back."

"Or can't," said Rosie. She looked at Sam, who was regarding her with a worried, questioning expression. "Jon, about the Gates," she said. "Lucas told me—while you were out on Friday night—that he thought he'd accidentally unlocked the Lychgate during that bad trip he had." She held up her hands, as Lucas had done. "Just a sliver."

Jon's face flickered with shock. "No. He would've told me!"

"He was frightened of the consequences, if he told anyone. He was kind of running away from what he'd done. He might've been mistaken, but do you think it's possible?"

Jon answered slowly, "The only way he could have cracked open the Gates is if Lawrence had lost the power." His velvet brown eyes flashed up at her. "Luc started telling me something when Alastair came . . . Oh my god."

They sat without speaking for a minute. It felt like a veil of mist coming down between them and the human world. "I'd go and check, except I can't walk."

"I could take a look," she said. "I'm going to Oakholme anyway."

"Hold on," said Sam. "Reality check. Running off to look for cracks in Freya's Crown—isn't that a little crazy? Lucas is *here*."

"You sound like Matthew."

"Sam's right," said Jon. "Even if Luc had unlocked the Gates, even if you could follow him into the Spiral, what would be the use?"

"You'd be first in if not for the broken ankle," she said.

"Of course," he said, eyes wild. "But look at me. There's no way."

Rosie studied Jon and wondered if it was fear she saw in his face. Devoted all his energy to the locked Gates, but never thought what he'd do if they were suddenly open? "Just an idle thought," she said softly. "Anyway, I really have to go home and check on Faith now. I'll see you both later."

"Hold on, love." Sam was on his feet. "You're going nowhere without me."

She looked straight into his eyes, challenging him. "Is that right?"

From the far end of the ward, Sapphire stood watching them. Rosie and Sam and Jon. They were a little clique, talking intently, completely absorbed in each other. It meant nothing to them that she wasn't with them. They didn't see her absence as a missing element, and never would.

She took in their shining hair and graceful movements, the Aetherial glamour that clung to them. They were unconscious of it themselves. Few humans could see it, but she could.

And she was jealous.

Aetherials would always exclude her, never let her in.

Was this what had destroyed her father—the obsessive need to break through the veil and grasp them, control them, *become* them?

That really was why she hated Rosie. Sapphire didn't care about Sam—disliked him, yes, but didn't envy him because he'd never made an issue of his Aetherial nature. Jon she could control. But Rosie was untamable, and had all the intangible qualities that had mesmerized Sapphire's father, and was still never satisfied.

Rosie was Aetherial. And still not happy.

There they were, oblivious, whispering of Aetheric matters as if she, Sapphire, didn't exist. Those matters were her business as much as theirs, but they'd never acknowledge it. It was always going to be like this. However hard she tried to outdo them with wisdom and glamour and sensuality, she was always going to be the outsider. The human.

She sympathized with Alastair. Unlike everyone else, she perfectly understood his motives. She thought, *We think we can live among Aetherials, be their equals—but in the end, they drive us to despair. What a pity I never got to know him. They even snatched that from me. I might have saved him.*

Sapphire set her perfect mouth. Part of her bled for Lucas, of course. Poor sweet, beautiful boy . . . Another part, however, couldn't help thinking that if Lucas were dead—brain-dead or otherwise—it would do them all good to suffer that lightning-streak of anguish across their privileged lives.

When Rosie entered Oakholme, she found no one there. The usual cars were on the drive, but there was no sign of Matthew, Faith or Heather. Strange. She explored the creaking corridors, calling out. The house stayed silent. The atmosphere was dense, dusky and full of glittering specks. Ghost figures flitted in the corner of her eye.

Oakholme was full of the Dusklands. Saturated.

There appeared to be no coats missing. In the kitchen,

there were scattered toys and dirty plates. Faith would never go out without cleaning up first. More disturbingly, the back door was wide open.

Rosie checked the gardens. As she came round to the front of the house, she crossed the grass lawn to where Sam waited in Lawrence's sleek black car. He'd insisted on bringing Rosie home, which on reflection was not the best idea in the world. *Take Sam into Oakholme where a berserk Matthew is waiting—yeah, great thinking,* Rosie had said to herself, and made him wait outside.

"What's up?" he called, lowering the window.

"There's no one home."

Sam climbed out. "D'you think they've gone to the hospital?"

"Maybe." She frowned. "How? Their cars are here. And the kitchen door's open."

He shut and locked the car. "Can I come in?" The mischievous glint in Sam's eye was subdued, but still there. "If Matt appears, I'll deal with it. Peacefully, honest."

"Yes, come on," she said anxiously. "I'd rather a fistfight than this *Marie Celeste* scene."

Sam took her hand. "Let's have a cup of tea. Don't look so scared, Foxy."

She led him through the front door. As they entered the hall, he stopped dead and said, *"Whoah."*

"It's really heavy, isn't it?" she remarked. The air was full of rippling veils, an aurora of blues, greens, autumn browns.

"Your house always like this?"

"No. We get the Dusklands, like you get Dumannios, but never this intense before." The light made Sam look strange, a luminous shadow with his eyes lit from inside, fiery aquamarine. Looking down, she saw the backs of her own hands covered in dappled tree shadows. "Come into the kitchen."

As she pushed open the door, there was someone in the center of the room. A wisp of a woman, green with flowing leafy hair. Holding out her arms, which were like thin tree branches, the dryad glared in horror at crimson blood dripping off the ends of her twig fingers.

"*I can't get the taste out of my mouth,*" said the apparition. One blood-soaked leafy arm floated up to point at the open door. "*You bring back our light, or I'll never get rid of the blood! Find him, bring him back!*" She shimmered, dissolving into the heat haze of the atmosphere.

"Holy fuck!" gasped Sam. "What the hell was that?"

"You saw her?"

"Yes, plain as anything."

"Oh," said Rosie, trying to breathe. "It was the Greenlady. The dryad out of the Crone Oak. She's been after me for years, complaining about blood on her tree . . . as if she knew it was going to happen and was begging me to stop it." Rosie sat down at the table and put her face in her hands. "Why the hell didn't I understand what she meant?"

"How could you?" Sam said, running a hand over her hair. "Even if you had, how could you have prevented it? Our light—d'you think she's talking about Lucas?"

"The name Lucas means 'light,'" said Rosie.

"Your idea about checking the Gates wasn't so idle, was it?" Sam said gravely. He was leaning on the table beside her and she longed to stroke his beautiful strong hand but she couldn't look at him without remembering the lust and the guilt and the crash and her parents' faces and Alastair dead and . . . it all came in a horrible circle back to Lucas dying on a machine.

"Erm," she said, swallowing the lump in her throat. "I wish Dad was here. He'd know what to do—but I daren't tell him what I'm thinking, because he'd forbid me to go. I can't stay around the hospital with everyone staring and blaming us. I need to be doing something. At least, I have to try, Sam. Greenlady's made the decision for me."

Abruptly, he moved away and started opening cupboards. "So, if you were going on a journey, is there anything you'd absolutely have to take?"

"Bottled water, toothbrush and clean underwear," said Rosie. "Why aren't you arguing with me?"

"It saves time." He found a canvas backpack, began throwing food items into it. "Grab what you need while I write a note."

"Saying what?"

" 'Gone on wild-goose chase,' " said Sam. "We'll be back here in twenty minutes' time, none the wiser, then it won't matter what I write. C'mon, move yourself!"

"Wow, you're bossy," she said flatly, but hurried anyway. She ran upstairs two at a time to her old room—almost afraid of the house in its capricious state—and seized a sweater and waterproof jacket. Would the deeper realms be icy cold or tropically hot? She had no idea. She borrowed a few of Matt's belongings for Sam, while she was at it.

Five minutes later, she and Sam were closing the kitchen door behind them. He hoisted the bag onto his shoulders. Outside, the Dusklands vanished. The surface world was ordinary; damp, chilly, the bare trees black against the greens of wet grass, laurel and holly. "You know, Matt and Faith are probably at a neighbor's," said Sam.

"I'm sure that's it. I won't lock the door."

"Why have we come out the back? We can drive up to Stonegate."

"Oh." Rosie hesitated. "On foot, though, we can sneak up there without being seen. And it feels right to walk— like treading a magical path. You think I'm crazy, don't you?"

"Goes without saying. Still, you're right. If we take the car, Lawrence or Her Ladyship are bound to spot us, and that's the last thing we need."

"Right," she said resolutely. "D'you think we'll need credit cards?"

Sam laughed; he looked captivating when he smiled spontaneously like that. They made for the deeper reaches of the garden and the gap in the hedge. Crossing the stream that ran along the boundary of Oakholme and Stonegate, pushing through the foliage of evergreens and winter-bare branches, Rosie felt a sense of freedom. It was almost possible to believe that the nightmare hadn't happened.

She wasn't even nervous as they climbed the rugged slope, since she had no preconceived notions about the Gates. She had to find Lucas, or rather his soul-essence; it was the only way to purge her guilt. Then she remembered Lawrence and a cold pulse went through her. Oh yes, a small matter of some terrible menace that was straining to burst through and devour them all . . .

Away to her right, she heard a roar.

She looked up and saw rocks, a lace of birch trees. A shape moved and was gone—only branches swaying. She climbed another two steps and heard it distinctly—a low snarl this time, from somewhere above them.

"Fuck, what was that?" said Sam. "Sounded like no dog I've ever heard."

"Dysir?"

"They don't make any noise that I know of." The sound came again. No animal native to the English countryside yowled like that. It had an undertone of human anguish. "Let's try this way."

They veered left, heading around the skirt of the hill, all the while looking warily for the source of the snarl. Then there was a whispered call behind them, "Rosie. *Rosie!*"

Freaked, she spun around. The whisper came from the deep banks concealing a curve of the stream. No one there . . . Instinct nudged her and she stepped slantwise into the Dusklands. At once she saw the top of a head below the dip, a glint of waterweed hair and dragonfly scales . . .

"Sam," she hissed, but he'd seen too. She ran and jumped down the steep bank, barely catching herself on grass clumps to avoid ending up in the stream. Sam rolled down beside her.

There was Faith in full Aetherial mode, hiding behind dead, yellow reeds, apparently terrified. Heather was beside her. The child, in pajamas, was human in shape with iridescent hues gleaming in her baby-pink skin. "We're playing hide-and-seek with Daddy," Faith whispered, pointing a shining scaled finger at her daughter.

"What?" said Sam.

"He pretends to be angry and we pretend to be frightened. Don't we, Heather?"

The little girl nodded. She was round-eyed, apparently having bought the story. Rosie was horrified. "What the hell's going on?" she whispered, pulling Faith round to face her.

Facing away from Heather, Faith's undine face collapsed into terror. She spoke quickly and so quietly that Rosie could only just hear. "Matt came home from the hospital last night, furious. He was raging about Sam and Alastair and everything. I tried to comfort him but he threw me off—I've never seen him like it. Heather must have heard; she started crying so I brought her downstairs—I thought if she was there, Matt would calm down. He didn't. I begged him not to shout in front of his daughter, but he got angrier and said it was me making her frightened, not him. So I picked her up—and he came at us. I don't know what he meant to do."

"Oh god, Fai . . ."

"I don't think he knew either. I panicked and stepped into the Dusklands—I couldn't help it—and of course, as soon as I did, he saw me change. Saw Heather as she really is. Oh Rosie, the look on his face . . . If I'd thought he was angry before, that was nothing. It was as if the last person in his life he trusted had betrayed him."

"So you ran away?"

"It's worse." Faith rose, anxiously scanning. "He came into the Dusklands with us. He changed too. As long as we stay in the water, he can't see us."

"You've been hiding all night?"

"Most of it . . . oh my god, he's coming." Faith slithered into the stream like a fish, taking Heather with her. The water was shallow but they both slid flat on their bellies among the rippling, freezing water and the glossy stones. They were fully submerged. Rosie was paralyzed, thinking Heather must drown—and then they disappeared. Became waterweed.

Sam gripped Rosie's arm, as if to stop her leaping up, which she'd no intention of doing. Above them, a creature was breathing. Its breath rumbled through a nonhuman voice box, a cavernous, toothed mouth.

She peered over the lip and saw him, stalking the hillside above them.

He was a beast walking on hind legs, predatory and terrible like a lion but stranger than any creature she'd ever seen. A pelt of thick fur covered him, a sandy gold striped with slate blue that darkened to near-black on the limbs. He held his heavy front paws like human hands. The facial bones were long and heavy, leonine but with still-human traits, the hair a long thick mane. The fierce head moved from side to side, scenting the air.

Rosie was transfixed. *Matthew?* She recalled the deformed furry hand she'd glimpsed. The paws were in full glory now, armed with thick black claws like sabers. His eyes were human-shaped but all black like an animal's, and they burned with predatory hunger. The hair flowing down his back fused with the ridged spine. Matthew was monstrous, horrifying, magnificent.

He roared again. The roar formed a plain word, *"Faith!"*

She saw the shine of curved fangs that would crunch through an undine's neck as if through a stick of celery. There was nothing in the eyes but psychotic rage. Could he even remember being human? What if he couldn't turn back?

The heavy head swiveled. He snuffed the air, then made his way along the stream bank in the direction of Oakholme. He prowled back and forth in the undergrowth there, cutting off their hope of returning Faith and Heather to the safety of the house.

"You look after Faith," Sam said urgently. "Go upstream, then head for Stonegate. Go that way," his finger traced the western rise of the hill, "past Freya's Crown, so that I can find you somewhere en route."

"What are you going to do?"

"Lure Matthew away long enough for you to get Faith and kid to safety."

"Be careful," she said, and Sam was away, running low behind rocks and bushes until she couldn't see him anymore. Rosie scrambled to the water's edge and touched the waterweed, which resolved into Faith as she slid upwards through the ripples. Heather popped up beside her, to Rosie's relief, unharmed but tearful. "Sam's trying to distract him while I get you to Stonegate."

"We fooled him again, didn't we?" Faith said to her daughter. Her voice broke on the false brightness. Heather started to cry. "Hush, hush. Daddy will hear."

"Fai, she's exhausted. So are you. You must be frozen."

"Can't feel it." Her friend climbed onto the bank, her child in her arms. Water rolled cleanly off them, like silver marbles off duck feathers. "What am I supposed to do?" said Faith. "I knew he'd find out. But I never—Ro, did you know Matthew could transform like that?"

"No," said Rosie, shocked. How had he kept it hidden all these years? "I had no idea. Follow me and keep low. If Matt reappears, I'll stall him while you keep going towards Freya's Crown, all right?"

Rosie began to circle the hill to their left, climbing paths through dead bracken, bare oaks and holly. Faith was behind her, carrying Heather, breathing hard with strain and fear.

Rosie had never been so frightened in her life.

Once or twice she heard the rumble of Matthew's voice, downhill to the east; but she kept going, deep into the belt of trees that surrounded the hill. Halfway, Rosie took Heather and discovered just how heavy a small child could be. At last she fought free of rhododendrons and came in sight of the bare peak with its crown of rock rearing against the sky. Her heart was pounding. Then she saw Sam running up from the other direction, wielding the backpack in one hand and looking all around him. No sign of the beast.

His lean body was all energy, his face contorted with

exertion. "Run!" he yelled, beckoning them towards the rocks. "He's coming!"

It wasn't far, but it was steep. The Dusklands, it seemed, reached out to envelop them and Rosie saw the Great Gates in their true, awe-inspiring form—shining, monolithic, like some mysterious ancient burial mound. Rosie saw the crack in the rock face. It was distinct; a narrow but obvious aperture.

"He's crazy, I couldn't hold him back," Sam gasped. "Get yourselves into that gap in the rock. Quick!"

She saw beast Matthew burst from cover on the far side of the clearing. Feral, raging, he came on like an unchained, slavering, furious guard dog. All that helped them was his lack of speed, because he ran on hind legs, not on all fours. "Sam!" she cried. Her voice hardly made a sound. She was stumbling under the weight of her niece. Sam was whirling the backpack like a slingshot to keep the beast away but it kept advancing, savage and relentless, forcing Sam back and back towards the Gates.

Sam sprinted, leaving Matthew behind, and held out his arms in a protective gesture to shepherd them towards the dark gap. It hadn't been her plan to dive in without caution, but suddenly there was no other escape. She ran straight in and felt the stone-cold alien air envelop her. Faith was on her heels.

Matthew approached, roaring guttural words that turned her blood to slush. His cries were full of murderous anguish, as if no one in the world had ever suffered like him and all must shed blood to pay for it . . . She turned her head to see the tall wedge of dusk-light behind her and, silhouetted against it, Sam swinging the loaded backpack. She heard the *whumph* as it connected with the beast's belly. Matthew fell with a grunt, lurching away and out of sight.

Then Sam was running after them, gasping, "That's slowed him up. Keep going, he's not following."

There were rock walls pressing on either side. Raven blackness and a thin breeze carrying waves of fear towards her. Behind was a raging beast roaming the hill . . . but ahead lay moving darkness, all the shadows of Lawrence's nightmares waiting for them. The breeze was their whispering breath.

Every fragment of her human skepticism fell away. The Gates to Elfland were real. And Lucas had unlocked them.

17

❦

Spiral Fire

The fissure in the rock was cold and ink-black. Rosie, in the lead, felt her way with her feet and one hand, the other arm holding Heather against her shoulder. The darkness was like a physical force pushing against her.

"What's there?" said Sam.

"I can't see a thing," said Rosie. "What if it's a dead end?"

"In that case we'll turn and go back, feeling a right bunch of idiots."

"Not with Matthew waiting," said Faith, her voice shaky.

"I won't let him hurt you," said Sam. "Keep going."

How ridiculous to be afraid of my own brother, thought Rosie. The sweat turned cold on her body as she squeezed onwards, driven by panic, slowed by fear and the narrow press of the walls. The passage ran in a curve. She found vertical rims of stone in the walls, smooth hand-sized patterns of inlaid metal. Her hand crept over a clearly defined symbol; a spiral, emblem of the Otherworld.

Heather reached at thin air and said, "Look at the sky, Mummy."

Rosie saw a brushstroke of navy ahead. She held her breath as if to plunge into deep water. "We're there," she said.

They stepped out of the fissure and into the flowing, indigo twilight of a forest. This was not the world she knew, not even under Dusklands glamour. Tall black trunks reached to the canopy far above and the undergrowth swayed like seaweed under the ocean. The forest was monumental, enveloping. Full of moving shadows. The air smelled delicious, fresh and moist, tangling her fear with wild excitement. *Elysion.*

"Get clear of the entrance," said Sam urgently, pulling her and Faith to one side. Thorns snagged her hair. The portal was silver-grey rock like Freya's Crown in miniature; the tall thin aperture framed by two fruit trees that leaned towards each other and clasped their branches above it. The flanks of the rock were clouded by bushes and briars. Before them, a green slope fell away, becoming a path that curved onto the forest floor and out of sight. The air rippled with ghostly shapes.

They waited. No sound disturbed the ocean rush of the forest. No Matthew came leaping enraged after them.

"Looks like Matt isn't joining us," Sam said grimly. "Take a good look around, so we can find the way back."

"Gods, we're really here," Rosie whispered. Heather was squirming in her arms, so she passed her to Faith, who kissed her and smoothed her hair, telling her, "It's all right, cross Daddy can't chase us anymore." She transformed before Rosie's eyes; scales fading, hair darkening, angelfish veils vanishing. Faith was her usual self again, wearing a brown dress patterned with tiny white flowers, barefoot . . . just as she'd run out of the house.

"Elysion," said Sam with a half-smile. "You're amazing, Rosie."

"I didn't do anything," she murmured. "So Luc was right, he unlocked the Lychgate . . . but where's the great peril that Lawrence warned us about?"

"Don't know," said Sam. "Maybe it's waiting . . . or invisible, or something."

A sense of watery movement all around disoriented her. From the corner of her eye, she glimpsed semihuman shapes. They seemed to be watching, circling. "Lucas?" she called out, in the wild hope that he might be among them.

As if in response, a low voice said, "*Unbranded.*"

"What the hell was that?" said Sam.

She caught his arm. "You heard it?"

"This feels creepy. I'm thinking we should head down the path . . . Looks like no one's been this way for quite some time."

They started downhill at a steady walk, anxiously scanning every direction. A thin silvery trail like a deer track threaded along the center of the broader path between the monolithic trunks. "We should stay on the track," Rosie said, nervously joking. "It's when you wander into the forest you get into trouble. My parents will go mad . . . I hope this isn't a horrible mistake . . ."

"Hey, you're with me," he grinned. "The master of horrible mistakes. It's too late now." He gave her a direct, firm look, as if to say, *We're in this together.* Her heart twisted hotly inside her. She returned the look, telling him, *Yes. I know.*

As they walked, the phantoms moved with them. "They're following us," Faith said uneasily.

Sam turned to her. "Let me carry Heather. We'll make faster progress that way. Don't worry, they're just . . . elementals, maybe."

Heather quickly fell asleep on Sam's shoulder. In pink teddy-bear pajamas she looked tender and vulnerable. "Never guessed you were Aetherial, Faith," he said. "You kept that one very dark."

"Long story," Rosie said softly. "It was what I couldn't tell you in the alley, remember?"

"Ah. No offense, but it wasn't in the plan to bring a child with us."

"What plan? Sam, we couldn't leave them behind!"

Faith said, "I'm sorry, I never meant to be a nuisance, but I didn't plan this, either. I don't even know where you're going, or why. Matthew's never going to forgive me."

"For being Aetherial?" Sam said in disgust.

"For deceiving him."

"He needs to get over himself. Pompous jerk."

"Sam!" said Rosie. "Shush. We're trying to find Lucas, Fai. Somehow he accidentally unlocked the Lychgate. We think his Aetherial essence fled through when he was injured, and he won't recover unless we find it. It's desperate, I know. I hadn't realized how mad it sounded until I said it."

"Needle, haystack," said Sam.

"I can't face my parents unless I at least try to find him," said Rosie. "You understand that, don't you?" Faith nodded. She looked pallid with exhaustion. Her heart, too, must be broken.

The twilight deepened. The darker it grew, the more solid the stalking figures became, keeping pace with them in the edge of the trees. The disembodied voice spoke again, *"Vaethyr. Virgin."*

Rosie caught a sharp breath. She was trying to convince herself she wasn't afraid but her hands were clammy, her heart tripping. The shadow shapes flowed into their path, charcoal on slate grey. A low, menacing voice came from all around them. *"You cannot come here unbranded."*

Encircled by dark, wavering specters, they halted. "This is not looking good," said Sam, clasping Heather firmly as he turned to Rosie and Faith. "We're going to run like hell, back the way we came. Ready?"

Then he gave a sharp cry. It was over before Rosie could react. He jerked as if shot and tumbled backwards, an arrow shaft sticking from his collarbone, the child shrieking on top of him.

She saw a pair of golden eyes staring at her, a transparent winged form sketched on the darkness, a glowing arrow poised in some kind of crossbow. A split second later she felt the elf-shot; a stabbing fiery pain in her ribs. Her sight and hearing vanished in a rush of stars. Through the fog, she was aware of Faith trying to wrestle Heather from Sam until she, too, convulsed and fell. There was a moment of incomprehension, *What the hell? No—this can't be happening—not now* . . . but pain dragged her down, across Sam's fallen body, into an ocean of shadows.

Rosie was drowning in another dimension; a blurred dim landscape that was Earth and Dusklands and Elysion and somewhere else entirely. She was running on all fours—knowing she was dreaming, which made running pointless, and had no time to waste on visions, but still desperately running as if her efforts could somehow influence the real world.

Sam ran beside her stride for stride, and Sam was a wolf. More than wolf—a dread, magnificent beast with bright cobalt eyes, blond-tipped dark fur. She was the same, and she could also see her wolfish *fylgia* from the outside—shadowy, silvery, an elemental or a small deity, an entity she didn't comprehend.

For a few intoxicating minutes in her dual being, Rosie understood. The Otherworld hunters fired divine arrows of a kind, delivering splinters of complex knowledge. She and wolf Sam looked at each other; no need for words. They had always been here, side by side, wild, instinctive, answering to no one. They ran for days; hunting, feeding, play-fighting, mating, racing onwards again.

Their human selves vanished.

She had left a dim awareness: that you could not come back from this and stay sane. It was a whirlwind. It must leave you demented. She rose on her hind legs and became a statue in a temple, and wolf-headed Sam was her priest. Rosie began to laugh manically. She heard her mother singing,

Let the Spiral take us down
Tread the Spiral, round and round
Dancing down the river's course
Spinning back towards the Source
Find the mirror at its heart

Merry meet, and merry part
We kiss the water and fly,
Kiss the water and fly . . .

Jessica's voice was a silver thread drawing her along the loop of time as it curved back towards its starting point. Suddenly, violently she was pitched into consciousness. A circle of pain burned under her left breast. The world was dark.

She felt Sam moving and groaning beneath her. He clutched her shoulders, trying to push her off him. Her mouth was rust-dry. She felt dizzy, as if she'd been drugged. Hauling herself into a kneeling position, she felt raw pain on her rib cage beneath her left breast. Her fingers found a hole in her sweater, and a two-inch circle of blistered flesh, weeping blood.

"Sam, are you all right?" Her voice came out as a sob. She clawed her hair back.

He stared at her, eyes unfocused. "What the hell happened?"

"Did you—were you with me? Wolf, but not?"

"Uh . . ." The glazed eyes widened. He drew a few shallow breaths. "Yes. We were there for like . . . months. But dream time, not real time."

She touched a frayed hole in his T-shirt below the collarbone, and her fingertip went through and found the flesh wound. Sam winced. "Ouch."

"Whatever shot us was real," she said, "but it's only skin-deep. More a stamp than a penetrating wound. Oh my god, I thought they'd killed you."

"They didn't, love. Feels like they stuck a hot coal on me. Jeez."

"Faith?" Rosie called out. "Are you there?"

Looking up, she was suddenly blinded by the flare of a swinging lamp. On the forest path ahead of them was a woman, cloaked and hooded in black, bending over something on the ground. She straightened, raising the lamp so its light washed over them. In the glow, Rosie saw Faith rising to her knees and beside her, thank heaven, stood Heather, sobbing but apparently unhurt.

"Where did you come from?" the woman called. Her voice was low, muffled within the deep hood. "I heard the little one crying. Come, you must go with me. It's not safe at night."

"Now they tell us," Sam said through his teeth. Rosie tried to stand up but the wound in her ribs burned so fiercely that she doubled over. Sam was no better. With an undignified struggle they made it to their feet, but it wasn't clear who was helping whom.

"I know it hurts, but it's not fatal," the woman said, rather impatiently. She helped Faith, giving her the lantern as she swung Heather up in a fireman's lift. "I'm surprised they didn't take the child. You are asking for trouble, bringing a youngster in here."

"They tried," Faith said shakily. "Unless I dreamed it. I hung on to her for dear life until they gave up." As she spoke, Rosie put her arms around her. Her friend was unyielding, distant, not the Faith she knew. She let her be, and fell back to Sam's side.

"You can rest with me tonight." The woman led them along the path, her cloak a black flare against the dancing sphere of lamplight. "I can't let you stay out here. You've come through the Lychgate, haven't you? How long has it been open? I didn't know. What on earth were you thinking, entering the Spiral without preparation?"

"That's a lot of questions," said Sam. "And I've got one: What business is it of yours?"

"Sam!" Rosie poked him in the ribs. "He doesn't mean to be rude, he was born that way. It's a long story. I have to find my brother."

"Well, you're going nowhere until morning." On every side, the forest flowed away into wilderness. Farther on, Rosie glimpsed a glade with a circle of standing stones, and wondered if Vaethyr used to dance there. She could almost taste echoes of it; animal masks, flower wreaths, wild music.

Exertion and pain made it hard to speak. Eventually she asked, "Who were they—the ones who attacked us?"

The woman answered without turning round. "I thought you knew. What have they taught you in Vaeth? They were Initiators. They recognized you as new to the Spiral and so they put the brand upon you. A toxic preparation of corrosive and hallucinogen—you will have had visions, I expect? And now be feeling a little rough."

"Yes." She and Sam glanced at each other. "It's true, we were never initiated because the Gates were locked . . . but I thought it would be more civilized than that. They hunted us down!"

Sam added, "And if I ever see them again, I'll stick their red-hot arrows so far up their . . ."

"You won't see them," the woman laughed. "You wouldn't recognize them. They are Aelyr who change shape and hunt down uninitiated Vaethyr. It's a trance state in which, it's said, the unbranded Vaethyr glow and so make themselves visible targets. Yes, the usual practice is for initiates to be brought through by their elders, so there's some element of guidance and ceremony. But, ultimately, you are left on your own to be hunted and branded. You were lucky. Traditionally you would have been stripped naked and turned loose in the forest first."

"Oh," said Sam. "I'm guessing that's not as much fun as it sounds."

"For some, initiation is ecstatic. For others, hideous. There have been deaths. It is really a stupid practice born of the Aelyr desire to put their stamp on those Vaethyr who have the effrontery to live on Earth. On the surface it says, You're one of us, but the subtext is, We own you. You came in uninvited, so they branded you anyway. It's the way they do things, unfortunately. Never mind. You survived."

She took a side path that brought them uphill, leaving Rosie too weary to ask any more questions. There was dense grass under their feet, trees to their left, a folded wall of rock on their right. The path began a steep descent. Over the shoulder, the trees opened out and below lay a small, hidden valley. To the right, a waterfall poured down the rock face into a stream. Along the stream bank to their left stood a cottage; an archetypal stone cottage with thatch roof and vines around the door. The scene was all in dark shades of sapphire and emerald. Firefly lights glanced on the water.

"Perfect," Sam said with a laugh. "There had to be a witch's cottage in the woods."

"Come in, walking wounded," said the woman, opening the door to a simple interior bathed in firelight. "I'll find something to salve those burns." She set Heather down, took the lantern from Faith and placed it on a hook. Unselfconsciously she threw off her cloak. Beneath it, she looked every inch the part of forest witch in a long figure-hugging dress of dark plum, with long tangles of black hair, a spare, bony face and penetrating eyes.

Rosie heard Sam make a noise in his throat, a sort of gasp. There was a thud as the backpack hit the ground. He said, "*Mum?*"

Lawrence stood looking down at the face of Lucas, his son. Still no improvement, the specialist had said. He couldn't identify what he felt. Clearly he felt something, if only a void, a sucking white emptiness too big to grasp. It was not a place from which tears came. Auberon could weep enough for them both.

"You're so gracious, Auberon," he said when the doctors had gone. "Gracious beyond words. You always have been."

The two men sat on either side of Lucas. There was no color in the room but black and white. Auberon had cleared up the doctor's confusion by quietly explaining that while Lucas was his son, Lawrence was actually his biological father. "I suppose a lad is lucky to have two fathers," Auberon said gravely. "Too many children have none at all."

"You're not jealous?"

"No, I'm not. It's me who's had the pleasure of his company all these years." Auberon paled as he spoke, as if aware of the obvious conclusion, *and these could be the last few days.*

"Well, I envy you that," said Lawrence. "But if a decision has to be made . . . about turning off life support . . . then I envy you not at all. Whatever you decide, I won't fight it."

"If they begin to pressure us, I don't know where we'll turn. What will it do to Jess? If his Aetherial essence can't die, where has it gone? Through the Gates, even closed? Or somewhere in the Dusklands, like a ghost . . . perhaps he'll attach himself to a tree or stone until he's ready for rebirth of some kind . . . but we'll never see him in this form again."

"So much of our existence is about saying farewell," said Lawrence. His voice was dry with strain. "Our losses are not as concrete as they are for humans, but that makes it the more painful. Not knowing. Our children shouldn't be able to fly through locked Gates—in physical or essential form—to vanish in the vastness of the inner realms . . . yet still they leave us."

Auberon met his eyes. "And there is the possibility," he said carefully, "that without access to the Spiral, our Aetheric essence will die. We'll become mortal. The Dusklands will fade from lack of sustenance, and we'll forget our true selves. Is that what you wanted all along, my friend?"

Lawrence gazed at Lucas's sleeping face. "No," he said hoarsely. "Never. The danger is real and terrible. What, you think I lied to you? I love the Otherworld."

Memories played across the back of Lawrence's mind. Masked Aelyr bowing to him as they presented the ceremonial staff of applewood. Albin, waiting for him by the stream that flowed from Sibeyla into Melusiel; Lawrence proudly presenting a casket of sparkling albinite that he'd harvested on Earth, saying, "All these, Father, in exchange for the one stone you took from me." Albin's fist flying upwards, sending the priceless cut gems cascading into the stream, lost. His contemptuous response. *"This is a sacred stone. To mine it and sell it on Vaeth is sacrilege!"*

Lawrence had realized, in that moment of despair, that nothing he did would ever incur Albin's favor. He was an impossible-to-please father who had marked his son as weak and flawed from birth. *And in the end, I fulfilled his prophecies,* Lawrence thought. *He was correct to despise me. He had all my faults pinned in a display case from the start.*

Not for a second had he blamed Albin for the existence of his nemesis, Brawth. Albin had not woken it or sent it. No, it was a horror entirely of Lawrence's own making and Albin would say, he knew, "*I told you that no good would come of defying me and following Liliana into the greedy corruption of Earth.*"

Here with Auberon, Lawrence found the confession spilling out. "It's strange. When they give you the power of the Gatekeeper, it's done with full ceremony. When they take it away, there is nothing. You are not even asked to clear your desk, as it were. Realization dawns and there is only a cold, dry emptiness."

Auberon leaned towards him, grasping Lucas's hand as he did so. "Are you saying you've lost the power?"

Lawrence nodded, eyes closed. "The Great Gates are blind rock to me now."

It took Auberon a few minutes to recover his composure. At last he said, "For how long? Have you told anyone?"

"Only you. I have not even been able to face going up there since . . . Tell no one, I beg you. The whole world has turned to bleak grey rock because of my failings and I am stranded in a granite tower looking out at my work and there is nothing to be done. I am being punished."

"For what?"

"For waking Brawth, the ice giant of the Abyss, and failing to destroy it."

Auberon paused, looking gravely at him like a concerned doctor. "How did you wake it?"

"I don't know. It defies reason. Simply by existing, I brought an enemy to life that grew greater as I diminished."

"Are you sure . . . that it is not all in your mind?"

Lawrence laughed. "When Aetherials dream, what do we create? I have asked myself that many times, of course, but in the Spiral, dreams become real. You have sensed it, haven't you? And Lucas has seen it. I have struggled all these years to protect my sons, to protect everyone from it . . . but now, if the lych-light's gone, it's out of my hands. My time is almost over, my friend."

"What are you saying?" Auberon had gone grey. "Don't talk like this. Promise me you won't think of harming yourself!"

Lawrence's bone-white finger traced Lucas's cheek. He murmured, "Bron, if the time should come to turn off the machine and you truly can't face it . . . I will."

Tears fell from Auberon's tired eyes. "Don't let's speak of that yet."

Lawrence hardly knew he was expressing his thoughts aloud until it was too late. "Will that be considered sufficient punishment? To be forced to destroy this beloved life? A sacrifice. Will anything pacify Brawth and make it sink back into the darkness, other than to consume my son? Not any son, but the most precious one. What could be more bitter?" He exhaled a long ragged breath and whispered, "Lucas, come back to us."

The woman was unquestionably Virginia Wilder. Once seen, thought Rosie, never forgotten. When Sam said "*Mum?*" she gave a puzzled frown, drew her head back and continued as if she hadn't heard. "Let me see to your wounds; they won't have branded the child, don't worry." She smiled at Heather. "What a pretty little girl. Come in, rest; you're safe here."

Sam and Rosie exchanged a look of astonished confusion. Virginia hurried through a dark archway at the back of the room, leaving them speechless.

Firelight washed rough cream walls. The floor covering was some kind of dry moss, springy underfoot, strewn with dried flowers and fragrant herbs. There was little furniture, only a basic kitchen—a water pump, a trestle of thick dark wood along the right-hand wall, cupboards. The large fireplace had a second archway beside it. In the center stood a low round table, like a big disk of lapis lazuli, with cushions scattered around for seats. Everything looked softly yellow and blue-green.

Faith collapsed onto a cushion with Heather in her lap. "Are you all right?" asked Rosie, kneeling beside her. "Where did they get you?"

Faith pulled down the neck of her dress and showed a weeping red blister just below her throat. Although swollen, the shape was a clear spiral. Rosie gasped. "Ohh. I've seen this before. Lucas had one, after he . . ."

Virginia came back with a brown glass bottle on a wad of gauze. "This lotion will ease the pain, although it will scar, of course; that's the idea." Sam only stared at her as she tended first Faith, then Rosie. It stung fiercely, making her eyes stream until it faded to a dull throb. Sam stood unflinching while Virginia dabbed his wound. When she'd finished, he touched one hand to her shoulder and snared her gaze so she couldn't evade him. Rosie sat back on her heels, watching. She saw them side-on, their profiles painted by firelight.

"Did you hear what I called you?" he said quietly. "Don't you recognize me? This is Rosie, Faith and Heather. You're Virginia Wilder, but they call you Ginny."

She blinked, green eyes darkening. "How did you know?"

"I'm Sam. Hello? Mum, I'm your flaming—" He caught himself and continued in a more measured tone. "I'm your son."

Her face froze, incredulous. "I had a son called Sam, but he was a boy . . . oh my god."

"Yes, I was eleven when you left, but that was fifteen years ago. Don't you know how long you've been away?"

Lotion and gauze fell to the floor. She put her fingers to her mouth. "Fifteen years? It doesn't seem it. Elysion plays tricks . . . Yes, you look like him, but—no, it's not possible."

"Bloody hell," he said, rubbing his hands over his hair. "We thought you were dead!"

"The life I had on Vaeth . . . it seems far away, cloudy . . . oh my god, don't do this to me. You can't be."

Sam caught her wrists and drew her hands away from her face. To Rosie's astonishment, he began to sing, *"There may be trouble ahead . . . "* Ginny's mouth opened; Rosie stared. Of all things, she had never expected to hear Sam singing an Irving Berlin song, 'Let's Face the Music and Dance.'

His voice was low, melodic, and slightly gravelly. Perhaps he wouldn't have taken the stage on the strength of it, but here it was a revelation. Rosie and Faith exchanged a startled glance. Ginny's face transformed. She appeared so dumbstruck that, when Sam spun her around in a jokey dance, she simply let him. He continued with, *"I get no kick from champagne . . ."* Cole Porter this time, 'I Get a Kick Out of You.'

Rosie started to smile. It was the most absurd, most moving thing she'd ever witnessed. Ginny's eyes opened wide and she gasped, "Oh—oh, Sam!"

She reached for him. He seized her in both arms.

Rosie had never seen his attention so completely focused on another woman before. Amid her relief, she felt a perfectly ungracious stab of jealousy.

"Oh, it's really you. My Sam. Gods—all these years— why are you here? And Jon, where is he?"

There were tears running down his face. "Not with us, but he's okay. You were trapped here. I knew you didn't abandon us on purpose."

Pulling away, Ginny sat down at the table next to Faith, covering her face with her hands. While she gathered herself, Sam sat cross-legged beside Rosie and said, "She loved those old songs. Didn't you, Mum? We used to sing them together, remember?"

Ginny let her hands drop. Her ice-queen face was a blotchy pink mess. "Yes—but when you're here a long time, the past fades like a dream. Still, I remember leaving

Stonegate as if it were yesterday. I fell over you and your brothers, Rosie, as I was walking out."

"You frightened us," Rosie put in.

"Oh, I was practically insane with rage that day. I came into Elysion, only to rest a few days while I decided what to do. Then I couldn't leave. The portal was blind stone. I might have known Lawrence would abandon the Gates."

"He didn't," said Sam. "He insists there's danger on this side. Is there?"

Ginny didn't answer. She shook her head, her eyes full of unspoken thoughts. "I'm a poor hostess; out of practice," she said, moving to stoke the fire and position a kettle over the flames. She fetched a patchwork quilt and wrapped it around Faith's shoulders, then brought cups and a jug of fruit juice to the table, followed by cakes, fruit and cheese. The juice tasted of strawberries and pomegranates. Although Rosie was bone-tired, food and drink revived her, reawakening her fears for Lucas.

"It's an Elysian tradition," said Ginny, "to wait at the portal with gifts for the Vaethyr around Earth's harvest time. Year after year I waited for you, but you never came."

"Wish we could have done." Sam's voice nearly broke. "Father wouldn't relent."

Rosie put in, "And the Aelyr can't open the portal from this side, I gather?"

Ginny shook her head. "One Gatekeeper was meant to serve both sides. Lawrence was never comfortable in the role." She added lightly, "How is he?"

A long pause. "He got married again," said Sam.

Her face turned to iron. "Did he?" she said flatly. "Who to?"

"A human called Sapphire who worked for him."

"Oh," said Ginny. "I think I remember her. She was at the New York store . . . I met her once, I believe."

"Very glossy and smiley, always telling everyone what to do."

"Oh yes, Lawrence loves being told what to do," Ginny

said acidly. "He must be ecstatic. Human, indeed. Is he happy?"

"When's Dad ever happy?" Sam said with a grin. As they were talking, Faith slipped lower until she was lying flat, her head pillowed on a cushion and Heather sound asleep in her arms. Ginny tucked the quilt over them. "They put on a brave front, but things have been frosty for a while."

At that, Ginny's mouth flattened with knowing amusement. "Ah. That's your father." She looked at Rosie. "He's the dream lover at the start—until you realize he's devouring you to warm the icy chasm in his soul. Only no one can. Then he turns away and crowns himself the Arctic Prince. He did so with me and with Jessica. He will with Sapphire, too." Her face lengthened and she breathed, "Oh, Rosie, I'm sorry. You won't have known about Lawrence and your mother. An unfortunate diversion."

"It's all right, everyone knows," said Rosie.

"Good," Ginny said crisply. "My humiliation is complete." She wasn't a warm or cozy person, Rosie observed, but the polar opposite of Jessica. "I have nothing against Lucas, of course. A beautiful boy."

"He's why we're here," Rosie put in, and gave a brief, bare explanation.

Ginny became somber. She brought a huge brown pot of tea to the table before she answered. Every move she made was poised, goddesslike. "It's true, the Aetheric soul-essence is drawn to the Spiral, drawn to the center of Asru, the Mirror Pool . . ."

"And can we go after him?" Rosie was fraught with anxiety. She felt Sam's hand on her knee. "It could be like trekking to Siberia, for all I know. I'm worried we're losing time."

"There's a specific way you must go, and I'm not promising it will be easy, but it is walkable. However, you can't go until light. You'd get lost, abducted or eaten. And you won't last five minutes unless you sleep off the initiation drug first."

Rosie knew she was right. She sipped the hot, honeyed tea, trying not to think about failure, or the chances of the Lychgate being relocked behind them.

"Did Lawrence ever explain why I left?" Ginny asked after a moment.

"Come on, we are talking about Dad here," said Sam. "Of course not. We suspected he'd murdered and buried you in the woods."

Ginny grimaced. "Even Lawrence wouldn't go that far."

Rosie put in, "I suppose seeing my mother and Lucas around can't have helped."

"Oh, that." Ginny swept her hair back over her shoulders. "We think we're above mortals, but we're not. We're every bit as prone to bad behavior and insane jealousy. Lawrence would always flee an argument rather than confront it." She shrugged. "We were at war for years, in the business of hurting each other. Neither of us was quite faithful. As for Jessica, I bear no grudge."

Ginny gave a thin smile. Sam stared, shocked. "No, the reason I left was rather more complicated. As Aetherials, we're sensitive to deeper layers of reality. Sometimes it can drive us mad. Lawrence wanted to live in Ecuador. For me, though, rain forest and Dumannios were all tangled together in nightmares. I had to come home, where the Dusklands were peaceful and kind. He thought it was fine to dump you and Jon in boarding school, but it wasn't."

Looking pale, Sam said, "Dad couldn't have lived abroad anyway, being Gatekeeper . . ."

"It wasn't that he didn't care about you," Ginny said, touching his hand. "Don't think that. No, it was being Gatekeeper that he wanted to escape. He couldn't, of course, but he resented me bitterly for making him face the truth. And I hated him for not understanding *my* fears, when he should have understood better than anyone. That was the problem, Sam. We each had a similar curse, yet we each refused to acknowledge it. We were both stubborn."

Sam frowned, eyes narrowing. "He's as paranoid as hell.

He insists there's some great force ready to burst through the Gates and destroy us. Some believe him, some don't."

"He always had that darkness," Ginny's gaze slipped down and sideways. "It drove me away. If I'd known I'd be trapped here, though, I would never have come."

"He must have suspected you were here when he sealed the portal, surely?" said Sam. "Bastard!"

"He must have had his reasons."

"He tried to find you, I'm certain," said Rosie. "I think he was in pieces, but just couldn't ever show it."

"I loved him," Ginny said simply. "I left because I was at my wits' end. I didn't mean it to be forever." They sat gazing at each other. After a minute, she lowered her eyes and asked softly, "And what about you, Sam? Look at you, a fine strong man. How are you, what's happened? Tell me everything."

"Hell, where do I start?" He sighed. Rosie saw his shoulders dip with the weight of memory. "Can't we sing some nice Cole Porter songs instead?"

"No, we can't."

"Shall I leave you to it?" Rosie asked quietly.

"No, Rosie, don't go." Sam caught her hand. "She's less likely to thrash me around the room if you're here."

"Shame. That would have been worth seeing," said Rosie.

Ginny was studying them, one eyebrow arched. "You two are an item, I take it?"

"Erm," said Sam, looking sideways at Rosie. "I'm working on it."

Rosie bit her lip, reddening. "It's why we're in this mess."

An hour or two later, Ginny showed them through an archway into a small dark passage with two rooms leading off. There were no doors, only a heavy curtain across each entrance. She drew back one of these curtains for them, kissed them good night, and was gone.

"My mother," Sam whispered. "I found my mother. Told

her everything, and she's still speaking to me." He couldn't stop smiling.

"I like her," said Rosie. "I love the way she's sort of acerbic. I can see where you get it from."

The room was strange, apparently taking no account of the cottage's outside dimensions. It was near-dark, soaked in a midnight-blue glow with walls and ceiling disappearing into shadow. The floor sloped slightly upwards towards the far end and was covered in a thick, dry carpet of mossy fronds. There was no furniture, only a cushiony dip in the center.

"I take it that's the bed," said Sam. "Kind of Freudian, isn't it? It looks like a mouth, or . . . something." He dropped the backpack and took off his boots. Rosie did the same, felt the carpet warm and squashy beneath her feet. A faint glow in the wall to her right led her to explore.

She found a narrow, curved passageway, lit by a soft glow, winding into a small cave. A spring flowed down the polished limestone curves of the wall and away through a hole into an underground stream. Aetherial plumbing, apparently. She availed herself of the hole—hoping that was its intended use—then stripped and showered under the chilly waterfall. A cleft in the rock held clouds of dry vegetable matter that could be torn off in clumps to dry the skin. Shivering, Rosie quickly dressed again.

"The weirdest en-suite bathroom ever is through there," she said as she came back. "No hot water, though."

Sam went to the passage and peered in. "Any towels?"

"No. Use the spongy stuff." As she waited for him, she felt nervous. She was on her feet near the doorway, staring at the strange oval sleeping area, when he came back.

"Not tried out the bed, yet?" he asked. He sat down on the lip, looking up at her. "Feels nice and soft."

Rosie wrapped her arms across her waist. She was suddenly frozen. He put his tongue between his teeth, gazed quizzically at her. "What's up? I'm not going to pounce on you."

"Really? Oh damn," she said, trying to joke and failing. She let her hands fall. "I know you're not, Sam."

"You weren't sure, though, were you? Good grief, Rosie, do you think I'm that insensitive?"

"Hey, I never said that."

"All I want to do is sleep," he said. "Not that I wouldn't want to—normally—but as things are, I can't. I'm not a machine. Of course it wouldn't be right; I know that. I'm not a complete Neanderthal, you know."

"Sam, will you cool down?" she said, kneeling in front of him. "I never suggested you were. I felt awkward, that's all. Never been in a situation like this with you before."

He exhaled. The hurt look bled away. "I'm sorry, love," he said. "Who the hell am I to get all indignant, anyway? Considering my track record of pouncing on you every chance I get, why should you trust me?"

"But I do," she said, and meant it—because if she couldn't trust him, they had nothing. "Let's not argue. We're both worn out and not thinking straight."

He gave a rueful smile, white in the dusk-light. "Come on, then. You sleep on the squishy thing. I'll take the floor."

"Okay."

Sam stayed fully clothed and so did she, ready for fight or flight. Carefully she eased herself into the dip. She found a quilt there, deepest violet in color and intricately sewn with tiny flowers. As she lay down on soft silk-padded moss with the cover over her, it felt like floating. She said after a moment, "It's unbelievably comfortable."

"Good."

Take a hint, damn it. "Sam, does no sex mean we can't even sleep together?"

"Erm." Lying a couple of yards away, he rose on one elbow. "Depends if you can control yourself, sweetie."

She gave a soft, tired laugh. "I can't sleep without you. Please hold me."

No answer, but a second later she felt him sliding into the dip beside her. His arms went around her and he kissed her forehead. "I thought you'd never ask. Go to sleep. I'm here. And tomorrow, we'll find Luc."

This was something they'd never done before; shared a bed fully clothed, holding each other. It felt strange and wonderful. Rosie turned on her side and, with Sam behind her and his arm over her, she fell into exhausted sleep.

Sam lay holding Rosie, his face in her hair. Her body molded to his as if she belonged there. Simply lying here with her was more than he'd ever dreamed of. It was wonderful beyond words. And unbearable.

At one stage she woke and he felt her shaking with suppressed sobs. He stroked her hair and held her more closely, letting her know with all his heart that he was there with her. He thought, *I love you,* but didn't say it out loud because he wouldn't be able to bear the silence if she didn't say it back. Eventually she slept again.

I need to know if this is the end or the beginning, she'd said.

Sam had no answer.

Love was meant to be noble and self-sacrificing and all the things he wasn't. And it had brought her to this.

She was right about him, he knew. He'd loved the mischief, the chaos, the sheer unkind fun of tempting her off her chosen path and into the dark thorny woods. Oh yes, so much gleeful pleasure at her fall. The truth was that he hadn't known any other way. She wouldn't give her love freely, so he'd stolen it. He truly wasn't good enough for her; he was cruel, selfish, a wolf who'd harried her until she'd given in. And this was the result.

His love was never going to bring her anything but pain.

If you get something you don't deserve, insisted a small voice at the back of his mind, *how can you possibly hope to keep it?* He tried to ignore the voice. His sweet dark red rose lay warm in his arms. For now, nothing else mattered.

18

Kissing the Mirror

Rosie woke with a sense of suffocation. She was in the strangest dream of following an owl, its flight leading her to climb a tree where she found a nest high up in the branches, and in the nest a silk bag containing a rosewood box, and inside the box an egg of pale rose quartz. The Greenlady seemed to be in the dream too, whispering an incomprehensible story. Rosie was stealing the egg and slipping it into her pocket as she woke.

Someone had called her name. She found herself lying in darkness under thick soft covers, with no sense of place or time but knowing something was terribly wrong . . . Then she remembered. Elysion. Lucas. She sat up and checked her watch. The light worked, but the hands had stopped. "Sam?"

"What's up, love?" he said sleepily beside her.

"What time is it? Have we been here two hours or two days?"

"I don't think they bother with time here. Not in any sensible fashion, anyhow."

The call came again, clear this time. "Sam, Rosie? It's light."

He sat up, smoothed her hair and kissed her forehead. "That's answered the question."

The glow spilling along the passageway had a fluid quality, as eerie as the deep ocean. Elysian dawn. Ginny was seated at the low table, with breakfast laid out. In a holly-green dress with ropes of amber around her neck and her hair flowing tangled down her back, she sat very straight; spare and poised like a dancer.

"Are you well rested?" she asked.

"Yes, thank you," said Rosie. "Just a bit . . . confused."

"That's normal." Ginny smiled.

"That was only one night, right?" said Sam.

"One night," she replied. "Night and day don't always fall when you expect them." She held out her hand to him.

"Okay, that's too cryptic before breakfast," he said. He took her hand, kissed her cheek. Rosie still felt awkward, witnessing their reunion. It was so intense and private; the knowledge of all the lost time between them, overwhelming. "Did I really tell you all that stuff last night?"

"Yes, dear," Ginny said dryly. "You did."

"Uh, well, it's not pretty but it is the truth."

Ginny looked down at the bread she was tearing between her long fingernails. "Come on, help yourselves."

"Where's Faith?" Rosie asked as they sat down.

"Still asleep. I put them to bed. They'll stay here while you find your brother, don't worry."

"Thank you," Rosie said quietly. "I really appreciate it. They've had such a hard time." As she looked at the food on the table—fruit, bread, eggs—she had a flash of intuition about the myth of faerie food. One meal would not bind you to the Otherworld—but years of imbibing the food and water and air might do it, as the Aetheric substance of the Spiral gradually became part of you.

"I've been thinking about everything," Ginny said, pouring tea. "Hardly slept for thinking about it. Something your father said once . . . That when humans dream, they create angels and vampires—but when Aetherials dream, what do *we* create?"

Sam leaned on the edge of the table, his sleeves rolled back. Disheveled from sleep, he looked so good that Rosie wanted to grab him . . . if only they'd been in a world where the crash had never happened. "Did he have an answer?"

"That's what I'm afraid of." She didn't elaborate. They were silent for a few minutes, Rosie doing her best to eat although she had little appetite. Then Ginny asked, "Does he still talk about Barada?"

"Rarely," said Sam. "He doesn't visit Valle Rojo anymore and says the mine's exhausted. He once spoke about Barada in a way that worried me—as if he'd transformed from nasty land-grabber to part of the nebulous threat. As if he sees all his enemies as joining the amorphous mass. Like I said, paranoid. That's the toughie, trying to work out if the threat's real or if he's plain mad . . . no one knows for sure, least of all me. Sorry."

"Don't be. Sounds like he hasn't changed."

"Has there been any sign of danger on this side?" Rosie asked. "Last night was scary enough."

"Oh, that's normal," said Ginny. "No, nothing clear . . . but I feel *something,* like the sultry pressure before a storm. Rosie, my ancestors were from the borderland of Melusiel and Asru, part watery and part spiritual, not quite one or the other . . . and I'm from a long line of women known as witches on Earth . . . so I should know the answer, but I don't. It's cloudy." She sighed. "If it is the case that the lych-light had been taken from Lawrence and bestowed elsewhere, only the Spiral Court could have done that. And if they've done it, they must want the Gates open again. Which means that the danger isn't real after all."

"Or that they haven't seen it," said Sam.

Rosie looked at him, startled by the thought. "Or aren't taking it seriously?"

"Or don't care," Sam added.

"The Spiral Court is a mysterious law unto itself," said Ginny. "It's said that only the most wise and ancient Aetherials are called to serve upon it, rather like being called to jury service. As the members change, so there are sways of political opinion and policy . . ."

"So maybe a bunch of doddering old idiots are in power just now?" said Sam.

Ginny laughed. "Still as disrespectful as ever. I like that. There are factions who want to maintain a peaceful connection with Earth, others who don't."

"Then there's my uncle Comyn, who's a good old anarchist," said Rosie.

"I remember him." Ginny smiled. "Lawrence never got on with him . . . but Lawrence got on with almost no one, really. He had such a difficult father in Albin, who was a particularly extreme Aelyr puritan and separatist. Myself, I keep out of the politics. I like my quiet life here. You know, it's hard to see you go, so soon after we've met. At least you're initiates now."

"I don't feel any different," said Rosie. "Just sore."

"Well, initiation isn't having a library of knowledge poured into your head. It's more an opening of awareness. The rest is up to you. You will already have had more glimpses of it than you realize."

"Oh, yeah." Sam gave Rosie a meaningful sideways glance that sent a thrilling rush of memories through her. *We've shared things no one else could imagine.*

"Aetherials are always drawn to the center, whether in physical or essential form," Ginny continued. "The realms aren't inside each other like the layers of an onion; the theory is that they're arranged loosely around a spiral, but the boundaries shift and change. The way is easy enough to find. Go back up to the path and turn left upon it. It will lead you across the Causeway of Souls, which cuts straight across the realms to the center. Anything you see on your way may be illusory—but it will have meaning, and possibly danger. Whether you'll find Lucas—I don't want to give you false hope."

Rosie exchanged a somber look with Sam. "We must try."

"I know. I can't promise you'll be safe, either."

"I like unsafe," Sam said, mouth curving. "It's what I'm best at."

Ginny rose to her feet. "Get ready, then. I've wrapped food for you to take."

"Thank you," said Rosie. "Give Faith a hug from me."

"Mum," said Sam, rising with her, "now the Lychgate's open—assuming it stays that way—will you come home?"

Her hesitation answered him before she spoke. "No, Sam. I've been here too long. This is home now." She turned away. Sam busied himself clearing the table, face expressionless, moisture on his lashes. Rosie tactfully avoided catching his eye.

"One more thing," said Ginny. "If you find Lucas—*when* you find him—don't come back here. You must lead him straight to the Gates. Don't leave the path and don't look back at him until you're safely on the other side. It's not superstition; it's said that the soul-essence is fragile, and the mere pressure of attention may unsettle it enough to make it flee."

"Hang on," said Sam, "I've only just found you and now you're telling me, don't come back? When am I going to see you again?"

"You will see me, don't worry." Ginny held his shoulders and looked into his eyes, her expression firm. "Concentrate on Lucas now. Remember, don't look back. Exactly as in the old myths. And remember, things you see on the Causeway may be illusory, but the meaning will still be important, and the danger real."

Sam and Rosie stepped out of the cottage to find the light of dawn limpidly soft and sparkling, fingers of gold infiltrating the aquatic blue. Rosie glanced back as they climbed the slope, but the cottage was already lost behind trees. Here was the clearest sign of all that they were in the Otherworld; it wasn't winter.

At the top of the hill, they found the silvery deer track once more. Anxiety hovered in her chest. Setting foot on the path, Rosie felt power zinging under her feet, an electric pull. Her head went up. A cold, haunting wind filled her lungs.

The way led them through green woodlands for a time. It was only wide enough to walk in single file, so she went first. Behind her, Sam asked, "How are you doing?"

"Not bad," she answered. "You?"

"Fine," he said quietly. "I still can't believe I found Ginny."

"Has she changed?"

"No, not really. More serene, maybe. What do you think of her?"

"I think she's wonderful," said Rosie. "Blunt and honest. Doesn't give a damn. I like that. She made me feel braver than I really am."

He smiled. "You are brave, sweetheart."

"I ought to be terrified, but I'm not, because I've no idea what to expect."

"Yeah, definitely best not to know."

"I'm glad you're with me," she said. "I wouldn't want anyone else."

"Nowhere I'd rather be, believe me."

Elysion shook off its intimate cloak of woods and orchards, unfolding into a landscape of rounded fells. The track took them up the largest hill, a sweeping curve like a turtle shell. Soft winds arrowed through the grass. Behind and on either side lay folded forests. Above, the sky was turquoise shading almost to midnight blue at the zenith, the sun an apricot yolk on the horizon. Daystars glittered like drifted snow. Rosie fancied she could hear their song, the white-noise hiss of creation.

Ahead, the path led them over the high curve of the hill, down a gentle slope on the far side. There it abruptly curled back on itself, terminating in the flourish of a large spiral gouged in the grass. They were on a cliff top.

Sam and Rosie looked over the edge in awe and dismay. The drop was breathtaking. A valley fell dizzyingly below them, rising again in the far distance to a ridged escarpment, softened by violet haze. A river glinted far below. The landscape was epic, as if painted by a visionary artist— but there was no way across. Rosie felt a rising flame of panic. If Lucas's essence was lost out there, how could they ever hope to find him?

"We're stuffed," Sam remarked. " 'Follow the path,' Mother said, but it fizzles out."

Rosie stared down at the spiral, pushing her hair behind one ear. "It's a map," she said. They looked at each other, frowning. "We haven't actually finished following it yet. This might be pointless, but let's try."

She set her feet in the curve and began to follow it round towards the heart of the spiral. Sam followed, one hand on her shoulder. "Yeah, this feels pretty daft, like dancing around a maypole."

Looking down at the track, she found that it looped on itself and came spiraling outwards again. On the outside curve, it straightened, heading towards the cliff edge. She experienced a disturbing change of perception. The track grew brighter, while their surroundings seemed to withdraw behind a thin veil of fog. Sam's fingers tightened on her shoulder. "Hey, look at that."

Stretching from the cliff top, there appeared to be a natural ridge of rock, running high above the valley floor. The path was taking them towards it. "The Causeway?" said Rosie. "How did it appear?"

"There all the time," he said. "I guess we couldn't see it until we approached by the correct route. It's all about perception."

The grass beneath their boots gave way to shale and then to the substance of the ridge, a smoky, semilucent quartz. They left behind safe ground as the narrow way climbed before them, with a precipice yawning on either side.

"Ah," said Sam, a few steps on. "Right, this is it, is it? Figures."

"Are you okay?" She glanced round. She'd never seen his face frozen like that that before. "Sam, are you scared of heights?"

"No! Well, yeah. It's just a thing." He looked to his left, swayed and closed his eyes, swallowing hard. "Oh, shit."

He appeared paralyzed. Rosie said in concern, "You can wait for me here, Sam. I'll manage on my own."

"No chance." His eyes came open, blue and fierce. "I'm fine."

"You don't have to act the macho guy, you know," she said gently. "Nobody's perfect."

He spoke through his teeth. "Shut up and keep walking."

In places, rock formations made a natural parapet and handhold beside them. In others, the ridge was exposed and uncomfortably narrow. She tried not to think about the height, or the possibility of falling. Below lay Elysion, with shimmering meadows, orchards heavy with fruit and hazelnuts, liquid birdsong—but they were far above that realm now, no longer part of it. It was like dreams she'd had, of a landscape monumental yet ethereal, a filament bridge too high to be real. The growing ache of her legs, however, was vivid enough.

It seemed a good two hours before the Causeway brought them to the far side of the valley, where it ran along the face of a chasm wall through a gorge. They sat down to rest, sharing food and water. Fog came down and she felt the air turn chilly. "You okay?" Sam asked.

"Soldiering on," she said. "You?"

"When you're this high up, it's not so bad. More like being in an airplane above the clouds."

She smiled at his offhand bravery. "I feel like shouting Luc's name into the void," she said, "as if he might hear me."

"Er, Rosie . . ."

She stood up and let her voice go in an impassioned yell, "Lucas!" The echo bounced off unseen surfaces until it was lost. The silence that followed was as deafening as machinery.

"I was going to say, you don't know what you might wake up," said Sam, rising to his feet. "Come on."

The ridge split away from the wall and continued its high, singular way. It appeared the gorge they'd rested in was a gateway; beyond, the scene changed dramatically. Thin cloud drained the sky of its riches. All around them was a foggy void full of vague shapes; mountain peaks, sketched in grey and white. They were inside a cloud.

"Sibeyla," he murmured over her shoulder. Turning, she could barely see him. She felt dizzy for a moment, almost losing her balance. Vague shadows circled them, arcing above, vanishing, reappearing to swoop through the archways beneath.

Rosie forced herself to continue along the slippery walkway, step by step. When the cloud thinned, the mountains were fully revealed, higher than the Causeway itself, their pale grey peaks capped with snow. Mountain flanks fell and plunged forever—never reaching solid ground, as far as she could see.

The airborne shadows were raptors the size of men, dark against the whiteness.

"Realm of air," said Sam. "Home of my ancestors."

"I don't like the look of these hawks," said Rosie. "They're easily big enough to—*Aah*." She dropped into a crouch as one swooped low, almost bowling her over. A small outcrop saved her from falling. The hawks continued to circle, playful but menacing. "Call your ancestors off!" she exclaimed.

Tenting air currents beneath its wings, the raptor came in again. This time, Sam swung the backpack at it, almost losing his footing as he did so. He clipped its wing, causing it to swerve and tumble a few hundred yards through the air. Rosie caught and held Sam's jacket for dear life until he found his balance. Crouching, they saw the bird rise and glide in to land in front of them.

Only it was not a hawk on the Causeway, but a man. He wore a cloak of greyish feathers and his hair was a pure white mane down to his waist. His pale patrician face looked no older than Sam's. He had bright blue irises, and a bright blue jewel in the center of his forehead, like a third eye.

"Travelers on the Causeway of Souls," he said. "Where are you from?"

Cautiously they walked towards him. There was just room to stand side by side on the ridge and Sam kept a firm arm around her. "Show me the rulebook that says we have to answer your questions." He pulled down the neck of his jacket and sweater to show the blistered spiral. "Look, we've been stamped. Let us past, please."

"In peace," Rosie added. "We don't mean any harm. We're looking for someone." She took an instant dislike to his icy, insinuating menace, but—real or not—she didn't want to antagonize him.

"You're Vaethyr," he observed with disdain. "Are the Gates open once more? I thought you were him, for a moment."

"Who?" said Sam.

"Lawrence. The worst Gatekeeper in history. He has cut the realms in half and some say that we will all wither and die as a result; but I say, good riddance. The Spiral will survive without the burden of Vaeth and those traitors who chose to live on its surface."

Sam's expression hardened. "Well, that's my father you're being so rude about. He's been protecting us and maybe if the Aelyr had helped him, he wouldn't have had to take those measures."

The Sibeylan smiled, a thin, knowing smile that made Rosie both furious and very frightened. "Lawrence only ever acted out of weakness. Protecting from what?"

"I don't know. Attack of the bird impersonators, maybe?"

"Funny, Samuel. You Vaethyr are very fond of your masks and of pathetically trying to recapture what you once had. You need to realize that entering the Spiral is all about stripping the masks off. Back to the bone."

Rosie felt Sam's arm tighten around her. For all his strength, she was horribly aware of how vulnerable they were, poised alone on the heights with a predator who, since he could fly, was fearless. "How do you know my name?" he said quietly.

"Work it out," said the Sibeylan, "unless you're as foolish as your father. Yes, a shade passed this way. It's no good shouting his name; he won't hear. Our soul-essence travels like an arrow to the heart, but you, brave idiots, will have to walk every step."

"And we're wasting time," said Rosie. "Please let us pass." Wings sprang from his shoulders with a *whumph*, star-

tling them; his face became a hawk's, uncannily like the
mask she'd seen Lawrence wearing. She thought it was
their last moment. The pale hawk slipped sideways off the
precipice, falling until the wind buoyed him up again. As
he rose back to their level, she heard his words, muffled,
"Violently separating your bodies from your souls would
not be half as amusing as watching you struggle to the end
of this pointless quest."

He tilted and wheeled away, joining the other hawks, the
wind of their flight stirring swirls of ice crystals, wing tips
dipping into the mist. She heard Sam murmur, "Oh, *shit!*"

"What?"

"I think it was Lawrence's father, Albin. My grandfather."

"He wasn't real!" Rosie said desperately.

"Seemed it. Never mind now. Keep going."

Rosie realized how hard she was shaking only once the
threat had gone. Cold burned her lungs and froze her fingers. She hadn't thought to bring gloves. Exposed, chilled,
with the treacherous path winding endlessly ahead, for the
first time she considered they might not actually make it.

"You want my jacket?" Sam said behind her.

"No. I work outdoors for ten hours at a stretch in worse
weather than this."

"Rough, tough and weather-beaten." His teeth chattered
slightly. "I like that in a woman."

The milky sea thinned. To her left she glimpsed the
sparkle of silver-blue towers. A city in the far-off cleft between two mountains. "Sam, look!"

"I'm not looking down, even for you."

"Not down. Across. Over there."

She heard his slow intake of breath. "The ancient towers
of somewhere or other," he said. "You never know what's
real and what's illusion in this place."

Presently the Causeway touched another mountain flank
and threaded through a vast natural arch of rock. Passing
beneath it, Rosie gazed up at its awesome height and reddish

glow. When she looked forward again, the sky had turned soot black.

This sense of disorientation was growing familiar now. She reached behind her and found Sam's hand. Heat sheathed their skin. Within seconds, their iced fingers were burning. "Naamon," she said. "Realm of fire."

She hadn't expected Naamon to be dark, but all she could see for a time was smoke shrouding an indistinct landscape. She had the impression of dark underground cities, backlit by smoldering fire. Warmth hitting her cold skin sent shivers all over her.

After a time, the sudden night faded. An amber glow crept over the scene, and she saw far below the remains of a rose-red town, with vines spilling over fallen towers. The Causeway bestrode the ruins like a colossal viaduct. The sight made her unbearably sad. She could sense the jostle of ghosts in silk and fur, the bright hair, the gleam of eyes behind ceremonial masks . . .

Gradually the sun climbed the sky and began to burn. The city was left behind, its edges crumbling away into an expanse of desert. On either side, scarlet rocks dotted tawny sweeps of sand. Volcanoes smoked on the horizon. The Causeway turned to orange sandstone, and the walkway became broader, more rugged, the strong central path forking into a confusion of smaller tracks around tall stones. "Wonder if Ginny ever came along here?" said Rosie. "It sounds like a line from a song. 'It cuts across the spiral, straight towards the heart.'"

"That's how the dead travel so fast." Sam's voice behind her sounded guttural, oddly accented, nothing like itself. The bizarre sound shocked her.

"What?" She whipped around. He wasn't there. "Sam?"

There was a faint cry below her. She looked over the edge, saw two figures locked together and rolling down the steep flank—Sam in a death grip with a heavy, sunburned man.

Rosie stood horrified for a heartbeat, then launched herself after them, finding the tiniest rough thread of a path to help her. She skidded down on her heels, tearing her jeans and skinning her hands. They'd come to rest about twenty feet down, where a ledge with a scooped lip had arrested their fall. Gasping in pain, she fell over Sam's feet and managed to stop her own descent by crashing into the sandstone lip. The impact winded her. Sam was on his back, fighting for his life.

The attacker seemed feral, with torn, dusty clothes, and a bald roast chestnut of a head. His fingers were locked around Sam's throat and he was snarling.

Rosie seized a medium-sized hunk of sandstone and brought it down on the shiny sphere of the wild man's skull. He uttered a grunt and flopped unconscious. Sam shoved him off and struggled up, coughing for breath. The rock fell from her hand. "Fucking hell," she said.

"That," Sam choked, pointing upwards, "is why I don't like heights. Falling off them."

"Where did he come from?"

"Jumped me out of nowhere."

"Oh my god, he's dead," she gasped. The man lying at her feet was waxen and blue-lipped, as if he'd been dead for days. There was a dark crimson hole in the center of his chest, and his shirt was a torn mess of blood.

"Yes, but you didn't kill him," said Sam. "Someone shot him—a while ago. Again, not real." He grabbed her hand, making her raw palm throb. "Leave him."

They'd fallen onto a half-eroded side path. A grueling scramble brought them back onto the ridge. "Less steep here," Rosie gasped through parched lips. "If you'd fallen in Sibeyla . . ." The words caught.

"Hey, you saved my life." He grinned at her. There was dust stuck to his face, blood tracking through it. Feet braced, he pulled off the scuffed backpack. "Bloody hell, everything hurts."

"Anything broken?"

"Only this." He held up a plastic bottle, split and leaking water. They shared what was left. Rosie looked down at the rock ledge below. There was nothing there. "What was he?" She pushed her hair back, wincing as sand scraped her palms. "Seemed human. A ghost corpse, like yours?"

"Maybe," said Sam, roughly wiping his face with one hand. "Absolutely *not* responsible for that one, I swear."

"I believe you. Are you all right?"

"Battered, bruised, half-strangled—it's like being back at school," he said. "Let's keep moving. That was the last of the water, by the way." They resumed their journey, sore limbs shrieking at every step. Rosie thought, *The Otherworld is testing us.*

The blinding apricot sun cast mirages in the liquid gold mirror of the desert. Rosie imagined she saw Malikala's fiery army, deluged by the unexpected rush of Jeleel's river, the King of Sibeyla's sky boats drifting in to rescue drowning soldiers. Soon her mouth was parched, her head aching.

"I'm missing something," she said. "The qualities of the realms are symbolic; they're supposed to strengthen us, not punish us." She thought she was speaking out loud, realized the words were only in her head. They walked in a trance of heat. After a few hours of it she was exhausted to the point of collapse but still her feet kept moving . . .

Violent change shocked them both out of the trance. From nowhere, sheets of rain hit them.

Without noticing, they had passed into the realm of water, Melusiel. As one, they put their heads back and drank the rain. Through curtains of soft silver they saw the cloudy shimmer of lakes far below, rivers lying like branched lightning across inky swamps. The Causeway turned to grey slate.

Rain washed away dust and blood, plastered their hair to their heads and ran down their necks. As Rosie's feet slipped on wet stone, she realized how weary she was. She couldn't control her legs anymore. How many hours had they been walking? The wind was growing so strong it was hard to breathe.

"Ought to rest a few minutes," said Sam.

"Bit further," she answered, pointing up the slope of the

·

path. "Some rocks there." A hurricane rose as she spoke, battering them with walls of rain. Rosie dropped to her hands and knees. The wind was pushing her towards the edge. She felt her legs going over, couldn't stop herself, felt the slate sliding like wet glass under her palms with no handholds . . . the pure terror of the moment sucked out her breath and she couldn't make a sound.

She felt Sam's hands grab her wrists. With his help she scrambled back, and together they crawled along the exposed ridge to the shelter of a tilted slab protruding from the Causeway's edge. They huddled there, blinded by rain. She had no thoughts left, only despair that they'd come so far and failed.

Rosie closed her eyes and endured. A long time later, she felt Sam's arm tighten around her shoulders. The storm had abated. She looked up and saw a clear black sky with a perfect, huge white moon. Melusiel was all silver and black.

As they rose, crabbed with weariness, they saw, in the center of the Causeway before them, a doe.

Snow-splashed by the moon, the creature regarded them. Rosie trod the last few yards and stopped, looking into the creature's round dark eyes. Beyond, the Causeway became a bridge proper, its slender span arching into the darkness. The doe stood guarding the threshold.

"Every realm so far, something's tried to stop us," Sam said hoarsely.

Rosie had no idea what to say or do. You could not thrust a guardian out of the way and the small pale deer looked so delicate . . . but if she didn't move they were going nowhere. Then the doe's mouth opened and spoke with a human voice. "What are you seeking?"

Rosie answered, stumbling, "A young man, Lucas. My brother."

"Our brother," said Sam over her shoulder.

"We think he came this way . . . towards . . ."

"Towards the Source," said the doe.

"I—I think so," said Rosie. "His body's still alive on

Earth and he's not ready to die. He must come back. Have you . . ." She shrugged helplessly. ". . . seen him?"

Before their eyes, the doe changed. She rose on her hind legs, becoming a petite young woman and wrapped in a full-length coat of the same creamy, dappled fur. She had a heart-shaped face, hazel eyes, fawn-colored hair.

"Daughter of Elysion," said the doe lady. "Son of the Gatekeeper-that-was. I know you. And Lucas—also an opener of ways. He's here."

Hearing the words, Rosie felt her heart race, sweat trickle down her neck, tears spill down her face. Sam's fingers dug into her arm, holding her up. "He must come back before it's too late."

The heart-shaped face was composed. "If he wants to. We would be loath to lose him."

"Please." It took all her strength to stay calm. "There may not be much time. Can I see him?"

The girl paused. "It won't be easy. You can try, of course. Follow me over the Frost Bridge. Beyond is Asru, realm of spirit."

Taking doe form again, she led them across the spun-glass arch of the bridge. Rosie glimpsed slender hills and chasms, trees of gnarled beauty clinging to rocks. Sam was so quiet behind her that she glanced round to make sure he was still there. His eyes were fixed straight ahead. He said, "Don't worry, if I fall you'll hear the scream."

Bright under moon and starlight, she saw elaborate roofs enameled with kingfisher colors. As the bridge curved onto the far side, all views were lost behind the foliage of a garden. The path continued as stepping-stones across a lawn, with tangles of briar roses and weeping willows on either side.

In human shape again, the doe lady led them along the final few curves of the path. Sam walked alongside Rosie. She felt the warmth of his arm around her and his quick sigh as he kissed her wet hair; his relief at being on firm ground again.

In the heart of the garden stood a temple the size of

Oakholme. It had no walls, only an azure-tiled roof supported on peacock-blue pillars. Inside, a soft green light glowed. The doe lady led them over the threshold and into a cool, lofty space with a floor of leaf-green marble, pillars rising like stylized trees to a celestial ceiling. This space stretched on and on, forming a broad cloister that curved gently down and round upon itself. In echo of the realms, the colors changed as they wound inwards. The greens of Earth faded to chilly violet and white for air, into amber and flame-red for fire, then to cloudy blues for water. Symbols were inlaid into the pillars like hieroglyphs; many were unknown to her, but she saw the spiral endlessly repeated. She touched the sore place on her ribs, the brand that connected her to this.

The doe lady brought them to an inner temple; a circle of silver columns around an obsidian floor, some forty feet across. The ceiling was a night sky emblazoned with a spiral galaxy of stars. The columns hung reflected in the floor as if in a still black lake, and in the very center of the floor was a sunken round pool, flashing with brilliant carp. The water within it appeared bottomless, the shimmer of fish hypnotic.

Again she heard Jessica singing, *"Find the mirror at its heart, Merry meet and merry part, We kiss the water and fly, Kiss the water and fly . . ."*

"The Mirror Pool?" Rosie whispered.

"No," said the doe lady. "The temple is the Spiral in miniature, the pond a tribute to the Mirror Pool, which lies in the most sacred grove of Asru's deep forests." She smiled. "No, this is the Spiral Court. Welcome."

"There's no one here," said Sam, looking around. "Where are the judges, the ancient ones, who look down on our little lives on Earth?"

Rosie stiffened. The heights of the court were hard to see clearly, but gave the impression of tiered galleries full of movement. She glimpsed figures like barely seen reflections in dark glass; hints of jeweled robes, shining hair, fierce all-seeing eyes like those of serpents . . . A moment later, the illusion vanished. The temple sighed with emptiness.

"No one here," Sam whispered. "It's deserted."

The girl paid no attention to his remark. "Ancient or dead or dying Aetherials pass through the Court on their way to the Mirror Pool, where they go to reflect, to immerse themselves in the pure water and consider their rebirth . . ."

"Is Lucas there?" Rosie's voice broke. "Are we too late?"

The black eyes met hers, kind and grave. "They rarely go to the Abyss itself. We shall all fall into the darkness at the end of time, but until then we can't say what lies beyond. From the Abyss there is no return. However, I cannot prevent any soul from going there."

"He went to the Abyss? And it's . . . final?"

"I've tried to persuade him away from the edge," the doe lady said sadly. "He won't listen. Perhaps he'll listen to you. He should return with you, since he is the Gatekeeper now."

A whirl of fear and exhaustion darkened her vision. Through it, she saw a pale figure drifting across the temple; the hawk man from Sibeyla, his hair white against the soft feathers of his cloak. She had the disturbing impression of a triangle of blue fires floating towards her.

"Since when?" exclaimed Sam.

The white-haired man said, "Since your father threw off the responsibility."

"No—hang on—he did nothing of the sort. The opposite. He was exercising his powers to protect us."

"Unless the Gates are open," said the girl, "Aetheric essences cannot travel from Vaeth to the center. Instead they haunt the Dusklands until they fade to nothing. Living Aetherials lose their memories and powers. Even humans suffer. Vaeth itself suffers. So the Spiral Court took Lawrence's power from him and gave it to Lucas. That is their judgment."

"And perhaps the young man should decide for himself," said the white-haired man.

"Albin." Sam named him grimly, as if it were a spell to bind him. "How can you look younger than me? You're supposed to be my grandfather. That's just wrong."

"Ah, finally, you know me. No doubt Lawrence poured poison on my memory."

"On the contrary, he rarely mentions you. It's all Liliana."

This clearly struck a nerve. Albin's lips and eyes narrowed. "And I say to hell with all Gatekeepers." He looked up, arms outstretched as to address the galleries. "The failure of Lawrence and his successor tells us that the Great Gates should stay sealed! Let Vaethyr traitors take their chances on Earth with the mortal rabble. Leave the Spiral to Aelyr of pure hearts."

"What the hell are you doing?" said Sam.

"Addressing my argument to the Spiral Court. They will decide whether to let you go to the Abyss."

"What?" He turned to the doe girl. "Tell my grandfather to get off our case, will you? Whose side are you on?"

"I take no sides," said the girl. "I only observe."

"Right," said Sam, squaring up to Albin. "Can I *respectfully* suggest that you step aside and let us see Lucas, unless you want to be using that third eye to look out of your backside?" He looked up at the glassy shadows above and shouted, "As for you lot, who haven't even got the guts to show yourselves, what are you thinking by disrespecting Lawrence's judgment and putting the burden on poor Luc instead? Have you any clue what you're doing?"

"Sam," Rosie whispered.

There was a moment of awful, echoing silence. Albin stared back at Sam with such icy lack of compassion that Rosie saw why, with such a father, Lawrence was as he was. Her hopes sank.

The doe lady only smiled and said, "The decision is made. Lucas must be given the chance to return to Earth. If ever you serve the Court, Albin, then you'll have a say, but not now. Let us pass."

Rosie almost cried out with relief. "Where is he?"

"Come with me." The doe lady beckoned, turning her back on Albin.

Stony-faced, he watched them go. "The Court itself will come to regret this pro-Vaeth bias," he said after them. "You will all be sorry."

When Rosie glanced back, Albin had vanished into shadow.

The doe lady led them out of the temple, between rows of pillars until they entered the darkness of a wild midnight garden. A cool wind breathed against their skin. Ahead, a reddish glow outlined the grass and rocks beneath their feet, masses of foliage on either side. A leaf scratched Rosie's hand. All the shrubs were barbed, she realized. Wild rose, bramble, spiny exotics she didn't recognize. She was wet, aching and exhausted, but none of it mattered, if she could only see Lucas again.

"Their arguments are beyond me," said the doe lady, a pale shape ahead of them. "Lucas matters. He reminds me of someone I loved."

"You sound as if you don't want him to leave," said Rosie.

"I would miss him, it's true," came the sad reply. "Here we are."

Where the thornbushes ended there lay a wide landscape of rock. The infinite night sky vibrated with the thunder of a waterfall. Following the doe girl, Sam and Rosie clambered over rocks until they reached the end of the shelf and saw the chasm, plunging straight down into blackness.

It was like standing on the edge of the world. Rosie instinctively reached for Sam's hand. Tears burned her eyes. There was solid ground and then there was nothingness. The full impact of the sight was veiled by a fine rising mist with a red glow at its heart.

She took another step forward. The Abyss went down forever. The thought of falling sent a pulse of terror through her. Looking up to her left, she saw the tangled branches of a huge leafless tree with stars netted in its twigs. Its thick roots clung deep in the rock and the trunk leaned out above the Abyss. Pale lichen sheened the iron-grey bark.

"The World Tree," said the doe lady.

"Lucas?" Rosie called softly. Panic rose in her. As she spoke, she saw him. There was a figure high up in the tree, far out on a limb that stretched above the Abyss. A small, gangly, unmistakable silhouette.

"Oh, god," she whispered. "How long's he been there?"

"Since he came. A hundred years. Or however long he's been missing on Vaeth." The girl's face was sad. "I have promised him stories if he comes down, but he still won't."

"What's he doing?"

"Deciding whether or not to fall."

Rosie ran towards the tree, stumbling on roots and rock. Sam was after her, calling, "Hold on—"

"Tree-climbing I can do," she said. She touched the trunk. It was not lichen that crusted the ridges of bark, but frost. As she reached out for a handhold, she heard the doe girl shout a warning, "Claws, beware the Claws!"—and something came rushing at her out of the wild garden.

A scarecrow creature, all twigs and spines, flung itself at Rosie and embraced her. Thorns snagged her clothes and pierced her flesh. She cried out and struggled to free herself, but the harder she fought the tighter it bound her, scratching and stabbing until she couldn't breathe, had to hold still to stop the spines going deeper.

"Sam?" she gasped at the end of her breath.

He was there, smashing the clawed creature with a branch. It clung stubbornly. He struck again and again until it began to disintegrate. Finally it let go, leaving her bleeding from a dozen punctures. She saw more Claws coming, tearing themselves out of the bushes to form semihuman shapes.

"Go!" snarled Sam. "I'll deal with them."

Rosie climbed, finding swellings in the bark to start her off, swinging her way up to the thick lower branches and then upwards into the crown. Her hands were so raw, cold and bloody she could hardly feel anything with them but pain. Below, Sam fought to protect her. She could hear the savage fight, the crunch of green wood.

As she climbed above the Abyss, she saw down into it. The chasm wall was thick with ice. A glacier issued from somewhere inside it and rolled ponderously down the rock face, falling towards infinity. A column of ice mist rose. Now she could see that the chasm had a far side. Lava flowed down the rock wall opposite, painting it scarlet. That was the source of the bloody glow. Between the two vast canyon walls lay the absolute blackness of the Abyss.

By the time she reached the limb on which Lucas sat she was sobbing for breath. He had his back to her. She braced herself against the trunk and looked at him, poised there with the branch bending under his slight weight. His clothes looked strange, vague and greyish, but he appeared real enough, substantial enough to fall. His dark hair blew about his shoulders. He was real, alive.

"Lucas," she called softly.

He looked over his shoulder and saw her. "Rosie?"

As soon as she saw his face, she knew this was a ghost after all. His face was shiny grey. It looked wrong, white where it should have been shadowed. It was his face in silver halide, a negative.

Sitting astride the branch, she shuffled along it towards him. "I've come to find you," she said. "Do you know where you are?"

"The Abyss," he answered, looking away from her again. "The Cauldron. The beginning, the end."

"Why, Luc?"

"It's peaceful here. All I can remember is fear and shattering glass."

"That was only the accident. It's over."

He didn't reply. He went on staring down into the void. She was as close as she dared go now without the limb bending dangerously beneath them. "Come with me," she said. "Let's go home."

"After you've looked into infinity, home is meaningless. There's no such place anymore."

Ice thickened in her stomach. "Please. You're still alive. You can't give up, you're the Gatekeeper now."

"I know," he said softly. "That's why I can't go back. I can't do it. Look what it did to Lawrence. It's too much."

"But you won't be alone. At least come back and talk it over."

He was quiet, then he said, "Once you look down, you can't look away. I came here in my visions. I can't stop wondering, how would it feel to let go and fall forever?"

"I don't know," Rosie said grimly, "but not as good as dancing on grass with bare feet. Not as bad as seeing the look on Mum and Dad's faces when I tell them I couldn't bring you back."

Lucas made a sound, perhaps a sob. Rosie was desperate. If she tried physically to seize him, they would both know how it felt to fall forever. "Don't make me angry," she said more assertively. "I have walked bloody miles to find you and I'm not going back empty-handed. You stop here, I stop here. That's going to be pretty annoying for both of us, don't you think?"

"If the Gates stay closed, the realms will fade. If they're opened, we'll be destroyed. How can I make that choice? It's too great a responsibility, Ro. I can't do it."

"So you'd rather die?"

"I've seen the shadow Lawrence fears." His soft tone chilled her. "There's nothing you can do in the face of it."

"That's his shadow, not yours."

"He and I are the same."

"No, you're not. What, never taste chocolate again, or see Mum and Dad, or Jon? Never lose your virginity?" He looked round, scowling with indignation. She smiled. "I swear, Luc, I'm not moving until you do."

"Where am I?" he asked, looking uncertain.

"In hospital. Haven't you any idea how much everyone loves you?"

He turned his head again to look down, sitting motionless. She gulped shallow breaths, her mouth as dry as Naamon, thinking, *What more can I say, what will make him listen?* Then Lucas said, "Look. Down there. Can you see it?"

Where the ice mist thinned, she saw a mass on the chasm wall opposite, several hundred feet below them. It was a gigantic black statue, poised there as if hewn from the basalt of the rock face itself. The shape was humanoid, heavy, hinting at both animal and demon; ice crusted its great limbs and vapor rolled slowly over its vast bulk as if down the sides of a mountain. Its head was indistinct and sinister. Frost sketched highlights on heavy, scaled features and the eyes were two empty, utterly black voids.

It was magnificent and hideous. The sight of the statue, poised there as if it had been there from the beginning of time, filled her with awe. She could easily imagine that when it woke, it would bring the end of the world. "What is it?" she murmured.

"Brawth," said Lucas.

As he spoke, the statue turned its great stone head and looked up at him. A hollow voice said, "*Lucas, come back to us.*" Rosie almost screamed, but no sound came. It was solid, frozen rock again—but it had moved, and seen Lucas, and fastened its empty stare upon him.

"Oh my god," he breathed. The growing fear in his voice told her, at last, that he wasn't ready to die after all. "Christ, it's seen me. Rosie, we have to go."

"Come on, then," she said urgently. "Don't rush. Be careful!"

Her heart was in her mouth as he turned, swinging his legs over the branch until he was fully round and facing her. She almost fell in relief as he started edging towards her. "Wait for me," he said.

"That's it, steady." She wanted to give him a hand, but instinct told her not to touch his Aetheric form. As she turned, already planning their descent, she stopped short. The doe lady was in front of her, sitting in the hollow where the branch joined the trunk. Below, Sam was still fighting the thorn creatures. The girl was like a china princess with her fur coat pooled around her. "Please, may we pass?"

"I will miss him."

Rosie was beyond politeness. "Have you seen what's down there?"

"It has always been there." The girl appeared unconcerned. Her doll-like innocence and refusal to acknowledge their urgency struck Rosie as sinister. "It can't pursue or harm you."

"Whatever, if Luc's fear of it will make him come home, I'm not arguing! Tell whoever's responsible to call off the Claws and let us go!"

"I can't. Something in your own mind is shaping them."

Looking down, Rosie saw Sam battling the Claws. As soon as one fell apart, another came. He had a technique now of thrusting the branch in to tear each one apart with a single wrench. "What are you saying—that they're my fear?"

"Something deeper than that." The doe girl sighed. "I know Lucas must leave. He's not mine. Still, you should leave something precious in exchange for him. Those are the rules of balance."

Rosie felt the lifeblood draining out of her heart. There was only Sam and herself. Leave him in Luc's place? Unthinkable. The girl, however, aimed her ivory finger at Rosie's breastbone. "You want me to stay in Luc's place?" Her heartbeat rushed in her ears.

"Would you?"

"Yes." Her throat and eyes hurt. She swallowed. "Yes, if you promise he'll return safely to life, I'll stay here gladly."

"No, Rosie," Lucas said behind her.

"Such self-sacrifice makes the best stories." The girl smiled. "That's a noble offer, but I only meant your crystal. One jewel for another."

Rosie exhaled, her hand flying to the crystal heart at her throat. She fumbled to unfasten the chain. "Yes." As she placed it into the doe lady's hand, she did so with a firm intent that the Claws would cease to exist, that she wouldn't be afraid anymore. Albin's desires had no power. She visualized the thorn beings dismembered and heaped on a bonfire. "Take it, gladly. Now may we pass?"

"Go, take him home," said the girl. She fastened the chain around her own neck, her eyes turning silver with tears. "Don't forget the rules. As soon as you set foot on the Causeway, you must go ahead and Lucas must follow. Don't stop, don't speak to him, don't look back until you are safely through the Gates. Otherwise you may break the invisible thread that draws him after you." The doe lady left the branch, flashing into the shape of a white owl and flying suddenly straight at Rosie, passing so close that she almost lost her balance and fell. For a moment, her world was full of whirring white feathers, wing tips and claws brushing across her from hip to shoulder. Then the owl soared free. "Farewell, brother of light," she called as she flew into darkness.

By the time Rosie had descended the tree, with Lucas close behind, the last of the Claws had fallen and Sam was leaning on the trunk, blood-spattered, getting his breath back. "Sam, will you go first? Once we start, we mustn't look back."

"Yes, I heard," he said matter-of-factly. "Come on."

They began to retrace their steps, Sam in the lead, Rosie fixing her gaze on his shoulders, Lucas silent-footed behind her. Back through the temple and garden; across the Frost Bridge to the Causeway. At first it was dark, with clouds covering the stars and a fine grey drizzle falling all the way through Melusiel.

Rosie hurt all over. Thorn scratches, bruises, skinned palms, blistered feet. Her throat was sore and her head ached. She ignored it and kept walking. Miles to go and they must not stop or speak or look back. She hardly dared to breathe.

"Don't you know who she was, the doe girl?" Lucas said behind her. Rosie opened her lips, quickly closed them again, resisting the natural urge to reply. "She's Estel, Lady of Stars. Her lover was Kern, who takes the form of a forest god, covered in green leaves. Perseid of Sibeyla was jealous and he tricked Kern and tore him to pieces, scattering him all across the Spiral as an autumn gale tears a tree apart. Ever since, Estel has been trying to gather the pieces of him back together. She's lonely. That's why she didn't want me to leave . . . but I'm not him. She knew that. She told me stories while I was in the Tree. All about the Spiral."

As they passed through Naamon, night remained and the desert was cold. Rosie watched nervously for the sun-burned ghost corpse, but nothing stirred.

Sibeyla was narrow, precipitous and chilly. Sam never faltered. He marched as doggedly as a soldier, drawing her on. All the way, Lucas was talking softly behind her, repeating the stories that the doe lady had told him. It was agony, being unable to respond. Silently she willed him to keep speaking so she knew he was still there.

By the time they reached Elysion, a faint colorless dawn was beginning. She was cold to the bone, but her spirits rose. As they reached the cliff top, she could have danced for joy to feel grass under her feet again. Around the spiral they trod until it wound outwards again, over the fells, up and down into the woods and past the fold where Ginny's cottage lay hidden . . . She didn't remember it being so far. They came through the sighing forest and at last up the gentle slope towards the trees embracing above the portal. It was only as they entered the aperture that she realized Lucas had fallen silent.

Passing through Lychgate was the worst thing. So dark and narrow, a burial chamber. Her hands were like dead things as she felt along the sides to guide herself. She could sense Lucas close behind her. The temptation to reassure him was overwhelming, but she resisted. "I don't know," she heard him say, very faintly. "That smell . . . twisted metal and petrol. The light's blinding."

It's all right, we're nearly there, she thought, willing

him on. At last she saw a wash of light, and her heart swelled with anticipation.

Sam stepped out of the crack in Freya's Crown, and she went stumbling out after him. It was dawn in the surface world. A wintry breeze ruffled the trees and blew her hair about wildly. For a moment she could see nothing through the strands. They stopped in the dip and turned as one to look back at the Gates. Sam's hands came up to catch Rosie as she collapsed against him.

There was no one there. Only blind rock and the wind blowing through the grass.

19

Snowfall

Rosie was barely aware of returning to Oakholme. Sam had to help her down the path. There was an iron shaft through her heart and it was all she could do to walk.

The kitchen door was unlocked, as they had left it. She looked blankly around at the Aga cooker, plates on the draining board, the sturdy farmhouse table. It looked as if nothing had been touched, except for Sam's note, which had disappeared.

"How long have we been away?" Her voice was a dry leaf. "What day is it?"

"I don't know, but look, everything's the same. Hang on . . ." Sam went into the hall, came back with a newspaper in his hand. "Apparently it's Tuesday. We were gone two days. It's okay. Time ran the same here."

Rosie nodded. One less thing to worry about, but she was too numb to feel actual relief. She sat down at the kitchen table. Sam, grey-faced and silent, occupied himself making tea, but she couldn't drink it. He sat quietly beside her, watching her. It was plain in his face that he felt completely helpless. There was nothing to be said. Her hands were pushed into the chaos of her hair and the mug of tea sat congealing in front of her.

Eventually she spoke. "Where did I go wrong? I did what they told us. I didn't speak, didn't look round. He was right behind me inside the Gate. What did I do wrong?"

"Nothing," said Sam. "You did everything possible."

"And it still wasn't enough." Her breath shuddered out of her. "Of all precious things in this world, the one person I would have wanted to save was Luc. I put nothing above him, nothing."

"I know, pet."

"I wonder where Matthew is?" The memory of his feral state was a vague anxiety behind veils of fog. It was difficult to feel anything beyond the leaden weight of grief on her shoulders.

"He'll turn up. Don't worry about him."

"That's one more thing for my parents to deal with. How can I tell them? I can't face any more."

"I'll speak to them," Sam said gently. "Love, we're both exhausted. Why don't you have a sleep? I'll stay down here in case Matthew—"

The phone rang, making them jump. Sam rose to answer it, spoke softly for a few seconds, hung up. The weight on Rosie's heart grew suddenly heavier, crushing her to nothing.

"That was your father," he said. "They need us at the hospital."

Rosie and Sam walked the long corridors of the infirmary like a pair of air-raid survivors. Everything looked bleached and dreamlike. People turned to stare as they passed along the ward. Through glass doors they saw Jessica, Auberon and Phyllida grouped in a corner, anxiously watching the doctors and nurses gathered around Lucas's bed.

The ward sister, Kate, stepped into their path and stopped them, her face full of grave compassion. "I don't know if Mr. Fox explained," she said.

Sam shook his head. "He just said, get here now."

"It's the last test we do for brain-stem function," Kate said gently. "We lift sedation and take him off the ventilator to see if he can breathe for himself."

"The last test?" said Sam. "He failed the others?"

"The neurosurgeons are with him. They test for various reflexes, but I'm afraid he's shown no response so far. The apnea test can take at least fifteen minutes . . . I'm sorry, I know this is hard for you."

Rosie felt herself sliding into darkness. The world disintegrated; her head whirled with murmuring voices. She came round sitting on a plastic chair with Sam's arm around her, Kate offering a glass of water. Pushing free of them like a swimmer escaping a dark flood, she rose to her feet, forced herself to go on walking unsteadily towards the room. The glass doors hissed open. The scene was crystal-clear; surreal. Chrome and plastic, monitors winking. Her mother and father turned to acknowledge her and she saw Lucas lying pale on the bed beside them . . .

Looking at her.

She hardly registered the medical staff around him. The sight of him cut between everyone like a beam of white light. He was propped up on pillows and the breathing tube was gone. He blinked and tried to smile. In a hoarse whisper he said, "There you are, Ro."

Her parents were holding on to each other, the desolate exhaustion of their faces sheened with amazement. Their eyes were red. Auberon held out a hand to usher Rosie forward and Sam came after her with a chair. She felt her father's hands on her shoulders as she sat down. The doctors were examining Lucas, asking questions which he answered slowly but lucidly.

"What happened?" Sam asked.

"When they switched off the ventilator, he kept breathing," said Jessica. "Then he opened his eyes, started coughing on the tube . . ."

The doctor smiled at her. "It is rare to see a spontaneous recovery in this situation, but the brain can be incredibly resilient. A law unto itself, at times."

"And this means—he will recover, won't he?" Jess's voice was rough.

"We'll need to keep him for a few weeks, but yes, it looks good. He'll need plenty of rest, but you can sit with him for a few minutes."

It was as if the entire world woke up and basked in sunlight. The doctors and nurses were grinning as they went out, tangibly elated. Phyllida went with them, smiling as she whispered, "I'll leave you to it."

"Weeks?" Lucas croaked. "No way."

"Hello, you," said Rosie. She held Lucas's hand, never taking her eyes off his face. He was pallid and bruised, but the light had returned to his eyes. The strength of his grip surprised her.

"Why's everyone staring at me? How long have I been here?"

"A few days," she choked. "We thought . . ." Tears began to flow out of her. She couldn't hold them back.

Lucas looked alarmed. "Stop it, Ro. What's the matter with you all?"

"You nearly died, idiot." She wiped her eyes. "They thought you were brain-dead. An easy mistake to make."

"Rosie!" said her mother.

Lucas pulled a face at her, clearly in possession of his wits. Then he paused, frowning. "I was at the Abyss . . . but you and Sam brought me back."

His gaze met Rosie's again, and locked. Her breath caught. "Do you remember?"

"Sort of . . . I was in the tree . . . then you came for me." His eyes widened. "Oh my god, the ice giant . . ."

"It's all right. Estel said it was just a statue."

Worry flickered in his eyes, but he didn't argue. "That

was a hell of a walk, Ro. I thought it was a dream, but—you're still wearing the same clothes."

She glanced down at herself. She'd forgotten what a shocking state she and Sam were in; cut, bruised and grimy, jeans ripped. All they'd done before coming out was rinse blood and dirt from their faces. No wonder people were staring. "It wasn't a dream," she said, squeezing his hand. "When we got to the Lychgate, you vanished. I thought it was over."

"I was trying to follow, but it went dark. I was scared that I was still in the car. The next thing I knew, I was here, having a tube yanked out of my throat and everyone staring at me as if I'd dropped out of a flying saucer."

"Of course, your essence came straight to your body," Rosie breathed. "I'm such an idiot! I should have realized."

"What's this about?" Jessica asked, not taking her eyes from Luc, "Rosie, where have you been? We've been frantic, trying to get hold of you and Matt. Bron slipped home to look for you and found this . . ." She produced the note, crumpled. "Something about 'an unexpected trip, not sure how long, don't worry?' What were we supposed to make of it?"

"Mum, I'm sorry." Rosie couldn't say any more. She didn't expect to be believed, and she wanted no credit. The nightmare was over. All she wanted to do was sleep.

Lucas cleared his throat and said simply, "She and Sam came after me into the Spiral to bring me back."

The sheer astonishment on her parents' faces, added to their exhaustion, made them seem childlike. Rosie's eyes stung again. She'd never been in this position before; of knowing something they didn't, or of experiencing an Aetheric adventure not sanctioned or even imagined by them. "They did *what*?" said Auberon. "Explanation, please."

Sam told most of it, as succinctly as he could, with occasional interjections from Lucas and Rosie. Jessica sat with tears streaming down her face. In the end, she came to Rosie and wrapped her arms around her. Rosie felt awkward, not wanting an embrace of gratitude that she didn't deserve. "Don't, Mum. If not for me, Luc wouldn't have been here in the first place. Anyway, it was your songs that gave me a hint; the ones about returning to the Source?"

"I haven't sung those songs for years," Jess murmured.

"All the same, I keep hearing them. Dad, we think it's best Lawrence doesn't hear any of this. Not yet, anyway."

Her father sat with his chin on his hand, the fingers occasionally moving to smooth his beard, his eyes introspective. He said, "I know that Lawrence has lost the power; he told me so himself. But to believe it's leapt to you, Luc—that's a very hasty assumption to take at face value. Let's keep it strictly to ourselves, shall we? We can discuss it when you're fit again."

Rosie looked up and saw Lawrence hovering outside, a long dark shadow. Lucas stiffened, all the light draining from his face. "I don't want to see him. Don't let him in. And please don't mention the Gates."

"It's okay. We won't," Rosie said quickly. Sam was already on his way to intercept his father.

"I'll speak to him," said Auberon, rising. "We should let you sleep now, in any case. Here comes Kate to throw us out."

They parted from Luc with kisses, Rosie last. As she leaned over him, he whispered, "That's why I nearly didn't come back. Becoming Gatekeeper—I can't do it. Brawth saw me. If it wakes, I won't be able to control it."

"Shh." The fear in his eyes disturbed her. She stroked his cheek. "Like Dad said, don't worry about it yet. Rest, honey. We'll see you later."

In his long black overcoat, Lawrence resembled an undertaker, motionless and watchful. Auberon fixed him with a hard gaze. "He needs to sleep."

"I won't disturb him. I only wanted to see for myself."

"Well, you can see from here. He's conscious, and recovering."

Lawrence was looking through a glass panel, so Rosie

couldn't see his expression. His voice sounded as hollow with relief as her father's. "Thank the gods for Aetheric powers of recovery."

"So your services will not, after all, be required," Auberon added. The two men exchanged a long, enigmatic look.

Lawrence, always pale, turned ashen. His voice shook. "I only meant that if it had to be done, I would."

"Of course. However, you might ask yourself how much Lucas could hear while in his coma, since he now refuses to see you." Auberon's face was grim; the others stared. Lawrence took a step backwards, turned, and began to walk away, his coat flaring behind him and his footsteps echoing faster and faster along the length of the ward as he went.

"Got some brilliant news, mate," said Sam, sitting down at Jon's bedside. "We made it."

Jon stared, eyes huge within their dark circles. "Christ, you look like you've fallen off a battlefield."

"Lucas regained consciousness. We found him."

Jon's head fell back, the long-lashed eyelids sweeping closed in relief. "Oh my god. I knew he'd come back. I have to see him."

"Later." He gripped Jon's uninjured wrist to hold his attention. "And I'll tell you all about it, but there's something else that you must swear on your life you won't tell Lawrence or Sapphire."

"I wouldn't tell them their shoelaces were undone," Jon retorted. His vehemence took Sam aback.

"Okay, well, I also found our mother."

Jon went white. His eyes turned liquid. "No. You can't have. How?"

He wasn't someone who had ever cried easily, if at all, but now, as Sam explained, he lay with tears flooding freely down his face. After a while, when the story was told, Jon spoke. "Virginia Wilder. She was like a film star, wasn't she? Joan Crawford or Vivien Leigh, poised but a bit crazy. She always had ropes of amber or turquoise around her neck and wrists. She used to love singing old jazz songs and you'd join in and I always felt left out, but I miss it. It was the only time she looked really happy. And one day she was just—gone."

"Yes." Sam struggled, at a loss. "But it wasn't her fault. She was trapped there, and the Otherworld does strange things, distorts time. She didn't mean to abandon us."

"And for all my efforts, you're the one who found her, not me . . . because even when the Gates were open, I wasn't brave enough to grab a pair of crutches and say sod it, I'm coming with you."

"Believe me, we had enough trouble without you, Long Jon Silver. It doesn't matter."

"Yes, it does." Jon grabbed his arm, distraught. "How can I face her? You don't know the half of it. Sam, swear on your life you won't repeat this, but I've got to tell you about Sapphire . . ."

Later, back at Oakholme, Jessica, Rosie and Auberon finally caught up with desperately needed sleep. Unearthly stamina had kept them going, but even Aetherials had their limit. Sam had come with them, helping Rosie to break the news about Matthew. Her parents took it with grim stoicism; it all seemed part of the same chaos pattern now. Luc's recovery at least made it bearable.

Rosie vanished into her old bedroom—a room Sam had speculated about, but never yet seen. He lay down on the huge squashy sofa in their front room, convinced he was fully alert to deal with anything, should a hostile Matthew return.

The next he knew, he woke suddenly in darkness. The curtains were open, the windows glimmering indigo against black. It felt strange and wrong to be here. Auberon and Jessica had been civilized towards him—they were always gracious—but he sensed their coolness and suspicion. Helping to save Lucas—had that redeemed him in their eyes? Could anything? *Yeah, great,* he thought, resting the back of one hand on his forehead. *I shamelessly wreck*

Rosie's marriage then try to creep into their good grace. That's got to impress them. Meanwhile, if my brother isn't filling Lucas with drugs, my father's causing havoc over him—no wonder we're so fucking popular in this house.

And then, Jon's confession earlier. He bit the tip of his thumb, his mood blackening. He still couldn't take it in. Sapphire was going to be sorry. If he found out she'd laid a finger on Lucas as well, there wouldn't be a grave deep enough to bury her.

A shadow took flesh and moved. Sam was on his feet in a second, heart pounding. A lamp flicked on and Auberon stood there, facing him across the hearthrug. "You and I should have a talk," he said.

"Yes, er—Mr. Fox, you scared the sh—the life out of me. I thought you were . . . Matthew."

Auberon shook his head. "I've been out looking for him. Been all over Cloudcroft with a torch. Hopeless. It's turned bitterly cold, as well."

"I'm sorry. You should have woken me. I'd have helped."

Auberon exhaled, sat on the arm of a chair. Usually gentle, in near-darkness he looked every bit as threatening as Lawrence. "I think you've done enough."

Sam opened his hands. "Look—sir—I know what you must think of me. I've ruined Rosie's life."

Auberon's face darkened. He trembled slightly. "She was a married woman. Could you not keep away from her? What the hell were you thinking?"

"I know, but I was desperate—I love her more than my life, I've loved her for years. And she wasn't happy. Do you think she would have looked at me twice if she'd been blissful with Alastair?" He lowered his voice. "She came to me because she was unhappy. She was going to leave him. That's why he did what he did—not because she slept with me—sorry—but because she wouldn't go back to him."

Sam half-expected a bayonet or some other ancient weapon to be seized; Auberon's face became thunderous. He said bitterly, "Alastair may have acted in grief or anger, but that doesn't excuse what he did. It was monstrous. I'm guessing he was the sort of man who, if they'd had children in a custody dispute, might have driven the children to a remote spot and gassed both them and himself in the car."

Sam was shocked into silence.

"I know she wasn't happy," Auberon went on. "She told me. Even before the wedding I half-suspected she was going along with it to please everyone around her and not herself, but I was too craven to say anything. What I wish to the very gods I had known was what sort of unbalanced individual Alastair proved to be. I don't blame Rosie for what happened, of course I don't. I don't even blame you. Only one person was responsible for the reckless act that nearly destroyed my family, and that was Alastair himself. You, however . . ."

"I've never blamed anyone but myself," Sam said hurriedly, "but, whatever else I've done, I did not drive that car into that tree. Knowing it was her special tree, as well."

"I was going to say that you're not such a bad person, Sam. You proved that by going over the Causeway. Even I have never been to the Frost Bridge. What you both did was incredibly brave."

"It was for Rosie. I'd walk to the ends of the earth and throw myself into the Abyss for her."

"Yes, I get the picture." Auberon became stern. "People think I'm a soft touch, but I'm not. As I say, you're not a bad man and may even be a decent one in time. However, that doesn't alter the fact that you behaved irresponsibly, or that my son-in-law is dead. I think a period of reflection is in order, don't you? Matthew is still absent. We each need to attend to our own families. Rosie needs to rest."

"You want me to make myself scarce?"

"I want you to do what you know to be right," Auberon said pointedly. "You must see that it would hardly be appropriate for you suddenly to be here in Alastair's place, after all that's happened. Rosie herself wouldn't want that."

"No, no," said Sam. A chill went through him. "Of course she wouldn't."

"Also, we would like some time with our daughter—in a

peaceful atmosphere with no further emotional disruption."

"Message understood," Sam answered. Arguing would only be pointless and undignified. "I'll get out of your hair. There's stuff I need to sort out, anyway."

"Thank you."

"Can I ask about Matthew? Did you know about him . . . changing shape?"

"No, I didn't." Auberon shook his head. "I've tried to live a peaceful life, Sam, in harmony with everyone. However, now I find that I've been not so much living on the Earth as with my head stuck in it. I didn't see, no, any more than I saw the depth of Rosie's unhappiness or the fact that Lucas appears to have inherited the lych-light of the Gatekeeper from Lawrence."

"You really think he has?" said Sam.

"I fear so. Fools like Lawrence and me try to hold the world still, only to find it's moved on without us."

After Auberon's visit, Sam couldn't sleep. He left early and returned to Stonegate before Rosie awoke, taking time to shower, put on clean clothes and order his thoughts. He guessed they'd be visiting Lucas in the morning. Mid-afternoon, he gathered his courage and walked downhill again to the friendly, beamed solidity of Oakholme. There was a distinct chill in the air, a heavy promise in the clouds.

Rosie was in the front room, sitting cross-legged on the sofa, wearing jeans and a cranberry-red sweater. Her freshly washed hair fell beautifully about her shoulders, with rose and gold lights in the burgundy. When she looked up at him, she gave only the faintest tired smile. Her eyes were empty, as if she were miles away.

"Hey, gorgeous," he said. She half-smiled but her eyes stayed ghost grey; he realized that she was in delayed shock. So was he. He sat down at the far end of the sofa, feeling unable to touch her. "How are you feeling?"

She groaned. "Like I've been flattened under a steam roller. Everything hurts. Covered in cuts and scrapes."

"Lucky we heal fast. How's the brand?"

Briefly she lifted the edge of her sweater to show the red spiral on her creamy flesh. "We went to see Luc," she said. "He's doing really well. Uncle Comyn was there too." She paused. "It's so hard to look at Luc without thinking what nearly happened . . . The whole thing was only a cat's whisker from complete tragedy. Alastair is still dead."

"Yes. I know."

"I should go to the funeral. But how do I face his family, the Scottish uncles and cousins?"

"Don't go," Sam said firmly. "Let them take his body home and deal with it themselves. You never have to see them again."

"It's such a mess. I feel I've let everyone down."

"No, it's my fault," Sam said quietly. "It was a game but when games go wrong, it's no fun anymore. Wish I could take it all back."

"No, you don't."

A dry smile lifted one side of his mouth. "It was incredible, but it wasn't worth seeing you like this."

"Now we have to live with what we did." She tilted her head. Her hair hung down, so beautiful he longed to stroke it. He thought of what Auberon had said to him, and felt cold. There was always going to be this imbalance between them; that Rosie felt too much shame, and Sam felt too little. "The Otherworld changes you. I realize that now. There's a saying that if you look into the Abyss, the Abyss looks back into you. I understood Luc's fascination with the void. It's the last thing to fear, isn't it? If you could let go of that fear and jump, you'd never fear anything again."

"No, plus you'd be dead," said Sam. "I don't think about stuff like that. It can drive you crazy."

"Can't deny I'm a little crazy today," she smiled. "You're the sensible one."

"Didn't mean . . ." He sighed. "Hey, what happened to your crystal heart? You were wearing it when we set out."

"Oh, I gave it to Estel, the doe girl. Seemed a tiny price

to pay in exchange for Lucas. And she was so sweet and childlike—not to mention incredibly scary."

"I'll get you another one."

"No albinite," she said quickly. "If sparkly glass is good enough for the Lady of Stars, it's good enough for me."

They sat in silence for a minute. Rosie's state of shock, and his guilt in the face of her pain, thickened between them like an ice wall. He longed to put his arms around her, but couldn't; she was closed off and spiky, plainly in no frame of mind to be comforted.

"Anyway," he said, "I'm going to make myself scarce for a while. Your father doesn't want me around and I don't blame him. You need your family around you, and I need to sort a few things out."

She stared at him, her expression tearing his heart out; stunned and serious and resigned all at once. "What things?"

"When I was in prison I met this amazing man."

"Wow, I didn't see that one coming."

He grinned. "Yeah, six foot five with a big ginger beard, just my type. He works for a crime-prevention charity; helping ex-cons find work, keeping young offenders out of trouble and so on. I started helping him, counseling the younger prisoners and that. Well, he's offered me work. I haven't been unemployed, Rosie, I've been taking college courses. Once I pass, I can go and work with him. Teaching skills to problem kids so they don't turn to crime, that sort of thing."

Rosie looked thrown. "I didn't know you were so soft-hearted."

"I'm not, but I am very effective. The little bastards won't get anything past me."

"You've known about this for ages, haven't you?" she said, eyes narrowing. "Why didn't you tell me?"

"Well, being seen to do something worthwhile isn't good for my image, is it?"

"Far from it. I'm sure you'll be their worst nightmare."

She smiled, looking genuinely pleased for him. "Sam, that's wonderful."

"Yes. Only I could be sent to another part of the country." He paused to gauge her reaction; her smile vanished, her lips parted in a silent *Oh*. At that point, the conversation stalled on an unspoken tangle of uncertainty. Did she think he meant he was leaving *her*? Did her silence mean she accepted him going? Or did it mean that she wanted him to stay but wouldn't admit it, because she assumed he was letting her down gently? Or . . . Sam sighed, wishing he hadn't said it.

"I hope you're not doing this to be noble," Rosie said quietly. "I'd hate Sapphire to think she was right when she told me you wouldn't stick around."

"Oh, she said that, did she?" He caught his breath, ran his hands over his hair. "She's poison. She's the other thing I need to deal with, before anything else. Jon told me something about her yesterday so vile I can't repeat it."

At that, she raised smoky eyes to his. "Oh my god, you know about them?"

"*You* know?" he exclaimed. Rage clouded his vision with black and white stars as Rosie haltingly explained that she'd seen them kissing, that Luc had told her the full story. "You knew about her, and didn't tell me?"

"You were planning to go away, and didn't tell me?" she retorted.

"Not quite the same, is it?" he said. This was going horribly wrong. It should have been a time to console each other. Instead, fraught with exhaustion, they were veering into an argument.

"Sam, I've been in agonies about telling you. I tried to blank it out. I wish Luc hadn't said anything, but it's like Pandora's box—once the lid's open, the horrors fly out."

"Until they reach every corner of our little world."

"I can't believe you never suspected."

"Never noticed a thing," he said sourly. "Wasn't there half the time. I should've paid more attention, but it's the last thing I expected." Pictures fell into place with new, sinister meaning. Sapphire pushing Jon's wheelchair, hovering by his hospital bed. Farther back: fussing over him, helping with homework, wanting to teach him yoga, the perfect substitute mother, and Jon going along with her like a lamb . . . He felt sick. "How could she do that to my father? I can't let her get away with it."

"What are you going to do?"

"Find out who the hell she really is, for a start."

"I told you everything she told me, in my secret agent mode." Rosie sat up, suddenly businesslike. "Wait there." She left the room and ran upstairs, reappearing a minute later with a small framed photograph in her hand.

It was a wedding photo of Lawrence and Sapphire. Sam looked at it in distaste. "What's this?"

"I found it when you sent me for the photo of Virginia. It was an accident; I grabbed it first and looked at it afterwards. Also I took the back off to see if there were any more pictures inside."

Puzzled, Sam bent back the metal tabs and removed the backing of the frame. Inside was a small passport-sized photo of a young Sapphire with a man he couldn't place but was certain he'd seen before. "Is it any help?" Rosie asked.

"I don't know." He slipped the tiny photo into his wallet. "Maybe the best thing to do is confront Sapphire and see what shade of white she turns."

"Sam, be careful," she said, perching on the edge of the sofa as he took his jacket. "And I'm sorry . . . about everything."

"Yeah, me too," he said, and gently kissed her hair as he left.

After he'd gone, Rosie sat stunned, as if she'd been slapped awake from a dream. *What happened?* she thought. *Did Sam just tell me he's leaving—permanently?*

The whole scene had washed over her like a tide. She'd let it happen because she was too numb from the aftermath of disaster to behave in a normal manner. She felt too horribly overwhelmed to let anyone near her, and far beyond being comforted. The numbness wouldn't last forever, she knew, but at the moment she couldn't see a way through it.

Of course, it had been a mistake not to reveal her suspicions about Jon and Sapphire—but such a huge risk to have told him. Either way, she couldn't win. So he was mad at her, and she was mad at him for not telling her his plans— but why should he have done so? They'd been too busy playing sexual cat-and-mouse. They'd barely reached the talking stage before Alastair interrupted.

Dull pain settled over her, stinging her eyes and throat. Yet she couldn't cry. There was no point in crying until you understood what had happened, and she didn't understand yet.

She went up to her old bedroom and examined the torn clothes in which she'd entered the Otherworld. Were they worth saving? No, best bundled up for rag recycling. She went through the pockets, excavating tissues and sweet wrappers. Pushing her hand into the jeans pocket, she found something hard and rounded. She drew it out and found it was a rose quartz egg the size of a hen's egg, a delicate translucent pink and beautifully polished. It was full of iridescent planes, with a cloudy whitish center.

Rosie looked at the object, bemused. She remembered a vague dream about finding it. Most likely Ginny, or even Estel, had slipped it in there—but why, or how they'd done so without her noticing, she had no idea. Then she remembered how Estel in owl form had flown at her, confounding her senses for a few moments . . . was it she who'd placed the egg in her pocket, as deftly as a magician?

Eventually she sat looking out of her old bedroom window, absently cupping the egg between her palms. It felt soothing. Twilight came blue and luminous and with it came snow. Big light feathers danced past her window, beginning to clot in the corners and pile up on the sill. All evening the snow fell and fell, turning the air grey and her windowpanes icy. So cold was the glass that when she touched it, a chilly draft poured over her fingers.

She thought about Sam, Lucas, Faith, Matthew, everyone, while outside the garden and the hill beyond turned ghostly, glowing white.

At Stonegate, Sam stood in the rooftop conservatory and watched the estate softly vanishing under snow. The translucent roof above him was covered, turning the room dim and eerily luminescent. Condensation fogged the edges of the windows. His only companions were the shadowy *dysir* and the background echo of Dumannios pressing on air-thin boundaries.

Sapphire and Lawrence had checked into a hotel in Leicester, since it would be foolish to start home in this weather. So, with no trace of conscience, he'd done something he'd never dreamed of before; sneaked up into her apartments, rooted through cupboards until he'd found a metal cash box. It was locked, but he hadn't spent three years behind bars for nothing. Inside were papers. A sheaf of letters, two passports, one American and one Brazilian, a birth certificate in the name of Maria Clara Ramos. The Brazilian passport, too, was in that name but the American belonged to a Marie Clare da Silva. Each bore a photo of Sapphire. There were other documents, too, in the name of Marie Clare or Sapphire da Silva.

He compared the names. Rosie had told him Sapphire's story of Brazilian poverty and rescue by a rich father, so a name change was feasible. When he began to read the letters, though, he grew confused. This couldn't be right. He looked again at the small photograph Rosie had found. This was impossible.

"Fucking hellfire," Sam had said to himself.

Then he'd put all her papers back as he'd found them, slipped the photo into his pocket, and made his way to the conservatory to watch the snow and think. A glass of his father's whiskey helped to keep out the cold.

He knew he couldn't tell his father about Sapphire; the

confession must come from her. That was, the confession of her true identity. Better Lawrence never, ever found out about her abuse of Jon. He couldn't tell him about Ginny, either, since she didn't want to be found.

Sam hadn't been truly angry with Rosie. All he'd really wanted was to put his arms around her and hold her. Perhaps he should have ignored his instincts and done just that.

No. He grimaced and took another swig of whiskey. Grabbing Rosie with protestations of love—while she was sitting there crushed, Luc barely out of critical care and Alastair's swollen body vivid in her mind—no, it was the last thing she'd needed. Doing the right thing, however, even though it was killing you—perhaps that was about growing up. He feared that her guilt would never let her love him, and the more he persuaded, the more she'd push him away. Wisdom was having the sense to make a graceful exit for once.

The pain lay across his shoulders, like torn muscles. It was also like a broken knife stuck through his chest, with a couple of metal spikes through the eyes for good measure. You could learn to live with it, he supposed. Eventually.

Snow piled and drifted on the parapet outside. Clouds and hills were all the same grey-white, whirling mass. Far below, on the white lawn, he saw something move. He went to a window, rubbed the condensation away. No good, he couldn't make it out. There was definitely someone out there, a smear of shadow struggling towards the house.

Sam put down the whiskey glass. He made his swift, light-footed way through the inner rooms, along the gallery and downstairs. All the lights were off and the great hall was full of cold grey light.

Something was out there. He saw the pale shadow turn darker and more solid as it came to one of the tall leaded windows near the center of the wall. He heard it scratching at the pane. Sam went closer. The lead and glass were shiny-new, a restoration. It was the window through which the burglar had thrown himself, trying to escape Sam's wrath.

He went softly to the casement, so close he could see the fog of the creature's breath. There was snow clotted thickly on its shoulders. Its features were indistinct, but he recognized the shape of it.

Sam listened to its guttural breathing, the horrible scratching of its nails. Finally its harsh voice came, muffled by the glass. "I know you are in there, Samuel. Come out into the cold and face me. Come out. Let us end it."

Calmly he answered, "I'm coming, Matthew."

20

❦

Winter Light

Sam could see nothing but cloudy whiteness. He stumbled through knee-deep snow, breath stolen by the cold. Snow drifted high up the house wall and turned the lawn to a swirling arctic plain. Rocks and shrubs became blurred humps.

Low, labored breathing came from all around him. He stopped, unable to pinpoint it. Perhaps if he entered the Dusklands . . . even as he made the transition, a blanketed bush shifted and rose in front of him. A ghost in the snow, it shook a blizzard from itself as it came lurching towards him.

He lunged to meet it, tackling the creature across the abdomen. Violent impact, then powerful arms seized and held him. Falling, they rolled together down the slope of the lawn, over and over through drifts. Snow plastered Sam's clothes and face.

His attacker was snarling, its furry clawed fingers reaching for his throat. Was it even Matthew anymore? It was like nothing he'd ever seen. A long, heavy head sheathed in slate-grey fur, glaring black eyes, carnivore fangs. Muscles like steel hawsers beneath the matted coat. Not human, not animal. Something from Dumannios.

The Dusklands turned the sky royal blue, the snow luminous. Sam changed too, Aetheric light glowing from him. Enough to freak a human, not enough to intimidate an enraged Matthew. They wrestled, gouging troughs in the snow. Human Matthew had fought aggressively, all those years ago, but Sam had beaten him with ease. Now he was impossibly strong. Sam didn't want to fight anymore, but had to.

The beast dragged him over like a puppet and pinned him down, breath steaming into his face. "You evil bastard." The words spilled rough and guttural from the carnivore mouth. "Years, you've had this coming."

"Yes, all right, we're even now," Sam gasped. "Enough." He tried to wrench free but the beast held him. The iron bands of its grip burned like the chill of the snow.

"Ruined my sister. Murdered Alazh-dair." The name emerged thickly distorted.

"No. Wasn't me drove his car into a tree. He did that himself."

The black eyes were glazed. Sam knew then that Matthew was going to kill him. "You took Faith. Where is she?"

"You were hunting her down." Sam spoke through his teeth, fighting for breath. "You don't give a damn about her!"

Matthew howled, deafening him. "*Where is she?*"

Jerking a hand free, Sam punched him in the temple. Matthew grunted, losing control for the second it took Sam to overbalance him and reverse their positions. He got astride but it was like trying to hold down a cheetah, a sinuous writhing creature that was all bone and muscle. Sam felt his own Aetheric strength swell through him. The beast's head thrashed with rage, denial.

"That's right," breathed Sam. "I'm stronger than you. I've had to be. See, I was in a place full of brutes who want to rob you, shag you or beat you up for the fun of it—and that was just boarding school. So I'm stronger and always will be. That's what you can't stand."

"No," came the bubbling roar. "Not anymore." Matthew's biceps flexed, resisting the pressure of Sam's hands. With trembling slowness the arms rose. Sam fought to press them back down, couldn't. He daren't let go or try to change his grip. Both men shook with the strain of exertion. However hard Sam resisted, Matthew's arms kept rising, bending inwards, claws questing for his neck.

"Your family destroyed mine." Although thick with exertion, every word was precise. "Thought you'd never pay?"

Sam was on top but it was Matthew who had control. His hands found Sam's throat and locked. None of Sam's usually effective tricks could shake the hold. He tried to return the favor but his own hands wouldn't even meet around the furry brawn of the neck. It was like trying to strangle a bull.

"You don't deserve a wife," Sam wheezed on the end of his breath. "Finish me, then. Feel good about it. Rosie won't thank you. Alastair won't come back."

Matthew's hands tightened. His forearms were like iron; Sam couldn't prize them away. The two men strained in counterpoise, the effort turning his sight red with painful starbursts.

"Faith will never love you," he finished, and made a desperate, two-fingered jab into Matthew's eye sockets.

Suddenly the pressure ceased. Matthew's hands went loose and slid away. Sam began to cough and gag, eyes streaming with the pain of his crushed throat. As his sight cleared, he looked down at the beast and saw it changing. Fur fading back into skin. The overgrown bones of the skull melting back into their true shape. Unnatural strength gone.

Matthew lay naked under him. His handsome face was pale and bewildered, his eyes bloodshot. He was crying.

Sam rolled off and rose to his hands and knees, snow swallowing him up to his elbows. They were back in the grey-white sweep of the surface world. Sam lurched to his feet and held out a hand to Matthew, who let himself be helped up without a word.

Sam swallowed and managed to whisper, "You'd better come in the house."

Inside, Sam sat Matthew down in the kitchen and put a towel around him. Then he ran upstairs, returning minutes later with a dressing gown and a duvet to wrap him in. Thus bundled up, Matthew sat silently on the chair, white and shivering.

Sam switched on the electric kettle. His red, cold fingers began to throb as feeling came back. For a while Matthew said nothing, only sat trembling and chewing at his lower lip, cradling his own frostbitten hands under his arms. Sam leaned against the countertop and watched him. Eventually, tilting his ravaged face slightly towards Sam, he hissed, "You bastard."

"Yes, I know," Sam said wearily. "You all right, mate?"

"I am not your 'mate.'"

"Do you remember what happened?"

Matthew squeezed his eyes shut and didn't answer. Sam went on, "You must have been wandering in that state for three or four days. You were hardly rational. Were you even aware of what you were doing?"

Eventually, he answered painfully, "Yes. I was aware."

"So that was a good plan, was it, scaring the crap out of everybody?"

"Faith—" It was a gasp of anger. "You've ruined us!"

"Oh yeah? How's that?"

"My best friend's dead. Your father, with my mother. You, with my sister. My family in ruins, my wife this—this *thing*—" He ran out of words and shook his head, fingertips pressing into his eyelids.

"Uh," said Sam, "I see how that must look, but I swear there's no master plan to ruin anyone. You spot the common factor in that list? My, my, my. Your family's all your personal property, is it?"

"Don't twist my words. Your family's a nest of serpents, all you do is destroy."

Sam smiled thinly. "Well, you're entitled to your opinion, and I've had a few moments with Dad and Jon myself, but there are two sides. Jessica's a pretty strong lady; I can't see anyone, even Lawrence, persuading her to do anything she didn't want. Same goes for Rosie. You ever asked yourself why she kept jumping on me, if she was getting what she needed from kilt boy?"

The chair scraped and Matthew came flying at him. Sam stepped aside and Matthew's hand landed instead on the boiling kettle. He recoiled with a yell. Sam grabbed the sides of the dressing gown and pushed him backwards, gently but firmly, against the marble lip of the island.

"It's a shame about Alastair, but I did not kill him," Sam said firmly. "He chose that himself. All Rosie and I did was discover a mutual taste for incredible, hot sex. Yes, it was wrong, but did it really deserve three deaths in revenge? Is that a fair exchange, d'you reckon? Don't you wish they'd had kids, so he could have killed them too? Yes?"

"No." His rage blurred into doubt. He whispered, "Deaths?"

"The world moved on while you were having your tantrum, Matt. You haven't once asked me about Lucas."

Matthew's face changed. A whole reality he'd forgotten on his rampage unveiled itself and dazzled him. He looked like a terrified twelve-year-old. "Is he . . . ?"

"Alive. Recovering."

Matt stared. "I don't trust you," he said gruffly.

"It's the truth. I can't be bothered to torment you. But where were you, when your family needed you?"

"Looking for my wife."

"Hunting her."

"Where is she?"

"You saw where she went," said Sam. "However, for all your fangs and bluster, you were too much of a coward to follow."

Matthew tried to lash out again, but his strength was gone. "Come on." Sam hauled the dead weight of him onto the chair and tucked the duvet around his shoulders. "Have you quite finished? Good man. Hot chocolate okay?"

Defeated, Matthew sipped at the mug Sam handed him. When he spoke, his voice was weak but lucid. "You're not going to redeem yourself by playing the boy scout. I don't like you, Sam. You're a villain."

"And you're such a great judge of character. Must be right."

"I knew it, from the moment we met. First thing you did was attack my sister, for god's sake!"

"I know, and I've been wearing a bloody hair shirt about it ever since. But didn't it occur to you that Rosie and I were capable of sorting it out ourselves? She got her necklace back. She even forgave me."

Matthew made a fist, then flexed the strawberry-red fingers, wincing. "I should have got it back for her. I failed."

"Oh, is that what this is about? *Your* failure."

"I spent my life trying to keep my sister away from people like you."

"You can't control your siblings. They never thank you for it."

"Away from people like *me*."

"What, self-important twits?"

"Aetherials! Monsters like me."

"You're not a monster, Matt. You're not nearly scary enough."

"Everything's a joke to you, isn't it? Even Rosie's marriage." Matthew pulled listlessly at his sleeves. "This force that takes us over—it's obscene."

"Hence, let's play humans? Pretend it's not there and it'll go away? And terrifying the life out of poor Faith?"

"She deceived me."

"You moron!" Sam cried. "Who the hell do you think you are? You've got a wonderful wife who adores you and you don't even see it. She's been terrified for years, in case you uncovered her little secret. You should be ashamed of yourself. God, this makes me so mad I can't speak." Matt was staring. Sam went on, "She's not your property. She doesn't exist to shore up your illusions. Notice your first question, 'Where is Faith?' Not, '*How* is Faith? Is she all right? What about Heather?' No. She's done nothing wrong. You should love her, no matter what. You should be on your knees begging forgiveness. Yet all you think about is yourself. You've got a loving wife and darling daughter and you don't even care. You don't deserve them! If you'd seen how frightened that little girl was—fuck, I can't speak to you anymore."

He turned to leave, but Matthew said in a small, gruff voice, "Sam? Are they all right?" His face was blotchy with tiredness and confusion.

"Yes. They're safe and fine. Whether they want to be found is another matter. You want me to call Oakholme?"

"No! No. I don't want them to see me like this." Matthew bent over and put his head in his hands, tears dripping between the fingers. "The beast that takes me over—I can't endure it."

Sam handed him a paper towel. "I see that. How long's it been happening?"

Matthew blotted his face and began to shred the damp tissue. "I must have been seven or eight . . . I'd go into the Dusklands and the change came so easily—the world turning dark and weird, like a dream. I wasn't even afraid at first, but as I got older the horror grew—because it felt wrong, and I couldn't control it."

"Didn't Auberon tell you, it's an Aetheric trait?"

"I never told him. I was too horrified. Instead I learned to avoid the Dusklands. Tried to keep Luc and Rosie out, too."

"But we all have a tendency to transform into something other than our everyday selves. Some change a little, others a lot. Other realities reveal different aspects of us. It's normal, apparently."

"Normal?" Matt gave a hollow laugh. "I knew the theory, of course, but it bore no relation to reality. It was so extreme. So *animal*. I thought, if this is being Aetherial, I want no part of it."

"So you turned a blind eye," said Sam.

"I thought Faith was human and then I saw . . ."

"I can see that must have freaked you out, but . . ."

"You've no idea how relieved I was when they said the Gates were locked, end of story. Best thing for everyone. That helped to stop the change happening . . . but if the Gates are open again, what will happen to us?"

Sam hesitated. "I don't know. There's nothing wrong with you. You can learn to control it."

"I thought I had."

"No. You suppressed it. That never ends well."

"But it doesn't happen to you, does it?"

"Yes, it does."

"Only a glow under your skin. You don't become a beast. Why don't you change?"

Sam shrugged. "Maybe it's because I'm not having an identity crisis."

Matthew's laugh became a convulsion of sobs. "Not long ago I thought I'd rather slit my own throat than ask you this," he said roughly, "but Sam, will you help me, please?"

Sapphire looked out of a hotel window at snow whirling in the streetlights. Soft white layers muffled the city. The roads were clogged with stranded vehicles. She and Lawrence were trapped here, as if in a spun cocoon.

They had made love, for something to do. Lawrence was not cold-skinned and passive like Jon, but skilled and athletic. As long as she closed her eyes and pretended she knew nothing about him, he was a wonderful lover.

Afterwards, she rose from bed and came to sit at the window, leaving Lawrence to his thoughts. His stern face, the eyes that looked into the distance with a near-psychopathic glitter—she'd almost grown to hate him. Still, there was a strange addiction in being close to such a man. So close, yet not touching what lay inside. If that carved, emotionless face were the very last thing you saw as you realized you were about to die—how terrible. The thought gave her a violent shudder.

The snow was a catalyst. No situation could endure forever. She felt changes in the cosmos, like the shifting of great ice floes.

Lawrence was never going to change. He would go on using her for as long as she let him. She thought, *Should I forget my mission and stay the polished, quiescent wife he wants, running his life and business so he's free to brood on his demons? Or should I take what I can and walk away? Or should I force him, finally, to tell me the truth?*

A touch on her back made her start. Lawrence was behind her, wrapping her pashmina around her shoulders. "You were shivering," he said.

"Lawrence," she said carefully, "why haven't you seen Lucas since he came round?"

"What can I say to him? I offered to switch off his life support. I only meant that if it had to be done and they couldn't face it, I would do it. Auberon, however, believes Lucas heard and misunderstood. Since they're all determined to think I'm the devil, it was inevitable. I decided it would be tactful to keep away."

"It's easy to project such beliefs onto someone who never reveals his true thoughts," she remarked acerbically.

His hands on her shoulders felt like claws. "What do you mean?"

"I'm not a life belt to hang on to into the darkness, Lawrence, but that's how you've treated me."

His hands dropped. She heard him sigh. "I know. You've been so patient. I should not have dragged you into this. Forgive me."

She turned and reached up to touch the angle of his cheekbone. "Do you actually want me?" she asked quietly. "The only way we have a chance is if you agree to be honest with me."

Lawrence moved away. She heard the chink of glass as light from the minibar spilled briefly into the dark room. "What do you want to know?"

There it was. A chance for them both to end the cold game they'd been playing for years and begin a genuine relationship at last. Sapphire shivered; the prospect was more frightening than she'd imagined—perhaps for them both—yet wildly thrilling, like standing on the edge of a precipice.

"Two things. Is it possible for a human to enter the Otherworld? And that old enemy of yours, Barada, whom you said disappeared—is it possible that he went through?"

Lawrence was silent for a while. The snow continued its thick, weightless descent. Eventually he murmured, "In theory, an exceptional human might pass through, if they had the will to do so. But Eugene Barada, no. I shot him dead."

Rosie needed space to think, and the snow gave her that. While snowplows worked their way along main routes, the lanes of Cloudcroft remained impassable. For three days, more snow fell and winds blew fresh drifts across any path that had been cleared. Snow-light filled the house with a flat pearly glow.

At least they knew Matthew was safe. Sam had phoned to say he would be staying at Stonegate until the weather lifted. Auberon was ready to go straight there until a combination of blizzards, thigh-deep snow and Matthew's own insistence dissuaded him.

For now, life was suspended. They spoke to Lucas every day, promising to be at his side the moment the roads were clear. Lawrence and Sapphire were stranded in a hotel in Leicester. Phyllida was staying at the hospital itself, so Luc had his aunt there at least.

Strangely peaceful, those eerie days inside the snow-bound house. Rosie entered a state of tranquillity. In the afternoons, she and Jessica would sit cuddled up on the sofa, looking out at the bleak snowscape of the garden. "We'll be reduced to tins of soup by the time they dig us out," said Jessica. "I can't wait to get everyone home."

"Me, too," said Rosie. "That's all I want, life to be normal again. But it can't be. It's all changed."

Jessica asked cautiously, "Has Sam called you?"

"We've spoken," Rosie said with a sigh, "but we haven't actually *talked*. Neither of us quite knows what to say. We're trying to be dignified. He said he might leave altogether, claims it would make my life too difficult if he stayed . . ."

Jess gave her hand a squeeze. "I'm trying to ask without sounding nosy—was it a mad fling, or serious?"

Rosie hesitated. "Mum, it was so exciting—but that might not be a basis for anything."

"That happens," Jess said dryly.

"He's flippant, caustic, hotheaded and drives me crazy. And I can't stop thinking about him. When I used to visit him in prison, we'd talk and talk. He'd always wind me up, but I was sort of addicted to it, you know? Searching for Luc, he was so courageous. Never left my side, never flinched. I miss him."

"Tell him, then. The real question is, can you trust him?"

"The problem is I don't trust *myself*." Rosie groaned. "My judgment's shot. I've been grossly mistaken about everything. I thought Jon was my angel and soulmate, but the truth was the complete opposite. I thought Alastair was a decent and steady human being—how did I get that so monumentally wrong? He was right there in front of me, but I wasn't paying attention! I had Faith in her little box with a label—how blind could I be? I believed Sam was a malicious sadist who got off on tormenting me. Wrong again. Turns out he'd walk to the ends of the Otherworld for me. Every single belief I held turned out to be false. I can't trust my own judgment, Mum. Now I know what she meant."

"Who?" Jessica leaned forward, puzzled.

"Estel, the doe lady. She said that it was my own mind that had shaped the Claws, the thorn creatures. Only it wasn't my fear—it was my buggered judgment. My lack of belief in myself. I realized that when you enter the Spiral, ideas can become solid and claw you to pieces."

Her mother's frown deepened. "I didn't know you felt like this."

"Mum, I'm not blaming anyone or asking you to fix it. I didn't realize the problem until it crashed in on me. Now I see that the Greenlady was trying to open my eyes, but I was sleepwalking and didn't wake up until it was too late."

Jessica's eyes narrowed. "Rosie, I know you. There's nothing wrong with your heart or your instincts. When you heard me singing, it was your own voice you were hearing. The voice of your *fylgia,* the pure instinct which ties you to the Otherworld and only ever tries to show you the right path."

Winter gloom filled the windows, but inside the ward fluorescent lights blazed and the heat was tropical. Lucas sat beside Jon's bed and they looked at each other. There were wispy lines of worry around Jon's brown eyes. "Hey, you're supposed to visit me," said Lucas. "I'm the one who nearly died."

"You're on your feet. I'm in plaster."

"You're malingering. Apparently I should be facing months of rehabilitation. They refuse to believe I'm fine, but I am. Aetheric constitution, Jon. I bet you any money your broken bones have healed already."

Jon looked down at his hands, hair falling around his face. "If you'd died, I wouldn't have wanted to live."

"God, don't be such a drama queen. I'm alive. What Sam and Rosie did was amazing."

"What was it like?" Jon's voice was husky. "The Spiral?"

Lucas struggled for words; all he could find were terrifying, haunting images. "Weirder than any trip. So vast, you can't get your mind around it. The Abyss . . ."

Drawing up his uninjured leg, Jon rested his arms and head on his knee. "When Sam and Rosie talked about going through, I was paralyzed with fear. I didn't dare go with them. I've never been so grateful in my life for a broken ankle. I'm such a useless coward."

"Jon, we were all terrified."

"It should have been me that saved you."

"Why? Not exactly the heroic type, are you?" Lucas said

it without malice, realizing too late it was not the most tactful remark he could have made. "I didn't expect it. Don't beat yourself up."

"No, you don't get it. What am I going to do? Years, I've devoted myself to breaking through the Gates. Now what's left to strive for? Nothing. They're open, and I'm frightened to go through. That's the whole purpose of my life, up in smoke. What the hell am I going to do?"

Lucas gasped. "*You're* scared? How do you think I feel? Don't you understand, I've had this power landed on me and I don't know what to do with it! Jon, you don't know what I saw in there . . ." He stopped, because his throat had closed up. Vivid memory hit him: the colossal statue on the cliff face. The way it had slowly turned its head and *looked* at him . . . He caught his breath against a sudden image of falling.

Jon was staring at him, spooked. "What?"

"I saw Brawth." Luc struggled to describe the statue, but words weren't enough. "Estel dismissed it as something that had always been there. Estel, the Lady of Stars . . . first conscious spark out of the Abyss . . . the goddess to end all goddesses . . . She was there, and even she didn't realize."

"I know who Estel is," Jon said, frowning. "But people don't just *meet* her. You sure you didn't dream it?"

Lucas gave an impatient laugh. "While I'm tripping, you're telling me it's real, and when I see something real, you tell me I'm dreaming? The point is that even Estel didn't recognize the danger, and neither did the Spiral Court. That's why they're ignoring it. They don't realize that Brawth could wake at any moment. It's still waiting for the Great Gates to open, and Lawrence has only kept it quiet by sealing the Gates . . . oh my god, what have I done?" He glanced outside at the iron sky. "This snow is the start of it, Jon. It's the ice giant breathing through the Lychgate as it starts to wake up. Oh god, I must have woken it—it saw me—I have to close the Lychgate, but I don't know how!"

"Luc, stop it," said Jon. "This is really disturbing. You've just come out of a coma. Don't get worked up. You need to relax and take your mind off it."

"What do you suggest?" Luc retorted. His heart was beating too fast, the sense of peril so strong he couldn't express it. "A game of Scrabble?"

"No, but we could talk about the future. We could start up the band again."

"And lie around in a haze of drugs? I can't go back to that. All that ever did was to suck the spirit out of us!" Once Jon had seemed glamorous and wise, a guru; now he looked scared, diminished, helpless. Luc had flown far ahead of him, into a realm he'd never wanted to see. Despite the heat, he was shivering. He saw Albin's cold white face and heard him whispering, *The cold of Brawth will pierce your brain and strip the very skin from your bones.* "This is real, Jon. I found something real and you don't believe me."

"I don't want to believe you," Jon said stubbornly. "It's too much. All you're doing is scaring yourself, and I don't know what you want me to say. Hey, where are you going?"

As Lucas stood up, Jon caught at the sleeve of his dressing gown, but Lucas pulled away. He felt frozen, dizzy, isolated by terrible knowledge. "Even if you'd believe me, you can't do anything. It's all on my shoulders. Who is going to listen to me, except Lawrence?"

Faith's head broke the surface of the water. Strange, even while she swam—her undine form flashing through the waterfall pool, finned hands propelling her like an arrow through dives and turns—she still felt echoes from the surface world. Momentary visions of snow, faint voices, gone before she could capture them. On Earth, she'd often grasped at brief visions of the Spiral. Now it was happening the other way.

Heather surfaced beside her, a tiny mermaid. "Again, Mummy, again," she said, kicking the crystal water to foam. Faith murmured, "We should get out, poppet."

They slithered onto the bank, hair flowing like the leafy tendrils of sea dragons. Ginny, in a long lavender dress, was sitting on a flat stone with her arms around her raised knees. In Elysion there was no snow, only mist softening the luscious greens of the hidden valley. Effortlessly, Faith slipped back into her human shape. Water rolled off, leaving her dry. "I never want to come out," she said quietly. "I forget everything when we're swimming."

"That's the danger." Ginny shook back her hair. "I let Elysion seduce me until I almost forgot who I was. That's fine if you want to forget, and become fully Aelyr, but not if you still have ties of love to the Earth."

"Watch me," said Heather. She was straight back in the water, a tiny undine again. Smiling, Faith sat beside Ginny and left her to splash. "I'd like to shake off the past. Start fresh."

"Initiation doesn't mean enlightenment—it only reveals a new layer of mysteries. You're experiencing your undine nature as a pleasure and not a guilty secret now. It's overwhelming, and it should be. Still, I won't let you forget your Earth-self, Faith. When the time comes, you'll be glad."

At first, she'd been in awe of Virginia Wilder, with her proud and abrasive beauty. She was a panther, and Faith a mouse—but Faith was feeling less timid by the day. "Do you remember my mother? She used to be your cleaner?"

"Yes," Ginny answered ruefully. "She worked hard but unfortunately helped herself so freely to our drinks cabinet that I had to let her go. I'm sorry."

"Don't be." Faith's head dropped. "Everyone in the village knew. The question is, why did no one see she had Aetherial blood?"

"Even pure Aetherials can pass for human," said Ginny. "And many humans have a trace of Vaethyr blood, but it's rare for it to be strong enough to manifest. You, and they, are quite unusual."

"I wish they'd had some awareness," said Faith. "Instead, they lived like the worst, unhappiest kind of humans. And that's what Matthew wants for us? Never. I tried to go along with him, but I can't. It's wrong."

"Are you still afraid of him?" Ginny asked.

Faith looked up at the plunging waterfall. There was a brooding quality to the sky, purplish clouds streaming against amber, as if the Spiral held its breath in wait for a storm. "Not sure. If I remember how the terror felt, it twists me into pieces . . . but I'm not the old Faith anymore."

The snow began its surrender to milder air, falling into fantastic shapes in a last show of glory before its decline. On the fourth morning, the lanes became passable and Sam had a nostalgic sense of being released from prison. He headed into Leicester on his motorbike to visit Jon.

Matthew had just returned to Oakholme, having spent the last few days at Stonegate recuperating on the living-room sofa, watching TV and steadily consuming their store of food and drink. At first he'd slept around the clock; then he and Sam had talked; finally, when they started sniping at each other again, Sam knew he was well enough to be sent home.

As he walked the slushy, gritty path from the car park to the hospital entrance, he phoned Rosie and said, "Did you receive the special delivery?"

"Yes, Matthew's here," she said, with a smile in her voice. "Thanks for looking after him. He isn't talking yet, but at least he's back. Where are you?"

"On my way to see the patients. Thought you might be here."

"We're going later. Comyn and Phyll have come round to see us. It was quite nice, hibernating for a few days. How about you? Anything happened with Sapphire yet?"

That was their "safe" subject. A few phone conversations hadn't been enough to pierce the wall of snow between them. They had to be tactful and not flaunt their affair, for her family's sake—that went without saying. Now Sam was at pains to show he was capable of maintaining a dignified separation. Actually, it wasn't hard; he only had to recall Rosie's devastation after the accident. He knew that if he gave the merest hint that he wanted to see her, she might view it as pressure she didn't need. And if that pressure forced her to tell him it was over—he couldn't bear it.

He didn't want to leave, the way he had when his bid to make Rosie jealous with the Pit Bull had backfired so horribly, but he was coming to terms with the possibility that he might have to.

"Haven't seen her," he said, "but I found out something very interesting that I'm guessing she does not want my father to know."

"Can you tell me?"

"Not yet. Schrödinger's Cat. It's neither dead nor alive until you open the box."

"What? You're being very mysterious."

He laughed. "Tell you later. One thing I know, I can't stay at Stonegate much longer. I've arranged to share an apartment in Ashvale with other students until I finish my college course in spring."

"Oh. And after that?" she asked, her voice soft and noncommittal.

"I don't know. Have to go, love . . . I'll call you later, okay?"

As he entered the hospital, he walked straight into Sapphire.

Her hair and fake-fur coat were damp, her fashionable boots tide-marked by salt. She quickly covered her shock at seeing him with a faultless smile. "I take it the roads are clear?"

"Yeah, just about," he said. They moved to stand near a coffee bar inside the entrance to avoid the endless stream of people. "Where's Dad?"

"He took the train to London last night to visit the store. He'll be back later today. And there's good news; we can bring Jon home in a few days. He'll need motherly care until he recovers."

Sam's mouth opened in a soundless gasp. Her hypocrisy was breathtaking. He stared at this poised, polished stranger and remembered how swift she'd been to call the police that fateful night; her calmly triumphant face as they'd taken him away in handcuffs.

She made to move past him but he stood square, blocking her. "We all struggle to see you as a mother, Sapphire. Lines get blurred."

"Excuse me?" She looked genuinely bemused.

"Don't you find me even a bit attractive?" He held out his arms, palms open. "Come on, what about it?"

Sapphire flushed. Her eyes burned with annoyance and a trace of confusion. "Have you gone mad? Get out of my way, Sam."

"Father, sons; from what I've heard, you're not that fussy. Apparently Jon's good enough for you, but I'm not. I'm hurt."

Her full lips thinned. Then she expelled a sharp breath. "I don't know what the hell you're playing at, Sam. I suggest you get therapy. Let me past."

He leaned towards her and said mildly, "You and Jon, I know all about it. He told me."

She went red. She went white. Sam laughed coldly and said, "That's good. Can you do candy stripes?"

"Jon is an attention-seeking fantasist with an unfortunate drug habit," she said, icily furious.

Sam tutted. "So it's all in his head, and when Rosie and Luc saw you in action it was a dream? I know my brother and, for all his quirks, I know when he's telling the truth. Can't say the same for you."

Sapphire stepped close to him, fierce and unafraid. Her eyes burned bright, like armor. "This is a repellent accusation."

"And what, you'll see me in court? Oh, that would be fun. He may have been over the age of consent, just, but don't tell me it was a case of irresistible mutual passion. He was a kid! You knew it was wrong. And you can't have done it for any reason but a vicious, calculated attempt to hurt my father. Fuck, if you were a man, you'd be begging for your life by now."

"And if *you* were a man," she hissed, "I'd say, just try it."

"Don't tempt me, Maria Clara Ramos."

As consummately as she disguised it, she was shocked. He saw the questions flashing behind her eyes. Her breath hissed through her teeth. "You're on extremely shaky ground, Sam. Criminal tendencies run in your family, of course. If you've touched anything of mine—"

"Accusing me of going through your secret papers would mean admitting you had secret papers to go through," he said flatly. "All I care about is my father. Either you tell him what you're playing at, or I will."

"Oh, I'm not playing. I changed my name—so? I've nothing to hide." She was good, he gave her that. She faced him down, tough and unafraid. "Why would you tell Lawrence anything? I'll deny it and so will Jon. You can't prove a thing. If you spread false rumors, you'll look a fool and be despised for it. If it's true, you'll break Lawrence's heart—assuming he has one. You've nothing to gain and everything to lose. You'll tell him nothing, Sam. Now let me pass."

He stepped aside. Round one to Sapphire. "You're right, it would break my father's heart," he said after her. "How about we keep it secret, for Jon's sake? I'm not asking you to reveal your sordid habits. I am suggesting you tell Lawrence who you are."

She paused. The glass doors hung open, admitting a chilly wind. "There's nothing missing from your papers," he said, a little louder. "Only one tiny item anyway, which, dammit, I seem to have mislaid. You come clean with Lawrence and I'll remember where it is. Otherwise . . . you had better hope you find it before he does."

Sapphire strode on her way, showing no sign that she'd heard him.

Walking the cold streets outside the infirmary, Sapphire felt a rising sense of urgency. She knew her game was nearly up, but the end had to be on her terms. She had to find whatever incriminating item Sam had left before Lawrence found it—and she must have Jon in her power.

Thinking that she and Lawrence had a chance had been a moment of weakness. Once he had confessed to murder, it was over for her. She hadn't reacted, only listened; afterwards, Lawrence had slept; but she had lain awake most of the night, feeling cold inside, and remembering the man to whom she had made her promises. Lawrence drove everyone away—but she wasn't going without delivering a death-blow.

Patiently she killed time for an hour or so, hiding behind a newspaper in the hospital coffee bar until she saw Sam leave. Then she made her way back to Jon's ward.

Whenever Lawrence returned to Stonegate, the house seemed to be bearing down on him, watching. The judges of the Spiral Court knew his every move and that was why they'd taken the lych-light from him and left him defenseless. This time, the atmosphere was worse than usual. He felt unseen currents shifting darkly around him. Hadn't sensed anything like it since the last time the Gates were unlocked—but that was impossible. Unthinkable.

Arriving by taxi, he'd noted his own limousine parked on the half-moon drive in front of the house where Sam had left it. Sapphire's car was behind it. Inside the house, there was no sign of her, so presumably she'd retreated to her own rooms.

Lawrence knew he should rejoice at Jon's imminent homecoming, but he felt no emotion that was appropriate. Other people seemed to him like smears of light on a distant piece of glass. An irritation. He wanted to be alone in this vast dark silence.

The house felt disturbed, and after a while he put his finger on it. Everything had been subtly moved. Coats and shoes in the cloakroom slightly out of place, kitchen cupboards rearranged, objects repositioned, a sheaf of letters on a mantelpiece taken out, shuffled, and put back . . . not by the cleaner, for there was a smudging of dust and no scent of polish. No. Someone had been searching.

Upstairs, too, there were signs that his bedside cabinet had been explored. He felt mild puzzlement, nothing more. He stared at the big, stark bedroom and it seemed not even to belong to him.

In London, he'd visited the store and broken the news to his staff; that he had sold the business. The buyer was American. They would continue as an exclusive jeweler, but there would be no more albinite. He'd found it hard to dredge up any regret or emotion for them; the greater his torment, the less he could express it.

These were the last days of his empire. He knew, and couldn't face it.

It was lunchtime. He had no desire for refreshment except a shot of whiskey. He headed into his study for a drink and there was Sapphire—still in her coat, riffling through the top drawer of his desk. At the sight of him she jumped guiltily.

"Can I help you?" he asked.

"Lawrence, I didn't expect you back so early," she said. "You made me jump." At once she was breezy again. "I was looking for your diary. To check our work schedule." Her expression softened, asking for understanding. "Sorry, but the sooner we get back to normal, the better we'll all feel."

His large black desk diary was in clear view. As he sardonically passed it to her, the pages flapped and a slip of paper fell out. She pounced to catch it. It was a bookmark he'd been using; clearing her throat, she pressed it back between the pages.

"Normal?" he said.

"I've got a surprise. Jon's been discharged early. I've just fetched him."

"What? Where is he?"

She set the diary down and sighed. "He's sitting in the car, refusing to come into the house."

"Why?" He hadn't paid enough attention to notice his son sitting behind the tinted windows.

"Oh, Lawrence, think about it. You threw him out, not so long ago. This is the first time he's been back and he's got cold feet."

"Well, persuade him to come in. This is ridiculous."

"You persuade him!" she retorted. "He's your son. No, I've tried. Arguing with him only makes him more stubborn. Leave him to stew, he'll come in when he's cold and hungry enough." Her gaze was still on the desk, her fingernails picking at the corners of stacked papers.

"Aren't you taking your coat off?" Lawrence went to his liquor cabinet and took a fresh bottle of whiskey from the shelf. "You seem nervous," he said. "When I confessed I'd once killed a man, it was a long time ago. It's not something that will ever happen again. Please don't take it to heart."

She gave him a look, but said nothing. Turning back for a glass, he found something lying on the shelf where the bottle had been.

It was a small passport-sized photograph. The colors were fading, pinkish and washed-out. The image was a head-and-shoulders shot of a girl posing with an older man; her smile shiny-bright and happy, his more guarded and complex. Her face was young, her hair in eighties-style big curls, but clearly recognizable as Sapphire. The man had the air of a hunter who'd just returned from safari with trophy kill over his shoulder; beefy, arrogant, sun-red. The thick eyebrows had a demonic quirk. Lawrence knew the face as well as his own. It was Eugene Michael Barada.

Enemy, nemesis, demon. Barada and Sapphire. Together.

He stood cupping the photo, staring at it in complete incomprehension. It was such an impossible juxtaposition that he couldn't take it in. A white storm was building up behind his eyes. He glanced up and saw Sapphire facing him across the desk, poised as if she'd turned to stone.

"What is this?" He turned his hand to show her the image. Her face lost its color. Her mouth tautened. "It appears to be a picture of me."

"And this man you're with—do you know who he is?"

She paused. He saw a dark flame racing behind her eyes; trembling horror and defiance mixed. Then, in a beat, her game was up and battle lines drawn.

"Of course I know who he is," she said evenly. "He was my father. He was the man you killed."

21.

Pandora's Box

"Ro, can I have a word?" Matthew's voice came hoarse and quiet from his doorway as Rosie passed his room.

"Yes, of course," she said, slipping inside. The bedroom he'd shared with Faith was bigger than hers but otherwise similar, with ivory walls, oak paneling, leaded windows and a big dark oak bed. She noticed with shock what an incredible mess it was. Strewn clothes, unmade bed, empty beer cans. "Oh my god, Matt . . ."

"I know. I'll get round to it. Without Faith here, there didn't seem any point."

"You're like a bear in a cave. You need to come out."

He nodded, looking at his feet. As he pushed back his hair, his hand shook. "When you helped Faith and Heather escape, you were frightened of me, weren't you?"

"On their behalf."

"I would never have hurt them!"

"That's not how it looked. You have to face it, Matt; you were out of control."

"I know that. I've had nightmares all week. I've been thinking about everything Sam said and I know he's right, but I can't get past it."

"So let us help you. Don't fall apart on us."

"Why don't you change?" The confusion in his eyes disturbed her. "In the Dusklands. You don't become a beast, do you?"

"Actually, I always wanted to. Felt I should become a fox, an owl, a wolf. You think you're abnormal because you change, and I think I'm abnormal because I don't." Rosie chewed her lip. "I'm in no position to preach, Matt, but how about you try helping your family instead of feeling sorry for yourself?"

The old Matthew would have come back with a sarcastic remark. The new one seemed too wounded to try. "Sam said that to me, as well."

"You know what? He's the wisest person I've ever met, after Dad. You treat him like an idiot, but he isn't. He's worth ten of Alastair." She was ready to walk out on him, but he caught her elbow.

"Rosie, please." He gave a quick sigh. "I need to tell you. This isn't easy. I knew about Alastair."

"Knew what, exactly?"

Matthew sat on the edge of the bed, head dangling. "That he'd had issues with women in the past. Big chip on his shoulder. That last girlfriend of his—when they broke up, there were things he did in revenge . . . destroying her clothes, having her cat put down . . . that went way beyond normal. And we all had a good laugh at the time, good old Alastair, that's taught her a lesson—but in my heart I knew it wasn't right. He went too far. He'd be as placid as anything but when he lost it, he totally lost it."

"*He had her cat put down?*" She nearly shrieked the words. For seconds she couldn't get her breath properly, thought her heart would explode.

"I didn't realize how bad it was until I said it," Matt answered very quietly. "I remembered that story of his, how hurt his mother was when he accidentally dropped a bike on her dog. He must have decided it was an effective policy. Sick, I know."

Rosie looked into his cloudy, troubled eyes. "You knew, and didn't tell me?"

"I thought he just needed the right woman."

"Maybe he did, but it wasn't me."

"He'd never hurt a person before. I thought it would be all right."

"Well, it wasn't!" she exclaimed. "So you knew he was unstable and decided to keep it quiet? Because that marriage wasn't about me and Alastair at all, it was all about you. Your way of controlling us."

Matt shook his head, baring his teeth. "Nobody made you marry him, Rose!"

"No, they didn't. That's true. And there were warning signs: I knew he had a temper, I knew he would sometimes drink when he was upset, but, god, I never saw him do anything worse than break a plant pot! I should have been paying more attention. But I still wish you'd told me."

"Me, too. I'm trying to say I'm sorry." He groaned. "Don't you think I've been going mad with guilt? I shouldn't have tried to push you together. But he was everything I wanted to be—normal, human, ordinary—so I thought. Rosie, I'm so sorry."

She'd rarely known him apologize sincerely in his life before. To see Matthew, the golden prince, brought low like this was horrifying. His face was webbed with pain. She took his hand. "I'm sorry too, Matty."

"Never dreamed it would end like this."

"Me neither," she said. "I screwed up horribly."

"Not like I have." Reaching under a pile of shirts he pulled out a small blue journal. "I found this. It's Faith's diary." He pressed it on her. "I had no idea she was so unhappy." Rosie turned the book in her hands. She let it fall open, saw a line in Faith's sloping handwriting, *What is love, anyway?*, and quickly closed it again. Matthew looked at her, pale and bewildered like a young boy. "Are Faith and Heather truly all right?"

"Yes, I promise." She looked at the unkempt room. "It's like a bachelor pad again," she said softly. "You can't tell Faith was ever here."

"She's better off without me," Matthew replied.

"Don't be so defeatist. You've been through the worst. Now think about how you're going to put things right. Auntie Phyll and Comyn are here; won't you come and say hello?"

As she spoke, her words were half-drowned by a noise outside; the chugging of a car engine in severe distress, followed by a frantic pounding on the front door. By the time she'd run downstairs to the hallway, Auberon was already opening the door, Jessica beside him.

Sapphire was on the doorstep, Jon behind her on crutches. They both looked ash-faced and disheveled, as if they'd stumbled out of wreckage. Sapphire's blue cabriolet was parked crookedly on the side of the lane.

"I need to call a taxi," she gasped. "Please."

"Oh," said Jessica, startled. "Come in. But your car's there. Are you all right?"

"Flat tires." As Sapphire stepped over the threshold, her self-control seemed to desert her and she reeled, her shoulder colliding with the wall. "Oh my god." She stood shaking, one hand pressed to her face.

Rosie had never seen her fall apart before. It shocked her.

Jessica touched her arm, concerned. "Sapphire, what ever's happened?"

"Lawrence has gone mad. He wrecked the car. He's completely lost his mind."

Sam, after his encounter with Sapphire, had run a few errands, seen a few people. Now he was riding his motorbike back to Stonegate, slowing as he approached Oakholme and thinking, *Should I stop? Is it too soon to see Rosie, will I make it worse?* Then he saw Sapphire's car, did a double take and braked hard.

He left the bike and went to look. The windshield was a shattered hole, the tires in ribbons, bodywork gouged and dented. "Fuck," he said. The front door was open, Jon on the doorstep apparently about to head inside. Running up the path, Sam turned the startled Jon to face him and said, "What the hell happened?"

Disheveled hair swung around his face as he swayed on the crutch. "I don't know."

"Yes, you do. Calm down and tell me."

The others had gone inside, leaving them alone. Jon panted for breath. "Sapphire fetched me from hospital, but when we reached Stonegate, I couldn't go in. First time I'd been back since Dad threw me out. I knew he didn't want me there. So she got mad and stormed into the house, and I was left sitting there, trying to work up courage to go in. Then Dad shows up in a taxi, but doesn't see me. About fifteen minutes later, I hear them arguing. I mean, they never argue—it's all icy silences, right? But they burst out of the house shouting at each other. I mean *yelling*.

"Father's practically foaming at the mouth—demented—and Sapphire's standing up to him but starting to lose it. He starts roaring at her to get out. Suddenly he dives back inside the porch and Sapphire comes running to the car—I'm trying to wind the window down to ask her what's going on—and she runs round to the driver's side and says, 'He knows everything, we have to go.'"

Sam held his upper arm. "Slow down, it's okay."

He swallowed painfully. "So Sapphire's in a complete panic, coat and hair flying, trying to start the car and turn it round. Father comes running out and he's got a fucking ax in his hand! He opens my door and tries to pull me out of the car, and I'm fighting him and I can hear myself pleading that I'm sorry and it's over and it was her fault, all that. He loses hold of the door, so I manage to close it, and the car's sliding on gravel and slush. Then I hear him yell and he brings the ax down on the hood—so hard it goes right through to the engine—then starts hacking the tires, literally chasing the car while Sapphire's turning it. Then the ax hits the windshield, *bang*." Jon stiffened at the memory, eyes widening. "Glass explodes all over us. She puts her foot down and we're gone. I look round and Father's standing on the drive behind us, staring, with the ax dropping out of his hand . . ."

Jon leaned against the wall, shuddering. "So we manage to get down the hill on flat tires before the engine seizes up . . . You should have seen his face, Sam. Not just angry, but dead white, completely deranged. I was so scared. He's going to kill us. I can never go back. I can never look him in the eye again."

Sam asked softly, "Did Sapphire say what he'd found out, exactly?"

"What do you *think*?" Jon said in anguish.

"I didn't tell him!"

"I know you didn't. *She* did. To hurt him like he'd hurt her, she said."

"But what started it? Did she mention a photo?"

Jon frowned though skeins of hair. "What photo?"

"I'm sorry," Sam said quietly. "I thought you were safe in hospital. Never meant you to get involved."

"How could you help it? You could put most things right in my life, but not this. You think I'm scum, right? So whatever Dad thinks, it's a billion times worse."

"I don't think you're scum." Sam sighed. "You're as dumb as a hatstand, but Sapphire—she knew exactly what she was doing. There's stuff you don't know about her. I left Dad a clue and it looks like he found it."

"I don't know what the hell you're on about."

"Let's go and see what madam's got to say for herself, shall we?"

Jon's head jerked round and he cannoned off the wall, almost falling over his plastered foot. "Oh my god, there's Dad's car. Let's get inside, lock the door!"

Sam took a firm grip of his arm and pushed him into the house. "Go in there and keep calm. I'll speak to him."

Sam saw the sleek black roof cruising past the hedge. Reaching the gate, he glimpsed his father's head turning, the pale face and impassive eyes fixed on Oakholme. The limousine, however, kept going. Sam went out through the gate and saw the vehicle turning farther down, where the lane widened. Then it came back at the same sinister walking pace.

"Dad!" Sam shouted, waving. He expected his father to stop, meant to intercept him before he went storming into the house. Lawrence's narrow arctic gaze slid over Oakholme and the wrecked car, over Sam himself. His expression said it all. Utter, freezing contempt.

Just as Sam thought he was going straight past, he braked. The electric window slid down an inch. "So you're all here," he said. "Even you."

The air smelled of melted snow. Their breath smoked. "Dad, she was never going to tell you," Sam said urgently. "I left the photo—to make her confess—I didn't think you'd—" He pointed at the damaged car.

"It must have pleased you to uncover the betrayal and reveal to me the depths of my own stupidity," said Lawrence.

Sam's jaw tightened. "No. That wasn't the idea at all. I warned her to tell you herself. I didn't expect you to lose it so drastically. Best you don't come in unless you've calmed down."

Lawrence looked away. Quietly he said, "I have no interest in speaking to anyone. Tell them all to go to hell."

"Did she explain herself?"

"She said enough. She married me for revenge, and by god, she's taken it. Persuaded me in the snowstorm to confess that I had shot and killed Barada. Now tells me that she plotted for years to take the mine and the business from me. I answered that there's nothing to take; the mine is dead, the business sold."

"Sold?"

"So I told her that there is nothing she can do to hurt me, and she answered that there is—and that it is already done." A spasm of pained disgust crossed Lawrence's face. "She, with my own son—I can't even say his name. Barada once said to me that there's a type of fairy who thieves and steals—but she only does it to those who deserve it, because they are so careless of their possessions. How was I to know he was talking about his daughter? My fault, for taking her at face value."

"No—you were lonely—" Sam put his fingertips on the hard edge of the window. He couldn't keep his father in the dark forever, about the Gates or Ginny. "Dad, we need to talk."

"There's nothing to say." A glaze came over Lawrence's face, obdurate withdrawal. "Of course she's part of it—part of Barada, part of Brawth. Of course. The shadow was there in my very bed." He stared sideways at Sam, his irises circled by white. "My enemy feeds and absorbs everyone and grows ever more powerful. You're all part of it. I want none of you under my roof anymore. Do you understand? Keep away from me. Damn you all to the Abyss."

The window closed, almost trapping Sam's fingers. "Dad!" he shouted, but the car moved off. Frustrated, he could only watch as it gathered speed, dwindling along the curves of the lane, as sleekly sealed as a coffin.

Sapphire settled in the middle of the sofa, jaw taut, hands opening and closing. She called on all her inner strength. Lawrence would have to get past seven people—she didn't count Jon—to attack her. No need to fear him. He was not going to make her flee a second time.

It was a big room with windows on three sides but she couldn't bring herself to look out. Lawrence had genuinely terrified her. She hated to lose control, to be stripped raw in front of all these glowing Aetherial eyes. They'd all come in, of course: Jessica and Auberon, Matthew, who frankly looked a bit crazy, even Comyn of the dark Celtic looks and cunning eyes; and Rosie, perched on the arm of a chair, straight-backed and petite with her glossy plum-brown hair, who had nothing to look so prim about. Only in down-to-earth Phyllida had she ever sensed a kindred spirit.

"He's gone," said Rosie.

Sapphire looked up. A few seconds later, with a waft of cold air from the front door, Sam came in, grim-faced. She saw the way Rosie's gaze went to him. "Well, he refuses to speak to anyone, unsurprisingly."

Auberon, Jessica and Phyll had been hovering defensively between Sapphire and the door. Almost sweet, the way they leapt to protect her, a mere human. Now there was a loosening of the atmosphere. "Hardly appropriate for him to come in, anyway, after what he's done," said Auberon.

" 'Damn you all to the Abyss' were his exact words." Sam exhaled.

Sapphire pinned him with wide eyes. "What did you expect, Sam? You couldn't let matters lie."

"You should know all about lying," he said thinly.

"Are you proud of what you've done?" Everyone looked at Sam. For a few glorious moments she had total control. "Made your father crazy, broken up his family, rendered your brother homeless? A day's work to be proud of, is it?"

Sam didn't like that. His expression darkened. He had an expressive face and couldn't hide his feelings at all. "Excuse me, I think that was your doing, not mine. I warned you to tell him."

"And I warned you that it's none of your business. You're nothing but a mischief-maker, Sam. I hope Rosie knows what she sacrificed her husband for."

She saw Rosie's mouth fall open. The girl looked soul-sick. "Don't drag her into this," Sam said in a low voice. "This is about you, no one else."

"And I've done nothing to be ashamed of."

Jessica brought her a cup of coffee. Sapphire sipped at it, letting the warmth of relief steal through her. She sensed the others dying to know what was happening but too polite to ask. Otherworldly they might be, but still so very English in that respect.

Phyllida said, "Sapphire, if you and Jon have nowhere to go, you're welcome to stay with us. I'm sure our farmhouse is no draftier than Stonegate."

Sapphire was astonished. The offer was made so easily and warmly, as if they were friends. She began to express her thanks. Jon made no objection, only sat sullen and bedraggled in a corner.

"Hold on," said Sam, "before you get too cozy, Jon and I are still waiting for an explanation."

"Sam," Jessica said quickly, "Sapphire's very shaken, and under no obligation to tell us anything."

"No, he's right," Sapphire said evenly. "I'm happy to explain, and I don't mind who hears it." She held Sam's frosty gaze in unspoken agreement: *I won't mention Jon if you don't.* No one wanted that unsavory matter aired in public.

"Fine," said Sam. "We're listening."

Their eyes fairly shone with anticipation. Sapphire rose to her feet, clasping her arms loosely around herself.

"I'm human; I can't help that," she began. "Can't you forgive me for a certain fascination with Aetherials? I absorbed it from my father, who told me about an ancient race of shining demon-angels who walk in other worlds and gave rise to a thousand myths. I've hardly kept my background secret; even Rosie knows."

Rosie put in, "You told me your mother was a Brazilian maid, your father a rich American who came back for you when your mother died. That's all."

"Ah, I never said he was American. Eugene Michael Barada was from a South African mining dynasty. Many years ago he bought some land in Ecuador, and when he went to explore he stumbled on a hidden valley in the rain forest." Sapphire smiled, remembering his tales. "He spoke of beings with hair like flame and cloaks or wings of orange fire, an alabaster man with raven hair, dark females who were somehow also lynxes with golden eyes, blue-green mermaids. Fever dreams, he thought. He followed these visions to the source of the creek, and saw them mining a red cleft in the rock. He was entranced.

"The next he knew, the pale one with raven hair was pointing a rifle at him. Lawrence. He called Barada a trespasser, a thief. He wanted to know how he'd found this secret place. My father quite reasonably pointed out that since he was the legal owner of the land, the mine belonged to him and Lawrence was the trespasser.

"That was how the feud began, but Lawrence never understood that Barada's obsession was about more than ownership. It was because he'd fallen in love with the idea of these secret beings."

She paused, allowing herself to glance at their faces. Satisfyingly, they appeared spellbound. "He wove such a tapestry for me of Aetherials—and this was a tough white South African without a fey bone in his body. I know he was arrogant. If he couldn't get his own way, he hung on like a bull terrier—he and Lawrence are very alike in that. He loved and hated Aetherials, and he worshipped and envied them. All the years the feud continued, he visited and wrote to me. Then, seventeen years ago, the letters stopped. I knew he was dead. I knew Lawrence had killed him."

"Have you any proof?" asked Auberon.

She laughed dryly. "He admitted it three days ago."

"And it's tormented him," said Sam. "If you knew him, you should have realized that."

"What do I care for his torment?" Sapphire lashed back. "That was my father he shot dead! Others only saw the bully, but to me Barada was a wonderful man. How many others would come back for an illegitimate daughter, like a big, sunburned guardian angel? He took me to New York and I left my old self behind like a shed skin. When I was old enough, he took me to England and Europe. I changed. I became a chameleon. I could pass for Brazilian, American, English—but the one thing we could not be, the only thing that mattered to him, was Aetherial.

"He would take me to Lawrence's store in New York to see the albinite jewels glittering on black velvet. I was the archetypal child outside a sweet-shop window. He promised me that one day it would be ours; in turn, I promised that if anything happened to him, I'd continue the fight. In time, I took a job there; sales girl, manager, marketing director. I don't know that I had a plan, until my father disappeared. I simply made myself indispensable to Lawrence.

I didn't lie to him about my father's identity; Lawrence wasn't interested enough to ask."

Jessica was frowning. "So you married him . . . to take revenge?"

"More than that. To fulfill my father's dream. To understand the obsession that had taken him from me. To possess the Elfstone mine that was rightfully his. I know I did wrong to deceive Lawrence, but I acted out of love and passion. Lawrence only ever acts from cold, selfish arrogance."

At that, she could sense their sympathy swaying towards her; all except Sam. "So you planned to take Lawrence for everything, yet still consider yourself the injured party?" he said. "Tell me I was wrong to leave him a little photo of you with your daddy."

"I couldn't keep up the pretense forever. But you must understand that when Lawrence destroyed my father, he destroyed my world."

Jessica asked, "Did you love him? Lawrence, I mean."

She laughed. "I began to, stupidly—until he killed my feelings, as he'd killed my father. He's more than adequate in bed—as you'd know." Jessica flushed red, to Sapphire's satisfaction. "When we first became lovers, he couldn't get enough of me . . . but I never guessed he'd turn cold so quickly. I didn't realize he was mad. Some naive part of me thought I might forgive, and save him. *He* thought I could save him. But no one can."

"No," Jess murmured, bowing her head.

"He carries such guilt, such nightmares. When he realized that a shiny new wife couldn't redeem him, it hit him hard. He blamed me. Only what I deserved, but strangely, it still hurt. He has no heart—only a sucking hole in his chest. He wanted a meek human wife who'd mother his sons to stop him feeling guilty. Instead, he got me. I guess we were both disappointed."

"What will you do?" Phyllida asked in genuine concern.

"Survive, as always," Sapphire answered, with a small thrill of triumph to see that she had won over Phyll and Comyn, at least. "I leave Lawrence as I arrived; with nothing."

She smiled into Sam's hostile blue eyes. "Do you think your father so honorable? I told him I'd take the mine and everything he had in the divorce settlement. He laughed and replied that he had never divorced Virginia. Think what you like of me; even I couldn't compete at that level of cynical deception. I should take him to court for bigamy, perhaps? He knew all the time that we were never truly married."

Rosie sat on her bed, her chin resting on her drawn-up knees, one thumb pressed between her teeth. She couldn't relax. Their visit to Lucas this afternoon had disturbed her. Outside, torrents of icy rain were eroding the snow.

Phyllida had taken Sapphire to stay at the farm and Jon had gone with them, despite Sam's attempts to persuade him otherwise. Then Sam had returned in haste to Stonegate, to talk to Lawrence. *Or,* Rosie wondered, *to avoid talking to me?* He had looked so good, all in black with the leather jacket he'd worn the day of her wedding, and she'd caught him glancing at her constantly . . . but he'd left, with hardly a word to her.

She felt him drifting away. *I know we behaved disgracefully,* she thought. *It's awkward for everyone if he hangs around. If he goes, we can heal and move on. All of that may be true and so what? I don't care. I just want his arms around me.*

She checked her watch. It was nearly midnight and everyone else was in bed. Several times this evening she'd selected Sam's number on her mobile phone, only to stare at it. Now the phone lay like a hand grenade beside her. Her heart began to accelerate and her nerve almost failed. At last she snatched it up, dialed, heard Sam's soft voice at the other end, "Hi, Rosie."

"Erm," she began, trying to sound casual, "are you at Stonegate?"

"Yes, still here."

"Have you spoken to your father?"

"Not as such." He sounded preoccupied. "He's gone into

shoot-the-messenger mode; shut himself in the library and won't talk."

"Do you regret making Sapphire tell him?"

"Not for a moment. I'm only sorry it hurt my father and Jon. As for her performance, that deserved a bloody Oscar, that did. Sorry about it happening in your front room. You okay, Foxy?"

"Fine." She swallowed. "It's only that I can't sleep. I'm concerned about Lucas—he's doing well physically, but he's not himself. I think the shock of the accident has hit him. I know he's safe but I can't stop worrying. So much has happened . . . I don't want to be on my own. Can you . . . come round? Only for tonight, then I'll be fine."

There was a silence she couldn't interpret. When he answered, he sounded impersonal and quite unlike himself. "I don't—don't think it would be such a good idea, Rosie. You've got people in the house, haven't you? It's them you need, not me. It wouldn't be right. Your parents wouldn't want me there." He was letting her down gently but firmly. "Try to sleep. I'll call you tomorrow."

"Oh," she said faintly. "Okay, yeah, you're right. I'll try. Night."

She dropped the phone and sat motionless, deflated. For ten minutes she hardly moved. If she let herself breathe she would start crying and she couldn't, wouldn't, give in to self-pity. Then her feet began to tingle and a rush of anger surged through her, almost lifting her off the bed.

She snatched up the phone and redialed, stabbing the buttons. "Sam, don't give me any more crap," she growled. "Get your ass over here *now*!"

His voice came back sounding quite different; shaky with exertion and cold. "Well, can you come down and unlock your back door? It's absolutely bloody freezing out here."

She saw his face pressed white against the glass, and as she opened the door he spilled through the gap in a surge of cold wind and rain. They grabbed each other and held on. Her head was in his shoulder, his cheek on her hair.

Then they separated enough to gaze at each other, breathing hard. He held her face between his hands and kissed her.

"Sam," she gasped, surfacing. "You ran down the hill . . ."

"I've been trying so hard to keep away from you," he said. "I can't. I missed you like hell."

"Me too, it's been killing me. Come up to my room."

"Are you sure?"

"Yes. Take off your wet boots. There's a bottle of wine up there, and TV—we can watch a film. I don't want to be on my own."

"If it won't upset your folks. Whatever you want, love. If you just want company, that's fine."

"Yes. No. I don't know. We need to talk." She grabbed his hand and pulled him with her. "Come on."

Entering her bedroom, Sam looked around, taking in the pale cream and dark oak of the room, the framed Waterhouse prints, all softly gilded by lamplight. "Rosie Fox's bedroom," he breathed. "The bedroom of Foxy Rose."

She lit a joss stick, found a DVD and switched on the small television that sat on a chest of drawers. "Is it how you imagined?"

"I thought it would be flame-red satin and crimson roses," he said, removing his jacket. Underneath he had a burgundy shirt open over a black T-shirt. "Can't think why. I was right about the Pre-Raphaelites, though."

"You fantasized about it, did you?" She was amused. "I bet you've spent hours fantasizing about my bedroom and what you'd like to do in it. You pervert!"

"Man's got to have a hobby." Sam threw himself headlong on the bed, turned onto his back and stretched out on the creamy satin. "It's lovely. Warm and welcoming. Perfect place to . . . watch a film."

They made a nest of pillows against the headboard and sat with their arms around each other, trying to concentrate on a quirky gothic animation. And it was all right. The horror began to fold away into the past. They were at ease, difficult conversations swept aside and the future suspended, at least for one night. Rosie told herself that the night would be platonic, even though it was all too easy to kiss and touch as they watched the film.

"So, what's with Lucas?" he asked after a while.

"He's out of bed and walking around," said Rosie, "but he's really moody. Doesn't want to smile or talk. Even mentioning coming home doesn't cheer him up."

Her mouth soured with tears as she spoke. Sam kissed and stroked her hair. "Don't get upset. I think I know what's wrong with him."

"Really?"

"Apparently he and Jon had an argument. Jon's really cut up about it."

"Oh, great," Rosie sighed. "Why didn't he say? It's not like him at all."

"Hey, give him time. It could take him months to recover properly. When Aetherials start thinking they're superhuman, that's when problems start."

Rosie relaxed against him, her head in the hollow of his shoulder. They drank red wine and talked idly about Luc, Matthew, Ginny. When the film ended, they were still wide awake, her hand resting lightly on Sam's forearm. As he reached for the remote to find another channel, the sensation of muscle hardening under her fingertips was amazing. She walked her fingers to his upper arm and said, "Tense your arm."

Sam obliged. "Like this?"

"Oh," she said, running her hand over the contours. The silkiness of skin over taut biceps was sensual beyond belief. She let her palm slide downwards over his chest and abdomen. "Now your legs, please."

He tensed, grinning. The strength of his thighs, even through jeans, made her lose control. She took both hands to one leg, moved down to press her cheek to the firmness. Gently she bit him, not to hurt, only to feel the vigor of his thigh through her teeth and tongue. Sam started laughing. "Are you enjoying yourself?"

"Oh, god, I'd forgotten how nice you feel," she gasped,

pushing hair out of her face. "Well, not forgotten, but not appreciated all this lovely . . . firmness."

"Plenty more where that came from." His voice was unsteady, his interest becoming obvious. It was an impossible temptation. She traced the swelling fabric with her fingertip, heard him catch his breath.

Caressing her hair, he drew her up and they began to kiss, gentle yet hungry. After a minute, he pulled back and whispered, "Don't do this if you're going to feel bad about it in the morning. Let's stop while we still can."

That sobered her and she drew away. "Sam, will you really leave? I don't want to keep you from your new career, but . . ."

She felt his breath warm on her scalp as he sighed. "Think what it's going to be like if I stay, love. 'There's that no-hope son of Lawrence Wilder, that convicted killer who broke up Rosie's marriage, caused all that grief—what's a nice girl like her doing with *him*?' I don't care about myself, Rosie, but imagine how it's going to feel, all the bitching and backbiting."

"I don't care what people think," she said heatedly. "That's not who you are. You're a man with a good heart who made a couple of mistakes. You show me one person in this village who hasn't screwed up in their time! They've no business condemning us. Unless . . ." She trailed off. "Sam, are you using this as an excuse to run?"

"No, it's the last thing I want!"

"Because if you are, be honest. If you're bored and want out, just go. Don't make a production of it. I'll get over you."

He stared at her, floored. "Rosie, you're the love of my life. What have I done to make you think otherwise?"

"Then think what it's going to be like when we meet again, which we're bound to do." She spoke softly, stroking his chest. "We might be with other lovers by then. But we'd still be looking at each other and remembering . . . maybe stealing a touch here, a kiss there . . ." She felt Sam stiffen and draw breath, picturing it. "Next, we'd be sneaking off together. Devouring each other in dark corners. We could hurt other people all over again. And whatever we did, we'd be hurting ourselves."

His arms grew tight around her. In a low voice he said, "The bottom line is, I can't stay with someone who's ashamed of me."

Rosie gasped, pulling back to stare at him. "I'm not ashamed of you, Sam. I love you."

The admission startled her as much as it did him.

"No, you don't," he said by reflex. Then, less certainly, "Do you?"

"Yes, I do. I wouldn't say it in a million years if I didn't mean it."

"Oh, my god." He laughed in wonder, held her so tight she couldn't breathe. His simple, overwhelming joy made her start crying. "For how long?"

"It started when you were in prison, I think. Despite the X-ray eyes and inappropriate suggestions. Or because of. Much longer than you think, anyway."

"Bloody hell, why didn't you say?"

"I couldn't get the words out. I thought they might be the incantation that makes it all vanish in a puff of smoke." He wiped tears from her cheek with his thumb as she spoke. "I was in denial. I wasn't supposed to be having feelings for you, so I pretended I wasn't. Then I didn't know if I could trust you. Still less, trust myself. I've screwed up so much by following the wrong instincts. Then it was never the right moment. I was afraid you wouldn't believe me, and hey—you didn't."

"No—I do—it takes a while to sink through my dense skull, that's all."

"Do you still love me?"

"Always. That never changes." He kissed her mouth. "I love you, Rosie."

"So if we haven't officially split up, we must be officially together."

"I like your logic."

"You can't lavish me with all this pleasure, then leave," she said. "That's got to be illegal."

"So it should be," he agreed. "Tell me again."

"I love you, Sam," she said, laughing and crying. "You must have noticed."

"There were clues. I daren't believe it. I don't deserve it."

"It's not about deserving it, but still, I am proud of you. Coming to the Abyss with me . . . Until then, I always suspected you were only chasing me for the excitement."

"Oh, that was desperation, love. Even with the risk that I was always going to be second-best to Jon, I had to give it my best shot."

She fixed him with a firm look. "You can put that idea out of your head. What I thought I could have with Jon—it was my own fantasy. It wasn't real."

"Yeah, well, you'd've made a beautiful couple but he was too stupid to realize it. His loss is my gain."

"I'm over him, Sam. I promise. I hated him for a while, but not anymore. Take a guy who stares into the distance when you talk to him and makes you feel about as sexy as cardboard, and then take a man who treats you like the center of the universe, can't take his eyes off you, makes you dissolve into a molten puddle every time he touches you—oh, which one am I going to fall for? Mm, that takes some working out."

He grinned, lifting her so that she lay along the length of his body. "Ha, my evil plan worked."

"You play a long game, Sam." She licked and bit his neck.

"And what isn't sexy about a cardboard Rosie? You haven't seen the life-size cutout in my bedroom."

"Shut up, for heaven's sake. Shh."

Slowly and gently their clothes came off. Then there was silken flesh to be worshipped, all the more ravishing for being familiar now. An infinity of kisses to bestow with lips and delicate tongues.

Time ran slow, like syrup. Rosie had to taste and kiss him all over, exploring every inch of his body. Sam let her have her way, lying with arms flung back and eyes closed in rapture like a naked god. No need to rush. Dreamlike, they flowed together and she found herself sitting across his thighs with her head thrown back while his lips feathered all over her neck and rose-tipped breasts. She pressed herself to his hard warmth, which was hot with the joy of life, demanding yet infinitely giving. All for her. The earthy musk of pleasure enfolded them like incense.

Time ceased, holding them in a sphere of honey light. Now they stretched along the bed together, Rosie falling back, Sam rising over her. She gripped the wonderful lean strength of his arms. She felt him filling her and cried out with bliss. It was raw and animal, transcendent. They would be here forever, in this altered state, a flow of perfect, tender ecstasy . . .

Until they collapsed in a hot tangled mess, gasping. They lay unable to speak. Only staring astonished into each other's eyes.

Finally, they lay back on the pillows, arms around each other. The television still babbled meaninglessly in the background. Rosie found the remote and flicked it off. Sam kissed her again, his lips and tongue warm between hers, as if they hadn't kissed enough. She felt ineffable fires dancing all through her and knew that they were both transformed. They'd entered a different realm, somewhere golden and soul-changing, and there was no coming back.

They slept at last.

She woke once near dawn, slipped to the bathroom, came back and smiled in wonder to see Sam there, so beautiful and serene, like an angel asleep in her bed. She sat and watched him for a while.

It wasn't that my instincts were ever wrong, she thought. *The trouble was that I went against them. Always knew Jon didn't want me, marriage would be a disaster, but I didn't listen. This time . . . I have to trust my heart. Take a risk. Jump.*

When she woke again, it was eight o'clock and daylight was glowing behind the curtains. Sam was leaning on one elbow, looking sweetly at her. His face was almost luminous against the light, eyebrows dark against the paleness, the blond tips of his hair sticking up in a delightful mess.

"Morning, beautiful," he said languidly. "Didn't dream it, did I?"

Rosie knew what he meant. "No, honey. I love you."

She stroked his cheek and he pushed into her palm, like a cat. "Will your parents go crazy that I'm here?"

"Of course not," she sighed. "They like you. We'll explain, and they'll be fine. Stay. Just stay with us for a while."

He dropped his head. His forehead touched the curve of her shoulder. "Oh, that's tempting. I love it here. Stonegate's cold and hard so I grew up cold and hard to cope with it. But I'm not, inside."

"I know that, Sam."

"I've been a rotten boyfriend. I'll try to behave like a civilized being in future. I can do it."

"No more rough sex in alleys?" She pouted.

"Well . . ." He leaned in to kiss the cushion of her lower lip. "I don't think we'll get too comfortable, do you?"

"No," she said thoughtfully. "You being such a mischief-maker."

His mouth curved. "And you, a colossal fetishist."

"Oh, you've seen nothing yet."

"Is that right?" He grinned, his hand shaping her waist and hip. She moaned as he took the hand from her, reaching out to take an object from the bedside table. "Hey, what's this?"

It was the rose quartz egg. "Oh, I found it in my pocket when we came back from the Spiral," she said. "A gift from Estel? I don't know. It opens, look . . ." She found the invisible crack that ran around the egg, twisted off the top half to show him a tablet of whitish, translucent stone within.

"In exchange for your crystal heart?" Sam took out the white stone and it turned to amethyst at his touch. Spirals and other symbols caught the light in flashes of blue and green. "Albinite," he said. "More a primitive cut than the sparkly stuff my father produces. Still worth a bit, though."

The color vanished from the gem as he put it back. Rosie

replaced the top hemisphere, making the egg a seamless whole again. "Worth fighting and killing for?"

"I always guessed Lawrence had killed Barada." Sam lay back with his arms around her. "And you know the ghost-corpse-illusion thing that attacked us in Naamon? It was him. That's how I recognized him in the photo."

"God, it was so real," she whispered.

"Sapphire made him out a victim, neglecting to mention that Barada was bringing groups of armed men against my father on a regular basis. It was nasty. I think one day Lawrence had had enough. He didn't want to harm Barada; I reckon he enjoyed the conflict, the mind games. But he reached the end of his tether."

"Is it why he's so reclusive? Guilt?"

"Or because he couldn't move on. Dad convinced himself that when Barada died, he went into the Spiral and joined forces with the shadowy demon, Brawth. I think he *knew,* rationally, that it wasn't the case and Barada was simply dead—but the paranoid part of him insisted otherwise."

"Brawth—the shadow of Qesoth," said Rosie. "First beings? Creation myth? God, that's scary."

"He deduced, wrongly or not, that Brawth had sent Barada in the first place. So now he finds Sapphire's another offshoot, infiltrating his home, seducing his son—bound to feed the paranoia, isn't it? He lost the plot years ago, love. Wish I knew what to do. I should go back and check that he's okay."

"Phone him."

"If he answers. No, I need to have a proper talk to him about Ginny and everything." He stroked her cheek. "Rosie, I'd better not stay again tonight. One night might be excusable, but two looks as if I think I've moved in."

"I know." She sighed. "Will you stay at Stonegate?"

"No, can't face it anymore. I've fixed to stay with college mates in Ashvale. Just for a while."

"And I've got a house standing empty, but I can't go back. It never felt like my home. Now it only makes me think of him." *Alastair.*

"Maybe you and I could . . . no, too soon."

She turned towards him, her hands resting on his chest. "This feels so strange—standing at the crossroads—I feel I know you inside out but I can't rush anything—not until I've put some distance between myself and the awful marriage. I'd drown, Sam."

"I know, sweetie," he said gently. "D'you think I want to ruin this when we've come so far? We'll take it slowly."

"I'll stay at Oakholme, at least until Lucas has recovered."

"That's the Holy Grail, isn't it?" said Sam. "Bringing Lucas home. Then I'll know you're a happy Fox."

The taxi pulled away, leaving Lucas alone on the sweep of the drive, gazing up at the walls of Stonegate Manor. He couldn't stop shivering. He'd grown used to hospital heat and now the raw cold pierced him, and the house looked as welcoming as a cliff face. It was eight o'clock in the morning and no doubt his family was still warm in bed, not dreaming that he was anywhere but safe on the ward.

He lifted the heavy iron knocker and tapped, hearing the sound boom inside the hall. No one came. Melting snow dripped off the porch roof onto him. The sky was raggedly grey, and just down the hill was his cozy home . . . but he couldn't go back. Even Rosie, even Auberon couldn't help him.

He hugged himself, trying to find warmth in his thin black trench coat. Despair had driven him from the hospital. He'd been too restless to stay, couldn't stop thinking about the Lychgate and what might happen if it stayed open. He knocked again, the iron freezing his fingers, then stepped back to look up at the fortress windows.

Just as he gave up hope, the door opened. Lawrence stood there, his face chalk against the soot of his hair and his eyes winter-grey under dark brows. There was no hint of warmth in his expression, or even recognition. Lucas quailed. "What do you want?"

"Lawrence—Father—you have to help me."

"Jon isn't here. Everyone has gone." His fingers tightened on the edge of the door. "When were you discharged from hospital? I want no one here."

Lucas stared at him, confused. He was too cold, too desperate to care what this meant. "But it's you I need to see. Please."

"Why?" The word was a dark whisper from the Abyss.

"Because I opened the Lychgate . . . I think the powers of the Gatekeeper have passed to me and I don't know what to do. There's absolutely no one I can turn to, except you."

Lawrence was motionless but for the changing expression of his eyes. Ravenous light flamed in them. A bone-white hand came out and seized his shoulder. "Show me."

Snow patched the ground and Lucas's boots were water-logged. Breathless from the march uphill, he delivered his stumbling explanation as Lawrence hurried him through the half-wild garden and naked woodlands to Freya's Crown.

The pleated rock stood bleak against the sky. It looked impervious, but when he shifted into the Dusklands he saw the split in the rock face. Cold wind abraded his throat. Lawrence stopped short, roughly catching Luc's arm to halt him.

"I see it now. Why didn't I see or sense it before? Are my perceptions so utterly ruined?" His face was grim, set solid with anger and dread. His mood alarmed Luc more than the open Lychgate. "How did I miss it? *How?*"

"I don't know." Lucas felt six years old, on the brink of tears. "I told you, it was by accident. I imagined it in a vision, and . . ."

"No one saw fit to tell me. Not even Sam."

"They're all frightened of you."

"And they are all blind fools!" The eyes were glinting razors. "Frightened of me, when all I've ever done is protect them? Are you sure *nothing* came through?"

It was the tenth time he'd asked. Lucas shook his head.

In hospital he'd felt fine, but outside he realized how weak, unfit and bruised he actually was. "Only the cold."

"Close it."

"I don't know how."

"It's the simplest thing—" Lawrence huffed in exasperation. He gripped Luc's shoulders and aimed him at the rocks. "Stay in the Dusklands as you approach. You'll find a spiral engraved on the right . . . there, at shoulder height . . ."

Lucas went to the mass of rock, noticing how it glimmered against the indigo Dusklands. As his hand found the symbol, silver light spilled under his palm. Suddenly it became obvious; simply turn it counterclockwise, feeling bright energy sing through his hand and his whole body. There was a sigh, a shiver of light inside him. The crack in the rock was gone. Only a faint quartz shimmer marked the seam.

He stepped backwards into the surface world, dizzy. His palm burned.

"You see, it's easy," said Lawrence. A visible shudder of relief went through him and he nearly smiled. "I should have guessed it would pass to you. I knew you were born for a reason. Come back to the house. You're cold. Surely the doctors have let you out too soon?"

"No," Lucas murmured. "Aetherials heal fast. I'm fine."

"Well." Lawrence slipped an arm around his shoulders and guided him down the hill, suddenly talkative. "The lych-light passes down the House of Sibeyla in a traditional line of responsibility, but not strictly from parent to child. It came to me from my grandmother Liliana and now, obviously, since I've been unwilling to use it, it has passed to you."

"Why me?" Lucas spoke faintly, stunned. "Why not Sam or Jon?"

Lawrence exhaled. "Too flawed by an insufficient upbringing, I fear. Too corrupted by the surface world. It takes a soul that is close to the Spiral."

"But I don't want it," Luc said anxiously. Alone with

Lawrence, the woodlands seemed unutterably eerie. "It's your power, not mine. I didn't steal it, sir, I swear."

"I know you didn't." The arm tightened around him. "The lych-light is taken or bestowed by the Spiral Court. And they've transferred it, apparently, because even they don't understand the threat. You think I barred the Gates to be difficult?"

"No. I never did."

"Then will you trust me?"

"Yes, I . . . I need you to teach me. I'm in the dark and scared to death. I don't want to go home. They'll wrap me in cotton wool and talk about the 'future,' but it's meaningless and I can't face it. All I can think about is the Gates. Can I stay with you . . . Father? For a few days?"

Lawrence was smiling, his teeth white in the winter gloom. "Yes, you must stay with me." Stonegate rose above them as they came down the last sweep of the estate. Shadowy *dysir* came out to welcome them. "It will be just you and me, Lucas, my one true son."

22

Persephone's Chamber

"What do you mean, he's discharged himself?"

Auberon paced around the kitchen, phone in one hand, the other dancing on the air to hush Jessica's insistent questions. "Yes, obviously he's got the right to do that, but . . . he wouldn't, without telling us . . . Obviously against your advice . . . Well, where's he gone? No, of course he's not here, or I wouldn't be asking, would I?"

Rosie and her mother exchanged glances. By the time

Auberon ended the call, they knew the essence; Lucas had signed himself out of hospital early that morning and apparently taken a taxi.

"Why didn't they let us know?" Jessica exclaimed.

Auberon stood shaking his head. "They assumed he was coming home. So now they phone to suggest we take him back in, and it's the first we've heard of it!"

"Didn't they try to stop him?"

"Of course, but he wasn't a prisoner. He signed a disclaimer that he left against medical advice, and that was that."

Rosie remembered how moody Lucas had been the previous day. Sam's presence and graceful apology this morning had earned no more from Auberon than a caustic remark, "I see the period of reflection lasted as long as the snow did." After that, her parents had been fine with him. Then, about an hour ago, he'd headed to Stonegate to see his father. When the doorbell sounded, she rushed to answer it, hoping it would be Lucas safe on the step with a damned convincing explanation.

Instead, Sam was there, holding a bouquet of crimson roses. In his black leather jacket he looked luminously sexy. "You're back," she said. "Are these for me?"

"No, they're for Matt," he said dryly. "Of course they're for you, Foxy Rose."

She took the roses from him, put her face among them and inhaled their delicate, dewy fragrance. "They're gorgeous. Thank you. Wow, they smell amazing." She kept her face there for a few seconds to hide the fact that this simple gesture had made her cry. Sam looked pleased and a touch embarrassed.

"Hoped you'd like them," he said softly. "Dark red and passionate, like you. By the way, what on earth is Lucas doing at Stonegate?"

Her head jerked up. "He's where?"

"I couldn't get in. Lawrence had bolted the doors from the inside, which is odd, considering he's usually pretty careless about security. So I'm on the front drive, shouting at him to let me in, and the next I know, an upstairs window opens and my bag comes hurtling out and lands on the drive beside me. Dad repeats that he won't see or speak to anyone. I start arguing but the window slams shut. And then—in the next window along, I see another face behind the glass. It's Lucas."

"Are you sure?"

"Positive. I called to him, but he only moved away from the window and vanished. Is he supposed to be out of hospital?"

Rosie and Sam stood with Jessica and Auberon, looking up at the walls of Stonegate. They'd tried phoning, but there had been no answer.

"D'you want me to break in?" Sam offered.

"No, no." Jessica shook her head. "That seems drastic."

"Well, we're not going until we've seen him," said Auberon, hands thrust in his overcoat pockets. They had rung the bell, pounded on the door, shouted Luc's name; nothing.

"Let me try," said Rosie. She slipped around the broad walls of the house into the back garden. The sloping lawn with its islands of rock and rhododendrons reminded her of the time she, Matthew and Luc had broken in. It had been like entering a castle of ice. The snow clung, here on the heights.

Rosie tapped gently and insistently at the kitchen door. Something moved inside. "Lucas?" she called. "Are you in there? It's me. Come on, speak to me."

To her surprise, the door opened a sliver and Lucas stood, looking gaunt and sheepish, in the gap. From the corner of her eye she saw Sam and her parents at the corner of the house. She waved them to keep their distance. "What?" he said.

Kid gloves, she thought. "Just making sure you're okay."

"I'm absolutely fine." His dark hair hung in his eyes. "Don't let Mum and Dad start on me. If you do, I'll shut the door."

"Don't," she said quickly. "They'll stay put, honestly. No

lecture about leaving hospital, either. I just want to know why you're here."

"Come on, Rosie." He folded his arms. The sleeves of his overlarge white shirt were rolled up and his long pale forearms bristled with goose bumps. "You understand about the Gates. No one can help me except Lawrence."

"Dad doesn't think you're safe with him."

"That's rubbish. He's my father."

"Did Lawrence invite you here?"

"No," Lucas sighed. "He wouldn't even let me in at first. I need to be with him for a while, that's all."

"He's not making you stay, then?"

"No, of course not! Look—I can walk out now if I want, but I don't."

Rosie longed to put her arms around him, as a prelude to dragging him physically out of the house. She restrained herself. "You look frozen and underfed. This is not the best way to convalesce. Why don't you come home and get warm? You can see Lawrence anytime."

His face set. He wouldn't meet her eyes. "Rosie, you may think I'm still thirteen, but I'm an adult. If I want to stay here, I will. Please. All I'm asking is to be left alone to make sense of things."

"For how long?"

"As long as it takes!"

She drew back. One more exchange and the conversation would deteriorate into begging and door-slamming. "Promise me that if you don't feel well, you'll make Lawrence call the doctor and call us, too."

"I promise. I'm all right."

"I'd better bring you some clothes. Anything else you'd like? Guitar?"

He looked startled. "Would you mind?" He lowered his voice. "If I come myself, Mum will be at me to stay and I can't face it."

"You know, if you want to be treated like an adult, you'll have to face difficulties like that eventually," she said aridly.

"Yeah." He lowered his head, hair flopping forwards.
"Give me a few days, Ro. I'm fine, really. I'll come home
when I'm ready. Just keep Mum and Dad away from me,
okay? I'm sorry." He raised one hand in a vague wave as he
closed the door. She heard bolts slide into place. Stepping
away, she went to her family.

"I take it you heard all that?" They nodded. Jessica was
pale. "He's right, we can't force him to leave. Let's go
home."

What is love, anyway? Rosie read in Faith's diary. *I know
Rosie doesn't love Alastair. He loves her, I think, but it's not
what she wanted. Yet she drifts along as if it's all she can
expect, making the best of it. I love Matthew but he doesn't
love me. It's all I ever dreamed of except for that one little
fact, he doesn't love me, and it's like walking through every
day with your feet hobbled and one hand tied behind your
back. It hurts so much you can't move properly but you still
have to pretend. Now Heather—she is love.*

*I wonder if my parents loved each other? No, their souls
were dead. They were part-Aetherial and didn't know it.
They would go into the Dusklands, even Dumannios, and
change into scaly demons and fight each other, without
even being aware! How is that possible? Could they have
become fully Aetherial if they hadn't lost themselves in the
human world and killed their own souls with drink and
bitterness? When I think about them I want to cry and cry.
I don't want Matthew and me to be like that but I see it
happening.*

Rosie flipped the pages to an earlier entry.

*Had a lucky escape tonight. M. walked in while I was
bathing Heather. The bubbles were almost gone and she
was green in the water, pale green, shimmery like a butterfly wing. Suddenly he appeared, and I thought he must
see her—she was sitting in plain view. I panicked and
threw a towel over her, only I was clumsy and it landed on
her head. He stared at me and said, "What on earth are
you doing?" and I said, "She has soap in her eyes," and I*

couldn't believe he didn't see anything because her tummy was clearly visible—but he didn't. He only shook his head and walked out. And then I was furious because she is so beautiful and he couldn't see it and I couldn't share it with him. And Heather kept asking why I was crying.

Rosie bit the end of her thumb. Faith's sadness pervaded every line. She felt guilty reading it but couldn't stop. *Had a lovely talk with Jessica today,* said a typical entry. *She is so nice. If it wasn't for her, I would probably just go.*

What does it mean, that I'm not human? I thought I felt human, but maybe I don't, because this is all I've ever known. Realizing you're Aetherial shouldn't mean being ashamed and trying to hide it from the one person who should understand. Never mind M—what does it mean to me? I see images of silver-blue lakes that go on forever. I swim and swim. There are marvellous underwater caves. When I climb out on the far shore, I see—oh, it's so clear—

The kitchen door opened. Rosie looked up from the diary and saw her mother standing there disconsolate. She was wearing a khaki walking jacket and her hair was tangled from wind and rain. "Mum?" she said, hardly needing to ask. "What's up?"

Jessica stirred, shouldering off the damp jacket. "I've been up to Stonegate."

"Oh, Mum." Rosie hung the garment on a chair and hugged her. It was painful to see the shadows around her eyes. "We talked about this."

"I didn't try to see Luc," Jess said stiffly. "I went to Freya's Crown. I meant to go and find Faith. To see she's all right and bring her back. Only the Lychgate's closed." She held up an unfastened bracelet of white gold and albinite, which sparkled faintly purple in response to her. "I was looking for the flash of green that indicates an open portal. Nothing."

"Oh, my god. You shouldn't have gone on your own!"

"Well, it's academic now. There's a sort of silver freckling where it was, but it's firmly shut again."

"Oh?" Rosie leaned against the table, arms folded. "Would it close without help?"

"No. Either Lawrence has done it, or he's forced Luc to. Faith's trapped. I miss her so much."

"So do I," said Rosie. Fear crept through her, a feeling she'd been trying to deny because she'd already had enough. Faith beyond reach—that was unthinkable, but what did Lawrence care? Jessica's face held a bleak, angry look Rosie had never seen before. "My biggest fear was always that Lawrence would get his claws into Lucas, and now he has. I'm close to thinking that Phyll and Comyn are right. There's nothing to do with Lawrence but bring him down."

Rosie stood before the Crone Oak and looked up into the naked branches. Winter was fading, snowdrops shining, daffodil shoots pushing up. It was the first time she'd brought herself to visit the site. The debris was long since cleared, but evidence of the crash was still apparent in tire marks on the road, newly sawn stumps shining white where fractured branches had been amputated. Glass fragments glinted on the tarmac.

People had left bunches of flowers. Most were from colleagues at Fox Homes. That floral shrine, more than anything, gave her a visceral shock. She hadn't expected the scene to affect her so badly, but a horrible, hot feeling crept over her and she could hardly breathe.

She wondered about the dryad who had insistently warned about blood. There was no whisper of her. "Greenlady?" Rosie spoke quietly. "You must have foreseen this. You asked me to prevent it, but I couldn't. I'm sorry."

Nothing stirred. The tree looked abandoned.

When spring came, Rosie began to create a garden. She'd started it some time ago in the neglected rose arbor where Oakholme bordered the Stonegate estate; the place where, years ago, she'd found Matthew hiding after he'd fought with Sam. Then she hadn't quite known what form the garden should take, but now it was clear. A restless spirit possessed her. Despite slaving all day at Fox Homes, she spent the remaining hours of daylight constructing this special, secret bower.

She designed a path that spiraled inwards and surfaced it with flakes of silvery slate. The curves were delineated by granite-edged beds that she filled with silver foliage and black flowers; tulips, pansies, iris, hyacinth; every variety she could find with near-black petals. Against the silver, they bloomed like waxy ebony brushed with the merest hint of purple.

The middle of her garden was slightly sunken, so it drew you down as it spiraled in. At the very center she placed an egg of black and grey polished marble, two feet in height. It was so heavy that she needed Sam's help to position it. For the past few weeks he'd been living with college friends in Ashvale, and she at Oakholme, but they saw each other every day. Often she would stay with him, but they were still treading very cautiously towards a future together. In front of her family, they downplayed their relationship and acted with tactful decorum. Somehow that made the private intensity between them stronger than ever, a spellbinding fire.

"What's this all about, anyway?" he asked.

"It's my ambition to design a garden for the Chelsea Flower Show," she answered. "This is my tryout."

"A spiral," said Sam. "I like it. Monochrome. Very contemporary."

"The secret, which you can't see until you walk it, is that where the path reaches the egg, it curls back on itself and brings you out again. Like death and rebirth."

"A garden about the Otherworld," Sam said, smiling. "I get it."

"Yes. A garden about the Spiral."

He gave her a candid look. "Other people write poems or paint pictures. My Foxy expresses herself in a medium that involves backbreaking hunks of rock."

"Thank goodness I've got you to massage my strained muscles." She slipped close to him, her arms folding around his waist. There was nothing sweeter than the radiant pleasure of holding each other, with no prison guards to stop them.

"Rosie, come away with me," he said softly in her ear.

"I'd love to, Sam, but I can't, not yet." She dug her fingers into his ribs. "How can you think of it?"

"Easy. I'd cheerfully walk away and leave them all to it. If we wait for everyone to get their lives into perfect shape, we could wait for bleeding eternity!" He sighed, rested his cheek on her hair. "Really, we have to stick around to the bitter end, don't we?"

What is love, anyway? Faith asked in her diary. Seated on the marble egg in the center of the spiral, Rosie pondered the question. The evenings were lengthening, the sun glimmering low to bathe her in cool golden light. She was finally beginning to grope towards an answer. Love wasn't one thing. It had many faces, many moods. It wasn't being infatuated with Jon's pretty face and flowing hair, that was for sure.

Alone, she sat and read the journal again, hoping her friend would forgive her. She realized that she'd never known Faith at all.

Matt thinks I'm a mouse. Even Rosie thinks it, albeit one to be loved and protected. They think I'm sad and fragile. That I only care about cooking, cleaning and mothering. If they knew what I really think about, they'd call me mad.

Rosie heard footsteps crunching behind her; someone taking a naughty shortcut across the beds. "It's beautiful," said Auberon. "Very unusual. I tried not to peek while you were working."

"I'm glad you like it. You're supposed to walk around, but I'll let you off."

"Walking a spiral is like treading a magical path," Auberon said dryly. "It invokes the Otherworld. I suppose you know that, or you wouldn't have built it."

"In that case, jumping over the flowerbeds is bound to annoy the Spiral Court," she retorted. "There's no causeway, it would have spoiled the lines."

"Quite." He perched himself on a small hunk of granite nearby, forearms resting on his knees. "It's very peaceful. Like a Zen garden."

Rosie opened the diary and said, "Dad, listen to this."

I see a city of gleaming black stone that shines with jewel-colors; crimson, royal purple and blue. I see labyrinthine passages and rooms where you can lose yourself for days, months.

Lofty pillars. Balconies onto a crystal-clear night full of stars, great sparkling white galaxies like flowers. Statues of winged men looking down with timeless eyes. I want to stand on those balconies and taste the breeze and hear the stars sing and be washed in the light of the moon. There will be ringed planets, and below—the tops of feathery trees blowing gently. An undiscovered land full of streams, with birch trees in spring green, and oak and hazel—and their elemental guardians, slender birch-white ladies with soft hazel brown hair—and mossy banks folding into water.

And through this citadel walk graceful men and women with lovely elongated faces and calm, knowing eyes—with a glint of mischief—and they are perfect and know it and they are imperfect and know it. They have seen too much. They might wear robes of medieval tapestry or jeans and a shirt but you would never mistake them for human. It's so much more than beauty. Look at them once and you can't look away. These are Aetherials in their oldest city, Tyrynaia.

They have been building the citadel for thousands of years and it will never be finished. Upwards it spreads, and outwards, and down into the rock below. Their seat of power. Their home.

They take the names of gods, on occasion.

And sometimes they are heroic and help the world.

And sometimes they are malicious and turn it upside down.

Some might be vampires. It's hard to tell.

In the deepest depths of the citadel, a ceiling of rock hangs over an underground lake and here is Persephone's chamber. She welcomes and cares for those who come,

*soul-sick with despair, seeking solace, rest and sleep.
Here they need not speak, only sit on the black marble lip
with their feet on the thick glass, and watch the lake and
the luminous fish beneath, which is like a reflection of the
sky far above. If you lie down in despair, Persephone will
lie down with you.*

Rosie stopped. "Can you believe that Faith could write
something like that?" she said.

Auberon shook his head. "How does she know about it?
That's the question."

"Is she talking about somewhere real?"

"There are said to be cities, Tyrynaia and Celadon . . .
What would the ancient Aetherials, the Estalyr, be without
a fabled city?" He looked down and tapped his foot, preoccupied.

"Dad, are you okay?"

"No, not really. I'm contemplating failure. I've always
tried to be the father figure who sorts out everyone's problems. Then you come to something you simply can't put
right, and it makes you admit you're as hopeless as anyone."

"Honestly," she said. "You're the least hopeless person I
know."

"Ah, it's all an act. I suspected for years that Matthew
had problems, but because he didn't ask for help, I thought
he was coping. Now, when I finally get to the root of it—I
realize I *can't* help him. No one actually can. I'm not om-
nipotent after all. Not that I ever thought I was, but you
know, one tries to maintain the illusion."

She smiled. "You've always been King of Elfland to Luc
and me."

"I thought I could tame Lawrence, but no. Couldn't even
keep Jess happy. Work took me over and I was too busy
building my little empire to remember that she had the
spirit of a wild Aetherial, and if I wasn't there, she would
run to the forests with someone like Lawrence, instead."

"She came back."

"Yes, she did. And never sang another note, as if to say,
look, I've clipped my own wings. I never wanted that. I

wouldn't be without Lucas for anything. She had no need to punish herself."

"You don't, either. We need our father, not Superman."

Auberon laughed softly. He leaned forward, bracing his hands on his thighs. "When Lawrence first locked the Gates, I was horrified and dismayed, as you'd expect of any pure-blood Aetherial. However, part of me was glad. I love the Earth, Rosie. My roots are deep in it. This guilty side of me thought that if Elysion were out of bounds, perhaps my wife and children wouldn't feel its pull, or vanish into the wilds of the Spiral. That's partly why I didn't fight Lawrence too hard."

"Partly?" Rosie watched her father intently. His eyes were dark under lowered lashes; a hint of sweat dewed the black curls of his beard. She held her breath as if the faintest sound might derail his confession.

"The initiation of a young Aetherial can be an ordeal. For as long as the Gates stayed shut, I thought I'd never have to worry about my children facing it."

"Dad, we know."

He gave a resigned laugh. "I was wrong to overprotect you, but I've seen how raw it can be. Lawrence . . . Although he was born in Sibeyla, his grandmother brought him to Earth quite young and that means, when you go back, the Aelyr will treat you like a Vaethyr initiate and brand you anyway. It's a small revenge on those who have the cheek to leave. His father Albin was particularly difficult about his leaving, I understand. Lawrence didn't actually have to come with me when my initiation fell due; but he did, because we were friends."

"Something bad happened?"

"That's the thing; it's so unpredictable. When it was my turn, yes, it hurt, and yes, it was terrifying, but I survived, obviously. What Lawrence saw, however, drove him mad."

"What was it?"

"I don't think he could explain, even to himself. He confronted whatever it is that has always haunted him. I came out of my own trance, there in the meadows of Elysion, and saw him. We were alone—the initiates are left to their own devices, as you know—and he was some way ahead of me, running blindly and tearing at his skin as he ran. I ran after him. He paused on the edge of a gully and I shouted, but he didn't hear. Then he threw himself over.

"When I reached him, he'd gone over a twenty-foot drop and landed on rocks in the edge of a river. There was blood. He was unconscious in the water. So I scrambled down and pulled him out, gave him the kiss of life, stopped the flow of blood from his side until he came back to himself."

"You saved his life."

Auberon sighed. "This one, anyway. And he was distraught. He raved about a shadow beast and said he couldn't live with it; why hadn't I let him die? What was I supposed to say to that? I reassured him it was only a vision—but initiatory visions can be a distorted picture of reality, which he knew full well. Anyway, he picked himself up and we went back and never spoke of it again."

"Ah," Rosie breathed. "So he's never forgiven you for saving his life, is that it?"

"Exactly." Auberon gave a sour smile. "I could never confront him or hate him—not when Comyn urged me, not even about Jessica—all because of that. I'd saved him. That made his life forever of special value to me, so that whatever he did, I could never hurt him back. As if, by that action, I'd signed up to safeguard him forever."

"Why didn't you tell us before?"

"Oh, it was always very personal, private. Apart from Jess, I told no one. Lawrence and I never spoke of it, but it was always there between us. Comyn accuses me of being too much of Earth, and he's right."

"I don't blame you for that." She frowned. "I love you for it."

"I've colluded in trying to keep you from your heritage, because I couldn't rise above being a protective father and treat you as independent adults."

"For all you did to prevent it, we got hunted down and

branded anyway. It happened to Lucas even before he opened the Lychgate. We survived."

Auberon lifted his hands. "And the plots and schemes of possessive old codgers are ultimately, utterly futile."

"Codger? You?" Rosie gasped. "I'll keep that to tease you with. But if Lawrence *had* died . . . if Luc had . . . you know what I'm trying to ask."

"It's said we can go on indefinitely, in one form or another. No return from the Abyss, they say—but we can't even be sure of that, since it's also the Source. The Mirror Pool, on the other hand, is about accepting transformation. Elysion may heal the physical body, but if that fails, we may revert to an elemental state for a few years or centuries. It's hard when someone close does that, because it's like touching a ghost; you have to accept that they aren't the same person, but in a state of transition."

"Like the Greenlady in the Crone Oak."

Auberon said quietly, "I didn't know you knew about her."

"She always used to leap out and utter dire warnings about the crash, which I didn't understand until it was too late. But she would be kind, too. She was strange and wonderful. And now she's gone."

Auberon let out a heavy sigh, his expression so dark she wondered what she'd said. "Rosie, the Greenlady—when she was in her human shape—she was my grandmother. I'm quite sure she would have known you were her great-granddaughter. And, in whatever distant way elementals are still capable of caring, that she cared about you."

After a time, when Rosie had let the knowledge sink in, she said, "And what now? Lawrence can't keep Lucas at Stonegate forever. It feels as if the world's holding its breath."

She felt her father's hand on her shoulder. "I also didn't fight Lawrence about the Gates because I always sensed that he is right. He has been protecting us from destruction."

"Luc and I saw something in the Abyss," Rosie whispered. She shivered, remembering. "It looked like a colossal statue, but it was more—like a living creature, petrified or frozen to black ice. I don't know. But I remember thinking, it only stays quiet while Lawrence is vigilant. And it looked at Lucas. Turned its head and stared right at him."

"Our imaginations spin solid realities in the Spiral." Auberon exhaled. "How useless were my schemes to shield you from all this. So if Lawrence is training Lucas in the same vigilance . . . that's understandable . . . but what kind of life is that for Luc? I wouldn't wish it on anyone. It needs to end, Rosie, but I don't know how."

The white walls of the farmhouse were covered by ivy and vines. Behind it stood a long modern barn like an industrial unit; in front was a glorious view of fields folding down into the valley of Cloudcroft, rising again on the far side to High Warrens. The farmyard to the side of the house was rutted with reeking green mud that clung to Sam's boots as he approached.

He was trying to remove the worst of it on a boot-scraper when Dr. Meadowcroft—he could never think of Rosie's aunt as Phyll—answered the door. "Jon's in the kitchen," she said briskly. "His turn to wash up; a little something to help earn his keep." She gave her friendly-but-formal smile. "I'll leave you to it."

Jon was leaning against a big oblong sink, lethargically drying plates on a red and white tea towel. He was dressed in his usual grunge style, and the strapping was off his leg and his wrist. Sam glanced around. The room was large, unpretentious and shabby, filled with the earthy smell of animals and damp coats. Cooking pots hung from a ceiling rack. There was a confidence about the place that made him feel strangely nostalgic.

"So, what's going on?" said Sam.

His brother jerked like a startled deer. "Nothing."

"Well, good." Sam raised his eyebrows. "I wasn't accusing you of anything. Just wondering how long you plan on hiding away here?"

Jon sighed, slinging the towel over his shoulder. "Got nowhere else to go, have I?"

"Where's the wicked stepmother?"

"Gone out. She lunches with friends so she can bitch about Father."

"I'm amazed she's still here at all." Sam jumped up to sit on a counter.

"I suppose she's waiting to see what she can get out of him. She's hired this solicitor . . . I'm sure she's screwing him."

"Jealous?" Sam said thinly.

"Hardly." Jon looked disgusted. "I told you, that's long over. I wish to god it had never happened. We've got rooms at opposite ends of the house—I'll show you if you don't believe me!"

"All right, don't have a fit. I believe you. Did you know Lucas is at Stonegate?"

"Mm." Jon became interested in putting cutlery away. "Yeah, I heard."

"You spoken to him?"

"No. He can call me if he wants."

"Aren't you even curious as to what he's doing there?"

"No," said Jon, tight-lipped. "He can fuck himself."

"I'm sure he will," said Sam. "There's nothing else to do at Stonegate."

A silence. Then Jon asked, "How about you? Still shagging Rosie?"

Sam smiled broadly. "Yes, thank you."

"I can't believe it. I thought her parents would drive you out of town with shotguns. I thought you and I might go on the run together."

"Her parents like me."

Jon laughed. "Did you hypnotize them?"

"Let's say I'm on probation."

"I'm pleased for you. Got your life all sorted out."

Sam exhaled. "You could too, if you put your mind to it. It's not bleeding quantum physics."

"You think it's that easy? Our mother couldn't leave fast enough, Father hates me, best friend turns on me, nutcase jealous husband tries to kill me—I thought Sapphire gave a damn, until I realized I'm only useful as a thing to torment Lawrence with. Yet that's all I've got left—her."

"You've got me." Sam was more sharp than sympathetic. "But you won't let anyone near you. Have you spoken to Father since you left?"

Jon frowned at him. "No. What am I supposed to say? 'Oops, sorry about doing unspeakable things with my stepmother—the very memory disgusts me, if that's any consolation?' I can never speak to him again, Sam. I can never be anything, or do anything, with Lawrence hanging over me like a death vulture."

Jon's hollow tone shocked Sam. "Don't talk about him like that. I think he's ill."

"He's not ill. He's plain evil."

"No. I think—if he knew about Mum—he'd see reason."

Jon threw knives into a drawer with some force. "The only way we're going to see our mother again is if we take Lucas away from Lawrence and make him reopen the Gates."

Sam groaned. "How? Burst in with a hand grenade? Don't be daft. You won't do anything, Jon; you never do. You're just angry. We need to be patient until Lawrence relents and starts talking. Shit, I sound like Auberon."

"You're still on Father's side, aren't you?"

"There are no sides." Sometimes, Sam thought, the temptation to slap Jon was practically irresistible. "I'm pretty furious with him, but still, if anyone attacked him, I'd defend him to the death."

Jon's eyelids fell. His mouth was grim, his body rigid. "Auberon never did a thing to help the Vaethyr. At least Comyn's heart is in the right place, even if he is like a bull at a gate."

"Anyway, just wanted to be sure you're all right," said Sam, jumping down off the counter. "I'll go. So you'll be here for a while, will you?"

"Looks like it." Jon shook his hair back and gave a defiant smile. "Give my love to Rosie."

"Sure." Sam pursed his lips. "D'you realize, this is the most work I've ever seen you do? You want to be careful. Comyn will have you outside feeding cows and shoveling shit next."

Sapphire liked the farmhouse. She appreciated its solid honesty. She'd spent a great deal of effort with new fittings and decor, trying to brighten Stonegate's atmosphere, but nothing had worked. Its chilly, sour nature always bled through, like a stain that could not be painted over. Phyll and Comyn's house might be plain, but it had no secrets.

Their kindness to her had restored her faith in Aetherial nature, to some extent. They'd taken her in because Lawrence had hurt her; they trusted her, and she appreciated that. They had little in common but hatred of Lawrence, yet it was a surprisingly strong and motivating bond.

Jon was in a bad mood at supper. Apparently Sam had visited, but Jon was tight-lipped.

Comyn had called a meeting that evening. Dissatisfied Aetherials were coming from other parts of the country, even from overseas. It was to be held late, in secret, as if they were rebels in a police state. Just before it was due to begin, the kitchen lightbulb blew. It seemed an omen. Phyllida made a fruitless search for a spare, voicing exasperation that she and Comyn might work all hours but surely *one* of them could remember to stock up on such a basic item? With visitors beginning to arrive, she set a monster of an oil lamp on the table instead.

Should Aetherials be slaving like humans, as doctors, farmers, builders? Sapphire wondered. Didn't they have the charisma and wealth to let others slave for them? Why did they do it? Even Lawrence, with a team of workers to command, was only truly happy shut in his workshop cutting gems with his own hands. Strange people.

Soon the oily glow lapped the faces of thirty Aetherials, leaving the corners of the room in shadow. Sapphire felt out of place. She was the only human here yet she'd won their trust because she wanted what they did: to destroy Lawrence. That knowledge gave her confidence. She could match their poise and purpose—and anything she couldn't match, she could certainly fake.

Jon, seated next to her, looked drawn and shaky. Comyn's eyes sparked like hot iron. Phyllida was unemotional and deathly serious.

The others, Sapphire barely knew. She remembered some from the ill-fated Christmas party long ago; they'd all been among the crowd that had heckled Lawrence. Flame-haired Peta Lyon and her sisters, the Tullivers, the Staggs and others. Lamplight drew out their otherworldly sheen, a mother-of-pearl glow. They wore no masks, yet she faintly perceived their animal affinities, which startled her. A feline tilt to an eyebrow, a bird-of-paradise flounce to the hair. Something of Stonegate, the energy of albinite perhaps, had penetrated her after all.

The table seated eight. The rest stood around in the shadows. Some stood behind her, which made her skin prickle.

Comyn folded his hands and sat in pointed silence for a minute. Then he said, "Most of you have been with me from the beginning. We welcome Sapphire since, in her commitment to our cause, she's proved a truer Aetherial than some I could name."

Sapphire felt a small glow of pride, but suppressed it. This was . . . a strange kind of treason. Like planning the assassination of Caesar. "Do you all understand that, from this moment, you cannot back out?" He continued, "We require your vow not to speak a word of this to those we can't trust, specifically Sam Wilder, any member of Auberon Fox's family, and Lawrence himself. If anyone objects, let them speak now." No one did. "It is an ancient ritual, not enacted for centuries. It will take Lawrence completely off guard, but he'll know precisely what it means. Every Vaethyr will know."

Phyllida said, "At Cloudcroft Show on the fifth of May there will be hundreds of people gathered in the village.

The Beast Parade, which Comyn and I have organized for years, will provide the perfect cover."

"Once it begins, it cannot be stopped," Comyn went on. "Others will be drawn into the wake, like a flood."

Phyllida added, "Every Vaethyr here has a dozen others who, although they won't be told our precise objective for security reasons, will be poised to join in."

"Lawrence must surrender," said Comyn. "He will have no choice. And Lucas will be in friendly hands again. According to Jon, he is the solution to this stalemate."

Jon seemed to glow pale in the spotlight of their attention. His shoulders were raised, his head bowed. "It's true. Luc is the new Gatekeeper."

"And you're certain you wish to take part?" Phyll asked carefully. "Lawrence is still your father. After this moment, you can't withdraw."

"I'm certain! I'm no longer his son." Jon spoke with animal fierceness. Sapphire imagined them all as a wolf pack, sighting their prey with moon-yellow eyes and focused intent. She quivered with grim excitement.

Comyn caught her gaze for a split second. "Now's the time for us to make our vows." He folded his weathered hands on the table. "Every person present will swear secrecy and fidelity. Not to breathe a word to any who would oppose us. To follow the ritual through to its bitter end. Any who betray their vow will face bitter punishment."

Phyllida had a pretty green-glazed rice bowl and a scalpel. With medical efficiency she went around the circle, making a small cut in each left wrist and catching the drops. Once the blood was mixed, Comyn rose and made the second circuit, dipping his thumb to paint each forehead with a smudged red spiral.

Sapphire felt sick as she submitted. The blood was cold and sticky. She wondered, *Does this make me one of them?* No going back now. It felt, irrationally, like a horrible betrayal. How much worse it felt for Jon, she couldn't imagine.

"I'll be the huntsman," said Comyn. "Who will be the hunted?"

"I will," said Jon.

"Oh—Jon dear, are you sure?" Sapphire said, before she could stop herself. She shouldn't have spoken. Of course it must be Jon.

He responded to her concern with a look of sullenly blazing anger. "Yes, who else but me?"

"He's your father," she said quietly. "It will be on your conscience for the rest of your life."

"Yes, and so it should be! Who should bring him down, but his own son? It's poetic justice," he said bitterly. "Who can do it, but me?"

23

The Tears of the Caged God

Lucas was frightened. It had taken him weeks to admit it to himself. Admitting it made it real.

Lawrence was teaching him, indeed; lessons in sheer terror of the Gates and what lay beyond. He instructed Lucas in every trick of opening Lychgates, half-gates, aligning portals within the labyrinth to enter any realm directly . . . but more than that, the arts of sealing, protecting, locking. Once the Great Gates were fully open, Lawrence told him, every portal on Earth would open along with them and nothing would hold Brawth back.

The teaching was all theory. Lucas wondered if he'd ever be allowed actually to touch the Gates. Lawrence seemed compelled to pour all his knowledge into him, at the same time warning him constantly against the dangers of putting theory into practice.

At these times, Lawrence would talk late into the night.

Luc had to bring him coffee and food, otherwise he would consume nothing but whiskey. They would usually sit in the library, with only a desk light to soften the cavernous gloom, and the tall net curtains shifting with every draft.

"I've often thought of the ice giant as a figment of my deranged mind," Lawrence told him. "But in the Spiral, dreams become real. I dreamed a mythical enemy, and woke it. Everything I have done is to protect my sons, especially you, from its wrath."

"I've seen it," Lucas told him, and described the great figure in the Abyss, the ice mist rolling off its mountainous flanks. When he reached the part where it had turned to look at him, Lawrence's face went grey.

"Brawth has seen you. Marked you. It knows you're my son. Thank the gods it didn't wake and pursue you. Your presence, and the open Lychgate, weren't enough to rouse it. I believe it will only wake in response to me. As long as it remains in stone form, we are safe."

"Estel said it had always been there," said Lucas. "Perhaps it really was just a statue, and I imagined it moving."

"Of course Brawth has always been there." Lawrence fixed him with glowing, ice-grey eyes; the pupils were pinpricks. "It is the shadow from the beginning and end of time."

At first Lucas had found these sessions thrilling. Lawrence was powerful; he seemed the lord of the universe, yet all of his precious attention was focused on Lucas, as if no one else in the world mattered. It was flattering. Initiation was bound to be hard but it meant he was special, chosen. A few weeks in, however, the gloss was wearing off. Instead, Lawrence's intensity became grueling and disturbing.

There were gentler moments, when Lawrence let him into the workshop behind his study where he cut albinite gems. Even there, his contemplation of individual jewels verged on obsessive. When Lucas asked about it, he received a long silence and a cryptic answer, "Someone once showed me a perfect stone that was rightfully mine, only to snatch it away from me. Ever since, even knowing I'll never find it, I keep on searching. Like a gambler forever placing his final bet. I cannot stop."

When Lawrence had talked himself to exhaustion, he would vanish to bed and Lucas would climb the stairs to Sapphire's zone. It felt friendlier than the rest of the house. There he would lie in bed, but he often couldn't sleep and would only stare at the ceiling, listening to the voice in the attic murmuring to itself.

Lawrence was always up before him. Often his mood was black, and he'd closet himself in his workshop, leaving Luc to his own devices. He explored halfheartedly or read books in the library. The shadowy *dysir* would pad around him; protecting or guarding him, he wasn't sure. He ordered groceries on the Internet, paid with Lawrence's credit card, and received them at the kitchen door. Each time Lucas looked at the outside world, he thought about simply walking away. And then he would close and lock the door again.

As spring came, he thought more often about leaving. Yet the more he considered, the less he seemed able to do it. Lawrence had flooded him with paralyzing terror. He felt he hadn't learned enough yet, was terrified of missing some vital secret. And, after all, he simply couldn't abandon his father. If he left, Lawrence would surely starve to death.

Still, the urge grew. He needed permission; that was it. One lunchtime, at the kitchen table, Lucas shredded a bread roll with trembling hands and announced that it was time he visited his family.

Lawrence froze. "I can't stop you," he said, "but I'd advise against it, Lucas. It's too dangerous."

"I won't go anywhere near the Gates."

The pallid face was heavy with disapproval. "It's not that. Don't you realize that our enemies are out there, itching to get their hands on you?"

"On me?"

"You understand the danger, but they don't. Comyn and his crew will force the Gates open at any price. Don't you realize that if you set foot outside, you are liable to be kidnapped?"

Lucas was shocked. "That sounds . . . dramatic. They wouldn't."

"Oh yes, they would. They'd stop at nothing. Our self-imposed exile here is no fun, but that's the sacrifice we make for keeping the Earth safe!" Lawrence went on, in soft-voiced anger, describing what horrors awaited Luc if he left.

"And what if something happens to you?" Lucas cried, jumping up. "What if the Court takes the power off me and gives it to someone else? What then? You can't keep the Gates closed forever!"

Lawrence shot to his feet, overturning the table. Dishes crashed and food spilled. "Don't speak of it! Don't you dare even suggest it!"

Lucas fled.

Later, when he'd stopped shaking and uncurled himself from the corner of his bed, he felt plain despair. There was no escape. He actually thought Lawrence might murder him sooner than let him go—but the hardest thing to bear was his disapproval. Again he heard the scratching and crying of the ghost in the attic. He growled, and threw a pillow at the ceiling.

Luc sat hopeless on the edge of the bed, staring at his feet. It wasn't the first time his father had lost his temper. Lawrence would right the table and clear up the mess; then, although he never apologized, everything would go on as before.

I'm as mad as him, thought Lucas. *I'll grow old in this place, I'll turn into a scratchy mad wraith like that thing in the attic . . .* "For fuck's sake, *shut up!*" he said out loud. It ignored him.

Despairing panic came over him. He craved escape, but the only place to hide was above. Perhaps he could jump off the roof. Numb, he went along the landing until he found the little door to the attic. He climbed the narrow stairs and felt for the light switch he remembered at the top.

Brownish light caressed the roof space. Old chests, boxes, fabrics; it appeared nothing had been touched since he was last here so many years ago. The oil painting of the collapsed angel stood facing him. The crouched figure with its trailing hands and hidden face made him sad. It was exactly how he felt. Fighting tears, he sat cross-legged in front of it. He felt safe here. Lawrence never ventured to Sapphire's rooms, let alone any higher. "Is it you crying?" he said. "I wish you'd stop. What's wrong?"

Lucas reached out to touch the textured surface. In answer, the angel's hand lunged out of the painting and grabbed him.

Sam lay in bed watching Rosie, who was on her feet with her back to him, on the phone to Lucas. She was wearing nothing but one of his shirts, which hinted deliciously at the curves of her bottom as she moved. Sam pushed the cover down to his hips to let his body cool. They were in the apartment he was sharing in Ashvale. He'd apologized for his room being cramped and shabby; she insisted she didn't care, since it was their sanctuary.

"Well, you keep telling me you're fine, but I don't believe you," she said. "The lack of detail makes me suspect otherwise . . . No, nothing's changed, Luc. Mum's still worried. We still want you home . . . Sorry, but I *will* keep on. I'm sick of treading on eggshells with you. If you keep saying the same thing, so will I!" Her tone took on a let's-change-the-subject brightness. "So, are you going to Cloudcroft Show on Saturday? Oh, the usual; cows, horses, big tractors, Morris dancers, Beast Parade, all that stuff."

Sam heard the scratch of Lucas's voice, saying no.

"Come on, you'd enjoy the music."

There was a rueful laugh at the other end. "Brass band? I don't think so. I'll call you next week, Ro."

Rosie glowered at the phone. "He's hung up." She turned towards Sam, the open shirt offering a tantalizing glimpse of soft dark curls between her thighs. "What are you grinning at?"

"At you," Sam said affectionately, "naked in my room. And the times I lay in my prison cell, fantasizing about this."

She brandished the phone at him, mock-annoyed. "I don't think you're taking this seriously."

He leaned on his elbows. "I am, love, but Luc's got a point. Village carnivals, not my scene either. How about we go elsewhere for the day?"

Her eyes glimmered. "Where?"

"Shopping, dinner, romantic walk—anything and everything you want, sweetie."

"*Ooh,*" Rosie breathed, her eyelids falling. "That sounds so tempting. To escape . . . it feels almost wicked."

"That's what we'll do, then." He smiled, basking in the tingle of conspiracy. Rosie parted her lips, moistened them with the pink tip of her tongue. The shine of her eyes became so intense that he felt its heat trailing over him. "Ah," he said, "you seem to have turned fully human. You've become aroused by the word *shopping.*"

Rosie launched herself, and he fell back laughing under the force of her. She lay full length on him, her teeth and tongue playing hungrily over his skin. "Not shopping. You," she said into his neck. She raised her head, trying to see through the wild mess of her hair. "You know, if you lie in bed with your naked chest on display, you are going to get jumped on."

Lucas ended the call to Rosie and looked up at the ceiling. What should he have said to her? Help me, Ro, I'm going mad, please come and get me? His heart jumped in his throat. He picked up a grocery bag and softly made his way to the attic again.

The angel was still out of the painting. The first time had frightened him half to death. The creature had come with him as he leapt up, unfolding from two dimensions into three; and there she stood eye-to-eye with him, a specter engraved on darkness, the face as wild with astonishment as his own.

Once he'd overcome his shock, he realized that she was the more terrified; that she was harmless, insubstantial like an elemental. She wouldn't speak, only knelt on the floorboards and hid under her hair. The second time he returned, she'd melted back into the canvas and he'd had to coax her out again.

Now he approached carefully, trying not to startle her. She was willowy, drawn in sienna shadow, with creamy highlights on her flesh, long rippling bronze hair covering her naked form. The canvas behind her was an indigo blank. The shape of wings was sketched in the air above her, a faint high curve that moved when she did.

"Hello, it's me again," he whispered. "I've brought you some water, and food . . . uh, there's a cheese sandwich, and some cake. I don't know if you eat, but . . ."

She raised her head and stared at the items he was taking from the bag. Her face was delicate, perfect, a true faerie face. The eyes were solid golden globes; un-human, timeless and wary. "It's all right," he said. "I'll sit with you. You're not on your own."

To his surprise, she reached out and took the bottled water from him. She tipped her head back and poured it on her face, opening her mouth. The red curl of her tongue was startling in the gloom. She took a bite of bread and spat it out; the cake seemed more to her liking. She licked and nibbled at it.

"So sweet," she said. Tears swelled in her eyes.

It was the first time she'd spoken. Lucas sat on the floor next to her, pulse racing. "Don't cry," he said. "Or at least tell me why."

"Lucas," she whispered, touching his arm with long, thin fingers.

"That's me. Do you have a name? I don't know if you're literally made of paint, or if I'm dreaming this, but you need a name."

She paused, putting her fingertips to her mouth. "Iola."

"Iola. That's nice."

Hesitantly she explored her face with her fingers. Her voice was faint, rusty with disuse. "I am not made of paint.

I'm like you." He began to ask if she meant Aetherial or something else, but she interrupted, her gold-leaf eyes widening. "Is he still here?"

"Do you mean Lawrence?"

The angel shivered. "Yes. Lawrence."

Lucas's heart sank. "He is. Why?"

Her lips opened; she froze, like a sculpture. "Then I can't come out."

"No." Lucas caught her arm, afraid she would vanish into the canvas again. She winced. "Sorry," he said, letting go. "Didn't mean to startle you. Please stay with me. He won't come up here, he never does. Why are you hiding from him?" Iola bowed her head and wouldn't answer. "You're obviously afraid of him. Me too. You've been here years, haven't you?"

"You're warm," she sighed. "I'm so cold."

"Come downstairs with me. You shouldn't be up here alone."

She only shook her thigh-length ripples of hair. "I can't leave. As long as he is still in the house, I must hide."

Each day Lucas took her food, and each day Iola became more substantial. She began to move around the attic, testing her feet and legs. Her wings were now only a spectral hint, if there at all. He brought her clothes, but she wouldn't wear them. She ran her fingers through her hair, gazed for a full hour at her reflection in an old pockmarked mirror, spun round so that her hair whirled in a fan. Lucas tried hard not to stare at the ivory flesh this revealed, and failed miserably.

She still looked gilded and fantastical like some opium dream of a faerie, but she was now too solid—he hoped—to fade back into camouflage. She let him plait and play with her hair. There was a sad serenity about her as she began to speak more freely.

"How long have you been here, in the painting?" he ventured.

"I don't know. Time stands still, but the memories are bright."

Skeins of silk ran deliciously through his hands. "It's said that when Aetherials die, we don't so much die as change. Become elemental and attach ourselves to a tree, a rock, or a stream. Is that what happened to you?"

"In a way." She fixed her eerie golden eyes on him. "I am like you, Luc. Aetherial."

"Did Lawrence . . . kill you?"

She smiled for the first time. The cosmos rearranged itself inside him. She was indulging his innocence. This was not a frightened fawn of a girl at all but an age-old creature beyond his comprehension. "He hasn't told you," she said. "I hear your conversations, when the house is quiet. He won't admit it."

Luc tried to take this in. She must have heard everything that went on in the house for years. "I knew he was keeping something back!"

"I'm from Asru, the realm of spirit," she went on. "The Spiral Court sent me to Liliana, and I stayed to help Lawrence. They always send a guardian to aid the Gatekeeper. We stay in the shadows, not quite secret, but not seen, either. I was mistress of the *dysir*."

Lucas was confounded. "Never heard such a thing. Did you have . . . authority over him?"

"No, the guardian only comes to offer guidance, protection. We offer a connection to the inner realms. My first few years with Lawrence were difficult. I was always there, helping him find his way . . . but he rejected me. A black madness came over him. I tried and tried to help, but there was nothing I could do and in the end I was overwhelmed. His dear wife went too and I was powerless to bring her back. He drove us away. I'm ashamed to admit my failure but by the end I was mad with fear, so I fled."

"Why here? Couldn't you have returned to Asru?"

"Why here?" she echoed. "You're here too. This is where he drives us."

"Oh." His mouth fell in shock, but she smiled.

"I couldn't leave him, Lucas. He was still my Gatekeeper. I was still bound to him. So I hid myself. Faded away."

Lucas thought of the weeping he and Jon had heard on and off for years. "You were heartbroken."

"Oh, the pain in the house. I could never shut it out."

"Does he know you're here?"

"I don't think so. He closed his ears to me years ago."

One shoulder appeared between the waves of her hair. Lucas instinctively went to kiss it, stopped himself just in time. He cleared his throat in embarrassment. "Er, Iola, I'm the Gatekeeper now. So they tell me."

"I know." This time her smile was girlish and sweet. "That must be why I came back into the solid world. You called me out."

"Then you have to come downstairs with me." Hope danced in him. "We can face Lawrence together."

She turned to him and placed her hands on either side of his face. "I can't."

He was pushing her too hard. She was still as fragile as smoke. Lucas was no good at being forceful, either; Lawrence could blow him over like a straw. How could he hope to defend Iola, if he couldn't look after himself? Frustration brought tears to his eyes. "I can't leave you up here."

"You must, dear friend. I'm used to it."

"I'm not leaving without you. We're both his prisoners."

"Don't weep. You brought me to life," she said softly, and kissed him.

The sweet surprise of her mouth on his ambushed him. Lucas was lost. He whispered, "Is this usual—with your Gatekeepers?" and her mouth warmed his ear as she breathed, "No. Never before. I need you . . . to make me real . . ." And he was falling into soft golden fire, falling through one exquisite sensation after another.

Snatches of memory touched him like electric shocks. Those knowing human girls who'd hung around the band, their solid flesh reeking of cigarettes and stale perfume; he'd never let them near him. There had been no one. Drugs had thrown a muffling veil over any desire for love. There was always Jon, of course, and the quiet release they offered each other since they had no one else, and which they never spoke about in daylight; but that didn't count. He'd never been inside anyone. Never imagined the feather-soft perfection of an angel's body or the tenderness of her mouth and hands moving over him, drawing him deep into her.

It lasted forever, and it was over in an instant. She took his breath away like a fall into the Abyss. Spasms of ecstasy possessed him, hurled him out of himself, lashing like lightning.

As pleasure trickled away, he found there was no one beneath him. He was embracing the folds of a dusty blanket.

Lawrence woke from the toils of a nightmare and the angel was there again at the foot of his bed, her stone finger pointing at him, her blank golden eyes staring. *"You will wake the Shadow,"* she hissed. *"I could have helped you, but you turned your back and drove me out. Now the beast is too hungry."*

"No," he gasped. "I control the Gates!"

"Too late, Lawrence." Lightning flickered around her. A hot wind caught the rippling hair. *"You woke Brawth with your anger. The great Shadow at the beginning and end of time."*

"Please." He writhed and his voice was raw. "How can I lay it to rest?"

"By losing whatever you love most," came the savage answer. *"When your pain is more powerful than your anger—that is all that will satisfy Brawth."*

"No!" he cried, starting up. He woke properly then, sweating in a tangle of sheets. There was no one there. The guardian, Iola, had fled and vanished years ago; he'd driven her away, believing that she was an infiltrator, in league with his enemies. Certainly not believing she could help him, for no one could. Yet still she haunted his nightmares, a wraith of ill omen, her stone finger piercing him with wintry cold and terrifying knowledge . . .

In the feverish aftershock of the dream, Lawrence suddenly knew, in horror, what she was telling him. *It must end. And I* . . . He trembled as all the years of fear, denial and icy self-control forged themselves into a torrent of rage. *I must be the one to end it.*

The morning of Cloudcroft Show was dry and fine. Jessica and Auberon were up early, ready to take full part in selling tickets, stewarding, or whatever duties they'd agreed to. Even Matthew dragged himself from bed despite an apparent hangover. Rosie felt a little guilty at running out on them; not guilty enough to change her plans, however.

Sam took her to Birmingham. Not the most exotic venue, but the city center had changed in recent years. Grimy industry had given way to the faux crystal glamour of shopping malls. At the entrance to the Bullring Center stood a great bronze bull statue that reminded Rosie of Brewster as she stroked the smooth metal; beyond were high viewpoints from which to admire the city skyline. They drank coffee in a bookstore. Sam bought her a blood red crystal heart on a black leather cord. They discovered the unexpectedly sensual pleasure of buying clothes for each other—sliding silk and cashmere and cotton against each other's skin, flirting with the danger of discovery in changing rooms—and later, after a lengthy meal with champagne, they walked hand-in-hand along the canal basin, which had been renovated and lined with trendy bars. Late sunlight sparkled on the water. No one knew them here. Rosie, with her arm wrapped around Sam's lean waist, had never felt more perfectly that she belonged.

"This has been the best day of my life," Sam said in wonder.

"And mine," said Rosie. They stood with their arms around each other, not wanting to break the spell. "Do they have designer stores in Elfland? Where would you get a cappuccino? Do they have an economy at all?"

"Nah," said Sam, amused. "You're supposed to find your true self up a mountain or in a sacred grove, aren't you? Instead it turns out to be here, in a grim old midlands city beside a canal. Perfect happiness. Perfect peace. Who'd have thought it? I like this world."

Fun and hot dogs and the flutter of bunting; it was all a masquerade for human benefit. Sapphire felt detached from it, tense all day as if with stage fright. When evening fell, it would begin; a carnival procession, traditional folkloric revelry, a perfectly natural part of the day's activities. In isolation, the Beast Parade would have looked as weird as hell. In context, no one had reason to suspect a thing.

They costumed in a back room of the Green Man. It was like dressing up for a village play, except that everyone was deathly quiet. Comyn and Jon were in another room. No one spoke to Sapphire. It was when she slid the hound mask onto her face that a sense of ritual strangeness and unreality hit her. The mask was stylized, with staring eyeholes; a fetish object.

I'm not myself anymore, she thought, looking at her animal reflection in a mirror. *Not little Maria Clara Ramos, not Marie Claire Barada, not Sapphire da Silva or Mrs. Lawrence Wilder. I don't know what I am.* She felt calm, focused, intent.

The costumes were in shades of green, part-medieval and part-fantastical. With their masks, the gathered Aetherials became hunter and hound in one. She couldn't tell who was who anymore. They were . . . a pack.

Comyn alone was dressed in red, complete with a Victorian-style huntsman's jacket in scarlet. He wore a simple black highwayman's mask. When he brought Jon in, Sapphire started. It was like a beast from another world lumbering in.

Jon towered, and the hide that covered him reeked. When she went closer and tried to see his face, he only smiled vacantly, horribly back at her. He'd obviously taken something, but who could blame him? It was what shamans did. For this night, it seemed appropriate.

The air felt humid as they stepped into the evening and made their way onto the village green. Sapphire felt the fire of vengeance quivering through her. This was what she'd lived for her whole life; the end of Lawrence.

Violet-blue dusk fell gently as Sam and Rosie drove back to Cloudcroft. The festival lingered on. It was a fine evening, with crowds of people outside the Green Man and all over the road. They plainly considered the day not done and the highway a traffic-free party zone. Sam had to crawl to avoid running anyone over. At the far corner of the green, there was activity. People were drifting in that direction, entirely blocking their way.

"Great," said Sam, drumming the steering wheel. "I thought they'd be done by now. Haven't you got bleeding homes to go to, people?"

"Must be the Beast Parade. It's usually long over by now." Rosie wound down her window and called to a man standing near the car, "What's happening?"

"Dunno, love," he said happily. He reminded her a bit of Alastair. "There's some idiot dressed up as a deer. These folk customs, all about fertility, aren't they?" He winked.

Rosie grinned back. "Er, yeah. Thanks."

The crowd began to stream up through the village, following the attraction. Rosie heard the thump of a ritual drum. Sam crawled after the procession in the car for a few yards, then swung into a side road and parked. "Be quicker to walk," he said.

The evening air felt warm. There was a pink flush to the sky, but the light was fading towards slate grey. She saw the spark of lanterns and torches concentrated at the front of the column.

As the lane rose in front, the head of the procession came into view. She glimpsed costumed dancers in green, perhaps thirty or so. At their head was a figure with massive antlers on his head. The antlers shook and dipped, making their wearer seem a mad, shamanic figure. Behind the core ran a looser group of a hundred or so folk, also mostly in green—and Aetherial, from their light, tireless pace.

The mass of human revelers ran to keep up. Ahead, others lined the road to watch. She heard the bright notes of a horn.

"They're hunting him," said Sam. He and Rosie began to run. It reminded her of something she couldn't bring to mind. A hidden intent, an age-old ritual.

The Beast Parade was different every year, but the dancers normally went around the village in a circle to complete the enactment on the green. There was often some daft theatrical climax. Instead, the procession took the left fork that led past Oakholme and ultimately out of the village altogether. Human followers were starting to grow tired and drop out by then.

Rosie glanced into the windows of Oakholme as they passed. The only light was in Matthew's room. Still the procession continued. There was nothing up here, no reason for them to come so far. She glanced at Sam but he only shrugged, puzzled.

"Are they drunk?" she asked. There was, however, nothing frivolous about the participants. They ran with serious intent. When they gave voice to hunting cries, the sound was raw, dirty, savage. The hunting horn sounded again.

"They're heading up to Stonegate," said Sam.

Twilight soaked the landscape in eerie gloom. The hunt took on the feel of a tribal rite. The stag sacrifice whirled and staggered in a trance. The huntsmen pursued in wild excitement like hounds after scent, their real selves subsumed. Sapphire was one of them—possessed, on another plane of consciousness, where all was narrowed down to their goal.

Even the human followers were caught up without understanding. Their shouts of encouragement were savage. Heaven knew, the villagers had no reason to love Lawrence either. The same dark blood hunger infected everyone.

The stag ran now as if exhausted. He staggered under the weight of the hide on his shoulders and the crown of antlers. He pushed himself into a brief burst of energy, running and feinting, then stumbling again. The hunting horn sounded, urging him on. The quarry must not fall too soon. Sapphire's heart was in her mouth as it seemed he would collapse halfway up the drive; but the antlered head rose again and he struggled on.

There on the step before the double doors of Stonegate Manor; that's where it would end.

Lucas was in the rooftop conservatory, resting his forehead against the glass. The incident in the attic had left him profoundly disturbed. He'd crept up once and found no one there; now he daren't return, in fear of what he might or might not find. Had he fallen in love with a hallucination? If so, he'd lost his mind without even noticing. Was it some conjuration of Lawrence's, designed to keep him at Stonegate? There was one way to find out; ask Lawrence what he knew of Iola the guardian, and watch his reaction. But then—if Iola *was* real—Lawrence would want to know how he'd found out, and that might place her in danger.

His confusion sank towards despair. He thought he'd discovered a wonderful living secret in this tomb. Then it proved to be dust, or some cruel trick. The landscape below was velvety green, but he was isolated from it. All day he'd been hearing snatches of music and loudspeaker announcements from down in the valley. He'd sneered, but now he longed to be part of it. He and Rosie, eating ice cream as they trailed behind their parents, children again.

As dusk fell, Lucas saw the procession coming up the drive. The sight shook him out of his torpor. Why the hell were a couple of hundred people suddenly flowing towards Stonegate? They must be drunk. It must be a joke, but Lawrence would be incandescent.

He could make out only a shadowy mass, carrying lights. A horde of villagers with flaming torches, come to oust the fiend from the castle; that was the image, but there was something darker and quieter in their intent. As they came level with the walls beneath him, he saw they were dressed up, masked. A figure cloaked in deerskin dodged this way and that, branched antlers swaying, in symbolic flight. The hunters mimed pursuit.

Lucas stared, confused. Human spectators must see this as enacted folklore, but it wasn't. There was a sinister, hidden meaning. Whatever it was, it would be nothing entertaining.

"Lawrence!" he shouted, running through deserted rooms until he reached the gallery.

Lawrence was already on his way downstairs. He crossed the great hall, switching lights on as he went. Luc followed him, alarmed. As they entered the lobby, a terrible sound came through the door; a muted ululation like the baying of hounds. Through the windows, they saw the crowd milling on the half-moon drive in front of the portico. "What do they want?" said Luc.

Lawrence's face was limestone. "Traitors," he said thinly. "So it comes to this."

Lucas saw the stag framed in the portico, turning to confront his pursuers, rearing to his full height as they held him at bay. He saw the red-coated huntsman raise a longbow and take aim. The arrow flew. The stag bowed his antlered head and fell, hitting the doors with a tremendous thud. Lucas jumped. The doors shuddered.

Lawrence's hand turned the key and began to slide back the bolts.

"No, don't!" Lucas cried.

"I must," said Lawrence.

He opened both doors wide. Light spilled out. Lucas saw dozens of pairs of glowing eyes staring back, red like the eyes of wild dogs. Only the huntsman had a human face, with a simple black mask, and he had a huge curved knife in his hand.

As Lawrence opened the door, the huntsman's huge butcher blade rose and fell. Blood spurted. The stag collapsed in a red lake. The scene froze for a heartbeat, a tableau. In the space while no one moved, Lucas recognized the scarlet huntsman as his uncle Comyn.

Lawrence stood expressionless, staring. Panting, wild-eyed and defiant, Comyn glared back. "Out," he said. "You are out, Lawrence Wilder."

"What the hell is this?" said Lawrence, his voice raw and shaky. "What the devil is the meaning of this cha-rade?"

"You know the meaning." The huntsman stood with the blood-soaked blade raised near his face. "The stag bears your crime and is slaughtered."

Lucas half-screamed, "Oh my god, it's Jon!"

He lurched forward, but Lawrence gripped him and shoved him back. For a few moments the world spun into nightmare and all he could see was Jon, the fallen quarry, dead in a pool of blood.

"You recruited my own son to act this out?" Lawrence whispered. "Jonathan?"

The air caught in Lucas's throat, raw. Then Jon raised his head. There was blood all over him, but not issuing from his body. Fake. He'd had a bag of pig's blood strapped to him. His face was barely visible under the stag's head. He was panting, eyes unfocused. Drugged; how else could he have done this?

"I'm not your son," he rasped. "You're not my father."

Sam and Rosie finally reached the head of the procession where the drive met the house. A chaotic mass of people roiled in the dusk. Impossible to make sense of the scene. There were some humans looking confused and asking each other what the hell was supposed to be happening. Others, drunk, were cheering. The hard core of costumed hunters clustered around the front doors.

"What the fuck do they think they're doing?" Sam hissed, outraged.

"The door's open," said Rosie. They pushed their way around the edge until they got somewhere near the front. The throng at the door wore forest greens and had the masks of hounds. Rosie felt the world shift like quicksand.

How come so many Aetherials had known about this—but not her, or Sam, or her family?

Suddenly she spotted her parents—but they were on the fringes, not costumed. Jessica was in a tie-dye skirt and caftan of sunburst yellows, Auberon in grey flannels and jacket, and they looked every bit as shocked as Rosie.

Finding gaps to peer through, she and Sam watched the scene on the doorstep. The stag was on his hands and knees, awash with crimson blood. Lawrence stood on the threshold, his face white and terrible, with Lucas at his shoulder. She recognized Comyn's voice.

"The slaughter of the stag upon your doorstep marks you as a pariah, Lawrence. It states the disapproval of the community. The stag is your crime. The stag is *you*. We sacrifice the old king and welcome the new."

Lawrence was rooted like a standing stone. Sam started forward, but Rosie grabbed his arm and stayed him. He let her, seemingly at a loss. Finally Lawrence spoke. "I know what this absurd ritual means. I never thought I'd see the day when it was enacted against your Gatekeeper."

"Then you know that the accepted procedure is to step down and leave," said Comyn.

Lawrence laughed. "You can't make me leave my own house."

"No, we can't prize you out of the old shell, it's true. The condemnation of the Aetherial community is something else. It is a vote of no confidence. It's the stripping away of any position and respect you had left."

Lawrence turned grey. He began to shake slightly. Rosie felt horrified for him.

"This is blasphemy!" he said. "Let me see the faces of those who would drive me out. I know you, Comyn—this is no surprise from you—but the others? At least have the courage to show me your faces!"

A moment of uncomfortable stillness, then the masks began to come off. Sapphire and Phyllida were among them. All the Aetherials stared flatly at Lawrence. His attention in return flicked over their heads straight to Auberon. "Even you?" He gave a horrible laugh. "Of course you! You were only ever biding your time! I can't stand against this wholesale condemnation, can I?"

"You brought it upon yourself," said Comyn.

"You traitors," Lawrence whispered. "You wretched, backstabbing traitors, all of you. Idiots!"

"You can see from our clothes that we took no part in this and knew nothing about it until it began," called Auberon. "Nor do I approve of it. However, you know this can't go on. Lawrence, please. For the sake of peace, step down."

"Have you come to kill me?"

"Of course not," said Comyn.

"What do you want me to do?"

"Let Lucas go," said Comyn. "Hand him over to us. Let us have our Gatekeeper again. What you do after that, no one cares."

Rosie saw Luc's face open up in terror. He looked at Lawrence and said, "Father?"

"Hand him over?" Lawrence's tone was contemptuous. His hand crept around Lucas's shoulders, drawing him forward. "He's not a hostage. He's not your slave. What makes you think he can open the Great Gates without my help, or indeed my permission?"

"So you've spent these weeks brainwashing him, have you? A desperate attempt to cling to your power? Give him up, Lawrence. It's over."

A chorus of Aetherial voices rose. *Lucas, Lucas, Lucas!* Lawrence waited sourly for it to subside. Both his hands rested on Lucas's shoulders, fingers tapping a spidery rhythm. His eyes were glinting ice. "Yes, it is over," he said. "You've got your way, Comyn. What do you want him to do for you?"

"To open the Gates, obviously."

"And you are certain that is what you want?"

"Yes," Comyn answered steadily. "Free access. It's our right."

"Even after due consideration of my warnings?"

"We don't recognize your warnings." Impatience edged his voice. "Whatever the danger, we'll face it, fight it and defeat it!" There were cheers and yells. "The Great Gates must be opened!"

Lawrence paused for a few heartbeats, staring bleakly at them. "If that's what you want—then so be it." Lawrence seized Lucas's arm and manhandled him from the house, sidestepping the fallen stag and pushing roughly through the front lines of the mob. They were taken by surprise. Lucas exclaimed in protest, but let himself be marched in the direction of Freya's Crown.

"Follow us, then," Lawrence called over his shoulder and suddenly, despite everything, he was in command again. "Then we'll see if this is what you want. Come on. Are you afraid?"

Sam and Rosie followed on the edges of the crowd. They were somehow caught in the tug of the current, unable to intervene, not even sure they should. She saw her parents trying to remonstrate with Lawrence, only to be shouldered aside and crowded out by Comyn's mob. Rosie couldn't get near them.

Reaching Freya's Crown, Lawrence gripped Lucas by the shoulders and turned him to face the rocks. Rosie caught a glimpse of Luc's expression; white, startled, way out of his depth. Instinct told her this must not happen, but she couldn't make a move. A spell lay over them, a force born of their massed will. They were no longer individuals but a single surging entity. Rosie couldn't be the one to step out and stop this. Even Sam couldn't.

The Dusklands shimmered softly around them and the gate mound found its true form; towering, shining. The crowd gathered in the dip. Among them she saw lavender glints of albinite. Lawrence was speaking to Lucas, whose voice came back faint. "I can't do this."

"Yes, you can."

"But you said . . ."

"What I said doesn't matter. We must serve the will of

the mob. Comyn is right; I cannot hold it back any longer. Let them have their way. Let it be over."

Sam made a move forward, yelling, "Dad, no," only to be stopped dead by Comyn's arm shooting out like a steel barrier across his chest. The blow knocked him to the ground; Rosie went to help him up but too late, no one now could stop the ritual.

"I don't know how," Luc was protesting.

"Yes, you do. As I told you. Work calmly through each stage, then your instinct will take charge."

"The apple branch—"

"Is symbolic. Your heel will do. Begin."

Visibly shaking, Lucas stepped up to the Gates. His hands flew over the surface, pressing here and there, drawing runes. From within the rocks came a deep grinding and rumbling. Lights glowed; pressure in the air made Rosie dizzy.

Lawrence yelled suddenly, "Come then, and do your worst!"

At the same moment, Lucas shouted an incoherent word, and stamped on a rock with his boot. The blow was almost triumphant. Dazzling light spilled out. All the points of albinite flared blood red. Lawrence screamed.

Against the glare, Rosie made out the rock shells of the inner gates grinding one inside another until all the gaps came into alignment. No subtle crack of a Lychgate, this, but a triumphal archway. Armies could have marched through it. The night lit up. There were cries and gasps all around.

In her mind, she had an image of a vast black statue carved into the wall of the Abyss. It raised its great head at Lawrence's call, responding to the pull of the Gates. Its solid form was turning liquid and flowing upwards from the Abyss, its silhouette towering against the night . . .

In the huge bright archway of the Gates, something was coming—a spindly darkness, taking shape against the brilliance, flickering and changing as it came; a vast blackness rushing towards them from a very great distance.

With it came a crescendo of sound, like the roar of machinery and tornadoes. Against it, Lawrence was screaming and sobbing on his knees, "I'm sorry—my sons, I'm sorry." Then the light and darkness came rushing out together, and the world was torn away into a firestorm.

24

Last Days of Empire

Pain split Rosie's head apart. An image of bright-edged blackness filled her vision. She couldn't see or think. The world roared.

She became aware that the steel band around her forearm was Sam's hand, that he was dragging her along with him as they ran for their lives downhill among a mass of moving shadows. A violent thunderstorm ravaged the sky. All around there were shouts and screams, snatched away on a tornado. Ferocious blasts of wind ripped branches from the trees, nearly swept them off their feet.

Rosie cried out as flying twigs lashed her. Something was coming after them. That was all she knew. The scar on her ribs was a circle of fire.

She glanced back over her shoulder. Through a jagged, blinding aura she saw humps that could have been rocks or fallen Aetherials. No rain fell; the atmosphere was heavy with electricity. Lightning drenched Freya's Crown, making it jump between light and dark. The towering, burning shadow that was Brawth could not be seen clearly—it was simply everywhere, inescapable.

". . . get off the hill before we get fried," Sam was saying; she could barely hear him. Fleeing figures scattered like cockroaches retreating from light. She heard their fading cries of alarm. She recognized no one.

"Where's Luc?" she managed to say.

"Don't know," Sam answered, breathless. "Couldn't see Dad either."

They stumbled downhill, bending low like swimmers against a current. Roof slates flew. The sky was full of thunderheads that glowed reddish black like plumes from a volcano. Rosie felt energy rushing up from the ground, heat haze or invisible flames. The wind screamed. It was a terrible noise, like machinery—trains roaring and the zing of overhead cables strained to breaking.

By the time they entered the tree line they'd lost everyone. Rosie fought snagging branches in a state of pure panic. The look on Sam's face, she'd seen before only when they began to cross the Causeway; blank, suppressed terror. Pain knifed her skull. With it came fear, psychic certainty that the vast, unseen enemy was in pursuit. They were running in slow motion as it crossed the sky to claim them. Brawth, the great ice shadow whose destruction helped create the Aetherial race . . . who now came again to unmake them.

The moment Lucas felt the Gates open—felt all that massive resistance give in to his will—the wrath of the universe fell on him. A bolt of lightning flung his mind into Asru. He saw a huge basalt statue poised on a black mountain above the Abyss; saw it come to life, raising its head to hear Lawrence's summons. He saw it rise up and come half-striding, half-flying along the Causeway, ponderous with menace yet weightless, as black as space and as blinding as multiple suns—a paradox that turned his mind inside out.

He saw the spectral ancients of the Spiral Court fleeing in panic, Estel in owl form perched on a branch of the World Tree, simply watching the end of the world as she'd watched the beginning, and Albin a streak of white on the darkness, head thrown back, screaming . . .

The scream was coming from Luc's own throat. He

came back to reality amid howling wind and thunder, to find his father pinning him to the ground. Lawrence's face was contorted with anguish, his eyes crazed. Luc's blind instinct was to run, but powerful arms held him rigid.

"It's here." Lawrence's voice was a rasp of torment. "Now do I throw you into its path as a sacrifice, my dearest son? Will that appease it? A loss great enough to lay it to rest? If it consumes the last Gatekeeper, will that bring us peace? Can I do it?"

Lucas opened his mouth but couldn't speak. Lawrence's questions were unanswerable. He thought he was about to take the last plunge into the Abyss after all—and he rejected it. Screaming soundlessly, he fought with every atom of his will, but his body was pinioned. Pain racked his limbs as the madman that used to be Lawrence twisted him to face the Shadow in the sky, offering him up . . .

"No," choked Lawrence. The words were savage sobs. "I can't. Not you, never. I won't let it take you! Go, Lucas. Run!"

He was released, almost thrown onto his feet. The sensory assault overwhelmed him. He fled, struggling through a sea of people, all stripped of identity by terror. For a few moments Lawrence was running beside him—then the writhing chaos separated them, and Lucas was fleeing alone, lost. It was the last he saw of Lawrence.

On the hillside, Sapphire had been squeezed to the edge of the crowd, no Aetherial caring that she was there. Well, they'd done it, forced Lawrence to his knees. Strange, she felt no sense of triumph after all. Her head ached. She heard the voices of Luc and Lawrence—the latter's words raising the hairs on her neck, *"Let them have their way"*—but Freya's Crown appeared only as a plug of sheared rock to her. What did they see that she could not?

Pressure built in the air, so powerful that even a human sensed it. She felt the static tension of thunder rising. She caught her breath on a thrill of terror as reality deformed around her and suddenly she *saw*. The landscape was bathed in reddish storm-light. In a rush of exhilaration she knew that Lawrence had misled her; a human *could* enter other realms, if only for a heartbeat.

The rock split, the storm broke. The effect upon the Vaethyr was astounding. They were crying out, clawing at their heads and eyes. Fleeing, they scattered in all directions as if a bomb had exploded among them.

Sapphire was almost knocked over in the rush. She dropped behind a rock and clung there, while lightning tongued the clouds and a humid gale snatched her hair. Although she couldn't see what had panicked them, she felt *something*—an invisible freezing veil brushing over her, almost unraveling her sanity in a single touch—then gone.

Within seconds the hill was deserted. Between dazzling light and darkness, she couldn't see, couldn't stand up against the gale. The air whirled with flying debris. The creaking and ripping of sapwood sounded horrific. She sat tight, waiting for the storm to subside. This was what it came to, dealing with Aetherials. Disaster.

She was looking straight at the pleated face of Freya's Crown when she saw movement in the dip below. In dark intervals, she lost it, but when eerie light bleached the landscape she saw it again, each time closer to her, as if stop-frame animated. A big man, skin burnished red-brown, heavy eyebrows quirking up like goat horns, scruffy khaki shirt and shorts . . .

She stared at this impossible creature moving towards her. Where could he have appeared from . . . except the Gates? Time froze. She knew him. *No.*

He staggered the last few steps towards her, hands raised as if to propitiate the storm. She saw the bleeding bullet hole in his chest. Then he collapsed. Sapphire tried to shout, but no sound came.

When she reached him he was near death, eyelids flickering, a groan issuing from his lips. "Papa," she whispered.

"My Maria Clara." His voice was rusty. "My princess."

"It's all right, Papa." She stumbled over the words in her urgency, knowing this was her one chance. "I did everything we planned. Ruined Lawrence, destroyed his family, draped myself head to foot in his wretched jewels. He killed you, but you took him with you. We won. We won!"

He was too weak to answer, but a smile broke on the dying face. He pawed at her arm, as if to say he understood. "Papa," she said, her tears falling onto him.

With the next blaze of lightning, he was a corpse—no, a carcass, flesh vanishing from his bones as she watched. Lawrence's monstrous enemy Barada, emissary of the implacable ice giant Brawth—meat for wild animals. When the lightning flared again, he was gone.

"Rest, Papa," whispered Sapphire. She bent forward over her knees with her arms around herself to hold in the grief, hold his spirit to her. "We can rest now."

Sam and Rosie broke from the trees and covered the last stretch of garden towards sanctuary. They glimpsed distant figures fleeing down the drive. Gaining the rear corner of Stonegate, they folded themselves into the back wall to find some protection from the wind. Rosie gasped for breath. Her mouth tasted of metal.

"Did you see where Luc went?" she said, when she could speak.

"No." Sam spat out a leaf, wiped his mouth. "Everyone was yelling and running. The shock wave from the Gates was incredible. All I could think of was hanging on to you."

"Did you see my parents?"

"No, love. Sorry. It was chaos." He rubbed his forehead. "Feels like someone cracked a rock on my head. Can't see properly."

"Me too, and the spiral brand's burning like hell."

"I saw Brawth come out," he said. "A moving darkness—like a piece of the Abyss that had torn itself loose. Now we know that my father wasn't mad or paranoid. He was right all along."

Red lightning cracked, making them duck into the shelter of each other's arms. Surfacing, Rosie gasped, "I can't believe Lawrence would do this just to tell Comyn, 'I told you so.'"

"I'm sure he didn't," said Sam. "He wouldn't. I think he was exhausted from keeping it back and this was the end of the road."

"And where is . . . Brawth?" she said. Ragged cloud layers raced like smoke over their heads, swollen thunderheads towering thousands of feet above them. Around the edge of the garden, vegetation thrashed madly as if caught in a hurricane. A couple of deer burst from cover and bounded across the lawn, ears flat in terror. "I'm scared, Sam. I feel like we're being hunted. I can't shake it off."

"Storms create an electromagnetic field that messes with your brain. Makes you feel ghostly presences and irrational terror."

"I saw that documentary, too," she retorted. "This is more than a storm."

"I know," he answered. "I'm saying that Brawth has the same effect. That doesn't mean it's not real. It means it's making us very aware that we can't escape, wherever we go. So it's everywhere, like a hologram image, or a quantum field, or something."

"We should get inside." Rosie felt her way along the wall towards the kitchen door. The sense of imminent danger almost paralyzed her. She found the cold slickness of the door handle, but it snapped back into place, unyielding. "Damn, it's locked."

"Knowing Stonegate, it will be worse inside," he said, grimacing. "We'll wait it out." They crouched against the wall, the force of the gale sucking their breath away. Sam's warmth against her was the only reality. Even at the Abyss she hadn't been petrified like this. When she closed her eyes, she could sense Brawth coming for them, a wavering, dazzling blackness. As mindless and deadly as a missile. She jumped, eyes flying open.

"What if it doesn't stop? What if Lawrence has unleashed the end of the world a little sooner than expected?"

"At least we'll go together, Foxy," he said seriously. "We

have to find Lawrence. This won't stop unless we find him—but that's the catch, we can't look until it stops. And even if we find him, then what?"

"Sam . . ." She pulled his sleeve. There was a figure moving beyond the end of the lawn, half-concealed in thrashing undergrowth. He ran like a drunk; staggering, panicking, getting nowhere.

"Holy fuck, it's him," said Sam. He rose to his feet, against his own warnings, and yelled, "Dad!"

Lucas had no idea where he was going. His mind was blank, like a panicked animal's. Anything to escape Brawth. Blood rushed in his ears as he ran. Instinct took him to Stonegate.

By the time he reached the front door, reason was returning. His lungs were bursting, but at least he knew where he was and realized he'd been utterly out of his mind for a few minutes. How could he be so astonished that Brawth had burst through? He'd seen it in a dozen visions.

His first clear thought was of Iola. He forgot that she'd vanished; he could only think that she was alone and terrified in the house at Brawth's mercy.

There was a figure slumped beside the step, half-covered by stag skin. Lucas bent down and shook his shoulder. "Jon." No response. "Jon. Come on, wake up!"

Jon groaned. He was unconscious; mouth slack, eyes closed. Lucas made an attempt to drag him towards the door, but fear had drained his strength and he couldn't do it. He gave Jon a rougher shake. "Wake up, damn it!"

Nothing. Summoning a desperate reserve of strength, Lucas grabbed him, dragged him like a sack of wet sand across the threshold and dumped him in the hall. Panting, he forced the door shut and bolted it, left Jon where he lay and plunged into the great hall. The lights were off, the power gone. The air was shockingly cold, and the walls shifted as if full of ghosts trying to come to life. He shivered as the atmosphere frosted through his clothes.

Iola was in the center of the great hall. Lightning filled

the tall leaded windows and she was caught in its strobing glare, an ethereal figure cloaked in the bronze ripples of her hair. She'd put on a long dress, one of Sapphire's, endearingly too big for her. She resembled a bewildered dryad, wincing at the hard floor beneath her feet. He ran to her. She felt real in his arms, solid and warm as any human.

"Where were you?" she said, her slender arms strong around him.

"Where were *you*? You vanished!"

"I thought it was you, not me . . . I don't know. The world isn't stable for me, Lucas. I went into Dumannios without realizing."

"And now we're both there," he whispered, understanding that the manifestations around them were just that; the fabric of Dumannios searing away the gentle surface of Vaeth and Dusklands. "This is my fault," Lucas choked. "I've done this."

"No," said Iola. "It had to happen."

"Brawth is coming. I couldn't stop it."

"It's the darkness Lawrence always feared," she said. "I might have helped him, but he pushed me away, and let it grow more powerful until it was too late . . ." She looked up at the high ceiling, which swirled with moving shadows. "It's coming for you. For all of us, but especially for you, his son."

When Lucas looked up, he saw it. A blinding silhouette; the Devil itself, roaring towards him from a very great distance. Cold pain pierced his head. He heard Albin's voice, *Its cold will sear the flesh from your bones* . . . "What can we do?"

Iola's golden eyes opened wide with despair. "Only Lawrence can stop it." The house trembled as lightning clawed the windows. "All we can do is make a shield."

"What do you mean?" he said. "Oh my god, my parents, Rosie . . ."

"You can't help them," she said, and called out a string of words he didn't understand. He saw the four *dysir* appear as if from nowhere, darkening and growing in size. At Iola's command, they went to each of the great hall's four corners and took up position like four guardian lions, huge, glowing like hot coals. "We can only protect ourselves."

She made him think of a goddess, standing in the center with four dark familiars at her command. Their defiance spun a fragile shield of protection. The amorphous power of Brawth surged towards the house only to be continuously repelled, like a stream of flaming oil pouring onto thin glass. The shield must crack eventually; but while it endured, Iola would not give up. And because she was so brave Lucas stood with her, resisting Brawth, refusing to let the burning arctic coldness or the fear take him down. The storm raged, shaking the chimneys. The fabric of Stonegate trembled, and all around them the world shuddered and crashed and dissolved like a nightmare ocean.

Dusklands narcotics had carried Jon far away from himself; he'd observed the pantomime of the stag hunt as if from a great distance before collapsing. Even the storm didn't rouse him. It intruded upon his stupor, however, turning uncomfortable dreams into nightmares. Voices washed in and out like the tide. There was something wrong, horribly wrong with the universe. It came to him that he must run for his life, but his body wouldn't respond.

A ghostly half-human gargoyle appeared before him, and its arrival was no great surprise amid the chaos. It fired a glowing arrow at him. Piercing white pain struck his hip. He thought he'd been hit by lightning and he tried again to rise, but a weight held him down.

There was a creature sitting on his chest. He saw it clearly against a vague landscape of pale grey stone; a beautiful youth with white skin, black hair, a huge pair of soot-black angel wings curving above his shoulders. He looked down at Jon with entirely jet-black, liquid eyes.

"Do you know who I am?" asked the youth.

"No," said Jon.

"Everyone knows Eros." The voice had a cruel edge.

Jon laughed, as best he could with this weight upon him. "I thought your voice would be more beautiful."

"The voice of Eros is said to be lovely, it's true. However, I am his brother, Anteros. The god of unrequited love." The youth leaned down and covered Jon's mouth with his. "This is what you could have had," he whispered.

He spread his wings and covered Jon with soft feathers. At first the kiss and caress were delicious; a moment later they began to suffocate him. He was being crushed, choked. He was dying.

Gasping for his life, Jon came back to the real world lying in the entrance hall of Stonegate Manor, slumped in a pool of congealing animal blood, covered in a stinking deerskin, entirely alone.

Bruised and bleeding, lungs heaving for breath, Auberon and Jessica had fled home, but even Oakholme did not feel safe. They'd found it by blind instinct; wherever Auberon looked, all he could see was the migraine-dazzle of Brawth. Comyn and Phyllida followed, and Matthew was there too—he'd been already in the house when the storm broke. Auberon bundled them all into the front room and slammed the door. The walls, though, were like cobwebs. Intangible shapes tried to form in the ether. Wind and thunder deafened them, and through it all Brawth attacked without mercy, driving spears of black ice into their skulls . . .

Comyn stumbled and fell, lay on the floor with his face contorted in terror. "Lawrence did this," he rasped. "He brought this on us."

"And he warned us!" cried Phyll. "And you swore we could defeat it, but we can't!"

"You can't fight it physically," Auberon gasped, holding Jessica to him, "because it cuts straight into our minds."

Helpless against pain, terror and sensory assault, they couldn't fight at all. If it did not stop, Auberon knew, Brawth would burn them to nothing, as it had already ripped away the surface world and Dusklands and stranded them in Dumannios. He convulsed with cold, trying to keep Jessica warm against him.

"I won't let it take you," said Matthew, his voice gruff

and strange. Auberon felt himself being dragged to a corner, Jess and Phyll and Comyn being pushed in with him. Around the moving edges of the blind Brawth-spot in his vision he saw Matthew, transformed: seven feet high, a leonine beast with a heavy mane and thick black claws. And Matthew placed himself in front of his family like a bodyguard, as if to absorb all the horror of Brawth into himself.

Sam and Rosie fought the push of the wind to cross the sloping lawn. An airborne twig glanced viciously off Rosie's forehead, drawing blood. Entering the rhododendrons at the other side was like plunging into a river torrent.

Lawrence, on folded knees, raised a ghastly colorless face to Sam. Rosie was horrified. She'd never expected to see Lawrence Wilder like this, broken. She'd never thought he would be even more frightened than she was.

"Dad." Sam knelt, extending a hand to his shoulder. "What are you doing?"

"Brawth is coming for *me*," panted Lawrence. "I can't let it take Lucas. Must draw it away. I have to keep running."

"No," said Sam. "It's all right. We're with you now."

"Why wouldn't they believe me?" Lawrence's voice was shredded raw with despair.

"Hey, Rosie and I weren't part of the lynch mob. They didn't let us in on the plot. I tried to stop it—really pathetic last-minute effort, I know—but I did try."

"You couldn't have stopped it. Nothing could. It was time. I must . . ." He lurched to his feet, took a stumbling step and fell. Sam caught hold of him. "Let me go!" He struggled for a few seconds, but Sam held on until he slumped to the ground, defeated.

"Dad, stop it. What are you trying to do?"

"I have to run. To draw it away. It's coming. Can't you feel it?"

"Yes, we feel it, but running isn't going to help. You're only in our back garden. You must have been going in circles."

"I know." Lawrence squeezed his eyes shut, his face all

lines of pain. "It's everywhere. Inside my head. I thought I'd be braver than this." The wind took on a mourning note and the clouds grew thick and dark, lit from inside by lashing fires.

"No one's feeling very brave, believe me. We'll help you."

"You can't. I unleashed it. Now it won't be satisfied until it finds me and I thought I was ready to meet it but I'm not—I must, but I don't know how . . ."

Rosie knelt beside him. Her instinct was to console him but he was still Lawrence Wilder; she couldn't touch him. "What will happen if you don't face . . . Brawth?"

"It will rage until it's consumed everything," said Lawrence, "leaving only the dry husk of Dumannios behind. It will pursue me forever—I must face it or it will consume my sons to reach me. I thought I was strong enough but I'm weak. The fear disables us. That is its strength, using fear on us as spiders use poison—to paralyze us."

"And if you confront it?" said Sam.

"Then . . . Brawth might be satisfied." His voice was raw and broken. "If I could make it fixate only upon me, it might pass over my dear sons and all the others. If I dared to meet it—if I were strong enough—if it burned out its rage upon me, then this might all be over."

"And you might stop being afraid," Sam breathed.

"No." Lawrence raised himself and pushed back his wild hair. "Although, in fact, my fear doesn't matter. To stand and face it, that's the important thing. The degree of terror I feel in that moment is irrelevant. To stand . . ."

"I'll fight it with you," said Sam.

"And me," Rosie added.

Lawrence gave a short laugh. "You can't fight it. I have to . . ." His hands, white claws, opened and closed. "Have to take a stand, but I don't want it to take me without warning. I need to be ready for it."

Rosie and Sam looked at each other. She saw that Sam, behind his composure, was completely distraught, but she knew he never shied away from hard decisions. Raising her voice above the thunder, she said, "Mr. Wilder, is there a place that would help you feel strong against it? Stone-gate?"

"No, not there." He gasped, shook his head. Rosie sensed any suggestion she made would be hopeless. "I need a place that would draw it to me yet slow its progress as it came, so that I could be ready. Somewhere that would bind us to each other, so that it can't stop coming towards me, but I can't escape, either. I don't know what I'm thinking of."

"There is somewhere," she said.

Lawrence grinned, mirthless and condescending. "You can't help me, my dear."

Rosie's lips tightened. "The spiral garden," she said, knowing with clear intuition that she was right. She described it. It was difficult to speak coherently against the roar of the wind but Lawrence seemed to understand. "My father said the spiral invokes the Otherworld. If nothing else, it's a calm space. You might feel better there."

"Why did you build it?"

"I don't know," said Rosie. "Inspiration. Compulsion."

"You built it for me," he said, almost accusing. "You knew."

"No." She drew away from him, unnerved.

"Take me there. Quickly." He was rising shakily as he spoke. "Must keep moving, I can't stay here."

They helped him down the hill as if dodging enemy fire. Lightning seared an oak tree two hundred yards away with a detonation that left her ears ringing. Flames leapt into the night. Sam urged them step by step down the bracken-lined tracks, supporting Lawrence between them. Still the black-bright image of Brawth pressed painfully on her vision. Rosie's eyes streamed and she felt faint from pain and dread, but it was only a grim background to the urgency of helping Lawrence.

The wind was fearsome even in the valley, clawing at them as they fought through the gap in Oakholme's hedge. A hail of twigs and leaves battered them. Within the spiral garden itself, however, the air turned absolutely still.

Their feet made a soft crunching on the gravel as they

led Lawrence around the spiral path to the egg at the center. As soon as he was there he became calmer. He stood up straight and Rosie saw the terror fall physically from him. Her headache eased, and she even forgot to pay attention to her fear.

Lawrence sat down on the stone egg at the center and released a long, deep sigh. Above, the sky crazed with forks of liquid fire. "Thank you, Rosie," he said. "This is where I need to be. You must have known."

"I didn't." She gave an uneasy laugh. "Not consciously, anyway."

"Still, this is why you built it, even if you weren't aware. Thank you. Sam, I regret that you should ever have seen me like this. I'm so ashamed."

"Dad, no. Don't be ashamed." Sam's voice cracked. "No one said you weren't allowed to fall off your pedestal, except you."

"You can leave me now. I'll wait here."

"No chance," Sam said. He knelt at his father's feet. "We'll stay with you."

Lawrence smiled. He looked up. "Here I am, poised over the Abyss."

The scene was colored dusty red and the wind circled ominously around the still eye. They sensed the unseen giant roaring its steady, inexorable way towards them. Rosie stayed on her feet. Sam reached up to clasp her hand where it rested on his shoulder.

"What is it," Sam asked, "this shadow, Brawth?"

"It's my *fylgia*," Lawrence answered. "It's part of me. When Aetherials have inner demons, they manifest on a cosmic scale."

"Are you sure, though, that it's all from you?"

A frown creased the high, pale forehead. "We can't be sure of anything, but I work from that theory. If it's more, it's still my fault. My *fylgia* attached to Brawth, or absorbed it or woke it or became it . . . the result is the same."

"So only you can control it?"

His father smiled thinly. "I can't control it. That's the

point. It took me years to understand that it's not separate but part of me, and that's why it persecutes me and my blood."

"Explain," said Sam. "Quick, while we're still alive."

"When I left Sibeyla, part of me was torn out and kept hostage in the Otherworld." Lawrence's voice was rapid and faint. "It's Albin's revenge. Not that I hold him responsible; I only blame myself, because I spent years running from it."

"Revenge for what, Dad?" He took his father's hand. Rosie had never seen that happen before.

"Albin resented Liliana's power bypassing him and coming straight to me. He held the belief that Aelyr are superior to Vaethyr, that we degrade ourselves by leaving the Spiral. He wanted me to stay in Sibeyla, but I followed Liliana to Earth and he never forgave me. Before I left, he showed me a piece of Elfstone carved with spirals and symbols of binding. He told me that my soul-essence was trapped within it and would always remain imprisoned in the Otherworld. And it's true; I have no heart, no soul, no core, have I? I never cared for my family as I should. I couldn't love. But the essence is not the *fylgia*. The *fylgia* is the shadow-self. The essence is the part of me that would have kept the shadow in balance; but because it was missing, the shadow was able to grow monstrous."

A piece of albinite carved with spirals.

Rosie's free hand flew to her face. The Greenlady's voice whispered like a lost memory, *Haven't you heard the story, girl, about the soul trapped in a jewel in an egg in a box in a bag in a nest in a tree* . . . "Oh my god," she said.

"Rosie?" said Sam, but she'd already torn her hand out of his and was running up the spiral—tempted to take a sensible shortcut, but knowing she must not disturb the energy—and across the garden and bursting at last through the back door of Oakholme.

The inside of the house was writhing. Walls were unstable, shadows moved, ghost forms of grotesque beasts thrust out of surfaces only to melt back again. Even the floor was treacherous, rising and falling in waves. Her breath condensed on the freezing air.

Rosie put out her hands to guide herself. This was Dumannios, she realized. It was the writhing horror that lay under the skin of reality, in the subconscious. *It can't hurt me,* she thought, but couldn't convince herself. Reality and the gentle Dusklands had been flayed off, leaving the raw ugliness of nightmares to break through, there inside Oakholme, which had always been safe.

Perhaps for humans none of this was happening. Perhaps their surface world was still intact, and it was only Vaethyr who'd been torn out of it. As she entered the hallway she wondered where her parents and brothers were—but there was no time to find them.

Hall and stairs and landing tilted around her in flashes of lightning as she ran upstairs to her room. Although the walls moved like cobwebs, the bedroom was still the shape she recognized, her belongings in the same place. She explored her bedside table until she found the cold smooth solidity of the egg. It glowed as pink as a living heart in the gloom.

As she retraced her route, the stairs swayed and dropped under her so that she nearly fell, narrowly saving herself on the banister. The kitchen had almost gone, replaced by a roiling cavern of demons—images of Brawth in a shattered hologram. She struggled across like a sailor across the deck of a pitching ship. Sightless she groped her way to the door, found her way out and made another frantic, stumbling run across the lawns.

The whole world had become Dumannios, she realized. Fire and ice. She tried to shake off the chaos, to sidestep into the Dusklands or the surface, but there was no escape. The red sky cracked with terrible pressure.

Brawth was close. She felt it all around her, a sparkling blackness that deformed the air. She must reach the center of the spiral before it came. A lightning bolt detonated near the house and she ducked, her ears ringing.

Inside the hedge, she halted. She was too late. She saw the

dark featureless form—flaring like an eclipse, yes, that was what it resembled, the inky center and the blinding corona—but the shape of it was humanoid, broad as a bull at the top, horned—a minotaur figure. Slow yet unstoppable, it drifted around the first curve of the spiral towards Lawrence.

Her heart threatened to burst.

"Lawrence!" she yelled. "Sam! Here—catch!"

And she threw the quartz egg.

Sam watched Brawth coming. He rose to his feet and stood behind his father with his hands protectively on his shoulders. Lawrence felt bony, and he was shaking. He remained seated, his feet planted and his spine straight.

"Go, Sam," he said.

"I'm staying," Sam answered.

"I have done nothing to deserve such a son."

"I could take that one of two ways."

"Then take it in the best way," his father said quietly.

A muscular breeze began to buffet them, as if the eye of the storm had moved. It was like a hot wind from a bonfire. Ever-changing, the shadow giant came. Thunder rumbled, but Brawth itself was silent. Sam's gaze was riveted to it. Flickering darkness and brightness. It was elusive, like spots dancing in the vision after a blow to the head. It was there and not there, hallucinatory, a weird artifact of the storm, the Devil conjured from Lawrence's nightmares. His heart started to thump. He had nothing to fight it with but still, no one would ever say he'd left his father to face it alone.

Then he heard Rosie's yell. Lawrence didn't react, but Sam did. He turned, saw the flying missile, reached out and felt it smack into his palm. He had no idea why Rosie had fled or why she was throwing stones at him, but it must be for a reason. The moment he opened his hand and saw the rose-quartz egg, he knew.

"Dad." He shook him. "Look!"

Lawrence turned his slow gaze to the stone without comprehension. Sam found the invisible line around it and fumbled to twist it open. It wouldn't shift. The vast silent black-flame entity came steadily curving around the spiral towards them.

"Fuck!" Sam yelled, and in desperation cracked the egg on a hunk of granite. It split. Sam plucked the tablet of albinite out of it and shoved it into his father's hand.

"What is this?" Lawrence stared. The symbols carved in the stone shone. "Where did you get it? *How?*"

"Long story. Oh, shit . . ." The blackness that came rushing softly towards them was a door into the Abyss. Sunfire flared around it. Sam was abruptly, mortally terrified. "Come on, what do we do with it, for chrissakes?"

Lawrence said nothing. He opened his mouth and put the jewel on his tongue. He swallowed. Then he stood up, arms spread wide as if to embrace Brawth, and all Sam saw after that was two great columns of light, the second the negative of the first, a bright core within a black corona. Meeting, merging.

He felt his hair stand on end, the air vaporize around him. A millisecond later there was a blast of heat, a deafening crack, a spear of white fire. Then utter darkness.

The blast threw Rosie into the air and she hit the ground yards away. She landed with her hip on a rock. The pain was so excruciating that she couldn't breathe.

Sight returned. She felt tears and dirt streaking her face. After that, she noticed that the red glow of Dumannios had dimmed to grey; and then, that huge drops of rain were beginning to spatter around her.

Groaning, she managed to get onto her hands and knees, and finally onto her feet, trying very hard to breathe through the pain so that she did not actually start crying. Clouds rolled thickly above her; lightning still glimmered but distant now, drifting away.

"Sam? Lawrence?" she called, picking her way towards the center of the spiral.

No answer. Only silence.

"Sam," she sobbed, losing her breath.

Lawrence and Sam both lay where they'd fallen beside the stone egg. Rosie knew they were dead, even before she took Sam's lifeless hand. Although there was no mark on the ground around them, the bodies themselves were blackened, the eyes slightly open in thin slivers of white against the soot. There was nowhere for Lawrence's essence to have gone, Rosie knew, except into Brawth: into the Abyss. And Sam . . . he would never leave his father.

Rosie bent over their bodies with her head in her hands. The rain quickened, drops becoming rods, drenching the world, washing it clean.

25

Dawn

When the rain eased at last, Sapphire looked up through the silvery gloom. Her hair hung plastered in wet strings down her back; she was soaked through, numb. It was over. She gazed up at the torn, paling sky, and thought how sweet and fresh the world smelled after a storm.

So she'd had her revenge, fulfilled her promise to her father, and what did it mean?

"Nothing," she said. She rose to her feet, realizing suddenly that she never had to see any of them, ever again. She smiled.

"So I leave you, Lawrence, as I arrived," she said. "With nothing." She took off the jacket of her ritual costume and threw it down, leaving it behind like a shed skin as she walked away. "Goodbye, Lawrence. Goodbye, Stonegate. Goodbye, dear Papa."

Stumbling into Oakholme, Rosie couldn't find anyone at first. The living room was a mess; the last bolt of lightning had blown out a window. Then she realized that a strange, heaped mound in the corner, covered in fallen plaster and broken glass, was a tangle of people. A transformed Matthew was lying across her parents and her aunt and uncle, for all the world like a feline mother protecting kittens. His fur was thick with dust.

"Help me," she said.

They stirred. Debris fell from them as they slowly disentangled themselves. Matthew looked up and stared at her, settling back to his ordinary human shape again, a dazed expression on his face. They were all alive, she saw. Pale, shocked, bleeding from various wounds—but they'd survived. Dumannios had gone; the world was solid again.

Stumbling, her mother rushed to embrace her. "God, Rosie. What happened?"

She could barely get the words out. "Sam and Lawrence . . ." She pointed to indicate the outside world. "Please, help me."

Lucas and Iola were in the sitting room off the great hall, pressed up against the French windows to watch the rain. The garden was a mess of broken trees and torn foliage. The sudden, abrupt end of Brawth's attack had left Luc too stunned to think. "Stay here," he said. "I'll make us a drink. I've actually gone past being scared, haven't you?"

"With you, I'm not afraid," she said, turning her gold-leaf eyes to him.

In the kitchen, Lucas lit a candle. Since the electric kettle wouldn't work, he set a saucepan of water to boil on the gas burner. While he waited, he tried to call Oakholme, but the line was dead, and he had no cell phone.

"Luc?" called a voice. Jon appeared, looking horrible. Sallow skin, bruised eyes, congealed blood all over him. He staggered in and slumped into a chair opposite.

"You came round, finally," said Lucas. "You all right?"

"I'm sorry." The words came out painfully. "Please forgive me."

Luc's mouth opened. His hands shaped antlers on the air. "What the hell was that, with the stag?"

Jon rubbed his eyes. "Some crazy nightmare. That's it, Luc. I'm never touching any drugs, ever again."

"Yeah? That doesn't include coffee, does it?" He got up to make drinks. Jon followed him.

"I'm serious. You're right about me, I've wasted my whole life acting like a prick. Couldn't see what was in front of my face. I'm truly sorry."

"Me too, Jon." Lucas turned to him, meaning it. They looked at each other and hugged, tight and close. Luc couldn't remember Jon ever hugging him like that before, in simple affection—almost desperation—with no ulterior motive. It was hard to end it.

"Can we wipe the slate clean?" Jon said as they let go, a little awkwardly.

"Sure. Why not." His mouth dried as he asked the hardest question, "Have you seen Lawrence?"

Jon shook his head. "I don't know what happened. I was out of it."

"You missed all that?" Lucas studied his befuddled eyes, reached up to tidy Jon's tangled hair. "We opened the Gates. The world went mad. Shadow giant, hurricane, huge storm. Thought it was going to tear the house down. I'm still shaking."

"I had the worst trip of my life." As Lucas made coffee, Jon stood at his elbow. "While I was out there—something shot me with a hot arrow and then there was this huge god called Anteros sitting on my chest . . ."

"You were stoned. I get it."

"But it's important. He was talking about unrequited love. It made me realize . . ." Jon shadowed him as he found sugar and milk. "I'm absolutely useless at loving people. Even if I do, I can't show it. I don't even know how it feels, because I'm frightened it might hurt. It made me realize . . . look, I don't want to waste my life being scared and cynical. I don't want to lose you because I never said anything."

Lucas turned round to him. He couldn't believe what he was hearing. "We're brothers."

"Only half. And so what?" Color came into Jon's cheeks. When he smiled, his beauty reappeared through the grime. "What does that matter to Aetherials? We were always close. We did things together that we never admitted to, but still, we did them. And we weren't always stoned."

Luc felt blood rising in his face. "That was—I don't know—different. Just because we were lonely, and too bloody sad to get girlfriends."

"I was never lonely with you. You're the only person I've ever felt safe with. That's what Anteros was telling me. This bond between us—it matters. When it's just you and me, it's simple, isn't it? You understand what I'm saying? We were lovers. Admit it."

"Yes," Lucas said, flustered. "I don't know. We were close, Jon, but you really messed up my head."

"That's in the past. It'll be different." Jon paused, grinning. "You've made three mugs—can't you count? Luc, I'm trying to tell you—"

Iola came into the room. Gilded by candlelight, she'd never looked more strange and exquisite, the more so because Luc saw her as Jon must, in complete amazement—unexpected and brand new. She came to Luc's side, raised her fingertips to his cheek and kissed his mouth.

"You're Jon," she said, turning to regard him with gentle recognition.

He stared back in bewilderment. "Okay, who's this?"

"This is Iola," said Lucas. His awkwardness was tempered by a strange feeling of pride, a sense of finally growing up. "She's a sort of guardian to help the Gatekeeper . . ."

"I see." Jon's gaze dropped.

"She was hiding from Lawrence, but I found her and . . ." Lucas found himself stammering to explain, to smooth the atmosphere, but Jon only gazed stonily back at him with eyes full of soured dreams. As he ran out of words, he looked past Jon and saw Rosie in the doorway.

She was a mess, her clothes damp and singed, her face colorless, her eyes empty. She looked like a waxwork of herself. "Thank heaven I found you," she said quietly. "I've got a lot to tell you both."

The hill stood grey and silver in the dawn, strewn with torn branches, scoured clean by rain. Grass and bracken were moistly fragrant. The scent of the air, fresh, raw and vibrant, was overwhelming.

Rosie walked up to Freya's Crown with Jon and Lucas and the Aelyr girl, Iola. Returning to the Great Gates to view the war zone at least gave them something else to do and think about. As long as they kept moving, the talons of pain couldn't find a purchase. She daren't stand still.

Lucas had cried. Jon hadn't; he'd only stared, his pupils black and dilated. He looked like an angel who'd been dragged through a bramble hedge. He had only whispered, "I always thought Sam was indestructible."

So did I, thought Rosie. She'd left her parents recovering at home. The damage to Oakholme from the lightning was a mess, but not a disaster; it could be repaired. As for herself—she could not and dared not cry. If she started, she would never stop. She had to be strong now, as Sam would have been.

Through the silvery light a woman came walking towards them, wearing a slate-blue cloak over a long black dress. Raven hair flowed around her shoulders. She might have formed from the shadows of Freya's Crown itself. It was Virginia. Jon saw her, and stared, and went to her without a word into the embrace of her arms, her cloak. Rosie guessed, from the stark expression on Ginny's face, that she somehow already knew everything.

"I sort of knew," Lucas said suddenly, his voice a rough whisper. "I knew, the moment we opened the Gates, that it was the end for Lawrence."

"He forced you," said Rosie. "We all saw that."

"I was scared of him." Lucas's black lashes swept down to veil his eyes. "I shouldn't have been. I wish . . ."

"It had all been different. Yes, I know."

The rocks stood solid against the sky, as if nothing had happened. Rosie reached out with her Aetherial senses; yes, the Dusklands were returning, like mist, which could be torn away by the wind and just as easily return. Letting herself blend into them for a second, she saw that the Gates were closed except for the narrow aperture of the Lychgate. Turning as she returned to surface reality, she saw Matthew walking tiredly up the hill, and a few yards behind him, Comyn, Phyll and a trailing handful of Vaethyr—the stricken remnants of the stag hunt.

"Matt?" said Rosie, going to her brother and touching his arm. "Where are you going?"

"To look for Faith and Heather, of course."

"But there might be dangers, Aelyr predators seeking to brand you . . ."

"If there are, they'll have the sense to leave me the hell alone," he said savagely. "At least until I find Faith."

He was in front of her, human; she saw the beginning of the change to his Otherworld self, a hint of striped tawny fur and liquid, animal eyes; then he was gone into the Dusklands, into the Lychgate. Rosie let him go. She lacked the energy or will to do otherwise.

When Comyn came limping up the hillside and into the dip where Rosie was with the others, Lucas went and blocked his path to the rocks.

"Well?" said Comyn, his voice gruff. "After all we endured last night, Lucas, are you going to prevent us inspecting the Gates for ourselves?"

"I'm asking for some respect, Uncle," Lucas said. His voice was emotional, but clear and assertive. Everyone turned to listen. Rosie looked at her brother with astonished pride. He was suddenly no longer a colt but a handsome, self-assured man. "I'm asking you not to enter the Lychgate yet. The Gates will be sealed until tonight. Then there will be a simple, quiet procession in tribute to Lawrence."

"Quite rightly so, but the Night of the Summer Stars—"

"Is not until July, two months away," said Luc. "Yes, it will take place, but it will be a restrained event. D'you think I'm going to throw the portals wide open, after what happened last night?" Comyn began to grumble, but Lucas stared him down. "What, did you expect to push me around, Uncle Com? I'm not a child. You don't control me!"

"Obviously." Comyn's lips thinned, the expression of an old hand impatient with the self-delusions of a novice. "But neither are you initiated. None of you younger ones are. You can't go in there unprepared. No fault of your own, but there are procedures, trials, traditions."

"Really?" said Rosie. Approaching Comyn, she pulled up her sweater to show the spiral on her ribs "It all seemed pretty haphazard to me, as if the Aelyr are going claim their own whether you want them to or not."

Lucas undid buttons to reveal the long-healed silver scar on his breastbone. "I've had mine for ages," he said. Even Jon turned to Comyn, one thumb pushing down the edge of his jeans to show a red-raw burn on his hip.

"Will this do?" said Jon. "I think you'll find we've all got them. We didn't get our ceremony, but they branded us like cattle anyway."

Comyn surveyed their wounds and was satisfyingly lost for words. Finally he said, "So you understand, Lucas, that we all belong to the Spiral as much as we belong to Vaeth. The Gatekeeper's duty is to let us roam freely and not hinder us."

Lucas inclined his dark, tousled head. Rosie noticed that he and Iola had joined hands. She smiled. A ghost of hope pushed through the heavy glacial mass of her heart, a tiny ray of sunlight. "I've no intention of hindering anyone, Uncle Com. You've got what you wanted, the Great Gates open and a new Gatekeeper—but before you say one more word about duty, remember that the fact we're standing here alive this morning is only because Lawrence sacrificed himself. He went into the Abyss to save us. Whatever he did wrong, he's paid for it."

Comyn stood like a wounded bear. "Finally did the right thing by destroying a demon of his own making," he growled.

"He did the bravest thing I've ever seen!" Rosie exclaimed. "And so did Sam. Lawrence was trying to protect all of us. He threw himself on his sword so we could have the precious Gates back, and he did it to save his sons—but Brawth took one of them anyway."

"Rosie's right," said Lucas. "I believe we could have helped Lawrence and avoided all this, if you'd given us time, Uncle, but you didn't. I don't believe that Brawth was ever Lawrence's fault at all. It was more than that. It was real, it was always real. It was the shadow giant from the beginning of time. Lawrence was wrong; he blamed himself but he shouldn't have done that. His *fylgia* did not create or wake Brawth. Just the opposite—his *fylgia* attached itself to Brawth in order to hold it back. That's what I believe and always will. Everything Lawrence did was to protect us! Now my duty is to guard the Gates as best I can to protect both Vaeth and the Spiral. And that's what I'll do, with Iola's help, as Láwrence taught me."

In Elysion the storm had spent itself in a last surge of wind. Faith was hypersensitive to its moods now. She'd felt the wrench of the Great Gates opening, seen in her mind's eye a great statue detach itself from the wall of the Abyss and stride towards the outer realms, churning the skies of the Spiral to chaos in its wake. And she and Ginny had talked and sung and played games with Heather, while a hurricane threatened to tear off the cottage roof above them.

The world hadn't ended. They'd been spared.

Afterwards, Ginny headed for the portal, but Faith took Heather to the waterfall pool, where she felt safe. She looked up past the lush gardens of the cottage, up through the knotted woods of the valley, through all the rich greens and moist shadows, to the high land above. The sky was still wild, moodily violet and ragged with cloud.

"Mummy," said Heather, "he's found us."

As she spoke, Faith felt a shiver of awareness. She was sensitive, but Heather was always ahead of her. Seconds later, he came into view, a man-beast with a lion's mane of hair, running disheveled down the steep path towards her. Holding her daughter close, she stood her ground. Waves rippled through the fur like the wind through wheat and the beast was gone, morphing into plain human shape.

Matthew.

"Shall we hide in the water?" Heather asked.

He appeared ordinary, unkempt. Something in his demeanor made him seem raw, vulnerable and boyish. At Heather's words, he looked simply aghast. "Faith," he said, halting feet from her and holding out a hand, as if to a shy fawn. "I'm not going to hurt you, I promise."

"I know, Matt," she answered.

He frowned. "Is it really you? You seem different."

"Yes, it's me," she answered. She was barefoot, in an ankle-length dress of teal cotton that clung to her slim body; her form was human, apart from blue-green tendrils among the brown fall of her hair.

"You look beautiful. And Heather . . . god, she's grown." His voice cracked. "I don't know what to say." He dropped to his knees in front of her and started sobbing, incoherent. She stood and watched. She felt strangely detached from this display, curious as a mermaid might be when confronted with emotion for the first time.

"I'm sorry for everything. For the way I treated you, taking you for granted, not loving you like you deserved. I wish I could take it all back. I love you, Faith. I never told you, because I was a contemptible ass. You're my whole life."

"But I'm not the same person."

He looked up, blinking, as if he couldn't believe her lack of reaction. "You're still my Faith. Aetherial, human, I love you. Please. I don't expect you to forgive me. How can you? But I had to tell you I'm sorry. So much has happened. Sam made me see . . ."

His head dropped and sobs shook him. A thread of pity tugged her heart. Her throat began to ache and her eyes to burn. She reached out and stroked his hair. Her tears dropped onto him. Her arms crept around his head and his around her hips and they clung to each other, one of his arms enfolding their daughter too. Heather hugged him back without inhibition, her blond head pressed to his.

"Come on, get up," Faith said after a while. He obeyed and stood shakily before her. He'd lost weight. Every shred of mocking arrogance had gone out of him.

"I know I can never make up the time I wasted, but I want to try." He took her hand, his fingers slippery with tears. "I need to explain—about the changing—and why I was angry—so much to talk about, if you'll listen. Will you come home?"

The words cut her in half. The old Faith would have traded her soul to hear them . . . but the old Faith hadn't known how to embrace a relationship of equals. "Matt, you don't know what you're asking. I've changed. I'm not afraid of you anymore."

"Thank god! I don't want you to be!"

"You will never bully me again. And if you ever frighten Heather again, I will kill you."

Anguish passed over his face. "And you'd have every right, but I won't. I've changed, too. Let me prove it."

"You don't know me," she whispered.

"I know. I never did. All I want you to be is the real Faith. As for the real me—I'm a hopeless idiot, but I'd give my life to make you happy."

Faith looked back at the cottage and the tumbling waterfall. She let her hand slide into Matthew's palm, tight and close. "Come on, Heather. The game's over now."

When night fell, there was a procession in the dark. Lawrence and Sam had been placed on makeshift stretchers of poles and canvas, their bodies draped with black cloth embroidered with silver moons. Rosie and Matthew, Faith and Jessica were pallbearers for Sam; Lucas, Auberon, Virginia and Jon bore Lawrence. Together they carried father and son home to the Spiral.

Behind them came Iola, bearing a lantern; and trailing some way behind, Comyn, the Lyons, the Tulliver clan and a long procession of Vaethyr from the hunt. Everyone paid their respects. Lawrence, for all the conflict, had been the pivot of their existence.

Their clothes were somber. No one spoke. They were shadows drifting through the darkness. Instinctively they blended into the Dusklands so that a human eye would see no more than ghosts. The night shone more deeply and the grass became netted with silver webs. Freya's Crown appeared in its true form, a silvery dolmen majestic against the sky. The Lychgate that Lucas had opened was narrow but distinct; the mouth of a burial chamber.

Jon hesitated. Ginny spoke softly to him, and after a moment he found his courage. The procession passed into the labyrinth.

On the far side were clasped trees, a winding path and forests moving softly like the rush of the ocean. Rosie was glad to find Elysion as she remembered. It was dark this side, too, as if the Spiral had sunk into mourning ready to receive them. Physically, no one shifted out of human form.

The path forked and they followed an unfamiliar branch through the forest, which took them far from the valley where—assuming the landscape played no tricks—Ginny lived. No one said which way to go. They simply knew, as if their ancestral memories had awoken with the Gates.

The ground rose. The forest cleared. There was a rugged hillside studded with rocks and low-growing vegetation. This plant cover was in bloom, each flower a tiny blue star. Their blue-lace shimmer lay in drifts up the sides of a big oblong stone lying on its back. It was a big, solid block of lapis lazuli. Rosie was beginning to know the runes carved in it; symbols for Elysion, Sibeyla, Naamon, Melusiel and Asru, other symbols that meant source, and mirror, and rebirth.

There was another beside it. Farther on, another. Rosie

saw lapis biers set at irregular intervals all along the undulating hillside until it curved out of sight. All appeared to be empty.

Here they laid Lawrence and Sam side by side. Auberon turned back the black cloth, uncovering their faces. Their sculpted features pointed impassively at the stars. Exposing them to crows and vultures; that was how it felt.

Jon took Iola's lantern and placed it on the dais at his father's feet, then knelt on the ground, face hidden behind his long veil of hair. Candles were lit around him. The company stood all around the biers, watching over Lawrence and Sam in silence. That was all. No words, no ceremony. They simply stood and watched until night began to fade. This was the Aetherial custom.

Rosie looked up at the sky. Stars hung as thick as snowflakes, hissing with cosmic white noise. It was so like Earth yet so clearly, eerily not, that she felt her soul-essence would leap out of her with awe. When she closed her eyes, she could see two wolves running through a slanting, silvery light. *I thought you were indestructible too, Sam,* she thought. *I refuse to cry, because that would be giving in. I'm just going to wait, okay? Like you waited for me finally to realize I love you.*

As dawn came, they made a silent farewell and began to move away. Rosie walked beside her father. "What does it mean, that we don't die like humans?" she whispered. "It looks final to me. What will happen to them?"

Auberon squeezed her shoulder. The grip hurt. "The borders are all tangled up for us." His voice was rough. "I suppose that is the defining difference between us and mortals."

Rosie shivered, feeling the cold. She looked back through the trees and thought of the cliff edge beyond and the high Causeway. She imagined Sam crossing it; a swift flame arrowing towards the heart. Was he still worried about the height? "The soul-essence flies to the Mirror Pool but forgets its previous life and loves," she said. "And if Lawrence went into the Abyss with Brawth, to end the pain, because he felt he'd brought misery to everyone around him . . . ?" Her voice was the faintest whisper. "How are Jon and Lucas supposed to live with that?"

"They're strong," said Auberon.

"Not Jon."

"He will be."

"What will I say when people ask me about Sam?" she breathed. "I can't say the word, *dead.* I'll just tell them that he had to go away with his father. Then I can believe it, too."

As they ascended the slope towards the embracing trees and the deceptively narrow cleft of the Gates, Rosie looked back and glimpsed the hill and the lapis slabs. It was impossible, from this distance and angle, to see bodies lying upon them. They looked empty. Strangely, she was relieved.

In the deep cobalt of early morning, Virginia remained at the mound. She'd embraced Jon and told him she was staying; he accepted it with sad grace. She needed to watch alone.

She kissed Sam's closed eyes, then turned to Lawrence, who lay like an effigy with his bone-white face pointing up at the sky. It had been such a shock to see him. His face was so familiar, even though she hadn't set eyes on him for years. She fitted one palm to the angles of his cheek and jaw. The skin felt gently cool, more like paper than ice.

"You bloody fool," she said. "What are you doing? Running away again?"

The wind stirred her cloak. She pulled it more tightly around herself.

"As if I'm one to talk," she sighed. "I ran. I hadn't understood that the horrors are attached and come with you. I understand now. And you—have you grasped the lesson yet?" She touched her fingers to the thick inky hair. Her eyes began to sting. Teardrops splashed onto his closed lids. "I think you must. Finally you stood and faced it, and it finished you, as you knew it would. Brave you."

She sat with her husband and her oldest son in silence for a while, watching the sky pale. Then she leaned down and kissed Lawrence on the lips, tasting the salt of tears.

From somewhere came the faintest whisper, *Ginny*.

26

❦

When We Dream

"You read my diary?" said Faith, openmouthed. "*You read my diary?*"

"Sorry." Rosie was shamed. It was July, two months on from the fateful day of the stag hunt; that was how long it had taken her to admit it. She and Faith were in her room with Lucas, the three of them sitting cross-legged on her bed. "Matt came across it—he was so genuinely astonished, I couldn't help myself. In retrospect, it was a crappy thing to do. Can you forgive me?"

Faith lowered her head, her hair tumbling forward. "Nothing to forgive. I'm only embarrassed at people seeing that nonsense."

"It wasn't nonsense, Fai. What you'd written was amazing. Painful, but wonderful. I'd no idea . . ."

She looked up, smiling. "I can put things on paper that I could never say out loud."

"Matt cried over it. So did I. It was as much transformative magic as anything that happens in the Otherworld."

"It helped change his mind?"

"Yes. To change *him*," said Rosie. "Things are better between you, aren't they?"

"Completely. Now I can be proud of Heather instead of hiding her away." Her smile widened. "*Everything* is better

between us. Tonight, the Night of the Summer Stars . . . I
never dreamed I'd be part of it, still less that Matthew
would be. I'm nervous."

Lucas pulled a face. "Not half as nervous as I am."

Rosie felt a dull pain, knowing she wouldn't be with
them. She didn't want to spoil their mood by admitting that
she couldn't face the celebration, however sacred.

"Oh, don't say that. You'll be fine," said Faith.

He bit the end of his thumb. "I know it won't be like . . .
that night again, but still . . . what if I forget what to do, or
open the wrong configuration and spill everyone into the
Abyss?"

"Luc!" Rosie cried. "Thank heaven you're not an airline
pilot! Some self-belief, please. You need to leave Stonegate, it drives people mad."

He looked enigmatically at her, eyes half-closed and
gleaming. "I'm not leaving. I want to stay there."

"Do you?" She was astonished. "But—how can you?
Lawrence presumably left a will. It might have to be sold."

"I don't know," Lucas said quietly. "I only know that the
Gatekeeper belongs there, and so does Iola."

"And that will be another tale for my diary," said Faith.
"At last I've found something I'm good at. I'm going to be
a writer, or at least give it a damn good try."

Rosie looked into her earnest eyes. "What will you write
about?"

"All about us," said Faith. "All about Elfland."

In the sepia glow of the barn, a cow groaned and her calf
came slithering, tumbling from the birth canal. Comyn
heaved it onto the straw, where it lay in a heap of slick, dark
flesh and viscous fluids. His old green coat was soaked.

"A beauty," he said, as he and Phyllida cleared mem-
brane from its head. He turned in triumph to Auberon,
who was watching over the rails. "Look."

As the calf raised its nose, questing for its mother, they
all saw the marking on its forehead; a white spiral.

"A new bull calf with the mark of Elysion on him,"

Comyn said gruffly, wiping blood and slime from his face with his sleeve. "The Gates are open and Brewster comes again."

"It's a fine calf," Auberon agreed quietly, "but at what cost?"

There must have been many evenings like this, Rosie realized, when her parents had been secretly preparing for some Otherworld festival, leaving her and her brothers blithely oblivious of their plans. Never a clue. How strange.

Rosie found Jessica in the main bedroom, twirling in a colorful peasant skirt. The wardrobe was open and the bed piled with clothes. "Mum, what are you doing?"

Jessica stopped in mid-spin, blushing. "Sorting through my old stage clothes. They're hopelessly dated. I need new things, really."

"Thank goodness, I thought for a moment you were packing." Rosie sat on the edge of the bed, fingering the edges of bright skirts and gossamer shawls. "You're not, are you?"

Jessica looked at her with cautious eyes. A smile pulled the corner of her mouth. "Rosie, I'm getting the band back together. It's time. I've missed it so much; being on stage, the festivals . . . the music."

"Wow." Jumping up, Rosie hugged her. "How exciting. What does Dad think?"

"Oh, I'm sure he'd prefer it, everyone would, if I stayed home being a mother like I always have . . . but that's not who I am, Ro. It's not *all* I am, anyway." Her eyes had a fierce, faraway light. Rosie realized she'd seen it before, but had never understood it until now.

"I'm proud of you," Rosie said quietly. "But it will be strange. Everyone's changing, or leaving."

Jessica spun again, hands above her head, skirt and golden hair flaring. "Will this do for tonight, do you think? Then we should decide what you're wearing."

"Mum," Rosie said faintly, "I'm not going."

Her mother came to her and put her hands very gently

on either side of Rosie's face. "It's our most special, sacred night. You can't miss it."

She felt the familiar push of loss in her chest. She'd never yet allowed it to dissolve into tears. "Without Sam there, it won't mean anything."

"You think that, but it's not true. Rosie, you can talk to me, you know. It's all right to cry and grieve."

"There's nothing to say." She heaved a breath and tried to smile. "I talk to Sam all the time, in my head. He's always with me. I don't need to cry. Sam taught me to be strong."

"So, be strong and come with us tonight." Jessica held her with a firm, serious gaze. "If not for yourself, for me and Auberon and Lucas—you must come, Rosie."

The bulk of Freya's Crown reared above them, dark against the extravagant glow of the stars. Rosie had never known such a clear night, crisp and milky with the brilliance of an entire galaxy, as if the sky itself knew this night was special.

The Night of the Summer Stars.

Rosie stood close between her parents, reassured by their presence. Around them, scores of Aetherials were gathered. She sensed their tension, the light rustle of their clothes. The colors were somber; sable, dark sapphire, wine. Rosie had chosen a long dress of black velvet, with a fitted bodice and panels of plum-red satin shining through black lace. Her hair swung loose around her stylized fox mask, which was decorated with gold, copper and ruby. Around her neck glittered the blood red crystal heart that Sam had bought her, that last sweet day in Birmingham. There was no sign of Jon; perhaps he'd found this too difficult after all.

A wave of anticipation bloomed through her. The brand on her ribs, although healed, burned suddenly as if tugging her towards the Gates.

Their masks were new; metal-leafed and embellished with hypnotic whirls of enamel and crystal. Artistic Peta

Lyon had made them; foxes, sea serpents, birds and all the menagerie of their affiliations. She didn't need to see the faces of her parents, or of Matthew and Faith, to sense their coiled tension.

In position at the rocks, Lucas looked magnificent, with a grey velvet tailcoat over charcoal trousers; the somber effect was enchanting. His unmasked face gleamed beneath the black cloud of his hair. Iola, standing opposite him to flank the portal, looked eerily exotic; a slender column of bronze and gold gossamer. Rosie couldn't help feeling suspicious of this unknown creature who'd taken her brother away.

"Tonight we gather to celebrate this night of nights," said Luc, so softly that someone shouted at him to speak up. He went on with greater confidence, "The Night of the Summer Stars. A time to celebrate trust and friendship between Vaethyr and Aelyr, peace between Aetherials in all realms, inner and outer. Out of respect for Lawrence, the Gates will not be thrown wide, only a single way to Elysion opened. As you go through, remember those who have passed through before us and let all hurts be healed."

He had no ceremonial staff, so he struck the rock with his heel. The grinding of stone on stone began and Rosie felt a flash of dread, remembering Brawth. A dark aperture appeared. No horrors burst through; there was only the soft static of two realms intersecting, Dusklands and Elysion. Rosie heard sighs of relief all around her, and realized she was shaking.

"The way is open," said Lucas, and from the gathered Vaethyr came a patter of applause, a swelling wave of joy.

Auberon and Jessica led the procession, the rest falling in behind. Lucas smiled at Rosie as she passed through; Iola offered a glass bowl filled with hazelnuts, symbol of passage into the Otherworld. Rosie relished the savory-sweet crunch on her tongue. It helped her focus against the darkness, the press of stone walls around her. She couldn't resist trailing her fingers over the walls as they went, caressing the sigils carved into them.

They stepped out of the portal and Elysion opened to embrace them with a sky so vast it seemed that they were on a cliff edge about to be swallowed by the universe.

She stood in wordless amazement. Someone jostled her from behind, reminding her to keep moving, but she couldn't take her eyes off the heavens. It was like the sky of Earth, magnified; stars clustered in drifts across the vault, falling in icy veils to the horizon. The forested landscape shone in this delicate silvery light. Planets could be clearly seen; the disk of Mars as red as Naamon, the marbled face of Jupiter, cloudy Saturn with its tilted rings—all as large and clear as moons.

She descended the hill amid the drifting mass of animal-faced deities, clothed in light, hardly able to believe she was part of it. To her increasing wonder, crowds of Aelyr were waiting for them, all along the path among the trees. Firefly lights glimmered among them. Shining hair, jeweled eyes; masked and unmasked faces equally alien. She saw tall beings with skin and hair like snow; brilliant green irises shining from faces of black obsidian; small, slender creatures as brown as bark with bright blue eyes. She glimpsed wings, haughty animal faces that might or might not be masks. The thousands of lights they carried sparkled softly like dandelion seeds.

Caught up in enchantment, barely feeling the spring of grass beneath her soles, Rosie grasped at the truth: the Spiral was the intersection of dozens of realities. The dark sister of Mother Earth.

The Vaethyr followed the way through the forest, emerging at last into a clearing where hundreds of Aelyr stood waiting within a circle of standing stones. The stones were deep blue flecked with gold, like lapis. As the two groups met, they paused to face each other. Then, as one, all masks were removed.

Rosie felt more than ever that she was in a dream. She saw her father unmasked as his transformed, bear-fox self; her mother like some translucent golden bird; Matthew, a striped beast who carried himself proudly, afraid no longer;

Faith, the exquisite water nymph. Comyn was something like a minotaur and Phyll, an avian spirit like her sister—and all of this felt so familiar and so right, she realized it had been there behind a veil all her life. Tonight, at last, the veil was torn aside.

She looked down at her own hands. Still human, but shining like starlight. She glanced at Lucas and he, too, was unchanged but glowing like ivory lit from within.

The crowd of Aelyr parted. Along the avenue they made, a woman came walking to greet the visitors. She had a long, pale, ageless face beneath a fall of icy hair. Her white robe was bisected by the embroidered stem of a lily that grew from the hem and flowered at her breasts. Rosie heard gasps around her, *"Liliana."* She held a pale, polished wooden staff across her outstretched hands.

Propelled by Auberon, Lucas went to meet her. As he knelt at her feet, Liliana bent to kiss his head, smiling and whispering to him. When he rose again, she placed the applewood staff into his hands. A long look passed between them; great-grandmother and great-grandson.

Rosie felt tears stinging. Sam and Lawrence should have been here to see this.

With a ripple of ghostly applause, the two groups began to flow forward and mingle. Rosie lost her own family entirely. She was adrift in a whirl of enigmatic faces, smiling lips brushing hers. It was a delirious feeling, the unearthly newness of it; knowing she was part of this dance of light and velvet. She sensed an exhilarating buildup of excitement, heard voices whispering to each other, "Will you join the Great Dance tonight?"

Iola passed, handing out wine in goblets. The liquor burned Rosie's throat and she felt her spiral scar flare in response, so raw it stole her breath. She examined the craftsmanship of the vessel; silver stem, silver vine leaves molded to entwine a flute of ultramarine glass. She found a tiny, perfectly made snake among the leaves. The wine tasted of elderflowers and honey, and went straight to her head.

Musicians gathered by the central stone of the circle, weaving songs with guitar, drums, violin and flute; somber at first out of respect for Lawrence, gradually gathering pace. Even the music was telling a story. Couples began to dance; she saw Jessica and Auberon among them in a close embrace, reminding Rosie again that they had an entire, hidden life that was only about each other. What did it mean to them, to come back again after all this time?

In a floating dream she watched them. They were in human shape again, she realized suddenly, but full of Aetheric light and grace. Presently Jessica joined the musicians and began to sing, her voice clear and strong. Auberon claimed Rosie for a dance. She laughed as he twirled her, finding her feet nimble even while her head spun. If Jon had sought this sensation through drugs, how could she blame him? "The Great Dance, what is that?" she asked, breathless.

Auberon held her tighter and spoke so softly, she could barely hear him over the music. "It's the culmination of the night. No one's forced to take part; it's an experience from which some don't return. But every Aetherial should take part at least once, Rosie."

His words sobered her. When the music changed, she worked her way around the edges of the crowd, needing fresh air and solitude. There was a rising meadow to the far end of the clearing with several great oaks on it. She climbed halfway and sat down on a thick tree root. The celebration below became a jewel box of colored light, miniaturized by the arc of heavenly bodies above. Tiny pale flowers in the grass echoed the stars. She breathed the fragrant air and tried to convince herself that she could live the rest of her life without Sam. Even if he still existed, as a spark of consciousness or an elemental—even if he remembered her—without his body, without the fusion of flesh and personality that had made him his shining, vibrant self, he would not truly be her Sam anymore. That Sam was gone.

A shadow stumbled out of the dark and sat down next to

her; Jon, of all people. He was clutching an Aelyr wine bottle, an attenuated object of blue glass and silver. She saw in shock that his hair had been chopped to collar length. That was why she hadn't picked him out at the Gates; she hadn't seen that long wavy fall of chestnut. "Oh my god, your hair!" she exclaimed. "Who did that?"

"I did." He shrugged. "I was sick of it. Sick of the old me, really. Does it look awful?" He shook the butchered hair, loosening it to a silkier mass around his face. He looked sideways at her. He hadn't lost the angelic beauty that had ensnared her young heart.

"It'll be fine when you've had it styled," she said. "And when we've got used to it."

Jon offered her the wine and she took a mouthful. He put his head back to look at the stars. "We should have got together, you and me," he said. "We missed out, somehow."

Rosie's jaw dropped. *"What?"* she mouthed.

"I sort of wish we had, now," he went on, blithely oblivious of her disbelief. "Why didn't we? I can't even remember."

After a couple of hollow gasps, she managed to speak. "You found me hideously unattractive, apparently."

"No, I didn't," he said with a frown. "I just never thought of you like that. My mind was on other stuff. If only I'd realized . . ." He put his hands around his knees. "You might have saved me from going off the rails."

"I doubt it. You'd have dragged me off with you."

"Still." He gave a slight smile, bitter nostalgia. "I feel like we missed out on something because I didn't appreciate or even realize it existed. You did like me, didn't you?"

"God, Jon, I worshipped you," Rosie said candidly. "In my own defense, I was very young and didn't get out much."

He laughed. The painful heave of her heart shocked her. It wasn't anguish for her present self, but for the dreams and disappointments of the young girl she had once been. Those feelings, or the memory of them, could still be taken out and unfolded like an old love letter.

"I loved what I *thought* you were," she added.

"Ouch." Jon sounded genuinely wounded. "That's harsh."

"Wasn't meant to be. It was all about what I wanted to see in you, but the fact that it wasn't real, or that you didn't feel the same—it's no one's fault. You weren't obliged to like me back, were you? I got it wrong, too. I need to be passionately wanted. Not to trail around like a groupie after someone who's staring at the distant horizon."

Jon smirked. "Yeah, you're right, I am like that. I'm lazy. It was weird at school, people used to follow me around like I was some messiah and I didn't care, I just let them believe it, but they never knew what a screwed-up mess my life was in."

"Sapphire?"

He pulled a sour face. "Among other things. Gross, isn't it? I should have stopped it but I wasn't strong enough. If you'd known about that, Rosie, you wouldn't have thought I was quite so wonderful, would you?"

She answered honestly, "I suppose at fifteen or sixteen, I would have found it hard to understand. Although it might have helped me realize you were only human, so to speak."

"Yes, to have had something pure and sweet instead, that would have been so much better . . ." He trailed off. "You're right, though. I'd have been no good for you, Rosie. I am passionate, but not about the same things as you, obviously."

"So what's brought on this orgy of wishful thinking?" she asked, and knew the answer even as she spoke. "Oh. *Oh.* This is about someone else, isn't it? Not about 'us' at all." He sighed. His head dropped. After a pause, she said, "It's Lucas, isn't it?"

"Why do you assume—?" Jon snapped. Then he groaned. "Yes, okay, of course it's him. I'm such an idiot."

"Why?" His honesty startled her.

"Because I treated him horribly and he's so loyal. I never realized how I really felt until I saw him with someone else—not messing about but serious. *Hers.* No one's ever got to me like he has, male or female, and now I've lost him—god, sorry. Sorry. Not good at tact."

"It's all right," she said gently. "We have to bear it, somehow."

"Aren't you going to give me the 'he's your brother' lecture?"

"Why, would that make you feel better? No, I'm not."

"I took him for granted," Jon went on. "I thought we'd always be together. I didn't even *think*, I *assumed*. Suddenly I wake up and he's gone, like it never meant a thing."

She touched his shoulder. His pain pierced her. "He does love you, Jon. Lots of people do." She smiled. "Even I still do, in a strange way. You get under people's skin."

He scoffed. "Like a splinter. What do I have to offer back? There's only one thing I'm good at and that's drugs."

A flurry of dismay filled her. "Oh, no, Jon, don't go down that road again."

He grinned at her, shaking his head. "I didn't mean that. I meant, I'm great with plants and potions. If I learned properly, I could do something constructive, like botany or pharmacology."

"Oh," she said. "At university?"

"Maybe, but there's Earth knowledge and Spiral knowledge. When the Initiator fired that brand into me, it must have been dipped in a perfect drug, one that tears down barriers and shows you a truth you weren't expecting. The Aelyr must have the most incredible store of herbal wisdom. I might stay in the Spiral to learn."

"Sounds like a plan."

"Or I might just become a famously debauched rock star." He gave a quick, soft laugh. Almost on the same breath he added, "How do you not break down?"

"Just can't let myself," Rosie answered steadily. "If I did, I'd never get back up. We have to believe that Sam's always with us, wherever he is."

"Told you he'd fight to the death for you." They were silent, then Jon added, "Anyway, first I'm going to spend some time with my mother."

"Ginny's an amazing lady," said Rosie. "When are you going?"

"Right now," he said. "You want to come with me?"

The words, thrown down so lightly, snared her heart. How easy it would be just to sneak away with Jon in the dark . . . She glanced down at the pool of light and revelry below and her eyes blurred. "No," she said. "Thanks, but I need my family now. You go. Take care."

He turned his head and smiled at her. "Give me a kiss, Rosie. To wish me luck."

She leaned in and kissed him on the mouth. It was the first and last time. Jon's lips were soft, dry and gentle; the kiss sweet and warm. When it ended, they put their arms around each other; his body felt lean, almost birdlike within the press of her arms. "I love you, too," he said. He kissed her on the cheek; then he rose and slipped away into the night, turning to give her a brief salute as he went.

She wondered if she would ever see him again.

He'd left the wine bottle in the grass, so she drained the last few honeyed mouthfuls. Leaning back, she took a deep breath of Otherworld air. It was too fresh and potent, filling her with strange sensations. Elysion appeared gently pastoral, then seized you with sudden dark coils of revelation. A serpent lurking in the vines.

Rosie stood up, light-headed, and picked her way downhill. At last she found her group seated on the grass; Faith and Matt, her parents, Lucas, Iola and Phyll. She'd almost reached them when the band fell quiet and everyone's attention was drawn to the center stone. Comyn was on his feet there, his glass raised in the air.

"A toast," he shouted. He was swaying, the faint taurean glamour over his human shape making him seem more Aelyr warrior than the farmer she knew. Rosie had seen him in an interesting variety of grim moods, but never before exuberant. "Let us drink to victory, to the overthrow of dictators, the unseating of those dark elements who would place barriers between Aetherials and their birthright! A curse on them! Victory to us!"

There were cheers, but Rosie was struck by pure outrage

on Sam's behalf. Dazzled by fury, she strode up to Comyn, landed a punch on his jaw and felled him.

Uproar. Younger Aetherials whooping and laughing, the older ones exclaiming in muted disapproval. Comyn was flailing to get up again, rubbing at his jaw, stunned and gasping in indignation. Auberon was on his feet, hands raised, trying to command their attention.

"Everyone—let's not forget that to bring us back here, Lawrence gave his life. He struggled for years with a darkness we can't begin to comprehend. No more toasts. Some respect, please."

Meanwhile, Rosie turned and walked away. She slipped into the cover of a beech wood with only the thinnest deer track to lead her, starlight gleaming softly between the trunks. She breathed the fragrance of sap, herbs and wildflowers, aware of how very easy it would be to get lost, how seductive. This was where it all unraveled. She couldn't hold it together after all, had been mad to think she could . . .

Someone was following. She swung round, expecting it to be Auberon—but it was Comyn there, breathing hard, dark eyes glittering. Blood flowered from a split lip and he fingered the contour of his jaw. "I hope you feel better for that, Rosie."

"It was for Sam, not me!" she said. "If you don't get it, Uncle, shame on you."

"But I do." His voice became gruff with contrition. "I don't ask that you forgive me, but you must admit that Lawrence had become an obstacle to the flow of life. Nothing would change unless we forced it. You must know that I didn't intend anyone's death. I bitterly regret the hurt it caused, but I can't undo what happened. Can you accept my apology?"

"That would be for Sam to decide."

She was too angry for tears, but Comyn was looking at her with a deep, serious, persuasive expression, just like the one Jessica had worn as she swayed Rosie to come to Elysion. "I understand," he said, "but come back to the circle, Rosie, please. Not for our sake, but for yourself."

"Why?"

"The Great Dance is just beginning. This is what the Night of the Summer Stars is all about. You young ones know nothing, and you owe it to your heritage at least to be curious. Not everyone is ready, but you are. I want you to understand what the whole struggle was for!"

Her uncle walked away and, after a moment, she followed him. Through the trees she could see the gathered Aetherials moving in a whirl of color. The musicians struck up a new, intense rhythm. Her anger was spent and there was no emotion left inside her, only an abyss she couldn't look into, and a sense of fate that drew her into the flow of the dance, careless of how it might end.

In the glade, Aetherials were joining hands and moving in a huge circle counterclockwise inside the stones. Two Aelyr broke their grip to catch her and pull her in. Now she was part of a chain that was stepping faster and faster, carrying her along. She heard drums pounding, heard her mother's voice,

> *Let the Spiral take us down*
> *Tread the Spiral, round and round*
> *Dancing down the river's course*
> *Spinning back towards the Source*
> *Find the mirror at its heart*
> *Merry meet, and merry part . . .*

Not everyone joined in; she glimpsed Auberon, Matt and Faith with the musicians in the center, and all around the outside of the glade there were Aetherial spectators, clapping and chanting in time to the rhythm. They became a blur as the dance swept Rosie along. All the standing stones began to glow and columns of light rushed up, connecting each stone to the stars. Rosie felt a thrilling fire ignite inside her.

> *Only on this night of nights*
> *Drink the stars and drink the light,*

Taste the fire that sets us free
As we will, so shall it be
We kiss the water and fly,
Kiss the water and fly . . .

Faster and faster the dance whirled around the center stone. The rhythm grew ever more urgent and now Jessica's voice became a chant, *"Elysiona, O Melusina, O-ah Sibeyla, Naamon-a Asru . . ."*

Rosie could no longer feel the ground beneath her feet. She glimpsed the faces around her and saw that they were washed in an inky light, their eyes golden. She looked down at her own joined hand and saw that it, too, was turning deepest blue with stars shining deep inside the flesh. She thought briefly that it should have been Sam's hand joined with hers—then it didn't matter anymore. The dancers had become a whirling circle of fire, blue, gold and silver. Fire and light-energy filled her. She was airborne, weightless, and soaring up into the sky.

Beneath, she saw woods spilling onto an open slope with a stream flowing through a gorge below. The folded valleys of Elysion rolled under the vault of stars. In the distance stood the spidery shadow of the Causeway.

She was flying.

Others were rising with her but she couldn't see them clearly. They faded into the night, leaving her utterly alone. She looked around and saw only the glassy indigo of the night sky, the amazing whorls and drifts of stars above her; glimpsed the wonder of her own transformed body. Her flesh was darkest midnight blue and yet transparent, full of stars. She had wings! Great, arching demon wings formed from the universe itself.

Being alone gave her no concern at all. Like a deity she simply observed and accepted. All human emotion was gone. She felt powerful and all-knowing. And as she tested the muscles and felt the air currents tenting under her strong yet delicate wing tissue, she felt the most overwhelming, soaring ecstasy.

She was Estalyr—the most ancient form of the first Aelyr.

This was it. A taste of her deepest nature, her true, primal self. Always there, buried deep inside, never truly experienced until this moment. And she knew why her family had wanted her to come, and yet not wanted her to. Every Aetherial should taste this, even with the danger that they might never return . . .

Rosie flew among stars and planets. The whole of the Spiral unfolded itself to her, and she knew then how tempting, how wondrous it would be to fly free like this forever, never to go back . . . to go back where? There was only this.

She was gliding over a jet-black city. Its towers stood in powerful silhouette against the stars; and there were great statues of winged beings, looking down from spires and terraces onto the labyrinthine streets. It was the city of Faith's vision, Tyrynaia, a glory of polished black onyx. In a wave of extreme bliss she felt she'd come home.

Her Estalyr-self alighted on the wall of a balcony and saw a white figure standing there, as pale as the city was dark. It was Albin—a masculine version of his mother Liliana, hair flowing pure white around a sharp, angular face. She saw a resemblance to Lawrence, the same pitiless beauty. The triangle of blue eyes and blue gem watched her. Those slotted eyes were the coldest she'd ever seen.

He was speaking, and she felt she'd been perched like a statue, interrogating him for a long time; as if past, present and future all flowed together. His hand came up to touch her face, only it was not a hand but the head of a snake, glistening with silver scales. She saw the glint of its sheathed fangs. Its tongue flicked out, sampling her skin.

"This primal form—is it not wonderful? You could stay here, experiencing the ecstasy and power forever. All I want is for the Vaethyr to open their eyes and remember where they belong. They'll always be less than Aelyr. Tainted. Inferior."

"Who are you to judge that?" her Estalyr-self asked coolly.

"How do you think Aetherials took on mortal camouflage? We tasted them, stole their breath, sucked their sap and seed, dissected them. Painted their blood on our skin. Ate their organs. We are thieves, predators, plagiarists."

"So are many artists."

"But on this night of nights, you can leave all that, come back to your origins and be pure again."

In her dream state, her fear of Albin was gone but her Estalyr-self demanded answers. "Is that why you stole Lawrence's soul-essence?" she asked. "To punish him for daring to leave you and follow Liliana to Earth?"

Albin responded with the merest tilt of his head that conveyed all the menace in the world. The snake tongue flicked over her mouth. "He told you I did that?"

"He said you showed him a tablet of Elfstone and claimed you'd trapped his heart, soul and core inside and would hold it hostage unless he came back."

Albin smiled. "And you took that at face value?"

"We had proof. We had the gem. When we returned it to him, he became his true self again."

"I did what you describe, it's true."

"How could you be so callous as to steal your own son's essence?"

"But I didn't," Albin said patiently. "Of course I didn't trap his soul inside a piece of mineral. How could I? Such a thing would be impossible."

"You told him you had, and he believed you."

"Exactly so. It was what he believed that did the damage."

"Then the effect was the same! You told him a cruel lie, and he trusted you."

"He chose that path himself," Albin replied, unmoved.

"You punished him for disobeying you!"

"Haven't fathers always done that to their sons?" His head shifted minimally and she reread the coldness of his eyes as desolation.

"You were jealous of him."

"Not so. His mother, my beloved Maia, vanished long ago into the Spiral. I needed Lawrence to help me find her, but he turned his back on us, greedy for the riches of Earth instead. I meant only to remind him that his heart belongs here. The symbol I chose was trifling."

"No; it destroyed him. I hope you felt he'd been punished enough by the end."

"Don't be so quick to pass judgment." The snake reared and rubbed its dry cheek across hers. "I tired of the game. It was I who asked Estel to bring you the egg. It took you long enough, with Earth-deadened instincts, to work out its purpose. Child of Vaeth, don't go back. You may not see your loved ones again, but you won't care. Caring is a curse, when we live too long, and spend eternity like galaxies drifting away from each other."

A cascade of strange feelings spilled through her. A strange coldness tugged her heart, like a distant call, or something urgent she had forgotten to do. The urge to fly was irresistible. Time shifted and she was airborne again, Albin a small pale figure looking up from the pooled shadows below. "Lawrence locked the Gates to protect Vaeth from terrible danger." His voice was faint as the wind took her. "Are you so very sure that the *true* danger has yet shown itself?"

"I'm very sure you're a trickster," she called back. "Ask yourself if Maia left you for a reason, and doesn't want to be found."

Her Estalyr-self was flying again, tossed on high winds and gazing down on steep mountains and jeweled roofs below. She saw the temple with its curving seashell chambers. She saw the silent eternal wood, the sacred glade with trees standing like columns around the Mirror Pool. There was a figure at the water's edge . . .

She folded her wings and went into a dive, saw her own reflection coming at her in the water; a great angel-demon carved from the night sky, full of whorled galaxies. She stared into her own alien eyes of liquid gold.

"No!" called a voice.

At the last moment she swerved aside and tumbled onto the bank in a heap of silken wings like a broken kite. The small, milk-white face looking down at her was that of

Estel, the doe girl, the Lady of Stars. The crystal heart was still around her neck. "No, you mustn't kiss the water yet," Estel said softly. "It isn't your time."

"Sam," said her Estalyr-self, suddenly knowing why she was here. "Have you seen him?"

"No, sweet sister, he hasn't come here," said Estel.

"Then where . . . ?" She was on her hands and knees, the awful cold pull growing worse by the moment. "Not the Abyss . . . ?"

"Go back to the human world," the doe girl said gently. "Live your life. Don't waste it on hopeless searching. Your Estalyr-self sees everything. Your *fylgia* will show you the way."

Rosie saw the small silvery shape of a wolf, indistinct and far below her as she swept into the night sky for the last time. The landscape rushed and tilted beneath her. She thought of nothing, simply kept her gaze fastened on the running wolf below. And sometimes it seemed there were two wolves, the other darker and gold-tipped, guiding her onwards as she flew, tired now, towards the dawn.

"Where are you going?" Lucas asked, falling into step beside Jon. They followed a narrow, starlit path through a forest that swayed like anemones around them, blue-green on violet.

"To see my mother."

"Can I come?"

Jon looked sideways at him. "Why? Haven't you got to go and be ceremonial?"

"There's nothing else for me to do," Lucas sighed. "Iola's looking after everyone. I came away when the Great Dance started—as Gatekeeper, I can't go into some mad trance, and anyway I'm not ready, and it was all just too . . . intense. I need space to think. Someone said they saw you leaving and I had to see you." It was harder to explain the compulsion he'd felt to follow the path itself. It was a pull, an unheard voice calling to him. He kept glimpsing the small dark cat shape of his *fylgia,* leading him on. And Jon's: a shadowy brown hare.

"Come on, then," said Jon.

As they descended into the valley, Ginny came through the trees to meet them, stunning in a long amethyst dress with her black hair loose. Lucas felt awkward as she embraced Jon; but when she looked at him there was only warmth in her expression. She hugged him too, then linked her arms through theirs and said, "I hoped you'd come. I knew you would."

The rush of water grew loud. Lucas saw the waterfall pouring into its mossy cup at the base of the rocks, the shining ribbon of the stream. Stars and planets washed the landscape as bright as day. And there was someone there, hard to see against the white frothing veil of the waterfall.

A tall man in simple ivory shirt and trousers, his hair stark black against the foam.

Lawrence.

Lucas and Jon stopped in their tracks, but Ginny coaxed them on through grass and ferns until there was no doubt. Lawrence looked straight at them. It wasn't exactly a smile on his face, more a radiance. Years had fallen from him. His face was relaxed, his posture one of complete peace.

Lucas ran forward and flung his arms around him. Lawrence staggered a little under the impact, proving himself solid and real. His hands came up to embrace Luc in return, and to hold Jon too as he came more hesitantly to join them.

"Oh my god, Dad, how the hell did you do that?" cried Lucas.

"And Sam?" said Jon, his voice hoarse. "Where is he?"

Lawrence said nothing. Ginny, turning pale, only shook her head. Then Jon almost fell and Lucas had to help him sit down on the mossy rocks by the waterfall pool. "What happens to each of us is different," she said. Her voice cracked and tears spilled down her face. "If his essence fled his body and went to the Mirror Pool, we will not see him for a very long time . . . if ever."

Ginny and Lawrence sat on a boulder facing them; her arm around his waist, his around her shoulders. His lips touched her hair. Lucas felt Jon trembling beside him and put a hand on his arm to steady him. "What happened?" said Luc. "We thought you . . ."

"The Abyss was tempting, it's true," said Lawrence. "But there's a blinding moment when you see the lies of the dark predator in the psyche for what they are. I couldn't let it win, could not let Albin's lies win. When I confronted and reclaimed the shadow, it ceased to exist. I could have fallen in self-loathing, but Ginny was there to draw me back."

"Self-loathing, why?" said Lucas, his throat on fire.

"It took my son, as it threatened."

"But he gave himself for you," said Jon. "He was always doing that. And always going too far."

"I should have given *my* life for his," said Lawrence.

"But you did!" said Lucas. "Don't argue with me. Rosie told us everything."

He could see the subtle changes of Lawrence's expression, as if he were continually remembering things he'd forgotten. "Rosie, where is she?"

"Last saw her in the Great Dance," said Luc. "She just threw herself in, as usual." He looked anxiously at Ginny. "She will come back from it, won't she?"

"No guarantees," said Ginny. "I hope so. For every Aetherial, the Estalyr experience is different."

"Everything's changed," Lucas whispered.

Jon looked at his mother and father. "You're not coming home, are you?" he said, the bare truth dawning.

"No, dear," Ginny answered. "We belong here now. Where I hope we will see you often."

"If you can forgive your wretched father for the utter wreck I made of our lives on Earth," Lawrence said quietly. "My jewelry business, I sold some time ago, when I knew I couldn't go on. I donated the money to build a school in Ecuador. You, my dear sons, don't need it, and it would be no compensation for the lost years."

"And Stonegate?" Lucas put in. "Will it be sold? I can't bear to think of strangers living there. It would be so wrong."

Lawrence laughed. "Lucas, I don't own Stonegate. It is held in trust for the Spiral Court through certain intermediaries on Earth. It is the home of the Gatekeeper, whoever he or she may be. It's yours now. You will be content there, won't you?"

"Yes. It's all we want," Lucas answered, astonished.

"You and Iola," said Jon.

Lucas turned to him. "You don't have to leave, you know. It's your home too." They held a long gaze, sharp and painful as knives. Then Jon gave a faint smile and looked away.

"Thanks, Luc. I know, but I'm going to stay here, just for a while." He went on with fervor. "You know, everything I did was aimed at finding you, Mum. I screwed up gloriously in the process, but that's what it was all for. I *knew* you were here!"

Virginia looked back at him through tears. "I hope it's not too late. I'd do anything to change things, Jon, but childhood is long over and can't be relived."

"There's time." Jon gave a tired grin. "We have more lives than cats, don't we?"

Rosie's last memory was of crashing through tree branches, rolling painfully over roots and stones. She came to herself, lying in a grove of silver birches, her black velvet dress soaked with dew and a violet dawn dazzling her. Every sinew and bone of her body ached. She had no idea where she was. Raising her hands to her face, she saw that they were her ordinary, human hands once more.

Dazed, she got to her feet. Pain clamped her head and she seemed to have the worst hangover in history, yet she remembered every detail of the previous night, sharp as crystal and as painful. She started downhill and after a minute or so heard the rush of water beyond the trees.

Emerging from the birch grove, she found herself in a

valley. To her right, a waterfall rushed down a rock face. The shining ribbon of a stream ran between gentle banks until it vanished to her left in front of a cottage half-hidden behind masses of foliage. She was in Ginny's valley.

She took a few unsteady steps forward, only to be assailed by a vision from the previous night, as obscure yet painfully vivid as a nightmare. Her Estalyr-self was circling down towards the stone bier on which Sam lay. He was a perfect wax effigy of death, yet she reached right inside and pulled his Estalyr-self out of him and they floated eye-to-eye and he had looked so beautiful, his eyes liquid gold against the ink of his skin, his hair luminous white-blond. She'd seen her own hand against his face, transparent ultramarine, her fingernails brushed with gold. God, she even remembered that as his head came straining forward to kiss her she'd teased him by resisting, allowing him only the lightest taste of her before she surrendered, giving him full possession of her mouth . . .

So real, she could still taste the succulence of the kiss. Rosie gasped aloud. Cruel hallucination—what else could it be? Unless she, too, was dead?

"Rosie?" The voice startled her out of her trance. Virginia Wilder was there in front of her. Rosie was so shocked and so glad to see her that she couldn't speak, and thought she would pass out from the exhaustion and confusion of all her senses. "My dear, what's happened to you? You were in the Great Dance, they said. It can be a very exhilarating and terrifying experience . . ."

"Yes," Rosie gasped. Then, "Who told you?"

"Come with me," Ginny touched her elbow, but Rosie couldn't move. "Dear, there's a lot to tell you. Jon and Lucas are here. And Lawrence."

"Lawrence?"

She stood like an ice statue, knowing by the too-gentle tone of Ginny's explanation that when she added the soft question, "And Sam?"—unable to resist asking, even knowing the answer would be torment—that Ginny's face would turn pale and her eyes would stream with tears.

And they did. Ginny grasped her arms and held her up, whispering, "I know it's not fair. But the strength and wisdom of your Estalyr-self; that will never leave you . . ." She broke off, looking past Rosie's shoulder. Her eyes became glazed, her face suddenly frozen but for the slow parting of her lips.

"Hey, sweetie," said a voice behind Rosie.

She turned and Sam was there. His hair was a mess, he had the same clothes as when she'd last seen him and he looked wrecked and almost as baffled as she felt. She started to reach out, but stopped, her hand poised in mid-air. She daren't touch the ghost in case he vanished. No words would come out of her.

"What the hell happened to you?" he said. "You were there, and then you . . . Rosie, are you okay?"

"Oh my god, I thought you were dead," she gasped, her voice breaking.

"Do I look that bad?" He reached out and touched her face. The touch was real. "But I . . . I only saw you last night, didn't I? We changed shape, we were flying . . . Hang on, was that a dream?"

"I don't know."

"It's a blur. What happened? We were right up there in the night sky together . . . then the next I know, I'm stumbling down some hillside as if I've just come round from a drunken stupor . . ." He pushed his hands through his hair, messing it up further. "Fuck! The end of the storm—with Brawth and my father—that was only yesterday, wasn't it?"

"Sam, it was two months ago!" she cried.

He turned white. "Oh my god—time plays tricks here—god, Rosie, I didn't know—"

They seized each other and then nothing hurt anymore because he was real and solid in her arms, holding her so tight that the strength of him forced all the pain out of her. She tried to scream but it came out muffled against his shoulder. "You were dead!" The flood of tears broke and Sam held her, letting it all soak into him.

When she opened her eyes she saw that Ginny was crying

too, with her arm around Sam's back and her forehead leaning on his shoulder blade.

"I wasn't dead, I was resting," he said into Rosie's hair.

The last of her sobs turned into a choke of laughter. "But how, what woke you?"

"Well, obvious, isn't it? You did. I must have been waiting for you."

"But your *fylgia* led mine to you," said Rosie. "I saw them—us—two wolves . . ." She was struggling for words; perhaps Faith would find the right ones, in time.

"Come on," said Virginia. "Come with me. There are people who want to see you."

Sam couldn't remember seeing his mother and father close and touching before, let alone with such easy, deep affection. They sat by the waterfall in the dew and mist, saturated but not caring, because the water of Elysion was part of the healing. He'd never been embraced so many times in his life, least of all by Lawrence. As a family they had never hugged, but that was changing, like glaciers melting. Now Sam's arms were firmly around Rosie, and hers around him. He'd noticed she was still wearing the crimson crystal heart, his first real gift to her. And that the scar on her throat was gone, healed at last.

"I stayed a long time by the stone biers," said Ginny. "Lawrence says he heard my voice, calling him away from the Abyss. He opened his eyes and I took his hand and led him here. He was dazed, like a creature newly born, but after he'd bathed in the waterfall, he came into my arms and wept." She sighed. "All the hostility between us was gone, like spring frost. Absolutely meaningless. We talked, finally, after all these years of misunderstanding."

Sam grinned. "It sounds like love."

"Many people never get a second chance. We're blessed."

"Now I understand why my parents and Comyn were so insistent that I took part last night," said Rosie. "It was only by becoming Estalyr that I managed to reach Sam.

My best chance, if not the only one. And they knew that, but they couldn't tell me, in case it gave me false hope."

Sam looked at his parents, serene in their surroundings, finally at peace with each other. "You're staying here, aren't you?" he said.

"Yes, we are," Lawrence answered.

Sam accepted the answer, but Rosie tensed against him. "Are you compelled to stay in the Otherworld, because you died on Earth? Sam?" She turned her anxious face to his. "Are you trapped here?"

"I don't know," he said, frowning. "If I was, would you stay with me? Or just visit in the winter, like Persephone?"

She stared at him, her beautiful silver eyes full of light and tears. "I'd stay. If you think I'm letting you out of my sight again . . ."

He was becoming aware of a change within himself. Nothing tangible, but you didn't lie for two months on the healing lapis, absorbing the saturated green energies of Elysion, without emerging transformed. Wondrous insights into the humans who might need his guidance? He'd barely begun to explore the feeling. Most of all he felt grounded, more himself than he'd ever been.

"You're welcome here, of course," said Ginny. One corner of her mouth curved. "How can you call it trapped, in a place full of wonders? But no, choice hasn't been taken from you. The privilege of being semimortal is that we can come and go through the Gates as we please. The Spiral is said to be a gateway to other Spirals in turn. It's ours to explore. Perhaps it is time for you to move on from Vaeth, too."

Sam thought about the Otherworld, so treacherous and gloriously seductive. The scarlet fire of Naamon and the dewy beauty of Melusiel. Running in wolf form, with wolfy Rosie running beside him. The wonder of flesh turning night-blue, translucent and full of stars. The lure of ancient cities, Estalyr secrets. Of Rosie in that primal form, clinging tight and hot around him, her lips and tongue hungry for his, her eyes on fire and her head falling back so that her hair rippled like dark blood . . . he shifted as the memory threatened to stir a physical reaction. What was the surface world, compared with that? Cities full of hopeless louts, corruption and war and climate change . . . it all seemed pointless and far away. He felt spray from the waterfall dewing his hair and skin and it was wonderful, soothing. *Maybe it's the water,* he thought, *that reels Aetherials in and seduces us like opium.* He remembered late sunlight slanting gold onto a mirror surface.

"Sam?" said his mother. "What are you thinking about?"

"Birmingham," he replied.

She blinked. "Pardon?"

Rosie was laughing. Sam grinned, stroking her damp hair. "Look, there is a dirty, nasty world out there, full of young offenders and ex-cons and low-life scum who are crying out for me to come and help turn their wretched lives around. Elysion is all very pretty, but does it have a decent pub? No offense, Mum, but I'd be bored shitless in a week if I stayed here. What do you say, Rosie?"

"I like it on Earth," she said. "I'm not ready to give up on it. I know Sam likes to get down and dirty in the real world and so do I. That's what I like about him."

"There's just the small problem of you having told everyone I'm dead," Sam said wryly.

"No." A stray tear fell as she shook her head. "I couldn't bring myself to say it. I told people you'd had to go away with your father. It was the truth, after all. We can slip back through the portal, Sam, make a new start, and no one will be any the wiser—except us."

"So, it took us a while to answer your question," he said quietly, just to Rosie, looking into her rain-silver eyes.

"But it was worth answering," she said. "It's the beginning. Not the end."

He hated goodbyes—remembering those awful times in prison when Rosie had left after visiting time—and it was as hard, giving a last embrace to his mother and father, to Jon and even to Lucas, who promised he would follow on later. Of course, he would see them all again. With the Otherworld, however, you could never be completely sure.

A breeze cooled their skin as he and Rosie climbed hand-in-hand up the rugged path out of Ginny's valley. Birch trees shivered around them, their trunks ghostly white against the rough velvet of the grass. "So I missed the Night of the Summer Stars," said Sam. "How was it?"

"Fantastic," said Rosie. "Jon kissed me."

"Right, that's it. I'm going to kiss Matthew. With tongues."

"It was a goodbye kiss—after he informed me that he's in love with Lucas."

Sam rolled his eyes. "I told you Jon was as gay as a nine-dollar note and you didn't believe me."

"Could've gone either way, I think." She grinned. "Also, I punched Comyn and nearly knocked him out."

"What?" Sam was delighted. "Why?"

"Because it's what you would have wanted. In fact, when I did it, I *was* you."

"You were always talking to me," he said quietly, another memory waking. "You never left me. I never left you, either. Our *fylgias* were always together. You know, don't you, that if you hadn't pulled me out, I would have pulled you in?"

His words lit an eerie flame in her eyes. "Sam, you didn't miss the best part of the night," she murmured. "We were Estalyr together. When Aetherials dream, what do we create?"

"Right now, my dreams are creating a hot bath with a naked woman, lots of coffee, and several days in bed—not all of them sleeping. Oakholme, sweet Oakholme."

By the time they neared the top, the horizon was liquid gold, and the valley behind them entirely lost in the folds and foliage of the landscape. Although bone-weary, they climbed the rest of the way with renewed strength until they rose over the valley rim and into the oceanic glow of dawn.

Rosie stretched, arching her back. "God, it's been a long night," she said with a heartfelt sigh.

He raised a suggestive eyebrow at her. "So how about you let me take you home?"

"Best offer I've had . . . since the last time I saw you." Her sleepy eyes were beautiful, her face pale but softly radiant, rose-petal mouth curved in a slight smile.

"And all this time—you've been waiting for me, Foxy?"

"All my life, Sam." She rose on tiptoe to kiss him. "I was always waiting for you."

*An exciting new
contemporary fantasy series*

INDIGO
SPRINGS

❧❦❧

A. M.
DELLAMONICA

Indigo Springs is a sleepy town where things seem pretty normal...
until Astrid discovers that magic flows, literally, in a blue stream
beneath the earth, leaking into her house. When she starts to use the
liquid to enchant everyday items, the results seem innocent enough:
a watch that ensures you're always in the right place at the right time;
a pendant which enables the wearer to convince anyone of anything.
But as events unfold and the magic's true potential is revealed, Astrid
and her friends unwittingly embark on a journey fraught with power,
change, and a future too devastating to contemplate.

**"I loved this. An original and terrific apocalyptic
fantasy set in the real world,** *Indigo Springs* **is terrifyingly
insightful, sprinkled with bits of humor for leavening."**

—PATRICIA BRIGGS,
#1 BESTSELLING AUTHOR OF
THE MERCY THOMPSON NOVELS

tor-forge.com

978-0-7653-1947-0
TRADE PAPERBACK